SILENT TRUTHS

Susan Lewis

WILLIAM HEINEMANN : LONDON

Published by William Heinemann in 2001

1 3 5 7 9 10 8 6 4 2

First published in the United Kingdom in 2001 by William Heinemann

The Random House Group Limited
20 Vauxhall Bridge Road, London SW1V 2SA

Random House Australia (Pty) Limited
20 Alfred Street, Milsons Point, Sydney,
New South Wales 2061, Australia

Random House New Zealand Limited
18 Poland Road, Glenfield
Auckland 10, New Zealand

Random House (Pty) Limited
Endulini, 5a Jubilee Road, Parktown, 2193, South Africa

The Random House Group Limited Reg. No. 954009
www.randomhouse.co.uk

A CIP catalogue record for this book is available from the British Library

Papers used by Random House are natural, recyclable products made from
wood grown in sustainable forests. The manufacturing processes conform to
the environmental regulations of the country of origin

Typeset by SX Composing DTP, Rayleigh, Essex
Printed and bound in the United Kingdom by
Mackays of Chatham PLC, Chatham, Kent

ISBN 0 434 00938 5

To Fan

Acknowledgements

A very special thank you to my friends Ernie Back and Don Tait for their invaluable support during the writing of this book. The financial aspects of the story were patiently and expertly overseen by Ernie, and I must stress that any inconsistencies or errors are solely the responsibility of the author. Not for the first time Don came to my rescue with help and guidance for the legal parts of the story, and again I claim all responsibility for any inaccuracies that might have inadvertently occurred.

A very warm thank you to Melinda Speck for so generously inviting me into the W Hotel in Los Angeles. An absolute must for anyone visiting LA! And to Andrew Solum and Stephen Kelly for allowing me to 'use' their gorgeous house in docklands.

My thanks also go to Pamela Salem for introducing me to the wonderful villa in Mexico that hasn't only served the characters in this book so well, but so many fortunate friends too! And last, but by no means least, thank you to my agent, Jonathan Lloyd, for his loyalty, support and wonderful sense of humour.

Chapter 1

'Mrs Ashby? Uh, I've come about your husband.'

Beth Ashby looked at the slight, scruffy blonde whose anxious eyes and half-flushing cheeks made her seem younger than she probably was. Twenty-six, twenty-seven, Beth guessed. Certainly not yet thirty. By comparison, at thirty-eight, Beth felt depressingly overcooked. She also felt too tall, gangly, like a scarecrow whose limbs were longer than its body, and immediately envious of the girl's natural femininity. However, despite the display of nerves and embarrassed hesitation, this was no fey miss, Beth thought, or she wouldn't be here, would she?

What was the girl thinking of her, Beth wondered. Would she like to swap that flimsy blonde topknot for Beth's copious brunette curls? Some said Beth's hair was her best feature. Others preferred her almond-shaped eyes, while a number of men had commented on her wide, shapely mouth, seeming especially to admire the pointed twin peaks of the full upper lip. No prizes for guessing the thoughts behind those particular compliments – male subtext might be unspoken, but it still managed to deafen most women. Personally, Beth favoured her nose, simply for being unremarkable. She didn't like to stand out, which was why she dressed in dark, shapeless clothes, like the olive baggy pants she'd just dragged on, and oversized brown linen shirt, but now, confronted by this phosphorescent blonde, she felt like the afterburn of a forty-watt light bulb.

So, who was she – this girl standing on the doorstep in a shiny blue raincoat and frayed denim jeans? The embodiment of Beth's unending nightmares? The long-term mistress? The

1

HIV carrier? The flighty little trollop with oversized tits and a firm, but fleshy bum? Why had she chosen now, today, to come? Was she pregnant? Is that what she wanted to discuss? Or had Colin chucked her and, in a fit of seething vengeance, she'd rushed over here to expose everything from his infidelity to his secret embezzlement of government funds?

The thudding of Beth's heart was silent but hard. She knew this was going to hurt and had no idea yet how she would handle it. In a sudden bid for survival her mind swerved from the obvious and seized the doubt of this girl being a mistress at all. She wasn't exactly Colin's type, although those noticeably ample breasts and big blue eyes no doubt made her every man's type, at least for a night.

Maybe she was a plain-clothes police officer come to tell her that Colin and his black, two-seater Mazda had been flattened by a juggernaut on the M25. That would hurt too, though probably him more than her. Did policewomen wear their hair in such juvenile disarray? Was it possible for them to have such tremulous mouths and guileless eyes?

He might have won something. Or inherited a fortune. Maybe he'd flashed himself at this innocent young mother while she was playing with her child in the park. So many thoughts whizzing around in her head, stirred up by panic, shying away from the obvious, alighting on the comfortingly absurd.

No more than a second had passed and already Beth felt like a she-cat purring over the instinct to kill. She took a breath to answer, not knowing what was going to come out.

'I'm not married,' she said, startling herself.

The blonde wasn't listening. She was looking over her shoulder at the car that had just screeched to a halt against the kerb. A young, balding man in a Barbour and black jeans leapt out. Beth couldn't see his face behind the camera he was pointing at her. *Oh God, no! No! No!*

She tried to close the door, but the blonde jammed a foot against it. 'You are Mrs Ashby,' she said. It wasn't a question.

The man was still clicking.

Another car pulled up.

'What's going on?' Beth demanded, her voice bubbling up through a vortex of fear. 'Who are you? Stop doing that,' she shouted at the photographer, who was now focusing his lens on the front bedroom window.

'Will you stand by your husband over this?' the blonde hastily demanded.

Beth's heart was skipping beats so fast she could hardly breathe. She should have been ready for this. Then she remembered she didn't know what the girl was talking about, so how could she be ready? She was distracted by another car arriving. Everything was happening so fast. A small crowd was gathering at the gate, a mere six paces from where she was standing. They were reporters, of course, all shouting and clicking at once, starting to scale the wall, about to burst through the gate. The blonde was trying to block her from view, a desperate attempt to hold on to her exclusive. After all, she'd got here first.

Inside, the phone was ringing incessantly.

'Mrs Ashby! Have you spoken to your husband?'

'Will you be going to see him?'

'Did you know the girl?'

Beth's eyes were wide and scared.

The blonde was watching her closely. 'You don't know, do you?' she whispered. 'Oh, my God.' Then before Beth could stop her the blonde was pushing her inside the front door and slamming it behind them.

'Through here,' the girl urged and, grabbing Beth's hand, she tugged her along the narrow hall to the kitchen, as though she knew her way round. The mistress suspicion flared up again. Had she been here with Colin while Beth was out? But no. These Victorian terraced houses were all the same. Everyone knew the layout.

Fists began hammering on the front door. An ugly chorus of voices called her name. Phones all over the house repeatedly rang, stopping when the machine picked up, then starting again.

The blonde shut them in the kitchen, rushed round the table to lock the back door, then whipped the curtains closed.

'Is there access to the rear?' she demanded, peering out.

Beth only stared at her. This was surreal. Less than five minutes ago she'd been coming down the stairs, returning to the computer. Now she was practically hunkering down in the kitchen, hiding like a *Résistante* from a bunch of murdering Nazis. She'd seen a film, recently, with a scene much like this, yet how bizarre that it should come to mind now, and make her feel sad all over again, that the hero and heroine had been caught and killed.

'You are Beth Ashby aren't you?' the blonde said. 'I recognize you.'

'What the hell's going on?' Beth demanded. There was no need to be hostile, but fear was hard to control.

The phone was ringing again. She reached for the kitchen extension, but the blonde stopped her.

'No,' she cautioned sharply. Then more gently, 'It'll probably be a reporter.'

Beth almost screamed. 'For God's sake! *What* is going on?'

The blonde glanced over her shoulder at the back door. 'You really don't know?' she said, turning back.

'Do I look like I'm acting?'

'No, you don't,' the blonde conceded.

Beth waited.

The blonde fixed her with cautious, watchful eyes. 'Your husband's been arrested,' she said.

Beth opened her mouth, but no sound came out. Then a sudden spurt of laughter broke free of her throat. Arrested? That's what she'd said. *Colin* had been *arrested*.

The blonde looked uneasy.

'What for?' Beth finally managed.

The girl's lucid eyes seemed to be seeing too far into her own. Beth forced herself to hold the gaze. Suddenly her heart felt like a dead weight struggling to stay alive. But she had nothing to fear. She was his wife, she had every right to ask questions.

The girl no longer seemed willing to speak.

Beth wondered what she should say or do now. She had to think fast, but her brain was sluggish and bewildered. Then suddenly she grabbed the girl and began to shake her. 'What for?' she seethed. 'Tell me what for.'

'Murder,' the blonde answered.

Beth's hands were still on the shiny blue raincoat as she stared into the girl's face. Arrested for murder? Was the girl mad? Dimly she was aware of the noise outside shrinking

4

back to a distant place. Her eyelids blinked up and down as time seemed to halt its journey and transport them to another dimension. There was the odd breath from the girl, whose beautiful ocean eyes watched her closely, whose collar was still bunched in Beth's fists.

'I – I'm sorry,' the blonde stammered. 'When I came . . . I presumed . . . Did no one call? The police? Your husband? Didn't anyone let you know?'

Beth let her go. Her eyes drifted to the pitted surface of the table where that morning's mail was still half open. There was no going back from this.

'Stupid question. We wouldn't be standing here now if they had,' the blonde mumbled.

Beth blinked, refocusing her eyes. She turned them back to the blonde. This time she saw her for what she really was – a reporter. Beth's defences instantly rose. Whatever she said or did now she had to remember she was in the presence of the enemy.

'Who?' she said. 'Who did he kill?' Her tone was dull, devoid of emotion.

The next day, when the question was quoted, in the newspaper Beth always took, it was made to sound like a presumption of guilt. There were no protestations of, 'He would never kill anyone, they must have got the wrong man,' or even, 'Who is he *supposed* to have killed?' Simply 'Who did he kill?'

'Sophie Long,' the blonde answered now, looking and sounding so apologetic that she might just as well have added, 'his mistress', or 'his piece on the side'.

'Who is Sophie Long?' Beth asked stupidly.

'You're shaking,' the blonde told her. 'Why don't you sit down? Let me get you a drink.'

'*Who* is Sophie Long?' Beth snapped.

The blonde looked embarrassed. 'I don't know exactly,' she answered.

'You know her name. You say my husband's been arrested for her murder. So you must know who she is,' Beth pointed out savagely.

'I'm not sure yet. I think she's someone he was . . . seeing,' the blonde answered.

'Fucking!' Beth corrected crudely. 'You mean she's some-one he was fucking.'

The blonde didn't argue.

Beth looked away. She sensed the crowd outside growing, billowing up around the house like a marauding army. They were going to smash in through the windows, break open the cracks round the door. They were determined to reach her and she was afraid. She could hear them yelling. 'Beth! Mrs Ashby! Did you know about your husband's affair?' 'Will you stand by him over this?' 'Did you ever meet Sophie Long?' 'How long had Colin known her?'

They called him Colin because they knew him.

Maybe she should tell this girl that she didn't believe it was true. She wanted to say those words, but her tongue was leaden. Nothing she said was going to make a difference now. This was the end. In her mind's eye she could see him falling into an abyss. She was standing on the edge, her hand outstretched to his as she watched him disappear. She wasn't able to help – or could she? *Colin! Oh God, Colin!* Her hand went to her mouth to stifle a sob.

All the time the phone kept on ringing. The machine was picking up the calls. Was he trying to get through?

She slumped into a chair.

'Can I get you something?' the blonde asked.

Beth looked up. 'What's your name?' she asked.

'Lorraine Forbes. My friends call me Laurie.' She paused awkwardly. 'I'm really sorry about this,' she said.

I'll bet you are, Beth thought nastily. *It must be terrible being the first on the scene, getting to break the news to the wife, and then managing to force your way into her house. Oh, I can imagine how sorry you are landing this opportunity to make a name for yourself at my expense.* 'Which paper do you work for?' she asked.

Laurie told her and Beth's eyebrows rose. She'd never have put her down for a serious broadsheet; if anything she seemed more of a tabloid trainee who'd somehow managed to get lucky.

The phone was still ringing.

'I should answer,' Beth said. 'It could be him.' But did she want to speak to him with this girl here?

6

Laurie Forbes glanced at the phone. 'Would you like me to take it?' she offered.

Beth buried her face in her hands.

'Hello?' Laurie said into the receiver. 'No, it's not Mrs Ashby. Who's speaking?' She paused, then said, 'I'm sorry, she has nothing to say. Please don't call again,' and she hung up.

'There's some whisky over there, in the pantry,' Beth said.

Laurie poured them each a double shot, then sat down too.

Beth's sense of the bizarre heightened. She became fixated on the way the two of them were sitting here, like a couple of foxes under siege from the hunt. But she had to remember that as innocuous as this girl seemed, she was even more dangerous than those outside, by very virtue of the fact that she was here, on the inside.

'Do you have someone you can call?' Laurie asked. 'A mother? Sister? Friend?'

Beth thought of her mother and shuddered. Then her heart jarred on the image of Colin's mother, whose devastation was going to be a spectacle horrible to behold. The scandal. The horror. However was she, an ex-local magistrate and dedicated churchwarden, going to cope with being the mother of a killer? She'd be booted out of her bridge club, voted off all those well-meaning, self-serving committees, and daily made to choke on all that galling pride of her son that she'd shoved down everyone's throats.

As quickly as Beth's hostility rose, it vanished. She was being too cruel. Colin's mother, for all her silly pretensions and self-importance, truly loved her son and, despite the unparalleled disgrace, Beth suspected the old woman would stand by him.

'Has it made the news yet?' she asked.

'It's probably been on Sky,' Laurie answered.

'She doesn't have Sky,' Beth mumbled.

Laurie didn't ask who.

Beth's mind returned to her own mother and father. What would they be doing right now, down there in Southern Spain? Four o'clock here made five o'clock there, so they'd probably be strolling off the golf course, skin all crinkled and bronzed, heading towards the clubhouse. In less than an hour they'd have imbibed enough of the peppery local wine to forget they even had a daughter, never mind to wonder how she was. Why had she always been such an irritant to her mother? She'd given up trying to please her long ago, but the pain of her failure still cut deeper than she'd ever want to admit. It gave her a moment's malicious pleasure to think of how affronted her mother would be by this scandal. What it might mean for Colin or Beth wouldn't be a major concern for Joyce Winters, who only ever measured events by how they affected her. Beth could picture her parents an hour or two from now, all cosied up in oblivion, false teeth clacking as they snorted and snored their way through yet another hourly Sky News airing of their son-in-law's terrible day. Rather like flying over an earthquake, she thought. Perhaps she should call and break it to them herself. If nothing else it would give her mother an early chance to blame her for Colin's disgrace.

'Why am I finding out like this?' she suddenly cried. 'Why didn't anyone call me?'

'I don't know,' Laurie answered. 'They're probably trying.'

Beth looked at the phone that had hardly stopped ringing. Was it odd that she hadn't been more forceful about answering? It seemed so to her, but what did Laurie Forbes think? *What the hell did it matter what Laurie Forbes thought?*

Beth looked at her helplessly. 'Where is he?' she asked.

'I think they're holding him at Notting Hill.'

Beth was confused. 'Why there?'

'It's near where it happened.'

Beth felt agitated and afraid. Her mind wasn't functioning well. What should she say next? She must get rid of this girl. Maybe then she could breathe.

'Sophie Long's flat is in Ladbroke Grove,' Laurie expanded. 'It happened there.'

Beth's eyes closed as images of Colin brutally slashing a female body to shreds began closing in on her. She pressed her hands into her eyes, and saw blood splattering unfamiliar walls, spurting into her husband's handsome face. 'Oh my God,' she gasped.

'Have some more,' Laurie said, indicating the whisky.

The reporters were still shouting outside, banging on the

door. The phone hadn't stopped ringing.

'I should check the machine,' Beth said dully.

Neither of them moved.

'Did you know about the affair?' Laurie asked.

'Not really. I mean . . .' Realizing what was happening, Beth got abruptly to her feet, spilling the whisky. 'You should go now,' she said. 'Thank you for . . .' For what? 'Please go.'

Laurie stood up. 'You shouldn't be alone,' she said, sounding as though she cared.

'No. But I don't know you, and I have nothing to say to the press.' *You're devious and conniving, and I know very well that you want to trick me into saying things you can twist into shameless lies that'll hurt my husband and degrade me . . .*

Laurie was just inside the hall. 'What will you say to the PM, if he calls?' she asked, turning back.

Considering who Colin was, it was a question the girl had to ask, but Beth didn't have to answer. 'Just go,' she responded.

'Beth! For God's sake, are you in there?' a voice called above the others outside. 'It's me, Georgie! Let me in.'

'Georgie!' Beth shoved past the blonde and ran down the hall.

'Wait!' Laurie shouted, before she could tear the door open. Beth turned back.

'I'll let her in,' Laurie said. 'They'll be all over you otherwise.'

Beth stood aside. A few moments later Laurie Forbes had gone and Beth's closest friend, Georgie Cottle, white-faced and trembling, was pulling her into an embrace.

'Why didn't you call me?' she demanded. 'I've been trying to get through since I heard. Are you OK? Oh my God, what a stupid question. Of course you're not. How could you be?'

'What are you doing here?' Beth said, squeezing her tight. 'I didn't even know you were in London.' The comfort of holding someone she loved was like finding soft ground in the middle of a long, terrifying plunge to disaster. But it was only temporary, for the reality of why Georgie was there wrenched her brutally back into freefall.

'I drove up with Bruce this morning,' Georgie answered. 'Just thank God I did. I came as soon as we got the call.'

'What call?'

'From Colin. Telling us he'd been arrested.'

Beth drew back. 'He called you and not me?' she said, baffled.

'Not me, Bruce,' Georgie corrected. 'His lawyer,' she added, by way of reminder.

Beth's hand went to her head. It was icy cold. 'Yes, of course. I'm sorry,' she mumbled. 'I can't seem to grasp any of this.'

'You're in shock,' Georgie told her.

Beth nodded. 'I know that, but it's not helping. Everything's so disconnected. I don't feel as though I'm doing or saying any of the right things.'

'There are no right things in a situation like this,' Georgie assured her. 'Have you spoken to him at all?'

Beth shook her head.

'So who told you?'

'The reporter who just let you in.'

'Are you serious?' Georgie groaned in dismay.

Beth turned away, then started as someone thumped on the door. A sudden anger flared inside her. 'It's the damned press,' she seethed. 'They're all over this already, blocking my phone, bombarding my house. If it weren't for them . . .' She shivered with revulsion. 'They make my skin *crawl. Just go away!*' she shrieked as another fist threatened to break through the panels.

'Sssh, it's OK,' Georgie soothed. 'We just need to get you out of here. Let's go and pack a bag.'

Beth started towards the stairs, then suddenly stopped. 'I should have known before the press,' she raged, spinning round. Her eyes were glittering, her fists were clenched at her sides. 'He didn't call to warn me. Why didn't he call to warn me?'

'Maybe he's been trying.'

'But he should have called me *first*! Not Bruce. Not you. I'm his wife, for God's sake.'

'Who threw him out a week ago,' Georgie reminded her gently. 'Maybe he thought . . . Well, I don't know what he thought.'

'I'm always throwing him out,' Beth cried hotly. 'He knows

it's not serious. When has it ever been serious? And when have I ever not taken him back?'

Georgie looked at her bloodless face. There was nothing she could say. All she knew of the current break-up was that Beth had called last week to say she couldn't take any more. Georgie had lost count of how many times she'd heard Beth utter those words, so this new drama had come as no surprise, and had caused no alarm. The endless parting and making-up was as much a feature of the Ashby marriage as the wedding bands and shared name. So, sadly, were Colin's affairs, every one of which broke Beth's heart. Yet she always forgave him, and still she loved him, though God only knew what was going to happen after today. If he really had killed that girl – and things weren't looking good – then Georgie just couldn't see how Beth could forgive that.

She followed Beth up the stairs, watching her long, slender back while trying to imagine how she was feeling inside. Part of her had expected more questions than this, something closer to panic, or hysteria, though Bruce had warned her that shock was likely to cause a temporary rewiring of the brain. So whatever Georgie might consider an appropriate or understandable response would have no bearing on the disjointed, delayed reactions and emotional trauma going on in Beth's mind. Just these first few minutes were proving Bruce right and, caring for Beth as deeply as she did, Georgie was determined not to judge, only to support.

On the landing, where an ironing board and iron partially blocked the way, Beth took a large holdall from the top shelf of a linen cupboard, opened it to check it was empty, then carried it into the master bedroom – the inner sanctum of a marriage. Georgie wondered how many shared bedrooms had such a pervasive air of intimacy as this one. Everything about the room was redolent of the couple who slept here, from the cologne-scented air, to the music centre built into the shelves, to the untidy collection of blues and soft rock CDs; the jazzy ties draped over the top of an open wardrobe door, the exquisite iron bedstead they'd bought at a French antiquities fair, then had Georgie and Bruce rent a van to come and help bring home; the eleven years' worth of photographs that were on every surface, some partly obscured by

11

fancy perfume bottles, coloured feathers, or pearl beads, or the kind of silly notes lovers wrote. Several pairs of Colin's shoes made a disorderly pile against one wall; his trouser press was open as though awaiting a fresh pair. A tangle of clean laundry spilt from a basket over in one corner, Beth's tights entwined with Colin's socks, her bras wrapped around his boxers, their shirts, tracksuits and shared towels. It was no wonder Beth had expected him back, when just one glance around this room made it hard to believe he'd even gone.

The brief anger Beth had shown at the foot of the stairs had vanished. Now she seemed tightly wrapped up in herself, fiercely guarding her emotions, suppressing her pain. Georgie could only guess at the extent of her dread and confusion. How strange her life must seem at this moment, not only because of what had happened today – though God knew that alone was enough to derail anyone from their senses – but because of the whole new world Colin and his ambitions had catapulted them into during these past three months, since his long-awaited government appointment. Becoming a public figure had been the most natural and smoothest of steps for him, with his easy charm and intellect, as well as his multiple Oxford honours and Establishment connections. He was born to it, unlike his shy, intensely private wife who'd lately been showing signs of the strain. And who could blame her, when this public path wasn't one she'd ever have chosen for herself, despite knowing how passionately Colin coveted it. Not that she'd ever tried to talk him out of it – she knew better even than to try – she'd just wanted him to understand how deeply she resented the intrusion into their private life, which to Beth was more precious than any amount of power or success. The worst part of it, at least so far, had been having to measure virtually every word she uttered for fear of how it might be construed, by his colleagues and their stiletto-tongued wives, and, of course, the press, a couple of whom had already dubbed her rude or standoffish for turning down their requests for interviews or comments.

What the hell were the next few weeks going to be like?

Georgie looked at Colin's photograph on the nightstand and wondered what was happening to him now. It was utterly bewildering to think of him being read his rights, handcuffed and locked up in a cell. Despite the seriousness of the situation, and his understandable dread of how Beth would take it, Georgie couldn't help wondering why he hadn't called her first. As a journalist himself, who until recently had been editor-in-chief of one of the leading nationals, he would know very well what kind of press barrage she was facing now. And there had to have been a window somewhere between his arrest and the inevitable media tip-off, when he could have got through to her. So maybe he'd taken their recent rift to be more serious than Beth realized. When Beth had told Georgie she hadn't made it sound any different from the previous bust-ups, though unusually there hadn't been any mention of an affair. This time, if Georgie's memory was holding up, it had been about some function Beth had refused to attend because he'd told her about it too late, and as it was the anniversary of the first time they'd made love she'd already prepared a candlelit dinner at home. Apparently Colin had gone to the function anyway, so Beth had called the twenty-four-hour locksmith she was by now on first-name terms with, and when Colin had returned in the early hours he'd found his keys defunct and a pile of his dirty laundry providing a bed for someone's cat on the doorstep. Whether they'd spoken at all since, Georgie didn't know, though it had seemed an irony to her that Beth had thrown him out of a house that they were both due to leave at the end of next week. No more turn-of-the-century, yuppified mid-terrace in Fulham for one of the Prime Minister's right-hand men. The entire upper storey of a Philip Gruben converted warehouse, with all the fancy lancets and loggias the stocky Italian was famous for, three en-suite bedrooms with gazebo-style bathrooms, and a view of the Thames that stretched from Wapping to Waterloo was much more like it. Georgie hadn't asked where all the money was coming from, and now, with a sinking dismay, she couldn't help wondering what connection it might have to what had happened today.

But she was jumping to conclusions, thinking the worst, when there was every chance that by this time tomorrow they'd be celebrating his release and raising a glass to the PM

13

in much the same way as they had the day he'd called to ask Colin to head the Downing Street Press Office. In truth the call had been a formality, since Colin had already privately been promised the job, and no one had worked, or angled, harder than he had to get it, first as a reporter on one of the better tabloids, then as a TV news producer, then as the editor-in-chief of one of the nation's leading broadsheets. And over the years he'd done everything in his journalistic power to elevate his old university chum Edward Carlyle from the relative obscurity of the back benches to the hallowed interior of the nation's most famous political address.

Not surprisingly Colin's appointment had received several scathing attacks from the far right, though none so bitter as those from the previous incumbent, Alan Dowling, whose fall from grace had been much more ignominious than it need have been, largely because he'd publicly vowed to bring Colin down too. Considering that threat, today might not be a good day for Dowling either, Georgie thought, if he didn't have an alibi. And God only knew what the bullish, ruthlessly ambitious Edward Carlyle and his icily glamorous wife, who now reigned at Number Ten, were making of it all, particularly when they'd already come to rely heavily on Colin's inimitable gift for damage control. When had they ever needed him more – Colin Ashby, the silver-tongued hero of blundering politicians, unskilled leaders and unworkable policies? What kind of spin would he have put on this, Georgie couldn't help wondering. Anyway, it was going to be interesting to see just how the PM handled this awkward little snag in his new party image.

'I should check the machine,' Beth suddenly said.

Abandoning her packing she started back down the stairs.

Together she and Georgie listened to the endless messages. None was from Colin.

Beth's eyes were burning as she turned to Georgie. 'Don't you think it's strange?' she demanded. 'How could he not have called?'

'Maybe there's still a rule about only one call,' Georgie said. 'We can ask Bruce.'

'Is Bruce with him now?'

14

'I'm not sure.'

Beth's gaze drifted with her thoughts. 'How much do you know?' she said finally. 'I mean, they've arrested him, so the police must think he did it.'

'I don't know any details,' Georgie answered. 'When we got the call I came straight here.'

'Maybe we should turn on the TV.'

'I wouldn't advise it. Let's just get you away from all that out there, maybe then we'll be able to think straight.'

Beth didn't move. 'I'm not saying I foresaw this,' she said, staring at nothing. 'How could I? How could anyone? But ever since he got that job . . .' Her voice became husky with emotion. 'I've had a feeling something bad would happen.' Her dark eyes met Georgie's. 'How am I going to get through this?' she whispered, her mouth trembling with the effort of holding on.

'You will,' Georgie said, hugging her. 'And I know it might not look good right now, but by this time tomorrow it could all be totally different –'

The phone rang, cutting her off. Without thinking she picked it up. 'Can you speak to who?' she said, watching Beth turn away. 'I'm sorry, you've got the wrong number. Well, yes, that is the right . . . No, there's no one here by that name. Yes, I heard what you said, but there's no Ava Montgomery here . . .'

Beth spun round and took the receiver. 'Hello?' she said, almost breathlessly. 'Yes, this is Ava speaking.' Her eyes avoided Georgie's as twin patches of colour rose up in her cheeks. 'I'm so glad,' she said. 'Yes, of course I'll be there. Would you tell me your name again, please?' She wrote it down, then a time and a date, and after thanking the caller she dropped the phone back in its cradle.

For a moment neither of them moved. Then Beth clasped her hands to her cheeks and started to shake.

'What was that about?' Georgie began. 'Who on earth's –'

'Don't ask,' Beth interrupted. 'Please. Just don't ask.'

By the time they were ready to leave the house, several uniformed police had arrived and a couple of detectives, who agreed, after a few perfunctory questions that established

Beth had been at home all day apart from a short trip to the stationer's, to delay further interrogation until she came into the station tomorrow. The uniformed officers helped clear a path to Georgie's car. Nevertheless, the crush was terrifying and despite keeping her eyes lowered Beth was blinded by flashguns and jostled so hard against one of the officers that a flower of blood bloomed on his lip where her head banged it into his teeth. Everyone was shouting at once, but she forced herself not to listen. Small satellite dishes were sprouting up like electronic daisies, news-gathering vehicles cluttered even the pavements, while reports were yelled live from the scene of Colin Ashby's home where Mrs Ashby was just leaving, presumably to go to see her husband.

'Mrs Ashby! Beth! Do you have any words for Sophie Long's family?'

'When did you last speak to your husband?'

'Can you tell us what he told you?'

'Is it true your husband is claiming he's innocent?'

'Have you heard from the Prime Minister?'

'Do you think this is the end of your husband's career?'

'How did you feel when you found out?'

Beth hunched her shoulders, fixed her vision on her feet and made herself think about the weather. Georgie and a policeman guided her through the mayhem. Tears scalded her eyes as she reminded herself that rain hadn't been forecast today, but there had been a brief shower around lunchtime. She tried to reconnect with the calm, early summer warmth she'd felt earlier, while walking, unmolested, along this very street. She imagined the blue sky, and struggled with the dreadful weight in her heart. If they'd stop shouting she might hear the birds, or a jet passing overhead en route to Heathrow, or the traffic speeding up and down the Fulham Road. Had she remembered to pop into the stationer's earlier?

A sob lodged in her throat halting her breath. Yes, she'd got the paper she needed for her printer. She'd kept the receipt for her accountant.

Oh God, Colin! Colin! Colin! It was her own voice, screaming inside her. But mercifully no sound came out, so nobody knew just how afraid and alone she was feeling. *Why hadn't he called?*

16

'It's OK, we're here,' Georgie said, opening the door of her Mercedes estate.

Beth got into the passenger seat. Someone rapped on the window. 'Lock the door,' the policeman warned.

Bodies, cameras, faces loomed up over the bonnet as the car pulled away. The police were battling to gain control, but the mêlée was a near-impenetrable mass.

'Someone's going to get hurt,' Georgie murmured.

'They're bound to follow us,' Beth said, not even daring to look back as they reached the end of the street. 'Where are we going?'

'To my house, I think. Get the mobile from my bag, will you?'

After she'd spoken to Bruce, Georgie passed the phone to Beth.

Beth froze. 'Is he with Colin?' she asked.

'I don't think so. He didn't say.'

'Bruce?' Beth said softly.

'Are you OK?' he asked.

'I'm not sure. How's Colin? Can I talk to him?'

'I'm not with him.'

'So what's happening?'

'A lot. Too much. Did you call Inspector Jones?'

'I've just seen him. He's asked me to go to the station tomorrow. What's he going to ask?'

'It's mainly procedure. He'll probably want to know if you knew about Sophie Long before any of this. Did you?'

'No. Did you?'

Avoiding the question, Bruce said, 'I'm trying to get hold of Giles Parker to see if he'll take the case.'

Beth's mind reeled away from that. 'Giles Parker? The QC?' she said. 'Does that mean he did it?'

'No. It just means he should have a good barrister. Hang on.' A muffled sound told her he'd put his hand over the receiver.

She looked out at the familiar shops and restaurants of the Fulham Road; the flower stall at the end of Callow Street, the Pan Bookshop, the cinema, the scaffolding around the Royal Marsden Hospital. It was as though she was travelling through it in a dream, because nothing seemed real despite

17

the fact she knew it so well. How many times had she and Colin driven this road, eaten at the restaurants, gone to see a film, chosen a book, chatted with the lady on the flower stall? Just last week, the day of their special anniversary when he'd ended up going off to that damned party, he'd actually stopped on the way home to pick up some roses. She'd known where he got them because she'd recognized the wrapping. Besides, they never bought their flowers anywhere else.

It had been hard to believe that twelve years had passed since their first fumbled, though glorious time on the sofa bed of his Pimlico bachelor pad. They'd known each other for five weeks by then, having met because Beth had called his office to complain about the reporters who'd started hanging round the kindergarten where she worked. They were hoping to snatch some shots of the child of a celebrity couple who'd recently joined the school. It turned out that the journalist she'd cornered had lied about which paper he was with, but somehow she'd been put through to Colin Ashby anyway, who had generously offered to see what he could do. To her amazement, the wolves vanished the next day, so she called again, this time to say thank you. She'd then ended up spending the best part of her lunch hour laughing and chatting to him on the phone as easily and flirtatiously as if they actually knew what each other looked like and approved. Before he rang off he invited her for a drink that evening. She didn't even hesitate, despite the fact she already had a boyfriend whom she'd been seeing for the past four months.

Memories of that evening now flooded her with such an awful sadness she could hardly bear to visit them. How delighted they'd been with each other. Not even in those first moments of setting eyes on him had she minded that he had to be at least ten, if not fifteen years older than she was. As it turned out, at the time she was twenty-six and he was thirty-nine. He was very distinguished and good-looking, with intense, humorous eyes that took almost no time at all to lull her into believing that she might just be the most special and fascinating woman alive. How many women had fallen for that charm before, and since? She had no idea, but she did know that she'd never, in all their years together, been able to

18

resist it. Nor back then had she been able to believe he wasn't married. Finally, to convince her, he'd made their seventh date a drive to Worcester to meet his parents, who had laughingly sworn that there was no wife that they knew of, nor any long-term girlfriends. There was only Jane, whom he'd been with for almost seven years, before they'd broken up back in February – and they'd recently heard that Jane was already planning her wedding to somebody else.

Where was Jane now, Beth wondered. Had she heard the news yet today? Would she consider she'd had a lucky escape? Or had she thought that a long time ago?

That night, after the visit to his parents, Beth had made no attempt to stop Colin making love to her. She wanted him so much and now she was ready to give herself completely. Though she hadn't been a virgin, she was nowhere near as experienced as he was, which had made her shy and awkward at first, until somehow he'd made her laugh and relax until he was filling her so gently and so powerfully that it was as though her entire existence had never been about anything more, or anything less, than being with him.

She'd never met his father again. The old man died a few weeks later, and Beth had often wondered if it was Colin's grief that had prompted him to propose soon after the funeral. She'd asked him once, and though he'd agreed that it might have made him ask sooner rather than later, she'd surely known by then that it was only a matter of time. She guessed she had known, since they'd become virtually inseparable, and were already allowing their views on marriage and children to start creeping into their love talk. And the truth was, she'd never really doubted his love, not even through all the bad times that had followed – and, God knew, there had been plenty of them . . .

'Beth? Are you still there?' Bruce said into the phone.

'Yes,' she answered.

'I'm sorry, I have to go. Tell Georgie to take you to Charlie Sheldon's.'

'Your partner, Charlie Sheldon? Why?'

'Because the press know we're good friends. They're bound to turn up at our place if they aren't there already. Charlie's wife is expecting you.'

'Bruce, before you go, I still don't know what happened. I mean, how did she . . .?' Dread of the answer made it impossible to finish the question.

'She was strangled,' he answered.

Beth's hand moved unconsciously to her throat. It wasn't easy to strangle someone, or so she'd been told. 'Do you think he did it?' she whispered, picturing her husband's long, elegant hands and wanting to cry so hard that God would take pity and turn back the clock.

'He says he didn't,' Bruce answered.

'But what do you say?'

'That he didn't.'

A lawyer's answer, which told her that maybe he did think Colin had done it, but it was his duty, his job to defend him. 'Why do they think he did it?' she asked.

Bruce hesitated. 'Look, I'm sorry. I have to go,' he said finally. 'Tell Georgie to take you to Charlie's. I'll be there as soon as I can.'

Beth rang off and relayed the message to Georgie. 'Apparently the girl was strangled,' she said, after a while.

Georgie's expression was steeped in sympathy as she glanced over at her.

'I guess that means no blood. Did you imagine blood?'

'I'm not sure,' Georgie answered.

Beth covered her face with her hands. 'Where's Blake?' she said suddenly, referring to Bruce and Georgie's one-year-old son.

'In Gloucestershire with my mother. We might need to take you there for a while until all this dies down a bit.'

Beth turned away. Georgie's words were a bewildering reminder that this wasn't going to look better in the morning. It was only going to get worse – and worse. 'When will I be able to see him?' she asked.

'I don't know. You'll have to ask Bruce.'

A few seconds ticked by. 'Tell me, does he strike you as someone who could commit murder?' Beth said.

Georgie shook her head. 'No.'

'But even serial killers look normal until you know who they are.'

Georgie's hands tightened on the wheel. 'Does that mean

you think he *could* have done it?' she said incredulously.

Beth's face was colourless. Her eyes were blind. 'No. I don't know what it means,' she said. Then, after a pause, 'I wish I didn't have to speak to this detective. I'm afraid it's going to make it seem too real. Right now, it still feels like a dream.'

'It's probably best to get it over with,' Georgie said.

Beth turned to look at her. 'Did you know about Sophie Long?' she asked.

'No. I never heard her name before today,' Georgie answered truthfully. 'What about you?'

Beth shook her head. 'I've no idea who she is,' she said, 'but he wasn't exactly in the habit of telling me their names.' A vague note of bitterness had crept into her voice.

'It might not be what we're thinking,' Georgie offered lamely.

Beth made a noise like laughter. 'I won't hold you to that,' she said.

After a while her eyes filled with tears. The foreboding in her heart was becoming so black it was as though it was shutting all the light from her life. 'I should call his mother,' she said. 'She's bound to have heard by now. I wonder why she hasn't called me.'

Georgie had no answer to that, so she said nothing as Beth picked up the mobile and dialled Phyllis Ashby's number.

'Phyllis?'

'Oh. I wondered when you'd get round to calling me.'

Beth's eyes closed. How could the woman keep up this absurd competition of who called whom first when her son had just been arrested for murder? 'Have you spoken to Colin?' she asked.

'Of course. You don't think he'd call his mother?'

Beth's heart tightened. So he'd managed to ring Bruce and Phyllis, but not her. Why not her?

'I suppose you're happy now,' Phyllis snapped.

'What are you talking about?' Beth cried. 'How the hell can I be happy about something like this?'

Phyllis was silent, then Beth realized the old lady was crying. 'He didn't do it,' she spluttered. 'I know he didn't.'

'Of course he didn't,' Beth reassured her.

'He told me she was already dead when he got there.'

Beth allowed herself to imagine the body lying on the bed, twisted, blue and lifeless, while Colin approached in his navy Savile Row suit and Cartier cufflinks. 'Do you know what he was doing there?' she said abruptly. 'Do you know who she was?'

'No.'

'He didn't tell you?'

'We couldn't speak for long. He just wanted me to . . . He was concerned about . . .'

Beth was hardly listening. 'Would you like me to come and see you?' she offered.

'No. I'm fine. You'll have enough on your plate without worrying about me.'

'Has the press found you yet?'

'I've had a few calls. I've got nothing to tell them.'

'Maybe you should go and stay with your sister Dolly for a while.'

'Yes, I'll probably do that.'

There was a long pause, then Beth said, 'If he calls you again . . .' Phyllis waited, but Beth's throat was suddenly too tight to say more. 'Nothing,' she finally managed. 'I just . . .' She knew she was going to break down. 'I'll be in touch soon,' she said hastily, and ended the call.

For several seconds she struggled to steady her breathing and reduce the swelling emotion in her chest. Then to Georgie she said, 'All I've ever done is love that woman's son, and she treats me as though I'm the worst thing that ever happened to him. Does she have any idea how he's treated me all these years? Does she even care?' Her breath had become ragged again as fear whipped up her anger and pushed tears on to her cheeks. 'He can do no wrong as far as she's concerned, and if he can't stay faithful then it must be my fault, because God forbid anyone should suggest there might be something wrong with her precious boy, like sex addiction, or serial adultery, or some psychotic kind of misogyny! Jesus, she's as bad as my own mother,' she seethed, banging her fists on her knees. 'Poor Colin, married to that boring, unaccomplished kindergarten teacher, who never was going to amount to anything. She doesn't even know how to dress properly, never mind hold her own in Society.' She was sobbing now.

'But if I was so wrong for him why did he keep coming back? Answer me that. Why didn't he stop loving me? Why didn't he just divorce me? We don't have any children, so it wouldn't be hard.' Struggling for breath, she dashed away her tears. 'No one gets it, do they?' she cried. 'Despite everything, all our differences, our rows, his adultery, my insecurity, we've always loved each other, and nothing's going to change that. Not even this is going to change that.'

'I know,' Georgie said softly. 'And no one's ever doubted how much he loves you.'

'But everyone's so critical! So damning of me and the way I hold him back. At least that's how they see it; just because I hate the limelight and despise his colleagues means I'm standing in his way. But he's right at the top, for God's sake. Do they seriously think he got there without my support? Even he says he couldn't have done it without me, so who the hell do they all think they are, spouting off on things they know nothing about? For Christ's sake, I love him. I've always been there for him, just like he's always been there for me. They're all so damned quick to judge, accusing me of resenting his success, wanting him all to myself and I don't even want to think about where all this is going to end, because I just can't imagine my life without him.' She gasped and choked, and her voice became a thin, high-pitched whisper as she said, 'The bastard. Doesn't he ever think about anyone but himself? He has to know what I'm going through. So why doesn't he call? For God's sake, it's making me think he really did do it!'

'He didn't,' Georgie assured her.

'But he was there, wasn't he? Whatever he did or didn't do, he was there, in her flat. So tell me, how the hell's he going to explain that away?'

'I don't know,' Georgie answered. 'Maybe someone else was there too. Someone we don't know about yet.'

Beth pressed her fingers to her eyes and held them there until she could feel herself starting to calm down. 'I'm sorry,' she said finally, her voice thickened by tears. 'It's just that I'm so afraid . . . I suppose I'm trying to prepare myself for the worst, when really I should know he could never have done it.'

'Of course he couldn't,' Georgie said warmly. 'We both know that. You're still trying to get over the shock of it all.'

After a while Beth gave a dry, anguished laugh. 'What makes you think this is all?' she said, closing her eyes.

Georgie frowned. 'What do you mean?'

Beth shook her head. 'Well, Colin obviously knew the girl, or why else would he have been at her flat? And whoever killed her must have done it for a reason. So maybe what I should be preparing myself for now is just how messy that reason is going to get.'

Chapter 2

Colin Ashby was thinking about irony and coincidence and symmetry, and how they related to the last time he'd been in this very cell. Was it twenty-five, maybe even thirty years ago? It had been the morning after a rock singer who was still famous today had been banged up for the night for trying to steal a police car. Having got an early tip-off to the story, Colin, with his young reporter's dubious flair for the different angle, had thought it would be interesting, after covering the judicial process, to write about the cell that had housed this icon. So a friendly officer here at Notting Hill had indulged his request and allowed him to see for himself what the cell in question looked like. He remembered now how severely it had tested his powers of description, since there'd been nothing to describe, beyond the knobbly grey-green walls whose graffiti, over the course of time, had been painted over and over, leaving only faint shadows of its existence, ghostly reminders of its writers who had long since been discharged back into the mêlée of life, or death or other, more permanent, prisons. Then there was the small meshed window cut into the wall above eyelevel, a stone sarcophagus-looking slab which was covered by a thin, waterproof mattress, and the inevitable steel door with its built-in food and communication trap. In the end the cell article had been cut anyway.

How ironic that he should find himself in that very cell all these years later, reflecting on how simple life had been back then, in the starting paddock of the ambition race. How utterly complicated and frightening it was now.

It was probably some time between two and three in the

morning, he guessed. Bruce and Giles Parker had left hours ago, looking almost as haggard as he felt. Since they'd gone, there had been little distraction beyond the inevitable sound-only entertainment of a couple of drunken arrests, and the occasional scrape and clatter of his communication trap, as the duty officer checked to make sure he hadn't hanged himself. Since they'd confiscated his belt, shoelaces and Hermès tie on arrival, checking for that eventuality was a perversely morbid waste of time.

It was hot and airless in the cell. Earlier the moon had thrown enough light for him to see the bleakness of his surroundings, just in case he should forget. It was darker now, but his eyes, swollen and sore as they were, could still make out some of the scratched graffiti on the walls. Not exactly *The Ballad of Reading Gaol*, but parts of it were witty or graphic enough to make him conjure up a profile of who'd written them, which was one way of trying to escape the horrors he was cooking up in his own head – horrors that were all too likely to succumb to reality in the coming weeks and months.

The usual neatness of his slightly greying dark hair had been wrecked by the continuous anxious sweeps of his hands; he was unshaven, crumpled and grubby. Hunger rumbled quietly through his gut, though he knew he'd be unable to eat, even if food were available. His long limbs ached, his teeth felt furry and he needed a drink. He wouldn't ask for one though; he was trying to get used to how it would be not having his needs on tap. What would be the worst, he wondered. Being unable to use a bathroom in private, or being prevented from seeing or contacting those he loved whenever he chose? How was he going to deal with losing everything he'd worked for all these years: his position and reputation, the power to make a difference as he had as a journalist and an editor, as well as a government adviser – as a husband too? Dread was a burgeoning monster inside him.

He wondered if Beth was asleep now, or if, like him, she was torturing herself with what might happen next. He knew she'd be upset that he hadn't called, but he wouldn't – not yet. He had to find out what was really going on first; decide how much he should tell her.

There was so much more to this than even he knew, so until his worst suspicions were confirmed or denied it would probably serve him better, beyond asserting his innocence, to continue to stay silent. Already his failure even to suggest who *might* have murdered the girl was frustrating the hell out of Bruce and Giles Parker. A defence had to be built on something, but Colin certainly wasn't going to tell them yet that from the moment the cleaning woman had blundered into Sophie's flat, catching him in the most incriminating, not to mention humiliating scene of his life, he'd known beyond any doubt that he'd been set up. If he told them that much he'd have to go further, and if he went further then God only knew what would happen to those he loved. Sophie's murder had been the most effective warning he could ever receive, he didn't need another.

Hearing footsteps trudging down the corridor, he looked over at the door. Adrenalin immediately began pumping through his system. There was something different about this. He sat straighter, his senses rapier sharp, his heart a thick, pounding mass of fear. He'd been expecting this visit, in the dead of night, when no one would know except those who were ordered to forget.

The door opened, a dim overhead light was switched on and a man he'd never seen before, wearing an expensive-looking tracksuit and top-of-the-line trainers, stepped into the cell. He was clean-shaven, around fifty, with a silver-grey crew cut, prominent cheekbones, and a jaw like an iron wedge. Of course, Marcus Gatling, the faceless, voiceless power behind the Carlyle throne, would never come himself; Colin had been a fool even to think it.

His uninvited guest didn't bother to introduce himself, but Colin knew very well who he was; Gatling wouldn't think twice about availing himself of the services of Special Branch. *Shit!* How the hell had he managed to get himself mixed up in this? From as far back as their Oxford days he'd loathed and feared Marcus Gatling, and over the years those feelings had only grown. Life dealt strange blows to those who opposed the stout, angry-faced man with his killer intellect and chilling genius for persuasion. His quest for power had always been lethal, and resoundingly effective, which was why Edward Carlyle had convinced Colin, during those early days, that they needed him on their side. Back then Colin had neither the sense nor the power to resist, but even if he had he shuddered to think where it might have got him. Now, all these years later, despite the fact that Gatling's name was virtually unknown to the public, there wasn't a senior newspaper editor, high-ranking politician or top-level financier in London who wasn't aware of exactly who he was. Each would have had to deal with him, and Colin knew only too well that Gatling's unerring talent for never setting a challenge he couldn't win or granting a favour without a high price was unparalleled. It was at the very core of his success, and what made him the single most powerful ally anyone at the top could have – or the very deadliest foe.

The Special Branch detective kept his questions brief and to the point. Colin answered the same way. Yes, he did understand the concerns of their mutual friends. No, he had not seen anyone else in Sophie's flat. Yes, he had gone there for sex. No, he hadn't taken anyone into his confidence over matters regarding the syndicate. Not his wife. Nor his lawyers. No, Sophie hadn't known anything either. Yes, he was sure. No, there was no one she could have told. He had never discussed anything with her, so she had nothing to tell.

The man hesitated. The air in the cell became clammier, edgier with tension, making it hard to breathe. Colin watched him, waiting, knowing there was more to come. He was at this man's mercy. The rest of his life moved forward from here.

The man's eyes were like granite. Sweat trickled down Colin's back.

Then came the question that took the floor from under Colin's world. If Sophie Long knew nothing, why had he killed her?

Fear filled his head like a cloud of hot ash. He understood only too well what he was being told, and he had no words to protest.

The man spoke briefly again, then he turned and left. As the door closed Colin's breath was still skimming the top of his lungs. This was the first time the force of Gatling's will had been levelled at him, and it was like standing in the path of a

28

wrecking ball with his feet anchored to the ground. He was on his own now – the detective's parting words had made that abundantly clear – and he knew very well that no one who could make a difference would be fool enough to run up against Gatling even if they wanted to. For one wild moment he considered making contact with Elliot Russell, perhaps the smartest reporter around, but not even Russell was going to take this on.

So he had no friends in high places now, only enemies, and until he figured out how to fight this, the only way he was going to keep those he loved safe was to stay silent and take the rap.

Beth was in the basement kitchen of Charlie and Sandra Sheldon's lavish Maida Vale mansion. It was still only eight in the morning, but Bruce and Charlie had left an hour ago, and Georgie's mobile had already started ringing.

The morning papers were spread out on the huge glass-topped dining table, where solid shafts of sunlight streamed in through the bay windows like spotlights on the many and various pictures of Colin and the cute, twenty-two-year-old Sophie Long. Every front page carried the story, the tabloids crowing with sanctimonious outrage at all its scandalous glory, while the broadsheets had taken a slightly more tempered, though none the less outspoken, approach. None was in any doubt of his guilt: he'd been caught red-handed and the only confusion seemed to be over whether or not he had denied it. Some papers claimed he had, while others were insisting he'd confessed either at the scene or under early interrogation. As for motive, the general opinion seemed to be that the evil Svengali, whose reputation as an adulterer and womanizer spanned at least two decades, had been systematically abusing his recently achieved power to seduce young girls with promises of high-paying jobs and the kind of flashy, celebrity-studded parties that would turn the head of anyone with a small income and social ambition. Where it had all gone wrong with Sophie was that she had threatened to go to Ashby's wife when he'd repeatedly failed to deliver.

Plausible, Beth supposed, if you didn't know him. Highly implausible if you did, since you'd be only too aware of his wife's pathetically long history of tolerance and forgiveness, so why go to the length of killing someone to stop her telling Beth a story she'd heard countless times before?

Dimly she wondered where the reporters had got the story from, for she'd been unable to find any interviews or statements from Sophie Long's friends or family, but maybe she just hadn't looked hard enough. Nor would she, for going through the papers like this, seeing her husband connected in such horrifying circumstances with a girl who should only ever have been a stranger, was a perversely self-punishing exercise that was doing frightening things to her mind.

'Here,' Sandra said, a clean, lemon smell wafting from her freshly washed hair as she set down a pot of coffee and warm croissants. 'I know you're not hungry, but you should try to eat something.'

Beth smiled weakly, then forced herself to show more warmth. After all, she really was touched by Charlie and Sandra's kindness, for not everyone would be willing to shield the wife of a suspected killer from the press, even if it was only for one night.

Georgie walked in from the garden, still talking into her mobile phone. 'I know, Elsa,' she was saying, 'but I'm sorry, I can't tell you where we are right now. It's not that we don't trust you . . . Oh, come on, Elsa, you're a really good friend, and we know you wouldn't . . . Listen, I'm just saying, as long as we tell no one . . . No, we're not in Gloucestershire. Nor in the London house. Elsa, stop it! I know this is hard, but try to think of what it's like for Beth. OK, I'll send her your love.' She paused, then through gritted teeth said, 'Just tell them the truth, Elsa. For heaven's sake, what else would you tell them?'

After she'd rung off she sat down at the end of the table and took the mug of coffee Sandra was passing over. 'It seems the police are contacting just about everyone you know,' she told Beth, taking a sip. 'And Elsa's about the fifth who's asked me what she should say. What do they think – that we want them to lie, or something?'

Beth's haunted, tired eyes came to hers. Her insides were like lead weights. 'I wonder who'll be the first kiss-and-tell,' she said hoarsely. At least one of the many mistresses would speak out, that much was certain, and dread of it was already piling up with everything else. 'Not that half of Fleet Street doesn't know already what he's like,' she added. 'I suppose it's a measure of how popular he is that no one's exposed him before this. After all, his new position made him a prime target.'

'They don't seem to be exhibiting much loyalty here,' Sandra commented bleakly, looking down at the papers. 'Did you see this? They're trying to say here that *you* think he did it.'

'Is that the Laurie Forbes piece?' Beth said.

Sandra nodded. 'She's obviously completely misquoted you.'

'Or she used words you said and put them together her own way,' Georgie declared. 'What's the matter with these people? Don't they understand shock?'

'She practically forced her way in,' Beth told them, staring down at her coffee. 'I hardly knew what I was saying, but the chances are she's right, I did ask her who he'd killed. Obviously, I meant to say, "Who's he *supposed* to have killed?" but I wasn't actually thinking of the precise words I was using, or how she might read them.' Her eyes closed for a horribly anguished moment. 'Do you think Colin's seen it?' she said in a whisper.

Sandra and Georgie glanced at each other. In their own ways they too were feeling disoriented and bemused, for neither had ever had to deal with anything like this before.

'Probably not,' Sandra answered. 'I don't think they deliver the papers with breakfast where he is.'

It was a poor joke that made no one laugh.

Somewhere deep inside herself Beth wanted to cry and maybe never stop. But her eyes remained dry as her tormented mind searched this madness for a road back to safety. Instead, it only returned her to last night, when she and Bruce and Georgie had sat up talking until long after midnight. Bruce had brought no message from Colin, nor had he been able to explain why Colin hadn't called, except to say that it was difficult for him to get to a phone, and the police interrogation had been tough and extremely long.

However, she now knew how Colin had been discovered

31

by a cleaning lady, sitting on the bed beside a naked Sophie Long, with the tights that had presumably choked the life from her still wrapped around his hands. The extra detail, that he'd been wearing only a shirt, jacket and tie – no trousers or underpants – had yet to come out in the papers. When Bruce had first told her that she'd felt sick. Then quite suddenly she'd started to laugh, breathlessly, almost dementedly until she'd fallen sobbing into Bruce's arms and clung to him hard. He was such a solid, dependable man. Why couldn't she have married someone like Bruce? Why did *her* husband have to repeatedly deceive and humiliate her? What was wrong with her that he should feel the need to do that? Yet, despite everything, she loved him. *Dear God in heaven, nothing was making any sense.*

Her breath caught on yet another wave of fear. Whether Bruce or the other lawyers actually believed in his innocence, she didn't know. It was their job to say they did and, to his credit, last night Bruce had sounded convincing. He was certain, he'd told her, that new evidence would come to light in the next day or so that would, at the very least, cast some doubt on Colin's guilt. Beth didn't confess that she was afraid of what the new evidence might be, or where it would lead them. She just instinctively knew that the best thing she could do right now was stay silent, for there was so much more to this than any of them knew.

'What time do you have to go to the police station today?' Sandra asked.

Beth glanced at Georgie as the dread of it drove hard into her heart. 'One o'clock,' she answered. 'I wonder if they'll let me see him while I'm there.' How was she managing to sound so calm?

'Will you be back later?' Sandra asked.

Georgie shook her head. 'I don't think so. The plan at the moment is for us to drive down to Gloucestershire later today. We'll probably stay there until all the fuss dies down.' As she finished she clicked on her mobile to answer it. 'Hello?' she said. 'Oh, yes, hi,' and getting up from the table she took the phone back out to the garden.

'I don't think you should read any more,' Sandra cautioned, as Beth picked up another paper.

Beth stared blindly down at it, then let it go. 'You're right,' she said. 'It could become an obsession, and, God knows, I don't want to find out any more through the press. One murder's enough.'

Sandra smiled sadly. 'I don't think there'll be any more,' she assured her.

'No,' Beth said, and allowed her eyes to follow the curving stem of a beautiful flowering orchid. She was thinking of the one in her bathroom at home. She desperately wanted to go home now, sink herself in a warm, comforting bath and wait for Colin to join her.

Georgie came back. Her face was pale, her eyes anxious as she looked at Beth. 'That was Bruce,' she said. 'Colin's in front of the magistrate at two fifteen.'

Beth was powerless to speak. Georgie's words were like crumbling rocks at the start of an avalanche.

'He'll plead not guilty?' Sandra said.

Georgie nodded. She was still looking at Beth.

'I wonder what that journalist Laurie Forbes will read into me not being there,' Beth said flatly.

'I'll get Bruce to make sure everyone understands that the times of the hearing and your police interview coincided,' Georgie assured her.

'And Colin? You'd think he'd want me there to show I was standing by him.'

'It's not an option,' Georgie responded. 'You have to see this inspector, and I can't imagine it'll be over in time for you to get to the court.'

'No,' Beth said, standing up. 'I'm going to take a shower.'

As she reached the door Georgie said, 'Bruce has had a call from Laurie Forbes. She wants to know if –'

'No!' Beth said sharply. 'I'm not talking to anyone from the press. She'll just twist everything I say. They've got so many tricks . . .'

'But if it'll help Colin . . .'

'No. Tell Bruce to tell her no. The same goes for all of them. I just want them to stay away from me.'

Chapter 3

Even though Bruce had called to warn them that the press would be waiting when they arrived at Notting Hill Police Station, Beth's heart still sank in dismay when she and Georgie rounded the corner and saw the clamouring mass of humanity no more than fifty yards away. She watched them as Georgie edged the car forwards, tension mounting as she waited for them to notice who was in it. That they were there simply to get a glimpse of *her* seemed so strange. Though she hated it, she realized there was a part of her that was vaguely intrigued by it. They were making her famous, treating her like a celebrity – and were it for any other reason, she thought it might be exciting. She wondered what it would be like to stand in the limelight alone, free of Colin's shadow. It wasn't a position she'd ever sought, but it crossed her mind to consider it now, as she attempted to detach herself from the reality of what was happening in order to get through the next few minutes. She could pretend she was a film star arriving for a premiere, a great humanitarian come to be honoured, a miracle-worker whom everyone wanted to know and touch.

Even before Georgie brought the car to a halt they were surrounded. It was like being trapped inside a capsule with faces, hands, cameras and bodies magnetized to every window and door. The car was rocking and jerking. They were zoo animals; items on display, helpless prey.

'This is a nightmare,' Georgie muttered. 'How the hell are we going to get through?'

Beth looked at the frustrated, cajoling, reddened faces. What damage were they doing to the car, as if they cared? Flashbulbs were popping faster than corn, elbows were digging in like oars. The voices were muted, but it wasn't hard to read the bobbing, twisting mouths. Beth's celebrity persona had vanished in seconds, leaving her to cope with the stark reality of who she actually was and why she was there. Fear slithered through her. It was horrifying to be the focus of so much demand, and so unqualified to handle it. How had it been for Colin when he'd left for the court? Had they put a coat over his head, the way they often did with high-profile killers? Had he been handcuffed? *Her dignified, elegant husband, handcuffed!* What sort of things had they shouted at him? Was any amongst them prepared to give him the benefit of the doubt? How quickly and readily they had all turned. Like his government colleagues. She'd heard from none of them, and Bruce said Colin hadn't either.

Georgie was on the phone, speaking to someone inside. Minutes later they were plucked from the middle of the circus, ushered to the station doors, then being led through drab, winding corridors to the interview rooms in the depths of this Victorian institution. It was the first time in her life that Beth had been beyond the front desk of a police station. The feeling it gave her was almost dizzying. Or was it that her senses were still reeling from the ordeal outside? And now, as the noise receded, and their footsteps filled her ears, her heart began pounding so hard she was afraid she'd never get through this without breaking down.

At the top of a small flight of stairs Georgie was taken off in another direction. Beth was unsettled by the fact that they were questioning Georgie too, or any of her friends, when they couldn't possibly know anything. Or could they? Maybe one or even more of them had met Sophie Long, but had never wanted to tell her. Maybe everyone knew more than she did and over the next few hellish hours, days, weeks she was going to find out just how much more.

'Through here,' a uniformed policewoman told her, smiling as she stood aside for Beth to enter a dingy room with cheap grey lino tiles on the floor, and matching paint on the walls. 'Can I get you something? Coffee? Tea?'

'Nothing, thank you,' Beth answered, looking at the window where light was struggling to shine through the painted-over panes.

'Mrs Ashby.'

She turned to find a kindly-looking man with a horseshoe of frizzy red hair wrapped round the base of his skull, standing right behind her. She almost jumped, for she hadn't been aware of him even drawing close.

'Detective Inspector Jones,' he reminded her, even as she recognized him. He held out a hand to shake. 'Thank you for coming to the station. I know this must be a difficult time, so we appreciate you taking the trouble.'

Beth took his hand.

'It shouldn't take long,' he assured her, gesturing for her to continue on into the room.

She glanced round at the sound of voices further along the corridor, then turned towards a chipped Formica table and an odd assortment of fibreglass chairs. To her dismay, Jones was joined by a stout, smartly dressed woman who looked to be in her early fifties, and a casually attired man with a bright grey US marine-style crew cut, dark flinty eyes and a heavy-set jaw.

'This is Detective Sergeant Freeling,' Jones said, introducing the woman.

Freeling smiled politely, though with little warmth.

Beth looked at the man with the crew cut, expecting Jones to introduce him too.

'Please, sit down.' Jones smiled pleasantly.

Beth perched on the edge of a chair and clutched her bag on her knees. Jones and Freeling set themselves up at the other side of the table, while the man with the jaw retreated to a corner and positioned his chair so that he had a clear view of Beth's face. Beth glanced at him nervously. Who was he? Why had no one introduced him?

Freeling was setting up a tape, speaking the time, date and all their names into the built-in mike. Beth looked at Jones. Though she was afraid, she was reasonably calm, she felt, and hopefully ready to convince them that she believed utterly in her husband's innocence. The thought of Colin sent a bolt of dread shooting through her heart. He must be at the court now, preparing to make his plea. *Not guilty*, he would say, and her breath almost caught on the image of his pale, handsome face as he spoke. What would he be feeling? How afraid he must be.

36

Jones looked up from the dossier in front of him. 'I apologize for the necessity of having to put you through this,' he began, sounding as though he meant it. 'Please be assured it's not our intention to cause you any more distress than you must already be suffering.'

Beth looked at him with wide, burning eyes. She made no attempt to speak for her emotions were embarrassingly close to the surface and his unexpected kindness had caused a tightness in her throat.

'I know you're aware that we searched your house yesterday,' he continued.

She nodded. Tension had stiffened her neck.

'Would you mind speaking your answers?' he asked, indicating the tape deck.

'Yes,' she responded, tilting her face towards the machine.

'We've removed several items,' he told her. 'Some of them are your diaries.'

She flushed, and felt the heat sinking to the base of her pores. A beat later she was panicking about how her private thoughts might be construed. Lawyers were even more skilled at twisting facts than reporters.

Jones's eyes were imbued with understanding as he said, 'Married life is rarely easy.'

The colour in her cheeks deepened as sweat began prickling her armpits. What had they found in those diaries? What were they misreading already?

'Do you have any idea how long your husband had been seeing Sophie Long?' he asked.

She shook her head. 'No.'

'But you did know he was seeing her?'

'No. I'd never heard of her until yesterday.' Her lips felt dry and cracked; her voice was hoarse.

'The women you've written about in your diaries – wasn't one of them Sophie?'

'I suppose it's possible,' she answered. 'I rarely knew their names.'

'So he could have been seeing her for some time?'

'I really don't know.'

He nodded, seemingly satisfied with the answer. 'Your husband moved out of the house a week or so ago?' he said.

The question made her feel horrible inside 'Yes,' she said. 'We had a row. I changed the locks. It wasn't the first time.' But he'd know that, having read her diaries.

'What was the row about?'

He must know that too. 'A party he wanted me to go to,' she answered. 'I'd already cooked dinner, so I wanted to stay at home. He went anyway, and I got someone in to change the locks.' She wondered what they were all thinking – that she was hysterical, or that more women should have the guts?

'Have you spoken to your husband since that night?'

'No. Yes. He called me the next day to say he was sorry.'

'But you didn't allow him back in the house?'

'He didn't ask to come. He knew I needed more time to calm down.'

'So where was he staying?'

'I don't know.'

'He didn't tell you?'

'No.'

Jones seemed genuinely surprised. 'And you didn't ask?' he said. 'You didn't need to know, for emergencies, say?'

'He has a mobile phone. I could have called him on that.'

Now Jones was really curious. 'Was it usual for him not to tell you where he was during these periods of estrangement?'

'Sometimes he did. Sometimes he didn't. There were certain friends he'd go to; I presumed he was with one of them.'

'What friends?'

Her eyes showed confusion and unease. 'Friends he's had for years,' she answered.

'Can you give us their names?'

Reluctantly she began listing them. But what harm could it do? The police probably already knew about them anyway. After all, they'd never been secret and were all entered in Colin's palm-pilot. She knew because she'd set up the address book herself, before giving it to him for Christmas last year.

When Freeling had finished writing the list, Jones said, 'Other than friends' wives there are no women here. Does that mean you didn't think he was with another woman?'

'Yes, it crossed my mind,' she admitted, feeling herself colour again. 'But like I said, I don't know their names.'

He nodded, as though thanking her for the reminder. 'On average, how long would you say your break-ups normally last?'

'A week or so. They aren't that frequent,' she added defensively.

'But more frequent than most.'

Shame caused her mouth to tremble. 'It was a feature of our marriage,' she said. 'You shouldn't read anything into it.'

His smile was benign. 'Did you know that he had an arrangement to see Sophie Long at midday yesterday?'

'No. I'd never heard of her until yesterday.'

'Do you have access to your husband's diary?'

'He doesn't usually hide it, if that's what you mean.'

'But he hadn't been in the house for almost a week, so presumably the last time you saw it was prior to him leaving?'

She nodded. 'I imagine so. I don't really remember when I last saw it.'

He glanced down at the notes in front of him.

Beth watched him closely, then started as Freeling suddenly said, 'Where were you at midday yesterday, Mrs Ashby?'

Beth blinked with surprise. 'At home,' she answered.

'You don't work?' Her tone was almost scathing, telling Beth precisely what she thought of women who didn't.

'Not exactly. I used to, but I left,' Beth responded, 'to write a book.'

Freeling didn't disguise her disdain. 'Did you leave the house at all yesterday morning?' she said curtly.

'No.'

'Did anyone visit you?'

'No. Except the cleaner, Mrs Tolstoy. She was there.'

'What about phone calls?'

'I don't know. I don't remember. I don't think anyone called.'

'Did you ring anyone?'

Beth shook her head. 'Not that I recall. Won't the BT records –'

'There were no calls,' Freeling butted in, 'so how do we know you're telling the truth?'

Beth's eyes widened with alarm. She turned to Jones. 'I was at home,' she insisted. 'Mrs Tolstoy was there, cleaning. I was working on my computer. I'm always at home in the day . . .'

'Can you give us Mrs Tolstoy's number?'

Beth gave it, shaking with indignation and fear.

'So she will confirm that you were there between eleven a.m. and twelve thirty p.m.' Freeling demanded.

'Yes, of course,' Beth cried.

'You didn't go out at all?'

'No! Yes. Hang on, yes, I did go out. I went to get paper for my printer. The stationer's isn't far. I bought paper, and a packet of pencils. I've got a receipt,' she said, scrabbling in her bag. 'It's here somewhere. I know I kept it. I can claim those kinds of things against tax, so I always keep . . . Here it is! I don't know if the time is on it, but I'm sure the boy who served me will remember.'

Freeling took the receipt and looked it over. She then handed it to Jones, who read it before passing it to the man in the corner.

After a while, like a weather vane, Freeling's brief storm retreated into the shadows as Jones's warmth returned to the light. 'Do you have any idea, Mrs Ashby, why your husband would have killed Sophie Long?'

Beth's eyes were bright with confusion. 'No,' she answered truthfully. 'None whatsoever. He's not a violent man. He never has been.' Then realizing her answer had suggested a doubt in his innocence, she hurriedly said, 'He wouldn't have done it. He couldn't. If you knew him . . . He'd never hurt anyone . . .'

Jones looked at her, his eyes a reminder of what he'd read in her diary.

'I mean physically,' she said. 'He'd never hurt anyone physically.'

'Has he ever told you anything that might have been . . . instrumental, or perhaps in any way linked, to Sophie Long's death?'

Beth frowned. 'I'm not sure I understand the question,' she said. 'I haven't spoken to my husband since it happened, so how could he have told me anything –'

'I mean before it happened,' Jones interrupted. 'Did you

ever get the impression that your husband was, well, holding something back from you?'

'He often did that,' she reminded him.

'Of course. But I wasn't actually referring to the, er, other women in his life. I was thinking more of his professional, or financial affairs. Did you ever feel that there might be something there that he was, perhaps, in with too deep?'

Again she frowned. 'No, I don't think so.'

'Nothing he might have been involved in, or knew about, or was trying to cover up?'

She was shaking her head. 'I don't know what you're getting at. If you could be more specific . . .'

Jones looked down at his dossier again. 'Does your husband discuss his colleagues with you?' he asked. 'I mean those since his recent appointment?'

'Occasionally. Some of them have been friends for many years.'

He met her eyes again. 'You're aware of the Official Secrets Act, I'm sure.'

'Of course. And if you're asking if he ever broke it, then the answer's not with me. Or not that I was ever aware of.'

Jones looked round as the man in the corner passed him a note.

Beth waited. The silence was too long for Jones just to have read a few lines. Something was happening, but she couldn't work out what. It was unnerving her. What kind of subtext were they picking up from her answers? What had they understood that she'd had no intention of saying? She was starting to perspire even harder, and the desire to get up and run almost overwhelmed her. But there was nothing to run from. They were only asking her questions that she wasn't even finding hard to answer. It would be over soon. She'd be able to get up and walk out, knowing that she had nothing to hide and nothing to be afraid of. Dear God, she had to stop feeling so guilty and defensive . . .

'That's exactly how I felt,' Georgie confided later as they swapped stories while speeding down the motorway. 'There was a moment there when they almost had me thinking I was involved! For God's sake, we're talking about murder! They

41

shouldn't be allowed to force people to behave as though they're guilty when they didn't even have anything to do with it.'

'I suppose it's one way of trying to find out who did do it,' Beth mumbled. Then swallowing hard she said, 'I hope to God we never have to go through it again, but I think we will, don't you?'

'I think it's more likely that you will, considering I was in the Cotswolds at the time. Just thank God for Mrs Tolstoy, eh? And that receipt.'

'I wonder if they'll let me have it back,' Beth said. 'I still need it for my taxes.'

Georgie glanced over at her, and after a moment's uncertainty they spluttered with laughter.

'Isn't it weird?' Beth said after a while. 'The tale of two cleaners. While he's getting caught at the scene by one, I'm at home getting protection from one. Just thank God it wasn't today or Wednesday – I'd have been alone then, with no alibi at all.'

'I still don't think they'd have seriously suspected you,' Georgie responded. 'Like you said, they have to be tough to make sure they're getting all the facts.'

Beth nodded, and watched a Jaguar go flying past. 'You know what?' she said. 'It struck me that they think Colin might be involved in something else besides all this. Or that's linked to it, maybe.'

Georgie frowned. 'Like what?'

'I'm not sure. It wasn't clear. Something financial, maybe. Or professional, they said.'

'Do you think he was?'

'Not that I know of.'

Georgie hesitated, then decided to say what she was thinking. 'What about the flat you're buying? That must be a lot of money.'

Beth groaned and closed her eyes. 'What's going to happen about that now?' she wailed. 'We're due to complete next week. We'll have to pull out. Oh God, I'm going to have to sort out the removers from our house too. I'll have to put everything in storage. *Shit!* I've got nowhere to live! Do you realize that? I'm actually homeless! And whatever profit we

42

make from the house will no doubt end up paying his legal fees, and some.'

'You're not homeless,' Georgie assured her. 'You've always got a place with us, which is where you should be right now anyway, not somewhere out there on your own.'

Beth was quiet as she considered the daunting prospect of the practical and emotional nightmares she was now facing. Every minute, every hour seemed to be bringing some new problem.

'So what about the money for the flat?' Georgie prompted.

'We're taking out a massive mortgage,' Beth answered. 'Or we were. There's no way I can manage it on my own. I'll have to call the bank. Oh God, I can't bear this. Colin, why are you doing this to me?' Her hands were clasped over her face as she dropped her head towards her chest.

A while later she was gazing blankly out of the window as she said, 'I wonder if he *was* into something, you know, crooked or whatever? Some kind of scam, or cult, or porn thing.' Suddenly the idea was too much. 'Oh God, please don't let him have been,' she implored, 'or this is only going to get worse. It'll go on and on and on . . . I have to see him. I have to know what's really happening. I take it Bruce hasn't called yet?'

'No. He will, as soon as he's got some news.'

Beth's head fell back against the seat as she wondered which was hardest to bear – not being in the court with Colin, or waiting to hear what had happened. She was so close to the edge now, it was probably only exhaustion that was holding her back.

Georgie glanced at her sympathetically, then pulled out to overtake a convoy of slow-moving lorries. 'You know, I wouldn't go worrying yourself too much over this other thing,' she said, when finally they'd returned to the centre lane and seventy miles an hour. 'Remember, he's pleading not guilty, so it's going to help their case if they can back it up with some kind of motive. That'll mean exploring every angle just in case.'

Beth was thinking about the man with the crew cut. 'He didn't utter a word,' she said, after describing him, 'but there was something about him . . .'

'There was someone sitting in on my interview like that too,' Georgie said. 'He didn't say anything, just watched the whole thing and listened. I thought he was probably some kind of assessor. You know, one of those psychologist types who's working on new interrogation techniques.'

'Could be,' Beth responded. The idea of there being anything sinister attached to the two men's observation wasn't one she was willing to run with right now so Georgie's answer would do. Life was already complicated enough.

After a while Georgie said quietly, 'They seem pretty convinced he did it, don't they?'

Beth sighed wearily. 'Can you blame them, when from what we've heard so far they've got enough evidence to throw away the key?'

'So why would he?' Georgie asked.

Beth took a breath and held it. 'I wish to God I knew,' she said finally. 'But if he did, I can tell you this much: it wouldn't have been because he was afraid of me finding out about his affair, the way the press currently seem to think.'

Georgie didn't respond to that, for knowing Colin as she did, she strongly doubted that motive too.

'What about you?' Beth said. 'Why do you think he might have done it?'

'I've got no idea. But if he didn't, I just wonder how on earth he's going to prove it when they found him right there.'

Beth's eyes closed as though to block out the image of Sophie Long's lifeless body lying on a bed, and Colin's ridiculous semi-nudity as he sat beside her, having throttled her with a pair of tights. Dear God, it was so burlesque it might actually be comical were it not so tragic.

'That could be Bruce,' Georgie said as her mobile rang.

Beth answered it.

'Hi, it's me,' Bruce said.

'It's Beth,' she informed him, her insides stretching with nerves. 'What happened?'

'It went the way we expected.'

'You mean –'

'I'm afraid so.'

'So where is he?' she said, the words barely making it past her throat.

44

'They've taken him to Wandsworth.'

She pictured him in a sealed prison van, travelling through the city he knew so well, unable to see out, not knowing when he would again. She opened her mouth to speak, but suddenly she had no breath. She gulped for air, but her lungs wouldn't work. She looked at Georgie with bulging, panicked eyes.

Georgie swerved the car fast on to the hard shoulder. 'It's OK,' she said, grasping her. 'Just take it steady. One breath at a time. That's it. Slowly. Slowly. In. Out.'

Beth's skin was like ice, while her head roared like a fire. Some air was getting through now, but still not enough to speak. Then her limbs started to judder.

'Beth!' Georgie cried. 'Oh my God, what's happening to you? Is it your heart?'

'No,' Beth managed to gasp. 'I'm OK. It's just . . .'

'Take it easy,' Georgie insisted. 'Don't try to speak. I'll call an ambulance.'

'No, I'm OK,' Beth whispered. 'I'm sorry . . . I don't know what . . . I'm not dealing with this very well . . .'

'You're still in shock,' Georgie declared forcefully, as though to convince them both. 'It's shock!' she repeated. 'You'll be all right.'

Beth nodded, and continued to fight for air. The struggle was becoming easier now, the terrible shaking slowly subsiding. 'They've taken him to prison,' she said finally.

'Oh God,' Georgie murmured, stroking Beth's hair. They'd known it would probably happen, but being prepared had obviously not lessened the blow. 'I'm sorry,' she soothed. 'I'm so sorry.'

Beth looked down at the phone, still there in her hand.

Georgie took it. 'Bruce?' she said.

'What's going on?' he demanded. 'Is she all right?'

'She'll be fine. I think it was some sort of panic attack.'

'Speak to Dr Howard when you get home,' he told her. 'There might be something he can give her. Are you OK?'

'I'm fine. More to the point, how's Colin?'

'Between you and me, he was pretty shaken up by it too.'

Georgie kept her eyes away from Beth. 'What happens next?' she asked.

45

'We should know the date for crown court by the end of the week. That's where he'll be committed for trial unless it can be demonstrated that there is no case to answer. Unless, by some miracle, we can prove he didn't do it. All hope at the moment is on the results of the forensic tests.'

'When are they due?'

'Your guess is as good as mine. Weeks probably.'

Georgie shifted the phone to her other ear. 'Are you coming home tonight?' she asked.

'No. I'll stay in London.'

'Then call us later. Beth'll want to talk to you again.'

'Of course. There's one other thing you should know,' Bruce said, before she could ring off. 'The press have got hold of Colin's state of dishabille when the cleaner walked in. They're going to have a field day with it, we know that, and it won't be pleasant, so it might be a good idea to keep Beth away from as many papers and TV as you can.'

'Of course.'

'How was it with the police, by the way?'

'Not an experience I'd care to repeat. It was worse for Beth.' She glanced at Beth, and squeezed her hand. 'We'll get through it, though,' she said to them both.

Beth took the phone. 'Bruce, will he be allowed to make any calls?' she asked, wiping tears from under her eyes.

'He should be able to. We're taking him a supply of phone cards tomorrow.'

'What about visits?'

'I think he'll be allowed two or three a week. I'll check.'

The need to touch him, hear him, smell him suddenly rose up in her with such urgency she couldn't bear it. 'When you see him,' she said, failing to keep her voice steady, 'please tell him . . . Tell him I don't care what he has or hasn't done. It's not important. What matters is that I see him, or at the very least speak to him.'

'I'll tell him,' Bruce promised.

An hour later Beth was gazing blindly out of the window as they joined a small stream of traffic heading off the motorway towards the roundabout that opened south towards Bath, and north towards Stroud. Georgie indicated right, and circled round to the north. They stayed on the main

46

road for some time, passing through the centre of a large, rambling council estate, where Beth watched the rows upon rows of identical houses passing by and wondered what the women inside would say if she told them how she envied their uncomplicated lives and faithful husbands. Her assumption was no doubt as wrong as it was condescending, but whoever those women and their husbands were, behind all those ruched net curtains and tidy front lawns, she knew they would almost certainly have an opinion on her husband, and her life, by now, thanks to the press. She wondered if it would even occur to them that they might be wrong.

Soon after the estate Georgie steered the car off the main road and began winding through the narrow country lanes that would eventually lead them to her and Bruce's South Cotswolds home.

Beth was thinking about her mother now, as she watched the passing green and yellow fields, turning gold in the early evening sunlight, and the lusciously dense hedgerows and trees that occasionally hemmed them into a sparkling tunnel of leaves. Joyce had surely heard the news by now, but as far as Beth knew she'd made no attempt to call. Nor had Beth any inclination to either. But she wasn't going to worry about it when she had plenty to worry about already. Just thank God for Georgie and Bruce, or she'd be truly alone right now, since there were no other friends she felt as close to, and no relatives who'd care.

Not wanting to wallow in the depressing truth of how few people there were who mattered in her life, she turned her thoughts to someone she'd hardly allowed herself to consider during this nightmare twenty-four hours. Thinking about her now she felt a tremor of anticipation coast through her heart. She was someone, Beth felt sure, who'd be able to help her through this in a way maybe no one else could. She'd discuss her with Georgie later, certain Georgie would have confidence in her too. In the meantime, as they pulled up outside the gates of the smart, double-fronted Queen Anne house, she felt a renewed and comforting sense of safety enfolding her.

As they moved slowly along the gravel driveway Beth looked around at the high stone peripheral walls, and thick, shimmering green foliage of the overhanging oaks and horse

47

chestnuts. Even if the press were to find her here the walls would keep them at a distance, while the house itself would protect her from all those brazenly invasive lenses. She grimaced inwardly, and ironically, as she recalled her earlier pretence of celebrity. She thought of how easily and readily Colin had always risen to the reality of it, and how desperately he must be cringing from it now. She wondered if that was how it was going to be: as Colin sank into disgrace she would soar to her own success, show the world that she was someone who mattered too. She smiled wryly to herself. What fanciful roads opened up to a mind in crisis. She'd taken so many since all this began. They were like escape routes, and though they might eventually turn into dead ends, how much easier they were on her psyche than the despair and fear that were almost constantly overwhelming her.

A sudden screech of delight broke her reverie. It was Blake, Georgie's adorable year-old son, who'd appeared at the front door and was teetering dangerously on the first step. Beatrice, Georgie's mother, was right behind him, showing her pleasure too that Georgie was home.

As she watched them Beth felt the unbearable ache of her own childless state – years of IVF that had resulted in two devastating miscarriages. Then seeing Beatrice coming towards her, she made herself smile.

'Hello, dear,' Beatrice said, embracing her warmly. 'Isn't it jolly pleasant weather we've been having?'

Just those few words were enough to bring tears to Beth's eyes even as she started to laugh. 'Beatrice, it could be dangerous to be nice to me right now,' she warned.

'I wouldn't dream of it,' Beatrice assured her, her dense brown eyes, that were so like Georgie's, glowing with mischief. 'Come along in now. I expect something stronger than tea is required. I hope so, because it's time.'

Beth turned to Georgie and only just caught Blake as he suddenly launched himself into her arms. 'Hello you,' she cried, kissing his mop of tousled blond curls. 'What have you been up to?'

'Mummy,' he gurgled happily. 'Mum, mum, mum.'

Beth laughed, then laughed again as he cried, 'Meh! Meh. Meh,' which was his best attempt so far at saying Beth. But now wasn't the time to be thinking about the babies she'd lost, or she never would get through this.

'I've prepared your usual room,' Beatrice told her, leading the way inside.

Beth smiled her thanks. It would be the room she and Colin always shared when they came to visit. It was even known as Colin and Beth's room, and had its own en-suite bathroom, combined TV and video unit, king-sized bed, antique wardrobes, chests and dressing tables and a private telephone line.

The TV, she noticed almost as soon as she entered the room, had been removed. She guessed Bruce had called ahead to tip Beatrice off. They were doing it for her own good – she knew that, and even appreciated it, despite the near-frantic desire to immerse herself totally in all the debates, updates and wall-to-wall coverage the case was currently receiving. How peculiar it felt, to know that her husband's life, and her own too, were being discussed, analysed, criticized and no doubt horribly vilified by the world at large while they remained remote from it all. Everyone would have an opinion, many would even claim to be experts, on psychology, criminology, the law in general, the law in precedent, the law in anything they could make fit. Marriage, mistresses and all aspects of infidelity would become red-hot topics. Absolutely nothing would be missed. By now they'd probably even dragged someone in from her kindergarten, her old school, previous jobs, even from her aerobics class, or her dentist's surgery. Had they found any of Colin's other mistresses yet? If not, they'd be there by tomorrow, or maybe they were being whipped up into Sunday exclusives. She knew how it went: no comment would be viewed too trite, and no source left untapped.

She thought of Colin and felt a debilitating sadness sweep over her. It was as though something huge and intransigent was rising up between them. They were both a part of this – he much more than her, it was true – but it was as though they were being pushed inexorably apart by a force that was running out of control.

She sat down on the edge of the bed. Outside the tall, half-open windows the garden was basking in the nostalgic

49

warmth of a mid-evening sun. She could hear the birds singing, and smell the pungent scent of jasmine and roses. She looked at the phone, and tried to imagine herself picking up the receiver and doing what she had to.

It was already past seven o'clock, so there wasn't really much chance she'd get through now. Before trying, though, she had to get the number from the notes at the back of her dog-eared Filofax. Having found it, she lifted the receiver and listened for the dialling tone. To her surprise it was there. So they weren't cutting her off from the outside world entirely.

Taking her time, she punched in the number, then turned to the mirror and held her breath.

After the fourth ring a female voice answered.

'Hello,' Beth responded. 'Am I too late to speak to Robin Lindsay?'

'Not at all. Can I say who's calling?'

Beth hesitated, then staring hard at her reflection she said, 'Yes, please tell him it's Ava Montgomery.'

Chapter 4

Laurie Forbes was at her desk, a slight, focused figure in the midst of newspaper bedlam. Shouting, phones, printers, TV and radio broadcasts swirled around her in a deafening cacophony, though she barely heard it as she rapidly pounded her computer keyboard reworking and researching the many megabytes of information she'd gathered on the Ashbys since Colin's arrest. From the moment she'd received the tip-off her life had been consumed by the affair. Even now she could hardly believe her luck, finding herself first on the scene, ahead of the tabloids, *and* the police. Actually, it was *only* luck that had got her there, since she'd been covering a thwarted robbery at a nearby convenience shop – which might have made the smallest paragraph of page seven – when her mobile had rung, so she probably hadn't received the first call, she'd just been closest to hand.

Well, that was the way it went, and she certainly hadn't wasted any time worrying about how she'd got her break, when this story was about as front page as they came. So far it had everything except drugs – and she was still working on that. But as far as sex, politics, glamour, crime, passion and intrigue were concerned, it was so far out there she hardly knew which angle to take next. She was literally wallowing in a surfeit of scandal, not to mention personal fame, for her by-line had appeared every day since the murder had happened, and other reporters and newscasters were calling her regularly to interview her about how she'd broken the news to Mrs Ashby and how Mrs Ashby had taken it. And all this for the new kid on the block, who'd only just got her stripes as a full news reporter after five years' graft out in the sticks, then a year's frustration at a desk in this glossy Canary Wharf tower, where not only one respectable broadsheet was housed.

Laurie knew very well that stumbling into such an exclusive could easily put her on the fast track to big time, provided she handled it right. Of course, all the heavyweight politicos were on the case too, so were the department editors, crime correspondents, features writers and any number of guest columnists. And then, of course, there were the tabloids, and since the broadsheets didn't have the kind of resources their smaller friends could boast, the two reporters from news who'd been working with her had now been reassigned to the daily grind. But battling on alone was OK with Laurie. She could handle it, despite the snootiness and noncooperation of her more experienced colleagues, who, frankly, were just plain pissed off that she alone had shared that intensely traumatic moment with Beth Ashby when she'd learnt of her husband's arrest, while those far more seasoned and acclaimed than she had clamoured at the door, pleading for just one word, one shot, one small piece of the private hell.

OK, it was true she hadn't exactly managed to get much out of Beth Ashby, which she was seriously hacked off about now, but, boy, had she managed to spin those few minutes into a sensation. *Who did he kill?* With those four immortal words Beth Ashby had all but condemned her husband and launched Laurie's career. Of course, getting caught in the act had done considerably more to incriminate Ashby than Beth's words, but that unpremeditated question had told the world that even his wife believed he was capable of murder. What the world and Laurie Forbes didn't know yet, though, was what Ashby's boss thought.

'Hello,' she snapped into the receiver, the speed of her hand sending a pile of cuttings cascading to the floor.

'Hi. It's me,' the voice at the other end responded. 'Bingo. Tonight. Six o'clock at Benitos. Do you know it?'

'Yep. I'll be there. Who are we talking about?'

'The bloke you were looking for.'

Laurie frowned. 'Remind me.'

'Minicab driver?'

'Laurie! Five minutes. My office.'

She gave the thumbs-up to Wilbur, the news editor, then ending the call returned to her computer. As she read the screen she absently slid a scrunchy off her already messy ponytail, stuck it in her mouth as she scooped up a few loose strands, then twisted it back on again.

'Flaxie just called,' she told Gino as he slumped into his chair and let his heavy bag thump to the floor. 'He's found the minicab driver.'

'Isn't he supposed to be covering the decay of some South London hospital?' Gino said, loosening his tie. 'Shit, it's really warming up out there.'

'Like you're meant to be getting the lowdown on some plagiarist in the efashion world, whatever the hell that is,' she reminded him. 'Anything on Sophie Long's parents yet?'

He shook his head. 'My sources tell me that *no one* knows where they are. Not even close family.'

'Someone must,' she corrected.

'Yeah, well, you find that someone, because I sure as hell can't.'

Laurie paused for a moment and rested her chin on her hand. 'It's weird, isn't it?' she said. 'The same day as their daughter gets murdered they just up and disappear.'

'Personally, I'd call it survival,' he responded, catching a high-five with one of the sports subs as he passed.

'I'll tell you what else is weird,' she continued, her large blue eyes narrowing in thought. 'I mean, I actually lie awake at night thinking about this. For a man who was so smart, who always knew what he was doing every step of the way ...' She shook her head. 'He had his whole life mapped out. He'd just achieved a lifetime goal, and until two weeks ago he had to be one of the most popular men in politics, not to mention journalism. And then he goes and does something like this.'

Gino looked up, his dark, irregular features drawn in a frown. 'He's not the first man to screw up when sitting atop the world,' he remarked. 'So what's your point?'

'I don't know,' she answered, still trying to make the links. 'Except, after all this delving into his life I feel I know him pretty well by now, and this ... Well, it just doesn't add up.'

'What about the evidence? That more than adds up.'

'I know. And as I've personally interviewed Mrs Come-

53

clean-with-everything-but-the-size-of-his-willy, and the gay couple across the landing who heard raised voices around the crucial time, I'm not about to argue over whether or not he did it. There's just something about it that's bugging me, that's all.'

Gino's attention was shifting to his computer screen. 'Has his wife been to see him yet?' he asked, keying in his password.

Laurie jumped on it. 'No!' she cried. 'Which is something else that's weird. The statement the lawyers put out makes it clear she's going to stand by him, so why hasn't she been to see him?'

'She might already have gone in on the floor of one of their cars,' Gino suggested.

Laurie shook her head. 'Milly over in crime's got an inside source at Wandsworth, so if she had we'd know by now. Not that Milly would tell me, of course. But she'd hardly omit it from her own reports.'

'So where is the wife?'

'She was in London yesterday, but it was in one of the tabloids this morning that she went back to the Cotswolds last night.'

'Any idea what she was here for?'

'Funny that, but she didn't call to tell me,' Laurie responded.

Gino's bushy eyebrows arched. 'And I don't suppose the Prime Minister's returned your calls yet either,' he commented, over the squeal and crunch of Internet connection.

'Oh, I'm sure there's a message on my machine somewhere,' she replied, mimicking the absurd response she'd got from Diana Cambourne, the political editor, when she'd plucked up the nerve to ask her if she'd had any contact with Downing Street.

'And there's something else you can put on your weird list,' Gino told her. 'A deafening silence from Number Ten that seems to be extending even to the political insiders.'

'That's top of my list,' she informed him, 'along with the whereabouts of Sophie Long's family.'

Gino took a call, then, turning back to his computer screen, said, 'Of course you know who could be hiding the Longs, getting the inside scoop all to himself.'

When Laurie didn't respond he looked up. Her pretty face had darkened with anger.

'I didn't mention his name,' Gino cried defensively, though his eyes were simmering with humour.

'It might be funny to you,' she retorted, 'but that man is nothing less than Satan to me, and you know it.'

She was right, he did know it, and since he was one of the few who was aware of the history behind her loathing of Elliot Russell he felt bad now for mocking it. 'Sorry,' he mumbled. 'But it still doesn't mean I might not be right.'

'Even *he* wouldn't be able to whisk a murdered girl's family off to a secret address before the police had spoken to them,' she snapped.

'How do you know the police haven't spoken to them?'

'I'm not saying they haven't. In fact, I'm damned sure they have.'

Gino's eyebrows went up. 'So what are you saying? That the police could have them holed up somewhere?'

She shrugged. 'It's possible. Even probable, considering the timing. And if they have, I want to know why. It's certainly not normal procedure.'

His interest was more than pricked. 'What does your chap at the Yard say?'

Her eyes gleamed. 'Wouldn't you like to know?' she teased.

'Yeah. I would.'

'I don't know,' she said, deflating. 'He's stopped returning my calls.' She glanced at her watch. 'OK, my five minutes are up. I'm off to see Wilbur.' He probably wanted to find out what angle she was taking for tomorrow, so she'd better start coming up with something fast. Not that she was even close to running out of material, since there were innumerable ways of skinning this cat, though it had to be said that even the tabloids appeared to be drawing blanks where anything new was concerned, and some of them would have sixteen people to her one working the story. Come to think of it, that was another interesting point. Nothing new had come out of this for over a week, which was early days for such a potentially rich source to dry up.

As she waited for Wilbur to finish his phone call, she turned her back on the office mayhem and went to stand at the window, hands plunged deeply into the pockets of her baggy dungarees as she stared out at the dramatic, sun-splashed view of London that shimmered all the way upriver to the House of Commons. It was so clear today she could even make out the tower of Big Ben. After staring at it for a moment she allowed her eyes to drift back down over the rooftops, roads, historical monuments and grey, glistening snake of water. That vibrant, beloved metropolis was so many things to so many people, whose lives were interconnected in so many ways that even they couldn't know them all. However, there was one connection they could never be in any doubt of. She looked again at the vast, splendid palace on the horizon, made small now by distance. Therein, she thought, resides the highest power in the nation; a comparatively small, but select group of people whose decisions, ambitions, personal agendas and human failings affected millions of people's lives in almost every conceivable way.

It was awesome. So much so it could almost make her quiver, particularly since she, like every other journalist worth a column inch knew only too well how rabidly corrupt, malign, and very, very dangerous it could be, though in ways that, mercifully, were more often felt by those within than those who had helped put them there.

'OK, in here,' Wilbur shouted.

As Laurie turned to walk round his glassed-in cubicle she heard someone guffaw, then snigger, and guessed that a couple of the more senior members of the news team were once again having a joke at her expense. But it was OK. Let them. It was their problem if they felt threatened by someone as young and inexperienced as she was. Besides, twenty-eight wasn't even that young, though it probably didn't help that she looked closer to twenty. She had no idea what kind of pressure they put on Wilbur to make sure she always got the dross but, give Wilbur his due, he hadn't even attempted to take the Ashby coup from her. To the contrary, he'd backed her all the way, and hadn't even demurred when she'd chosen Flaxie and Gino, two fellow members of the junior team, as her support crew. Of course, everyone had been waiting for them to screw up, but so far all they'd earned from Wilbur was praise and encouragement, along with an apology when it had become necessary to reassign Flaxie and Gino. But he'd left her on the case, hadn't he? And though he had to know Gino and Flaxie were still helping her out where they could, he'd uttered not a squeak of reproof. So let the sniggering baby-boomers, with their superiority chips and depowered flowers, stuff that in their worn-out peace pipes to puff over in cruddy Strand pubs.

'Are you OK?' Wilbur said, leaning his long head curiously to one side as Laurie closed the door.

'Yes, why?' she asked, knowing very well that the little incident outside had probably turned her lips pale. That was what happened to her when she was upset, or stressed, or just plain tired: the blood fled her lips, leaving her looking strained and unwell.

'Just checking,' he responded, waving her to a chair. 'Now tomorrow –'

'I've got an in with the estate agent who was selling them the flat just along the river here,' she said. 'There's also –'

'The designer warehouse was done last week in the *Mail*,' he interrupted.

'It was the *Express*,' she corrected. 'And they did a ware-house next door that's similar and also for sale. I can get us into the one they were actually supposed to be buying.'

As usual Wilbur's hooded eyes were darting about like flies, giving the impression his attention was too. 'What time's your appointment?' he said.

'Two.'

'Then you're after just about every other paper in town,' he told her bluntly.

Her face drained. 'She told me I had an exclusive,' she mumbled, wanting to kill the agent. She'd also like to know who'd gone to Wilbur with the information, though she probably only had to look just outside the door.

She was on the point of telling him about the minicab driver Flaxie had managed to track down when he said, 'Anyway, this warehouse thing's not for us. We're a serious paper. We report the facts and move on.'

Laurie frowned her surprise. This was the first time he'd sounded anything less than keen to keep the Ashby story going, whatever the angle. 'There are hundreds of different ways we can go with this,' she reminded him, 'and I thought –'

'Let it drop,' he said. 'The wife's kindergarten has been photographed more times than the Taj Mahal; the tabloids have still got the empty house in Fulham under siege despite the fact no one except the removers have come or gone in a fortnight; the eighty-year-old mother's going to collapse under the strain if we hound her any more –'

'Wilbur, I'm not the one who's been hounding her,' Laurie cut in.

'And there's a limit to how many so-called friends and mistresses have actually got anything valuable to say. Now unless you can come up with something that's going to set us apart –'

'I can!' she interrupted. 'I just need some time, that's all.'

He glanced at her sharply. 'Impress me,' he challenged.

'I'm working on finding the Longs,' she replied.

'We've got other people out there on that.'

'I've also got the name of a minicab driver who regularly drove Colin Ashby.'

'Drove him where?'

'Anywhere he was going, I suppose. I haven't talked to him yet.'

'What's his relevance?'

'I don't know until I talk to him.'

'Forget it. If he had anything worth saying the police or one of the tabloids would have found him by now.'

'The police have found him, but he hasn't talked to the press yet.'

'And you think you're going to get him?'

'Flaxie's found him. I'm seeing him tonight.'

His eyes shot up and down the office outside. 'No,' he said, shaking his head.

'But *Wilbur* . . .'

'No, come on, Laurie. I know you've got an attachment to this story, but we've milked it so dry we're not even making Marvel any more. When it goes to trial you'll be assigned. Until then, let it go.'

'What if I told you I think there's some kind of cover-up going on?' she cried, before he could dismiss her.

His eyes were suddenly unnervingly still. 'Go on,' he said.

Momentarily thrown by the abrupt shift of gears, she said, 'Well, right now it's just a feeling. No! It's more than that,' she added hastily as his eyebrows started an ascent. 'It's the fact that no one, except his lawyers, has spoken out in his defence.'

'And you call that a cover-up when he was found with the tights in his hands and his trousers *in absentia*?'

'No, listen. The Longs have disappeared. His wife hasn't been to visit him. Not one of his colleagues is owning up to a friendship with him when it's well known that in some cases, such as the *Prime Minister's*, they go right back to Oxford. No, OK, no one would seriously expect the Prime Minister to comment, but there are others who knew him. They could at least say something. But not a single one is stepping up to the plate and admitting even to having had coffee with the man. All right! All right! We then come to the fact that he's pleading not guilty, despite the kind of evidence he doesn't have a hope in hell of refuting. And let's not forget, the man's extramarital affairs have been going on for years, most of which, according to the friends we've spoken to, his wife knew about, so why would he kill a girl who by all accounts wasn't much more than a one-night stand?'

'All of which amounts to . . .?'

'I don't know. I'm just asking for more time. Wilbur,' she pleaded, as he began shaking his head, 'there's more to this, I'm telling you.'

'You're not hearing me, Laurie,' he said, his voice deepening with authority.

'I am. I just –'

'Laurie.'

She met his stare, held it and only then did she begin to hear him. She had no choice in this: he was *ordering* her to back off.

Apparently satisfied she'd got the message he said, 'Features are looking for someone to do a piece on mistresses and political scandals. It's yours if you want it.'

Her mind was elsewhere, still dealing with this veiled, and exciting order to back off.

'Did you hear that?' he asked.

She looked at him.

'Did you *hear* it?' he repeated.

She nodded. Then her eyes widened as she really came up to speed. He might be ordering her to back off, but in assigning her to a feature he was, unofficially, giving her at least some of the space she was requesting. 'Yes, I'll take it,' she said.

'Good.'

And she was dismissed.

'The most intriguing part of it,' she said to Gino as they stepped off a Docklands Light Railway train later and headed out of the station, 'is who gave Wilbur *his* order?'

'God, presumably,' Gino answered, referring to their editor-in-chief.

'Because I'm treading on the political or crime boys' toes? Or because I've inadvertently stumbled upon something that's making someone, somewhere nervous?'

'Good question. But who would it be making nervous? We don't know, unless we can find out what it is you might have stumbled upon.'

After flashing her travel pass she waited for him to slot his ticket in the exit machine, then fell in beside him again as they walked out into the sunny, noisy splendour of rush hour at Tower Hill.

'If I'd found something,' she said, 'I'd know. Do you agree with that?'

'I'll go along with it if you want me to,' he responded, dodging from the path of a speeding pedestrian.

'I mean, I wouldn't be all questions and no answers,' she explained. 'Or at the very least I'd have a new set of questions.'

'Makes sense,' he conceded. 'Where are we going, by the way?'

'St Katharine's Dock. Benitos. Flaxie's meeting us there with the minicab driver.'

'Any chance *he* could be what you've stumbled upon?' Gino asked, as they descended into the labyrinthine tunnels of the underpass that would take them beneath the frantic intersection of five major roads to the relative calm of the river.

'We won't know until we talk to him. Interesting, though, that the order to back off came minutes after Flaxie's call.'

'You're going way out there with that one,' Gino warned. 'It presupposes a tap on your line to begin –'

'I know,' she interrupted, 'and there's a good chance I'm getting too Washington DC here, but I've got to tell you, Gino, the more I think about it, the more convinced I am that there really is some kind of cover-up going on.'

'If there is, you won't be the only one who's thought it,' he warned.

'Of course not. But who's ahead in the game? We don't know, but we can make a good guess. Elliot Russell's cream-team will have had this inside out, upside down, laid out on a couch and tested for prints so many times by now that if there is another dimension he won't only know it, he'll have sold it.'

'No. You've just gone from A to C there.'

'B being?'

'Between knowing and selling, has to come proving. And as we haven't heard a single peep about another dimension, from anyone, we have to conclude that if there is some kind of cover-up then Elliot Russell, or whoever, is still working on it.'

'Mm.' She frowned thoughtfully and hitched her backpack higher. This deduction had enough merit to be transmitting some stimulating frissons of challenge through her brain.

They walked on in silence for a while, weaving through the fast-paced commuters and map-reading tourists, until finally they found themselves up close and almost personal with some pretty swanky yachts.

'It's impressive what they've done with this place, don't you think?' she remarked, looking round at the expensively converted dockside apartments and arcades of lord and lady muck shops that hugged the marina.

'Isn't this where the Ashbys were supposed to be buying?' Gino asked.

'No. Their place was further along towards Wapping.' She gazed up at a huge arched window and watched the reflection of a plane cutting silently through a clear blue sky. 'Mirrors,' she murmured. 'Funny, isn't it, how they make things appear as though they're moving in one direction, when reality is totally reversed?'

'Are we still on the Ashbys here?' he asked. 'Or are we taking some kind of philosophical side trip?'

'I was just thinking how often things aren't what they seem, and that's how this case is. It's just not what it seems.'

'So you hold a mirror up to it and what?'

'I don't know until we put it there, but we will.'

They walked on, passing a news-stand where Beth Ashby's anguished face was emblazoned on the front page of every copy under the headline 'Beth's Personal Pain'. Laurie picked up a copy and scanned it quickly. Nothing new, except a lonely-looking stroll with her friend's golden retriever. The rest was a rehash of a very private woman's public torment. How she must be cursing the slow news days that were turning a mere walk in the woods into a front-page sensation. And God alone knew how horrible it might have been if she'd taken the friend's baby instead of the dog, now everyone knew about the two she had lost. Anyway, she still hadn't talked to any press, which was what mainly concerned Laurie, for that was an exclusive she'd do the proverbial for.

'I wonder how she must be feeling,' she said to Gino, as they walked on. 'All those glad-to-blab mistresses, and the kind of friends you'd only want so's you'd have someone not to piss on in a fire. Talk about "fuck me in the good times, fuck you in the bad times"! Then there's the failed IVF and miscarriages, and you can just imagine what kind of support that revoltingly narcissistic mother was in time of her daughter's crisis. I can't see the mother-in-law being much better either. And to cap it all, here's her husband, whose best chance of survival right now has got to be an insanity plea. Tell me, what does one person do to deserve that much bad luck? And she seemed so nice to me. Not that I speak from long association, you understand.'

Gino was pondering it all as she spoke. 'Interesting, isn't it?' he commented eventually, 'how she hasn't let anyone from the press near her since it happened. Not even those she must have known for years.'

'It's still early days,' Laurie reminded him. 'It only happened two weeks ago.'

He shrugged. 'I'm just making a point. No luck with the lawyer, I suppose?'

'You mean Bruce Cottle? I call him every day. He swears he passes my messages on, but he's never got any to pass back.

Besides, my name's probably way down there at the bottom of the list, after the *Who did he kill?* zinger. But it won't stop me trying. I've also requested a visit with Ashby.'

Gino gave a shout of laughter. 'I've got to hand it to you, Laurie, for a woman, you've got balls.'

Grinning, she pushed open the wine-bar door. 'They haven't got me anywhere, though, have they?' she shouted over the noise as they looked round for Flaxie. 'At least not with the Ashbys.'

Spotting their colleague hemmed in at a small round table at the back of the room, she began pushing through the happy hour crowd. 'So where is he?' she demanded, squeezing herself into one of the chairs he was fighting off the masses for.

'I'm great. How are you?' David Flaxton responded, his quirkily handsome smile appearing between the upper fluff of a moustache and lower frizzle of a beard.

'Very funny. Gino, that's my foot you're standing on.'

'You can feel that, through those steel toecaps?' he cried.

'No, you just got taller, that's all. While you're up there, get a waiter over here, will you?'

'You imagined I was here for the view?' he responded, waving frantically as a waiter's head momentarily bobbed above the tide.

'Could you have found anywhere noisier?' Laurie asked Flaxie.

'I tried, but this was the best I could do.'

'So, I repeat, where is he?'

'He'll be here.'

'What's he going to tell us that we don't already know?'

'That he drove Ashby to Sophie Long's flat more than once.'

'Please tell me one of those times was the day of the murder.'

'Yep.'

Her eyes widened in surprise. That was not the answer she'd been expecting. 'So,' she demanded, sitting in even closer.

'So he drops Ashby off.'

'And?'

'And that's it.'

'Jesus Christ, Flaxie. You got me –'

'Wait! Wait! There's more, much more, but not about that day.'

'Go on,' she said, drawing out the words.

'Quick, what are you having?' Gino demanded.

'Lemonade,' Laurie answered.

'Another Kronenbourg,' Flaxie added.

Laurie's eyes hadn't let go of Flaxie.

'The driver's name is Pinkton,' he told her. 'Brad Pinkton. He's got his own minicab, just one driver, namely him, just one account, namely . . . Well, he's not prepared to grass 'em all up, but basically, he runs a taxi service for some of the highest ranking civil servants our fair land can boast, who he takes to certain shall we say, Bacchanalian events around our fair city and beyond.'

'No kidding,' Laurie murmured, liking the sound of this a great deal. 'And I suppose there are girls at these Bacchanalian events?'

'Oh yes, lots of them.'

'Who are paid to be there?'

'Very possibly.'

'And I presume many of Mr Pinkton's clients are married men?'

'I think that would be a fair presumption.'

'Is he prepared to name any of them?'

'Any of who?' Gino said, finally sitting down. 'What are we talking about?'

Laurie quickly filled him in.

Gino's eyes goggled. Then feigning ecstasy he sighed, 'A prostitution ring. The feather bed of all scandals. And Sophie Long was one of the girls?'

'According to Pinkton,' Flaxie replied.

Gino and Laurie looked at each other. 'It still doesn't tell us why Ashby would have killed her,' she pointed out.

'But it does open up the possibility of another motive *and* a cover-up,' Gino countered.

Laurie was nodding. 'So does this Pinkton know anything about the murder?' she asked Flaxie.

'I don't know. If he does, he's either staying shtoom, or saving it for you.'

Laurie looked at her watch. 'It's a quarter past six,' she

declared. 'You said he'd be here at six.'

'He's probably stuck in traffic. I'll try his mobile.'

As he dialled Laurie turned back to Gino. 'Whether he knows anything about the murder or not,' she said, 'this is a story we definitely want.'

'It'll be connected, somehow,' Gino assured her. 'It has to be.'

'I'm sure you're right.' She grinned widely. 'Boy, this is really going to piss off the boomers. The upstart Laurie Forbes gets another Ashby exclusive.'

Gino cocked an eyebrow. 'You're right, it will,' he agreed, 'but just don't make too many enemies. The boomers have been at it a long time, and you never know when you might need them.'

She snorted. 'As if they'd do an SOS on me! Bastards!'

'No reply,' Flaxie said, clicking off his phone. 'Probably in a tunnel, or one of the multistoreys parking his cab.'

Laurie stared at him harshly.

'He'll be here,' he promised. 'He's a good bloke. You'll see.'

Tearing her eyes away, she struggled to her feet. 'Fill Flaxie in on what we think about a cover-up,' she said to Gino, 'and Wilbur's instruction to back off.'

As she forced a path through to the ladies room she was trying to come up with a feasible scenario that would start with the procurement of young girls – a crime in itself – for the titillation and fantasy fulfilment of ugly old geezers – possible crimes here too depending what the old goats were into – and ended with one of the girls being throttled with her own tights by the youngest and handsomest of the old geezers, who could have got sex anywhere without paying for it. However, that, once again, depended on what he was into, though none of the many mistresses so far had mentioned anything particularly bestial or barbaric.

Clearly, in order to help connect the opening scene of procurement to the dastardly denouement of death they needed Pinkton, who, though he might not have all the answers, could certainly put them on the right road. Already he'd thrown a whole new light on Sophie Long, whose only claim to fame prior to all this was as runner-up to Miss Essex at the age of nineteen. Since then, as a victim she'd been the darling of the press, her image squeakier than holy, despite having an affair with a married man, but of course she'd been corrupted so that didn't count. Laurie wondered what this new little grenade was going to do when she took out the pin and let fly. Well, one thing was for certain: Sophie Long's new persona as a professional escort, if she wanted to put it nicely, wasn't going to change the fate of Colin Ashby, for his goose had been stuck in a thousand-watt microwave the minute the cleaner burst into the room. No, Laurie wasn't in any doubt about the fact that he'd done it, it was the *why* that was intriguing her now – in fact, it was outright fascinating her. So please, God, don't let Pinkton turn into a no-show because if his story panned out there was no way Wilbur, or anyone else, would hold up the order for her to back off, and the glory that could come with the exposure . . .

'Have you tried him again?' she demanded, sliding back into her chair.

Flaxie nodded. He was looking uneasy. 'He swore he'd be here,' he said, 'and he seemed like a really good bloke. Something must have happened.'

They looked at each other, and in less than a heartbeat all three had arrived at the same alarming scenario. Gino was the one to voice it. 'You don't think he's going to turn up face down in the ferry lane, do you?' he said shakily.

'No, don't be ridiculous,' Laurie snapped. 'This isn't a Bond movie.' She looked to Flaxie for something more convincing.

'If anyone wanted to silence him they'd have done it before he spoke to the police,' he pointed out reasonably.

Liking the logic of that Laurie was about to speak again when Flaxie's mobile started to ring.

'That'll be him,' Flaxie declared, snatching it up. 'Hello,' he bellowed down the line, while blocking his other ear. 'Yeah, it's me.' He gave the thumbs-up. 'Where the hell are you?' He listened, screwing up his eyes as though it might improve his hearing. 'What!' he suddenly exploded. 'You're kidding me. Tell me you didn't do that. Oh shit, man. Oh *shit*. No, I don't fucking well understand . . . We had a deal . . . Yeah, I hear you.' He listened again, then said, 'You've really stitched me up here. Why didn't you . . . ? No, tomorrow's no good.'

As he snapped off the call Laurie's heart was thudding.

'Someone else got to him,' Flaxie said, sounding as wretched as he looked.

'What do you mean?' Gino demanded.

'I mean, he's been paid for his story. We had diddly to offer, so he went to someone who had dough.'

'That someone being . . . ?' Laurie said, feeling the icy burn even before his eyes told her the answer.

'I'm sorry,' he said.

'Oh God, no,' Gino groaned.

They both looked at Laurie.

Not only her lips, her whole face had turned pale. 'What I'd like to know,' she said through her teeth, 'is if that bastard got to him before you did, Flaxie, or if he let you set up the meeting, then snatched him right from under my nose.'

'You're making it personal, Laurie,' Gino warned.

'You're damned right it's personal,' she spat. 'Where Elliot Russell's concerned everything's personal.'

'Laurie, he's a seriously heavyweight player,' Gino reminded her. 'I know you've got your issues with him, but professionally, you've got to face it, you're a minnow and he's . . .'

'A shark. I hope that's what you were going to say,' she butted in, her face tight with fury. 'But he's worse than a shark. So never underestimate him, Gino, and never, ever trust him.'

Knowing Laurie couldn't be rational where Elliot Russell was concerned, Flaxie said, 'Pinkton's willing to talk to us tomorrow, tell us everything he's told Russell. No fee.'

'By midnight tonight Elliot Russell will have sold the exclusive to the highest bidder,' she seethed, 'and every other paper in town will have it in time for second edition, including ours. He'll do a deal with one of the boomers who'll write it up as though it were his and we'll be sitting right there, sick as pigs, and twice as stupid. Well, to hell with that,' she snarled, grabbing her bag. 'This is war, and while he might have won this round, he's not going to bloody well win the next.'

Chapter 5

Did people think she was guilty too? As the murderer's wife she had somehow to be involved? Was that why they all stared? Or was it just that she *felt* guilty? But she mustn't allow herself to feel that way. Above all she had to resist that common failing in women, the way they assumed blame for events beyond their control. And they had been beyond her control, she must always remember that; if she didn't she'd be on a sure route to breakdown or something even worse. No, what she felt was tainted. Yes, tainted, because there wasn't much about the past three weeks that hadn't felt like a contamination.

Beth didn't think anyone had followed her from the station. She hadn't noticed anyone, but they weren't always easy to spot, like the day she'd taken Dillon, Georgie's dog, for a walk. She'd had no idea a photographer was stalking her until Dillon had suddenly run at him barking. He'd got his picture, though; it had made the late edition of the London evening paper, and had appeared in a couple of the tabloids the next day too. Since then there hadn't been very much, which might have been more of a blessing were she not so afraid that it was just a lull as the eye of the storm passed over.

She'd taken a taxi here, hidden behind dark glasses and a large straw hat, which was OK since it was the middle of June. She was wearing a long, pale blue linen dress, loosely belted at the waist, with a matching overshirt and brown leather sandals. She hadn't been sure whether to carry a briefcase or her usual roomy shoulder bag. Beth Ashby had never had much use for a briefcase, but maybe Ava Montgomery did. She wasn't sure, because she didn't know much about Ava yet. In the end she'd opted for both, though the briefcase was empty.

She was in the small reception area of a third-floor office suite in one of the large Regency buildings, just off Piccadilly. The shelves were stuffed full of books, brand-new glossy editions of the latest in commercial and literary fiction, travel and sports. A few were propped up on the coffee table, with an assortment of catalogues and magazines. She could hear the traffic outside, while along the hall telephones buzzed and disembodied voices answered. The receptionists, just a few feet away, behind their horseshoe desk, were trying not to stare. Were they wondering if it was really her, or did they already know? She considered doing something outrageous, like picking up a couple of the books and stuffing them into her briefcase; or launching into a tango with an imaginary partner. Instead, she crossed one leg over the other and sat primly waiting. She'd never had the courage to be extreme or eccentric, though she and Colin had frequently made each other laugh with those kinds of absurd imaginings.

These past three weeks had been the most peculiar time of her life. Nothing had ever affected her like this, not even the loss of her babies. There was so much that she no longer understood. It was as though she'd stepped outside of her normal self into a confusion of persecution and paranoia – and endless, persistent questions from Bruce, Giles Parker and the police. What had really happened in Sophie Long's flat that day? Why was Colin denying the murder when even he couldn't argue with the facts? They were convinced he was holding something back, and if she knew what it was, she must tell them. But what reason would he have to hold anything back? Surely if there was anything that might clear his name he wouldn't even hesitate to tell.

The police were leaving her alone now, but Bruce and Giles Parker had increased the pressure. They didn't seem to hear her answers. Why would she hold back *anything* that would help him, she'd asked them. He was her husband, she loved him, and she'd give anything in her power to turn back the clock. They kept asking *her* why he was refusing to see her, or speak to her, when they should have been asking him. Bruce still hadn't brought home even so much as a message, and no visiting order had been issued either. If Colin had any idea what his silence was doing to her, he either didn't care or it was what he intended. But why would he want to torment her like this? What reason could he have for pulling away when he surely needed her more now than he ever had? Since Bruce was asking her the same questions she was inclined to believe him when he claimed not to know why Colin was behaving this way.

'He just says it's for the best,' he told her each time she asked why Colin didn't call or let her visit. 'He won't discuss it any further than that.'

So now, in an effort to deal with a rejection that actually felt worse than all the others, Beth was trying to detach herself too. In the past, whenever she'd tried to move forward alone, her resolve would crumble the instant she saw him. But now she must consider only the extraordinary coincidence, and indeed blessing, of how Ava Montgomery's existence had achieved its first recognition a mere few hours after Colin had lost his freedom. There must have been some exceptional universal power at work that day, she thought, and all she could do was thank it, for in giving her Ava it had given her something to hold on to – some small chance of survival.

'Miss Montgomery?'

She looked up into the pale, quizzical eyes of a middle-aged man with dark wavy hair and florid cheeks.

'Robin Lindsay,' he said, smiling and holding out a hand to shake.

Ava rose gracefully to her feet and took the hand. 'It's a pleasure to meet you,' she told him, using a deeper, sultrier voice than Beth's. She wanted to be this person, Ava Montgomery, whom she saw as a confident, talented woman, with thoughts, behaviour, maybe even a look all her own. Ava should be an almost separate entity so that people wouldn't think of Beth Ashby when they saw her and feel pity, or discomfort, or worse.

'The pleasure's all mine,' he assured her, standing aside. 'Let's go through to my office, shall we? Would you like some coffee? Tea?'

'What, no champagne?' she teased.

He laughed, seeming to like the suggestion, while inwardly Beth was startled, though amused, by Ava's audacity.

Halfway down the drably carpeted corridor he popped his head in through an open door and spoke to a well-groomed woman in her early forties. 'Ruth, you wanted to meet Ava Montgomery,' he said.

The woman's face lit up. 'I most certainly do,' she declared, coming out from behind her desk.

'This is Ruth Pembroke,' Robin told her. 'She's already a fan.'

'Congratulations,' Ruth said, shaking her hand warmly. 'What you've achieved is stunning. Quite unique.'

'Thank you,' Beth responded in Ava's contralto. Pleasure was rushing through her like a river. 'I'm so glad you like it.'

'I love it,' Ruth corrected. 'And I'd love to discuss it some time, if you're willing. Maybe I'll catch up with you later, before you leave.'

'I hope so,' Ava replied.

Robin was smiling like a proud father. 'Come along,' he said, putting a hand under her elbow. 'My office is at the end here. I'll just introduce you to my secretary, Caroline, then we can get down to business.'

A few minutes later Ava had discarded her hat and over-shirt, and was relaxing on a hard leather sofa, a glass of champagne in one hand while the other lay limply beside her. Robin Lindsay, who was sitting in an armchair beside a floor-to-ceiling bookcase, was doing all the talking, never calling her anything but Ava, even though he knew very well who she was. She'd had to tell him in advance in order to avoid him spending time dealing with the shock of it when she got here. This way, he'd had the chance to assimilate the knowledge, and now the scandal of Colin Ashby's crime and arrest weren't impinging. So, for this brief hour at least, she could be Ava Montgomery the writer, not Beth Ashby the murderer's wife.

'Can I ask why you chose the name Ava Montgomery?' he said, taking a sip of champagne.

Her eyes sparkled as she said, 'Ava Montgomery sounds like the kind of person who knows how to have fun.' It was the answer she'd given Georgie when she'd asked, and it seemed to amuse Robin Lindsay just as much.

'Have you written anything before this?' he asked.

'Nothing that's complete.'

71

He nodded, as though it was an answer he'd expected. 'As I told you on the phone,' he said, 'your style, the story, are both highly unusual and compelling. I take it you know the Italian lakes well.'

'Not as well I'd like,' she confessed. 'I've only been once.' Once, with Colin, just the two of them, to a small, family-owned hotel on the western shore of Lake Maggiore. It was the one and only time she'd met Carlotta, the dark, mysterious woman who'd become the focus of Ava Montgomery's existence, and the nourishment of Beth Ashby's soul.

His eyes were watching her over the rim of his glass as he took another sip. 'The characters,' he said. 'Might they be drawn from people you know?'

'In some aspects.'

'Carlotta?'

Her smile became sphinxlike. 'Carlotta is an amalgam of the modern woman in reality and history's dreams in perpetuity. In other words, she exists today, even though she died two hundred years ago.'

He nodded slowly. He'd read the book, so he understood her meaning. It was a story like no other, for the fluidity of its journey between a created heaven and hell, through a world of brutal mortality and into a universe of temporary death, was as shocking as the violence it occasionally depicted, and perhaps even more powerful than the pain. Then there was the love, so unbearably sweet and intense, torturous and, in the end, as indestructible as time. He wanted to ask how much of the story was real, whether she had shared any of those potent feelings or experiences with her now infamous husband, if Carlotta had ever truly lived, or if it was all merely the creation of an extremely gifted writer's mind. But he didn't know her well enough yet, and, being a gentleman, he was too polite even to approach the boundaries he sensed she had drawn.

Caroline, his secretary, put her head round the door. 'You wanted me to let you know when Stacey Greene called,' she said.

'Ah, yes.' Robin glanced at his watch. 'Ask her to hold on for a moment, will you?' When Caroline had gone he said, 'Stacey Greene's an editor at Buchmanns. I'm sure you've heard of Buchmanns Publishing?'

Only Ava could have been capable of such composure as she nodded and smiled, for inside Beth was flustered with excitement.

'Stacey doesn't know that you're here with me,' he told her, 'but I wanted to speak to her now so that I can tell you right away what she has to say about your book. That's how confident I am that she'll love it.'

This was a wildest dream coming true. Beth's heart was singing, as Ava's cool, subtle voice said, 'She doesn't know who I am?'

He shook his head. 'Not yet. I kept my promise. No one will know who Ava Montgomery really is until the sale of the book has been finalized. I understand you want to know that you've achieved this on the book's merit, not because of your . . . shall we say fame?'

She liked this man. He was warm, understated and insightful. 'If possible,' she said, 'I'd like to keep the secret right through to publication.' She almost added *if it gets that far*, but those would have been Beth's words; Ava wasn't insecure.

'That will be harder,' he warned, 'but certainly we can try. Now, if you'll excuse me a moment, I'll go and speak to Stacey.'

He took the call at Caroline's desk, leaving Beth, Ava, to reflect on the way she was being eased from the protection of Colin's shadow into a warm, glowing space of her own. Not that she in any way courted fame – if it were at all possible, she'd prefer it never to be known that Beth Ashby was the true identity of Ava Montgomery. To the world at large Ava Montgomery should be a name unconnected to the scandal. To the public Ava's face should remain a mystery, unknown, unrecognizable. All they had a right to was the novel she had written, *Carlotta's Symphony of Love and Death*, the work that had brought her here, into the office of this high-powered agent. At least she would always know that Robin Lindsay's response to her work was genuine, for he'd had no way of knowing who she was until she'd called to tell him.

Looking down at her half-glass of champagne she couldn't stop herself thinking of how desperately she wanted to be sharing this with Colin. He was the only other person, until now, who'd read the book, though even he hadn't read the end. Nevertheless, his praise of her writing, the way she'd fleshed her characters, created a style and universe that was so unpredictable and unique, and her capturing of emotions that were so gently, yet powerfully consuming, had left him in no doubt that he was 'married to a genius'. She remembered how she'd glowed and laughed when he'd spoken those words. Thinking of that time now, when he'd seemed almost overawed by her talent, made her want to weep for what had happened since. That night had been so full of passion, wine, romance, and the kind of togetherness and understanding that only came after so many years of marriage. He was so proud of her, so certain of her success. She truly believed he'd wanted it as much as she had for he'd offered to introduce her to anyone she'd care to name. Even if he didn't know them personally, he'd be sure to know someone who would. But in the end she'd decided to submit her typescript under another name, just on spec. He'd understood and was glad, he'd claimed, because she'd find out then just how right he was.

Her heart twisted with longing. He needed to share this with her. She wasn't even sure at this moment if it meant anything without him. Yet it did. It had to. She must make herself believe that it was possible for her to exist as Ava Montgomery the writer she'd long dreamt of being, rather than as Beth Ashby, the wife who was trapped inside her own love and held back by her husband's unexplained rejection.

Poor Beth Ashby, with her broken heart and shambolic life. That was Ava thinking – Ava, whose inclinations were slightly wild and impulsive, and who was electrified enough by this meeting to want to start moving on.

Then quite suddenly her mind swooped off in another direction – to Sophie Long's infamous tights. Tights! Such an unexotic item for a mistress! One paper had asked, what kind of tights were they? She ran through some of the possibles: black Lycra, seamless, ten or fifteen denier, crotchless. Tights on the hands. Tights on the legs. Tights as a scarf. Her eyes closed. He was still swearing he hadn't done it, but how could he deny it when he'd been caught right there and so far there was no evidence of anyone else being present? Maybe, as one reporter had half-heartedly ventured, it had been an accident.

74

Asphyxia-induced orgasms had been given an airing after that – how she and Georgie had laughed when she'd phrased it like that. And then there were the side-splitting moments as they'd tried to work out why he'd been wearing only a jacket, shirt and tie, no trousers. Thank God for black humour. It had to be the greatest antidote to loneliness and fear, for those hysterical moments bobbed like life rafts in overpowering tides of despair.

A siren was whooping down Piccadilly as Robin Lindsay came back into the room. Beth's thoughts went to Georgie. She'd be on her way to the Ritz by now, where they'd arranged to drink cocktails while Beth recounted all the details of this meeting. She prayed silently that the siren had nothing to do with Georgie, and struggled to block out the horrible, gruesome images that were pushing their way into her mind. She'd become prone to these irrational fears since her world had turned inside out. She didn't feel anything was to be trusted any more. Everything was going to be taken away, mutilated, ruined; destroyed beyond repair.

'Sorry to have kept you,' Robin Lindsay said, lifting the champagne bottle from its ice bucket and topping up her glass.

Beth's, Ava's, eyes were shining as she watched him return to his chair and fix her with a satisfied smile. 'That call has just decided me on what we should do,' he said.

She waited, allowing a touch of flirtation to beautify her smile.

'I'd like to put your book up for auction,' he told her. 'Do you know what that means?'

Ava nodded calmly, while inside Beth became almost giddy. 'It means you'll give it to several editors and the book will go to the highest bidder.'

He smiled, his ruddy cheeks turning redder. 'I have five editors in mind,' he said. 'Stacey Greene has already put in an offer of one hundred and fifty thousand.'

Though Ava held steady, Beth's euphoria was quietly erupting. It was true that Colin's salary had always been substantial, but she herself had never had any real money of her own. In fact, since she'd left the nursery she'd been living on just over three hundred pounds a month, eking out a small inheritance from her granddad so that she didn't have to go to Colin for all her needs, like make-up and tights! He wouldn't have minded – he was generous to a fault, which was why they had no savings – but she'd just wanted to be able to pay for some things herself. She'd be able to do that now. One hundred and fifty thousand pounds was an unimaginable amount of money to someone who'd never earned more than twenty thousand in a year, and who until today had avoided even thinking about how she was going to manage in the coming months now she was homeless, husbandless and all but jobless too.

'That will be the starting figure,' Robin Lindsay said. 'It should go a lot higher.'

Later, with Georgie, she'd shriek, laugh and throw her arms around in girlish elation. Now, in this respectable office with its low-key ambience and dignified owner, she allowed Ava to suppress Beth's inclinations and smile her own catlike approval.

Robin Lindsay raised his glass. 'I'd like to tell you what a pleasure it is meeting you,' he said, thinking of the husband that had hurt and betrayed her, yet had always gone back to her. He thought he understood why, though it wouldn't necessarily have been for her beauty which, though understated, was exceptional; it would, he suspected, have been for the inner qualities that he could already tell existed in irresistible and mysterious abundance. 'I believe I'm going to enjoy having you as a client,' he told her.

Her eyebrows rose in a gently mocking manner. 'Why thank you,' she responded in a voice that was dark and sensual. 'I'm sure the enjoyment will be mutual.' Their eyes met, and after brazening out the innuendo she said, 'When do you think the auction will happen?'

'Maybe next Friday. I'll call to confirm. Would you like to be here?'

'Yes,' she said. 'Yes, I would.'

Half an hour later Georgie was slumped in a chair at the Ritz, fanning herself with a cocktail menu. 'I think I'm going to faint,' she laughed. 'All that money, and he thinks it'll go higher.'

Beth was laughing too. 'I wish you could have heard the

things he said about the book,' she said. 'They were incredible. If I weren't so modest, I'd repeat them.'

'Just tell me,' Georgie urged. 'I know it's brilliant, because Colin couldn't stop talking about it after he'd read it.'

Beth's eyes flickered away for a moment, but as Georgie touched her hand in apology she forced a smile, then recklessly told the waiter to bring them an entire bottle of Bollinger.

'There's something I need to tell you,' Georgie said.

But Beth wasn't listening. 'It doesn't look as though there'll be a problem with the identity issue,' she said. 'In fact I've asked for my own name to be kept secret at least until after the auction. Hopefully until after the publication too, though Robin Lindsay thinks that'll be harder.' She pulled a face. 'I just don't want people picking over it, analysing it, reading things into it, simply because of who I am. It's just a book. Nothing to do with Colin, or me as his wife. It's about Carlotta – and Ava.'

Georgie's eyes were twinkling. She didn't need to burst the bubble yet. 'So did you try out the Ava character?' she asked.

Beth grinned. 'Yes, a bit,' she answered. 'She has the potential to be quite outrageous, I think.'

'I always knew you did,' Georgie told her. 'She's you, or at least one aspect of you. And now her world is waiting, while the world of Beth Ashby . . .' Her smile suddenly lost its light, and her eyes fell away.

'What?' Beth said, her heart turning over. No more bad news. Please God, don't let anything spoil today. 'What is it?' she pressed.

Georgie took a breath. Her large blue eyes came uncertainly back to Beth's. 'Colin wants to see you,' she said. 'He's calling tonight.'

Beth's face drained. Everything was suddenly different. The road had abruptly ended again, and she could feel herself going into a slow-burning spiral of emotions. 'Why now?' she said. 'Why has he changed his mind?'

'I don't know. Bruce didn't say. I only got the call an hour ago.'

It was a while before Beth could speak, as she tried to imagine what it was going to be like, seeing him in prison, hearing what he had to say, feeling the devastation of his life as though it were her own. He was so much a part of her that it *was* her own. Yet lately he'd started to feel like a stranger. She couldn't quite envisage his face any more, or hear the sound of his voice. 'Why is he calling first?' she asked.

'I imagine to set up your visit.' Georgie paused, then said, 'Will you go?'

Beth blinked in surprise. 'Of course,' she replied. 'Why do you think I wouldn't?'

'What if it coincides with the auction?'

'I don't think that's likely, but if it does the auction can happen without me.'

Though Georgie wasn't surprised by the answer, it still saddened her, for she'd hoped that today's news might have helped Beth to start breaking away. It was what she needed to do for, Bruce was certain, if things continued the way they were going, they'd never get Colin off. Which meant they had to face the fact that he was looking at a life sentence, unless he changed his plea to guilty, and even then, striking some kind of deal with the prosecution wasn't likely. However, she was hardly going to tell Beth any of that right now.

'Will you tell him about the book?' she asked.

Beth was inside her own head. 'I don't know,' she answered distractedly. 'Maybe. But maybe not. I know he's read it, but he's never heard of Ava and, who knows, I might want it to stay that way. At least for now.'

Georgie smiled. On the whole it was an answer she liked, since it meant Beth was prepared to keep something for herself.

Beth smiled too and wondered if Georgie had any idea of how afraid she was now – of herself, of Colin and of what might have changed his mind about seeing her.

Just before seven thirty that evening Bruce and Georgie left Beth alone in the study of their London flat. It was a small room, full of books and papers on the law, with framed photos of Georgie and Blake on the roll-top desk. From the window Beth could see across the street to where a few people were crammed on to a terrace, enjoying the evening warmth and wine.

Ever since Georgie had told her Colin was going to call Beth had been trying to come up with all the reasons why he might have decided on now. Bruce was claiming not to know, though she could tell he was hopeful that this new contact might, in some way, improve their chances of getting him off. It was bizarre how Bruce seemed to want Colin's freedom more than Colin did. Her heart jarred on the thought of him in prison – not only now, today, but for another twenty-five, maybe even thirty years. Her hand went up, as though to stave off the horror.

She looked at the phone. The digital clock beside it showed seven thirty-one. It was already a minute past the time he'd said. Please God, he wasn't going to let her down. He couldn't have brought her to this point only to destroy her all over again. It was going to ring any second. Her heartbeat skimmed the top of her chest. She was so tense her whole body hurt. She tried to imagine what they would say. What did a wife say to a husband who was in prison for killing his girlfriend? A part of her wanted to run away from it, flee into oblivion, but nothing was going to make her get up and leave that room now.

The phone rang.

The noise jolted through her like volts. She stared at it, feeling sick with dread, and so full of relief and love that she wanted to cry. He was so close now, at the other end of the line. All she had to do was pick it up.

'Hello?' she said softly into the receiver.

'Beth? Is that you?' It was his voice, low and intimate, and so profoundly familiar it could break her heart in two.

'Yes,' she answered. 'It's me.'

'How are you?'

She took a breath, but for a moment her voice failed. 'I'm not sure how to answer that,' she finally managed.

'I'm sorry,' he said.

She swallowed hard, and dashed away the tears. 'How are you?' she asked.

There was a pause before he answered and she wondered if someone at his end was listening. 'We need to talk,' he said. 'Will you come?'

She wouldn't turn him down – she couldn't – but nor could she say yes right away. 'Why now? Why not before?' she asked.

'I'm sorry,' he said again. Then after a beat, 'I didn't kill her,

Beth.'

Tears were clogging her throat. She could see his face, tense, pale, needing her to believe him.

'She was dead when I got there,' he said.

She thought of his missing trousers, his hands on the tights, the lack of any evidence to say anyone else had been there before him. She didn't know what to say. Then suddenly all the emotion she'd been struggling to suppress broke through the dam. 'Oh God,' she cried brokenly. 'Colin. Oh God . . .'

'It's all right,' he told her. 'It's going to be all right. We'll get through this.'

But they wouldn't, surely he must know that. Even if he got out of this horrible mess nothing was ever going to be all right again. How could it be?

'Has anyone called you?' he asked.

'You mean from . . . No.'

He was silent, and once again her heart began filling up with despair. She wished she knew how to make this easier for him, but she couldn't. None of his colleagues had called, not even to ask where they might send his personal belongings. She wondered if Bruce had told him that they'd already cleared out his office, and that Alan Dowling had now resumed his former position.

'So will you come?' he asked softly.

'Yes.'

His relief was almost audible and her arms felt heavy with the desire to hold him. 'Bruce will let you know when,' he said. 'He'll bring you.'

They were silent for a few moments then, not knowing what else to say, but not wanting to let go yet. She wondered again who might be listening.

'Will you bring some things for me?' he asked.

'Of course. What do you need?'

'Cigarettes. Phone cards.'

'Is there anything else?' she asked, thinking how pathetic his needs were now.

'No.'

She waited, knowing he was going to tell her he loved her. But then the line went dead and his failure to say it was more heartbreaking than anything else.

Chapter 6

It was gaining fast on midnight and Laurie was exhausted. For more than a week now, whilst whizzing through all her official assignments, which had taken her up and down the country, over to Ireland once and to Holland twice, she'd been trying desperately to find out why no one had run the minicab driver's story. She knew for a fact that Elliot Russell had it, because Pinkton had confirmed it when she'd refrained from clocking him one the day after he'd reneged on giving her the exclusive. So where was it? Why hadn't it made a single paper or broadcast yet?

Obviously it didn't take Sherlock Holmes to deduce that someone was blocking it, but no amount of inveiglement, threats, or even limited begging had so far managed to extract a credible reason from Wilbur as to why Pinkton's story didn't make the grade. After all, she had it now, and if Elliot Russell wasn't going to run with it, there was no reason why they shouldn't. OK, she understood that since the man wasn't prepared to name names it might not be wise to start throwing mud when it might stick on the wrong faces. But it wasn't only about the high-fliers Pinkton claimed to pick up regularly from significant political locales, was it? It was about Sophie Long providing sexual favours in return for money. Now *that* was a story.

So why all the secrecy?

'Laurie, just leave it alone,' was what Wilbur had instructed when she'd taken it to him for the third time in as many days, twice on the phone, then in person. 'It's not for us.'

'Why?' she'd demanded.

'I'm just telling you, leave it alone.'

'Wilbur, for God's sake . . .'

His hawkish face came over the desk at her. 'You don't think someone out there,' he growled, pointing towards the politicos' desks, 'isn't already on this? You think the first time I heard it was when *you* brought it up?'

She flushed at the allusion to her junior, outsider status. 'So just tell me why you're not running it,' she challenged.

'I don't have to tell you anything. Just let it drop and go back to where it's safe.'

At that her eyes boggled. 'Safe?' she repeated.

'From them out there,' he snarled. 'They don't like the way you're treading on their toes, and I don't blame them. You're overstepping the mark, Laurie. You haven't earned your place yet, so don't screw it up before you even get there.'

Her face was taut. 'I come to you with a perfectly good story and you tell me to drop it, because one of those precious baby-boomers, who think they've got a God-given right to the world, might not like me getting there first?'

'I told you, I'm already aware of who, or what, Sophie Long was. It's not going to change anything, so –'

'You're in on the cover-up!' she suddenly cried. 'You're a part of it, aren't you?'

At that his head dropped forward in exasperation. Then sitting back down in his chair he said, 'Laurie, you've got to learn to hold some things in. You're too hot-headed, and outspoken, and it's not doing you any good. Now, take my advice and let this go.'

'What if I can find out who else Pinkton drove?' she challenged. 'If I can get some more names –'

'You'll be wasting your time,' he responded. 'You won't get them, and you could do yourself a lot of harm trying. Now take your backside out of here and don't let me see you again until you've got the five hundred words on Concorde I asked you for first thing this morning.'

And that was as far as she'd got, which wasn't quite a brick wall, but for the little it had told her it might just as well have been. However, it was interesting to know that others in the office were aware of Sophie Long's status, and Pinkton's taxi service, though no one, besides her, it seemed, was trying to get it its place in the sun. She wondered if any of her colleagues on other papers, or in TV were having the same problem, but she could hardly ask when it would be tantamount to tipping them off if they didn't already know about Sophie and Pinkton. So what she needed to find out was why the boomers were happy to sit on the story.

Stretching and yawning, she sat back in her chair, rubbing her tired eyes. She'd heard her parents going to bed a while ago, but knew even if she tried to sleep right now she'd be unable to, for her mind was just too fired up over this. Sophie Long's family had long since returned to their home in Essex, though no one had managed to get near them yet, which was weird when the family in these cases generally had something to say. She'd been calling their number day and night, but to no avail, and every trip out there showed the same thing – the place surrounded by press, but no one even getting close, since the police were guarding the front and back of the house, and there were rumours that not all the helicopters buzzing overhead were weather, traffic and news.

She yawned again. There was a real mystery going on there, with what had happened to that family, where they'd gone during those first days after Sophie's death, and why they'd been so heavily guarded since. She'd give anything to be the one to crack it, though she had to admit the chances of her getting to the Longs before anyone else were about as likely as her getting to the Prime Minister, with whom she wouldn't mind discussing his few decades of friendship with Colin Ashby. However, perseverance was the better part of valour, or something like that, so she wasn't going to stop trying just because she was a no one.

Flipping down the cover on her mobile, she dialled the number to retrieve her messages, and turned back to her computer screen. She needed to find out where she was supposed to be tomorrow so that she could work out how she was going to make it fit in with her Ashby investigations. Not that she'd been officially removed from the Ashby story, but Wilbur was piling her up so high with trivia and dross he might just as well come right out and admit he was blocking her. And sure enough, the first two messages she replayed were from Lucy, the news co-ordinator, telling her what she was down for the next day, which was something about some rat-infested tower blocks in Romford, and a new form of laser eye surgery being carried out at a clinic in Suffolk – both stories located out of London.

Throwing her pen down in disgust she began pacing as she moved on to the third message, which was from Andrew and Stephen, her gay friends from Limehouse, asking her to call back for an offer she couldn't refuse. Making a mental note, she moved on to the fourth message, from Rhona, her closest friend, asking where she'd been lately, and the fifth was from her contact at the Yard who sounded characteristically reluctant to see her, though to her inexpressible delight he was agreeing to.

She was just clicking off the line with a little victory punch into thin air, when she heard the bedroom door open behind her, and turned to see her mother, bleary-eyed and dishevelled from sleep, belting her dressing gown and shaking her head.

'Laurie, for heaven's sake, girl,' she grumbled, her gentle face only partially visible in the semi-light. 'You're driving me nuts, pacing up and down, then tapping away on that computer. Get some sleep, will you?'

'Sorry,' Laurie grimaced. 'Just another half-hour and no pacing. OK? I've still got some prepping to do for tomorrow. Shall I make you some tea?'

'No, I'll make you some cocoa. It might help you switch off. What are you working on, anyway?'

'Oh, just the usual stuff,' she answered, turning back to the screen and reclipping her hair. 'Is Dad awake?'

'No, but he will be if you carry on like this.' Mindy Forbes hesitated, then said, 'Did you call Greg back?'

'No.'

'Laurie, you can't treat him like this. He's –'

'Mum, it's over between us,' Laurie interrupted, 'which is why I'm here, remember? It won't be for long, though. As soon as I've got time I'll find myself a place nearer to the office.'

Mindy looked long into her daughter's face. How, she was wondering, did Laurie manage even to come into this room now, when just to stand in the doorway caused such an ache in her own heart it was as though that terrible event in their lives had happened a mere week ago, rather than a year. But Laurie had her own way of dealing with her twin sister's death, which seemed to entail shutting it out most of the time. It was what had made her choice to return to this room when she'd broken up with her boyfriend so surprising. Mindy had dared to hope that it might prove some sort of therapy, being back in the private world the twins had always shared, but if it had, she had yet to know about it, for Laurie still wouldn't discuss Lysette's death with anyone, not even her father, whom she'd always found it so easy to talk to.

Even without looking round the room Mindy could sense Laurie's chaos, spread out over the twin beds where she and Lysette had slept since they were old enough to have a room of their own. As children they'd been inseparable, even as teenagers they'd done most things together. They were so alike physically it used to turn people's heads in the street, though their characters could hardly have been more different. Mindy had often thought that it was their differences even more than their similarities that had made them so close. They could fight too, like any sisters, but Lysette was always the one to back down first, never Laurie, and it was always Lysette who gave in when they were making such crucial decisions as to which pop idol posters to plaster over their bedroom walls, or which university they should try for, Bristol (Lysette's choice) or London (Laurie's choice and where they'd ended up). But for all Laurie's bull-headedness and domineering ways, Lysette had loved her more than anyone else alive. And the same went for Laurie. Though only ten minutes older, she'd always been fiercely protective of Lysette, constantly shielding her from the beastly world out there that Lysette had never been able to see any harm in. Indeed, it had been as though Laurie's main purpose in life was to make sure nothing bad ever happened to Lysette, which was why this past year had been so very hard on Laurie, since Lysette had taken her own life.

'Mum?' Laurie said softly.

Mindy's eyes had drifted to Joe, her dead daughter's teddy bear, lying on the rose-coloured bedspread that never got turned back now.

Getting up from her chair Laurie came to hug her.

'I still miss her so much,' Mindy sighed tearfully. 'I know you do too.'

Laurie didn't answer, she just held her mother and waited for the moment to pass.

After a while Mindy pulled back, wiping her eyes with her fingers. 'Dad's not getting any better,' she said.

At that Laurie's heart turned over. She wished her mother wouldn't tell her these things; she couldn't bear to hear them. 'He'll be fine,' she said. 'You just fuss too much.'

Mindy smiled. 'I worry about you too,' she said. 'You work too hard. You haven't turned out the light before two o'clock in the last three weeks.'

'There's no need to worry about me,' Laurie assured her. 'I'm fine. I enjoy my work, you know that.'

Mindy cupped her cheek in one hand. Yes, she knew that, but it was an escape too, and Mindy wasn't sure how far she should allow it to go. Not that making Laurie face up to her pain would ever be easy, but the longer this denial went on, the harder it was going to be, especially when her beautiful, headstrong daughter had such a clever and wilful mind of her own. 'Life's for living as well as working,' she said, 'and even if it is over with Greg, there are others out there –'

'Mum, no,' Laurie cut in gently. Living at home was too hard. She had to find somewhere else soon.

Mindy's eyes were still watching her, seeing more than Laurie would want her to. 'Laurie, you know it wasn't your –'

Laurie's fingers pressed against her lips. 'Don't go there, Mum,' she said. 'Not now.'

Resigning herself for the moment, Mindy kissed her on the forehead. 'I'll go and make the cocoa,' she said. 'Try to be finished by the time I come back.'

Moments later Laurie was absorbed in her story again, typing furiously as though the speed of her fingers would somehow help her outrun those last few horrible minutes. She was making herself think about Beth Ashby now, wondering if the pain of her husband's betrayal had left her feeling as though an integral part of her had been damaged, or maybe even lost. That was how she herself felt about Lysette – damaged and unworthy, alone, incomplete, lost without a soul. But this wasn't about her and Lysette.

Nothing would ever be about her and Lysette again. It was about Beth and Colin Ashby, and the fact that Beth surely had to know, or at least suspect, that there was more to Sophie Long's death than was being reported, by the press and by the police. If only she could get Beth to see her, talk to her . . . but she might just as well put her wish list in to Santa for all the headway she was making with the Ashby lawyers. She wondered if anyone had told Beth about Brad Pinkton, or Sophie's real profession. Of course, Beth might not have to be told; she might already know.

'What Beth Ashby does or doesn't know remains locked inside Beth Ashby's head,' Chilton, her police contact, told her when she put it to him the next day. 'But even if she is aware of Sophie Long's real profession, what difference does it make? Her husband still killed the girl, and whether the victim was a sinner or a saint the crime and punishment remain the same.'

Laurie wondered how she'd feel in Beth's shoes, whether she'd want her husband's girlfriend to be a prostitute or a paragon. She thought probably a prostitute; it seemed, oddly, less of a betrayal.

'What about all this ferrying back and forth to orgies Pinkton claims to have done?' she said. 'How is that linked to the murder?'

Chilton shook his head. He was a large man in his mid-fifties, square-jawed and partially bald, with long, cumbersome eyebrows that gave him a permanent scowl. 'Pinkton dropped Ashby off at the flat,' he said, 'and less than fifteen minutes later he was picking up a customer at Paddington Station. There's your link.'

She watched him as he drank. They were in a secluded corner of a dingy North London pub, where they were currently the only clientele. They'd met here once or twice before; Chilton felt comfortable in the place as it was far enough away from the office, and close to his home. As a high-ranking administrative officer with the force, he was an extremely useful contact to have, though she was never in any doubt of how deeply he disapproved of their arrangement, which he would never have entered into were it not for Mindy, his beloved only cousin. It was why Laurie never pushed him too hard, for fear of losing him altogether. However, she had him to thank for the tip-off that had led her to Beth Ashby's front door, and for several other titbits since, so presumably something in him condoned their liaison or he wouldn't be here. 'Will you have another drink?' he offered.

'Tomato juice,' she said. 'What about Pinkton's claims that he drove others?'

'Nothing to support them,' he replied, while signalling the barman to bring another round. 'Which is not to say he's lying . . .'

Laurie waited, confused and vaguely annoyed. Talk about smoke and mirrors. 'So what does it say?' she finally prompted.

'Have you ever heard the name Marcus Gatling?' Chilton asked.

She wrinkled her nose as she thought. 'It seems to ring a bell,' she said. 'Why? Who is he?'

'A very good question. I'd say he's best described as a behind-the-scenes type with a lot of power in places it pays to have it. It's generally known by those who operate in his kind of circles that he's a close friend and adviser to the Prime Minister, but he seeks no publicity and seems to get very little.'

Laurie was immediately intrigued. 'Meaning he has influence with the media too?' she said. 'To keep his name out of lights?'

'Let's just say it's interesting how few people seem to have heard of him, considering how well connected he is.'

She was thinking of Wilbur now, and her thinly veiled orders to back off. Could this mean that they'd originated from a level so high that it made her giddy even to think of it? 'So what's this Gatling character got to do with anything?' she asked.

Chilton waited until the barman had finished setting down their drinks, paid him, then said, 'I want you to understand that you'll never be able to quote me on anything I say here today, not only because it's all off the record, but because I have absolutely nothing to back it up.'

She nodded agreement and understanding.

'There are certain of my colleagues,' he said, staring down

at the full head on his beer, 'who believe that the victims to fit Pinkton's story will be *chosen*.'

Laurie sat with that, slightly stunned that he was telling her something so crucial, and needing some time to assimilate it. 'So are you saying,' she ventured in the end, wanting to get this absolutely clear, 'that someone will decide which of Brad Pinkton's party-going politicians will be named? And even if others were involved, if it suits for them to stay in power, they'll be eliminated from investigations, and very probably from any kind of speculation in the press?'

Chilton's eyebrows were raised, as though impressed.

So far, so good. But she still didn't have it quite in her grasp. 'So Pinkton's story will break,' she said, 'just not yet, and when it does it will have been . . . managed?'

His eyebrows were still up.

Laurie frowned. Of course it was nothing new, stories being managed, or withheld, or even killed altogether. It went on much more than the public knew about, but it was the first time it had happened to one of hers. 'If this Marcus Gatling has the kind of power you're talking about,' she said, 'why doesn't he just stop the story altogether? I mean, why bother creating all these scapegoats when it's just drawing attention to a situation they'd surely rather went away?'

'Another good question,' Chilton commended. 'But we think he sent Brad Pinkton to us for the very purpose of getting the orgy story into the papers.'

Laurie's eyes widened. It took her only a beat to get there, and if she was right in the way she was thinking now, then they weren't looking at a whitewash as she'd suspected earlier, but a smokescreen. 'So by exposing the orgies and allowing a few carefully selected heads to roll as a result, people will think that Colin Ashby's most likely motive for killing Sophie Long was to protect his party-going colleagues from blackmail.'

Chilton watched the barman as he walked to the dartboard and plucked out a set of darts. 'It could certainly be interpreted that way,' he responded.

Laurie lapsed into silence again. This was all way beyond any kind of normal logic, so it wasn't really surprising that she kept lagging behind. And boy, was he making her work for this. Her mobile rang, but she let it go through to messages. Nothing was going to interrupt her now. 'So do you believe that's why Ashby did it?' she asked.

Chilton sipped his beer through the froth at the top of his glass. 'What we think,' he said, 'is what we've always thought – that there's more to this, and someone somewhere is trying to put us on the wrong scent.'

'So the orgy scene is a false trail?' She needed this spelt out.

'We believe so.'

'Which is being laid by this Marcus Gatling.'

'It's all conjecture.'

'Has anyone spoken to him?'

'There's no reason to. There's nothing to link him with anything.'

She was quiet again as her mind raced through just how extraordinary and inflammable this information was. But as Chilton had already said, she couldn't do anything with it when she had no sources to quote and no evidence to support it.

'Why are you telling me all this?' she asked in the end.

'Because you're interested,' he replied. 'And you'll probably find something to do with it, later if not sooner.'

His words sent the thrill of the hunt coursing through her veins. This none-too-subtle encouragement to continue her investigations was telling her: first, that the force must be dealing with its own frustrations with higher authorities and stone walls, and second, that they were prepared to work with the press to uncover what was really going on. She wondered how many more members of her profession were being secretly approached by Chilton's colleagues, for though she'd like to think this was an exclusive, she couldn't fool herself into believing it was. 'So who am I competing with?' she asked.

Chilton frowned.

'Who else is being tipped off about this?'

'As far as I know, no one. Of course I can't vouch for all the officers involved in the case, of which I'm not one, as you know . . .'

'That's a good point,' she said, jumping on it. 'How come you know all this when you're not a part of the investigation?'

He slanted her a look and waited.

'OK, I get it,' she said. They'd presumably chosen someone who wasn't directly involved to approach the press so that nothing could be traced back to the detectives themselves. And to her great good fortune Chilton was their man. Her adrenalin was really starting to flow now. So maybe this *was* an exclusive. Maybe she was going to get the chance to blow the lid off this and . . . And what? She had no Westminster or Downing Street contacts who'd be able to get her this kind of information, and no way could she call on Wilbur, or any of the boomers. Of course, Gino and Flaxie could be relied on, but even between the three of them, they just didn't have the kind of clout that was needed to get any of these allegations to the starting gate, never mind past the post.

As though reading her mind Chilton said, 'I do realize, of course, that you won't be able to go this alone.'

'Tell me about it,' she mumbled. No way was she letting it go, but right now, she wasn't coming up with too many bright ideas on how to get it going. Then something hit her. 'Have you spoken to Ashby's lawyers about any of this?'

He shook his head. 'There's a good chance they're already aware of it. Their client has to be telling them something to help in his own defence.'

'Do you still think Ashby did it?'

'No doubt about it. But the man's pleading not guilty, so we're going to need to be ready for whatever they might throw our way to try and get him off.'

'But you've got proof, material evidence, an eyewitness . . . And what about defence statements? Don't they have to tell you what they know before it goes into court?'

'Not until the case is ready for trial. By then, they could have come up with something that'll get the whole thing thrown out on some kind of technicality, leaving us with egg all over our faces. A powerful man gets caught choking the life out of a twenty-two-year-old girl and the police can't make it stick. How's that going to look? Ashby walks and an innocent girl's family goes unavenged.'

'Speaking of whom,' she said, 'is there any chance you can get me in to see the Longs?'

He shook his head.

She hadn't really expected a yes, but he might be able to tell her where they'd been during those early days. 'They've got to have been in police custody, or protection, or whatever you want to call it,' she said. 'It's the only scenario that makes sense.'

'They were,' he confirmed, 'but as to the exact location, and why . . .' His smile was grim.

'OK,' she said, 'so going back to Marcus Gatling. Who is he exactly, and why is he getting involved in this?'

'He's got business holdings all over the world; his main game is finance. Socially he's thick with everyone that matters from the PM down. He was at Oxford the same time as Ashby and the PM, but he's never pursued a career in politics himself. He's almost certainly behind the funding of the current regime's rise to glory, and as we all know, he who holds the purse strings holds the power.'

'Where's his base?'

'In London he's got two. One on Smith Square, the other in the City.'

Laurie's mind was ticking over so fast she could hardly keep track. 'So what's his plan for Ashby?' she wondered.

'The sixty-four-thousand-dollar question,' he responded with a sigh. 'What is Marcus Gatling up to? On the one hand we've got another Ashby motive looming on the horizon, which, on the face of it, isn't going to help the man at all. But on the other there are twenty-odd years of friendship to consider, which gives rise to anything from simple fraternal loyalty to the sharing of some seriously sensitive knowledge.'

Laurie was mulling it over fast. 'So, is he really planning to let Ashby go down,' she murmured, 'or is he engaging in the kind of illusion that'll have even David Copperfield whimpering in awe?'

Chilton picked up his beer. 'It's all a guessing game, I'm afraid,' he said. 'But I can tell you this: as far as we know Ashby's had only one visitor apart from his lawyers, and that was the night of his arrest. The man turned up in the early hours of the morning with enough credentials to get himself into Ashby's cell –'

'What kind of credentials?' she interrupted.

'Special Branch,' he replied.

Laurie's heart gave an unsteady throb. In Chilton's world it didn't get any higher than that, so this must mean that even within the force itself, secrets were being kept. 'But considering who Colin Ashby is –' she began.

Chilton cut her off. 'You're right,' he said, reading her mind. 'Given Ashby's access to government secrets it's only to be expected that he'd be interviewed by the big boys. They were in on most of the other interrogations too.'

'And it was presumably they who whisked the Longs out of harm's way within hours of the murder?'

Chilton nodded.

They sat quietly for a moment, digesting it all, until Chilton said, 'This has the potential to be big, Laurie. And I mean *big*. You're not going to be able to handle it alone – no one could – so I want to discuss who's going to handle it with you.'

Though she was nodding agreement, her mind wasn't quite with him. 'I'll start by putting more pressure on Ashby's lawyers,' she said. 'I need to see him, talk to him myself, if I can. At the very least I need a face-to-face with them.'

'Laurie, you're not experienced in this,' he said, staying with his theme. 'You've got the break, but you need someone to help you –'

'Gino and Flaxie –'

'Not Gino and Flaxie,' he interrupted. 'You need a *serious* player. Someone with the right contacts, the influence, the back-up –'

'No!' she suddenly broke in. Her eyes were glittering hard; her mouth was tight with anger. 'I know who you're talking about and the answer's, not even if my life depended on it.'

His expression was quite sober. 'It might,' he responded.

Her eyes flashed her surprise.

'Sophie Long is dead,' he reminded her, 'and frankly we don't know why.'

Laurie looked at him, unable to argue with that.

'There are likely to be a lot of risks involved in trying to find out,' he said, 'so what I'm saying is, let someone like Elliot Russell take them. He's used to them, the man thrives on them, and, believe me when I tell you, you'll end up being a serious liability, even a danger to yourself, if you don't get his help.'

Laurie's lips were pale, her hands were shaking. 'I can see right through this,' she seethed. 'You've played me for a fool, haven't you? You never had any intention of giving me this story. You're just using me as a way of making contact with Elliot Russell, so that no one in your precious outfit can be accused of leaking the information to him themselves.' Her temper was flaring out of control. 'So what do you do? You call in naïve, stupid little me with my big-time ambition and schoolgirl bravado and hook me up as the bait to land the biggest barracuda in newspaper history. My God, that *you*, of all people . . . Knowing what you know, what he did to my family . . . I can't believe you'd be this insensitive. Well, I'll tell you this, Chilton! You can forget it, because no way am I taking it to him. Do you hear me? No way. Never. *Not ever!*'

Chilton blinked his way through the outburst, then took another sip of his drink. 'So you still haven't forgiven him,' he commented, apparently unmoved by it all.

She was so angry now she was close to storming out, but with supreme effort she managed to keep her voice to a virulent hiss. 'Lysette would be alive now if it weren't for that man,' she seethed. 'You know that as well as I do. And my father wouldn't be hanging on to his life by a thread because of it.'

'How is Dennis?' he asked, referring to her father.

'I just told you, he's still suffering. He'll never get over it.'

Chilton's eyes were fixed on his drink. 'That was a terrible way to lose a child,' he said. 'Terrible.'

'So why are you trying to make me work with the man who caused it?'

'Russell wasn't –'

'It's a fact!' she cried. 'Everyone knows it.'

'OK. Have it your way. But I'm afraid the deal is, you either forget everything we've discussed here today, or you get Elliot Russell on your side.'

'Not him!' she snarled. 'There are others . . .'

'No one else has the resources or contacts.'

'Don't be ridiculous, of course they do.'

'Not in the freelance world, and we've already agreed that strings can be pulled in the Establishment. Especially in the Establishment, which *you* in your job are a part of. Now, I'm not going to sit here arguing. You either take this to Russell with your own set of conditions on how you can be cut in on the action, or we'll get someone else to do it. I've got to tell you

94

that giving any of it to you is against my better judgement, but I know how difficult they've been making it for you on that paper, and you deserve a break. So don't screw this up, because if you do, you won't even want to think about the kind of hell you'll be paying.' He drained his glass and got to his feet. 'I'll call you in a couple of days. And next time we meet, do me a favour, turn off that damned phone.'

After he'd gone Laurie ordered herself a large vodka and gulped half of it down in one go. She then took out her notebook ready to jot down the messages that had been piling up since she got here. Her blood was still boiling. Just no way was she going to Elliot Russell with this; she'd rather tie her head to a moving car and try running. But she damned well wasn't going to give it up either. She needed a conference with Gino and Flaxie. Between them, they'd surely be able to come up with some kind of strategy, a workable plan on how they could start infiltrating the hallowed corridors of power. She also needed to make yet another call to Colin Ashby's lawyers; also to Brad Pinkton; to Georgie Cottle in the vain hope of getting through to Beth Ashby; and she'd work out later whether or not she should mention anything to Wilbur, just in case he might have the odd contact or two he'd be willing to toss her way. However, recalling what Chilton had said about Establishment, Wilbur probably wasn't a good bet.

On the point of dialling up her messages, she took another fortifying sip of vodka, then barked into the receiver as the mobile rang.

'Laurie? It's me,' Flaxie said. 'I've just heard that Beth Ashby's due to visit the prison tomorrow at eleven.'

Laurie's heart tightened its beat. 'How do you know?' she said.

'I got a call.'

'From whom?'

He paused. 'Murray Cox,' he confessed.

Laurie's whole body stiffened. 'Are we talking about the same Murray Cox?' she demanded.

'From Elliot Russell's office, yes,' he confirmed.

Inside Laurie was screaming. Why did this man's name keep coming up? Wasn't it a big enough world to make sure they never saw each other again? 'Why did Murray call you?'

she demanded. 'Why would he give you that information?'

'I don't know,' Flaxie answered. 'He called here about five minutes ago wanting to speak to you, actually, but when I told him who I was he gave me the information instead.'

Laurie was still livid. 'Why?' she snarled. 'It doesn't make any sense.'

'We're asking the same questions,' Flaxie told her. 'I don't have any answers either. All I know is what I just told you. Beth Ashby's going to the prison tomorrow.'

'Then one of us should be there,' she stated.

'Not you. Wilbur's got you down for a happy birthday Eurostar.'

Laurie's jaw clenched in disgust. 'I'll work something out,' she retorted. 'What else?'

'Nothing. Oh, your mates Andrew and Stephen are trying to get hold of you. Apparently they're going to New York for three months and want you to take care of their house and cat while they've gone.'

Now that was the kind of news Laurie could float off to heaven on, since Andrew and Stephen's funky three-storey townie was not only like a second home to her and the rest of their friends, but was also a maximum ten-minute walk along the river from the office. 'I'll call them right away,' she said. 'Did my mother ring back, by any chance?'

'No.'

'Then there's probably a message on the mobile. My dad was going in for more tests today. Anyway, if Murray Cox or anyone else calls again, you can reach me on this number.'

'Where are you?'

'On my way to do a stupid piece on some stupid blocks of flats in Romford that're about to be condemned. Tell Gino we need to talk. I should be back at the office around five. Before you go, when did you say Beth Ashby was due to visit the prison?'

'Tomorrow morning. Eleven o'clock.'

She thought about the source, detesting it and not at all understanding it when there was no reason in the world why Elliot Russell would give her this kind of information. However, she obviously had to act on it, and if there was some kind of price to pay later, she'd deal with it then.

Chapter 7

Beth was lying on the floor in the back of Bruce's car. Her eyes were closed, her body jammed between the seats with the scent of new leather and carpet filling her nose. The unsteady motion, and jarring into her side, were making her feel sick. She detested the press for forcing this indignity on her, though in a way it was to punish them, depriving them of even the shadowiest shot as she entered the prison. God only knew who had tipped them off – probably someone inside, an officer, another inmate. Did they have any idea how miserable their constant intrusion was making her life? Did they even care? All that mattered to them was the fact that Beth Ashby was visiting her husband for the first time since his arrest. It should be all that mattered to her too, but she had to get through this humiliation first.

After a while Bruce brought the car to a stop and came round to open the door. She looked up at him, blinking at the sun's glare. She felt foolish and resentful, though anxiety was already moving in like a prowler.

'No one can see you here,' he told her. 'They let us park out of the way, but I'll have to wait outside. These are normal visiting hours – not for lawyers.'

Allowing him to help her up, she climbed out of the car and brushed herself down. She was wearing a long tan dress with a brown leather belt and sandals – nothing fancy, though she'd taken care with her hair and make-up, wanting to remind Colin that she could make herself beautiful, and that she wanted to for him.

Bruce led her to the gate lodge, where they were ushered into a kind of waiting room. There were at least two dozen people already there, and children too, waiting for their own snatched hour with cohorts or loved ones. Beth's heart twisted with dismay. She'd never encountered people like this at such close quarters. Almost immediately she was afraid of them, for their stares were hostile and mocking, and their sneering asides about her were obviously meant to be heard. A tall, fat woman with a shorn head, silver studs in her ears and nose, and tattoos on her arms, gave her a leering look, then waggled her tongue crudely. Beth blushed and dropped her eyes as several people sniggered.

Bruce's hand tightened on her arm.

There were others in the waiting room who appeared as well-dressed and awkward as she did, but none of them sought eye contact. Mainly they stared at the notices and leaflets on the walls, all of which seemed to bear aggressive reminders of who ruled this establishment. Wandsworth's prison officers weren't known for their humanity to inmates, or visitors, and already Beth could sense an undercurrent of violence that seemed to seep not only from the arrogant notices, but from the very walls they were hung on.

After a while two guards came to release the visitors from their temporary confinement. Bruce gave her a quick hug, then watched her as, white-faced and cautious, she moved forward with the group. Suddenly an elbow slammed into her ribs, and she grunted with pain. The woman with the shaved head stepped in front her, blocking her view as they continued after the guards. Beth held back, trying to distance herself from the woman, but was jostled and derided by those trying to get past her.

It was so horrible and terrifying and demeaning that she wanted to run back to Bruce. But she made herself think only of Colin and pressed on. She tried to concentrate on how she felt about seeing him, but now she was here she seemed to have lost contact with herself, as well as the world outside. She was suddenly horribly afraid of how he was going to look. Would she be able to keep the shock from her face if it was bad?

Dread was binding itself tighter and tighter round her heart as they proceeded along corridors and through double-locked doors. It was like tramping towards the dead end of a netherworld. She thought of the dazzling sunlight outside, shining down on the outer shell of this dreadful place. The eerie Victorian gloom was even worse than she'd imagined.

Then they were there, herding into the visitors' room. Twenty or more men, prisoners, were seated at small square tables, like oversized pupils at their desks. The air was rank with old cigarette smoke and stale body odour. Beth looked around as her group started to fracture and move out between the tables. *Colin. Colin, where are you?*

Then she saw him, on the other side of the room, at a table up against the wall. It was a man she didn't know who looked like her husband. He signalled for her to come forward. Torn between resistance and longing, she began weaving through the tables, excusing herself as she tried to pass, apologizing profusely when she accidentally bumped someone hard. Then she was standing over him, looking down at him, but instead of the prolonged, urgent embrace and breathless relief she'd expected, he merely took her hands and guided her to the chair on the other side of his table.

Her heart was so full she could only look at him, while inwardly she railed and recoiled from the gauntness of his cheeks and bruising shadows round his eyes. The laughter lines that seeped into his cheeks now seemed etched with pain, the touches of grey in his hair had become thick, burrowing streaks. It was badly cut, his chin was roughly shaved. She didn't recognize the brown T-shirt and dun-coloured trousers he was wearing. He'd never owned clothes like that before. She guessed Bruce had brought them, as this was no place for Colin's natural sartorial elegance. She wished she knew what to say, but for the moment she could only cling to his hands and stare into his unnervingly distant eyes.

'How are you?' he said.

She let her breath go, and tightened her grip on his hands. 'I'm fine. You look . . .' She bit her lips as they trembled.

'I know,' he said. 'It's one of the reasons I didn't want you to come.'

Odd memories began flashing through her mind: times of laughter, love, anger, excitement. The way he touched her face in affection, and gazed into her eyes with humour. The crazy way he'd twirl her round in moments of triumph, then

99

hold her close when desire arose. She saw their faces twisted with anger, heard their voices full of reproach. So much hurt, anguish, tears and reprisals. She felt suddenly giddy with the power of her love. What was going through his head now, she wondered. What was really in his heart?

There were so many words she longed to hear, but when finally he spoke all he said was, 'You've lost weight.'

She was suddenly finding it hard to breathe. She stared down at their hands and fought the surging dread inside her. *Please God, this wasn't how it was going to be from now on; only ever seeing each other in a place like this, never able to share anything beyond it again, always struggling to find the right words.*

He placed his fingers under her chin and tilted her face up to his. She could barely see him through the tears, though she forced a smile. 'I'm trying to be strong for you,' she said, 'but I don't think I'm doing very well.'

'Be strong for yourself,' he told her. 'I don't want you to worry about me.'

Her eyes were incredulous. 'How can I not?' she whispered. 'Thinking of you here, of what's happening . . . I never think about anything else.' She swallowed hard, then flinched as a woman nearby suddenly erupted from her seat and began screaming obscenities at the gorilla of a man she was visiting. The man loomed over her, threatening all kinds of violence, until a guard moved swiftly to break up the row, and the woman was escorted out.

Colin and Beth turned back to each other. 'That's another reason I didn't want you to come,' he said. 'It's a terrible place. I didn't want you to see me here.'

'But you won't stay,' she told him. 'You can't.'

His tired, bloodshot eyes were holding tight to hers. 'Beth, we can't pretend –'

She drew back. 'No. No. Don't say it.'

'You have to listen,' he told her harshly. 'This isn't going to go away.'

'It has to. You have to make it. I don't know what you've done . . .'

Anger tightened his grip on her hands. 'Do you think I did it?' he demanded in a whisper. 'Do you think I'm capable of killing another human being?'

She stared down at his hands and saw them strangling a young girl to death.

'Did you say that?' he urged bitterly. 'What it said in the paper? Was that really your first question, "Who did he kill?"?'

Her eyes came up to his.

His face twisted with disgust. 'That you, my own wife –'

'Of course I don't believe you did it,' she hissed. 'But what am I supposed to think when all I know is what they've told me.'

'And what did they tell you? That I was caught in the act? The tights wrapped round my hands, body still warm beside me, half my clothes missing?' His drawn, handsome face was paling as memory clouded his eyes. She could smell the familiar aroma that was him, feel the life pulsing through his veins, the anguish and fear drowning his heart.

'Yes, that's what they told me,' she said.

A lit match landed on the table between them. She heard someone snickering nearby. Without looking up Colin pinched the flame with his fingers, then returned his eyes to hers. 'It's all true,' he said.

Her heart caught on the words, but before she could speak he said, 'Except being caught in the act. She was already dead. When I found her, she was already . . .' He didn't repeat the word.

Her chest was tight, her mind was reeling, becoming entangled in the deafening acoustics of the hall, the scream and clatter of the children, garble of voices . . . 'Then what happened?' she said, struggling to keep herself focused.

He swallowed hard, then rubbed his hands over his face as though to push away the tiredness and confusion. 'This isn't going to be easy,' he said. 'I mean for you. For either of us. But I want you to know the truth, insofar as I know it myself.' He took several breaths, as though drawing in courage. Then, reaching for her hands again, he continued, 'I met Sophie Long at a party one night, six weeks, maybe two months ago –'

'I've heard the rumours of a prostitution ring,' she interrupted. 'Was she one of them?'

'The ring exists,' he told her. 'And yes, she was a part of it.'

101

'So you paid her?'

'Yes, I paid her. Sometimes. Not always.'

'Meaning you were so good she'd give it to you for free?'

'Beth, please, I know this is hard, but right now what I did with Sophie, whether I paid her or not, just isn't relevant.'

'It is if she was blackmailing you. Were you paying her for that?'

'She wasn't blackmailing me. She had nothing to blackmail me about.'

'You don't think this orgy scene was –'

'She wasn't blackmailing me,' he cut in. 'Not about that, or anything else.'

Her eyes were smouldering with resentment, but in the end she managed to let it go and told him to continue.

'When you changed the locks, that last time,' he said, 'I went to stay with Sophie. Just for a few nights. Her flat was –'

'I don't want to know about her flat,' she interrupted. 'Just tell me what happened that day.'

He nodded, then drew a hand over his face as though to loosen the tension. 'Sophie and I had developed this little – *game* I suppose you could call it, or routine. When she knew I was about to arrive she'd go into the bedroom to wait. Sometimes she'd undress and sometimes not. On that day she did. My role was to come into the flat, take off my own clothes, or at least some of them, and go to find her. So that's what I did that day. I let myself in at the front door, removed my trousers and underpants, and went into the bedroom to find her.'

Beth was staring at his neck, the dark bristles and bobbing Adam's apple, and thinking of how often she had kissed that neck, stroked it and loved it.

'Her eyes . . .' he said, his voice so low she could hardly hear him. 'I saw straight away . . . I knew something was wrong. Her face was . . .' He stopped, seeming unable to continue.

'I saw the tights,' he eventually continued, 'around her throat. I tried to unwind them. I thought she might still be alive. Then the door opened and the cleaning woman came in. She took one look at us and started to scream. I tried to calm her down, but she ran out of the flat, yelling that she knew who I was and she was going to call the police. I think she

102

went to the flat opposite, I'm not sure. I thought about getting out of there, but she'd recognized me, and if I didn't stay, well, how was it going to look?' He laughed bitterly. 'No better than it does now, I guess. So I dressed and waited for the police to arrive.'

Beth looked at him. Though her heart was pounding she was barely connecting to his words. She felt disoriented and sick. She knew she needed to respond, but she couldn't make her mind work. Suddenly a huge wave of longing and denial swept through her. She didn't want to lose him. She wanted only for none of this to have happened.

'It's the way it happened,' he said softly. 'I swear.'

She looked at him briefly, then gazed down at her hands.

'Do you believe me?' he asked.

She took a breath, nodded, then put a hand to her head. 'Yes, I believe you,' she gasped. Her breath was becoming ragged, her chest hurt, and she was suddenly afraid she was going to have another attack of the kind she had had in Georgie's car.

'Beth, are you OK?' he asked. 'Take it steady. Breathe deeply.'

'I'm OK,' she responded. 'I just . . . I keep getting these feelings . . . It's as though I'm losing control . . . Oh God, why is this happening?'

'Sssh,' he soothed. 'It's all right. Just calm down. Everything's going to be all right.'

Her eyes were suddenly harsh. 'Tell me how!' she cried in a whisper. 'You say you didn't kill her, you want me to believe you didn't kill her, but you were the only one there.'

'I swear, I didn't kill her,' he responded.

'Then tell me who did.'

'I don't know who did.'

She took a few more breaths, trying to keep herself steady. 'So who do you *think* could have killed her?' she asked.

'I don't know.'

Her hands went to her head in frustration. 'Then who would want to?' she cried.

'I don't *know!*' His eyes darted towards those who were closest, as though to check if they'd heard. 'I've got no idea,' he said. 'What about you?'

Her eyes dilated at she looked at him in horror. 'Me?' she cried. 'How would I know who did it? I'd never even heard of the girl until all this happened.'

'So no one's been to see you. Tried to contact you?'

'Like who? Oh my God, Colin! It's no wonder I'm losing my mind. *What* is going on? What about this prostitution ring . . .'

'It's got nothing to do with that,' he cut in. 'It's a red herring. I knew they'd use it.'

'Who're they?' she demanded. 'You say you don't know who'd want to kill her, then you start talking about *they*!'

He didn't answer.

'Colin, you have to tell me.'

He stared hard into her eyes, watching her search every line on his face as though in one she might find what he was concealing. In return he was wanting to be sure she was holding nothing back from him.

In the end she said, 'It's Gatling, isn't it? He's behind this –'

He cut her off swiftly, eyes shooting to one side to see if she'd been heard. 'Don't ever let anyone hear you say that,' he hissed. 'For your own good. Don't even let his name past your lips where this is concerned.'

'Do you think it was him who did it?' she asked bluntly.

'No. Just leave it!' he told her.

'Why would he do it?'

'Beth, please, don't get yourself any more involved than you already are.'

'But I'm not involved. I don't know what happened, except what you've just told me, and that doesn't answer anything.'

'You're involved because you're my wife,' he said harshly. 'They're going to assume you know things.'

'What kind of things?'

He only looked at her.

She looked at him too, her eyes showing frustration and anguish. 'So you're just going to stay here, in this place,' she said, as his head bowed, 'rotting away, while *that bastard* –'

'Beth, stop!' he hissed. 'Don't even think about him. Do you hear me? Forget he exists.'

'And what about you? Do I forget you exist too?' she snapped angrily.

'Yes,' he answered. 'That's exactly what you do.'

It took a moment for his answer to register. Then shock sent her mind reeling again.

'I want you to leave here and start a new life,' he went on. 'I want you to do it now, today.'

'You don't mean that,' she said.

'I've never been more serious about anything. It's over between us – it has to be. I have nothing left to give you that you need. I'm no good for you now. It's time for you to move on.'

Despite the horror of his words, their unthinkable meaning, her mind was suddenly blocked by Ava and the auction that was happening tomorrow. For one wild moment she almost threw it at him, wanting him to know that she already had a life and didn't need to be told by him to get one! But love and fear quickly overwhelmed the urge. She didn't want to hurt him. She didn't want to lose him either.

'You think I'd do that?' she said. 'Just walk out on you now?'

'You have to,' he responded. 'I want you to.'

Her face showed the strain of the hurt. 'You want me to?' she repeated. 'What does that mean?'

'It means what I said, that I want you to walk out of here now and start a life of your own. One that doesn't include me.'

'Why would I do that?' she cried. 'Why would I even want to? You're my husband, I love you. No matter what you did –'

His eyes turned stony.

'That doesn't mean I think you did it,' she cried hastily. 'I'm just saying, even if you had, it wouldn't change the way I feel about you.'

He was about to speak again when a small, scruffy woman in a skimpy Lycra top and torn jeans sauntered past them, saying to Beth, 'Why don't you get down on your knees and suck him off, bitch – give us something worth watching.'

Heat rose to Beth's cheeks.

'Unzip it, and I'll give him one,' another woman offered, and the room dissolved into laughter.

Beth's face was scarlet as she waited for Colin to open his eyes.

'I don't want you to come here again,' he said roughly.

'Because you think I can't handle that? Colin –'

'It would just be better if you stay away now, for your own good. I can't bear to see you having to endure this place. You mustn't ever come here again.'

'Then why did you tell me to come today?'

'Because you deserved to hear what happened from me.'

'I deserved to hear from you the day it happened,' she spat. 'And I deserve a full picture.'

They glared at each other, anger and pain loading the air, years of knowing each other linking them like chains. For a long time neither of them spoke, then suddenly a guard announced that visiting time was over.

Beth watched, dumbfounded, as Colin, her husband, the stranger, got to his feet. It didn't seem possible that someone could make him walk away from her, or that he had no choice but to go. Their lives were being torn apart and neither of them had the power to stop it. She wondered if she'd be allowed to embrace him, but when she tried to get up her legs were too weak to support her.

He was looking down at her. The guard was moving up behind him, watching.

'Colin, we can't leave it like this . . .'

'I'm sorry,' he said, touching her face. 'I never wanted to hurt you, but it's all I ever seem to do. Get a divorce –'

'No! Colin, wait . . .'

'Get it for your own sake.'

'I don't want a divorce.'

He was already turning away. At last she was on her feet. 'Colin!' she cried, lunging after him.

'Time to go,' the guard said, stepping between them.

'But I have to –'

'Next visit,' he barked.

She tried to move past him. Colin was still walking away. She called him again, but he didn't turn round. Several voices echoed hers, mimicking her distress. An ugly, scarred man blew her a kiss and rubbed his groin. Another wolf-whistled, then gave her the fist. Others were telling her graphically what they wanted to do to her. The women were laughing. The guards were shouting.

Ten minutes later she was lying on the floor of Bruce's car as he drove them away from the prison. This time the humiliation and anger were escaping her as she gazed at the threads of black carpet and thought of the fine stubble on Colin's neck. His parting words were still in her ears, but she wasn't fighting them now. She was simply numbed by them, exhausted from the emotional battle, lying still and limp, listening to the burr of the engine, the occasional swish of a passing car.

Bruce was speaking to her, telling her she could get up, but she couldn't think about what he was saying, couldn't make herself move. All she knew was the helplessness and confusion of having no control over events now. The power of whether or not she saw him again lay wholly with him, and she was terrified that he'd meant what he said. He didn't want her there again. She didn't understand it. Why was he withdrawing into that terrible place and shutting her out? Surely to God he wanted to get out, so why wasn't he fighting? Because of Marcus Gatling? Would he actually give up on their marriage, and his freedom, because of what that one man might do? But what could Gatling do? What the hell was going on between them that Colin would actually give up his life for, rather than tell? But it wouldn't just be Gatling, would it? It would be Gatling's wife, Leonora. Leonora, the statuesque, cut-glass beauty whose charm and ambitions curled like tendrils round her goals, choking the very life from whomever she used before slithering lethally on.

Elliot Russell was sitting with his feet up on his desk, hands locked behind his head, laughing as three members of his élite team spun a raucous tale from a story they'd been investigating on a rail scam that was going to make prior outrage over derailments and timetables look like a little boy's five-minute paddy. The other four members of the team, all journalists too, were out either following up leads Elliot had given them, or chasing contacts and stories of their own.

The spacious, river-view offices on Westferry Road, just a couple of streets from the Canary Wharf tower in Docklands, were on the third floor of a new, sand-brick block, facing west into the dazzling afternoon sun. Behind Elliot, Murray Cox, his persónal assistant and general manager, was lowering the blinds, while talking rapidly into the phone. Murray was almost never off the phone, generally fielding calls for Elliot, taking in information, or setting up various meetings and assignations his boss needed to attend. He was the lynchpin of Elliot's organization, so was treated with utmost respect by everyone from editors, to high-ranking police officers, to government officials, to gangland *hoi polloi* who occasionally forgot themselves and threatened to incapacitate his kneecaps or blow out his brains if he didn't put them on to Elliot *now!* Murray was rarely impressed. Working for Elliot gave him a standing and a security he'd never in a million years have achieved running the desk at a daily tabloid, from whence Elliot had plucked him, so there weren't many situations that could unnerve Murray Cox now.

Ending one call and immediately picking up another, he turned to his computer screen and accessed their twenty-four-hour Internet connection. Behind him Elliot was listening attentively now, as Gail, Jed and Jerome got down to the more serious elements of their findings. Murray already had three editors on ice for the story, but Elliot would conduct the negotiations that decided who got it in much the same way as he conducted everything around here – with a will of iron, and a manner of somewhat deceptive *laissez-faire*.

Right now Elliot's sloping black eyebrows were connected in a frown as he listened to Gail's suggestions on how they should angle the story. Beneath them his sharp grey eyes were narrowed in concentration, while his thin mouth pursed at the corners. He was a tall, broad-shouldered man with a shock of rough dark hair and a good physique, but his oddly chiselled cheekbones and crooked nose left him, in the classic sense at least, far short of handsome. However, his smile was a winner, as was his creditable lack of arrogance considering the kind of success he was enjoying in such a notoriously cutthroat business. That wasn't to say he couldn't be ruthless, difficult, demanding, and even downright aggressive when the mood took him, and everyone who worked for him knew, one mistake was OK, two you were out.

'So how're you going to back this up?' he said to Jerome, who'd just presented Railtrack's latest list of woes that were still, they thought, under wraps.

'We're working on the source to come up with more names,' Jerome answered, his taut, bearded face showing signs of exhaustion. 'We were out there at Didcot, Bracknell and Dorking last night. It seems to be happening the way he's telling it. Or not happening, as the case may be, so we've got our own eyewitness accounts.'

Elliot was pensive. 'I'll put you in touch with someone at Thameslink,' he said. 'He might be able to fill in some blanks. When do we need to move on this?'

'Soon,' Gail answered, using her copious red hair to fan the back of her neck. 'Two days tops.'

Elliot was about to respond when Jed, who'd been rocking back and forth on two legs of his chair, suddenly vanished over the back of it.

Murray's voice cut into the laughter. 'Elliot. Priority One, line three,' he shouted.

Elliot's eyebrows went up, as swinging his feet to the floor he reached for the phone. 'Elliot Russell,' he said into the receiver.

The others were silent. Priority Ones didn't happen very often. Elliot's eyes moved across their faces as he listened to the voice at the other end. Only he and Murray would know the identity of the person he was speaking to, though neither would ever speak his name.

The call was over in less than a minute. Elliot had scribbled two numbers on to the notepad in front of him. Ripping the page free he said to Murray, 'When was Sam last in here?'

'First thing this morning,' Murray answered.

Elliot looked round the large, airy room with all its hi-tech wizardry and low-tech necessities. With so many gizmos and gadgets out there these days, the electronic bugging of an office or a phone line was about as difficult to set up as the nightly news on a VCR. As a result he'd taken to having this place, along with his home and car, swept on a regular basis, for the rivalry, not to mention money, involved in news exclusives had turned more than one of his freelance colleagues into a budding James Bond.

'OK,' he said, satisfied that no one but those present could hear. 'We've got an in with Sophie Long's family, and a lead to someone by the name of Heather Dance.'

'And Heather Dance is . . .?' Gail prompted.

'Another mistress.'

They all groaned. There'd been enough mistresses in the Ashby affair to swell ten men's egos, and none of them had had anything interesting to say yet.

Elliot waited for them to remember that this had come from a Priority One source. That alone made it different. He then toyed with the idea of telling them *why* it was different, but took a quick decision not to. He'd keep it to himself while he puzzled out the reason he'd been given this information now. In fact, had it come from one of a dozen other sources he might not be so suspicious, but coming from this one it was hard to be anything but.

Telling them to go on with the rail story for now, he turned to Murray and spoke with him quietly, finding out how much the source had told him. It turned out Murray knew as much as he did, which was good. 'OK, get me a printout of the profile on Gatling, Mr and Mrs,' he said.

'Done,' Murray responded, already tapping in the relevant keys.

'Better still, transfer it to my palm-pilot.'

'Rerouting,' Murray confirmed, hitting more keys.

'It's going to take a few days to get this in the works,' Elliot continued. 'See if you can get anywhere with Ashby's lawyers. Keep trying for the man himself, or his wife. In this instance, we'd probably rather have his wife.'

Murray was typing up his orders.

After a moment Elliot said, 'Did you get any comeback from Laurie Forbes on the prison visit?'

'Negative,' Murray responded.

Elliot was pensive. 'Who covered it for us?' he asked.

'Liam. It's in today's *Guardian*. We've also had pick-ups from France, Germany and Australia.'

Elliot nodded, then turned back to his desk. 'Did Laurie Forbes get a by-line in her paper for the story?' he asked.

Murray's face was impassive. 'Yes,' he answered.

110

'So she was there. OK, put a call in to her tonight,' he continued. 'I'm going to the New Forest first thing, give her my mobile number and tell her to call.'

Still Murray's expression showed no sign of receiving anything other than run-of-the-mill instructions.

'What do you want to do about Sophie Long's family?'

'Leave it with me.' Elliot got to his feet, threw his jacket over one shoulder and pocketed his mobile and palm-pilot. 'I'm going to see a man about a dog,' he said. 'You know where to get hold of me.'

Only after the door had closed behind him did Murray allow an eyebrow to drift. Never, after all that had happened, had he imagined his boss having anything to do with the Forbes family again, but Elliot was nothing if not an enigma.

And that wasn't all that had Murray's curiosity piqued on this benignly sunny afternoon in June, while birds were singing in the trees outside and boats were gliding up and down the river. It was the information they'd just received from Priority One, not so much because of what it was, but because it had come at all. Obviously it was going to serve someone's purpose somewhere, and the mystery of who, and how, had to be perplexing Elliot every bit as much as it was Murray. However, that was nothing to what it was going to do to poor Beth Ashby, if what they'd just heard was true, and since Murray had no reason to believe it wasn't, he could only feel for the woman when she opened the morning paper a couple of days from now.

Chapter 8

'OK, are you ready?' Robin Lindsay cried, making ready to open the champagne.

'Ready,' Ava laughed, holding the pen over the last page of her new contract and looking into the camera Robin's assistant, Caroline, was holding.

'Stacey, move in a bit,' Caroline instructed.

Stacey Greene, Ava's new editor, stepped in closer to Ava, putting a proprietorial hand on her shoulder. Her shiny grey bob framed a jovial face with small brown eyes, apple cheeks and a permanently smiling mouth. Beside Ava's glamorous figure-skimming white dress, with its wide shoulder straps, low, but discreetly cut bodice and scalloped knee-length hemline, her own ankle-length wrap-over appeared quite lamentably drab. But she certainly wasn't there to upstage her new author, nor could she even if she tried. No one had told her quite how lovely Beth Ashby – or Ava Montgomery – was in the flesh, certainly none of the newspaper shots had suggested it, and it was unusual for Robin Lindsay, who had an eye for the ladies, to hold back on such detail.

'OK, Robin, make with the cork,' Caroline instructed, after clicking a few shots of the preparation. 'Stay with the contract and pen, Ava.'

The cork popped, everyone cheered, and Robin quickly filled the four flutes on his desk. After handing one each to Ava and Stacey, he picked up his own and went to stand between them. 'So here we go! The big signing!' he declared. 'Put the ink on the page, Ava.'

Ava touched the gold pen to the signature line. It was a Mont Blanc that Georgie had given her as a surprise that morning. *Amazing,* she was thinking to herself, as Caroline started clicking away. She was actually signing a contract with a major publishing house that wasn't only going to provide publication for her novel, but was going to turn her financial difficulties into financial dreamland.

'Great!' Caroline declared. 'The moment's suitably captured on film.'

'Then let's drink a toast to our new rising star,' Stacey suggested, beaming a smile up into Ava's face.

'To Ava and *Carlotta's Symphony,'* Robin said, holding his glass high.

'To Ava and *Carlotta's Symphony,'* Stacey echoed.

They clinked glasses, Caroline snapped some more, then picked up her own drink. 'To you, and your absolutely brilliant book,' she gushed to Ava. 'I was spellbound.'

Ava's smile was quietly dazzling. Her dark eyes were suffused with laughter, and her lightly tanned olive skin glowed. How wonderful and easy it was to be this other person when there was no one around who knew her. 'Thank you,' she responded, in Ava's lush, guttural tones. 'All of you, thank you.'

'The rest of the team is eager to meet you,' Stacey pronounced happily. 'Most of them have already read the book; the others will have finished by the time you come into the office. It's causing quite a stir. As I told you when we spoke on the phone, I was especially impressed with the way you've turned life itself into the villain of the piece, rather than death. Quite extraordinary. Mesmerizing. Well done, you,' and she clinked Ava's glass again.

'Thank you.' Ava smiled graciously. Then after sipping her champagne she said, 'The rest of the team, who are they exactly?'

'Sales, publicity, marketing. The top –'

'Publicity?' Ava looked at Robin. 'Didn't you tell –'

'It's OK,' Robin assured her. 'Stacey's not talking about personal publicity.'

'Oh, no, no, no,' Stacey laughed. 'We quite understand your reasons for shunning the limelight, though it has to be said, the sales –'

'I know what it would do to sales if people knew who I

really was,' Ava cut in, 'but if the book's as good as you say . . .'

'Oh, it is! It is!' Stacey cried. 'I was simply saying –'

'Does anyone at your office know who I am yet?' Ava interrupted again.

'Only those who have to,' Stacey promised, 'and I personally can vouch for their discretion. Of course, they'll be disappointed that you don't want to promote the book yourself . . .'

'We agreed, no publicity,' Ava stated, her smile turning chill. 'I don't want people, reporters, taking this book apart in an effort to find allusions or some kind of synchronicity with my husband's crime. It's not about him. It's not about me either, but they'll manage to turn it into something that is, and their analysis isn't likely to be favourable – it could even be damaging. So no, I won't promote it myself just to be gawped at, or pitied or vilified because I'm the wife of a celebrated killer, and that's what will happen, whether any of us wants it or not.'

'Of course, we understand,' Robin said, stepping in smoothly, though like Stacey and Caroline he too was slightly shaken by her candour. 'And you're right to be concerned, because conclusions will almost certainly be drawn, even though I, personally, can see no connection to current events at all.' He looked pointedly at Stacey. 'The only publicity will be for the book itself,' he said, 'not the author. Though I think you'll have to accept, Ava, that the secret's bound to come out sooner or later.'

'Then let's do everything we can to make sure it's later,' she responded, her eyes directed straight at Stacey.

'Oh, you have my word,' Stacey responded. 'We'll be a very small group who knows the truth. Just three or four of us. You'll meet the others when you come in on Friday.'

Ava sipped her champagne.

'Have you set up an editorial meeting yet?' Robin enquired.

'Yes, we must do that,' Stacey replied. 'As it's such an unusual love story we're rather hoping to publish in February in time for St Valentine's Day. I think it should be possible. There's really not much editing to be done – perhaps a few cuts here and there, but we can discuss that when we meet.'

114

Ava was regarding her with interest. 'Cuts?' she repeated.

'Just a few,' Stacey chortled. 'It's normal. And maybe a few points could do with a little clarification.'

Ava tore her eyes away and fixed them on Robin. 'So how long will I have to wait for the first cheque?' she enquired.

Grinning, he looked at Stacey. 'Oh, about a week,' he said, a roguish light in his eyes.

Stacey chortled again. 'Make that four,' she corrected.

Ava's perfectly plucked eyebrows rose, but she merely turned to greet several more agents who were piling in from along the corridor, come to join the celebration. Robin opened more champagne and Ava received her critiques and adulation with modest gratitude and enchanted smiles. Though right there in the moment, she was watching herself too, marvelling at the poise and elegance that seemed to come so naturally to Ava. Of course, they all imagined this was exactly how Beth Ashby dressed and behaved, but Beth had no such confidence, or style. If she had, maybe she'd have done a better job of satisfying her husband, who'd no doubt be as enthralled by Ava as he was by any woman who emanated such sublime sensuality. Where had all this been during the years of their marriage, she wondered. Why had she been so afraid of it then, when it might have saved her from so much pain? She had no answers right now, only a profound fascination with the miracles a little suntan, a French manicure, an expensive dress and newfound success were performing on a battered and bewildered psyche. How desperately Beth needed this, how fortunate she was to be able to reach inside herself and find it.

She left the agency at three when the taxi Robin had arranged came to collect her and take her to Paddington Station. The train ride to Swindon lasted no more than an hour, where another taxi was waiting to drive her back to Georgie's.

'So how did it go?' Georgie cried, bursting out of the front door in a bright red swimsuit, matching shorts and little Blake in her arms. 'God, you look fantastic in that dress. Who'd have thought one little trip into Bath could result in such a transformation? I feel like a fairy godmother. So, do I call you Beth or Ava?'

Beth was laughing. 'I think Beth,' she answered, scooping Blake into a hug and planting a big kiss on his cheek. 'How are you, you gorgeous thing?' she teased. 'Looks like you've been playing in your pool.'

Delighting in the attention, Blake bounced up and down and blew a few bubbles.

'You've got a visitor,' Georgie said, keeping her voice low.

Immediately Beth's heart turned over. 'Who?' she asked.

Georgie nodded towards the sleek black Mercedes that was parked under the trees at the end of the drive. 'You didn't see it on the way in?' she said.

'Whose is it?' Beth asked, shielding her eyes from the dazzling sunlight. 'Why is it parked down there?'

'To keep the chauffeur cool in the shade.'

Beth's heart was hammering as her eyes came back to Georgie's. 'Leonora,' she murmured.

'She's in the drawing room,' Georgie confirmed. 'She arrived about twenty minutes ago and decided to wait.'

'What does she want?'

'She didn't say. My mother's in there, keeping her entertained and probably in need of rescue.'

'Just give me a minute to change,' Beth said.

'Why? You look –'

'It just doesn't feel right, seeing her in something like this,' Beth cut in. 'I'll be two minutes.' And, dumping Blake back in his mother's arms, she ran quickly up the stairs to her room.

In less than two minutes she was fully transformed back to Beth just by putting on a thin rust cotton dress that flowed loosely round her slender body, and sturdy leather sandals. She looked in the mirror and was dismayed to see how far her earlier glow had faded with the nervous tension that was building inside her. Now she looked pinched and anxious, a woman of little self-esteem, who was no doubt about to be belittled and beleaguered by the supreme sophistication and Machiavellian intellect of the woman waiting downstairs. How she detested herself for being so unnerved by Leonora Gatling, yet she wasn't alone, for anyone who'd met the woman knew that only a fool underestimated that veneer of exquisite charm. Even Colin, who Beth was certain had slept with her, treated her with extreme caution and repeatedly advised that she, Beth, should do the same. Inwardly she shuddered. What she wouldn't give to avoid this encounter. She simply wasn't equipped to deal with Leonora's convoluted mind games, even though she might be able to use them to persuade Colin to let her visit again, for he'd surely want a blow-by-blow account of every word, every nuance and gesture.

Beatrice, Georgie's mother, had taken Blake up to his playroom by the time Beth opened the door to the drawing room. Almost instantly the overpowering scent of Joy confirmed that Leonora really was there. Georgie rose from one of the sofas, put a dainty cup and saucer back on a silver tray, then reached out to take her guest's.

'Leonora, what a pleasant surprise,' Beth declared warmly, surprising and pleasing herself with how relaxed she had managed to sound.

Leonora ascended from her chair, rising to a full six feet, which made her taller than Beth, though not quite as slender, nor as young. However, even at fifty Leonora was still the most striking-looking woman Beth had ever met. As usual her glossy, ebony hair was rolled in an immaculate pleat, her exotic, finely honed features were perfectly made up, and her light summer suit hadn't acquired a single crease. 'Beth, my dear. How are you?' she said in her low, velvety tones. 'I do hope you don't mind me crashing in like this. I've been so concerned. I simply had to come and see you for myself.'

Beth didn't remark on how many weeks it had taken, she merely kissed the air either side of Leonora's cheeks, as Leonora did the same to hers.

'You're looking a little thin,' Leonora remarked with a charming smile, 'but that's never a bad thing. Has it been terrible? Yes, of course it has.'

Clearing her throat, Georgie said, 'If you'll excuse me, I'll leave you to talk.'

'I was rather thinking a walk in the garden would be nice,' Leonora suggested. 'It looks so beautiful out there, and I'm sure that lovely high wall with those glorious roses climbing all over it will make us perfectly private.'

As Beth showed Leonora out through the French windows she glanced quickly back at Georgie, then stepped out on to the patio, with its exploding tubs of geraniums and fuchsias, which were nestled in amongst the deeply cushioned green wicker furniture and an assortment of Blake's cars, trucks and Lego bricks.

For the next five minutes, as they strolled along the gravel path that dissected the lawn, then ducked beneath a passiflora-covered pergola and wandered in through the beds and banks of chrysanths, begonias, dahlias and laburnum trees Beth found herself being schooled in all matters horticultural and arboreal.

'I had no idea you knew so much about gardening,' she remarked after a while.

'I don't really,' Leonora confessed. 'Just a few little tips I've picked up here and there. They come in useful when one is touring gardens, as one frequently does.'

Beth smiled and thought of how satisfying it would be to rub dirt in 'one's' smug little face.

'You know,' Leonora said, placing a hand on her arm, 'I really am sorry for what you're going through. It must be perfectly ghastly.'

'I think it's probably worse for Colin,' Beth responded.

'Of course.' Leonora's grip tightened a fraction, then she turned to stroll on, stopping finally to admire a walled enclave of vivid blue delphiniums. 'Giant Pacific Hybrids,' she murmured, touching her elegant fingers to the petals. 'Quite lovely.' She glanced at Beth. 'The PM sends his regards. He's very distressed about what's happened.'

Beth had no problem believing that, though didn't doubt for a moment that the concern was much more for himself than for his old and loyal friend Colin Ashby.

'He wants you to know that if there was anything he could do . . .'

The unfinished sentence hung in the air, its regret as empty as its effect.

'Of course he's counting on you to remain discreet,' Leonora said.

'Discreet about what?' Beth enquired.

Leonora turned to face her. 'Just discreet,' she responded. Then holding her eyes, 'I do hope I can be frank with you, my dear,' she said, continuing to perk and prissy the flowers.

118

'I'm sure you will be,' Beth replied sweetly.

Leonora's smile was as unshakeable as the sunlight streaming down in thick, misty bands through the trees. 'Please understand,' she said, starting to move on, 'I'm not only here because of Colin's long friendship with my husband and the Prime Minister, I'm here out of concern for you, my dear.'

Beth didn't bother to answer.

'It's important for you to realize that you have friends who care,' Leonora said. 'Of course, publicly we must be seen to keep a distance, but privately I want you to know that we're here for you.'

Beth's smile was suitably grateful, while inside she was already tying herself up in knots trying to work out where this was going.

'It's just too awful,' Leonora murmured, 'this situation that poor Colin finds himself in. Too awful. We've been so worried about him. I do hope he understands that. We're all so very fond of him. You too, of course. We've known each other a long time and friends really must stick together, don't you think?'

Beth wished she had the courage to ask just what Leonora's definition of sticking together was, but since the last place she wanted to be was on the wrong side of this woman, she took the safer option and refrained from comment.

'Yes, of course you do,' Leonora answered for her. 'And I'm sure you understand how very difficult it is for us to do anything to help Colin at this time, though of course we want to. We've discussed it over and over, but it's just too, shall we say, delicate a situation for any of us to become embroiled in. You do understand that, don't you?'

Beth nodded obediently.

Apparently satisfied, Leonora paused to coif a particularly vibrant rhododendron bush. 'Forgive me for asking,' she said, 'but do you have any idea *why* he killed the girl?'

Though startled by the abruptness of the question, Beth's cheeks immediately flushed with anger. 'You're assuming he did,' she retorted. 'He says he didn't.'

Leonora nodded. 'Of course, I'm sorry,' she responded. 'I suppose I was just going with the evidence, but I'm sure there's much more we don't know about yet, isn't there?' Her smile was benign as she stood back to admire her little bit of handiwork. 'Isn't there?' she repeated, when Beth didn't respond.

'Not that I'm aware of,' Beth replied. 'But in your position, it's possible that you know more than I do.'

Leonora's laugh was like delicately sprinkling glass. 'But you're his wife, my dear. I'm sure you'd be kept more informed than any of us.'

As they both knew how absurdly false that statement was, Beth merely said, 'Then I'm sure we have the same information.'

Leonora's lips maintained their upward curves at the corners as, blinking once or twice, she led them on towards the greenhouse and vegetable garden. 'As we both know what it is to be the wives of men in sensitive positions,' she said, 'I'm sure you won't mind me asking if we need to be concerned about some kind of scandal erupting from this that we're not prepared for?'

Beth was so surprised by the question that she almost laughed. 'You mean besides Colin being caught in the act of murder?' she asked.

Leonora's smile became thin.

Though pleased to have rattled her, Beth knew it wasn't going to help either her or Colin, so she said, 'I've heard that there's some kind of prostitution ring. Did you know about that?'

Leonora's head went back as she gazed up at the blazing blue sky through a tapestry of leaves. 'Such silly risks men take,' she commented.

'Surely not Marcus,' Beth protested.

Leonora's amusement seemed genuine as she laughed for several seconds. 'Was the girl blackmailing Colin?' she asked suddenly.

'You'd need to ask Colin that,' Beth answered. Then she added, 'Would she have something to blackmail him about, do you think?'

'That's what I'm trying to find out,' Leonora replied. 'As you know, Colin had access to many government secrets. We want to be sure that none has been passed on, or is being used against him.'

'If they were, the girl's dead,' Beth reminded her.

Leonora was quiet for a moment, then said, 'Yes. Of course.'

Beth followed her into the greenhouse where she began inspecting Georgie's prized orchids. It was almost unbearably humid inside all that glass.

'So Colin hasn't discussed any blackmail attempts with you?' Leonora asked.

'Only to say there weren't any,' Beth answered.

'Has he confided anything in you that you feel we should know about?'

'No. I don't think so. Maybe if you gave me some idea . . .'

Leonora turned her exquisite smile on Beth. 'I won't allow myself to disbelieve you,' she said, 'so I do hope, for all our sakes, that you're telling me the truth.'

Beth feigned surprise. 'Why wouldn't I?' she responded.

Leonora's expression remained pleasant as her eyes carried out one of the deepest probes Beth had ever undergone. She stared back, not faltering for a moment.

Finally Leonora looked at her watch. 'Well, I've probably taken up too much of your time already,' she said. 'I just wanted to be sure that you're coping, and to let you know that if there's anything you need, or feel you would like to discuss, my door is always open.'

'That's very kind of you,' Beth responded. 'I'll remember that.'

As they ambled back through the garden it occurred to Beth that she'd very likely been modelling Ava on this woman without realizing it. Now she did it made her feel oddly pleased and powerful, for it was as though, by usurping Leonora's character, she had some kind of control over her.

'I hear,' Leonora said chattily, as they arrived back at the house, 'that Colin has an excellent barrister. I know Giles Parker, of course, though not well.'

Was that a deliberate reminder that she'd once been an extremely successful lawyer herself, Beth wondered.

'Incidentally, how often are you managing to see Colin?' Leonora asked, stepping over one of Blake's toys as they walked up on to the patio.

121

'Actually, not often,' Beth answered feeling suddenly depressed and vulnerable, for the painful reality of Colin's refusal to see her again far outweighed the relief of getting through this past half an hour unscathed.

Leonora looked sympathetic. 'It must be hard,' she said, touching Beth's hand, 'especially when Heather's going so often.'

Beth's blood turned to ice. 'Heather?' she echoed, feeling the sky starting to tilt.

'Oh dear,' Leonora gasped, putting her fingers to her mouth. 'I thought . . . I assumed . . .'

Beth's eyes were wide with panic. 'Who's Heather?' she blurted.

'Oh, no one, I'm sure,' Leonora responded. 'I just heard . . . I'm sure it's nothing. I've probably got it wrong anyway.'

Leonora never got anything wrong, but whatever it was, Beth didn't want to hear it from her. 'Actually,' she stumbled, though trying hard to rally, 'I know who you mean. Heather is . . . Well, she's Heather.'

'Of course,' Leonora smiled. 'She's just Heather.'

At the French windows Leonora stopped and turned round so swiftly that Beth almost crashed into her. Steadying her, by placing her hands on Beth's arms, she said, 'I do hope they manage to get him off. I don't think I could bear to think of him being locked away for so many years. Such a brilliant man. So handsome too. It would be a terrible waste.'

'Not if he did it,' Beth said.

Though she instantly regretted it, it at least gave her the satisfaction of seeing Leonora's composure ruffled again.

A few minutes later she was standing at the end of the drive watching the black Mercedes inching carefully along the country lane and wishing she could just run up into the low, slumbering hills in the distance and lose herself and the pain in their timeless peace and stability. Heather. Who was Heather? She had to ask the question, even though, in her heart, she already knew the answer. She was another mistress. Another woman he'd loved while claiming to love her. A woman, if Leonora was to be believed, whom he'd rather see now than her. *Oh God, how much more of this could she stand?*

'So what did she have to say?' Georgie asked, taking a bottle of wine from the fridge as Beth came into the kitchen.

'Not much,' Beth answered, 'but they're obviously afraid of something.'

'Like what?'

'I only wish I knew.' Taking the glass Georgie was passing, she said, 'She seemed to think the girl could have been blackmailing Colin.'

'Well, we've all thought that,' Georgie commented. 'Did she have any theories on what about?'

Beth shrugged. 'Government secrets? I don't know. You know Leonora, she never lets anything slip if she doesn't want to. Anyway, he told me it was nothing to do with blackmail. That the girl didn't know anything she shouldn't.'

'Would he tell you if she did?'

'Probably not. He'd surely tell Bruce and Giles Parker, though.'

'Only if it would help his defence.'

Beth looked at her and felt the world sliding into chaos. 'Why do you think none of the papers has run the story about the prostitution scandal?' she said.

Georgie shook her head. 'Bruce and I were discussing it the other night,' she answered. 'He thinks they will, they just don't have the names, or the proof, yet.'

'I mentioned it to Leonora, but again she wasn't giving anything away. Colin says it's a red herring. That it's got nothing to do with that.'

'Then I wish to God he'd tell someone what it does have to do with,' Georgie remarked.

Beth took a sip of wine and tried again to wrest her mind from the devastation Leonora had left her with. She didn't want to face it; she didn't even want to think about it.

'Are you going to tell Colin about the visit?' Georgie asked.

Beth started to say something flip, but instead, in a voice choked with anguish she heard herself saying, 'Have you ever heard of someone called Heather?'

When Georgie didn't answer right away she looked up and her heart turned inside out to see the expression on Georgie's face.

'You know!' she cried.

'I was going to tell you,' Georgie said. 'Later, when Bruce gets home. He had a call earlier, telling him it's going to be in the papers tomorrow.'

Beth's eyes were so wide they hurt. She couldn't stand any more. *Please, God, she just couldn't take any more.* 'What is?' she whispered.

'Apparently this Heather – Heather Dance her name is. Well, apparently she and Colin . . . They have a home and child together. A little girl. She's three.'

'Oh my God,' Beth murmured, grabbing the edge of the table. There was such a horrible drumming in her ears that she hardly heard herself as she said, 'Who is this woman? She must be making it up. She *has* to be making it up.'

Georgie's anguish was almost palpable. 'Bruce has already spoken to Colin,' she said.

'No!' Beth cried, jumping to her feet. 'Georgie, it can't be true. If he had a child, I'd know.'

'I'm sorry,' Georgie said. 'Oh God, I'm sorry.'

Beth's eyes were darting about in a frenzy. Somewhere there was an escape from this, she just had to find it. Then Georgie took hold of her and pulled her into an embrace.

'It's OK,' Georgie said. 'You can get through this. We're here to help you.'

'Leonora said she's been going to visit him,' Beth sobbed. 'He's been seeing this woman and not me.'

'No, that's not true,' Georgie assured her. 'If it were Bruce would know, and the first he heard of the woman was when Elliot Russell, the journalist, called his office today to tell him the story was about to run.'

Beth was confused. She couldn't make herself think straight. It was going to be in the papers. Everyone would know. Robin Lindsay, Stacey Greene, everyone who called her Ava would know that behind that smooth, cultivated exterior was the wretched failure of a woman who'd been unable to give her husband a child, so he'd gone out and had one with somebody else. They would know that Ava was damaged, wrecked, a false image . . .

Then suddenly she realized what it was going to mean for him and she groaned aloud. 'They'll twist this into another motive,' she said. 'They'll say this is what Sophie Long was

124

blackmailing him about, and maybe it was. Maybe she knew about the child and was threatening to tell me.' Then shaking her head, she said, 'But why would Leonora get involved in that? What difference would it make to her? Or her husband? She just made sure to let me know she knew about Heather *before* it came out in the papers. Why would she do that? What was she telling me? That she knows about this woman, and doesn't consider her to be important? They're still hiding something, Georgie. They're afraid of something, and they think I know what it is.'

'Let it go,' Georgie advised. 'Don't even think about it. It's Colin's problem, and theirs. Don't let it hurt you any more than it already has.'

'I just wish I knew how to stop it,' Beth sobbed. 'I just wish to God I could run away and hide from it all.'

'What about going to Spain?' Georgie suggested. 'I know you don't get on with your mother, but maybe you should go away for a few days. The pressure here is just too intense.'

'I've got a meeting on Friday, with my publisher.'

'Then go after.'

Beth was shaking her head. 'She won't want me there.'

'Give her a call. I'm sure she won't say no.'

'I want to see Colin,' Beth suddenly cried. 'I have to talk to him.'

'OK. We'll speak to Bruce later, see if he can arrange it.'

Beth's heart and mind were in turmoil. 'What if he says no? What if he still won't see me?' she gasped. 'Oh God, I couldn't bear it. Which paper is it going to be in, do you know?'

'The *Mirror*, I think.'

Beth covered her face with her hands. 'Georgie, this hurts too much. It just hurts too much.'

'I know,' Georgie soothed. 'That's why I think you should get away. If you like, I'll call your mother for you.'

'OK, yes. You're right. I have to get away from this, because I'm just not handling it well. I need some space. I need some time to think before the next disaster explodes in my face.' Her eyes closed as the sheer dread of it swelled through her like a malicious wind. 'But there can't be any more,' she murmured. 'Please, tell me, there won't be any more.'

*

125

Inside the rear compartment of the black Mercedes Leonora was speaking to her husband on the phone.

'No, it certainly wasn't a waste of time,' she was saying. 'Nothing is where this is concerned.'

'But she doesn't know anything?'

'I don't think so, but I'm reserving final judgement.'

'Why?'

'The purpose of breaking the Heather Dance story is threefold,' she reminded him. 'First, to let our good friend Colin know that we're aware of her existence. Second, to provide a reasonable motive for the prosecution to work with. And third, to get Beth Ashby to show her colours. She might be trying to protect her dear husband right now, but that could change once she's over the shock of finding out he has a child, and a home, with another woman. If it does, and he was foolish enough to tell her anything, there's a very good chance she'll come to us for, let's say, help.'

'And what if she decides to go public instead? Leonora, we have to take whatever steps are necessary to prevent that from happening.'

'Marcus, darling, you're starting to sound like a gangster. Stop worrying. I truly don't think she knows anything, for the simple reason that if she did she'd have used it to get him out of there by now.'

'Unless he's told her not to.'

'She'd have done it anyway. Women are like that, believe me. We'll do anything to protect those we love, especially from themselves.'

'So where does that leave us?'

'Keeping an eye on her, but not aggressively so. She hasn't spoken to the press yet, and personally I don't think she will, even if she does know more than we'd like her to. After the Heather Dance affair she'll be looking out for herself more than him, and now that juicy income of his has dried up she's going to need money. Of course, she could sell her story, but she's not stupid, she'll know very well that no one in the media can even come close to what we can give her.'

'You're worrying me, Leonora,' he told her. 'You're making it sound as though she does know something.'

'Darling, relax. Please. We'll keep tabs on her over these

next few weeks, make sure she doesn't make any contact with the press, and by then, if she hasn't come to us either, we'll know that he never told her anything. By the way, has Sophie Long's family spoken to anyone from the press yet?'

'Not that I know of. They've been given the go-ahead, though. Apparently, the father's reporter of choice is Elliot Russell, but Mrs Long is putting up some resistance. I'm sure they'll work it out. Now, I have to talk to Kleinstein in New York in half an hour. What do I tell him about Beth Ashby?'

'That there's absolutely no need to worry.'

'He won't want her in on this if she does know anything,' Gatling warned. 'No one will.'

Leonora sighed. 'Darling, please, let's just stop getting excited,' she responded. 'First, this is far too big for Beth Ashby to fully comprehend, so she'll just want paying. And second, if she does want more, it simply won't be an option. So now, let's just settle down and wait and see if the Heather Dance story manages to live up to our expectations.'

Chapter 9

Elliot Russell was driving fast through the East End of London after spending the past day and night in Brussels talking to contacts at selected financial institutions. The primary subject for discussion had been Marcus Gatling and his multinational investment dealings. The man was a serious player in so many fields it was hard to keep track, but just as Elliot had hoped, a pattern of other names had started to emerge, of equally powerful men in equally strategic positions in such far-flung places as New York, Washington, Singapore and the Bahamas. There was no clear picture yet of what might be going on between them, but considering the nature of the protagonists it had to be both financial and political, and considering the lengths these men were going to to disguise their contact, never mind its purpose, he certainly wasn't drawing the line at criminal either. Nor was he ruling out a connection to Sophie Long's murder, since it was her untimely demise, and Ashby's curious denial considering the evidence, that had triggered these investigations in the first place.

Now, as he accelerated his Carrera past the East India Dock basin and down on to Aspen Way, he was trying to reach Heather Dance on the phone. Her story had broken that morning, and though he now knew why she'd agreed so readily to see him after her initial shock of being found, he was still curious to learn precisely how this little exposé was going to serve Leonora Gatling, who, albeit indirectly, had given him the lead in the first place. On the face of it, she'd just fixed Ashby up with yet another motive, which immediately begged the question, why? It also strongly suggested that she knew more about this case than she should, which might have been a surprisingly vulnerable position to have put herself in, had she made the call personally. As it was, an underling had made it for her, so she could always deny any knowledge of it ever taking place, and insist that the underling had acted upon his own conscience.

With a sigh of impatience he prodded a key on the dashboard again, and listened to the rapid beeps of Heather Dance's number redialling. This time he made the connection.

'Heather. It's Elliot,' he said into the speaker/mike. 'How are you?'

'OK. I think. I'm glad you called. It all feels rather strange.' Her whispery Welsh accent sounded even softer than he remembered, but though he couldn't hear her anxiety he could sense it.

'Has anyone tried to contact you?' he said.

'No, it's all been rather eerily quiet, considering.'

'How's Jessica?' he asked, referring to her daughter.

'She's fine. Oblivious, of course.' She paused for a moment, then said, 'I keep thinking about Beth. This has to have been very hard on her. How do you think she's taken it?'

He'd been thinking about Beth Ashby rather a lot himself since pulling this together, but not even warning her that it was about to break had reaped a response from her end. 'I don't know,' he answered. 'She won't talk to anyone. We can't get near her.'

'You know I wouldn't have done it if Colin hadn't insisted,' she said. 'I mean I'd never have wanted her to find out like this. Never. My God, I can hardly bear to look at it myself, so heaven only knows how she must be feeling.'

Elliot glanced down at the open newspaper on the seat beside him, where Heather Dance's almost wistful beauty and her daughter's exquisite elfin features were either side of Colin's laughing face in a perfect happy family shot. It was a photograph Heather had given him when he'd gone down to the New Forest to see her three days ago. The headline above it had been written by a sub, 'Colin's Two Good Reasons for Killing'. So Heather wouldn't be the only one wondering how Beth Ashby must be feeling right now, though what Elliot would really like to know was what the hell had made Ashby do this to his wife. OK, he wasn't the only man in Christendom who'd got himself a mistress and love-child, but he was the only one Elliot had ever come across who'd told the mistress to go right ahead and talk to the press. Or that was the way Heather had told it, when she'd finally agreed to see him. 'I've told Colin you've been in touch,' she'd informed him the second time he called, 'and he says I should see you and tell you everything. He thinks it'll be safer for me if people actually know I exist.'

Of course, when he got there he'd quizzed her relentlessly on the 'safer', but if she had any idea what Ashby had meant by it she'd put on such a convincing show of not knowing that he was actually tempted to buy it.

So now everyone knew of Heather and Jessica Dance's existence, that Ashby had been supporting and part-time living with them for the past four years, that Heather had no doubt whatsoever that Ashby had *not* killed Sophie Long, and that if Ashby, by some miracle, managed to get out of this, he was planning to marry her. In fact, according to Heather, he'd already asked Beth for a divorce. Since there was no line of communication with Beth, Elliot had no way of knowing if that was true, but from the way Heather had told it, it was clear she believed it.

Actually, what interested Elliot much more than all the marital wranglings was the visit Heather had been paid, just after the murder, by someone claiming to be Special Branch. Though Heather hadn't been able to tell him the man's name, she'd described him as looking rather American with a military-style crew cut and a harsh, jutting jaw. In fact there was an officer in Special Branch who fitted that description, so Elliot was inclined to believe that the man had been telling the truth, which suggested either some kind of government collusion surrounding Sophie Long's murder, or that Marcus Gatling was appropriating the services of élite police officials to carry out his private business. Either way, Elliot hadn't mentioned anything about it in that morning's story, so for the moment, other than those directly involved, only he knew about it.

'So no one's called you at all today?' he said to Heather. 'From the press, or anywhere else?'

'No. Apart from Colin and my mother you're the only one who has this number. But no, that can't be right, can it? Someone must have given it to you. Was it –'

'Have you spoken to Colin?' he cut in.

'Not since last night. He said he'd call again tonight.'

'Then get him to send me a visiting order. I need to talk to him.'

'Actually, he guessed you'd ask and he's already said to tell you no.'

'Well, try anyway. Now, tell me again about the man who came to see you from Special Branch. What exactly did he ask you?'

'Mainly if I knew why Colin would kill that poor girl,' she answered. 'And I just kept telling him that I didn't care what evidence they had, I just don't believe he did it.'

'Did he give you any idea why *he* thought Colin might have done it?' Elliot pressed.

'Not exactly, but he wanted to know if Colin had ever said he was being blackmailed, about me and Jessica, or anything else.'

'Had he?'

'No. I even asked him the next time we spoke and he swore he wasn't being blackmailed, by Sophie Long, or anyone.'

'Did you believe him?'

'Yes.'

Of course. She was in love with the man, she'd believe anything he told her.

'Did he ever mention anything about some kind of syndicate, or exclusive organization – a kind of financial consortium operating on an international level?'

'No. I don't think so.'

'Are you sure? Did he ever discuss investments, or currencies, or commodities?'

'Yes, quite a lot, actually. I used to be a stockbroker, so we'd often talk about his investments.'

'Does he have any offshore, that you know about?'

'I don't think so.'

'But it's possible?'

'I suppose so. Why?'

'Was he part of an investment group of any kind?'

131

'Not that I know of.'

Elliot paused for a moment. Drawing this many blanks always annoyed him, but reining it in, he said, 'OK. Let's talk about old friends.'

She sounded uncertain. 'Do you mean Colin's old friends?' she said.

'Yes. Tell me again what you know about one in particular.'

'Well, I've never actually met the man, but Colin used to talk about him from time to time.'

'In what context?'

'He'd occasionally tell me if he ran into him, or if he'd been invited to dinner at the Gatling estate. It's in Suffolk somewhere, I believe.'

'Yes,' Elliot confirmed, wincing at the mention of Gatling's name. His car had been parked at the City airport for the past thirty-six hours, so Sam the bug-buster hadn't got round to it since Leonora's tip-off. He made a mental note to send Sam down to Heather's place too, then said, 'OK, go on.'

'Well, as I told you before, there was that one time when Colin was a bit drunk and said that Mar – his friend had made him an offer he couldn't refuse, and he'd made the grandiose mistake of refusing.'

Just like the first time he'd heard her say that, Elliot's pulse quickened. Here was the link, he was certain of it. Gatling makes Ashby an offer, Ashby refuses, and now, inevitably, Ashby has information Gatling would rather he didn't have. The most obvious conclusion was that Gatling had invited Ashby to become part of this covert financial syndicate, and to do that he had to tell Ashby what it was. '*Shit!*' he muttered, braking hard and swerving to the left as he almost missed his turn-off. 'Are you sure he didn't tell you what the offer was?' he said to Heather.

'I'm sure. It was the only time he ever mentioned it, and that was two days before he was arrested. Do you think it's connected?'

'Yes, I do. So if you remember anything else about it, anything at all, I want you to contact me immediately. Can you discuss it with Colin when he calls?'

'I can try. But I think his calls are monitored.'

'Oh, they will be,' he assured her. 'In fact, on second

thoughts, don't bring it up. It'll only alert someone to the fact that you know there was an offer, and that might not be a good idea.' In fact, he was starting to see some logic now to Ashby's desire for her existence to be made public, for in its way it did make her safer. In other words, the Gatlings would find dealing with someone under the public spotlight a lot harder than trying to tackle them in the shadows of obscurity. However, he, Elliot, had to remember that it was Leonora who had brought Heather to his attention in the first place, which suggested she didn't view Heather so much as a threat, as some kind of weapon or tool. Whatever, there certainly appeared to be a war being waged between Ashby and the Gatlings, and so far Ashby's chances of winning weren't looking good.

'When you told Colin about me,' Elliot said, 'did he ask how I'd managed to find you?'

'Yes, actually, he did.'

'What did you tell him?'

'That I didn't know.'

It was true she didn't, but Ashby at least must have a pretty good idea. Putting the press on to his mistress was a shot across the bows, a warning to let him know that the Gatlings knew about her and would, if necessary, use her to keep him quiet. And Ashby had retaliated by telling Heather to co-operate with the press, thereby gaining their protection.

'Who's there with you now, besides Jessica?' Elliot asked, hearing a voice in the background.

'Just Gail, from your office. She's saying that it's only a matter of time before a neighbour, or someone from Jess's playschool, calls another paper to tell them where I am.'

'They've probably already done it,' he assured her. 'Is there somewhere else you can stay?'

'Yes. At my mother's. She's expecting us in an hour or so. I'd like Gail to come too, if that's OK. Just to keep me company on the journey.'

'No problem,' he said, responding to the nervousness in her voice. 'She's yours as long as you need her. And don't worry. You'll be all right. Nothing's going to happen to you. I've got another call coming in now, but I'll get back to you later, OK? And you know where to reach me if you need me.'

'OK.'

He clicked off the line, then picked up again. 'Elliot Russell,' he barked, speeding through an amber light, as he headed on to the Isle of Dogs.

'It's Laurie Forbes.'

His foot instantly relaxed, slowing the car as his mind performed a jarring change of gears.

'Laurie,' he said, keeping it light. 'I'm surprised.'

'I'm returning your call,' she said shortly.

'Of course. But I'm still surprised.'

'Just tell me what you want.'

'To help you,' he said. 'I know you're still working on the Ashby story and I've got something here that might interest you.'

There was only silence at the other end, but he could almost see her blue eyes flashing. How those eyes, so like her sister's, still haunted him.

'I can get you in to talk to Sophie Long's family,' he said abruptly.

There was another brief pause, then she said, 'If you're giving it to me it's because they've got nothing to say.'

'Wrong. I'm giving it to you because Mrs Long has expressed a preference for a woman.'

'As I recall you have at least two on your team.'

'One,' he corrected. 'Which goes to show what a male chauvinist I am, I know. So now we've got that out of the way, let's go straight to the bottom line, I don't need another exclusive, but I do need your forgiveness.'

'You'll never get that,' she hissed, 'and if this is your way of buying it –'

'OK! Have it your way. But before you turn me down, at least think about it.'

Her answer was to cut the line dead.

At her end Laurie was in a cold sweat. Her hands were shaking, her heart pounding. It was the first time she'd spoken to Elliot Russell in a year, and though she knew hearing his voice would affect her, she hadn't imagined it would be to quite this extent.

'Are you OK?' Gino asked, peering at her across the desks.

Laurie looked up, took a breath then nodded. 'Yes,' she answered. 'Just conversations with Satan can be a bit disconcerting.'

'So what did he want?'

Laurie told him.

'You're kidding me,' Gino responded. 'And you turned him down? Laurie, for God's sake . . .'

'All right! All right! You don't have to remind –'

'Laurie, five minutes,' Wilbur barked, appearing out of nowhere.

'Shit!' she muttered, after he'd closed his door. 'I need more time to think.'

'What's to think about?' Gino hissed. 'Do you want to keep at this, or don't you?'

'Of course. I just want to do it myself,' she replied, feeling foolish even as she said it.

'Then look on Russell as a source,' Gino advised. 'If this offer had come from anyone else, you'd be in Wilbur's office faster than you can say "hold the front page".'

'Hey, what's new?' Flaxie cried, swinging round the partition into their shared corner space.

'Elliot Russell's just offered Laurie an in with Sophie Long's family,' Gino told him.

Flaxie's eyes bulged. 'Well, I guess you know how Christ felt in the wilderness now,' he responded. 'Satan's temptations are always the hardest to refuse. Incidentally, did you two get back on speaking terms without telling me?'

'Absolutely not,' Laurie answered.

'So have you got any other leads on this tantalizing little scandalum magnatum? Because you missed out big time on the mistress and love-child.'

Laurie's mouth tightened. 'Thanks for that,' she spat.

'So what are you waiting for?' he cried. 'Principles are too high a price for ambition.'

Even feeling as she did, she couldn't help laughing at that.

A few minutes later she let herself into Wilbur's office and sat in the chair he waved her to. After he'd finished his call, he told his assistant to hold any others, then firing glances up and down the office outside, he said, 'I don't want you to pretend that you're not pursuing the Ashby story, contrary to orders –'

135

'I don't recall any direct orders,' she interrupted. 'And besides, I've been doing it in my own time.'

'Laurie, I'm not stupid. You're doing it on company time too, and frankly it's a shame your efforts didn't pay off with the mistress and child. Do you know how Russell found them?'

She shook her head.

'No, of course not. Who knows how the hell that man finds anything?'

'He has a whole team of researchers and more contacts . . .'

'. . . than an optician. I know, I know,' he said, waving for her to stop, 'and it was always expected that he'd solve the mystery, so now he has.'

'What are you talking about, solved?' she cried. 'It's anything but solved.'

'Laurie, how many motives does it take to convince you that Ashby did it?'

'I'm not saying he didn't. But I'm telling you, it's not as straightforward as Sophie Long blackmailing him over the mistress and child.'

'OK. What evidence do you have to back that up?'

'None, at the moment,' she confessed, 'but I've just been given a lead to Sophie Long's family.'

Wilbur scowled. 'By whom?'

'I can't tell you that. You know sources are sacred.'

'How reliable is this source?'

'Very.'

He stared at her hard, his eagle eyes constantly flicking sideways, though never seeming to release her. In the end he shook his head. 'We need you full time back on the news,' he said.

Laurie almost gasped. 'But I just told you, I had a lead,' she protested.

'The man's guilty, Laurie. Live with it and get on with your life. There's some kind of trouble expected at –'

'No, wait!' she said angrily. 'My source is Elliot Russell, OK? I spoke to him this morning. He's prepared to give me the Longs.'

Wilbur's left eyebrow went up. 'Why would he do that?' But before she could answer he said, 'No, the man's got an agenda where you're concerned Laurie, and I don't trust him. So forget it. If anything new comes to light on the Ashby affair –'

'It just has!' she cried in frustration. 'That's what I'm telling you. We can have an exclusive with Sophie Long's family.'

'Courtesy of Elliot Russell,' he snorted. 'Come on, Laurie, we both know things aren't entirely uncomplicated where you two are concerned.'

'But if I can get to the Longs, if I can find out something –'

'Laurie, are you watching my lips? Forget it.'

'But why? For God's sake, Wilbur, what you're doing doesn't make any sense –' She stopped, so suddenly that his eyes widened in surprise. Then he watched her, as she sat there, glaring at him, her young face flushed with anger, her shrewd eyes flashing the challenge he'd been trying to avoid. In the end she said, 'I'm not stupid either, Wilbur.'

He rested his forehead in his hand, pressing the frown lines out from between his eyebrows. 'OK,' he said finally, returning to his sweeping glances of the outer office, 'I'll give it to you straight, but it goes no further than this office, do you hear me? If it does it'll be me who pays, so don't forget I'm the one with the hundred-and-twenty-K mortgage and three kids in private school, so I can't afford the luxury of your principles, though God knows, in this case, I wish I could. Something's going on, and it's probably a lot bigger than you think. I don't know who's giving the orders, but I do know they're coming from way up, and I'm in no position to argue. Nor are you, if you want to keep your job. So do as they say, Laurie, ease up on the investigation and toe the official line of Ashby's guilt.'

Even though she'd known there was a cover-up, hearing it like this left her momentarily stunned. 'You surely don't think I'm just going to walk away from it now?' she said.

'No, you probably won't, but you should. As far as this paper's concerned we know all there is to know on this little calumny. The rest is going to be speculation, embellishment or more tabloid-style scandals, and in case you hadn't noticed we don't trade in those particular commodities.'

At that her eyes flashed. 'I don't deserve that kind of put-down,' she spat, 'especially not from you.'

'You're right, you don't,' he responded, 'but keep up the fire, because you never know who's watching. Most of those guys out there are prepared to do as they're told and back off. They'll have their own reasons – long-time friendships, called-in favours, whatever. The point is you're seriously pissing them off by not letting go too.'

'I'm not afraid of them,' she declared rashly.

'I know. That's half the trouble. But watch your step, OK? I can't cover you on this, nor can I sit here all day discussing it. So the official line is, you're off the Ashby story, and as I started to tell you just now, they're expecting some kind of disruption over at Lambeth Town Hall . . .'

'I already know,' she snapped, and, spinning on her heel, she stalked out of the room.

Later, as she sat at the back of the town hall with a group of other reporters waiting, apparently in vain, for something even mildly exciting to happen on the podium, she was reluctantly facing up to the unthinkable. If Wilbur wouldn't, couldn't, back her on this, then the only way forward as she could see it was to do as Chilton said and co-operate with Elliot Russell. Even to think it caused a violent rebellion inside her, since, at the very least it would mean calling him to accept his offer, and at the very worst . . . But no, she wasn't going there, because just no way in the world was she prepared to forgive him – it wasn't even up for discussion – so if that was his condition . . . More dismay engulfed her, for both Chilton and Wilbur had stated their cases so clearly and unequivocally that she really didn't have any choice but to accept that for the moment at least there wasn't an alternative.

Inwardly groaning she got up from her seat and crept outside into the sunshine. Along with everything else, Beth Ashby had been on her mind almost constantly today. She wondered if Elliot had given her any warning of the story, or maybe Beth had known for a long time that her husband was leading this double life. But even if she had, it still had to be pretty devastating, having it all come out like this, and in the light of her two miscarriages and all the failed fertility treatment there surely couldn't be a woman in the country who wasn't feeling for her today.

138

'Laurie Forbes,' she said into her mobile as it rang.

'It's Rhona Childs. Your closest friend. Remember?'

'Oh God, Rhona,' she groaned. 'I'm sorry. It's been such a hectic time. How are you?'

'Sizzling. How are you?'

'Surviving,' Laurie answered, starting out into the street to wave down a cab. 'Where are you?'

'Sunning my gorgeous self on the balcony at home. Can you hear me OK?'

'More or less. Wait, I'm just getting into a cab.' A couple of minutes later she was settled in the back seat on the way to Limehouse. 'So what's new?' she said.

'Actually, something that might interest you,' Rhona replied, her voice thickening with intrigue.

Laurie smiled. 'I'm all ears,' she responded.

'Well, would I be right in thinking you're still sniffing around for a scent on the Ashby trail?'

Surprised, Laurie said, 'Yes. Why?'

'Because we've just signed a first-time author for over a million.'

'And?' Laurie prompted.

'And the colleague who's been assigned to the publicity isn't allowed to use this author's real name anywhere, nor is said author going to make any public appearances. Of course, I couldn't tell you any of this if she'd been assigned to me, but since she hasn't, and since the last time we spoke you mentioned you'd been trying, with no success, to contact her . . .'

Laurie's heart rate was climbing. 'Rhona, coitus interruptus I can stand, tip-off interruptus I can't. *Don't stop now!*'

Rhona chuckled. 'Her author name is Ava Montgomery,' she responded. 'There's going to be a small reception for her at Buchmanns' main offices on Friday at three. It should be finished by four. Whether she'll enter and leave the building alone, or accompanied I've no idea. My guess is her agent'll be with her, though she might arrange to meet him here. No press invited. What am I saying? No one but a very select few are invited. It's all very hush-hush, so however you design your chance encounter you'll need to make it convincing.'

139

'Rhona, I love you,' Laurie laughed. 'If you had any idea how utterly spectacular your timing is . . .'

'It has been mentioned,' Rhona purred. 'What news on Greg?'

'Still history. I need a man who doesn't see my career as a threat.'

'Then you could be looking a long time. What about your parents?'

'They're fine.'

'Good. Send them my love. Dinner next Thursday? My club.'

'I'll check my diary and get back to you.'

Laughing, Laurie rang off and keyed in the code to replay her messages. Rhona was nothing if not grand, with her sultry airs and memberships to all the right places. The latest was the exclusive Home House on Portman Square, where all the fabulously successful young executives went to get blitzed on champagne and cosmopolitans after a hard day's graft on millionaire row. Exactly how Rhona, a lowly paid publicist, had managed to acquire herself a membership, Laurie had no idea, but ever since she and Lysette had met Rhona, at an art class Lysette had dragged Laurie along to, they had been constantly surprised and impressed by the kind of snazzy deals the high-born, but stony-broke, Rhona could pull off.

After listening to a message from Gino, who was on his way to Scotland and wanted her to do some background work on the story he was covering, Laurie skipped on through the list until she heard her mother's voice saying she'd just left the hospital with Dad.

'Nothing serious. He's all right, but he gave us a bit of a scare earlier. If you could –'

Laurie was already punching in her parents' number. 'Mum?' she gasped when her mother answered. 'What happened? Where is he?'

'Sitting right here on the sofa. It was just a funny turn. Nothing to get –'

'Then don't do that!' she cried. 'You scare me half to death, then you tell me he's right there.'

'Here, I'll pass you over,' Mindy said.

'Dad! Are you all right?' Laurie demanded, hardly waiting for him to take the phone.

'Of course I am,' he chuckled. 'You know what your mother's like. She fusses too much.'

'But you went to hospital.'

'It was just a dizzy spell. Nothing more. The old ticker's in good working order, they tell me, I just have to go for my regular check-up at the end of the month. So how's your day been? Where are you?'

'On my way to see Andrew and Stephen. I'm moving into their house at the weekend, remember? But listen, you don't have to help. They've said they'll come and get me . . .'

'That's good. The more the merrier.'

'Dad, you've got to take it easy. I know you hate it, but that heart attack was serious. We nearly lost you, and –'

'Oh, that's enough now,' he grumbled. 'It was over six months ago and Andrew and Stephen are always a bit of fun. You're surely not going to deprive me of that, are you?'

'No, of course not. But –'

'No buts. You just go on getting your by-line on the front page and the only thing this old heart'll be doing is bursting with pride. OK?'

Though she was still shaking and her face was bloodless Laurie managed a smile. 'OK,' she said, making a decision right there and then to stop telling him about the Ashby affair. After today's developments, all round, it would be better for him not to know.

'What time shall we expect you back tonight?' he asked.

'Nine. Ten at the latest.'

'We'll wait up then. And Laurie, don't shout at your mother.'

Ringing off before she shouted at him too, she quickly pressed in the password to continue her messages. Everything had been so tense at home, so unbearable and wrong since Lysette had gone, it was as though they weren't a proper family any more. But it was OK, she was moving out of there at the weekend; she wouldn't have to deal with the pressure on a daily basis any more. She might even find a way of making it up to them that they'd lost the most precious of their girls, because the other had failed them all so badly.

141

After checking her final messages and leaving a few of her own, she forced herself to sit quietly throughout the rest of the journey, as she tried to come up with a way to get the Long family interview without having to go through the detestable experience of dealing with Elliot Russell. The trouble was, if there were a way of doing it without him, she'd almost certainly have found it by now, for God knew how hard she'd already tried. So was she going to have to resign herself to calling him, or should she just let the Long interview go and follow up on Rhona's lead to Beth Ashby? That was good, it had to be said, but there were no guarantees with it, whereas with the Long family there were.

Half an hour later her taxi pulled up outside Andrew and Stephen's townhouse on Ropemaker's Fields, where the evening sunlight was pinging off the windows and the mouth-watering aroma of barbecued steaks and home-grown hemp drifted down from the roof terrace above. Shielding her eyes as she looked up and waved to Andrew, she felt a warming lift in her heart, for by then she'd come to the conclusion that there actually might be a way of getting to the Long family without having to go through Elliot Russell. It would never have been possible before today, but now that he'd called to tell her the option was there . . . She smiled slyly to herself. No, she didn't mind double-crossing Elliot Russell. In fact, after what he'd done to Lysette, it wouldn't only be a pleasure, it would be an absolute joy.

Chapter 10

Bruce was sitting across a graffiti-scratched table from Colin, in a room of solid grey walls and grimed, opaque windows. Giles Parker, the QC who was leading Ashby's case, was leaning his shoulders against the door, arms folded, head bowed as he listened to what was being said. It was late in the day for a legal visit, but Parker had been in court until now presenting legal arguments on another high-profile case, so this was the first opportunity he'd had to come since the story had broken on Heather Dance and her child.

'You surely realize how this is being interpreted out there,' Bruce was saying. 'So why the hell didn't you prepare us? We're on your side, for God's sake, but the press are making fools of us with what they know that we don't. Is that how you want it to go in court? Because that's exactly what'll happen if you don't start telling us what we need to know.'

Colin looked at him. There was a bruise under his left eye and a small cut on his upper lip.

'For God's sake, Colin,' Bruce cried, slamming the table. 'You want to get out of here, don't you?'

'Of course I do.'

'Then stop holding back like this. What's just happened, all this about Heather Dance, it doesn't need to be disastrous if you just tell us how she fits into your life, whether she's got anything to do with what happened.'

'She fits in exactly the way it says in the paper,' Colin responded. 'We've been together for four years, we have a daughter, and their home is mine too whenever I can get there. She had nothing to do with Sophie Long's murder.'

'How can you be so certain?' Parker demanded.

'I just know,' Colin answered.

Parker stared at him, his harsh, narrowed eyes and thin mouth showing his anger. Colin was the first to look away.

'Did Sophie Long know about Heather Dance and the child?' Bruce asked.

'No.'

'Did your wife?' Parker snapped.

'Don't be ridiculous. It was because of her that I didn't want anything about them to come out.'

'Well, it's certainly out there now,' Parker said shortly. 'Did you know that Heather Dance was going to be as forthright as she was in talking to the press? I presume you spoke to her before she spoke to them.'

'As a matter of fact I told her to be,' Colin responded.

Parker frowned. 'Why?'

Colin didn't answer right away, he merely turned his head and stared at nothing, almost as though he was alone in the room. His face, bony with weight loss and taut with fatigue, had aged ten years in less than ten weeks.

'Why?' Parker repeated.

'Because I want Beth to divorce me,' Colin said wearily, 'and since Elliot Russell was already on to Heather, I thought this would force Beth to do it.'

Bruce's eyes closed as he thought of the way Beth had suffered since the news had broken. God only knew what it would do to her if she heard him utter those words. 'That's a pretty despicable way of treating her,' he remarked bitterly. 'She's never done anything to deserve that.'

'No,' Colin answered. 'But I have a child with Heather. I'll always be responsible for Jessica. And I've let Beth down so badly. She's better off without me.'

Parker took a pen from his inside pocket, went to make a note on the pad he'd left on the table, then said, 'We established a few weeks ago that you're trying to protect those you love. I could comment that you have a strange way of doing it, but what is much more relevant is *why* you're doing it. I'm a busy man, Mr Ashby. I also want to help you, but if you continue to deny us the facts, I'm afraid you'll make that impossible.'

Colin looked down at his hand resting on the table. His

144

mind and body ached with the strain of holding back, but after what had just happened with Heather he didn't dare to weaken now. 'All I can tell you,' he said, 'is what I've told you before – that I believe Sophie's murder was set up to put me exactly where I am. Who was the mastermind behind it, and who carried it out, I can't say.'

'Can't or won't?' Bruce interjected.

'Can't, because I don't know.'

'But you have your theories.'

'Of course. But Sophie's dead, I'm here, and I have good reason to believe Beth could be in danger too.'

'Why?'

'They'll be afraid of what she might know.'

'*They*?' Parker repeated.

Colin's face went blank.

'Then what might she know?' Parker said, hiding his exasperation.

'Nothing. She doesn't know anything.'

'Are you certain of that?'

'As certain as I can be. There's also a very good chance they'll use her to put pressure on me to stay silent.'

'Use her? In what way?'

'They could threaten her. Or worse.'

'So to get her out of danger, you divorce her?' Parker stated.

Colin's eyes flickered to his, but he made no response.

Parker glanced at Bruce. Bruce was watching his friend, sensing how embattled and confused he was. He appeared to have no idea of the rules he should be playing by and, unless he opened up, he was likely to make some very serious mistakes.

'It won't surprise you to hear that there are plenty of journalists eager to speak to you,' Bruce said. 'Perhaps you'd be more forthcoming with one of them?'

Colin shook his head.

Quite suddenly Parker picked up his briefcase and began packing it. 'I'll continue preparing your defence,' he said brusquely, 'but as I've told you on several occasions, a defendant's unsubstantiated claims of unnamed other parties being involved in the killing, though admissible as evidence, is not going to carry any weight with a jury. In other words, we're getting nowhere, Mr Ashby.'

Colin looked at Bruce.

'You have to give us more than this,' Bruce told him.

'Can they prove I did it?' Colin asked.

'In a way that will satisfy a jury, undoubtedly yes,' Parker answered.

Colin's face turned paler than ever as he lowered his eyes and his shoulders seemed to slump. 'I should have just accepted their damned offer,' he groaned, burying his face in his hands. 'I didn't want to be part of it, but if I'd gone along with them, none of this would be happening.'

Parker and Bruce exchanged glances. At last something new.

'What offer?' Bruce said.

Colin was staring down at the table, shaking his head. 'It's no good, Bruce, I can't tell you,' he answered. 'All I can do is let my silence over time prove that I'm not prepared to tell anyone what I know.'

'But surely to God, man, it can't be worth losing your freedom for,' Bruce protested.

Colin looked up. 'By putting Elliot Russell on to Heather, they were telling me that they know who and where she is,' he said. 'In their language, that is a threat.'

Bruce turned to Parker. 'If this woman needs protection –' Parker said.

'She's got it, to a degree, now that people know who she is,' Colin interrupted. 'It's the best we can do.'

'What about Beth?' Bruce asked.

Colin's eyes, bleak and anguished, came up to his. 'How is she?' he asked.

'How do you think?'

Colin wiped a hand over his face. It was shaking, and bruised. That his life had been reduced to this, and he wasn't doing anything to help get himself out of it, was simply beyond Bruce's understanding.

'Can I give her a message?' Bruce asked.

'Just tell her I'm sorry.'

'She wants to see you.'

Colin shook his head.

'Then at least speak to her on the phone, man.'

Colin's eyes went down, as again he shook his head.

'You'll speak to your mistress, but not your wife! How the hell do you think that's going to make her feel?'

'She has to let go,' Colin answered. 'We both do.'

Parker was picking up his briefcase again. 'It's clear that you don't want this investigation to go through official channels,' he said, 'so perhaps you'll reconsider speaking to one of your former colleagues in the media, and let them try to help you. We're certainly prepared to work with them, so you know where to get hold of us if you decide to take this option.'

Colin rose to his feet. 'I'm sorry Heather and Jessica were sprung on you like that,' he said.

Parker shook his hand. 'Committal proceedings are scheduled six weeks from now,' he told him. 'September the third. Time is not on our side.'

Colin nodded gravely, and Bruce could see he felt sick.

Parker was still grasping Colin's hand. 'You're either a very foolish or very honourable man,' he said, 'I just hope you realize, before it's too late, that neither one is going to help you.'

The street on which Sophie Long's family lived was typical of that part of Essex, two facing rows of sixties orange brick semis, symmetrical lawns rolled out like flags, fussily clipped privets and the ubiquitous frills and folds of John Lewis nets at every window. There was no one about – not a neighbour, not a reporter, not even a dog. Even so, Laurie felt as though a thousand eyes were watching her, not least of all Elliot Russell's. Since she was about to steal his thunder she was struggling with a minor bout of conscience. However, she wasn't going to worry too much about that, since her plan, simple and obvious as it was, was hardly going to bump her off to moral Siberia even if it worked, which it just might not. Mrs Long had expressed preference for a woman, so she was here, as that woman, ready to claim Elliot had sent her. Which, in a way, he had. He just didn't know he'd done it today.

She detected no movement of the nets, either upstairs or

down, as she walked up the Longs' crazy-paved front path. Nor was there any sound from within after the resonance of the doorbell's four Beethoven chords finally died away.

She waited, listening hard and feeling much more apprehensive than she wanted to admit. Was someone watching her through the little brass peephole? If so, did she look friendly, or menacing in its distorting lens? What a terrible job this was really, trying to force her way into a family's private grief. It made her think of the time Gino had told her she had too much human decency to make a really good reporter, which had made them all laugh when he'd said it, but she was starting to wonder if he might have a point.

She pushed the bell again, waited for the percussive vibrations to fade, then turned an ear towards the door without actually touching it. Nothing. No radio, TV, voices, vacuums or even footsteps, just the whine of a strimmer in the next street and the sluggish subsong of a young chaffinch somewhere nearby. She wondered if the Longs were in the back garden, and if so could she get round there. There was a gate at the side, but it didn't only look locked, it had such an air of unscalability that surely not even a burglar would try. For one hilarious moment she had an image of herself tumbling into their back garden, bruised and dishevelled, startling them out of their wake.

'Who is it?' a male voice suddenly shouted.

Startled, she called out her name, adding, 'Elliot Russell said I should come.'

'Elliot who?' the voice called back.

'Russell,' she answered, her heart sinking with anger and dismay. This man, presumably Chas Long, hadn't even heard of Elliot Russell, so the bastard had set her up. He'd guessed she'd do this, had no doubt informed the world, and now she could already see the boomers' smirking faces as she walked back into the office. 'He said you'd prefer to talk to a woman,' she added, not quite ready to give up yet.

There was a long pause, then the same voice said, 'We was expecting you tomorrow.'

'Oh, I'm sorry,' she cried, taking heart. 'He said he'd called to change it to today. Didn't he speak to you?'

'Hang on,' the man said.

Silence resumed. She continued to stand there, waiting, burning in the sun's scorching rays and hardly daring to breathe as with all her might she willed those inside to let her in. *Please, please, please, God,* she fervently prayed. Any minute now her tabloid colleagues would arrive back from lunch, first one, then two, then in droves, ready to pick a fight on the doorstep, either to get in there first, or to ruin it for her. They'd surround the place, as they had for weeks, anything to totally decimate what little chance she stood of getting over that threshold.

Time ticked relentlessly on. Someone backed out of a garage down the street, threw her a suspicious look, then drove away. Her skin was on fire, there was no shade, not even from the small slab of an overhead porch. Maybe they thought if they kept her waiting long enough she'd just go away. Should she ring that dreadful bell again, remind them she was still there? She could call them on her mobile if she had their new number.

Then quite suddenly the door swung open and a short, narrow-faced man in his mid-forties, whom she recognized as Chas Long, told her to come in.

'He should have called,' he said grumpily. 'We're trying to get him on the phone, but the missis says we can't leave you standing out there in that heat.'

Laurie hid her horror well. It hadn't occurred to her that they might call Elliot to check. *Shit.* What was she going to do now? He would be bound to blow her cover, and she'd be back out the door a lot quicker than she'd managed to get in.

'Thank you,' she said, as Chas Long closed the door behind her. 'I hope it's not inconvenient. I didn't realize no one had got your agreement to the change.'

'Then it's lucky for you we was here,' he grunted. 'Go on through to the kitchen. The wife's holding on to speak to Elliot.'

Deciding that all she could do now was brazen it out, Laurie walked along the thickly carpeted hallway towards what must be the kitchen. Chas Long followed, then suddenly lunged awkwardly ahead of her to open the door.

'Thank you,' Laurie smiled.

The fake walnut wood kitchen wasn't large, but was

149

spotlessly clean and seemed to have all the modern gadgets and appliances, which included a cosy little breakfast niche over by the back door, where Daphne Long and her fifteen-year-old son, Simon, were sitting, almost huddled together behind two giant glasses of Coke.

Seeing Laurie, Daphne waved her to come in and pointed to the neat little cordless phone she had pressed to one ear, indicating she was on it. She was a petite, peroxide blonde with a sun-weathered face, a taut little body and chunks of gold jewellery on her fingers, wrists, one ear and throat.

Laurie looked at Simon, whose unfortunate spots and sullen expression weren't made any more attractive by the scythe of silver studs adorning one ear, or the tattoo of West Ham United on his upper left arm. She smiled at him, but his eyes merely slid off to nowhere, while he tapped an impatient foot on the floor and seemed to sink lower into his teenage slouch.

'Sit down here,' Daphne whispered, pointing Laurie to one of the empty chairs the other side of the breakfast niche. 'Chas, get her a drink. It's so bloody hot out there, innit?' she grumbled. 'Haven't had a summer for years, and now they're like bloody buses, all coming at once . . . Hello? Hello,' she said into the phone, her cockney twang more discernible now she'd stopped whispering. 'Who? Oh, yeah, Mr Russell.' She paused and looked at Laurie. 'That's right, Daphne Long. I know, tomorrow, but . . . No, I'm not cancelling . . . It's just we got your girl here – hang on.' She covered the mouthpiece and said to Laurie, 'What's your name again?'

Laurie told her.

'We got your girl Laurie Forbes here,' Daphne told him. 'She said you was supposed to call and change . . . What? Oh no, it's all right. I mean, we was here, so . . . No, well we wasn't quite ready for it, but she's here now . . . Oh, it's OK. No need to apologize. I just wanted to check. We've had so many people trying to trick their way in here. All right, cheers then.'

As Daphne hung up, Laurie didn't waste too much time feeling grateful to Elliot, since he more than owed her this. However, she was thankful that no one, including Daphne, could see her squirming inside as she wondered what Elliot was thinking now, if he was angry, or . . . Well, there was no

150

fathoming Elliot, and what did she care anyway? He'd obviously call her some time in the next few hours, so she'd just make sure her mobile stayed off.

Daphne Long was watching her with small, limpid eyes and an attractive, though sad little smile. 'I'm Daphne,' she said, touching a bejewelled hand to her chest. 'And this is Simon, my boy. Well, I expect you recognize us from all the publicity.'

Laurie smiled. 'I'm pleased to meet you,' she responded. 'And thank you for agreeing to this. There was obviously some kind of mix-up –'

'It's all right,' Daphne said, clipping a shiny gold ball back on her earlobe now she'd finished with the phone. 'Makes no difference really, does it? Today, tomorrow, we're still going to say the same things.'

Laurie thanked Chas as he placed a tall, frosted glass of Coke and ice in front of her. After gulping down several refreshing mouthfuls she thanked him again, then to Daphne she said, 'I understand what a very difficult time this must be for you. As if it's not bad enough losing your daughter the way you did, then all this attention from people like me . . . I'm really sorry you're having to go through it.'

'I got to tell you, it is you people who make it worse,' Daphne confided. 'We didn't want to talk to none of you, actually. I mean, this isn't the kind of thing you want people sticking their noses in, is it?'

'No, of course not,' Laurie responded with feeling.

'But I know you got a job to do. It's not your fault. I'm just saying . . . The way they all hang around out there . . . It's like vultures innit, Chas? Like bloody vultures. Poor Princess Di, is all I can say, because we've had a taste of it now so we know what it's like.'

Laurie's expression was a picture of understanding. 'What changed your mind about doing an interview?' she asked, reaching casually into her bag and taking out her tape recorder.

'They told us it was probably the only way of getting you to leave us alone. We had to say something, because that's the way it is, these days, innit? You people in the media, you don't go away until you've got what you came for.'

She was eyeing Laurie's little Sony player with such

marked distaste that Laurie said, 'I can use a notepad and pen if you prefer.'

'No, it's all right. I suppose we're used to them now, after all that time with the police.' Her eyes flicked towards her husband, who'd settled in next to her, creating an awkward and incomplete family picture of father, mother and son.

'We can't talk about our interrogation,' Chas said crisply. 'I told Elliot Russell that. It's private.'

Laurie's pleasant expression remained intact, as she wondered what other conditions she might blunder into.

She was about to open up the interview when Daphne said, 'She was a good girl, weren't she, Chas?' She dabbed away the tears that had welled in her eyes. 'Can't stop thinking about her,' she said woefully. 'We was so close, we was more like friends or sisters really, than mother and daughter. Where're *you* going?' she said to Simon as he got up.

'Let him go,' Chas advised as Simon scuffed sulkily out of the kitchen. 'This has been really hard on him, poor lad. Been hard on us all.'

'Of course,' Laurie responded. She looked at them both, then as gently as she could, she said, 'Did you know Colin Ashby? Did you ever meet him?'

'No, not personally,' Daphne answered, speaking over Chas who was saying, 'What I wouldn't like to do to that bastard.'

'Chas, don't,' Daphne said, putting a wifely hand on his arm.

Laurie gave them a moment, then judging it OK to continue, she said, 'Did you know Sophie was seeing him? I mean before all this?'

'Oh yeah,' Daphne answered. 'Me and my Sophes never had no secrets. We told each other everything.'

Laurie wondered how true that was, and hoped she was about to find out. 'So you know how they met?' she said.

'Course I do. It was like fate, that's what she said. Bloody bad fate it turned out to be, didn't it? But anyway, she thought it was special at the time. She had this friend, Brad, not boyfriend and girlfriend or anything, just mates, you know. He's a minicab driver. Well, there was this one night when he was giving Sophes a lift home after they'd been out clubbing or somewhere, and he gets a call from Colin Ashby asking him to come and pick him up at the Houses of Parliament. So Brad asked if he minded Sophes being there, cos he couldn't just abandon her, could he? Anyway, it didn't turn out to be a problem, so Sophes went along too, and that was how they met. In the back of a minicab, of all places. She said they hit it off right away. Chatting and laughing. He was a real easy bloke to talk to, she said. She always said that, didn't she, Chas? That he was real easy-going.'

Chas only grunted.

'She was right excited when he called Brad a couple of days later to ask for her number,' Daphne went on. 'An important man like that. Everyone knew who he was. She was dead chuffed, she was. Rang me on my mobile to tell me. "He just called me, Mum," she said. "That one I told you about. He wants to see me again."' Daphne's eyes were filling up again and, ripping off a square of kitchen roll, she added brokenly, 'If only she'd known how it was all going to end, she'd never have seen him.'

Well, she was certainly right about that, Laurie was thinking as she looked down at the small islands of ice floating in her Coke. She wondered if they genuinely didn't know that their daughter had been a professional escort, or if they'd been instructed to give this watered-down version of Brad Pinkton's role in it all. Since that particular aspect of Sophie's life still hadn't been made public, she dispensed with the idea of asking them straight out if they knew, because if they didn't, it wasn't going to help them, or her, to add to their suffering with such a painful revelation.

'Did Sophie know Colin Ashby was married?' she asked after a while.

'Yes. He told her straight away,' Daphne answered. 'It took her a few weeks to tell me, though, and I didn't like it one bit, when she told me, did I, Chas? I said to her, "You can't go getting yourself mixed up with a married man, it's not right, and you'll only end up getting hurt." I never thought it would be like this, though,' she added tearfully.

Laurie kept her compassionate face going, then bracing herself, she said, 'Do you know if they became intimate on their first date?'

153

Daphne's eyes shot to Chas, whose jaw went so tight it turned his face pale.

Daphne's hand moved back to his arm. 'Course they was,' Daphne answered. 'You've seen pictures of her. She was gorgeous. No man was going to resist her, was he? She called me after he'd gone. Full of it, she was. Said he thought she was the most beautiful girl he'd ever met, that he hadn't been able to stop thinking about her since the first time he saw her ... He had all the lines. Later she told me he said him and his wife weren't hitting it off. They didn't have no sex, or nothing any more. He'd had other affairs, he said, but he'd never felt like this before. I told her she was soft in the head if she believed all that, but there was no getting through to her. Still, for all that, he was good to her. Generous, you know. Bought her loads of clothes, but I haven't had the heart to sort through them yet. They're upstairs in her room. The police let us have them back after they'd finished, you know, whatever they have to do with them.'

Laurie nodded. Would they be worth looking at, she wondered. Possibly, but since she could imagine all too easily what kind of clothes they were, she didn't think she could bear to be there when Daphne unpacked them.

'She was besotted with him,' Daphne suddenly went on. Her tanned, leathery face was becoming much more strained now, reminding Laurie of how deep and real her loss was. 'She didn't want to meet anyone else. As far as she was concerned he was going to leave his wife and go and live with her. That's what he said, so she believed him. Well, why wouldn't she when he kept saying it, and in the end he did, didn't he? He left his wife and turned up at her flat in the early hours of the morning, saying he couldn't stay away a minute longer.' Her voice almost gave out then as she said, 'She was so happy when he came to her like that, then a week later she was ... dead.'

Chas put an arm round her shoulders. 'If I could get my hands on that bastard ...' he snarled at Laurie. 'She was just a kid. Less than half his age. He had a responsibility to take care of her. She didn't know nothing of the world, like he did. What did he think he was doing? I'd like to kill him, I would. Same as what he did to her.'

154

'Sssh,' Daphne sniffed. 'It don't do no good talking like that. They've got him, so at least we know he hasn't got away with it.'

'Do you have any idea *why* he might have done it?' Laurie asked gently.

'No. None,' Daphne said. 'We keep asking ourselves that. But what reason could there be? If he'd wanted to go back to his wife she could hardly have stopped him, could she? He's twice her size, never mind twice her age, and anyway, she wouldn't have stood in his way. She wasn't like that, hanging on to a bloke if he didn't want to stay.'

'Did the police give you any idea why they think he might have done it?' Laurie said.

Daphne looked at Chas. 'We don't know what they think, do we?' she answered. 'They don't tell you nothing. They just asks questions.'

'Did Sophie know about Heather Dance and her little girl?'

'What, the woman who was in the paper the other day? No. She couldn't have done. She'd have told me if she did.'

'So the suggestion that Sophie might have been black-mailing him –'

'Is bloody nonsense,' Chas growled. 'They make me sick with the effing tripe they come up with. Blackmail! Anyone who knew her would tell you what a load of bollocks that is.'

Daphne looked down at the kitchen roll she was shredding. 'Honest to God, I don't know why he'd have done that to her,' she said. 'It just don't make any sense.'

Laurie took a breath before asking the next question. It was probably one they'd heard before, and she wondered if, over the past few weeks, their answer might have changed at all. 'Do you think there's any chance it might not have been him?' she said tentatively. 'I'm sure you know he's denying it.'

Chas's face turned puce. 'The bastard was caught red-handed,' he practically shouted. 'He did it all right, and I'll tell you this much, they ought to bring back hanging for blokes who go round doing that to innocent young girls. I was never for it before this, but I am now. It's different when it's your own. Believe me. I'd do time just to get my hands on that bastard.'

155

Daphne's eyes were bleak. 'Yeah, we know he's denying it,' she said. 'Well, I suppose he would, wouldn't he? But he did it all right. They caught him right there, didn't they?'

Laurie nodded, for there was no disputing that. 'Did the police mention anything about blackmail?' she asked. 'I don't mean about Heather Dance, I mean about anything else.'

'We told you already, she wasn't blackmailing him,' Chas said testily. 'She wasn't that kind of girl.'

Laurie looked at Daphne again. 'So the police didn't mention it?' she prompted. 'As a matter of procedure, it would have made sense for them to.'

'Why don't you tell her?' Simon suddenly shouted, startling them all as he burst in the door. 'Tell her the truth, what's really been happening . . .'

'Simon! Shut it!' his father barked.

'Yeah, they reckon she was blackmailing him,' Simon cried. 'That's why they think he killed her. She knew something she shouldn't have and –'

Chas was on his feet. 'Simon, go to your room!' he bellowed.

The boy was already backing away. 'Why are you helping them?' he sobbed furiously. 'All they're interested in is protecting *him*. They don't care about us. They just want us to keep our mouths shut, that's all.'

'Simon!' Chas roared, advancing with his fist in the air. 'Don't make me do this!'

'Chas!' Daphne cried, scrambling after him and grabbing his fist in both hands. 'Stop it. Just stop,' she sobbed. 'I can't stand all this . . . Simon, just go to your room.'

'Not till you start telling the –'

'Simon!' she shouted.

The boy's face was twisted with rage and frustration. Laurie could see he wanted to say more, but didn't quite dare. In the end, he banged the door open again and stormed out, snarling 'Fuck off, all of you. Just fuck off.'

For several minutes after he'd gone there was only the sound of Chas breathing as he stood with his hands resting on the sink, and the muted whirr of the tape as it absorbed these moments of calm after the storm. Laurie sat very still, feeling desperately sorry for them in their confusion, while trying to decide how best to proceed from here.

'Maybe you'd better turn that thing off,' Daphne said, pointing to the tape recorder.

Immediately Laurie put her hand over it and made it click.

Chas's eyes were blazing with anger as he turned them on his wife. 'You're not going to tell her any more,' he snarled. 'Jesus Christ, woman, you know what they said . . .'

'Calm down!' Daphne snapped. 'I'm not telling her anything. Anyway, we don't know anything, do we? Not what it's about, anyway. We just know there was something . . .'

'And they don't want us telling people like her,' he raged.

'Well, it's a bit late now, innit?' she shouted back. 'She knows now, thanks to your big mouth son.'

'And where does he get that from?' he sneered. 'You've never been able to keep your mouth shut.'

'Fuck you!' she spat. 'Just fuck you.'

'Fuck you too.' He turned away, but not before Laurie had seen the tears in his eyes.

Daphne moved back on to the padded bench seat, and looked across at Laurie.

'If it helps,' Laurie said, 'I already knew there was some kind of cover-up, so you haven't told me anything you need to feel concerned about.'

Daphne nodded, then turned her head to stare out at the garden. It was several minutes before she spoke, and when she did she continued to look outside. 'They didn't threaten us, or nothing,' she said. She jerked a thumb towards Chas. 'He just made it sound like they did, but they didn't. They just made it plain that they didn't want us going into any kind of detail with the press about –'

'Daph*ne*!' Chas warned.

'Look, it all comes down to the same thing in the end, don't it?' Daphne cried. 'Sophie's dead and he killed her. What does it matter what she did or didn't know? She can't tell anyone now, can she?'

'Did she know anything?' Laurie probed.

Daphne shook her head. 'If she did she never told me. I mean not anything that could do anyone any harm. I don't know if they believe that, but it's the truth. She never told me nothing like that.'

'What about the police? Did they give you any idea what they thought she might be blackmailing him about?'

'No,' Daphne answered shaking her head. 'Like I said, they never told us nothing. They just kept asking us all these different questions. It was a bloody nightmare, I can tell you.'

'What kind of questions?' Laurie prompted, choosing to forget that she wasn't supposed to ask about their interrogation.

'I don't know. All kinds. If she'd ever met any of his friends. If they'd –'

'Had she?' Laurie interrupted, surprised that Chas hadn't jumped in yet.

'Some. You know, his colleagues, when he took her to show her the Houses of Parliament, and places like that. She met some of them then.'

'Do you remember their names?'

'Daphne!' Chas growled. 'This is the very stuff they told us not to talk about.'

'What difference does it make now?' his wife cried. 'It's not going to bring her back, is it? And we don't know none of their names anyway.'

Laurie could easily believe they didn't, but the kind of questions they'd been asked could tell her a great deal. She might make more headway were she able to get rid of Chas for a while, but since that wasn't possible she resigned herself to treading carefully through the minefield of possibilities she was now facing. 'These friends he introduced her to,' she said, 'did they ever go to her flat, do you know?'

'She said they did, a couple of times. With him.'

'And I suppose the police wanted to know what they all talked about?'

'As if I'd know,' Daphne responded. 'I wasn't blooming well there, was I? Did they talk about money or politics they wanted to know. Was there ever any mention of people who lived abroad? What kind of question's that? I ask you. Hundreds of people live abroad, for crying out loud. How am I supposed to know if any of them did? And I told them, if he ever talked about any deals with her, or anything like that, then I wouldn't have a clue.'

Laurie was frowning. 'Did they give you the impression they thought he might be involved in some kind of deal?' she

158

said. 'Something that might have been top secret, or even illegal, maybe?'

'Oh yeah, we got that impression all right,' Daphne replied. 'Top secret, anyway, because you only had to look at where we was when they was asking all their bloomin' questions. In this bloody great big house out in the country, with dirty great big fences and alarms and God only knows what. It was like being in a flaming prison, except you never saw luxury like it. All these paintings, and marble fireplaces, furniture straight out of a stately home. Well, it was a stately home. I've never been in such a posh place in me life.'

'Where was it?' Laurie asked.

Daphne shook her head. 'All we know is we went north out of here, after that . . .' she shrugged. 'We reckon we must have been somewhere in Suffolk, even Norfolk. We don't know, though. We was in the car a long time, anyway.'

Laurie waited for her to come up with more, but that seemed to be it, so she said, 'What about the people who were questioning you? I suppose they were police?'

'Good question,' Daphne retorted. 'That's what they said, but Chas reckons they was MI5 or something like that, don't you?'

Laurie looked at Chas, but his face was averted.

'Do you remember any of their names, or what they looked like?' she asked turning back to Daphne.

'I don't think they ever told us their names, did they?' she said again to Chas.

This time his head came round. 'Have you finished now?' he growled. 'Is there anything else you want to blab before she goes? We was supposed to say we was with relatives.'

'What relatives?' Daphne cried angrily. 'We've hardly bloody got any, have we?'

'But she don't know that,' Chas spat, jabbing a finger towards Laurie.

'I'm afraid I do,' Laurie interjected.

He glared at her with such menace that were it not for the underlying confusion in his eyes she might have been ready to leave. 'Who the bloody hell's that?' he snarled as the Beethoven chimes started ringing down the hall.

He lumbered off to check, and was back within seconds,

159

looking furious and pale. 'It's someone else from the press,' he snarled. 'I thought they said they was going to keep 'em away. Bloody parasites.' His eyes shot to Laurie. 'Excuse me,' he said, 'but that's what you are. You come here, trying to get things out of us . . . Well, we've had enough of it, do you hear me? Our girl's dead, and all anyone wants to do is talk about that bastard –'

'Chas, shut up,' Daphne interrupted.

He flinched as the bell went again. 'We're never going to bloody get rid of them,' he raged. Then to Laurie: 'We gave you what you came for, now you go out there and tell them to fuck off. Go on. We're finished here. She's told you all you're going hear.'

'Chas, where's your manners?' Daphne scolded angrily.

'If I were you,' Laurie said, slipping the tape recorder, which had continued to run, back into her bag, 'I'd call the police. I'm sure they'll help clear the street.'

Daphne walked down the hall with her. When they reached the front door Daphne said, 'Which paper is this going to be in?'

Laurie took a breath. It was a good question, but she would have to bluff. So after mentioning her own paper first, she added, 'The final decision hasn't been made yet. We'll let you know when it has.'

'Do we get to see it before it comes out? Elliot said we would.'

'Yes, of course,' she promised.

Daphne forced a smile. Then after a couple of nods, she said, 'Do you mind letting yourself out? I don't want them to see me. I hate the things they shout out.'

'No, of course not,' Laurie assured her. Then on impulse she pulled the small woman into an embrace. 'Thanks for talking to me,' she said. 'And I really am sorry about Sophie.'

'I know,' Daphne responded, wincing as the doorbell chimed again. 'She was a good girl. Everyone liked her.' Her eyes came up to Laurie's. 'She weren't no blackmailer,' she said. 'She might have been a lot of other things, but that definitely weren't one of them. I'd stake my life on it.'

Knowing how hard it was to think ill of someone you

160

loved, particularly when they were recently dead, Laurie hugged her again, saying, 'I'm sure you're right.' Now wasn't the time to tell her that her efforts to preserve her daughter's good name weren't only going to be smashed apart once the Brad Pinkton story broke, but were, in the long run, more likely to get Colin Ashby off than to send him down.

There were about a dozen reporters outside, most of whom surged forward as Laurie opened the front door and quickly let herself out. It took a moment for them to realize it was her, and their resentment once they did became almost palpable. She tried to ignore them, pushing her way through their aggressive jostling and banter, but they were making it increasingly hard for her to get past. As if being first on the scene at Beth Ashby's wasn't enough, how the hell had she managed this?

'So who are you sleeping with?' someone jeered, as she forced her way out of the gate. 'You've got to be sleeping with someone.'

'Come on, Laurie, give us a break,' Bill Krupps from the *Sun* shouted. 'We've been waiting round here for weeks.'

'What did they tell you, Laurie? Do you know where they went?'

'No,' she answered, still struggling to break free.

'She's not going to tell you anything,' a female voice sneered. 'She's going to keep it all for herself.'

'Did you tape it, Laurie?' Rob Phipps from the *Star* demanded, trying to grab her bag.

'Let go!' she cried, hugging it hard to her chest.

'Oh, she bites,' someone laughed.

'Come on, Laurie, let us all have a listen.'

'Stop it!' she shouted, as they began roughing her up even more. 'Let me go!'

'Just give us the tape! A little girl like you won't know what to do with it anyway.'

A few of them laughed, while others continued pulling her bag, and prising at her arms.

'She gets in first with Beth Ashby,' someone hissed, 'and all she comes out with is four fucking words. Call yourself a reporter.'

'Let me go!' Laurie seethed, kicking out and twisting her shoulders away from them.

'Let her go!' a new voice suddenly commanded.

Momentarily surprised, they all turned round.

'Now!' Elliot snapped. His harsh, craggy features were uncompromising and distinctly unpleasant.

'We were just having a bit of fun,' Rob Phipps said, releasing the bag.

'She's got to learn to take a joke,' someone else piped up.

Elliot brushed them aside, took Laurie's arm and marched her out of the fray.

'Well, now we know who she's sleeping with,' someone called after them, making the others laugh.

Rage and embarrassment swept through Laurie, turning her cheeks scarlet.

'Just keep walking,' Elliot muttered under his breath.

His Porsche was outside a house further up the street, where a woman was peering out through her nets.

'Get in,' he said.

'No,' she snapped, wresting her arm free. 'Thank you for the rescue, but I'd rather get the train.'

His eyes held no warmth. 'Just get in the car,' he responded.

She didn't move. She couldn't allow herself to think of how much she hated him. If she did she might start screaming it.

'Do you want everyone over there to watch this?' he demanded.

Worse than anything else she could imagine at that moment was the spectacle of him picking her up and stuffing her into the car, so, her face taut with anger, her heart pounding with dread, she descended into the passenger seat and held her bag close. As soon as he was in the driver's seat she said, 'Please, just drop me at the station.'

Ignoring her, he roared away from the kerb, turned left at the end of the road, and carried on along the high street, past the Renault garage where Chas Long's brother was a mechanic, the funeral parlour that had received Sophie's flowers, the station entrance where Laurie needed to get out, until they were heading out into the countryside on roads she didn't know.

'Where are you taking me?' she demanded.

'You'll see.'

'Just turn the car round and take me back to the station.'

He continued driving, revving the engine hard, squealing fast round bends, never taking his eyes from the road.

Were it anyone else she might have protested further, but with him she was afraid to. There was just too much emotion wrapped up in this situation, this man, for her to trust herself to speak, so she kept her eyes averted, not wanting to look at him even for an instant.

'It's OK, you don't have to thank me for getting you in to see the Longs today,' he said, finally.

She stayed silent.

'So, can I assume you've got something worth listening to?'

'The interview's mine,' she snapped.

His eyebrows went up, but he said no more until he'd pulled into the car park of a country inn and held out his hand. 'The tape,' he said, when she looked at his open palm. 'I want to hear it.'

'I told you –'

'Give me the damned tape,' he growled.

Knowing she had no choice, she reached into her bag, rewound the tape, then set her machine down next to the gear stick. No way was she handing over the actual cassette, he'd just have to listen to it like this.

It took no more than twenty minutes to replay. When it was over he sat staring out at the fields, his long fingers drumming tunelessly on the wheel.

'Do you know where they were staying?' she finally made herself ask. 'Do you recognize the description?'

'I can hazard a pretty good guess,' he responded.

'Well?' she prompted, when he didn't elaborate.

'Did you know that forensics have come up with some unidentified hairs and fibres?' he said, still staring straight ahead.

Her eyes widened. 'No,' she replied. 'How do you know?'

'I just do. Are you familiar with the name Marcus Gatling?'

Recalling Chilton asking her the same question she felt the stirrings of intrigue. 'Yes,' she answered.

'What do you know about him?'

'That he and Colin Ashby have been friends since their time at Oxford. That he's some kind of heavyweight in the business world . . . What do you know about him?'

'That it was probably his house the Longs were at. That he made Colin Ashby an offer, which Ashby refused.'

'What kind of an offer?'

'That's a question for Ashby.'

Inwardly she groaned. 'So you've managed to get an interview with him too,' she responded.

'Wrong.'

He turned to look at her and as their eyes met a horrible burning seared through her chest. Immediately she reached for the Sony player. He was just as quick, but as his hand closed over hers she drew back sharply, recoiling from the physical contact. 'I'm no longer officially on this story,' she said, turning to look out of the side window so he wouldn't see the heat on her face. 'That tape could get me back on it.'

When he made no comment more anger lashed through her. 'I did that interview,' she seethed. 'The tape belongs as much to me –' She stopped as he threw open the door and got out.

'Come on, let's get a drink,' he said.

As she walked into the pub behind him, memories of Lysette were tearing so painfully through her that she could hardly bear it. How could her sister have loved a man like this? He was a monster. A demon. He had no heart, no soul, no care in the world for anyone but himself.

'What'll you have?' he asked when they reached the bar.

'Bloody Mary, with ice.'

As he ordered she glanced round the shadowy interior with its gnarled wood furniture and small niche windows. A group of German tourists was gathered round a table next to an old-fashioned pinball machine, studying their maps and drinking lager, while a middle-aged couple who looked decidedly illicit, canoodled in a dimly lit corner booth.

'There are tables outside, on the patio,' Elliot said, nodding towards an open door at the back. 'Why don't you go and sit down?'

Though it was cooler inside, the view down over the valley to a red-roofed town and cathedral towers and spires in the distance was more pleasing than the throb of the jukebox, so selecting a long wooden table and benches in the shade of an oak she nodded to an old man who was just leaving, and sat down.

Elliot joined her a few minutes later with two bloody Marys and a couple of bags of crisps. 'In case you're hungry,' he said throwing them on to the table.

She was, but would be damned before she'd accept them.

'OK,' he said, after downing half his drink, 'we need to clear the air and this seems as good a place as any to do it. I know you blame me for Lysette's death, and believe you me, I've spent a long time blaming myself too . . .'

'I don't want to discuss it,' she said through her teeth. 'What you –'

'Laurie, listen to me. I had no idea she'd do what she did –'

'Stop it!' she cried, putting her hands over her ears. 'I don't want to hear your excuses. If it weren't for you she'd be alive now, and nothing you say's going to change that. You killed her, Elliot. It was *you* who killed her.'

His face had turned pale, and his eyes showed the anguish he felt at her words. 'I swear, if I'd known . . .'

When he stopped she rounded on him bitterly. 'If you'd known what?' she snarled. 'That she'd kill herself because you told her you'd met someone else, so she should stop bugging you now? That was the word you used, wasn't it? "Bugging." A year and a half you'd been putting her through all kinds of hell, taking advantage of her in a way any normal person would be ashamed of, then you tell her there's someone else on the scene now so she should get out and stop bugging you. Just what kind of man are you? No, don't answer that, I'll tell you. You're one who's not fit to tread the same earth as a decent human being.'

'Which is exactly how I felt for a long time after she died,' he responded.

'But you've let yourself off the hook now, is that it? Or no, you want me to do it for you. That's what all this is about, isn't it? Get me involved in what could be one of the most sensational stories of the decade, give my career a little boost, and I might just forgive you for killing my sister. Well, forget it! In fact, you can just go straight to hell. She was my twin, for

God's sake. She was so much a part of me that I only feel half alive now she's gone. Have you got any idea what that feels like? How it is to lose someone you're so close to you can actually feel their pain? And I felt hers over you. God, did I feel it. And the sick, sad part of it was, the worse you treated her the more she loved you. Dear God, why couldn't you have been kind to her? She was so sweet and good. She'd never hurt anyone. The whole world mattered to her, but no one as much as you, and you had to go and destroy her.'

He said nothing, only stared at the horizon and occasionally blinked. He'd thought nothing, not even her loathing, could make him feel any worse than he already did, but she was coming close. It didn't help either that he'd somehow forgotten how alike they were. A part of him was still reeling from the shock of seeing her when she'd come out of the Longs' earlier. She could so easily have been Lysette. They even sounded the same, though only the timbre of their voices. The words they used had always been different. But maybe this was what he wanted, why he was here – to suffer Laurie's hatred as though it were Lysette's, even though he knew Lysette had been incapable of hating a single living soul.

Laurie looked at his hand lying on the table, the tapering fingers, the dark hair curling over his knuckles and watch-strap, and for one insane moment she thought she might smash her glass into it. Why was God allowing him to remain on this earth, when he'd done what he had to her sister? It didn't make any sense. He should be dead and Lysette should be here. She deserved to live, while he didn't even deserve to be remembered. She pushed a fist to her mouth to stifle a sob. Why had he brought her here? Why was he making them both suffer like this, when it was over, Lysette was gone and nothing was ever going to bring her back.

'I'm sorry,' he said finally. 'I don't know what else to say, except I'm sorry.'

Laurie turned her face away, but the tears were coming so fast she could hardly catch her breath. 'I told you not to bring it up,' she choked. 'You're not decent enough even to utter her name, so just don't.'

'Can I ask how your father is?' he said quietly. 'I heard about his heart attack.'

'Just stay away from my family,' she gasped furiously, crying harder than ever. 'We've got nothing to do with you any more. Do you hear me? Nothing! As far as you're concerned we're as dead as my sister.'

He picked up his glass, but didn't drink. He'd truly believed he was ready to handle this, but now he wasn't so sure.

For a long time they sat in the difficult, memory-filled silence, barely hearing the traffic on the road nearby, or noticing the sun glinting on the leaves overhead. It was so hot and humid that sweat was beading on their faces, while the flowerbeds wilted and the grass turned to straw. All either of them could think about was Lysette with her gentle, poetic heart, angelic soul and total inability to see bad in anyone. Everyone who'd known her had loved her, so why couldn't Elliot? Why had he withheld what she'd craved so deeply that in the end, unable to stand the pain of his rejection, she'd driven her car so fast into a motorway bridge that she hadn't stood a chance of survival? She'd even told him she was going to do it, and his answer had been 'be my guest'.

Such a horrifically violent end, with such cruel words ringing in her ears, and still Laurie woke up gasping in the night as she saw the car hurtling at high speed towards the bridge, with her sister at the wheel. She could see Lysette's face, terrified, traumatized. Sometimes she even felt the impact, saw the chaos, heard the terrible crunching of metal and crushing of bones. And there was more, so much more but she couldn't deal with it now. She'd never been able to, and maybe she never would.

'I thought,' Elliot began, 'if we saw each other . . .' His hand tightened on his glass. 'I was wrong,' he said shortly.

Without finishing their drinks they returned to the car and started back towards London. The forty-minute journey passed in silence, until finally they reached West India Quay.

'I'm not going to the office,' Laurie said, eager to get away. 'You can drop me at the station.'

After pulling the car to a halt, causing the traffic behind to honk in frustration, he handed her the Sony player. 'The interview's yours,' he said. 'Play it to Wilbur. If he doesn't reassign you, and you decide to continue anyway – well, good luck.'

167

Chapter 11

The selection in Ava's new wardrobe was still small, but every item had been chosen to suit the dynamic and worldly kind of woman she aimed to portray. She wanted nothing that reminded her of Beth, none of the long, shapeless dresses or drawstring trousers. No more sloppy sandals or loose-fitting T-shirts. To quote Georgie, Ava was a woman of class and literary standing, whose style of dress should reflect her inner confidence and flamboyance. So they had shopped, mainly in Bath, with Georgie's credit card picking up the bills until Ava's initial cheque for her novel came through.

Today was Ava's first outing since Leonora had dropped the bombshell about Heather Dance and her three-year-old daughter. Beth's suffering during the days that had followed had driven her to the point where she no longer wanted to live. If the pain and devastation were going to be this bad then what was the point? The strain of it was all but annihilating her, so that all she wanted was for her mind to stop working, in the hope it would stop her heart from hurting. She wondered how many more times she'd have to lose herself in the woods so that she could scream and scream and scream and plead with God to make it all go away, before He listened and did something to help her. She couldn't decide which was worse: the child, or that Colin was in contact with the woman, while refusing to see her. She hated, loathed and despised the woman with such a passion it was almost insane, yet she could feel sorry for her too, since no one knew better than Beth Ashby how deeply Colin's betrayal could cut. And he had betrayed Heather Dance too, for where had he gone the last time Beth had thrown him out?

Not to his mistress and child, but to yet another one of his affairs.

But she wasn't going to go through it all again, not today. Today belonged to Ava and God knew how desperately Beth needed her, for emptying or stopping her mind, no matter how hard she tried, simply wasn't possible, whereas filling it with something, even somebody else, might provide at least some small respite from the hell.

Stepping into a buttercup-yellow shift dress with its elegant boat neck and slinky cut felt good. The expensive fabric was cool on her skin, and the way it touched her slim hips and settled closely, but not cloyingly against her breasts made her look stylish and sensuous, rather than obviously sexy. The vibrant colour, with its subtle frosting, seemed to turn her honey-tone tan a shade darker. Her legs were exposed only from the knee down, but their length and slenderness were subtly accentuated by the expert styling of the sheath dress. She looked in the mirror and tilted her head to one side in order to get a better view of the chic French pleat Georgie's mother had created. It was incredible how just the hair and the dress were already making her feel stronger. And all the time she was slipping her feet into the silver Magli sandals with their two-inch heels and sparkly straps, touching her cheeks with blusher and frosting her lips a delicate shade of peach, she could sense Beth's wretchedness withdrawing further and further into the shadows. She knew it was only temporary, but the gradual release was like taking in the first few gasps of air after being buried alive. It was as though her blood was starting to flow freely again, and her limbs were unravelling themselves from unbearable tension. It was true that flashes of panic were still snatching at her confidence, trying to trap it and smother it, but for the moment at least she was encouraged by the pleasing image she was presenting.

By the time she stepped off the train at Paddington, she found herself able to walk with a jaunty spring in her step as she tossed her bag carelessly over one shoulder and regarded her fellow travellers from behind dark glasses. Heads turned as she passed, not because they recognized her, she was sure, but because she was so fresh and lovely to look at. In fact, she doubted even her own parents would recognize this tall, graceful woman with her exotic tan and mysterious smile, so there was really no need to feel shy or afraid as she entered the familiar fray of London.

From the back of a taxi she watched the world outside. The weather was so glorious that Hyde Park was full of families, students, office workers and tourists, either strolling, boating, picnicking or bronzing in the dazzling afternoon sun. For a few daydreamy moments she pictured herself as Ava lying with a lover in the shade of a tree, teasing and laughing, kissing and caressing. Who would he be, she wondered, as a frisson of anticipation passed tantalizingly through her. Then darkness suddenly descended as somewhere deep inside Beth struggled to reach Colin. Ava's eyes immediately stung with tears, as her heart became so heavy with despair that she almost told the driver to turn back. But she'd sworn not to let Beth do this. Ava was stronger, more capable and courageous, so she mustn't allow the confusion of Beth's past to spoil the heady prospects of this brand-new future.

Nevertheless, this had been a lot easier at Robin Lindsay's office on Monday, before Leonora had brought the news about Heather. She'd really had the feel of Ava then, whereas now, she was like a light flickering in the darkness, apt to go out at any moment. But once she'd arrived and they were calling her Ava, the light would start to burn brighter and steadier, and their praise and attention would keep her confidence secure.

By the time the taxi came to a halt in Mayfair, she was breathing easily again, and the enigmatic smile was curving her lips. She kept her mind in the moment, thinking no further than the act of stretching her long legs out on to the street and of how pleasurable it was to hold her willowy body back for a moment, like a hidden promise. She was the kind of woman who would enslave Colin virtually on sight with her graceful movements and discreet promiscuity, so why had she never let him see her like this before? It surprised her then to realize that this time, instead of being weakened by thoughts of Colin, she felt almost empowered by the fact that there was a part of herself she could hold back, knowing he would want it, as he had so often held back from her.

170

Aware of how precarious her hold was on this small surge of power she took out her purse and paid the driver. She felt strangely vulnerable when the taxi pulled away, as though she'd been abandoned to a whim she no longer had the courage to fulfil. She turned to look up at the tall, glass-fronted building where Stacey Greene had her office, and Robin Lindsay was waiting with others to meet her. A throb of excitement strengthened her heart, and stepping forward she felt herself warming inside to the joy of being there. No one, especially not Beth, must be allowed to spoil this, for it wasn't only a dream come true, or an achievement to be proud of, it was proof that there was a God, for he was showing her that despite the current devastation of her marriage, she was someone who mattered, who had talent and a future.

The steps up to the revolving front doors were wide and shallow. A few people were coming and going, but none seemed especially to notice her. Standing aside as a motorcycle messenger exited, she was on the point of stepping into the revolving door when it suddenly spun round fast and someone rushed out clutching a heavy bag and a large brown package.

'Oh gosh! I'm sorry!' the young girl gasped, as she banged right into Ava. 'I was trying to catch the messenger. He left this . . .' She stopped suddenly and her head went curiously to one side.

Beth's heart was pounding for she'd recognized the girl immediately. It was the reporter who'd barged her way in the day Colin had been arrested.

'Mrs Ashby?' Laurie said. 'It is Mrs Ashby, isn't it?'

Beth, Ava, was so flustered she didn't know what to say. She wanted desperately to get away from this girl, but she wasn't sure how to do it.

'How are you?' Laurie asked, her pretty face appearing genuinely concerned. 'You look great.'

Beth's smile was shaky. 'Thank you. I'm, uh . . . You'll miss the messenger,' she said.

'Oh no,' Laurie groaned, as the motorcycle roared away. 'Well, I have the name of the company, I can always get in touch.'

'Yes,' Beth said. 'Well, I'm afraid I have to go.' Did she want to go inside with this journalist watching? Would she wonder why she was here, and start asking questions? Come to think of it, why was *she* here? Understanding suddenly hit her like a slap in the face. Oh God, what a fool she was. What a stupid, stupid fool. How many years had she been married to a journalist? And it had taken her this long to see through the ruse of the motorcycle messenger.

'I was just wondering,' Laurie was saying, 'how your husband is.'

Beth's confusion was now compounded by anger. 'If you'll excuse me . . .' she said tightly, but as she tried to push past Laurie held on to her arm.

'I'm sorry,' Laurie said, 'I didn't mean to –'

'Let go of me,' Beth seethed.

'I just wanted to let you know . . .' Laurie said, removing her hand. 'Well, what I'm trying to say is, I'd really like to help you.' Even as the words left her lips her face flooded with colour. It wasn't supposed to have come out like that.

'What are you talking about?' Beth cried scathingly. 'I don't need any help from you. All I need from you is to be left alone.'

'I understand that. But . . . Well, I just wanted to tell you that I'm not convinced your husband's guilty, so maybe –'

Beth suddenly rounded on her. 'I don't know what gives you the right to say things like that –'

'Please,' Laurie cried. 'This is coming out all wrong. I had it all prepared . . .' She stopped as Beth's eyes suddenly widened and her nostrils flared with fury. A beat later she realized what she'd just said. 'I mean, if I ever got to speak to you,' she added quickly. 'I had it all worked out, what I was going to say . . .'

'Don't you think you did enough damage after you pushed your way into my house and printed what I said the next day?' Beth snarled. 'Did it occur to you, even for a minute, that I might have been distressed, or shocked?'

'Of course it did,' Laurie jumped in. 'And I know you were. It was just . . . well, you said it, and –'

'And you printed it. Yes, we know. Now just get out of here, will you? Go wherever you need to go that's no longer a part of our lives, and for God's sake stop calling our lawyers.'

She turned away, daring to hope that was an end to it, but her entire body stiffened as Laurie said, 'Mrs Ashby, are you standing by your husband?'

Beth pushed against the door.

'You've only been to see him once,' Laurie called after her. 'Did you know about Heather Dance before it was in the paper?'

Beth kept on going.

'Mrs Ashby, do *you* think your husband did it?'

Why was the girl doing this? Why couldn't she just let go?

'I spoke to the Longs yesterday –' Laurie began.

Beth swung round again. 'Stop it!' she hissed. 'Just stop. Don't you realize how difficult this is, without having to deal with you too? My whole life is a shambles. I'm already living in terror of what the next day will bring, so I don't need you making it worse. Now just get away from me. Get away, and don't come near me again.' She pushed on through the door, trembling, furious and so agitated she couldn't think straight. The girl had ruined it, *ruined it*, damn her! How could she be Ava now, with those words ringing in her ears, those emotions making her head spin? Oh God, she just wanted to die. She had to get away from here before she broke down and disgraced herself.

Keeping her sunglasses on she walked over to the reception desk, announced her name and asked to be directed to the ladies. It would be all right. She could get herself together again. She just needed to take some deep breaths, repsych herself into being Ava, who could and would handle all this, if Beth would just let her.

Five minutes later she returned to the lobby, calmer, though still anxious that she'd run into the girl again. But there was no sign of her. Instead, to her unutterable relief, Robin Lindsay was coming towards, his friendly face beaming.

'Ava!' he cried. 'There you are. How lovely you look. That's quite a tan you've got going.'

'Robin,' she murmured, stepping into his welcoming embrace. 'Thank you.'

'Everyone's waiting to meet you. We're just up on the second floor, in one of the conference rooms.'

'How many people are there?' she asked.

'Only seven, including you. So how are you holding up in this heat?' he said chattily, escorting her towards the stairs.

'OK,' she answered. 'Yes fine. But I'm concerned about something that just happened. There was a journalist here. Outside. She recognized me and the scene wasn't pleasant. I want to know who told her I'd be here.'

'Of course,' he assured her. 'We'll talk to Stacey about it as soon as we get upstairs. But I should tell you that journalists are coming in and out of this building all the time. Dare I say it,' he chuckled, 'there are other authors who are published by Buchmanns –'

'I understand that,' she snapped. 'But this girl – she knew I'd be here. She tried to cover it up, but she knew.'

'I did try to warn you,' he said gently, 'that it would be very hard to keep your identity a secret.'

'I made it abundantly clear,' she declared hotly, 'that I don't want people to know. Now we either get this sorted out, or they can keep their money and I'll go somewhere else.' She was feeling much more like Ava now – imperious, demanding, unshakeably in charge.

'Oh, now I'm sure we won't need to do that,' Robin responded soothingly. 'And it wouldn't help anyway, because there really wouldn't be any reason for anyone here to keep your identity to themselves if you're no longer one of their authors.'

The fact that he was right didn't quell the fury she felt at having been betrayed before she'd even set foot in the building. However, to vent it any further wasn't going to help, and there was always the outside chance that the doorway collision really had been an unfortunate coincidence.

'I'm sure that's all it was,' he responded, when she voiced this hope as an attempt to convince herself. 'But I'll certainly mention it to Stacey before we leave here today.'

However, when the time came for her small welcome party to end, despite the three glasses of champagne she'd drunk and all the fawning admiration and praise she'd so graciously absorbed, she was still uneasy about leaving for fear that Laurie Forbes might yet be lurking.

'Then young Jeremy here shall go downstairs and check the coast is clear,' Stacey declared, putting a hand on the handsome young designer's arm.

'Of course,' he responded, clearly eager to do anything to gain himself the favour of the gorgeous creature he'd hardly stopped ogling since she'd arrived.

Ava treated him to a slow, grateful smile that brought a splash of colour to his cheeks. She had no idea if it was the champagne, the way she was dressed or his youthful fascination that was stirring the erotic thoughts in her mind, though she guessed it was probably all three.

Chuckling as Jeremy left, Stacey turned back to Ava saying, 'I really am sorry about that dreadful experience, my dear. Reporters can be such a bane sometimes, but we need them, I'm afraid.'

'Of course,' Ava responded.

'Just as long as you're satisfied that it really was an accident,' Stacey continued.

'Totally,' Ava assured her. Enquiries had been made, and it seemed Laurie Forbes had been in the building talking to one of the publicists about a celebrity kiss-and-tell that was currently causing a stir.

'So now, when are you off to Spain, did you say?'

'Next Tuesday,' Ava answered. 'I should be gone for a week.'

'Marvellous. I'm sure you could do with a little break. Then perhaps we can get down to a spot of editing on your return.'

The warmth drained from Ava's smile, but she made no comment. *Carlotta's Symphony* was all her own work, something she'd achieved herself, and Ava was not a woman who fell into the role of intellectual inferior as Beth had so often been made to do.

'I'm hoping to have a little surprise for you by the time you get back,' Robin chipped in.

Ava was immediately interested. 'I adore surprises,' she told him, 'so I won't attempt to persuade it out of you.'

His brown eyes were steeped in humour. She liked this man. He was someone she instinctively felt she could trust.

'Would you like to give me your number in Spain?' he asked. 'Or would you prefer to be left alone?'

'As it's you, I'll give you the number,' she replied, wondering if his thoughts were taking the same direction as hers. Not that she had any intention of pursuing an affair, but toying with it in her mind wasn't at all disagreeable.

'No enemy in sight,' Jeremy announced, coming back through the door.

'Excellent,' Ava purred, making him blush again. Then turning back to the others, who included three senior executives from sales, marketing and publicity, she said, 'Thank you so much for making me welcome. I've enjoyed meeting you all.'

One by one they stepped forward to shake her hand and tell her all over again what high hopes they had for her extraordinary book.

'I'll be happy to walk down with you,' Jeremy offered, his face turning crimson at his own temerity.

Ava's amused eyes moved to Robin. 'That would be splendid,' she responded. 'I'm being picked up by a friend, so I'll just call and tell him I'm ready to leave. His office isn't far.'

After using one of the conference-room phones, she kissed Stacey and Robin on each cheek, then inclined her head genially to Jeremy as he opened the door and waved her through.

As they walked along the corridor towards the stairs, she said, 'If you don't mind me saying, you look very young to be such a senior designer. Have you done many book jackets?'

'Quite a few,' he replied. 'I'm thirty next birthday, so maybe I'm not as young as you think.'

He was right, he wasn't, which added to his attraction. 'I'm looking forward to seeing what you come up with for *Carlotta's Symphony*,' she told him. 'Have you had any ideas yet?'

'Several.'

When he didn't elaborate she put a hand on his arm. 'It's OK, I understand how you artists don't like to discuss your work until you've got something to show.'

'It's true,' he admitted, putting his hand over hers as they started down the stairs.

The physical contact, though slight, was rather pleasurable

and evoked some wonderfully potent imaginings. She really would have to drink champagne more often.

They parted at the foot of the stairs and walked out into the stifling heat.

'You're lucky going to Spain,' he commented. 'London's so awful in this kind of weather.'

It was on the tip of her tongue to invite him, though of course she never would. She just liked the way she was teasing herself. 'Maybe, when I get back,' she said, 'we can get together and discuss some of your ideas.'

He was almost shaking as he said, 'I'd be happy to do that.'

'Good.' She smiled, and let her eyes roam suggestively from his eyes to his deliciously full mouth.

At the foot of the steps Bruce honked the car horn to let her know he'd arrived. Tearing her eyes from Jeremy, Ava went to get in the passenger seat, looking back at him as her skirt rode up over her thighs.

How liberating and exhilarating it was to be Ava. It was as though life had no barriers, and anything was possible: the publishing of a book, the flowering of her beauty, the game of seduction, the denial of Colin, even the shedding of Beth. For Ava there was no ugliness or pain, no rejection or betrayal. Ava's world was a pure, untainted page on which she could write anything she wanted for the future.

Then the car door closed, and as Bruce drove away from the kerb, he said, 'Colin's committal proceedings have been postponed to the beginning of October.'

It was such a horrible, crashing return to reality that it almost felt like a physical blow. 'Why?' she asked.

'Some new evidence has come to light.'

Her stomach turned over. 'What kind of evidence?'

'Fibres that haven't been identified.'

Her head fell back against the seat. Her chest felt horribly tight and her ears were buzzing. 'Oh, thank God, thank God,' she murmured.

Bruce glanced at her. 'Don't get your hopes too high,' he warned. 'They don't necessarily prove anything.'

'No, of course not,' she replied. She felt faint, weak, and in need of some air. 'Have you told Colin?' she asked, pushing a button to lower the window.

'Not yet. He's calling Giles Parker later. Giles will tell him then.'

Her hand went to her mouth, as though to stem the onslaught of emotion. 'You'll get him out of this, Bruce, won't you?' she said. 'You have to get him out.'

'Believe me, Beth, we're trying, but he's not doing much to help himself.'

'I know. But why doesn't he just tell you what's going on?'

'I wish I knew. It doesn't make any sense, except he says he's trying to protect you.'

'From whom?'

Bruce sighed. 'I wish I knew that too,' he replied. 'But we have some extra ammunition tucked up our sleeves that doesn't depend on these mysterious fibres.'

'Oh? What?' she asked.

He shook his head. 'I can't discuss it yet,' he told her. 'But believe me, if we use it, you'll be one of the first to know. Now tell me how it went with your publisher today.'

Somehow wresting herself from the stressful place she'd just been thrust into, Beth turned her mind around and began recounting the past couple of hours, starting with the ghastly encounter with Laurie Forbes at the front door. She made it sound almost amusing now, despite feeling bewildered and slightly out of kilter with the sound of her own voice. It wasn't easy being Beth, then Ava, then Beth – back and forth, round and round . . . It was no wonder she was looking forward to going to Spain, even if it did mean having to deal with her mother. At least she wasn't some sort of nemesis, like Laurie Forbes, who kept popping up at all the worst possible moments. What a horrible knack that was to have, though she had to admit that her mother's talent for turning her into the villain of the piece would, without question, be far superior to any of the distorted facts or half-truths Laurie Forbes would end up sending to print. And she knew very well that was how Laurie Forbes would tell it, for having been married to a journalist herself all these years, she was perfectly familiar with the kind of tactics that beefed up a story to make it sell papers. A little nuance here, a fragmented quote there, and the sense of what had been said could be altered to suggest something else entirely without any risk of libel. So no, she wouldn't have anything to do with Laurie Forbes, or any other reporter, because they were all of them, every last one, shamelessly self-opinionated glory-seekers with little or no regard for the truth unless it in some way served them, which immediately turned them into an avaricious, ruthless and conniving posse of soul-stealers who never spared a second thought for the lives they destroyed.

Laurie was sitting in the chrome-and-ebony-appointed office of Laurence Goldman, her editor-in-chief. It was rare for anyone of her lowly status to be invited into the hallowed territory of the executive floor – in fact, this was the first time she'd ever set foot here. The great man, whose balding head, vanishing chin and diminutive frame were strikingly at odds with his professional stature, was staring at her across the desk with impenetrable glassy green eyes as the tape recorder between them finished playing the Long family interview. Once or twice she glanced back, but no more than that, for it would seem disrespectful to hold his gaze. She didn't look at Wilbur either, who was perched casually on one corner of the desk, head bowed, hands deep in his pockets. For Laurie, the only good part about being here was that it was helping to distract her from that hideous encounter with Beth Ashby earlier. What an unutterable cockup she'd made of that. It was so excruciating she'd just wanted to run off down the street screaming gibberish at the top of her voice to prove she was mad.

Not even two hours had passed since then, and already two pretty monumental things had happened. First there was the summons to the mount regarding the Long tape, and second, just before Wilbur had come to escort her on the dead man's walk, she'd received a call from Giles Parker, Colin Ashby's lawyer. She was so stunned that at first she'd thought it was Gino or Flaxie playing a joke.

Goldman reached a well-manicured hand towards the tape deck and pressed stop. She knew, because Wilbur had told her, that this wasn't the first time he'd heard the interview, but for some reason he'd wanted to listen to it again with her in the room. She wondered if she was supposed to look nervous, or contrite now, or proud or simply expectant. It was hard to know when his eyes, like transparent peas, were so uninviting.

'How did you manage to come by this interview?' he asked, resting his pinstriped elbows on the desk in front of him.

'I . . . uh,' she glanced at Wilbur, 'I was given a lead.'

'One that you pursued after Wilbur instructed you to return to the daily news.'

She wasn't sure whether it was a question or statement, so she merely looked at him.

'Has Elliot Russell listened to it?' he said.

'No,' she answered, not quite sure what had prompted her to lie.

He nodded thoughtfully, though whether he believed her she had no idea. 'What is it about this story that so fascinates you, Miss Forbes?' he said.

Did she dare to mention a cover-up to him when there was a good chance he was a part of it – after all, Wilbur had admitted his orders had come from 'way up there' and this office was pretty high. Not that she at all considered it the final stop. 'It's just that there seems to be more to it than we're being told,' she responded.

Goldman's eyebrows rose. He looked over at Wilbur, then sat back in his chair and steepled his hands. 'What would it take to convince you that you have all the facts?' he asked.

Surprised by the question, she was momentarily flustered. 'If I were allowed to investigate further,' she said tentatively, 'and if I found that nothing panned out . . . maybe then I'd be more willing to accept that nothing's being held back.'

He frowned curiously. 'But what exactly do you think is being held back?' he asked. 'As I understand it, Colin Ashby was found at the scene, and no evidence has come to light that suggests anyone else was there. I don't believe Mr Ashby is even claiming that anyone was.'

It was on the tip of her tongue to tell him about the unidentified fibres, but instinct advised her to hold on to that for the moment. 'I'm not saying he didn't do it,' she responded, 'I just think there's more to it, and my chat with the Long family more or less confirms that, as you heard.'

'Mmm.' He tapped his forefingers against his chin for a

second or two, then said, 'I'd like to keep this tape, if you don't mind.'

Yes, she did mind, because, fool that she was she hadn't made a copy. 'Can I ask why?' she responded.

'I'd like to listen to it again.'

She could hardly press him any harder, considering who he was, but she couldn't give up so easily. 'I hope, sir,' she said, 'that you're not intending to give the tape to one of my more senior colleagues. I don't think that would be fair.'

'You're right, it wouldn't,' he agreed. 'And no, that isn't my intention.'

So what is? she wanted to demand, but didn't quite have the nerve.

'Do you like working here?' he asked.

Her eyes grew slightly wider. 'Yes,' she answered.

He smiled suddenly. 'Good,' he said, 'then you'll have no problem adhering to Wilbur's instructions from now on.' He looked at Wilbur. 'OK,' he said.

Wilbur got to his feet, gestured for Laurie to do the same, then opened the door for them to leave.

Laurie waited until they were in the lift going down, then said, 'Was that a threat? It sounded like a threat. He's going to fire me if I don't back off?'

Wilbur sighed. 'I don't know what it was,' he answered.

'He's a part of it, isn't he?'

'Laurie, just don't go there,' he warned. 'You're making this difficult enough for yourself, and for me . . .'

'I'm sorry, Wilbur, but I can't just pretend nothing's happening.'

'Then try, for God's sake.'

'I'll never see that tape again, will I?'

'I doubt it.'

The lift doors opened, but before they started down the corridor he took her arm and drew her aside. 'Don't go on with this,' he said quietly. 'For your own sake.' His normally jumpy eyes were boring straight into hers. 'Sophie Long's dead, remember?'

Laurie's blood turned slightly chill. 'Was that another kind of threat?' she prompted.

'Read into it what you will,' he answered, 'but remember it.'

As he walked away she remained where she was, still stunned and vaguely unnerved. It didn't seem quite real that anyone, no matter how indirectly, would be threatening her physically just for trying to get to the truth. Though it had to be said that history showed, over and over, the kind of lengths some people went to to keep the truth hidden, and prisons the world over were full of those who had failed. Anyway, nothing that had been said here today was going to stop her pursuit, especially not now she had a meeting with Giles Parker lined up for next Monday. She had no idea yet what might come out of it, nor had she quite got over the shock of her calls finally being returned, but if she did learn anything worth knowing, then the fact that she could be forced to turn to Elliot Russell to get it printed could prove the least of her problems – though the very thought of ever seeing him again, after that disastrous episode at the pub, filled her with all kinds of horrible feelings. She knew she'd hurt him that day, and she was glad, because she'd fully intended to, but it hadn't resulted in making her feel any better, in fact quite the reverse.

Anyway, she'd deal with that when it came to it. Meanwhile, she'd just have to be careful to whom she told what, and keep a check on whether or not she was being phone-tapped or followed. Bizarre, but she certainly wouldn't be the first reporter ever to have had his or her movements tracked, or to come under this kind of pressure to back off. It was probably happening to Elliot Russell all the time, though she doubted he'd have lost a crucial tape the way she just had.

Still, there was always this little exclusive about Beth Ashby having a book published under another name to give her heart. In the grand scheme of things it might seem rather a minor detail, but she'd stake her entire two-thousand-pound fortune that there were several people out there who'd dearly love to get their hands on that book before it hit the shelves, this mysterious Marcus Gatling no doubt being one of them. Needless to say she was another, though she didn't hold out much hope of Rhona doing the deed, not after the débâcle earlier, when Rhona had had to come up with an alibi fast in order get them both off the hook. Which circled her right back to Elliot, who'd no doubt have several cat-burglar contacts who could scale walls in the dead of night and manage to slither through barred and locked windows to claim the prize. But there was just no way she was going to him for help, and the very fact that everything, not to mention everyone, seemed to be pushing her in that direction, was just making her more determined than ever not to.

Bruce couldn't help noticing that Colin Ashby's face was becoming more and more drawn with each visit, and his shoulders seemed almost to slump under the weight of his ordeal. For a man who had always been so upright in his posture and self-possessed in his manner, it was hard seeing him like this, though, thank God, today they at last seemed to be making some headway in persuading him to do something to help himself.

He was sitting in his usual place for these visits, at the scratched central table with his back to the door. Giles Parker was seated opposite him, while Bruce stood against one cooling stone wall, watching and listening, and waiting as Colin mulled over the fact that Giles Parker had talked to a reporter, and was prepared to disclose what little information they had on the case, with Colin's permission. Better still would be if Colin himself would agree to see the reporter, and the fact that he hadn't, so far, dismissed either suggestion, was providing some cause for encouragement.

In the end, Colin's eyes remained fixed on the table as he said. 'So who is this Laurie Forbes? I don't know that name.'

'But you know the paper,' Parker responded.

'Of course. Laurence Goldman's –' He stopped, and changed tack. 'I worked there myself, a long time ago. It's got substance. Goldman's done a good job.' He rubbed his hands over his badly shaven face. 'Elliot Russell's asking to see me too,' he said.

'It's up to you who you talk to,' Parker told him, 'but I would strongly recommend you talk to one of them.' He had no particular loyalty to Laurie Forbes just because he'd met with her on Monday to check how far she was prepared to go for this story. Her answer had been encouraging, but his only real interest was in his client, and the preparation of a defence case that would eventually contain all, rather than just some, of the facts.

Colin's face reflected his inner struggle.

'Look,' Parker said, 'these unidentified fibres tell us that someone else was in the flat. That alone is cause –'

'But when?' Colin growled. 'Midday or midnight? Fibres don't tell the time, and matching them –'

'If they can be linked to someone who has no alibi at the time of the murder . . .'

'All right, I hear you. I just don't want any of us getting our hopes up on a few fibres that might well have been left there by the damned gas man, for all we know.'

'OK,' Parker conceded. 'So let's go back to Laurie Forbes. Or Elliot Russell. Or anyone else you'd feel more comfortable with.'

Colin inhaled deeply, letting the air puff out his cheeks.

'With you, or without you, both Russell and Forbes will continue their investigations,' Parker warned. 'You have no control over that, and it would be in your interest, presuming you want to get out of here, to help at least one of them.'

Colin's agitation was starting to show. 'Look, I just don't know how far they're prepared to go with this,' he said. 'The kind of risk involved –'

'They're prepared to take it,' Parker cut in.

Colin looked at Bruce. 'Do you know either of them?' he asked.

Bruce shook his head. 'I've heard of Russell, of course.'

'I know the man,' Colin said. 'Not well. But he's good. Damn good. He'll get this without my help.'

Taking that as a refusal to see either, Parker's eyes closed in frustration.

'OK, let's give this Laurie Forbes a chance,' Colin suddenly said. 'Russell's too high profile.' Then with a dry laugh: 'It'll be one way for this Laurie Forbes to make a name for himself, if he wants to.'

The door crashed open before Parker could correct him. 'Lunch, Ashby!' the guard snarled.

Bruce and Parker began packing up. Nothing interrupted prison routine, not even lawyers' visits, and neither of them

184

saw any reason to get into the gender confusion when it might endanger the yes.

As he reached the door Colin turned back to Bruce. 'What news of Beth?' he asked. 'How is she?'

'She's going to Spain tomorrow to stay with her parents,' Bruce answered. 'She needs to get away.'

Colin looked so dejected that Bruce was tempted to tell him about Ava Montgomery and the book, in an effort to show she was surviving. But there wasn't time, and it wouldn't be true anyway, for the depth of Beth's heartache was never going to be healed by a few smart dresses and a book deal, despite the brief respites they were managing to buy.

'I've been worried about her,' Colin said. 'Has she done anything about a divorce?'

'No, I don't think so.'

'She should.'

'*Ashby!*' the guard growled.

Parker handed over Laurie Forbes's address. 'Send the visiting order today,' he said. 'And make it for the next visit.'

'My mother and Heather already have it,' Colin answered.

'Then change it.'

Bruce held on to Colin's shoulder as he shook his hand, glad that Beth had no way of knowing that Heather wasn't only being allowed to visit, but that she was supposed to come with his mother. He didn't mention it to Colin either, for he couldn't find it in himself to make the man feel worse than he obviously already did. So all he said was, 'You're doing the right thing, talking to a reporter.'

'I hope to God you're right,' Colin murmured. 'I just hope to God you're right.'

Chapter 12

La Residencia d'el Sol was about seventy kilometres from Málaga, and five from the nearest beach, in a beautiful sun-drenched valley of vibrant feathery palms, powdery sand and lush cool grass. The two-storey buildings, with their exquisite Moorish arches, red roofs and bougainvillaea-clad walls, were grouped around an Olympic-sized pool, with half a dozen tennis courts, a clubhouse providing all facilities including two gourmet restaurants, and an eighteen-hole golf course completing the sprawling acreage of the luxury complex.

Beth's parents, Hal and Joyce Winters, had lived there for seven years. They spent their afternoons golfing, and evenings imbibing the local brew. Hangovers, and any shopping or chores that needed to be done, generally took up the mornings. They knew everyone in the complex, and might have been more enthusiastic about reintroducing their daughter to their friends, were she not embroiled in this embarrassing fiasco.

'Of course, we're always glad to see you,' her mother said, her words slurring into each other because it was now early evening and she'd already consumed the best part of a bottle of plonk, 'but we have busy lives and the world doesn't just stop because you've decided to turn up. I hope you understand that. Are you going to have some?'

Her father was putting a tray on the mosaic-topped table with three tall glasses, a dish of succulent black olives and a large pitcher of his home-made speciality, sangria. 'Of course she is,' he answered. 'She'll need one after that long journey.'

'So how is Colin?' her mother demanded, her leathery face

puckered with resentment. 'What on earth did he think he was doing? He surely didn't imagine he was going to get away with it? Well, of course he hasn't, has he? And no more should he, but I don't mind telling you it's not been easy holding our heads up around here, us being related to him and all. Right to the top, Hal.'

'Have you been to see him?' her father asked, passing a brimming glass of sangria to his wife.

'Only once,' Beth answered, watching him fill a glass for her. 'You heard about the other woman and the child, I suppose?'

'Makes you wonder how much worse it's going to get,' Joyce snorted. 'Here, cheers,' and she clanged her glass against Beth's. 'Anyway, enough about him. We've got some friends coming over at eight, so why don't you go and freshen up? You might want to go into the local town for a look round. Or you can stay here with us. Up to you, but I don't want to spend the evening talking about him.'

'I'll just get an early night,' Beth responded, wondering why on earth she'd come when she'd known full well it would be like this. It had never been any different where her mother was concerned – she was an irritant, a liability, a pathetic streak of nothing that had never got any further than being a kindergarten teacher, though, by some miracle, had managed to land herself the dashingly handsome and successful Colin Ashby, a man of impeccable character and social standing who'd presumably suffered some kind of aberration the day he met her. Of course, Joyce's high opinion of Colin had dramatically nose-dived now, though it would only be a matter of time before she got round to making Beth fully responsible for his disgrace.

She spent the first two days by the pool, carrying her book and towel as far from her parents' apartment as she could get, and setting herself up under a blue-and-white-striped parasol to read and sleep the time away. No one had mentioned Colin again, and though she wasn't surprised that her mother hadn't bothered to ask how she was coping, or what she might be planning to do now, she couldn't help feeling resentful of the neglect. But she kept it to herself. It never paid to get into a row with Joyce, and being in such a vulnerable state anyway she knew how unlikely it was that she'd be able to handle too many of Joyce's hurtful remarks. She hadn't even told her about Ava or the book deal, though the fact that she was using Ava's persona to defend herself against her mother hadn't gone unnoticed.

'What kind of outfit's *that*?' Joyce spat, as Beth stalked into the sitting room in a flame-red bikini and matching sandals. 'It's not decent. You can't go out there like that.'

Beth simply ignored her. As Ava she didn't even hear people like Joyce, never mind heed them.

'Cover yourself up!' Joyce cried after her. 'I've got to live here.'

Ava turned slowly on her heel to face her. 'Mother, this is a bikini,' she said. 'And out there is a pool. Why are you having trouble matching one with the other?'

'Don't you speak to me like that,' Joyce raged, her face turning puce. 'There's no backside in that thing, and no one else round here wears thongs, so I don't want you out there making a spectacle of yourself because it'll only reflect on me.'

'So this is about you, not me?'

Joyce's nostrils flared as her eyes bulged with fury.

'Or is it about the fact that my backside is small and firm, whereas yours . . . isn't?'

Joyce was so shocked that for a moment she looked like a fish. 'Just who the hell do you think you're talking to?' she demanded, saliva bubbling at the corners of her mouth. 'I'm your mother! You don't take that attitude with me.'

'Then don't take it with me.'

'You just get yourself back in that bedroom *now*, and make yourself decent,' Joyce shouted in panic as Ava started to move on. 'If you don't have a proper swimming costume you can use one of mine.'

'No thank you,' Ava responded pleasantly. 'I'm quite happy with this one. Enjoy your golf,' and off she stalked.

It was a small victory that made her feel good for a while, but as the day wore on, and she fell into the self-inflicted misery of composing letter after letter to Colin, she became increasingly unhappy and confused. She was so desperate to talk to him that the need swept through her like bolts of energy, readying her to go to the phone or the car, anywhere that would connect her to him. But for the moment at least, letters were all she had, and knowing she would probably never send them made their comfort very small.

On the third morning Joyce's hangover was particularly bad, so she had less to say about the bikini this time, though she couldn't let it go entirely. 'You look like a tart,' she sniped as Ava brushed past her in the kitchen to pick up her book.

'Thank you,' Ava responded.

'Why do you want to go flaunting yourself like that, a woman your age? You look ridiculous.'

'How kind,' Ava said with a smile. Then looking her full in the face, 'Would you like to tell me why you dislike me so much, Mother, or shall I just put it down to jealousy?'

'Jealous of you?' Joyce snorted. 'What's there to be jealous of? And where did this hoity-toity attitude come from, eh? Anyone would think you had something to be proud of, instead of more than enough to be ashamed of.'

Realizing that Colin's name was only a few seconds away, but forcing herself to think of the book, Ava said, 'Mother, if only you knew,' and draping a towel over one shoulder, she slipped on her sunglasses and walked out of the flat showing not a glimmer of the quaking hurt inside.

By mid-morning her mind was clogged with thoughts of Colin again. She felt angry and sad and confused that both he and her mother were treating her so badly. She didn't understand why. She wasn't a bad person, and she'd certainly never done anything to hurt them.

Looking down at her long, lean body, she thought of the way Colin always used to touch it. It was almost three months since they'd last made love, and it seemed the deeper the pain of missing him drove, the stronger her desire became. Sometimes it was almost as though the two were linked, for the harder she cried the more aroused she became. But it wasn't only crying; the agony of thinking and feeling could make her respond the same way. It was as though everything in her was so raw and charged by grief that her emotions were a physical mayhem.

Feeling a new onslaught of panic starting to rise, she abruptly got up from the chaise, picked up her keys and went to let herself back into the apartment. She couldn't remain alone with her thoughts any longer – they were driving her crazy. She needed some kind of distraction, something to remove her from the misery that was making it so hard to stay calm. After checking her parents weren't around she picked up the phone.

'Oh, I'm sorry, Ava,' Caroline said, 'Robin's out at a meeting. But I know he wants to talk to you. We've had some pretty exciting news.'

Beth's heart gave a beat of pleasure. This was just what she needed, to hear someone call her Ava, and have them tell her that one part of her life at least was good and free of the pain. 'I suppose you're going to keep me on tenterhooks,' she teased lightly.

'I'm sorry, but I know Robin wants to tell you himself.'

'Of course. When will he be back?'

'Not until the end of the day, but I'm sure he'll call before he goes home. Probably seven or eight your time.'

'I'll be here all evening,' Ava told her.

After ringing off she went to look in the mirror. Her tan was very deep now, and her glossy, dark chestnut hair had grown a lot these last few weeks. It didn't look too bad, actually, though now she came to think about it . . . She tilted her head to one side. No, something about it wasn't right. For some reason, it didn't quite suit her. Maybe she should go and get it cut. Or maybe . . . Yes! Of course. Why hadn't she realized it before? A woman like Ava would never have brown hair. She'd be seriously held back by such an incorrect feature, which had to be why she was having such trouble staying on top of Beth.

Returning to the phone, she pressed the button for the clubhouse, got put through to the hair salon, and two hours later she re-emerged into the sunlight with an exquisitely stylish blonde crop that framed her face in a way that made her features both sultry and elfin. Hearing someone whistle she smiled, then laughed, and was suddenly warmed by a feeling of more confidence and sexual power than she'd ever had in her life.

'My God, what have you done?' her mother cried, when she walked in, the horror appearing quite genuine.

190

'Isn't it fabulous?' Ava purred, pouting from side to side in the mirror.

Her father was watching from his balcony chair, though staying well out of it.

Joyce's face was twisted in rancour. 'Well, at least no one'll recognize you now,' she said acidly.

Beth's teeth were clenched; Ava's smile was dazzling. 'Time to go shopping,' she declared. 'Can I take the convertible?'

'As long as you bring it back in one piece. And while you're out, get yourself some decent clothes.'

'What's the matter with this?' Ava challenged, blousing out the copious folds of her white cotton dress that had a perfectly modest top with shoestring straps.

Joyce merely grunted and turned away, so Ava swept up the keys and went off to find the car.

The local town wasn't far, though most shops were still closed for the afternoon siesta. It didn't matter. She was content to stroll around the nearly deserted streets, catching wonderful glimpses of her glamorous new self in darkened windows, and stopping at a stall for ice cream. The vendor didn't speak English, but the look in his eyes easily conveyed the meaning of his words. Ava laughed in a girlish, flirtatious fashion, then, tossing her head like a diva, she walked off licking her ice cream, knowing he was watching her sensuously swaying hips.

Turning into a narrow, palm-lined street, she continued watching her reflection, falling more and more in love with her gorgeous new look. It was making her feel so alive and reckless, so gloriously detached from her mother's daughter, that she could almost be a brand-new person. How wonderful that would be to break away from the past completely, let all her problems and fears fade like bad dreams, and step into a whole other existence. Not one that was just temporary, the way Ava was now, but one that could take over entirely, transporting her to whole new experiences she'd never had before, places she'd never been and where no one at all knew her. There'd be no one to hurt her then, no one to tell her she looked like a tart, or that she should get a divorce. With Ava's glamour and self-confidence she could start a whole new life so full of fun and laughter that everyone, just everyone, would adore her.

Smiling at the fantasy she idled a while at the window of a perfumery before moving lazily on. There was no one else around, except the man strolling along behind her, and though there didn't appear anything particularly menacing about him, she decided that since this was a bit of a backwater she should maybe return to the main street. However, short of doubling back, she had no other way to go, for she hadn't any idea which of the narrow lanes she was passing might take her in the right direction. Then she spotted a shop that was open, just up ahead, all its wares displayed outside, from snorkels and flippers, to buckets and spades, to T-shirts and shorts.

Pausing to browse, she waited to see what the man following her would do. From the few glimpses she'd caught of him, she didn't think he was Spanish, but it was hard to tell in a distorted shop-window reflection. He was very close to her now, still ambling along, hands in his pockets, eyes mainly on the sky above as he whistled tunefully to himself. In fact he didn't even look at her as he passed, just continued on down the street, as though he were the only human being in the world.

She was about to turn back the way she'd come when the shop's owner appeared, and beckoned her inside.

'I have very beautiful dresses for the lady,' he told her. 'Very beautiful for the night and for the day. Come. You see.'

Well, that was what she was here for, to do some shopping, and though this didn't look at all like Ava's kind of shop, with nothing else open why not give it a try?

To her amazement, when she stepped inside she found she was in another world altogether. There was no touristy bric-a-brac in here, in fact there was hardly any clutter at all, with the exception of a couple of overstuffed dress racks and a small mountain of boxes. The rest of the carefully spot-lit interior was given over to an impressive display of women's clothing by many designers she'd heard of and some she hadn't. There was some expensive-looking beachwear too, and even a selection of designer shoes.

The owner was beaming with pride. 'Everyone have

192

surprise when they come in for first time,' he told her. 'But my special customers, they know about me. They come always to Antonio. I have the best dresses. Please, you look.'

Happy to, Ava turned to a row of exotic-looking sarongs that had already caught her eye. Taking one from the hanger, she wrapped it around her waist and turned to the mirror. Immediately her heart lifted at the blonde vision she now was, with her perfect golden tan and simple white dress.

'Please, you try anything,' Antonio insisted. 'You have very lovely shape. All dresses look good on you.'

Absorbing the compliment, Ava cast him a look from the corner of her eye, then carried on browsing. He was tall for a Spaniard, she was thinking, with a pretty good body of his own. His shirt was open almost to the waist, and his trousers were the customary hip-huggers the Latins often went in for. She guessed he was around the same age as her, though maybe a little older. It could be fun trying on clothes and having him admire her.

The first two dresses she slipped into were from the Armani day collection. Though elegant, they didn't set either her or Antonio on fire, so he began bringing in a slightly more colourful selection with more daring cuts and unusual styles. It was exciting her to leave the curtain partially open while she changed, so he could see her in her strapless bra and panties. The bra was only because the white dress was semi-transparent; she was hardly well-endowed enough to make one necessary otherwise. Then Antonio brought her a stunning gold evening gown that was cut very low in front and had no back at all.

'This is for you,' he declared with certainty. 'In this, you are the most beautiful woman in all of Spain.'

Laughing softly, she hung up the dress, feeling tiny frissons of excitement eddying through her as she failed to close the curtain fully. Her heart was hammering as she let the burnt-orange dress she was wearing fall to the floor then unhooked her bra. She had no idea if he was watching, but it was enough to know he might be. She looked at her dark nipples in the mirror, standing out large and proud. Then reaching for the dress, she slipped it from the hanger, undid the zip at the waist and stepped into it.

The shimmering gold top was a halter, and was cut lower in the front than anything she'd ever worn in her life. It was almost to her navel, and the view of her totally naked back with her new blonde hair curling in wisps around her neck was utterly exquisite.

'Ah, *Mamá mía*,' Antonio murmured, clapping his hands together as she came out of the changing room. 'Is very beautiful, no? Is dress made for you. We just need maybe to move the buttons here . . .' Turning her round to face a mirror, he pulled the halter top a little tighter. 'See. Is perfect now,' he said. And holding it in place with one hand, he swept the other down the front V of the dress, almost touching her, but not quite. 'Like this,' he said, letting the halter go slack, 'is too big. Like this,' he tightened it again, 'is perfect. And the length is good too. She stop at the knee, and we see the wrapover show us the legs. You like?'

Ava was entranced. She looked and felt like a goddess.

'We have shoes,' he told her, taking off to get them. 'You want try the shoes?'

They were gold mules with four-inch heels and two sparkly bands across the front. Slipping her feet into them she walked up and down the shop, admiring herself in the mirror and becoming more and more turned on by the daring that was electrifying her mind. 'I'll take the dress and shoes,' she said. 'And maybe a bikini.'

'Oh *sí*,' he agreed. 'We have fantastic bikinis. I show you.'

As he went to sort out the best, she returned to the changing room and removed the dress. She was slipping it back on the hanger when he opened the curtain and put two bikinis on one of the hooks. 'You try,' he said, not looking at her breasts, but surely noticing them.

Allowing the curtain to remain as open as he left it, she slipped her panties down over her long brown legs, then stood straight to take one of the bikinis from its hanger. It was lime green with turquoise polka dots, no straps and a thong back. After she'd put it on, she stepped out into the shop to look in the mirror. Antonio was right behind her.

'I don't think so,' she said, hands on hips as she shifted her weight on to one leg. Had he seen her naked? She hoped so, but just in case she wanted to be naked again.

'You try the other,' he suggested.

Leaving the curtain open again, she removed the bikini entirely, then reached for the other. Never in all her life had she been this brazen, nor would she be now, without Ava in control, and even Ava didn't know how far she might go, particularly with the door to outside still open. Anyone could come in at any moment, and the risk was so erotic it was almost making her faint.

Making a circle with his finger and thumb as she stepped out in the black bikini, Antonio said, 'Perfect.'

She turned to the mirror. The throbbing between her legs was intense; her nipples were like rock. 'I agree,' she said, her voice faltering slightly.

'Yes. I think you must take this one,' he told her, coming to stand very close behind her.

Her heart was beating wildly. She was certain she could feel his breath on her shoulder. She wondered what she'd do if he touched her. Did she want him to? She wasn't sure. She slid her hands over her hips, keeping her eyes away from his. It was as though they'd both become frozen in the moment, uncertain where to go from here. Then, hearing a noise, they both turned and looked at the door. It was the idly strolling man who'd passed her earlier, returned to browse through the tat outside. She half suspected that he'd been there for a while, had possibly even seen her naked too. Did she mind about that? She didn't think so, but she wanted to get dressed now, this had gone far enough.

Later, as she recalled the episode, and explored its wonderfully erotic potential, she realized that what was exciting her the most was the way Ava had managed, for those few precious minutes, to transport her out of Beth's misery into a whole other consciousness. If she could do it once, she could do it again, maybe for longer, with more courage and daring. It was what she wanted – to become so far removed from who Beth really was that eventually she could forget she even existed.

Her lips curved in a smile. She looked different, and even now, all these hours later, she still felt different, but she had to confess that the prospect of getting to know all sides of Ava's nature in order to become her completely was filling her with fear as much as excitement.

This was the third time in her career that Laurie had visited someone inside Wandsworth Prison, so the unwelcome interest, plus the crude gestures and comments were expected, though still offensive. However, she maintained a pleasant expression as she worked her way through the closely packed lines of tables towards Colin Ashby, whom she'd spotted in a far corner at the back of the room. Because it was so hot out she was wearing thin, yellow cotton trousers and a white T-shirt with an embroidered waistcoat buttoned over the top of it, for the last thing she wanted, especially in a place like this, was for the ampleness of her breasts to be noticed. Nevertheless, her ash-blonde hair, clear creamy skin and deep blue eyes made her look as fresh as a spring flower that had somehow wafted into a drab and dingy backyard.

As she neared him Ashby glanced at her, but didn't even seem to register her as he looked on past. She saw that his eyes were bloodshot and exhausted; he was badly shaven and his pallor was a ghostly grey. Though she hadn't imagined he'd create the picture of health, she was still shaken, for it seemed that his legendary easy-going charm and confidence had already been beaten into submission.

'Mr Ashby,' she said, stopping at the other side of his table.

He looked at her with vague surprise.

'I'm Laurie Forbes,' she told him.

At first he appeared confused, then his eyes closed tightly in what seemed to be frustration. 'I presumed you were a man,' he told her, his voice thickening with anger. 'Why the hell didn't they tell me you were a woman? All this time waiting . . .' He pressed his fists to his temples and clenched his teeth in rage.

Sitting down quickly, she said, 'I'm sorry. I didn't realize they hadn't told you. But please don't let it make a difference. I'm very interested in your story. I've already done a lot of work on it.'

'You don't understand,' he growled. 'I'm already trying to protect the women in my life, I can't take responsibility for you too.'

'I promise you, I can do that for myself,' she retorted.

His expression was almost derisive. 'Look at you,' he

declared. 'You're hardly out of pigtails . . .' His eyes closed again and for one startling moment she thought he was going to cry. 'I should have known, when I hadn't heard of you,' he seethed. 'The name Laurie Forbes. What a fool. I'm just not thinking straight. I can't in here . . . Jesus Christ, is someone having a joke on me somewhere?'

'Mr Ashby,' she said gently, 'I'm really sorry I've disappointed you. I swear I had no idea you thought I was a man, but it doesn't change the fact that I truly do want to help you. Giles Parker said you were ready to talk.'

He was shaking his head. 'No. Not to you.'

'Look, I don't believe you killed Sophie Long,' she told him earnestly. She wasn't entirely sure she meant that, but it just might go some way towards breaking down his resistance. She took a breath to continue, but was forced to wait for an uproar nearby to subside. Then, leaning towards him, she said quietly and urgently, 'Please let me help you. I'll do everything I can to make you forget I'm a woman.'

He looked at her sadly. 'At any other time that might be funny,' he responded, 'but here and now . . . Well, let me tell you this, naivety can be a good thing when you're starting out in the world, but it's not going to work for this. Does Wilbur know you're here? Of course he does. It's a coup –'

'No, actually, he doesn't,' she interrupted. 'I've been instructed to leave the story alone. Threatened, almost,' she added.

His eyes filled with dismay. 'Now why doesn't that surprise me?' he said, more to himself than to her.

'Why doesn't it?' she prompted.

His eyes returned to hers and he shook his head. 'No, do as they tell you,' he said bleakly. 'Laurence Goldman's not going to rock any boats, and certainly not this one. So go home, Laurie Forbes, and stop putting yourself and your boss's knighthood in jeopardy.'

'Would you walk away from this if you were me?' she challenged. 'No, of course not. You didn't get to the top by always toeing the line and bowing to every bit of pressure that came your way.'

'Laurie, you're a girl,' he said in a pained tone. 'You're not even a woman.' He looked at the annoyance in her lovely

197

young face, then, as though to temper his rejection, he said, 'You write well, though. I've been reading some of your articles since knowing you were coming.'

'You don't have to patronize me,' she responded.

He shook his head, and said, 'It's the truth. Your article this morning, about my wife . . . I didn't know about her success until I read your piece. She didn't – no one told me.'

Laurie looked at his hands on the table and was almost tempted to cover them with her own, for his misery couldn't have been more pronounced. It seemed he was genuinely hurt that he'd found out about the book in a newspaper, which in turn made her curious to know why his wife hadn't told him. 'I submitted the story a few days ago,' she said, 'right after I found out. Then I didn't hear anything until last night when Wilbur called to tell me it would be in today. I suppose, as exclusives go, it was pretty innocuous so they decided to let it run. Have you read the book?'

He nodded. 'It's good. Better than good. She's got talent.'

'Of course, everyone's going to be wondering now if any of the characters are based on you,' she said. 'Are they?'

He only looked at her.

'By the time it comes out,' she continued, 'everyone's going to be looking for things that might allude to what's happened.'

'It was written before,' he reminded her.

'I know, but that won't stop them looking.'

He was shaking his head. 'Beth doesn't know anything,' he told her.

She watched his eyes, wondering if that were true, but they told her nothing.

After a while he sat back and looked at her frankly. 'Beth and I are divorcing,' he said. 'There's an exclusive for you.'

Though surprised, she kept her expression neutral and fixed her gaze on his. 'Why?' she asked.

He gave a dry, almost bitter laugh. 'Why does anyone divorce? The marriage is over.'

'Was it over before this?'

'Of course. We just hadn't got round to admitting it.'

'So why now?'

'I've held her back for too long, and as your colleague Elliot

198

Russell informed the world, I have a child by another woman.'

She nodded. Somewhere in the back of her mind she was having difficulty with the exclusive on a divorce. It seemed a strange thing to offer, though right at that moment she couldn't work out why. 'Do you intend to marry Heather Dance?' she asked bluntly.

He said nothing, but as she looked into his ravaged face she got the impression that the answer was probably yes, if it ever became possible. 'You know, you owe it to those who love you,' she said, 'as well as to yourself, to do everything you can to get out of here.'

'Ah,' he responded, 'there speaks Giles Parker who sends me a girl-child to do the job of at least three grown men. Now why would he do that? I guess because he doesn't know what's involved.'

'So what is?'

He didn't answer.

'I'm not working alone,' she assured him. 'I have colleagues who are helping me.'

'Which colleagues? Do I know them?' There was a glimmer of hope in his voice. 'You've got some good people on your paper.'

Of course he was referring to the boomers whom he'd obviously know, and who would be as likely to work with her as they would to give up the front page for a fiver. Unfortunately, Gino and Flaxie's names would mean nothing to him, and besides, she hardly even dare mention them when they didn't know anything about Goldman's warning, or Wilbur's deepening concern.

For him her hesitation was answer enough. 'Ah yes, I forgot, they're being made to toe the official line,' he commented. 'Amazing the power of a mortgage and an offspring's education. So now tell me this: where are you intending to get the story printed, considering your own employer's reluctance?'

'There's more than one paper,' she reminded him. 'And, I imagine, once the whole truth is out, plenty will be more than eager to run it.'

'Now that's a fact,' he responded drily. 'So what are your theories on the truth, Laurie Forbes?'

'I have no theories, exactly, but I do know that Sophie Long was a professional escort who very probably entertained several of your colleagues too. I also hear that there are some fibres from the scene that have yet to be matched.'

He was nodding. 'Good,' he told her. 'But forget the professional escort link. It's got nothing to do with what's really going on. Doesn't even come close.'

'So why is the story being held back? It's still interesting, and immoral enough to excite the tabloids.'

'It'll run when they're ready.'

'When who's ready?'

'Amongst others, the *News of the World*. They've had the story prepared for a while.'

'How do you know that?'

'Elliot Russell told Heather, when he interviewed her. Do you know Elliot Russell?'

Deliberately ignoring the question she said, 'You still haven't told me why they're holding the story back.'

His brown eyes regarded her for some time as he debated which way to go. All his male instincts were warning him against getting her involved any further, but time was not on his side.

'If I trust you with any of this,' he said in the end, 'I want your word you'll take it to Elliot Russell.' She froze, but he seemed not to notice as he continued, 'If you don't know him, just call and tell him you've spoken to me in person and he'll see you straight away. Or get Giles Parker to make the call for you. Russell's got the experience, the contacts, the staff, all the back-up this is going to need. In fact, he's probably about the only reporter I know who's equipped to deal with this, now that the staffers' hands are being tied, and I'm not even sure how far he can get. Until today I was concerned about his high profile, but frankly, when compared to you and the kind of problems you present . . . well, I don't want to be rude, so let's just say, on your own you're going to be finished before you've begun. With Russell, you might just stand a chance. So, is it a deal? Do I have your word you'll take this to Russell?'

Laurie eyes were widening as she fought to keep out the resistance. He had no idea what he was asking, and now was hardly the time to tell him, when he'd just agreed to give her the biggest break she'd probably ever get in her career.

He was still watching her, quizzically, as though sensing he'd somehow hit a nerve.

'What about,' she said, hedging, 'letting me evaluate the danger for myself?'

His answer was unequivocal. 'Sophie Long,' he responded.

Her heart skipped a beat, for this was the third time Sophie's name had been used like a warning. 'Why was she killed?' she demanded, as eager to get him off the subject of Elliot, as she was to learn.

'Because of what I know. They either thought I told her, or they did it to put me right where I am now.'

She was shaking her head. 'It doesn't add up,' she responded. 'If you and/or Sophie Long have information they don't want you to have, then why not kill you both and be done with it?'

'A question I ask myself constantly,' he replied.

'Did she have the information?'

'Not that I was aware of. No. It's not possible.'

'Why?'

'It just isn't.'

'If you're so sure of that, how come someone else wasn't?'

'Another question I frequently ask myself,' he admitted. 'Now, before we go any further, do I have your word you'll take what I tell you to Elliot Russell?'

Her heart sank, but it was clear he wasn't going to give up on that, so deciding she'd work out later how to get out of it, she said, 'OK. You have my word.'

His eyes narrowed suspiciously.

'You have my word,' she repeated forcefully.

Still he looked at her, though whether he was concerned about trusting her, or having second thoughts about everything, she couldn't tell.

In the end he said, 'I want you to understand that there's enough money involved in this to make it worth everyone's while to get rid of you *and* Russell, if they have to, and that's a fact. You've probably been in this business long enough to have some idea just how many cover-ups there are in a year, particularly in areas of extreme sensitivity, such as

201

government policies and economic programmes. In other words, if certain people don't want certain information to get out, believe you me, it generally doesn't. And there's no one in this who's going to want this information out there. No one.'

She started to speak, but stopped when he raised a hand.

'I don't know how knowledgeable you are about high finance,' he said, 'or the kind of people who are key players in the international banking communities, currency markets, commodity exchanges and so on, but believe me, there are those out there who go hunting billions, and I mean billions, as though it were some sort of sport. It doesn't matter that they're already worth more than half a dozen small countries put together, this is a big man's game where all the big men stand to win and to hell with the little people who get hurt in the chase. I had no idea it was happening until I was invited to join.' His expression became bitter. 'And like a bloody fool I turned them down. Don't ask me why. I'm no more averse to making money than the next man, so maybe I'm just an old-fashioned bloke with morals who cares about his country and the people in it. And did I want to get out there as a government spokesman, spewing all that rubbish about why we're not joining the euro, why interest rates are on the climb, why the economy's taking a downturn, whatever I might have to say, knowing that I'm benefiting from whatever disaster's afoot?' He was shaking his head. 'I couldn't do it.'

Laurie's mind was buzzing, but only when she was convinced he'd stopped for the moment did she start asking the dozens of questions she had forming. The first had to be the most important, and the answer could be earth-shattering. 'Are you saying that the government knows about this, this –'

'Syndicate,' he supplied. 'It's an international syndicate. And no, I'm not saying that, because I don't know who's involved. Obviously there are only a select few, but if you're thinking about the Prime Minister, and I know you are – well, let's just say if he knows I still don't believe he's a part of it.'

'So give me some names,' she challenged.

He inhaled deeply, then shook his head. 'You need to speak to those whose strings are being pulled by the syndicate, such as certain brokerage firms, merchant banks, economic policy makers . . . There are a couple of people here, in London, that you could try talking to.'

Her pen was poised.

'Can you remember them?' he said. 'It might be better than writing them down.'

Her pen disappeared.

'Sandra Chettle,' he said, keeping his voice low. 'She's with the Bank of England. And Philip Buck. He's with Morton Shields. Have you got that?'

She nodded.

'I don't know how far you're going to get with them, but once you've told Elliot Russell all this he'll probably have some ideas of his own on where else to try. The fact that you've been here, talking to me, means that you should expect a visitor in the next day or so.'

'By "visitor" you mean someone wanting details of what we've discussed?'

He nodded. 'My biggest fear now, and it should be yours too, is that they'll dispense with the niceties and eliminate all risk by getting rid of you anyway. However, that's probably not too likely to happen when people know you're here – the coincidence would be too much – but it's another reason to go straight to Russell when you leave.'

'What about your lawyer? Where does he stand in all this?'

'He doesn't know as much as you do even, and that's the way I want it to stay. At least for now. If things get . . . Well, if anything happens to Beth, or Heather – or you, come to that – I'll know that it's not worth carrying on. In other words, what my lawyer knows he'll be obliged to bring up at trial, and that might not be a good idea.'

She took a moment to digest that, then said, 'Marcus Gatling is a name that has come up a few times recently.'

Ashby's eyes were instantly cautious. 'In what context?' he asked.

'Nothing really specific. But I know he's an extremely wealthy and influential man who's been a Party supporter all his life. He's also been a personal friend of yours and the Prime Minister's for many years. It seems to me that he's the kind of man the media is much more interested in than the public.'

He nodded. 'You're right about that.'

'So was it him who invited you to join the syndicate?'

He regarded her with something that looked like disappointment, until finally he said, 'Even if I told you who it was, you still won't get to them from where you are now.'

'But it was him who made you the offer?' she persisted.

'Actually, it was his wife. But with the Gatlings it's the same thing. Husband, wife, take your pick. They're in this together and you probably won't ever meet a more devoted or a more lethal pair in your life.'

'What's his wife's name?'

'Leonora.'

'Do you think they had something to do with Sophie Long's murder?'

His laugh had no humour. 'If they did, you'll never pin it on them, I can promise you that now.'

'But we can try.'

To her surprise he reached across the table and took her hands between his. 'I can't say this strongly enough: the Gatlings are *exceptionally* powerful people, which in itself makes them extremely dangerous enemies to have. But they're only a part of the syndicate, they're not the whole. This means there are others you need to search out, and people who move in that league don't enjoy being sought, believe me. Picture a fat Texan in his big game hunter's lodge when the prey gets wind of him and starts to move in. He won't even hesitate, and his aim will be sure, right between the eyes.'

Reflexively she blinked. 'So who else is in it?' she asked.

'I'd only be guessing, but in order to work it has to be international, and the players are almost certainly going to have close attachments to high-level government insiders. Take a look at those who make particularly large campaign contributions in the US. Study the trends in certain currency exchange rates over the past few years, particularly the euro and how it's been reacting to the dollar. There are many routes to go with this. Russell's bound to have some good suggestions, and the names I just gave you will hopefully come up with some too.'

Laurie's eyes were moving searchingly between his.

'What?' he said. 'What are you thinking?'

'Actually, I'm wondering how you explain being half undressed next to the body when the cleaning lady came in?' she said frankly.

At that he let go of her hands and buried his face. Then he told her about the sexual game he and Sophie had played, of him coming in the door, partially undressing, then going in search of her.

Laurie listened carefully. It was so incredible that she was almost tempted to believe it, but if he really had been framed, as he was claiming, the timing would have had to be so exact, she just couldn't work out how it could be done.

'Tell me a bit more about Sandra Chettle and Philip Buck,' she said, returning to the contacts he'd given her.

'Sandra's a senior executive with the Bank of England. She's given me several tip-offs in the past, when I was in the game. I don't know whether she'll come through on this, or not, but if you mention my name there's a chance she'll see you. Philip Buck's an old friend of my wife's – mine too, I suppose. His and Beth's families were neighbours in Devon. He's head of the foreign exchange at Morton Shields, which makes him pretty well informed on all matters of currency. Whether he'll be willing to help out on this . . .' He shrugged. 'You won't know until you try. Once again, can't stress this enough: the amount of money and heavyweight contacts this syndicate has to call on gives them more power than God above. You've only got to look at how the police are handling my case, and the press is keeping quiet. Someone knows the right buttons to push, and they're pushing. I'd like to say it would all come out in the end anyway, but I don't know how many years the syndicate's been going, and even if it did those running it will have their funds stashed away in places no one will ever think to look, and then we get started on the lawyers.'

There was so much more Laurie wanted to ask, but the visiting hour was abruptly pronounced over and the guard from hell was heading towards them. 'Can I come again?' she said quickly, as they got to their feet.

'If you need to, let Giles Parker know.'

She shook his hand. 'I really appreciate –'

'Call Russell,' he interrupted as the guard growled at her to leave. 'Call as soon as you leave here.'

Ten minutes later Laurie was in the back of a taxi with those words still ringing in her ears. She stared angrily and miserably down at her mobile, wishing she knew how the hell to get out of making the damned call. She was ready to accept now that she really couldn't handle this alone, but just what kind of forces were at play here, that seemed to be pushing her at Elliot Russell with every turn?

'Laurie Forbes,' she said into the phone as it rang.

'Hi. It's me,' Rhona told her. 'The proverbial's really hit the fan over here. Apparently someone broke in last night and stole a copy of the manuscript from the editor's office.'

Laurie's eyes rounded. 'You mean *the* manuscript?' she said.

'Tell me it wasn't you,' Rhona pleaded. 'Tell me you weren't behind it.'

'I wish I were,' Laurie confessed. 'But I can make a good guess who is.'

'Speak.'

There were two names in Laurie's mind, Marcus Gatling and Elliot Russell, but now wasn't the time to voice them. 'Later,' she said. 'I moved into Andrew and Stephen's house at the weekend. Can you come over?'

'Six?'

'Make it seven.'

After ringing off she tucked the phone back in her bag, then almost groaned aloud as she recalled her dilemma. However, since she hadn't actually answered when he'd told her to call Elliot as soon as she left, it couldn't be said that she was breaking her word by not ringing him now, could it? So, in fact, that got her off the hook for the next hour or two or three, and by later she might have come up with another way of getting round the problem.

Chapter 13

Heather Dance was a striking young woman with dark, shoulder-length hair that waved and wandered like a forties movie star's. Her large green eyes were fringed by long, naturally thick lashes, and her small retroussé nose was sprinkled with freckles. But best of all were her rosebud lips that were as fascinating to watch as she talked, as her lilting Welsh voice was melodious to listen to. Much like the first time they'd met, Elliot wasn't finding it hard to work out what Ashby saw in her.

They were sitting on a bench on a remote hilltop in Devon. He'd driven down early that morning, after speaking to her on the phone last night to arrange where they should meet. She was staying with her mother in a small town nearby until the press found out where she was, then she'd sort out somewhere else to go.

'But it might not be necessary,' she said, lifting her hair for the breeze to waft its coolness around her neck. 'The fuss is bound to die down sooner or later, then they won't be interested in us any more.'

Elliot looked at Jessica, the tiny three-year-old who was sitting on the grass, her glossy brown curls stirring in the gentle currents of air as she concentrated fiercely on mashing daisies into a chain. 'How much does she understand of what's going on?' he asked.

'Nothing, really. She's too young. Which is a blessing. I've got to decide whether or not to take her with me when I go to visit. Colin doesn't want her to see him where he is, but it's breaking his heart not seeing her at all, so he's left it up to me.' She sighed and gazed out to where a triangle of far-distant sea glittered like diamonds encrusted on the horizon. 'It seems strange, doesn't it,' she said dreamily, 'when you're sitting here on what feels like the top of such a beautiful world, that there could be anything wrong with it?' She smiled wryly to herself. 'You know, when I fell for him I wasn't a fool. I was aware of his reputation so I knew I was in for a lot of heartache, and I never believed he'd stay with me, even after Jess was born. But he did, in his way, and now we want him back with us, Elliot. We want him back very much.'

'When are you going to visit?' he asked.

'In a few days. It's been delayed.' She turned to look at him and engaged his eyes with the sheer loveliness of her own. 'Thanks for coming all the way down here,' she said. 'You didn't have to. I could have told you on the phone.'

'You did,' he reminded her.

'Yes, but not everything.'

He looked surprised.

'I spoke to Colin again last night. I told him you were coming, so he's given me another message which might be a little more useful than the one you got via his lawyers asking you to keep an eye on me.'

He smiled.

'You know why he asked, don't you?' she said.

He probably did, but he was interested to hear what she had to say.

'As he sees it,' she said, 'Beth's got Bruce and his wife, Georgie, to look out for her, while Jess and I don't really have anyone.'

'I guessed as much,' he replied. 'And it's not a problem. In fact, it's a good excuse to get out of town for a few hours. London's no place for a human being in this heat, and fresh air and landscapes don't come much more spectacular than this.'

'No,' she agreed, gazing out at the sun-drenched hills and valleys again. 'So,' she said after a while, 'have you heard from Laurie Forbes?'

'Not yet. I knew she'd been to see Colin, but I didn't know until you told me last night that he'd made her promise to come to me.'

'So why hasn't she?'

'It's a long story. It won't be easy for her, though, so I'll give her some more time. Then, if I still don't hear, I'll make the call myself.'

'So you two have a history?'

'You could say that.'

She nodded. 'Colin thought you might. What's she like? He said she's very pretty, but *very* young.'

His eyes filled with irony as he imagined Laurie's response to that. 'If it doesn't sound too unchivalrous,' he said, 'she's probably older than he thinks.'

'So she's in her twenties?'

Elliot laughed. 'Yes,' he said. 'And because I know she'd want me to tell you, she's not very far short of thirty. There aren't many women who have a problem with looking younger than they are, but she's definitely one of them.'

Heather was watching him closely, her eyes sparkling with humour as she listened. 'Are you married?' she asked.

His eyebrows went up. 'No.'

'Ever been?'

'Briefly, just after university.'

'Where is she now?'

'Canada. Married again with three kids. I see them whenever they're over.'

She nodded approval. 'That's nice, you remained friends.'

He didn't disagree.

'So you haven't met anyone since who you've wanted to marry?'

'No,' he answered, his expression full of laughter.

'Have you come close at all?'

'No.'

'I'm surprised. You're a good catch. But then, I suppose it's you doing all the resisting, which of course makes you all the more irresistible. Has anyone ever told you that you become quite gorgeous when you smile? When you don't you're positively scary. I actually trembled the first time we met.'

He gave a shout of laughter, which made her laugh too.

'How old are you?' she asked.

'Thirty-five.'

The corners of her mouth went down. 'That's about what I thought. Where do you live?'

'I've got a flat in the Barbican.'

'Very swish. Do you entertain many ladies there?'

Still laughing, he raised a hand in protest. 'Enough,' he declared. 'I'm here to talk about you, not me.'

'Thought that one might hit a wall,' she grinned. But undeterred, she said, 'I've got some good friends in London. Single, very eligible. Beautiful. Successful. I could offer to give you their numbers if your little black book isn't already full.'

'It's a palm-pilot these days,' he corrected.

'Full?'

'No vacancies,' he countered.

Laughing delightedly she let her head fall back and squinted her eyes against the sun. The warmth, the nostalgic smell of fresh grass with a soupçon of sea-salt in the air, and the sheer vastness of the wide-open space were the very best cure-all tonic there was. 'So now,' she said finally, turning back to him, 'which do you want first? The message or . . .' She stopped as Jessica trotted up with her mangled daisies and dropped them on Elliot's lap.

He picked them up, turned them over in his hands, then looked down into her big, expectant eyes. 'I'll wear it always,' he promised.

'It's not as good as Mummy makes them,' she told him.

'It's better than I make them,' he assured her.

'That's because you've got big fingers. I've only got small ones. See?' She put her little hand out and measured it against his. The entire span of her fingers fitted inside his palm. 'You've got even bigger hands than Daddy,' she cried, her eyes rounding with awe.

Laughing, he held them both out for her to smack, which she did, heartily, until Heather said, 'Why don't you get your crayons out of the bag and draw Elliot a picture?'

'What of?'

'Make it a surprise.'

Obediently she skipped off to the big raffia basket, tugged out a large white drawing pad and a packet of crayons, then lay down on the grass to begin her contemplation.

'So where were we?' Heather said.

'I was being offered the choice of a message or . . .' Elliot prompted.

'A glass of squash,' she laughed, reaching for the bag. As

she took out a Thermos flask and three plastic cups, she said, 'The message is that you should contact Tom Maykin. Colin says you'll know who he is.'

Elliot nodded.

She looked at him expectantly.

'He works for the *Wall Street Journal*,' he told her.

'Based here?'

'New York.'

She passed him a cup of orange squash, then went to give one to Jessica, who gulped it down greedily, then stuck her arm back out with the cup, not once taking her eyes off the page.

To his dismay Elliot found himself thinking about Beth Ashby's miscarriages and failed IVF. How painful it must be for her now, knowing this child existed, and how innocent the child was in all the suffering. 'Have you ever met Beth?' he asked.

To his surprise Heather went still for a moment. Then, smiling and frowning, she turned to him, saying, 'What a strange question. I thought you knew when you did the story that it would be how Beth found out. We even discussed it.'

'Of course,' he said. 'I'm sorry. I suppose I was just wondering if you'd ever run into her at all, maybe even before you and Colin met.'

Shaking her head she said, 'No. Our paths have never crossed. Everything I know about her I've got from Colin. He's very protective of her, you know. She's probably not half as dependent on him as he thinks, but men can be like that sometimes, can't they? Flattering themselves that a woman can't live without them? Actually, in Colin's case, I don't think it was flattery as much as frustration. He always said he'd have left her a long time ago if he hadn't been afraid she'd go to pieces without him.'

'So why would he want to hurt her by revealing your existence the way he did?' Elliot asked.

'I don't know,' she answered. 'It seems so cruel, doesn't it, which isn't like him at all, normally. Maybe, being in prison, he's resolved to make a choice between us. There'd be no kind of way of letting Beth go. Possibly, if she hates him, he thought, she'll be glad to be rid of him.'

211

Jessica was in front of them again. 'It's a bear,' she declared, plonking the crumpled drawing in Elliot's hands.

He studied the red squiggly circles critically. 'Ah, it's a *polar* bear,' he said, understanding now.

'I don't know what a polar bear is,' she confessed, hooking one foot up behind her and swivelling from side to side.

'Polar bears are white,' he explained. 'And this one looks white, except his outside skin's red. So maybe he's a *grisly*.'

'No, he's a polar bear,' she said definitely.

Elliot glanced at Heather, whose eyes were shining with merriment. 'Does he have a name?' he asked.

Jessica immediately ran round to the other side of her mother and whispered in her ear. Heather whispered back, then Jessica looked up and said, 'He's called Elliot.'

Laughing, Elliot said, 'That's a fine name for a bear.'

Laughing too, Heather put a hand on her daughter's soft dark head saying, 'Come on, Grandma will be wondering where we are.'

'Grandma Ash?' Jessica responded excitedly.

'No. Grandma Dance. Grandma Ash is coming tomorrow, remember?'

'Hooray!' Jessica whooped, and skipped off to get her artist's palette and sketchpad.

'I'm sure you gathered that Grandma Ash is Colin's mother,' Heather said as she packed up the basket.

'How long has she known about you?' he asked, passing her his empty cup.

'Actually, since before Jess was born. Colin was never going to tolerate her being a grandmother without her knowing it. She and Beth have never got on. She can be difficult, but having madam over there helps.'

As they walked back down the path together Elliot was reflecting on just how complete and cosy Ashby's other family seemed. It jarred with him slightly, for while it was impossible not to warm to Heather and Jessica, he could hardly respect a man who'd do this to his wife. Still, like most marriages, there was no doubt a lot more to the Ashbys' than anyone on the outside could even begin to guess, and quizzing the mistress wasn't exactly going to result in an unbiased insight.

'Are you OK for money?' he asked, putting the basket into the boot of her car.

She appeared startled at first, then chuckling she said, 'If that was an offer then it's really very deeply appreciated, but we're fine, thank you.'

He waited as she buckled Jessica into her seat, then said, 'If the situation changes –'

'I'll let you know,' she promised. 'But honestly, we're OK.'

He said no more, merely opened the driver's door for her to get in.

'Oh, by the way,' she said, 'did you see the story in the paper this morning about a copy of Beth's manuscript being stolen from her publishers?'

'I heard about it,' he said. 'I haven't read the story yet.'

'Who do you think would want it?'

'Marcus Gatling for one,' he responded. 'Laurie Forbes for another.'

'And you for another?'

'Of course.'

'But it wasn't you?'

'No.'

'Is Beth still refusing to see you?'

'She won't talk to anyone,' he responded.

She appeared thoughtful for a moment, then, brightening, she put her arms around him and gave him an affectionate hug. 'Thanks for coming,' she said. 'In a way you make me feel more linked to Colin. I hope that doesn't offend your male ego.'

Laughing again at her frankness, he said, 'Not at all.' He waited until she was behind the wheel then slammed the door closed. 'Call me any time,' he told her. 'You've got my email address too?'

'I have,' she confirmed.

He stood back, waved goodbye to Jessica, then, after waiting for them to drive away, he took out his mobile and dialled the office.

'Yes, boss?' Murray's voice came down the line.

'Anything on the manuscript?' Elliot asked.

'The story they're putting out now is that it wasn't stolen at all,' Murray responded, 'but that the editor had put a copy in

213

one of those famous safe places and forgot where it was. She now has it, and all's well that ends well.'

Elliot's tone was dry as he said, 'And we believe every word, of course. Any other messages?'

Murray quickly ran through them. At the fifth Elliot stopped him. 'Give me that one again,' he said, getting into the car and taking a pen off the dashboard.

'Simpson's in Paris,' Murray repeated. 'Call him on 331 12 16 15.'

Elliot wrote the number down, then told Murray to continue. There were eleven messages in all. None was from Laurie.

'OK,' he said, starting the engine. 'I should be back in a few hours. Anything happens, you know where to reach me.'

Dropping the phone on to the seat beside him, he turned the car round and began heading back down the track towards the main road. The roof was off, and the over-hanging trees were providing some welcome shade while he was moving so slowly. He was thinking about the fact that Laurie hadn't kept to the promise she'd given Ashby, and how he was going to handle calling her if she didn't get in touch by the end of the day. In truth, he'd welcome her thoughts on the way all this was unfolding, for there were several aspects that were making him curious and several more that were baffling him completely. However, the manuscript theft was something he probably had a good picture on, presuming the lame excuse didn't hold any truth. At first he'd been convinced Laurie had it, for he was well aware of her friendship with Rhona Childs, whom he knew fairly well himself, but after giving it some thought he just couldn't see Rhona putting her job on the line by taking an entire manuscript and smuggling it out to a reporter – particularly not one who could so easily be traced back to her. Tip-offs, yes; early proofs, yes; theft no. So that left the Gatlings, who, rather coincidentally, were in Washington DC right now. How smoothly and effectively they managed to put a distance between themselves and anything unpleasant, he was thinking. It was rather like pressing the red button then returning to a party, while havoc erupted elsewhere on the planet. Not for the first time he wondered where they'd been at the time of Sophie Long's murder. Since there had been no reason to question, or even link them, that missing piece of the puzzle wasn't going to be easy to find, but even when it did turn up it was almost certainly going to be stamped with Switzerland, or the Caymans or any other haven for the stupendously wealthy and politically discreet.

Suddenly his mind was full of Laurie again, though this time neither objectively nor professionally. Sure, he'd call her if he had to, but the thought of working that closely with her took him right back to how damned wretched she'd made him feel that day at the pub. It was coming over him again now so, pushing his foot down hard on the accelerator, he sped towards London, eager to get down to some work rather than continue being stuck here in a car, where the volume of his thoughts was drowning out the music, and almost making him wish he'd been born someone else.

It was time to leave Spain. Though Ava was having a fabulous time with her new blonde hair and growing bravado, Beth just couldn't stand being around her mother any more. The woman was a monster, and Beth was so easily upset by her that even Ava was failing to keep her afloat, especially now the tension had become so incendiary that their tempers were likely to explode like bombs at any moment.

There was also the problem of the manuscript that had been stolen, then mysteriously found. She was too out of touch here. It was unnerving her, for though the manuscript had apparently turned up in the bottom drawer of a filing cabinet, having gone nowhere, the fact that there had been any confusion at all was what actually mattered, for now the whole world knew that Beth Ashby had written a book under the name of Ava Montgomery – absolutely what she'd been trying to avoid, since being Ava was the only relief she was managing to get from what was starting to feel like everlasting hell.

However, Robin's surprise had provided some cause to feel good, for the fact that he had no less than three film producers vying for an option on the book was a bonus Ava hadn't even considered until he'd brought it up.

'And if we can swing it when we sign a deal,' Robin said

when they'd spoken on the phone, 'you can go and lose yourself in LA for a while, where no one's ever heard of Beth Ashby, or Ava Montgomery, so you can be who you like, whenever you like and to hell with whomsoever you like.'

This was what she adored about Robin – how understanding and non-judgemental he could be, and so ready with a solution. 'We can try to get you a story consultancy role, unless you want to tackle the screenplay?' he told her.

'Story consultancy sounds safer,' she laughed, 'but don't do anything until I get back, because I'm not sure I really want to go.' It was tempting to say yes. But maybe it was too drastic, too cut off and unknown. Ava could cope with that, but Beth might not, when LA was so far from Colin. However, the alternative, staying in England and watching her book turn into something about Beth and Colin, when it was only about Carlotta and Rodrigo was, in some ways, enough to make her never want to go back to England again.

Blowing on her nails to dry them, she stretched her long legs out to the balcony balustrade, allowing her flame-red sarong to fall open to the waist. Her skin had turned an exquisite walnut brown and looked as smooth and inviting as chocolate. She ran her hands languorously over her thighs, then was just picking a stray bougainvillaea bract from the sleeve of her T-shirt, when the apartment door crashed open and her mother stormed in like a bull. If Beth had been quicker she'd have whipped off her sarong and held it out for the charge, but Joyce was already yelling.

'I can't believe you'd do this!' she cried, slapping a hand against the newspaper she was holding. 'Just what kind of game are you playing, letting me find out from a neighbour who I don't particularly like, and a bloody newspaper, that you've been paid over a million pounds for some book that you never even bothered to tell your own mother about?'

Though it was rising fast, somehow Beth held on to her temper. 'I didn't think you'd be particularly interested,' she responded, blowing on her nails again. 'You never have been in anything else I've ever done. But then, there was never a million smackeroos before, was there? So silly me, I should have realized you'd want to know.'

Joyce rounded on her husband, who was quietly closing

the door behind them. 'Did you hear that?' she shouted. 'There she goes with that attitude again. I suppose she thinks being rich makes her better than us. Is that what you think?' she shouted at Beth, 'that you're above us all now?'

'Probably,' Beth answered.

'Well, let me tell you this,' Joyce snarled, starting towards her, 'they're only interested because of who you're married to, so you've got no cause for airs and graces around here, my lady. Who'd want to publish anything you wrote otherwise?'

At that Beth lost it. 'You are such a bitch!' she cried, leaping to her feet. 'It wouldn't even occur to you, would it, that I might actually be capable of writing a good book?'

'I told you, it's because of who you are. They're interested because your husband's a celebrity killer –'

'Shut up!' Beth raged. 'Just shut the fuck up!'

'Get in here now,' Joyce seethed. 'Don't you dare stand out there, using that language where everyone can hear.'

'*Just shut the fuck up!*' Beth screamed. 'Or I swear I'll do something we'll both regret.'

'Is that a threat? Did you just threaten me? Who the bloody hell do you think you are, coming into my house and threatening? Did you hear that, Hal? She just threatened me, her own mother.'

Beth was stalking into the room, her face glowing red with fury. 'For your information, *bitch*,' she spat, 'that book was accepted before anyone knew who I was.'

Joyce snorted. 'Don't kid yourself. They knew. Jesus Christ, look at you. You can dye your hair blonde and wear all the flashy clothes you like, but you're still Colin Ashby's wife, and it's him they're interested in, not you! It's always been him, because you're nothing! You never were, and you never will be.'

'Beth, no!' her father cried, grabbing her as she threw herself at her mother. 'Just leave it. Come on, both of you . . .'

'I hate her!' Beth cried. 'She denigrates everything I do and always has. Well, the truth is that they *didn't* know who I was, so I got paid over one million pounds for something I created without any help from you, or Colin or anyone else. So fuck you, Mother. Do you hear me? *Fuck you!*'

'There she goes with that vile language again,' Joyce

217

shouted, her face quivering with outrage. 'And if you've got so much money, Miss High and Bloody Mighty, then it's about time you started sharing it around, because we've never seen a red cent from you since the day you were born. You didn't even bring us a present from England when you turned up. You never think of anyone but yourself.'

Beth lunged towards her again, but her father still held her. 'Just listen to her!' she yelled. 'The most self-centred, grabbing bitch of all time. Talk about me only ever thinking of myself! What have you ever done for anyone except yourself? When have I, your own daughter, ever mattered? Where were you when I was growing up and needed a mother to make things better? What happened to the birds and the bees and the boyfriends you were supposed to tell me about? Where were our days out shopping? When did we ever do anything together? What have you ever told me about my grandparents, or my childhood, or all those little things you're supposed to share with your daughter? Where's the support now, when I've never needed it more in my life? Just what the hell kind of mother are you?'

Joyce's face looked about to explode. 'I'm the only one you've got, so you'd better learn some respect,' she hissed.

'For what? What is there to respect about you? Even Colin, who you thought the sun shone out of until now, couldn't stand you.'

'It was you he couldn't stand, you stupid cow!' Joyce shouted. 'Why else do you think he had all those mistresses? No man goes looking around as much as he did, if he's got himself a wife who's fit to call herself a wife. Why else do you think he's where he is now? None of it would have happened if he hadn't been stupid enough to marry – *get back*!' she yelled, as Beth wrenched herself free from Hal and towered over her like an animal ready to strike. 'Don't you dare touch me. Hal, grab her! She's gone mad.'

Beth's fists were bunched tight to her mother's head. Her teeth were bared, and a terrible fury vibrated in her throat as tears streamed from her eyes. 'He kills a twenty-two-year-old girl, and you manage to make it my fault!' she screamed. 'And do you know what's really sick about that? I knew you would. Your own daughter, your own flesh and blood, and you blame me. Just thank God you never had any other children, because I'd never want to inflict you as a parent on anyone else. I just wonder how Dad can stand being married to you.'

'At least he's here, providing a decent life for me, not sneaking round other women's bedrooms, or locked up in some prison cell. It even took someone else to give your husband a child because you were too inept . . . *Don't you dare!*' she shrieked as Beth's fury threatened to smash right into her. 'Hal, get hold of her. She's lost her mind.'

As her father's hands clenched round her wrists Beth jerked herself away, sobbing. 'You're not worth it,' she choked. 'You're just not worth it,' and, grabbing up the car keys and her bag, she ran out of the flat.

For hour after hour she drove and drove, too distraught to know where she was going, or even to care. Time after time she almost left the road, then, spinning the wheel, skidding and throwing up dust, she'd right the car and press on, up into the hills, down into valleys, while all the time tears coursed down her cheeks and sobs of utter despair racked her body. It was the worst scene they'd ever had, and though she'd sensed it building, she'd never dreamt it would be so terrible or hurt so much.

It was early evening when she finally registered the sign for a *taberna* and followed the winding dirt road out towards the cliff edge. By then the need for Colin's arms and comfort was swelling and threatening like another kind of storm. But that need was always there. It probably wouldn't ever go away until they could be together again, so she would just have to wait for it to pass, holding herself back from its might until the worst had gone. And it would go, she knew that, just as she knew they'd be together again, and then it would be as though nothing bad had ever happened, and only good would take them to the end. Oh dear God, she had to believe that. She just had to.

The *taberna* was nestled on a grassy knoll that overlooked the most breathtaking views of the Mediterranean. Parking alongside three others cars, she walked to the edge of the knoll and stood staring out to the horizon. It was so beautiful and peaceful, and she felt so unbearably alone, and afraid, that she didn't dare to move for fear of what she might do. The rocks below were a long way down, the noise of the waves rushed through her ears, while their power seemed to sweep her insides. She thought of Heather Dance, and for one desperate moment considered calling her. Maybe, in a sad, female way they could comfort each other, reach out in their shared pain and make the other believe that in the end it would all come good. But Heather had Colin to comfort her, so why would she need Beth? Or Ava? Why did anyone need Beth? But Beth needed Ava. Ava could make all this pain go away, even if only for short, blessed moments.

The light was beginning to fade as she walked back across the grass and into the bar. It was deserted, apart from a young boy, nineteen or twenty, bone thin and no taller than her shoulder, who was polishing glasses and watching a TV that was jammed into a shelf between assorted bottles of spirits and liqueurs. Catching her reflection in the mirrored backdrop, he turned and greeted her in broken English, which made her smile. It was funny how people could tell, despite her dark tan and Scandinavian blondeness.

She ordered a large vodka with ice, then perched on one of the bar stools. She didn't notice the half-finished drinks at the other end of the bar until the door to the gents opened and two men returned to claim them. To her surprise she recognized them both. One was Antonio, from the designer dress shop in the old town; the other was the taxi driver who served her parents' complex.

Immediately her heart started to beat faster, even though there was no coherence to the instinct yet. It was enough just to feel the power blooming and pricking like roses at the join of her legs. She picked up her vodka, downed it in one go, then signalled the boy to bring another. The drink was heating her from the inside, making her glow, dazzling all inhibitions into submission. She kept her eyes on her reflection, but she had Antonio's attention now, she could feel it. She waited a few seconds, then looked along the bar to where he was watching her curiously, seeming to ask himself if it was really her. She raised her eyebrows and his face instantly lit up.

'I tell myself it is you,' he grinned, getting to his feet. 'I say, it is the beautiful woman who try the gold dress and I am lucky enough to see her again.' He was coming towards her, so she swivelled on her stool to greet him.

'Are you alone?' he asked, looking around.

'It would seem so,' she responded, looking around too.

'You remember me, *sí*? Antonio.'

'Of course,' she replied, gazing right into his eyes.

'And this,' he said, indicating his friend, 'is Marco.'

'Hello, Marco,' she purred, as the short, stocky driver joined them. Funny, she'd never thought of men as pawns before, but that was what she was thinking now. She could use them, make them do anything she wanted, because she, Ava, had the desire and the power.

'We already meet,' Marco informed Antonio, while not taking his eyes off Ava.

Antonio looked interested, and said something to Marco in Spanish. Marco shook his head. 'No, I never take her in my taxi,' he replied, a slow smile curving the fleshy mouth beneath his moustache. 'But I like to.'

Antonio spoke in Spanish again, and from the way Marco's eyes began to bulge Ava knew he was relating what had happened in the shop. Marco looked her up and down, clearly surprised, but obviously hoping he might be treated to the same kind of show.

Ava picked up her drink, drank half of it, then stroked her bottom lip with the rim of her glass.

Less than ten minutes later she was naked on the bar stool between them, inwardly revelling in the abandon, and adoring the feel of the air, and their eyes on her flesh. It felt so exhilarating to be undressed like this, drinking her drink and absorbing their desire, while knowing they wouldn't dare to touch unless she allowed it. Maybe she would, maybe she wouldn't.

The boy served another round of drinks, then, trembling with excitement, did as Antonio told him and went to turn the sign on the door to closed. Her back was against the bar, one arm across her waist propping the other that was holding her glass. She watched the boy, while imagining the feel of Antonio's and Marco's hands on her breasts. The sting of lust between her legs was severe. She smiled and took a sip of her drink. Her eyes met Antonio's. He moved in closer. She looked down as his hand came towards her. How far would she let this go? He was touching her, stroking one distended nipple, while Marco began teasing the other. The boy was standing close by, transfixed by a scene he'd probably never even dreamt of seeing. She looked at him and quite suddenly everything changed.

'No,' she cried, as shame and nausea washed through her. 'No. Stop!'

Antonio and Marco drew back in surprise.

Her glass hit the floor as starting to panic she grabbed for her clothes.

'What is wrong? What happen?' Antonio said with feeling. 'We no hurt you . . .'

'No! I have to go,' she gasped, pushing past him and running for the door. To her relief it wasn't locked. She tore it open, closing her ears to their protests, but when she reached the car she didn't have the keys.

Quickly she pulled on her T-shirt and wrapped the sarong round her waist. There was so much fear inside her that her entire body was shaking. She couldn't go back in there, so what was she going to do?

'You forget these.'

She swung round to find Antonio holding her keys, offering them to her and smiling.

Cautiously she took them, tensed ready for his move. But where would she run? How could she possibly fight him off? Oh, dear God, what had she been thinking?

'We thought it was what you wanted,' he told her, letting his hand fall to his side.

She couldn't speak. The thoughts in her head were so jumbled she barely knew what they were.

It was quite dark now, with only the lights from the *taberna* flashing an occasional red and amber glow on their faces. Not far away the surf crashed on the rocks then sucked itself back. She thought he was going to speak again, but then he turned and walked away.

Half an hour later, as she drove through the pitch-black night, she was still trembling with the shock of what she'd done. It could have turned out so much worse. They could have raped her, for God's sake, and who would have blamed them. She'd been asking for it, at least Ava had, and in truth she couldn't even say now that Ava had any regrets, for there was no denying the incredible sense of power she'd experienced before Beth had snatched control. Her heart gave a painful twist as she realized that she had no clear idea of how she felt about any of it, for there was a part of her that was still turned on by what had happened, while another part was clinging to the fear and revulsion. Dear God, was this how it was going to be from now on? Had the struggle begun between the totally disparate sides of her nature? Who was going to win, Beth or Ava? Who did she really want to be?

Feeling suddenly nauseous and breathless she pulled in to the side of the road. Her heart was pounding, seeming to crush her lungs. Her skin was burning and sweat was pouring down her body. She rested her head against the wheel, forcing herself to take in slow, steadying gulps of air. She'd be all right, the world would stop spinning soon; the nausea would pass. It must be the thought of returning to Joyce that was making her feel like this, so maybe she should find a hotel and go back in the morning. Yes, that was what she'd do, and as soon as the decision was made she felt herself starting to relax.

After a while she looked around at the empty black night. There were no lights, no signs of life; no other cars on the road. She was in a lay-by. The roof was on the car; the windows were up to seal in the pre-cooled air. The harvest moon was one of the most beautiful she'd ever seen, big and round and such a deep buttery yellow it might actually start to melt. She wondered if they had those moons in LA, whether the smog would get in the way, or somehow contrive to make them even more beautiful than the one she was staring at now. She wished it could speak, or in some way convey a message of hope or understanding, or simply a small sign to show her that everything really was going to be all right.

Her eyes dropped to the side-mirror as it reflected the twin beams of a car's headlights coming along the road behind her. As they drew closer the car seemed to slow. She continued to watch, curiously, then anxiously, as it pulled up alongside her. She reached for the ignition key and started to turn, but as the engine caught, the other car came to a stop, blocking her way out.

Fear made her heart pound again. She couldn't see who was in the driver's seat. The windows were tinted. She was so remote and vulnerable here. There was nowhere to run, and if she screamed no one would hear.

She watched, frozen to her seat, as a man got out of the car and walked round to hers. Quickly she scrambled for the lock, making sure it was down. Her eyes were panicked as she looked up at him. His face was only just visible in the moonlight. He was saying something, then she realized he was asking if she was all right.

Still she only stared at him, fully expecting him to kill her, *the way Colin had killed Sophie Long*?

He backed off a little, and gestured for her to roll down the window. Shaking badly, she opened it a crack.

'Do you need help?' he asked in English. 'Have you broken down?'

She shook her head.

He nodded and smiled. 'OK. I just wanted to be sure. Good-night then.'

She watched him get back in his car and drive away. For several more minutes she continued to sit where she was, shaken, and disoriented by the coincidence that was making her feel as though she was in some kind of weird Buñuel movie, where people kept appearing in places they were least expected. First there was Laurie Forbes on the day Colin was arrested, and again at the publishers. Then there were Antonio and Marco, in the wine bar tonight. And now there was the man who had walked behind her in town, whistling and appearing more interested in the sky, stopping here to check she was all right. He'd shown no sign of recognizing her, but she'd recognized him. Her head was starting to throb. Did any of it mean anything? Was there some strange sort of significance to these coincidences that she was supposed to understand, and didn't?

Putting the car into gear she drove back out on to the road. She had no theories as far as Laurie Forbes and Antonio were concerned, but if the man who'd just stopped was who she thought he was, she needed to leave Spain right now, tonight, and when she got back to England she'd call Robin immediately and tell him to do what he could to get her to LA.

Chapter 14

'Laurie, it's simply too gorgeous an evening to be scowling like that,' Rhona complained from the kitchen terrace, where she was relaxing amongst Andrew and Stephen's lovingly nurtured pot plants and alabaster statues, with a freshly blended grey goose martini. Up above was the spectacular roof terrace where Andrew and Stephen barbecued and partied with almost the same regularity as most people ate lunch, but for this evening this little outdoor haven would do.

Laurie was in the kitchen, the phone pressed to one ear as she waited for Murray Cox to come back on the line. She was looking at Rhona through the open windows and was about to respond when Murray's voice suddenly said, 'Laurie, sorry to have kept you. It's a bit frantic here this evening. Now where were we? Oh yes. Elliot's on his way back from Zurich, but I spoke to him before he left. He says can you meet him early evening tomorrow?'

'Did you tell him what it was about?'

'He already knew.'

Laurie's face tightened, even though she'd guessed Ashby would have got word to him somehow. In fact she was surprised he hadn't called her by now, or maybe they were engaged in some kind of competition on who could hold out the longest. 'Tomorrow evening will be fine,' she said. 'Where?'

'He'll call you to set it up,' Murray answered. 'How are you by the way? It's been a long time.'

'Fine,' she answered, softening slightly. She had nothing against Murray – in fact she'd always liked him a lot. 'How are you?' she asked.

'Too busy to know,' he responded. 'The other lines are going berserk. Sorry, I'll have to go, but it was nice hearing you. Hopefully we'll get to see you before too much longer.'

'Mm,' Laurie answered.

After putting the phone down she picked up her own martini and looked at it appraisingly. It was bound to be lethal, knowing Rhona, but they were the best martinis in town, and no evening as balmy and tranquil as this should be without one, no matter the mood.

'Nectar,' she murmured after her first sip. 'Simply nectar.'

Rhona wandered to the door and leant against the frame. She was neither tall, nor slim, nor particularly beautiful, but her luscious curves and long, narrow eyes oozed the kind of sex appeal that had made more than one man leave home. 'So?' she said in the seductive, guttural tones she couldn't help.

Laurie was midway through another sip. 'This is too much,' she declared after letting it steal potently into her senses. 'You're just too good. He's en route from Zurich. I'm seeing him tomorrow.'

Rhona's eyebrows went up. 'And he knows what it's about?'

'Apparently. According to Murray.'

'Aaah, Murray,' Rhona purred. 'Is he still working there? Of course, the place would fall apart without him. How is he, the little darling? I've missed him. We used to have such good times, didn't we, dropping into that office unannounced? Do you remember how we used to plot to take on the world, put everything to rights? Amazing what we thought we could achieve after a couple of Murray's martinis, wasn't it? We were going off to Africa at one point, I remember, but we couldn't decide which country needed us most.'

'Lysette went to Uganda,' Laurie reminded her.

'Of course. With Elliot. He wrote some brilliant articles from there, as I recall. And Lysette got her heart broken a thousand times over. Wasn't she arranging to smuggle a child back here, until Elliot found out and stopped her?'

'Three children,' Laurie corrected, remembering that time only too well. 'She never really got over that experience,' she said. 'It crushed her, seeing all that tragedy. Then she and

Elliot broke up for the nineteenth time, because he couldn't make her stop pining.'

Rhona was smiling sadly to herself. 'They were always the most unlikely couple, those two, weren't they? Him, such a man of the world, hard-edged, down to earth, no illusions, and her so starry-eyed and gentle and full of dreams. Yet somehow it seemed to work.'

'If you call all that heartache working,' Laurie responded.

Rhona's eyes moved to hers. 'There were good times too,' she reminded her. 'Lots of them, as I recall.'

'Do they make up for the others?'

'Lysette would probably think so.'

'But she didn't, did she, considering what happened in the end?'

Rhona's eyes went down. 'Laurie, your sister was a saint,' she said, 'and that would be hard for any man to live with, especially a man like Elliot.'

'No one forced him.'

Rhona's eyes were imbued with feeling. 'Did it ever occur to you that it was in trying not to hurt her that he ended up hurting her so much? He really cared about her, Laurie. Deeply. That was why he found it so hard to break off the relationship.'

'Well, we all know how he did it in the end,' Laurie said sharply, 'so maybe we should change the subject and decide if we're going to order in. This kitchen is so pristine, I'm almost afraid to touch anything.'

They looked around at the immaculate shiny white and stainless-steel surfaces, and fixtures that boasted zero embellishments, such as fridge magnets, plants, hanging pans, dried herbs or pots of utensils. Everything was so designer-minimal that the dining room that was annexed to it seemed almost cluttered with its eight black-lacquered chairs, glass-topped table on a black marble plinth and three moody monochromes of Rubayat, the precious Persian cat, that had been taken by Stephen.

'It would feel like a sacrilege bringing anything as common as pizza into this place,' Rhona lamented. 'But we can always eat outside. Have you heard from Andrew and Stephen, by the way?'

'They called last night,' Laurie answered, sliding open a drawer that contained the local phone directories. 'Rehearsals are due to start next Monday for Andrew's play, and Stephen thinks he might have a commission to photograph someone's house out on Long Island. So they're off to a good start. Oh, who's that?' she said, as the phone suddenly rang. She scooped up the triangular chrome receiver. 'Hello?'

'Laurie? It's Elliot.'

The surprise was like a punch in the heart. 'Hello,' she said coldly, looking at Rhona, who frowned curiously at the tone of her voice. 'I thought you were on a plane.'

'It just landed. Murray told me you called. This is the first chance I've had to get back to you.'

'It's OK. I spoke to Murray just now. I'm free tomorrow evening.'

'Good. Is this Andrew and Stephen's number I've just rung?'

'Yes,' she confirmed. 'I'm looking after the cat and the house while they're in New York.'

He paused, then said, 'We'll need to discuss certain aspects of you staying there, but we'll leave it until tomorrow. Has anyone contacted you since you made the visit?'

Knowing what he meant she resisted the urge to be difficult and said, 'No.'

'OK. I'm hiring a private detective to keep an eye on you.'

'*What*!' she seethed. 'Don't you dare –'

'His name's Stan Bright. You'll like him. He's discreet, but good.'

'I don't care,' she said through her teeth, 'I'm not –'

'Have you been in touch with any of the names you were given?' he cut in.

Again through her teeth she said, 'I've been trying. I'm not getting anywhere at the moment.' It galled her no end to think that he'd probably have more success once he got on to it.

'How are things at the office?'

'They ran the manuscript story.'

'I saw it. Do you believe the lost and found?'

'No.'

'Does our mutual friend?'

Her eyes went back to Rhona. 'No,' she answered.

'So we're presuming someone out there does have a copy?'

'That's right.'

'Does the author know that?'

Again Laurie looked at Rhona. 'Our friend doesn't think so,' she answered.

'What about theories on who might have taken it?'

'She hasn't heard any.'

He went off the line for a moment, then came back saying, 'OK. Have you thought about how you're going to manage this, given the resistance you're meeting at the office?'

Anger flared like a firework in Laurie's head. 'If you think you're going to push me off this just because –'

'I have some suggestions,' he barked across her.

She stopped, and stood mutely glaring at nothing.

'Are you ready to hear them?' he asked.

'Actually I have some of my own,' she responded. 'I've put in for leave.'

'Have they accepted it?'

'Not yet. In fact they're trying to send me to Kenya on a story.'

'Well, there's a surprise,' he commented. 'I can arrange for Gail or Jed to cover for you. That way you manage to stay on this, and the stories get filed. They'll email them to you, you can rewrite them in your own style and forward them on to the office.'

'That's fraud,' she retorted. 'Or it's criminal, anyway.'

'It's a fine line,' he responded. 'The other alternative is that you resign and come and join my team.'

Her eyes expanded so large that Rhona's did too. 'No thank you,' she said in a tone that meant 'over my dead body'. 'I'll think about the offer of Gail and Jed, though. Anything else?'

'No,' and without saying goodbye he cut the line dead.

'Pig,' she said waspishly into the receiver.

'Well, that seemed to go well,' Rhona commented drily. 'Sounds like you've really made up.'

'I don't actually have a choice in this,' Laurie reminded her tersely. 'Were it up to me, I'd never speak to the man again in my life.'

'How could I have forgotten?' Rhona murmured and,

reaching for one of the directories, she began searching through. 'Now, are we going to have pizza, Chinese, Japanese or fish and chips?'

'Whatever you like,' Laurie answered distractedly. She was immersed in frustration again as she revisited just how difficult this self-appointed assignment was going to be now she'd been forced to share it with Elliot Russell.

'Then let it go,' Rhona advised, when she finally blurted it out over the crispy cod and chips that had been hand-delivered from a nearby chippie, complete with salt and pepper packs and wrapped in yesterday's paper.

'What do you mean?' Laurie demanded. 'This is *my* story. I'm the one who did the Colin Ashby interview –'

'I meant the anger towards Elliot,' Rhona cut in. 'It's time, Laurie. Really it is. What's passed is past, and you being like this isn't going to change what happened. It's just prolonging the agony.'

'But he was so *cruel*, Rhona, you know that.'

'Yes, a lot of men are, and not all of them were constantly having to deal with the kind of spiritual purity that used to make even me feel as though I had horns and a forked tongue half the time, and I wasn't with her anywhere near as much as Elliot was. Angels are hell to live with, you know that. You've even admitted yourself before now that Lysette's unshakeable belief in the goodness of man could, and very often did, bring out the worst in you. It's the kind of perversity we're all guilty of, to one degree or another, and Elliot's no different, nor is he any more proud of it than the rest of us. He was constantly failing her, he knew that, and how do you think it felt to be the source of so much anguish and disappointment all the time, even if she never saw it that way? Having someone making constant excuses for your shortcomings in the holy field, assuring you that you don't mean the bad things you say, or the unneighbourly things you do, isn't easy, especially when you mean them with knobs on. He's not a bad man, Laurie. At least, he's not the evil incarnate you make him out to be, and in your heart you *know* it. So, for God's sake, ease up on him, and give yourself a break at the same time.'

Laurie pushed her food away. 'What I know is the way he

230

treated her and what he said that night,' she responded tightly. 'I can't forgive it, Rhona. If I did it would be like saying it was all right, and it wasn't. It was so not all right that I can hardly express how bad it was.' She swallowed hard, but it was still a moment before she could speak with a steady voice. 'Have you got any idea how much I still miss her?' she said. 'And being here, in this house . . .' She couldn't go on.

'We all miss her,' Rhona said. 'We all loved her. It was impossible not to. She left a gap in all our lives, and I know how often you two used to come to this house, so I understand how difficult it must be for you now. But we have to move on, darling. It's what she would want, especially for you. She adored you, more than anyone. Maybe even more than she adored Elliot. You were everything to her –'

'Stop!' Laurie cried. 'Don't say any more. Please. It's hard enough without hearing you –'

'I know it is,' Rhona said forcefully, 'but, Laurie, you've got to face it. She's not coming back, and if she's up there watching you, which I firmly believe she is, then the last thing she'd want to see is you tormenting yourself *and* Elliot the way you are. So if you won't let go for yourself, then for God's sake, do it for her.'

Laurie's heart was unbearably full as her eyes turned towards the gradually darkening sky, where a plane was grazing across the pale orb of the moon, and recently lit streetlamps were reflecting in the small stretch of river that was visible between the buildings, over by Limekiln Dock. How many times had she asked herself if Lysette really was out there somewhere, watching and forgiving, and loving, the way she always had? She didn't know and she never would, so why keep putting herself through this?

'Don't let's talk about it any more,' she said abruptly. 'I'll find a way to handle it.' She looked down at her drink, took a sip, then said, 'Actually, he's making the inevitable joining of forces as easy as he can, so I suppose I'm grateful to him for that.'

Rhona's eyebrows arched. 'So much so soon,' she commented drily. 'Why? What's he doing?'

Laurie shrugged. 'Well, if tonight's conversation was anything to go by, he seems to be going straight into it. No preamble, or agonizing, or pussy-footing around what went before. There's a job to be done, we're both going to do it, so let's get on with it. In other words, his attitude is totally professional, not at all personal, and I know what you're going to say, I should be treating it the same way.'

'Hooray! I knew you'd get there in the end,' Rhona cheered.

Laurie slanted her a look.

Rhona's hands went up in defence. Then, turning serious, she said, 'Listen, I know you can't tell me everything that's going on with the story, and frankly I don't want to know, but from the little I've managed to glean, it seems pretty obvious that you really do need his help.'

'I've just said I'm going to take it. I've made the call. The meeting's set up. What more do you want?'

'I'm not sure,' Rhona answered. 'I think it might be trust. I wish you'd trust him, because you just might need to. These are powerful people you're dealing with –'

'How do you know that?' Laurie snapped.

Rhona threw out her hands in exasperation. 'Colin Ashby's not powerful?' she cried.

'Not where he is right now.'

'Don't you believe it,' Rhona scoffed.

'You're right,' Laurie conceded. 'In fact, there are all kinds of anomalies and peculiarities I've come up with since talking to him – even while I was there in fact – that are making me wonder if there isn't some kind of weird but brilliant master plan behind all this.'

'You could almost stake your life on it,' Rhona responded. 'Men in his position – well, they just aren't like us mere mortals. They play all kinds of games with rules that are about as easy to decipher as a Chinese thesaurus. And before you've even decided which way up it goes, you can bet your bottom dollar they'll have changed the system completely.'

Laurie's fingers were tapping on the table, as her thoughts ran back over the interview. 'There's something odd about his relationship with his wife,' she said impatiently. 'It's been bugging me since I spoke to him, and I'm still no closer to pinning it down now. Of course, if I could speak to her . . .'

Rhona groaned. 'Just don't get me involved in that again,' she pleaded.

232

Laurie's look was sheepish. 'Sorry,' she said, for the umpteenth time. 'Is she back from Spain yet, do you know?'

'Apparently, yes.'

'And?'

'And nothing. You know what a long lead-time there is for a book. She'll have a couple of editorial meetings, get shown the jackets, taken out to lunch a few times and if we're lucky we'll have proofs by the end of the year.'

'No chance before that?'

Rhona shook her head. 'After the break-in, or whatever it was, there's just no way I could risk it,' she said.

'What about reading it yourself, and telling me what's in it?'

'No one can get their hands on it now,' Rhona replied. 'There are probably a max of four copies, and they're all in Stacey's office. I hear they're being checked in and out like library books, but in this instance you have to put up a damned good case for wanting it. Someone told me that Stacey's even doing the copy-editing herself in order to keep the number of eyes to a minimum.'

'Then there's got to be something in it for all this secrecy,' Laurie commented.

Rhona shrugged. 'All I've been told is that Mrs Ashby is furious about the cat being out of the bag. She thought the pseudonym would help guard her privacy, so I don't expect you're her favourite person, now you've told the world she's Ava Whatshername.'

'Montgomery. I wasn't top of her love list anyway,' Laurie reminded her.

'No, I suppose not,' Rhona agreed.

They sat quietly then, listening to the distant sounds of boats on the river, the squawking of crickets, other people out on their verandas. Laurie was ruminating on it all again, until eventually she said, 'Have you ever heard of someone called Marcus Gatling?'

Rhona frowned. 'No. Should I?'

'Not necessarily. What about Leonora Gatling?'

Rhona shook her head. 'Who is she?'

'Marcus Gatling's wife.'

'Oh, well, I'm glad you cleared that up,' Rhona responded gratefully.

Laurie looked at her. 'They're an interesting couple,' she said. 'I've been doing some research into them these past few days . . .' She stopped, looked at her watch in the candlelight and groaned. 'I'm sorry, I've still got a piece to write for tomorrow's edition and it has to be in by nine. That gives me all of fifteen minutes. Feel free to stay if you like – if not, let yourself out quietly, this is a respectable neighbourhood.'

Chuckling, Rhona got to her feet and began clearing the table. 'Go on,' she said, 'I'll see to this, then I'll keep my street-carousing to a minimum and call you tomorrow. Sleep well,' she added, giving Laurie a peck on the cheek.

By ten o'clock Laurie had filed the story and completed over an hour's research on the web, trying to track down more about Marcus Gatling and his mysterious wife. There was almost nothing about her, except a few charity patron-ages and her connection to him, but once again his name was cropping up in all sorts of interesting places, such as the boards of obscure-sounding foreign banks, specialized insurance companies, specific types of brokerage firms, as well as several non-executive directorships in what appeared to be new, or developing companies, ranging from shipping to petrochemicals to telecommunications. In fact, as far as she could see it, if there were megamillions to be made, Marcus Gatling was very definitely out there making them. Curiously, though, she'd found nothing so far about his friendship with Colin Ashby, which was most surprising in that it didn't seem to have been mentioned by anyone in the coverage of Sophie Long's murder, when all the delving into Ashby's life should surely have unearthed such a long, and presumably beneficial, association.

After programming in a few more searches, she down-loaded her findings into the appropriate file, saved it, closed it, then called up the one that contained her interview with Ashby. The transcript, of necessity, had come straight from memory, which she'd done immediately after returning from the prison, and had been adding to ever since as missing details resurfaced in her mind. As she scanned through it now she wondered whether she'd put her own slant on it by making it read as though he was trying to mislead her, or if that really was how it had been. She didn't recall feeling particularly duped, or handled, at the time. However, she was aware that not everything had seemed quite what it should.

Getting up from the dining table, she went to answer the phone, which was ringing in the kitchen. A movement in the corner of her eye caused her to spin round quickly, but it was only Ruby, the cat, descending the wooden staircase that led to Andrew's top-floor study. She hadn't wanted to use the study herself; since everything was so polished and orderly she'd been afraid of leaving a smear on the desktop, or a footprint in the carpet. However, it didn't appear Ruby had any such qualms, and seeing him now reminded her that she should pop up and close the skylight before going to bed.

After talking to Wilbur about her next day's assignment, she rang Gino to see how much he could cover, then returned to her computer. By the time she'd read through the Ashby transcript again and made more copious notes, she was ready to admit that she'd actually welcome someone else's take on it now, and if that someone else had to be Elliot Russell, then she'd just have to suffer it. Indeed, if anyone had a theory on the wife-and-mistress aspect that still kept niggling her, he would, since he'd met the mistress, maybe even the wife, before all this had happened. He might even have discovered a link between the murder and this high finance syndicate. In fact, hadn't he just returned from Zurich? And wasn't one of the banks bearing Gatling's name on its board in that city?

Resting her chin on her hand she gazed out at the night, and wondered just how straight Elliot intended to play this with her. Maybe she'd wait to hear what he told her before she revealed too much to him. Actually, there was a chance he didn't even know about this syndicate yet, though she supposed holding its existence back from him wasn't going to get them very far – nor, come to that, was hogging any other details in her Ashby folder. She just wished it didn't all feel so horribly disloyal to Lysette, moving on ahead with Elliot, as though none of it mattered any more. Of course, Rhona was right, Lysette wouldn't want her storing up all this resentment, but it wasn't up to Lysette, was it? It wasn't Lysette who'd lost her twin in such a horrible, violent way. It wasn't Lysette who was having to cope with all this guilt and failure and longing, and worst of all, the empty place inside. Nor was she ever going to come back to tell them that she really did forgive them, or that she was in a much better place, so they must stop worrying and get on with their lives.

The ache circling round her heart was relentless as she got up to go and close the French windows. Thinking of Lysette was always painful, but tonight it felt particularly so, for it was reminding her of the suffering she had seen in Elliot's face the day they'd stopped at the pub. Obviously she didn't need Rhona to tell her that Lysette's death hadn't been easy for him either, but thinking of him, without anger and blame, was just too hard. She needed it to fuel the hate, for without it everything would fall apart. It was the real reason she was going to find it so hard to work with him, because she had no idea, if she was with him all the time, how long she could keep the hate going, and if it wasn't there to protect her . . . But no, she wasn't going any further with that, she was simply going to print out her notes and take them downstairs to the master bedroom, where she was still having problems with messing up the exquisite four-poster bed and all those feathered and fluffy cushions that just never looked the same when she arranged them as when Stephen had waved his pillow-scatter wand. Maybe she should have taken the guest room, further along the hall, with its minimal frills and fancies, though it was pretty nice having a walk-in closet and en-suite bathroom.

After checking everything was locked, she slotted the chain on the front door, double-turned the keys, then took them into the bedroom with her. It was one of the things she loved most about this house, its upside-downness. Bedrooms on the ground floor, sitting room, kitchen and dining room on the middle floor, playwright's study, summer kitchen and party terrace on the top floor. How many rowdy get-togethers and out-of-hand soirées had she and Lysette been to, up on that terrace? Too many to count. Elliot had always been there too, but that was something else she wasn't going to dwell on. She'd just put some music on the built-in sound system, cool herself down in the power shower, then climb into the mountainous feather bed with the TV remote, and review her notes.

It was probably somewhere around dawn when she woke with a start, to find the bedside light still on, and her notes scattered across the single white sheet that partially covered her. Not sure whether it was a dream, or a noise from outside that had startled her, she lay quietly for a moment to see if it happened again. Everything was perfectly still, except a few twittering birds and a car that crossed the end of the street. She heard a vague rumble somewhere in the distance, which was probably the first DLR train of the day. Yawning, she began stacking her notes into an untidy pile and was just putting them on the nightstand when she heard something again. It was a kind of muffled rustling sound. Frowning, she looked across at the door, which was slightly ajar. Whatever it was it didn't sound close, so it was either outside – or somewhere upstairs.

Adrenalin broke through her tiredness, and her heart began a dull sort of thud as, pushing back the sheet, she slipped gingerly from the bed. She was wearing only a thin pair of boxers and a matching crop top. Her dressing gown was in the bathroom, but she wasn't thinking about that as a faint clatter from what might have been the kitchen caused her to stop where she was. Her mind was suddenly racing, flipping over thoughts like pages in a wind: the stolen manuscript; the skylight she'd forgotten to close, a chance burglar, the private investigator, the visitor she'd been warned to expect. *The cat!* But before relief had time to distil she gasped as Ruby slunk past her legs and padded into the bedroom.

Her heartbeat was loud in her ears as she tried to make herself think straight. If there was someone upstairs, then there was a good chance they were here searching for her interview with Ashby. If she was right, the noises she was hearing was someone going through her computer and backpack. So how long before they came looking for her?

Fear was hampering her decisions. Could she get along the hall and out of the front door without anyone hearing? What about the bedroom window? But no, the underground garage made the drop too far. It had to be the front door.

Very carefully she eased the bedroom door wider, squeezing her eyes shut as the hinge squeaked. Stopping, she

237

listened again. The sounds continued. It didn't seem anyone had heard. Pleading silently and fervently with God to get her out of here before anyone found her, she started forward until horror suddenly froze her to the spot. The wooden floor of the sitting room was creaking, which meant someone was walking on it right overhead. She had to get out of here, now!

Swiftly she ran along the hall, her feet silenced by the thick pile carpet. Reaching the door, she frantically, but quietly turned the handle. To her horror nothing happened. Oh dear God, she'd locked it and put the keys next to the bed. Having no choice, she ran back to get them, trying not to hear the floorboards groaning. Her heart was erratic, and her hands shaking so badly it was all she could do to grab the keys. Then she had to sort out which one it was. Taking a breath to steady herself, she forced herself to look through, found the right one, then started back to the door. She was halfway along the hall, when she heard a heavy tread on the stairs. Her head jerked up. She saw two feet moving cautiously downwards. In panic she ran for the door. Suddenly the footsteps were thundering. Her fingers fumbled manically with the keys. She swung round. He was masked and dressed in dark clothes. She opened her mouth to scream, but no sound came out. She spun round again, trying to force the key in. Grabbing her, he flung her back against the wall. The keys fell to the floor. He stooped to retrieve them. Without thinking she slammed both fists into the back of his head. He staggered only slightly, but it knocked her laptop from his grasp. Quickly he scooped it up, then he was towering over her, eyes lasering through the slits in his mask. He didn't speak; she barely even saw him move, she just felt the blinding pain that shot through her head as he slammed her computer into it. For an agonized and blurred few seconds she was aware of being dragged and lifted before her senses were swallowed into a swirling, smothering ocean of black.

It was seven in the morning Monte Carlo time, making it midnight in Fort Worth, Texas. Leonora and Marcus Gatling were in the bedroom of their luxurious Monaco penthouse that overlooked a harbour full of rich men's yachts to the south, and confronted the imposing majesty of the Alpes Maritimes to the north.

Leonora was lowering the blinds against the early morning glare of the sun, diluting the vivid orange glow to a more muted amber wash, while her husband sat propped up against an avalanche of pillows, talking into the phone. In contrast to his wife's sublime elegance, he was a short, thuggish-looking man with receding wavy grey hair, dark spiky eyebrows, a pockmarked nose and moist fleshy lips. His voice was between alto and tenor, its staccato delivery scaled it to just short of rude.

'Where are you now?' he demanded into the receiver.

'At Hank Wingate's ranch in Texas,' Abe Kleinstein's voice responded. 'I'll be there by five your time tomorrow. What time's the meeting?'

'Seven, here at the flat. Is Wingate coming?'

'Yep, he'll be there. We're using his Gulfstream.'

'Do we need to organize a hotel?'

'My secretary's on it. Now before we get into it, what's new on Ashby? I don't mind telling you this situation's getting us all a tad worked up.'

'Then relax,' Gatling told him. 'We've got the reporter's computer. It's on its way here now.'

'Did anyone check the interview's on it?'

'Not yet. There hasn't been time.'

'What about Mrs Ashby?' Hank Wingate's Texan drawl demanded. 'How y'all coming along with her?'

Gatling's small, incisive eyes moved to his wife as she sat on the bed beside him. 'We got a report yesterday,' he answered. 'She's been engaging in some unusual behaviour.'

'And what would that be?'

'Sexual encounters with strangers. She's back in the UK now.'

'So what's with these sexual encounters?'

'We don't know. It's uncharacteristic. She's also dyed her hair blonde.'

'Any significance there?'

'She's starting to look and behave like somebody else. What does that say to you?'

'She's getting ready to start a new life?'

Gatling's eyes met Leonora's. 'She's already got the name,' he responded.

'So what's this adding up to?'

'It's our guess they're trying to throw out some kind of smokescreen with talk of a divorce, but how they're reckoning on getting him off this murder charge, or where this new promiscuity fits in, we don't know. It'll be interesting to find out how much Ashby divulged during his chat with the reporter.'

'What about the manuscript? Did anyone read it yet?'

'Leonora's taking care of it. Nothing to concern us so far.' His eyes were a question, so she nodded confirmation.

'So what're your instincts telling you here?' Kleinstein demanded. 'Does Mrs Ashby know anything?'

'About the syndicate? My instincts say yes. Leonora's say no.'

'Normally I'd trust the woman on instinct,' Kleinstein said. 'In this case I'll err on the side of caution, and go with you.'

'Y'all still keeping an eye on her?' Wingate wanted to know.

'Of course.'

'Good. So what's on the agenda tomorrow night? Who's going to be there?'

'We'll be five,' Gatling answered. 'Brunner's coming in from Hong Kong. Wesley's going to be here. He's completed his analysis of the latest reports on the euro from the French and German Treasuries.'

'Do you have a bottom line there?'

'Not yet. He'll give us one tomorrow, but we're still waiting for the ECB forecasts for the coming year.'

'So the euro stays down?'

'It might gain some ground in the next few weeks, but it shouldn't be anything to worry about.'

'And the mood in Britain is still anti?'

'Generally. Yes.'

'What about the Heiler-Janks investment deal? Are we pulling out of that?'

'Probably. We'll discuss it tomorrow. The US NMD programme's on the agenda too.'

'Ah, Son of Star Wars,' Kleinstein responded, giving it its colloquial name with the pride of a father. 'We've still got some way to go on that. What're your guys saying?'

'Still hedging. Manley's updated his long-term evaluation. It'll be on the table tomorrow. I'll email you a full agenda so you can look it over before you get here. I'll use the Fielding code.'

'Sure.' Kleinstein was on the point of ringing off when Wingate suddenly said, 'Y'know, I'm kind of concerned about this here uncharacteristic behaviour of Mrs Ashby's. I think y'all need to speak to her again.'

'We'll discuss it tomorrow,' Gatling responded and ended the call.

Half an hour later both Gatlings were in the enormous his-and-hers bathroom that ran alongside the bedroom, when the downstairs buzzer sounded, heralding the arrival of Laurie Forbes's laptop. No sooner had it been handed over than one of the mobile phones rang, bringing a call from London informing them that Ava Montgomery's agent was nego-tiating a deal with an interested producer to turn the book into a movie – and get his client out to Hollywood.

The Gatlings looked at each other as they digested this proposed new turn in Beth Ashby's curiously changing life.

'First,' Leonora said, 'I need to finish that manuscript to make sure it doesn't contain any nasty surprises. Then we should do as Kleinstein suggested and consider speaking to her again. I'm not really for it at this stage, but I can see your blood pressure is in danger of rising up against the angst.'

'Just remember,' he snapped, knocking her soothing hands away from his chest, 'we wouldn't be in this position if you hadn't had the brainwave of inviting Ashby in.'

Leonora smiled her surprise. 'Oh, now you know very well there's more to it than that, darling,' she said smoothly. 'But we won't get into another fight about it, will we? I'll just go and tuck myself away with the manuscript, while you open up that computer and find out what Miss Forbes has to tell us.'

Chapter 15

Beth was sitting on the edge of the lawn, watching as Georgie dug gently and precisely into the soil, lifting out the spring-flowering bulbs to place in her basket ready for winter storing. There had been a couple of showers while she was in Spain, which had softened the earth and apparently cooled the air for a while, but today the temperature was rising towards thirty again, and the garden could hardly have looked more beautiful, or felt more tranquil.

'So do you think this man was following you?' Georgie said, stroking the loose earth from a bulb.

'I don't know,' Beth answered. 'Maybe it was just the coincidence that shook me up.'

'But why would anyone be following you anyway?'

Beth gazed up at the high, rose-covered wall. 'I'm not sure,' she answered. 'But sometimes I feel as though there's a whole other dimension to all this. Colin was involved in something with Gatling, I'm certain of it, and Gatling's afraid I might know what it is.'

Georgie sat back on her heels and smeared dirt across her face as she swept the hair from her eyes.

Beth looked at her, then, hugging her knees to her chest, she said, 'I can't tell you how much calmer I feel now I'm back here. Hardly twenty-four hours and already I feel sane again. I swear, I was close to losing it while I was over there with her.'

'I'm sorry it went like that,' Georgie said. 'I'd hoped, when I didn't hear from you, that it was because things were going well.'

'We should both know better,' Beth responded. 'Especially after all these years.'

Georgie's eyes showed her concern, but the longer she looked at Beth the more her smile grew. 'I just can't get over it,' she laughed. 'You look so different. Gorgeous, but totally unlike you. I'm still getting used to it.'

Laughing too, Beth touched her hair. 'It was a mad moment,' she confessed, 'but I'm not sorry.'

'Nor should you be. It really suits you, and if it gets you into the kind of adventures you were telling me about last night – well, all power to you.'

Beth was still incredulous, not only of Georgie's reaction, but of the way she herself had embellished the stories of the shop and *taberna* to make them sound as though much more had happened. 'I honestly thought you'd be horrified,' she said. 'I was, after. Three men in one go, in the middle of a wine bar.'

'Don't, you're getting all my fantasies going again.' Georgie shivered. 'Not that I'd ever have the nerve.'

'I never dreamt I would either,' Beth confessed, 'but something really got into me while I was around that woman. My head just wasn't my own. First I was Ava, then I was Beth, then I didn't know who the hell I was. I wanted to kill myself, then I wanted to kill her. Then Colin topped the list. Then, when that man turned up on the side of the road . . . But you know how you can turn a simple coincidence into something creepy and sinister if your mind's not in the right frame.'

'Do you think he saw what happened in the shop?'

'He might have. He could have been lurking around the bar too, for all I know. So maybe he was following me, getting his kicks out of watching.'

'Probably,' Georgie responded. She felt strangely doubtful about all this, but wasn't entirely sure why.

Beth chucked her under the chin. 'Don't look so serious,' she chided. 'It was nothing, I'm sure.'

Georgie smiled, then looked down at her hands that were covered in dirt.

'Georgie?' Beth said, half-laughing, half-worried. 'What is it?'

'I don't know,' Georgie answered. 'It's probably just the heat.'

'Come on, we know each other better than that, so spit it out.'

Georgie sighed and looked over at Blake, who was screeching and splashing about in the paddling pool with her mother. 'It's hard to put into words,' she said, 'but I suppose it's the way everything seems to be changing. First Colin being where he is, doing what he did, or is supposed to have done. Then refusing to see you. Then there are you with your new hair and new career. And now there's this Hollywood thing . . . I don't know, like I said, it's hard to put into words.' How could she say that she felt Beth was hiding something from her, when she wasn't even really sure if that was how she felt.

'I thought you liked my hair,' Beth said.

Inwardly Georgie winced, for it was a surprisingly shallow remark for Beth, particularly in light of everything else Georgie had just said. 'I do,' she responded. 'It's lovely. It's just . . . Well, Hollywood seems so far away, and with everything you hear about it . . .'

'Oh, Georgie,' Beth laughed, hugging her. 'You don't need to worry about me. I'll be fine.'

'Will you?'

'Of course. And it's only going to be for a couple of months.'

Georgie's eyes looked searchingly into hers. 'What about Colin?' she asked.

At that Beth's heart turned over and her smile faded. 'Georgie, don't please,' she said. 'You know I wouldn't even consider leaving here if there was a chance he'd see me, but he won't. You picked me up yesterday, what was the first thing I asked? How is he, and has he changed his mind about seeing me? Have you got any idea how it feels every time I'm told no to that question? It's as though another small part of me dies, and if I go on like this I'm afraid there won't be anything left. So I have to try to do something to make myself survive. Getting the book published, and now this film – don't you see, it's telling me that there really is more out there for me. But don't think for one minute that I wouldn't throw it all away if it meant I could have him back where he belongs, as though none of this had happened.'

'I'm sorry,' Georgie responded, squeezing her hands. 'I suppose I just want you to know that you've always got a home here, so you don't need to run away if you don't want to. We love you and care for you. You're safe here with us.'

'I know that,' Beth said, holding tight to her hands. 'And I'm not running away. Well, maybe I am, but only in a good sense, because it might help me to get a better perspective on my life now, as Beth, as Ava, as a newly single woman, if that's what I am . . .' Her heart caught on those words, and her mouth trembled as she said, 'I wrote him a long letter while I was in Spain. I didn't think I'd send it, but I've got it here, and I think I'd like him to have it after all.'

'Then you must send it,' Georgie told her.

Beth nodded. 'I just hate the idea of strangers reading it first,' she said. 'That's partly what's held me back all this time. It's so intrusive. As if being apart like this isn't bad enough, having other people pick through all your private thoughts and feelings . . . I don't know if it'll change anything if I send it, whether he'll want to see me after, or even if he'll write back, but I really want him to have it. Do you think, if I asked, Bruce would give it to him for me?'

'Oh, I'm sure he will,' Georgie responded. 'He'll be home tonight for the weekend. He can take it back with him on Monday.'

Happy with that, Beth put out a finger for a ladybird to climb on to it. 'Three dots,' she said, looking at its back as it scuttled over her hand. 'One for each month Colin will be in prison? If it were, he'd be coming home any day. Maybe it's one for each year.' The ladybird's wings started to spread, then a moment later it flew away. Beth smiled at the symbolism. 'Three years,' she said softly.

Georgie didn't comment. Now wasn't the time to remind her that first-degree murder carried a sentence ten times the one she had mentioned, though, who could say, maybe Colin was going to end up on remand for three years before finally being acquitted? So she merely wiped her hands in her apron and reached for the cordless phone as it rang.

Elliot had just finished a call to his office when Rhona came into the kitchen. 'How is she?' he asked, putting his mobile down on the counter-top bar that separated the kitchen and dining room, and going to help himself to coffee.

'Still asleep. She's going to have one giant headache when

she wakes up, that's for sure. Are you going to report it to the police?'

'I don't think so,' he answered. 'It's probably not worth it when we've got a pretty good idea who was behind it. The only strange part was that they didn't go to the trouble of making it look like a chance break and entry.'

'You mean you're sorry more wasn't taken,' Rhona commented wryly.

His expression mirrored her irony.

'What time did she call you?' she asked, wandering over to pour herself a coffee.

'Around six, which means she was out for a couple of hours if it happened at dawn. They obviously came in through the skylight upstairs. Andrew's office is in a bit of a mess.'

'We can sort it out,' she said. Then, tilting her head to one side, she said, 'I'm glad she called you. Surprised, but glad.'

He didn't answer, merely clicked on his mobile as it rang.

'Elliot? It's Wilbur,' said the voice at the other end. 'Are you still at the hospital?'

'No. We got back about an hour ago.'

'So how is she?'

'She'll live. Don't expect to see her for a couple of days, though. Make that a week.'

'OK. I'm in a phone booth, down in the lobby.'

'Is that promotion?' Elliot enquired.

Wilbur didn't laugh. 'So who did it?' he pressed. 'Any idea?'

'Try asking Goldman.'

'Yeah, funny. I'm worried about her, Elliot. She doesn't get how serious this is. You've got to talk some sense into her.'

'If you couldn't do it, Wilbur, what hope is there for the rest of us?'

'You could close her out of this, and you know it.'

Aware of Rhona listening Elliot said, 'She'll need a new laptop. You must have a spare hanging around over there.'

'I'll have one sent over. What did she have on hers that they were after?'

'Your sources are better than mine,' Elliot countered.

Wilbur was silent.

So was Elliot.

'We don't all have your freedom, Elliot,' Wilbur said shortly.

'You could make your information flow a two-way street,' Elliot suggested.

'I don't have any information. I just get told to back her off.'

'What about the manuscript? Or was it just coincidence that a copy was stolen the day after your paper revealed its existence? The more people that know, the more culprits there might be. Is that how you got clearance to run it?'

Again Wilbur was silent.

'Call again when you're ready to make it two-way,' Elliot said, and rang off.

'Wilbur the concerned boss,' Rhona commented, biting into a chocolate biscuit.

'He's genuine,' Elliot responded, getting to his feet. 'Can you stay here? There's a meeting I have to get to.' He looked at his watch. 'I should be back by seven.'

Rhona's eyebrows were up. 'Will you be staying the night?' she enquired.

'No. But you will. You can get me on my mobile if you need me.'

He descended the stairs quickly, then quietly pushed open the door to the master bedroom. The curtains were blocking most of the light, but he could see Laurie's sleeping face on the pillow, still deathly pale, with patches of dried blood in her hair. She was going to have a hard time washing it for the next few days, but Rhona could always lend a hand.

Turning on his heel he let himself out of the house and got into the Porsche. He had to give this some serious consideration now, because Wilbur was right, she didn't understand what she was up against, and if the brief discussion they'd had earlier was anything to go by, not even this little episode had dented her resolve. In fact, it seemed to have fired her up more than ever, though he'd be interested to see how she felt once the shock wore off and reality kicked in. That could take a while, however, since the experience of having someone break into the house while she was sleeping, then slam her over the head with something as potentially lethal as a seven-pound computer was far more traumatic to the senses, never mind the skull, than she was currently allowing for. And the

247

situation wasn't helped by her stubborn refusal to give her emotions free rein. In fact, her struggle to hold back while they were returning from the hospital had been so absurd he'd almost shouted at her to just damned well let go. However, they'd already spent the best part of the day arguing by then, and he was getting tired of it, so he'd just let her carry on the struggle as though he didn't know it was happening.

But the good thing in all this was the fact that she'd called him first when she'd finally come round. As there was next to no traffic at that hour, he'd got to the house in ten minutes flat, to find her sitting at the bottom of the stairs with the phone, shaking and fighting even then to hold back the tears. Of course the intruder was long gone, and the private detective he'd threatened to hire, was still just that, a threat, though by the end of today he'd be a reality unless Elliot somehow managed to turn things round by talking her out of carrying on. He grimaced as he considered the battle he'd had just getting her to casualty. It was only when he'd pointed out that she had blood in her hair, which meant she could be haemorrhaging so could therefore die in the next five minutes and he didn't want to be the one to tell her father, that the fight had finally gone out of her and she'd meekly gone to get dressed.

The wait at the hospital had proved no easy time either, for she'd kept insisting he should go, that she'd be all right on her own. Like a fool he'd protested, until eventually he'd gone outside to use the phone, then came back to tell her he was leaving, but there was a taxi rank down the road so she could easily get home. That had gone down about as well as he'd expected, so she'd promptly buttoned up on that subject, turning instead to the sheer misery of losing her computer when it contained only a part of Ashby's life, but the entire twenty-eight years of hers.

'And what's more,' she'd said, 'it's probably not going to do them any good, because even if they can break my password to get into it, they'll have a hell of a time finding the right files under the system I use, and even if they do, they're all in code.'

At first, Elliot was impressed by that. 'What kind of code?'

'It's one that Lysette and I used to use,' she said, making sure not to connect with his eyes as she mentioned Lysette's name. 'It was a game, really, when we were kids, to see how good we were at reading each other's minds. She was always better at it than I was, but it became almost like a second language, so I tend to use it when I'm writing articles that are sensitive, or still being researched, and I don't want anyone to steal them. OK. I know it sounds paranoid, but you never know who can break into your computer these days, and they don't have to steal it to do it.'

'I don't think it's paranoid,' he told her. 'I think it's wise.'

It had taken him all of a minute to do a complete one-eighty on that, as he'd realized that if Gatling and his friends had a problem finding the information they wanted, there was a good chance they'd be back to access the source. So once this afternoon's meeting was over that little problem was going straight to the top of his priority list.

An hour and a half later, having woven dangerously through the interminable traffic that clogged up the City, West End and then the M4 to Heathrow, he finally snatched a ticket to enter the short-term parking, drove under the barrier and found a space on the uppermost level. It was four twenty-five now, he should have been there ten minutes ago.

Cooling his speed so as not to attract attention, he headed into Terminal 2, making straight for the gents on the arrivals level, while willing Edwards still to be there. The man generally never waited. As one of Europe's most prominent businessmen, his time was necessarily limited, so Elliot was fully aware of how great this favour was, even though it had been Edwards who'd contacted him.

Of the eight stalls inside the gents three doors were closed. Elliot relieved himself, then stood over a basin and washed his hands. In the mirror he watched the traffic behind him. By the time all three stalls had either emptied or switched occupants he knew Edwards wasn't there. Swearing under his breath he stabbed the automatic dryer and shoved his hands into the warm air. He was only guessing at what Edwards wanted to see him about, but if he was right he was never going to forgive himself for missing this rendezvous, when it was likely to provide the most promising leads yet.

Wanting to be sure he had the details right, he slipped out his palm-pilot and checked. The message read: 'Simpson's in

Paris, call him 331 12 16 15'. If he ignored the third digit, as arranged, what it actually meant was that Edwards would be in London on the third day of the third week of the month, and would meet him at the city's number one airport, Heathrow, Terminal 2 at four fifteen. That Edwards had used the elaborate code they'd devised between them, was indication enough of how important, and indeed sensitive, this meeting was. And now, thanks to the traffic, and Laurie's resistance to going to hospital, there was a chance he was too damned late.

'Elliot? Is that you, my friend?'

It was Edwards striding in through the door with a heavy briefcase and folding suitcase.

'Alan!' Elliot responded, mimicking the surprise. 'I heard you were in New York.'

'That was last week.' With a widening of his eyes and inclination of his head Edwards asked about the stalls, while saying, 'I've just come from Brussels.'

Nodding the all clear, Elliot said, 'Good tip you gave in the *FT* a couple of weeks ago. I'm getting rich.'

Chuckling, Edwards set down his luggage and began to soap his hands. His face was shaped like a rodent's – large eyes, elongated nose, thin lips and backward-sloping chin. He was still smiling as quietly he said, 'I'm told you're going into the Ashby story.'

Exactly what Elliot had hoped to hear. 'That's right,' he confirmed.

'So what do you know?'

'Only that there's more to it. Gatling's name is coming up.'

Edwards nodded. 'Don't only look here. Look in Washington. Tokyo. Singapore. Brussels.'

'Do you know what it is?'

'Let's just say something's going down, and it's not just the euro.'

Elliot knew better than to accept that as a lame joke. He glanced in the mirror as two Pakistanis came noisily in the door. They didn't even look in his and Edwards's direction as they moved over to the latrine. 'Give me somewhere to go,' he said.

'Watch the foreign exchange markets. There's a trend. Dollar and sterling against the euro.'

'What's all this got to do with Ashby, and the murder?'

'It's linked somehow, but you're not looking at someone who knows.'

'Who does?'

Edwards shook his head.

'What do you know about a syndicate?'

If Edwards was surprised Elliot knew about it, he didn't show it. 'You're on the right track,' he confirmed.

'Gatling's part of it?'

'Yes.'

'Tell me some more about it. How long are we going back?'

'Years. They've got some of the world's key policy-makers in their pockets. They can, and do, make things happen, my friend. So watch your back.'

'Give me some more names.'

'Brunner, Hong Kong banking. Kleinstein, international media. Wingate, Texas oil. Yoroshito, Japanese telecoms. There're a dozen or more of them, scattered all over the globe. Each of them heads up a powerful group within his own territory, the kind of groups that put their own boys in the driver's seat then steer from behind. You know how it goes. You've only got to look at the last US election.'

Yes, he knew how it went, since it was no secret that behind just about every political leader there was at least a handful of self-interested industrialists, financiers, or billionaire businessmen who pulled the strings in order to activate policies that most benefited them. So the only surprising part about the syndicate was that it had managed to insert itself been the power groups and the parliaments without anyone detecting its existence. The question now was, how legal were their activities, and how far would they go to cover them?

'Was Ashby part of this syndicate?' Elliot asked.

'Possibly.'

'Did he kill the girl?'

'Probably.' Edwards tugged a fistful of paper towels from the loader, dried his hands, then treating Elliot to a friendly slap on the back, he said, 'It was good running into you, my friend. If you've got anything in Heiler-Janks, take my advice, get it out now,' and picking up his bags he stalked back out into the mayhem.

It was gone five by the time Elliot drove out of the airport.

It would take him at least two hours to get back to Limehouse now, so he rang Rhona's mobile to tell her to expect him at eight. He had one more call to make this side of London, which was one he'd much rather avoid, but in the light of recent events he couldn't see how to. However, turning up unannounced wasn't the way to go, so dialling a number he hadn't used in over a year, he inched back on to the A4, heading towards Windsor.

'Hello?' a male voice answered.

Elliot recognized it immediately. 'Mr Forbes,' he said. 'I know this call might not be welcome –'

'Elliot?' Dennis Forbes interrupted.

'Yes,' Elliot confirmed. 'But before you ring off –'

'I'm not ringing off. How are you? We haven't seen you since the funeral.'

Not what Elliot had expected, such a direct reference to Lysette's death, and in a friendly tone. He had to admit it had thrown him. 'Uh, I've been busy,' he said lamely. Then, 'Frankly, I thought I'd be the last person you'd want to see.'

'You're talking about Laurie,' Forbes said. 'Mindy and I could do with seeing you. We've all got things we need to say. It's probably time we said them.'

Elliot balked. His reason for going was to solicit Forbes's support in getting Laurie to give up the Ashby story, which was bad enough, but hauling out all those buried emotions . . . 'Of course,' he said, hedging. 'I was hoping we could. When would be a good time to come?'

'Whenever's convenient for you,' Forbes answered. 'We're here.'

Elliot fell silent. Maybe he should go now. But no, worrying Dennis about Laurie's involvement in the Ashby story was not what the man needed, and he could only feel surprised at himself now for considering it at all. Besides, were Laurie ever to find out that he'd spoken to her father, well, he could handle Laurie, just, but Dennis he couldn't. At least not at this moment. So after promising to be in touch soon, he ended the call, made a quick U-turn and headed back into London.

By the time he pulled up in Ropemaker's Fields, the offshoot of Narrow Street where Andrew and Stephen lived, it was just after seven thirty and Stan Bright, the private eye he'd contacted en route, had already set up watch outside.

Inside, Laurie was propped up in bed drinking tea and watching the Channel 4 news, while Rhona chatted to someone on her mobile phone.

'I didn't think you were coming back,' Laurie remarked tartly, flicking off the TV as Elliot leant against the doorframe.

He raised an eyebrow. 'You're still dreaming,' he told her.

'You call *you* being in the room a dream?' she responded.

He couldn't help but laugh, and reluctantly she smiled too. 'So, where have you been?' she asked.

'To see a man about a syndicate.'

Her eyes rounded. 'And?'

He glanced at Rhona. 'We'll talk tomorrow,' he said. 'But I've got more names. Liam and Jed are our financial whizz-kids – they're working on the things I picked up in Zurich. We should have a bit more to go on once we've run a check on the latest players. At the moment euro seems to be the name of the game.'

'Was Gatling mentioned?'

'Yep.'

'Excuse me, darlings,' Rhona said, putting a hand over the mouthpiece as she slunk past Elliot, 'this is getting rather personal now, so I'll just pop upstairs.'

Elliot turned to watch her go, then looked at Laurie again. He didn't move any further into the room, nor did she invite him to. She simply leant over to put her cup on the night-stand, then groaned as a wave of nausea swept through her.

'God, my head hurts,' she grumbled.

He nodded towards the painkillers on the nightstand.

She took two with the tea, waited for the spinning to stop, then said, 'Any news on whether or not I'm likely to get my computer back?'

'Wilbur's sending over a replacement. Have you eaten?'

'I couldn't face it. What about you?'

'Starving.'

'The kitchen's upstairs. As I recall, you're a great cook. Just a minute, so you've talked to Wilbur about this?'

'Sort of. Weren't you supposed to be on an assignment today?'

'Yes, but –'

'Someone had to let him know you wouldn't be there.

253

Now, I think you should eat something. I take it you do have food up there?'

'Rhona went shopping while you were out.' She was starting to get panicky all of a sudden. This was too much like old times, too comfortable and friendly. She didn't want to look at him any more. He seemed too tall, overpowering, and painfully familiar. Her eyes closed as the intense throbbing in her head increased, and the tension in her chest started to hurt. 'Please, just help yourself,' she said quietly.

When she opened her eyes again he'd gone, but a few minutes later she heard him talking to Rhona in the kitchen. Wanting to avoid him coming back to the bedroom, she threw off the sheet, put her feet on the floor and gingerly stood. The dizziness wasn't too bad – it only took a few moments to pass – then she was making her way shakily across the room towards the walk-in closet. By the time she'd tugged a pair of denim shorts on under her giant T-shirt and cleaned her teeth, she felt so well recovered that the stairs might not have seemed daunting at all had she not caught sight of herself in the mirror and started to reel. She looked at her hairbrush and winced. Had any such instrument ever appeared more like a weapon of torture?

When finally she walked into the kitchen, twin patches of blusher on her cheeks and one half of her hair brushed flat while the other remained matted and on end, there was only Elliot, sitting at the counter-bar eating a sandwich.

'Where's Rhona?' she asked, shuffling over to get some water from the filter.

He raised his eyes towards the roof terrace. 'How many men does she have?' he said, taking another bite.

Laurie's mouth was watering as she looked at the double layers of fresh crusty bread, with a creamy dressing oozing out of the sides. 'According to Rhona, never enough,' she answered. 'What's in that?'

'Cheese, ham and coleslaw.' He took another bite and Laurie's mouth almost moved with his as he chewed.

'Shame you're not hungry,' he commented. 'This is good.'

She was staring at the other half, sitting like exposed prey on a plate. 'Well, I could probably –'

'Here,' he said, pushing it towards her.

254

She looked up and, seeing the mirth in his eyes, she might have withdrawn if she had the will. But hunger won out.

'So what about you?' he said as she positioned the two-inch-thick sandwich ready to bite.

She frowned. 'What about me?'

He watched her chomp down hard on far too big a mouthful. 'Men,' he said. 'Are you seeing anyone these days?'

'Mmm, hm, nnn, mmm hm,' she responded, pressing her fingers to her lips. 'Not really,' she finally managed. 'Well, nothing serious.'

'What about Greg?'

'That's over.' She took another more modest mouthful and wished Rhona would hurry up on the phone. This was getting too personal again. 'What about you?' she said after a while. 'Are you seeing anyone?'

'Nothing serious,' he answered.

She nodded.

He started to ask how her parents were, then, remembering the response he'd got last time, thought better of it, and said instead, 'You know, any time you want to talk . . . I mean, we don't have to at all, but if you feel the need to . . .'

Her heartbeat didn't feel steady. He was referring to Lysette, of course, but she wanted to tell herself it was Ashby. In the end she said, 'We shouldn't make that a part of this.'

'No. You're probably right.' He finished his sandwich then went to get more wine from the fridge. 'By the way, Stan's outside,' he told her. 'I'll give you his mobile so you can let him know when you're ready to say hello.'

She frowned. 'Stan?' But even as she said it she remembered and was about to protest, when the idea of being watched over for the next few days didn't seem quite so bad after all. 'I've started worrying about the code,' she confessed as he refilled his glass with a crisp-looking Australian chardonnay. 'If they can't work it out, do you think they'll come back?'

His dark eyes were expressionless as they looked at her. 'Just introduce yourself to Stan,' he said.

His failure to deny it made her heart contract and the dizziness was returning to her head. 'You think they will, don't you?' she said.

'It's possible. So we need to sit down tomorrow and go over

everything you can remember that was on the computer. I don't suppose you have back-ups?'

'Actually, yes. But they've gone too.'

He took a sip of wine and watched her over the rim of the glass. His eyes seemed suddenly relentless, as though they were boring right into her mind. She wanted to pull away, but even when her eyelids dropped she still felt bound by that invasive stare.

'I'm sorry,' she murmured, putting a hand to her head. 'Maybe I'm not . . .'

She didn't finish, nor did he say anything. He merely continued to watch her, until finally she rescued herself the only way she knew how. 'I've been thinking about the Ashby women,' she said, asserting herself on a professional level. 'The wife and the mistress, not the mother.'

His expression showed interest.

'What's the mistress like?' she asked.

'Down to earth. Friendly. Very open.'

'Have you ever met the wife?'

'Once or twice. I can't say I know her.'

'Do you know if they've ever met?'

'Heather says not.'

'Do you believe her?'

'I think so. Why?'

Laurie watched him as he drank more wine. Then, raising her eyes from his hand, she said, 'I've wondered if all three of them might be in it together, Colin, Beth and Heather, working some kind of master plan that'll rip off the syndicate to the tune of millions and buy them a safe haven somewhere in the sun.'

Though Eliot seemed surprised, he nodded slowly, mulling the suggestion over as he stretched his long legs out in front of him and crossed them.

'But even if that's true,' she said, 'how they'd pull it off is beyond my powers of deduction, especially when Ashby's on remand for murder.'

'And why would they need to kill Sophie?' he pointed out.

She had no answer for that, and was in fact noticing the white Lacoste shirt that Lysette had given him. She even remembered going with her to choose it, and thinking at the time how good he looked in white, being so dark. 'Is there any chance of you talking to Beth Ashby?' she asked abruptly, knowing it would be giving away the biggest part of this for her, but if he stood more chance than she did she'd make herself accept it.

'Not that I know of,' he answered. 'Did you know they're supposed to be getting divorced?'

Laurie nodded. 'Yes. He told me. I confess I found that very odd. Why would they do it now, at a time when most men would be trying to tie their wives to them as tightly as possible?'

'Heather Dance says he's wanted to end the marriage for some time.'

'Do you believe that?'

'I think *she* does. Certainly she's in regular touch with him, whereas Beth apparently isn't.'

As he raised a hand to comb his fingers through his hair Laurie's gaze moved to the watch on his wrist. It wasn't one she remembered. Then she looked at his scowl and suddenly remembered too much.

Finally his eyes came back to hers, but as he started to speak, he frowned again. 'Are you all right?' he asked.

'Yes. Why?'

'You've gone pale.'

'It's my natural colour,' she said, feeling strangely shaky and edgy.

He looked at her hard.

She looked back, and tried to summon her defences. Why was she suddenly losing it like this? What had happened? Where was her mind going?

'That's enough for now,' he declared. 'You need to get some more rest.'

Picking up his glass and plate he walked round the counter-top towards her.

She watched him warily, senses swimming. When he reached her he stopped and looked down into her eyes. He was so close she could smell the male scent of him, and almost feel him, though he wasn't touching her at all. For one breathless moment as he leant towards her, to put his plate and cup in the sink, she thought he was going to kiss her. Her lips parted as

257

she struggled for air. She had no idea what was happening. She couldn't make herself think straight. Then finally relinquishing the hold on her eyes he returned to his stool.

Turning away quickly she wondered if he'd known she'd wanted his kiss. Oh, please God, no he hadn't. This was insufferable. Unthinkable. She meant no more to him than Lysette ever had, and that she could still want him like this, after everything that had happened, and after so much time had passed, was so horrendous she could hardly stand it. She wished he would go. She wanted to scream and rant and loathe herself in private. She wanted to berate God and the world and the universe for the weakness she'd struggled so hard to overcome. But how was she ever going to when they kept being thrown together like this?

'You know, I think I might need to lie down again,' she said, somehow keeping her voice steady. 'You don't have to stay any longer. Rhona's here.'

He didn't answer right away, but she couldn't turn round. The air of professionalism had vanished. It was entirely personal now, and she knew he sensed it. It was as though everything they were avoiding was right there, waiting to be confronted, no longer willing to hide behind a pretence. This was getting out of hand. She wasn't in control and she didn't know what would happen if she looked at him again. With all her might she willed him just to leave, until finally, mercifully, she heard him get up and walk to the door.

'I know this isn't going to be easy,' he said, 'for either of us, and I won't ask for your forgiveness again. I just want you to believe that I never meant it to happen. If I'd known –'

'Don't say any more,' she sobbed, pressing her hands to her face. 'Please, just don't say any more.'

A moment or two later she heard the front door close downstairs behind him, followed by the Porsche roaring off down the street. By then all the tears she'd kept bottled up since early that morning were erupting in harsh, racking sobs and coursing hard down her cheeks. She knew it was the shock coming out, and she'd keep telling herself that, but she knew too that she'd just hurt him again, and she desperately wanted to go after him, and tell him she did believe it, because of course he hadn't meant it to happen, no one had, and the one who was really to blame wasn't him at all. It was her.

Chapter 16

Beth was looking at Theo Kennedy across the lunch table. For a so-called Hollywood producer, he was surprisingly softly spoken and had an air of dignity and integrity about him that she really hadn't been expecting at all, even though Robin Lindsay had told her what a respected and acclaimed filmmaker he was. Not being familiar with the movie world herself, she hadn't heard of him until Robin had first mentioned him, but it turned out she'd seen one of his films, which might have been helpful were she able to remember now what it was about. However, she needn't have worried, because the subject, so far, had centred round her book, which he seemed to have a genuine high regard for. Naturally, his praise was welcome, and his screen-adaptation proposals, though vague at this early stage, were interesting. But as he waxed on about special effects and story techniques, she was, for the moment at least, more intrigued by the man himself.

She guessed he was around forty, and even if the accent hadn't told her he was American, the look certainly would, for he had that shiny, yet rugged, sort of cleanness about him, that made his features appear freshly sculpted, and his body genetically enhanced to athletic perfection. His hair was probably naturally sun-bleached and curled, she decided, though she could easily imagine his super-white, dead-straight teeth on the front of some Hollywood dentist's portfolio of successes. And then there were his eyes, which were such a deep, lavender blue she had to wonder about tinted contacts, though they were so grave and intense, even when he smiled, that it made the idea of such artificial aids seem unlikely. In fact, he appeared to take himself very seriously indeed, and had, she noticed, either missed the few ironies Robin Lindsay had dropped into proceedings, or simply hadn't found them amusing at all.

Realizing he'd moved on to the subject of casting, she started paying attention again, listening to the various names he was considering for the role of Carlotta. Most were instantly recognizable, and, as he put it, guaranteed box office, though personally she found that more of a turn-off than a turn-on. However, she didn't voice her opinion, for she could see she was supposed to be impressed by these legends, and there was simply no point in making objections until the suggestions were promoted from a producer's hyperbole to the status of serious contenders, for even she knew that most of what was discussed at this stage fell into the category of blarney and bluster.

'But getting the script together is priority one,' Theo informed them. 'Obviously we can circulate a copy of the book manuscript to the potential leads, but if we can show them a red-hot script, they'll be more likely to commit.'

'Do you have someone in mind to write the screenplay?' Robin asked, sitting back as a waiter came to clear away their entrées.

'Mitzi Bower's my first choice,' he answered. 'She co-wrote *Heaven Came Down*, which won at Sundance a couple of years ago. She's done a couple of scripts for me since, both are in development, and I'm here to tell you she's good.' He turned to Beth, who blinked at the way his lavender gaze seemed suddenly to glow with feeling. 'You two should really get along,' he told her earnestly. 'She doesn't come loaded down with the kind of ego that'll get us stuck in the starting gate. She's easy, laid-back, and she'll welcome your input as story consultant. How soon do you reckon you can get out to California?'

Beth blinked again, then looked at Robin. 'Well, uh, I'm not sure,' she answered. 'When were you thinking?'

'Just as soon as you can make it,' he replied, picking up his glass of iced water. 'The quicker we get moving on this, the better chance we'll have of pulling in the cast and director before my option runs out. Did I tell you I've spoken to Eric Weston about directing?' he added, more to Robin than Beth.

Robin frowned. 'I don't think I know that name,' he said.

'He's got a film coming out in the fall. I'll try to get you an advance copy. Everyone's tipping it for an Oscar next year. He's young, kind of crazy, looks like a geek, but he's got an unusual style that could be just right for this. I'm waiting to hear back from his agent.'

'What sort of accommodation are you arranging for Ava once she gets to Hollywood?' Robin asked.

'I've got my PA on it,' Theo answered, returning his attention to Beth. 'We're looking into renting a house somewhere in Beverly Hills or West Hollywood. Not too far from the office, which is on Wilshire, west of Doheny. Do you know LA at all?'

Beth shook her head.

'Don't worry about it. It's not hard to learn, especially when you're going in at this level. If I can get Mitzi on the project, it might be a good idea for you two to move in together for the duration. Would you have a problem with that?'

Beth shrugged. 'It's hard to say when I've never met her,' she answered, 'but I'd be willing to give it a try.' It was amazing, she was thinking, how smoothly her words were going along with this when her heart, whilst not exactly resisting, was still there on the fence. But of course she would go, she knew that already, because apart from anything else she'd just signed the contract to say she would act as story consultant. Not that she was going to get rich on what Theo was paying her during the option period, but since that wasn't the point of the exercise, she was hardly going to make it an issue.

'Is there any more editing to be done on the book?' he asked. 'Anything that might change things from the way they stand right now?'

'No,' Robin answered, before Ava could speak. He felt it best not to get into the little tussle she was currently having with Stacey about the few cuts Stacey had suggested. 'Everything will be as per the manuscript.'

Beth treated him to one of Ava's dazzling smiles. How wonderful it was to be able to rely on his support. Picking up her wine she said, 'So, Theo, when are you going back to LA?'

'Friday,' he answered.

She mulled that over, then said, 'Maybe I could get the same flight.'

Both men appeared taken aback. 'Well, sure,' Theo said, 'if you can be ready that fast. It'll mean staying in a hotel when you first get there, but hell, there's no shortage in LA.'

Beth was smiling, amused by the speed of her decision, and pleased that she'd actually made it. After all, what was the point in delaying, when she needed to put as much distance as she could, emotionally and geographically, between herself and Colin – and whoever it was following her. Though she still hadn't spotted anyone since returning from Spain, someone was there, she could sense it, just like a bird could sense when danger was close.

'Who'll be paying for the hotel?' Robin enquired, ever the agent.

'We will,' Theo answered, meaning his production company.

'The Four Seasons?'

'Or equivalent,' Kennedy responded.

As she regarded them Beth felt herself flood with affection. It was so comforting, and enjoyable, having them take care of her like this. If it continued it might almost make up for Colin's neglect.

'What's the weather like in LA?' she asked Theo.

'Hotter than this. And don't expect too much in the way of humidity. You might hear Californians complaining about it, but in comparison to here, it's drier than paper. You'll need a great moisturizer at all times, and plenty of sunscreen. But don't worry, Mitzi'll get you fixed up with everything, including all the right spas and masseuses and manicurists and hair salons . . .' For the first time his smile seemed to reach his eyes. 'We'll turn you into a real California girl,' he promised.

Beth's eyebrows were up. 'What about the accent?' she said. 'I don't think I'd do too well with that.'

'Oh no,' he protested, 'your Englishness is going to be as effective a passport as your book, so no way do we want to lose it.'

She didn't respond to that, though the idea of Ava with a Californian accent was already starting to gain some appeal.

Later in the afternoon, after returning to Bruce and

Georgie's London flat, she stripped off Ava's neutral Armani sheath and stepped into a cooling shower. She was intrigued and slightly amused by the way she was going so effortlessly with the flow of this new stream of events. Was this how easy life could be if she just allowed it to happen? Tickets were now being arranged, hotels booked and houses rented, all in order to transport her from this turbulent yet familiar world to one where she hardly knew what to expect, apart from sunshine, luxury and the freedom to be, as Robin had put it, whosoever she wanted to be.

'Friday!' Georgie cried, when she came in from her workout. 'Isn't that a bit soon?'

Beth shrugged. 'Why wait? They want to get started, and what am I doing here besides trying to fight off an editor who doesn't understand no, and hanging around for a letter that's probably never going to come?'

'Actually,' Georgie said, pulling open a drawer, 'it arrived with the second post.'

It was suddenly as though day had turned into night, or the world had started spinning the other way. She'd been so convinced Colin wouldn't write back, so engrossed in her Hollywood plans, that she couldn't make the change. She stared at the prison envelope, so fearful, yet hopeful, of what it might contain that the conflict was making it hard to move. She'd prayed every night for a letter, but now it was here she wasn't sure she wanted it. She could see that it had come through regular channels, rather than through Bruce. Was that significant? Would it make it harder, or easier to read? If there was a visiting order she would see that first. She'd know then that it would be easier. But if there was, what would she do if it was dated after Friday?

Her eyes came up to Georgie's. 'I almost want you to read it for me,' she said in a hushed voice.

Georgie put it on the table. 'I'm going to have a shower,' she said. 'There's wine in the fridge if you need some fortification.'

Beth nodded, then realizing she did, she opened a cupboard and took out a glass. 'Theo Kennedy, the producer, doesn't seem to drink,' she said, her voice sounding oddly distant to her own ears.

'Probably in rehab,' Georgie commented. 'Half of them are.'

'What about the other half?'

'They're fun.'

Beth smiled vaguely, then poured the wine as Georgie went off to the bathroom. After taking a sip she sat down at the table and forced herself to tear open the envelope. There was no visiting order, just a single blue page.

My darling Beth,

I have read your letter over and over, and though I've tried many times I know I'll never be able to find the words to tell you how truly sorry I am for all the pain and anguish I have caused you, or for the times I've deceived you. No man could ever ask for a more beautiful, supportive and loving wife. I have been truly blessed in you, my darling, yet how do I repay you? By abusing your trust, dishonouring your love, and failing to appreciate your loyalty. And now, when I deserve your scorn and contempt, you are there, wanting to stand by me to show the world how deeply you believe in me. For that, and for everything else you are, I will always love you. But, my darling, I can't hold you to me any longer. You have a life to live, one that is just opening up with all the new and exciting challenges you told me about in your letter, which I'm sure will bring all the success and recognition you so deserve.

It filled my heart with pride when I read about Ava's achievement – and I love her name, by the way. I'd already read about her in the paper, which was hard, not hearing it from you first, but all the excitement you expressed in your letter more than made up for me finding out that way. Will you send me a copy when it's in print?

I don't know how long I will be in here now, but don't feel badly, darling, that you've doubted me. I didn't kill Sophie, but I can understand why you, and so many others believe I did, when the evidence looks the way it does. So yes, of course I forgive you for thinking the worst, though I'm relieved to hear that you no longer do. I've relented now, and am allowing others to try finding out what really happened that day. All the time I've been afraid for your safety, wondering if your association with me will bring you harm. I will tell you no more than that, because I don't want you to bear the burden of secrets that I only half know anyway. It won't surprise you to hear that I've turned to journalists for help. I just hope I've chosen the right ones. My own close colleagues appear to have deserted me, so I'm left with the girl who delivered the news of my arrest, and Elliot Russell, who we've both met once or twice in the past. He is not an easy man to intimidate, and has a way of getting to the truth that I hope will eventually return me to freedom.

If that happens, my darling, I want you to know that I will go to Heather and Jessica. Your offer to accept my daughter into our lives reduced me to tears, but, Beth, I can't let you sacrifice yourself any more. You deserve all the happiness and triumphs Ava can bring you, so, darling, seize your opportunities and know that I will always be there for you in spirit.

God bless and good luck,
    Colin

Beth was sobbing and laughing, twisting her hair, and trying to be strong, but this was so devastating she didn't know if she could hold on. The last thing she wanted now was to go to Hollywood. Ava was nothing, no one, just a false dimension of her battered mind that she was using to protect herself from the pain. But it wasn't working; the pain was still there, and it would never go away because in the end Colin was all that mattered – not a book, or a script, or even a new life. But he didn't want her. He'd chosen Jessica. *The daughter that should have been hers.* How was she going to bear this? Oh God, how could she change his mind?

She looked around the empty kitchen. What should she do now? Almost without thinking she shouted Georgie's name. Georgie needed to know this, she might be able to help.

Georgie's feet sounded in the hall. 'Oh no,' she groaned, seeing Beth's stricken, tear-stained face. 'What does it say?'

Beth passed her the letter. Georgie read swiftly, then turned to take Beth in her arms. 'I'm sorry,' she soothed. 'I'm so, so sorry.'

'I've got to see him,' Beth sobbed. 'I can change his mind if I see him. I know I can.'

'Of course, I'll speak to Bruce. I'll ring him right now.'

'Is she there with you?' Bruce asked after Georgie told him why she was calling.

'Yes,' she answered.

'OK. Well, I've got no reason to think he'll change his mind, but he's due to call here in the next half-hour. I'll put it to him, and get back to you.'

'Oh God, I can't bear it,' Beth groaned, when Georgie passed on the message. 'He's got to say yes. He's just got to.'

'Pour me one too,' Georgie said, as Beth refilled her glass.

Five minutes later the phone rang, making them both jump.

'Hello?' Georgie said into the receiver. 'Ava? Oh yes, she's right here. Who's calling please?' Covering the mouthpiece she said, 'It's Theo Kennedy.'

Beth was confused and panicky. She wanted to speak to him, but not now. Her head was in chaos and he just wasn't a part of this world, where she was Beth Ashby, a murderer's wife, who was afraid and vulnerable, desperate to speak to her husband and ready to abandon a future of riches and fame. But Georgie had already said she was there, so she had no choice. She had to speak to him now and somehow make herself sound like Ava, the super-cool siren he'd been with earlier.

Taking the phone, she said, 'Hello, Theo. How nice to hear from you.'

'Quick call,' he told her. 'I just need to know where to send the car on Friday?'

Frowning, she said, 'What car?'

'To take you to the airport.'

'Oh, uh yes . . .' she said, looking at Georgie and wondering if she should prepare Theo now for the fact that she might not be going.

'By the way,' he said, 'I just got word from Eric Weston's agent. He's agreed to read the manuscript.'

Who was Eric Weston? Then she remembered, it was the director he was after. 'That's good,' she said.

'It's great,' he corrected. 'So, the address . . .'

'Well, actually, Theo,' she said, 'I might have a bit of a problem –'

'Oh, hell,' he cut in, 'there goes my other line. I'll get back to you.'

After he'd rung off, Beth picked up her wine.

'Have you changed your mind about going?' Georgie said.

'I don't know. I suppose it depends if Colin will see me.' She took a sip of wine, then said, 'Everything in my life has always depended on Colin, one way or the other. I can't change it just like that.'

'But you're trying,' Georgie reminded her.

Beth smiled weakly and nodded. Yes, she was trying.

It was another forty minutes before the phone rang again.

'Bruce, hi, darling,' Georgie said, experiencing some of Beth's nerves on hearing his voice.

'Is she still with you?' he asked.

'Yes.'

'OK. Well, you'll have to find a way of breaking this to her, because he obviously finds it a lot easier to be brutal about her than to her.'

Georgie braced herself.

'He said, and I quote, "If this place doesn't do anything else for me, at least it'll get me out of a marriage I should have got out of years ago. So no, I don't want her coming here, and tell her I don't want her asking again." '

Somehow Georgie managed to keep the shock from her expression, though she turned away so that Beth could no longer see her eyes. 'I see,' she said. 'Well, that's a shame, but if it's not possible, I suppose –'

'Let me speak to him,' Beth demanded, reaching for the phone.

Reluctantly Georgie handed it over.

'Why's he doing this?' Beth cried into the receiver. 'I don't understand why he wants to keep hurting me.'

'I'm sorry,' Bruce said. 'I wish I knew what to tell you.'

'Then you tell him that I'm going to America, and unless I'm subpoenaed I won't be back for his trial.' And without saying goodbye she slammed the phone down.

Rhona yawned and resettled Ruby, the cat, on to the sofa beside her. It was too hot to be smothered in all that fur, no matter how silky and feathery it felt. 'You shouldn't be doing that,' she chided, as Laurie put a tray of hors-d'oeuvres on the polished walnut and chrome coffee table that had arrived from Italy two days before Andrew and Stephen had left. 'I'm supposed to be the one looking after you.'

'But you've been at work all day, whilst I've just been sitting here on the phone or the Internet,' Laurie reminded her. 'And besides, I've decided to renounce my invalid status as of now. It's getting on my nerves.'

'Well, I'll let you be the one to tell Elliot,' Rhona responded, helping herself to a savoury pretzel.

Laurie let that go, as filling up their glasses with her own speciality fruit cocktail she said, 'So go on telling me about Beth Ashby.'

'Ava Montgomery,' Rhona corrected. 'There's not really any more to tell. Just that she's dyed her hair blonde, looks outrageously chic, and stalks down the office as though she's already got six bestsellers on the shelves rather than one in the works. Stacey would never admit it, of course, but it sounds like she's turning into a real handful – won't make any changes to the book, totally disdained the jacket design . . . Is that mine?'

'No, mine,' Laurie said, picking up her mobile. 'Laurie Forbes.'

'Elliot Russell,' he responded.

'Where are you?'

'Stuck in traffic on Blackfriars Bridge. Have you spoken to Murray?'

'About Sandra Chettle and Philip Buck?' she said, referring to the contacts Colin Ashby had given her. 'Yes, I have, and he hasn't got anywhere either. But Morton Shields is right here at Canary Wharf. I'm thinking of going over there in person. If I call from reception Philip Buck might be per-suaded to come down for a moment.'

'OK. Just make sure Stan goes with you.'

'You're surely not suggesting a foreign exchange dealer is dangerous,' she protested.

'No, but I know what you can be like when you don't get your own way.'

Wishing it hadn't made her laugh, she said, 'So what's new your end?'

'Can I come over?'

If only she could make herself say no. 'Does that mean you've got something interesting?' she countered. 'By the way, Sam deBugger, as Murray calls him, appeared today and swept me clean.'

'Did it need it?'

'No, apparently.'

'Ah well, you can never be too careful. Yes, it does mean I've got something interesting. I've just spent a couple of hours with Bruce Cottle. There's a lot to tell, but how's this for coming attractions – Beth Ashby's taking off for LaLa Land the day after tomorrow. Apparently they're turning the book into a feature film.'

Laurie's eyes widened as they went to Rhona. 'You never told me that,' she said.

'What?' Rhona and Elliot said in unison.

'Rhona's here,' she said into the phone. 'Did you know Beth Ashby's book is being made into a movie?' she asked Rhona.

Rhona shook her head. 'It's the first I've heard,' she said. 'But I don't know everything. Why, is it a big deal?'

'I'm not sure,' she answered. 'Is it a big deal?' she asked Elliot.

'It could be,' he replied. 'Have you got the fax turned on? I need Jed and Liam to send over the stuff they've been working on today.'

'It's on,' she confirmed. 'What time should we expect you?'

'About half an hour.'

'We're ordering in food. Do you have a preference?'

'I won't be staying that long,' he answered.

Annoyed at her disappointment, she said, 'Then why not tell me your news on the phone? It'll save you dragging all the way over here.' But she was talking into a dead connection.

'I wish he'd learn the art of saying goodbye,' she snapped, throwing her mobile on to the cushion beside her.

'The man's a brute,' Rhona agreed, selecting herself a juicy little crab cake. Then chuckling as Laurie slanted her a look, she said, 'So, Ava's off to Hollywood. Does that confuse or clarify matters? No, don't bother to tell me, it'll only burden me with things I'd probably rather not know. Did you call

269

your father back, by the way? He left a message last night, after you'd gone to bed.'

'Yes, I spoke to him,' Laurie confirmed. 'He sounds on good form, actually, but I ended up snapping at my mother as usual.'

'What about this time?'

'Elliot, would you believe? Apparently he called a couple of days ago and spoke to my father, so now my mother wants us all to get together for a cosy little chin-wag.'

'Wow! That's a bit of a turn-up. What does Elliot say?'

'I haven't discussed it with him, nor will I, because it's not going to happen. At least not with me, it isn't.'

'Oh, go on, a good old purging of the soul, a bit of happy hand-clapping and thanks be to God – I can't think of a better way to spend a Sunday.'

'Who said anything about Sunday?'

Rhona shrugged. 'It just seemed like a good day.'

'Let's change the subject,' Laurie said irritably. It was bad enough feeling the way she did about him coming over here and not staying long, without having to go into the deeper implications of a get-it-all-out routine with her parents.

'What time did he say he'd be here?' Rhona asked, looking at her watch.

'In about half an hour.'

'Great. That should give me just enough time to shower and make myself gorgeous.'

Laurie looked at her in amazement, until the slow beat of suspicion turned her expression darker. 'I didn't know you –'

'Oh, for heaven's sake,' Rhona cried. 'Not for him. For Josh. I was thinking, if Elliot's going to be here, I can go out for the evening.'

Laurie gave a laugh of surprise. 'Elliot doesn't need to be here for that,' she told her. 'I'm perfectly OK on my own. I've got Sam Spade outside, remember?'

'Yeah, well, I just don't want you to be lonely, that's all.'

'Who said I was lonely?'

'No one. I simply meant I don't want you to be. You're very defensive tonight.'

'Am I?'

'Yes.'

'Sorry.'

'It's OK. You're allowed, once in a while.'

When Elliot arrived about twenty minutes later, Laurie was just coming down from Andrew's office, flipping through the twenty-page fax Jed and Liam had sent.

'Rhona let me in,' he explained, when she stopped on the stairs in surprise.

'Of course.' She returned to the fax, not wanting to prolong eye contact. 'Would you like a drink?' she offered. 'There's some fruit cocktail on the table in the lounge. It's got rum in it.'

'Sounds good,' he responded.

As he went to get one she carried on reading the fax, though her concentration was poor. This wasn't the first time she'd seen him since the night following her attack, but it was the first time they'd been alone, and she was feeling annoyingly on edge and uncomfortable with it.

'So what else did Bruce Cottle have to say?' she asked, when he came back into the kitchen. 'Actually, shall we go outside?' she suggested, realizing they were about to return to the positions they'd been in the other night. 'It's probably dried off after the rain.'

'Did it rain today?' he asked, following her out.

'Only slightly. Here's the fax, by the way.'

Putting his glass down on the table, he flicked quickly through the pages.

'The graphs,' she told him, 'reflect the past three-year trends in the currencies you requested. The tables are more detailed versions of the same, and the text is Jed and Liam's analysis of the whole. I've been on the phone with them half the day, so I've got a pretty good idea of what they've found so far.'

He was nodding as she spoke, then his eyes narrowed as he looked at the closing line. 'Inconclusive,' he said. 'Which is hardly a surprise. Are they calling in more experts?'

She nodded. She turned over a couple of pages, then pushed them towards him. 'Berlin's regained control of East Prussia,' she stated. 'Incalculable sums of money involved there, and who has it benefited most at this stage? We're working on the answers. Mitterrand's former foreign

271

minister and his corruption trial – is this the syndicate taking some kind of revenge on one of its own?'

'Chancy. He's likely to blow the lid if they back him against a wall like that.'

'Colin Ashby hasn't,' she reminded him. 'Jed's going to Paris tomorrow to talk to your contacts there.'

'Great. So, the Gatling syndicate's starting to go under the microscope.'

'Is that what we're calling it now?'

'Unless you've got another idea. Are you in a bad mood?'

'No. Why?'

'Just wondered. You look better, by the way. Pissed off, but better.'

The comment lodged straight under her skin. However, she made a valiant effort to smile which she followed with, 'Back to Bruce Cottle. What did you discuss?'

'OK,' he said, taking a sip of his drink. 'This is one of your best, by the way. I'd forgotten how good you were at these.'

She didn't answer.

'Right. Bruce Cottle. We discussed the fact that Beth Ashby – or Ava Montgomery – has got a Hollywood deal for her book, and how she's going to be acting as story consultant for the adaptation. She's planning to leave on Friday, having just failed in a last-ditch attempt to see her husband.'

Laurie looked interested. 'So what are we to deduce from that?' she said. 'The failed attempt first.'

'It's more what Bruce Cottle and his wife deduced,' he responded. 'He didn't have a copy of the letter Ashby recently sent to Beth, but apparently, to quote him, "It was certainly out of step with the tone Colin used on the phone when he said he didn't want to see her." In other words, the letter, so they tell me, was very loving and regretful, whilst the phone message was harsh to the point of being cruel.'

She was frowning. 'Is there any chance of talking to Bruce Cottle's wife?' she asked, picking up her mobile as it rang. 'Laurie Forbes.'

'It's Murray. I've got Mr and Mrs Long, Sophie's parents, on the other line, wanting to know when they can expect to see their story.'

Laurie swore under her breath, but was already thinking.

'OK, tell them it's part of a much bigger piece that's still being researched,' she said. 'It's not a lie, but it's definitely a fudge, and as they know there's something untoward going on it won't surprise them.'

'Got it,' Murray responded. 'Is Elliot there?'

'Yes. Do you want to speak to him?'

'No, just tell him his ticket's booked for the eight o'clock flight Saturday morning.'

'OK.' She rang off, relayed Murray's message, then said, 'So where were we?'

'Needing to talk to Mrs Cottle,' he reminded her. 'I've already put it to Bruce, on your behalf. He's getting back to us, but he's pretty certain she won't do anything unless Beth Ashby says it's OK.'

'Which is about as likely as Beth Ashby flying to LA on her own wings.'

He nodded agreement.

From inside the kitchen Rhona watched them, moved by the feeling of *déjà vu* that had come over her when she'd spotted them, sitting together like that, for how often had she seen them like it in the past, engrossed in whatever had their interest that day, oblivious to everyone else, talking, debating, questioning, laughing, connecting in a way it was impossible for an onlooker not to understand? Unless the onlooker happened to be Lysette, who'd always been so proud of the way the two people she loved most in the world got along so well. Had she ever known, Rhona wondered. In her heart of hearts, had she sensed it, the way she and Laurie always used to sense each other's feelings?

'Gosh, this looks like fun,' she declared, sweeping out on to the balcony as Laurie noticed her watching them.

Elliot got to his feet.

'Oh darling, you're so divinely old-fashioned,' she purred, pulling him into an embrace. 'And I don't know how you do it, but each time I see you I swear you look meaner than the last.'

'That's because I am,' he assured her.

'And how's the gorgeous Petra Wilson? I hear you're still seeing her.'

'Not any more,' he answered.

Rhona immediately perked up. 'Does that mean you're free?' she demanded.

Laughing, he said, 'Not exactly.' Then looking at Laurie, who was fully engaged in Jed and Liam's fax again, he glanced at his watch and said, 'I'll leave you two to your dinner. I just wanted to make sure you were OK, and keep you up to date.'

'Great,' Laurie said, lifting a hand to wave but not looking up.

'Oh, but, darling, you can't leave –'

'Rhona!' Laurie snapped. 'Elliot's got another engagement, so why don't we just decide what we're going to order?'

Rhona was about to protest again when she finally got what was happening. Laurie wanted Elliot to think that she had company for dinner. 'Oh, what a shame you can't stay,' she said to Elliot. 'Where are you going? Can you give me a lift to the station?'

Laurie's groan was almost audible.

'Of course,' Elliot responded. 'Are you leaving now?'

'*Tout de suite*,' she smiled in her inimitable fashion. 'I'll meet you down at the car.'

To Laurie he said, 'I'm going to New York at the weekend. Do you know Tom Maykin?'

'No,' she answered.

'He works for the *Wall Street Journal*. He's an Ashby recommendation, but I know him, he's worth talking to.'

'Then what can I say, but have a good trip?'

He looked at Rhona, who signalled him to leave. When the coast was clear she leant in closely to Laurie, just to make sure she couldn't be overheard, and whispered, 'You're on your own now, so be brave. There's no one to lie to except yourself, and it's high time you stopped.' And with a big, overdone hug, she wafted off into the night, leaving a trail of musky perfume in her wake and Laurie with an irrepressible urge to slap her.

However, by the time Rhona returned, just after eleven, Laurie had calmed down considerably and was even ready to admit that she was, in many ways, hiding from the truth. 'But you have to understand, Rhona,' she said earnestly, 'that sometimes it's better that way.'

'No, it's not,' Rhona told her, brushing her hair at the

dressing table, while Laurie sat cross-legged on the bed. 'It's never better that way.'

'You don't know. You weren't there,' Laurie said. 'It wasn't you she called minutes before she drove her car into a wall. You didn't hear her the way I did. He totally devastated her, Rhona. He couldn't have hurt her more if he'd tried. And then I . . . Well, what I did is just too –'

'But that's not the issue here, is it?' Rhona cut in. 'What you did or didn't do isn't the truth you're hiding from.'

'How do you know? I've never told you what was said that night.'

'You've told me enough for me to be able to put the rest of it together. And as for saying he couldn't have hurt her more, well he could, and you know it.'

'That's enough now.'

'No, it's not nearly enough. He could have told her he was in love with you, but he didn't. He spared her that. Or did he?'

'He wasn't in love with me,' Laurie cried. 'It was *me* who was in love with *him*. It was always that way round, never the other, never returned. Why else do you think I didn't show her any pity that night? I didn't care how she was feeling. I only cared about myself. She'd just told me he was in love with another woman, and all I could think about was how *I* wouldn't be able to stand it. I'd always believed that if it weren't for her he'd want me, but then there was somebody else, someone we didn't know, and we were both hurting so much . . . We both loved him, we both wanted him, but she didn't know that. All she knew was that she needed me that night. She pleaded with me. She was crying, sobbing, begging me to let her come. She told me she didn't want to live, but still I wouldn't listen. I didn't want to hear her any more, and now I never stop hearing her, calling my name, the way she did that night. I put the phone down then, but I can't put it down now. She's always there, in my head, calling my name and I want so much to tell her I'm sorry. I want her to come to me so I can comfort her and tell her it'll be all right. But she'll never come now, will she? She's dead now, thanks to me, and the way I only cared about myself.'

Rhona looked on helplessly as Laurie let the tears run unchecked down her face. In the end she said, 'Have you never discussed this with anyone? Not even your parents?'

'No, of course not. How could I? It's my fault she's dead, and they loved her so much, you know that.'

'But they love you too. They'd –'

'I know, but I wasn't there for her when I should have been. And then I let Elliot take the blame for what she'd done, because I couldn't stand for anyone to know it was me who'd let her down. It wasn't his fault, but I told myself if it weren't for him, and what a bastard he'd been to her, then none of it would have happened. She wouldn't have called me that night, and I wouldn't have hung up on her. So he deserved the blame. I let everyone else blame him too. I wanted them to hate him as much as I did. I wanted to ruin his life, the way he'd ruined hers. But I was the last one she spoke to, not Elliot. If I'd listened, if I hadn't been thinking only of myself and how much I wanted him, she'd be here now.'

'Oh my,' Rhona murmured, 'I didn't realize you'd been giving yourself quite such a terrible time. But, darling, you've got to make yourself accept that Lysette is responsible for what she did. Not you, not Elliot, not anyone but her. No, I can see you're going to argue, but I'm right, and anyway, it's Elliot you should be talking to, you know that, don't you?'

Laurie was shaking her head. 'No. I couldn't,' she said.

'Oh, you could,' Rhona corrected. 'You have to. He's suffered a great deal over this, just as you have, and as far as I can see you're the only ones who can help each other finally get past it. Did he ever tell her how he felt about you?'

'I told you, it was the other way round.'

'He feels the same way, and you know it. Now did he ever tell her?'

'I don't know.'

'Then you must ask him.'

'No! Never!'

'Laurie, you're not a coward so stop behaving like one. If she knew how he felt about you –'

'If she knew, I couldn't handle it, Rhona. If it turned out that she killed herself because of that . . . But she said she didn't know who the other woman was.'

'Then the chances are she didn't. But that's what you're

hiding from, isn't it? You're afraid of finding out that she knew.'

'Wouldn't you be?'

'And you're also,' Rhona continued, 'afraid of finding out that it wasn't you.'

Laurie looked away.

'Oh dear, I can see the dilemma all too clearly now,' Rhona sighed. 'You don't know whether to be afraid of him loving you, or not loving you. Poor thing. But it has to be faced. And I know this is going to sound hard, but I'm afraid if you don't tell him everything you've just told me, then I'll have to tell him myself.'

Laurie gasped. 'No. You can't,' she cried. 'That's not fair! It's not your –'

'If you were about to say it's not my business, then I'm here to tell you it is. I care about you both far too much to just sit back and watch what this is doing to you. It's been long enough, Laurie. You have to get over it, both of you. Elliot's at least trying. He's called your parents, and he's told you himself that he's ready to talk if you are. So it's up to you now.'

'I'm just not ready,' Laurie responded.

Rhona was unmoved.

Laurie's eyes were becoming desperate. 'Rhona, no. We have to work together now. You don't understand . . . The way I let him take the blame – it was such a terrible thing to do. He's never going to forgive me for that, and why should he?'

'Give him the chance.'

'No.'

'Then you leave me no choice.'

Laurie's head spun as she searched frantically for a solution, some way she could change Rhona's mind, or take back everything she'd said. But there was nothing she could say or do, no answers, no excuses, only the smallest, weakest of compromises that might not help in the end either, but for the moment it was all she had. 'OK,' she said, 'I'll tell him, but you have to let me do it when I feel the time is right.'

Rhona's expression showed little mercy as she said, 'All right. Just don't make it too long, or you might end up finding it's too late.'

Chapter 17

Ava was getting drunk. Not very. Just enough to stop her thinking about the last time she'd flown, with Colin, to Paris for a romantic weekend. And to stop her thinking about the letter that had all but destroyed Beth. After today she'd be able to say goodbye to Beth almost entirely, because people in LA would know her only as Ava. No one would have any idea that, given the choice, she'd take her life right back to where it had been a year, or even three months ago – except that would mean to a time before Ava, and she wasn't sure now how she'd ever manage to cope without Ava. She was always there, ready to come to the rescue when hell was calling; a shining white light at the start of the tunnel, rather than the end. She had a way of dealing with people, and emotions, and life's disturbing coincidences that Beth alone had never mastered. She was dazzling and reckless, and unfailingly courageous, especially when drinking vodka martinis, as she was now. This was her third since boarding the plane, so the shock of discovering that Marcus and Leonora Gatling were no more than eight rows ahead, in the first-class cabin, was starting to become more of a hazy confusion.

Theo Kennedy, the celluloid super-god of Hollywood production, was in the business-class seat next to her, snoring softly behind his black satin eye-mask, ears plugged with spongy yellow bullets, warming socks tugged over his size elevens, blanket snuggled under his chin and a good supply of water in the holder between the seats. He didn't drink alcohol when flying, it dehydrated the system. Poor Theo, he obviously hadn't read a book on how to have fun; and Ava was rapidly coming to the conclusion that he did everything by the book.

Personally, she felt like doing something outrageous, though not with him. Adonis-like as he was, he just didn't inspire the creative juices of passion, or much else, come to that. He was so methodical, sincere, knowledgeable, with a brain as orderly as an index and a permanent vacancy where humour should reside. She couldn't imagine him doing anything on instinct. Everything had to be studied, brainstormed, market-researched, evaluated, then possibly, after some further assessment, expert opinion and reconfigured industry analysis, produced. What was it like being inside his head, she wondered. Definitely not a picnic, or a day at the beach; more like a session with a librarian, or a tax audit. How had he ever come to be in entertainment? Still, for all that, she rather liked him. He was pleasant, considerate, and knew all the right things to say, probably because he'd read them in a book.

Picking the olive out of her martini, she bit into it and looked around at her fellow passengers. The cabin was less than half full and most seemed to be watching films on their personal screens. The first-class passengers had a wider and more up-to-date choice, she'd noticed when reading the in-flight magazine. So what were Leonora and Marcus watching? Actually, she couldn't imagine them doing anything that seemed such a waste of time, when they could be checking the markets or preparing details of their next multimillion-dollar deal. She wondered why they were going to LA. It seemed a trivial sort of destination for people like them, who'd hardly be interested in movie studio tours or rollerblading along Santa Monica beach. However, LA didn't make up the whole of California, whereas California did make up the world's fifth largest economy, which was why she was no longer so perplexed about them being on the same flight. Whether or not they'd spotted her, she had no idea. Maybe she'd ask a stewardess if she could borrow a tray to go and offer them a drink. *Surprise!* One more martini and she might.

Another hour slipped by. They were now somewhere over Greenland according to the constantly updating electronic map. Though it was late afternoon London time, since the films had finished everyone had lowered their shutters, and seemed either to be tilting off into a doze, or reading a book. Ava was still restless, thinking about LA, what it was going to be like there, the man over in the back corner whom she was considering joining for a drink, and Leonora Gatling, whom she'd caught a glimpse of earlier, when she'd gone to the bathroom. If it *wasn't* a coincidence that they were on the same flight, then what was the Gatlings' purpose in being here? To intimidate? To let her know they were watching? But surely they'd never put themselves to the trouble of going all the way to LA, just for that.

She'd had four martinis by now – any more would make her ill. As it was, she felt expansive, gregarious, in the mood for some fun. She liked the idea of doing something wild and shocking, right under the Gatlings' noses. It would add a sort of piquancy to whatever she chose to do. She sat quietly thinking it over, imagining coaxing the man behind into the bathroom and wrapping her legs round his waist, or going to offer the pilots a little mid-flight relaxation. It was interesting how all her urges were sexual, and with men she didn't know, when it was the Gatlings she was trying to affect. What did that say, she wondered. Theo and his textbook brain would probably understand. Were the strangers symbolic of her unknown future, while the act of sex was saying fuck you to the past? Maybe. It had a certain Jungian sort of logic.

Finally she got up from her seat, took off her black frock coat, and sauntered slowly along the aisle towards the first-class cabin. Her vision was slightly blurred, but her unsteady movements were covered by a few small judders of turbulence. She could easily picture how striking she looked, in her straight black trousers and tight white T-shirt top that hugged the dark, swollen peaks of her nipples. She thought, when she got to LA, that one of the first things she'd do would be to get larger breasts, nice big D cups that wouldn't need a bra and would make her feel sexier than Circe.

On reaching the front of the cabin she cast a sultry glance over her shoulder, but the man at the back wasn't watching. What the hell? She wasn't that interested anyway. So after checking with a stewardess that it was all right to go into first

280

class to say hello to some friends, she stepped in under the curtain.

The Gatlings' ten-thousand-dollar seats were in the second row. Marcus, who was closest to the window, was studying the finance pages of the *Wall Street Journal*, while Leonora appeared to be midway through Margaret Atwood's *The Blind Assassin*. It didn't surprise her to find them awake, for she couldn't imagine them ever sleeping.

'Hello, Leonora,' she said. The drone of the plane's engines might have drowned her voice, but someone stopping alongside them got both Gatlings' attention.

Leonora frowned. 'Beth?' she said. 'Is that you? My, how different you look.'

'Thank you,' she smiled, taking it as a compliment. 'How are you?'

'Very well. How are you? What takes you to LA?'

She chuckled. 'Oh, I'm sure you know,' she responded.

Leonora looked surprised, and glanced briefly at her husband. 'Why would I know?' she asked.

Ava merely looked at her, smiling.

Leonora seemed baffled. 'Are you all right, dear?' she asked.

'Of course. Why wouldn't I be?'

Again Leonora glanced at Marcus.

'Uh, how's Colin?' Gatling asked gruffly.

Ava looked at him. 'Colin who?' she politely enquired.

Leonora blinked, then apparently amused, she laughed. 'You seem to be in rather an unusual mood, my dear,' she commented. 'Maybe it's this new look of yours.'

'Maybe it is,' Ava responded, frowning as though the thought had only just occurred to her. Then brightening again, she said, 'So what takes *you* to LA?'

'We have business in Santa Barbara,' Leonora answered. 'Do you know it?'

Ava shook her head. 'Such a coincidence, isn't it, us being on the same flight?'

'Isn't it?' Leonora agreed.

Ava waited for her to say more.

Leonora wasn't easily discomfited and she showed no signs of it now, though she was the first to break the impasse.

'I read in the paper that you've written a book,' she said. 'When will we have the pleasure of reading it?'

Ava looked her straight in the eyes. 'You mean you haven't already?' she said.

Again Leonora frowned. 'Is it out?' she asked.

Ava laughed. 'Very good,' she commended. 'Very good indeed.'

Brushing over that, Leonora said, 'Has Colin read it, by any chance?'

'Yes. He didn't understand it either.'

The 'either' hung there, as heavily as the implication, until Leonora said casually, 'What exactly didn't he understand?'

'The murder.'

Leonora's eyebrows went up. 'Why? Is there something difficult about it?' she asked.

'I wouldn't say difficult. More, allusive.'

'To what, exactly?'

'Oh no,' Ava laughed, 'I can't tell you that, it would be cheating. You have to read it first.'

Leonora's eyes were sharp as razors.

Ava continued to smile.

'Well, do enjoy the rest of the flight,' Leonora said, returning to her book.

Ava remained where she was, moving her eyes to Gatling.

'I hear Colin's trial has been delayed,' he said, the overhead lights glinting in the moisture on his lips.

'Has it?' Ava replied. 'Ah, that'll be because of the evidence they've found that throws some doubt on who actually did it.'

Gatling's face darkened, as the air around them seemed suddenly to load with tension. 'What evidence?' he said.

Ava glanced down at Leonora, knowing full well that her ears were as alert as a rodent's. 'I'm not entirely sure,' she answered, wondering whether to mention the mysterious fibres, which they would already know about, or if it might be more entertaining to invent something new. In the end, she decided just to leave them guessing.

'Your games are a little tiresome,' Leonora remarked, turning a page, 'so if you wouldn't mind going back to your seat . . .'

Ava's eyes flashed, but her temper was under control. 'I'll go when I'm ready,' she told her.

At that Leonora seemed genuinely surprised. 'We would like to be left alone now,' she said, smoothing her annoyance with burred, velvety tones.

'Yes, so would I,' Ava responded.

Leonora appeared confused. 'Beth, what on earth has got into you?' she demanded. 'Have you been drinking?'

'Yes, as a matter of fact. I do a lot of it now, since *my husband was arrested for murder.*'

'Well, I'm sorry, I understand it must be very stressful,' Leonora replied, looking around to see who was listening. 'But there's really nothing –'

'You said, if I ever felt the need to talk . . .'

'But not here, dear. Really, it's hardly appropriate.'

'Then where? Sophie Long's flat?' Her eyes were glittering with menace.

Leonora's face was scarlet. 'Heavens above,' she muttered, looking around for an attendant.

Gatling was watching Ava closely, his steely eyes as lethal as bullets. 'Colin killed that girl and we both know it,' he said, pitching his voice so only she could hear. 'Now, if I were you, I'd go and sit down before –'

'Madam, please return to your seat,' a steward was saying as he tried to take her arm.

Ava shrugged him off. 'What we both know,' she said to Gatling, 'is that you're scared witless over this, and –'

'Madam, please,' the steward interrupted, taking hold of her more firmly. 'You're bothering other passengers . . .'

'And I can't promise,' Ava shouted, as he dragged her away, 'that your secret's going to stay safe with me.'

At the end of the aisle she wrenched herself out of the steward's grip and staggered back to her seat.

She was shaking with fury and shock. She hadn't expected to erupt the way she had at the end, and now she was afraid of what she'd said. They were dangerous people, much too dangerous to play around with like that, so what had got into her? Why hadn't she just given in to the sexual urges, instead of throwing herself straight into the lions' den, as though her new blonde hair and a bit of Dutch courage were enough to take on the whole damned pride. She obviously had some kind of death wish. What would Colin say if he knew? What would he do? She had to pull herself together. She needed another drink.

An attendant brought one. She had just taken a sip, when the man from behind leant down to speak in her ear. She didn't even look at him as she got up. Yes, she'd care to take her drink over to his seat. Yes, he could get her another. And while they waited perhaps he'd like to escort her to the bathroom.

The space was ridiculously small, though quite conducive to what he had in mind, once he'd stripped off her T-shirt and finished biting and sucking her nipples.

She laughed when he suggested it, then laughed and laughed. 'Oh no, no, no,' she told him, looking up into his vaguely handsome, though florid face. 'It's you, my friend, who's going into the prayer position, not I.'

His eyebrows immediately went up, but she could see he was turned on by her manner, and, after she'd removed her trousers and panties, he dropped meekly to his knees, putting his mouth at just the right level.

She parted her legs readily then gave an audible sigh of pleasure as his tongue found her. Colin had always been an expert at this, but Ava wasn't thinking about Colin. She was thinking only of herself. How easy it had been to assume control. And this time she wasn't going to let it go. Oh no, she was in charge here, not Beth, or Colin, so now her new friend could just get up off the floor and penetrate her from behind.

He was happy to oblige, but she wasn't interested in his happiness. All she cared about was the inner struggle with Beth that this time she was easily winning. She was allowing this man to plunge into Colin's private territory and Beth wasn't putting up as much as a murmur. Ava was exultant. She could do this. She could break free of Beth. She'd just stood up to the Gatlings, and now she was making this man pump with all his might because she wanted to come. And minutes later she did, while watching her face in the mirror. It was Ava's face, that only looked like Beth's as she started to come down from the high. But Beth was back home in England, while Ava was the one heading fast for LA.

'OK, yes, I'm still here,' Laurie said into the phone, while stuffing her purse and notebook into her backpack and hunting for her keys. 'What time is it over there?'

'Ten past five,' Elliot answered.

'In the morning? Have you turned nocturnal? Who was just calling you at ten past five in the morning?'

'Liam, from Paris. He was trying to reach you, but your line was tied up.'

'Talking to you. OK, so where were we? Yes, the *News of the World* ran the Brad Pinkton story yesterday. Gail and I called the fall guys on Saturday to warn them what was coming, but there were a couple of names we weren't expecting so there was no tip-off for them. So now we have a scandalized nation, a few more disgraced politicians, and Sophie Long's mother breathing fire and fury down the phone at Murray, trying to get hold of you or me.'

'You think she genuinely didn't know her daughter was on the game?' Elliot said incredulously.

'You heard the tape,' she reminded him, turning off the radio and sliding closed the window. 'Actually, I think she might have guessed, but the last thing she'd want is the whole world knowing, as they now do – which reminds me, when I speak to her I'm going to plead ignorance. It's just too horrible for her to think that all the time we were talking I knew and pretended not to.'

'Sounds reasonable,' he responded. 'What's on your agenda today?'

'Actually, I'm going into the office to check I still have a job, and I might pop over to Morton Shields to try and ambush Philip Buck. What did Liam want, by the way?'

'From me, a telephone number. From you, a call back.'

'OK. Sandra Chettle left a message on my mobile last night.'

'The other of Ashby's contacts? What did she say?'

'Just that she was returning my call. With any luck she'll try again. I left a message on her voice mail about an hour ago.'

'Sounds hopeful.'

'Could be,' Laurie responded. Then as he told her what had been happening so far in New York, which didn't amount to much more than a few phone calls, as he'd only arrived on

Saturday and Monday had barely begun, she shrugged on her backpack, picked up her borrowed laptop, sunglasses and keys, made sure the cat was in, and all was locked, then started downstairs to the front door.

'I'm seeing Tom Maykin at twelve,' Elliot said. 'There are a few others I've arranged to meet while I'm here too, and there's a chance I might pop down to Washington. I should be back on Friday. Saturday at the latest. Has Bruce Cottle come back with an answer from his wife yet?'

'Not that I know of. I'll call him later. Beth Ashby must be in LA by now.'

'As Ava Montgomery. I might see if Tom Maykin's got someone out there who can keep an eye on her.'

'Good thinking.'

'OK. That's it,' he said abruptly. 'Have a good day, as they say over here,' and the line went dead.

'Bye,' she responded, then, clicking off the phone, she slammed the front door, double-locked it and started across the road towards the cut-through in the snazzy new apartment complex that would take her down to the river walk. From there she'd stroll along to the office, stopping off to get herself a coffee and Danish, and, considering how buoyant this non-stop sunshine was making her feel, she might just kick up her heels and have a dance on the way.

She'd just reached the narrow blue house that some said marked where the fire of London had stopped, when she suddenly remembered Stan. Swinging round, she spotted him outside The Grapes, just starting up his engine, intending to follow. Waving for him to stay put, she trotted back along the cobbled street, swerving to avoid the handsome thespian knight who lived in one of the protected Queen Annes, scooted round Bootle's blackboard where the chef was chalking up today's lunchtime specials, then finally stopped to pet Truffles, the Rich Old Lady's chocolate lab, whose leg was cocked against Stan's front wheel.

'Morning,' she beamed in through his window.

'Morning,' he responded, his alarmingly bullish features cracking in a six-tooth smile. 'How are you feeling?'

'Great. I'm going to walk along the river, so I'll meet you outside the office. Shall I get you a coffee at Frescos?'

'Double Espresso, plenty of sugar.'

'Food?'

'I'm on a diet.'

Laughing, she started back down the street, paused to rebunch her hair into its band, and had just reached the cut-through in the flats when she heard someone calling her name.

Surprised, she turned round, and might have overlooked the Mercedes parked on the other side of the road, had the woman in the driver's seat not called out again.

'Are you Laurie Forbes?' she asked.

Laurie nodded. The woman's face didn't look familiar, but there was something about the anxiety in her middle-aged features, and the neatness of her bobbed brown hair and gold-rimmed glasses, that inspired nothing more than concern and curiosity.

'I'm Sandra Chettle,' she said as Laurie drew close. 'You want to talk?'

'Yes, very much,' Laurie responded. 'How did you find me?'

'I called your editor. I had to make sure you were who you said you were. We need to go somewhere private. Are you free to come now?'

Laurie's hesitation was only momentary. She hadn't actually told Wilbur she was coming in today so he was hardly going to complain if she didn't turn up. 'Where are we going?' she said, getting into the passenger seat.

'Actually, it's a little way out of London. There's something I want to show you. It should make a lot of things clear.'

'I'm intrigued,' Laurie responded, fastening her seat belt as they started down the street. When they passed Stan she waved and gave him the thumbs-up, letting him know it was all right. 'I got your message last night,' she told Sandra. 'I was hoping you'd call again.'

'I thought it was better to come in person,' Sandra responded. 'There's a lot you need to know, and it's not a good idea for me to be seen or overheard talking to you.'

Laurie's mobile rang. Digging it out of her bag she checked the caller ID, saw it was Stan and switched on. 'It's OK,' she told him. 'It's Sandra Chettle.'

'Is her name on my list?'

'It should be.'

Sandra glanced over at her, frowning.

'Just my minder keeping tabs,' Laurie assured her, putting the phone away.

Sandra's eyes returned to the road. 'Do you need one?' she asked.

'Not really. It's a long story.'

For the next few minutes they exchanged platitudes about the weather and traffic until, sensing her silence might be more appreciated, Laurie turned to look out of the window. She didn't mind; it was a good opportunity to clear her head and start structuring the many questions she needed to ask.

After a while she took out a notepad and began jotting things down, wanting to make sure she left nothing out. Then her mobile rang again. This time the ID showed a number she didn't know.

'It's Liam. I'm coming back on the four o'clock flight,' he told her. 'We all need to meet.'

Laurie's heart gave a skip of excitement. 'Does that mean you've turned something up?' she said.

'Possibly. Murray's calling in Sam deBugger tonight, so we'll make it for nine in the morning. At the office.'

'Can you tell me anything now?'

'Just that a couple of the people I've been talking to were responsible for the initial investigation into the ex-minister who's currently on trial. They've been working on uncovering the corruption for nearly three years, and some of the names we compared matched. There's more, I'll fill you in tomorrow.'

'Great,' she said, and rang off.

'Something interesting?' Sandra enquired.

'Maybe. It's connected to this, so I'm hoping whatever you're about to show me is going to move it even further along.'

'I'm sure it will,' Sandra responded.

Laurie looked out at the passing fields, hedgerows and scattered farms. They'd been travelling for quite some time now, and they were definitely out of London, so just how far out did they need to go?

'Not much further,' Sandra informed her, as though reading her mind.

'Maybe I could starting asking some questions?'

'I'd rather you waited. You'll understand why when we get there.'

They drove on, through towns and villages, more country-side, passing signposts that directed them to places Laurie had never even heard of. Were they in Essex, she wondered. Or had they crossed over into Suffolk? It wasn't a part of the country she knew, so it would all seem the same to her. In fact, she was starting to become vaguely uneasy now, and hoped Stan was managing to keep up, presuming he was there at all, after she'd told him it was all right.

This was ridiculous, she was thinking. Being too polite to ask again where they were going was like being too polite to exist. She had a right to know, and what was more, she was going to.

This time Sandra Chettle didn't answer.

Unsettled, and starting to get annoyed, Laurie was about to demand a reply when her mobile rang again.

'Laurie? It's Stan,' he said quietly. 'Don't say my name. Don't say anything yet, just make out I'm Elliot, or Rhona or someone. Nice and easy. Keep it casual.'

Laurie had become very still. Her heartbeat was a thick, dull thud. This wasn't good. It wasn't good at all. 'Oh, hi, Rhona,' she managed. 'I'm fine. How are you?'

'OK,' Stan responded. 'Now, you need to get out of that car as soon as you possibly can.'

Already fear was rushing at her in a way she couldn't handle for long so this was not what she wanted to hear. 'Uh, OK,' she responded. 'Um, why would that be?'

'The woman driving it isn't Sandra Chettle.'

Even though she'd known he was going to say that, his words were like an explosion inside her head. 'Oh, I see. Then who?' she asked sweetly.

'I don't know. We're still tracing the car. But Sandra Chettle drives a Volvo and is, right now, at her desk in the City.'

Absurdly, embarrassingly, she suddenly wanted to cry. 'That's nice,' she responded. 'So where are you?'

'Not where you want me to be. Is there any way you can tell me where you are?'

'Oh no, not really,' she said chirpily, her words sounding like a single high note breaking through the thunderous rush in her ears.

'Country? Town?'

'I'd say the first.'

'Did you go east or west out of London.'

'Again the first, then it seemed to go up.'

The woman was throwing her glances now, obviously becoming suspicious. 'OK, well, thanks for letting me know, Rhona,' she said. 'I'll see you later then.'

'Don't worry,' Stan told her. 'Just keep your head, we'll find you – and first chance you get, bail that car and call me.'

Laurie rang off and stared out at the passing scenery, her hands clasped tight to her mobile. Who the hell was this woman, if she wasn't Sandra Chettle? What did she want? Where was she taking her? She didn't look at her, nor did she speak. She was trying to force her mind round what she should do, how she was going to get out of that car. But they were in the middle of nowhere, for God's sake. How the hell was she supposed to know where to go even if she managed it?

Her chest was hardly letting in air as she looked round, casually, trying to spot the central door-locking button. She had to force herself to remain calm. She couldn't allow her imagination any freedom at all, or she'd start to panic. The fact that her life was flashing before her eyes had to be ignored. It was an overreaction. She wasn't really in any danger. The woman was probably some kind of government agent. The thought jarred in her brain, for there was no comfort in it at all – quite the reverse, in fact.

Get a grip, she screamed silently at herself. *Just think about the dashboard.* Logic told her the lock release should be somewhere in the middle, putting it well within her reach. But the connection between her eyes and her brain seemed not to be working, because though she was registering the buttons, they weren't meaning anything. And even if she managed to jab the right one, the car was going much too fast for her to jump out. Then there was her seat belt. And what about her bag, and computer? Should she leave them? Oh God, she had to think faster because the car was starting to slow down. She might get the chance to jump. But what if the woman was carrying a gun? And even if she wasn't, where the bloody hell was she going to run to? There was nothing but country lanes and fields, cart tracks, haystacks, isolated barns . . .

She noticed a car up ahead was pulled in to the side of the road. Please God, let there be someone in it she could signal to. She had to get the window down so they could hear her. She lowered her right hand to the panel between the seats, fumbling for the controls. The woman's presence was overwhelming her, making her afraid to move. But no, it was her own fear doing that. The woman was only looking at the road ahead. She looked too, and saw two men getting out of the parked car ahead.

She was about to push hard on the window control when she realized the Mercedes was stopping. She turned towards the woman, then back to the men. They were standing behind their car now. The Mercedes was pulling up alongside them; the two cars were so close that the wing mirrors touched. There was no way Laurie could get her door open.

'What are you doing? What's happening?' she demanded, anger breaking through her fear.

The woman's eyes were on the rear-view mirror.

One of the back doors opened. Laurie spun round as the two men got in. Something close to terror was hammering her chest. 'Answer me,' she cried. 'I thought we were going to talk.'

'It's all right,' the woman told her, accelerating away from the parked car. 'No one's going to harm you.'

Laurie's eyes were wild. 'What do you mean? Harm me? What's going on?'

'We just need to ask you some questions,' the woman explained.

'About what? Who are they?' Laurie's voice was turning shrill.

'Not much further now,' the woman assured her.

Laurie sat tightly in her seat, not knowing what else to do. This was about Ashby's interview, of course, and the code. They hadn't been able to break it, and now, just as she'd feared, they'd come to find out how much she knew. She could hardly believe how easily she'd walked into the trap. They'd set it up the night before with a phone call. Then this morning they'd just driven into her street, called her over to the car, right in front of Stan, and it hadn't even occurred to her that the woman was lying when she'd said she was Sandra Chettle. All she'd thought of then was how good she was going to feel when she told Elliot that one of the Bank of England's senior executives had talked to her. Dear God, what a fool! Just how naïve was she that she hadn't seen through something so simple? But berating herself now wasn't going to help. She had to think of a way out of here, and she had to think fast. Sobbing like a baby wasn't going to help, even though that was what she was very close to doing.

'If you don't mind,' the woman said, 'there's a blindfold in the glove compartment.'

Laurie gaped at her. The last thing in the world she wanted was to cover her eyes.

'Please,' the woman said politely. 'It'll only be for a few minutes.'

'Why? Where are we going?' Laurie demanded.

The woman's smile was thin as she reached over and popped open the glove box.

Laurie drew back. 'No!' she cried. 'I'm *not* putting on a blindfold.'

The woman brought the car to a stop. Laurie lunged frantically at the dashboard, trying to release the door, but the seat belt held her back. She looked at the woman in dread. Was she going to force the blindfold on her? Oh God, just how bad was this going to get?

'Please put it on,' the woman said, taking it out and holding it towards her.

Laurie stared at it, but didn't take it.

'I'm afraid you don't have a choice,' the woman told her.

Laurie looked at her again, then gasped as one of the men in the back seat clamped her head between his hands and held it still. 'Let me go!' she seethed. 'Let me go! I'll do it myself.'

Though her hands were shaking as she put the blindfold in place, real anger, for the moment, was staving off the panic.

The way Sophie Long's name had been used as a warning was now ringing in her ears, and that Stan hadn't been able to trace the car, they just weren't things she could allow herself to think about. She had to concentrate on how to handle this, try to get away if she could, and if she couldn't then she'd have to pray to God that they didn't resort to anything physical in order to extract information, when there was every chance she didn't know enough to make them stop.

Elliot was in a Greenwich Village bar, drinking Diet Coke through a tall glass of ice when Tom Maykin, a short, wiry man in his mid-forties, arrived.

'Elliot, it's good to see you again,' he said, appearing not in the least perturbed by the way Elliot's superior height dwarfed him. 'How's tricks?'

'Fair. What about you? What're you having?'

'Miller Lite,' Maykin said to the barman, while looking round to see who else was in. Since it was a small place, with only a couple of tables over by the pinball, it was a quick scan that told him he and Elliot were the only early lunchtime drinkers. 'So you've got wind of this euro business,' he said coming straight to the point.

Elliot picked up his drink and gestured for them to go and sit at a table.

'So how d'you pick up on it?' Maykin asked.

'Couple of different ways,' Elliot answered. 'One of them was a murder.'

Maykin slanted him a look.

'Colin Ashby's girlfriend,' Elliot expounded.

'Oh, yeah, right.' Maykin nodded grimly. 'Ashby's girl-friend. Did he do it?'

'I don't know. He says not.'

Maykin gave a short laugh, then waited for the barman to put down his beer before picking it up. He took a long sip, then said, 'This syndicate you mentioned on the phone – I've being making some calls. Very discreet, you know, a question here, surmise there . . . Tell me, how much do you know about it?'

'Just that it exists, and that its operatives or members seem

293

to reach into virtually every field of government and finance there is.'

Maykin sucked in his lips.

'What do you know about it?' Elliot asked.

'I'm not as up to speed as you are, but yeah, I can see your assessment has merit,' Maykin replied. 'And I get the feeling its upper echelon is going to consist of the kind of folk you don't go messing with just to get next week's headline.'

'Do you know who any of them are?'

'There are a few I'd find easy to suspect, but I don't know any for sure. What about you?'

Elliot listed the names he'd got from the businessman, Alan Edwards, and the handful of others that had come up as a result of the searches since. The last name he mentioned was Marcus Gatling.

'Ah, yes, Gatling,' Maykin responded. 'The great British bulldog as they call him here. It would stand to reason he was involved. And no doubt his lady wife too. Did you know they're here in the States right now?'

'No. Where?'

'Santa Barbara. Hal Drummond's got a place there. You know who he is?'

'Ohio Drummonds? Third-generation steel.'

'And big-time donor to the Republican Party. Apparently there's some kind of billionaire's convention going on at his Santa Barbara mansion right now, because Abe Kleinstein's there, the media mogul, Hank Wingate, Texas oil, Yoroshito, the telecom giant from Japan, Hans Brunner, the Hong Kong banker you mentioned, there are a couple of mining and chemicals hotshots in from Mexico, some other media guy from Asia . . . Hell, there's a dozen or more there, by all accounts.'

'How do you know?'

'A contact on the West Coast told me. No news in it, though; just a bunch of rich guys getting together for a party.'

'No politicians on the guest list?'

'Not that we know of. My guess is they get dealt with privately and individually.'

'Of course,' Elliot murmured, feeling curious to know what

kind of dialogue, promise and coercion was used at those meetings.

'So what about Ashby – was he a part of it?' Maykin asked.

'I haven't spoken to him personally, but he's claiming he turned the offer down.'

Maykin looked incredulous. 'Do you believe that?'

'Do you?'

Maykin shrugged. 'As I understand it,' he said, 'we're talking about the kind of money – and incentive, if you get my meaning – that no one turns down.'

Elliot nodded. That was the way he saw it too, and incentive was a good euphemism for the kind of intimidation they'd no doubt use as collateral on silence if anyone showed reluctance – like Ashby? 'Is anyone here investigating them?' he asked.

'I could probably put you in touch with some interested parties. But as for any kind of in-depth research, I don't know that anyone's really got into it.'

'Would you be prepared to?'

Maykin didn't even hestitate. 'Are you kidding? I want to live, man.' Then with a grin, 'Count me in, and I know a good lawyer if you want to make a will.'

Elliot drained his glass, then said, 'Have you come up with any thoughts on why Ashby put me on to you?'

Maykin frowned and stared down at his beer. 'Not really,' he answered. 'But I can tell you this, we go back a long way, him and me, and until now I'd have trusted him the same way I trust you. After this murder business –' he sighed and shook his head – 'I don't know any more.'

'We're getting a lot of cross-signals from him,' Elliot said. 'First he won't talk, then he tells a tale that's got more loose ends than story and gives us virtually nothing to tie them up with. The names he's delivered so far are proving uncontactable, with the exception of yourself, whom I already knew and would have been in touch with anyway. Would he have known that? Have you two ever discussed me?'

'Not that I recall. Maybe in passing once or twice.'

Elliot thought of Heather Dance, whom the message had come through, then of Beth Ashby. 'His wife's in LA,' he said. 'Apparently the marriage is over, or that's what they want us to think. There's some confusion around one of his mistresses too, that we're working on. Have you ever met Beth Ashby? Do you know her at all?'

'Not well. What's she doing in LA?'

'I'm told some film company's turning her book into a feature.'

'What book?'

'It's not out yet, but it's been the subject of some interesting events during the past month or so. Someone stole a copy of the manuscript from the publisher, and it's my guess that someone was working for Gatling.'

'Wanting an advance look at what's in the book,' Maykin stated. 'Do you know what is?'

Elliot shook his head. 'Not yet.'

'And now she's in LA?'

'With a whole new look.'

'What's your theory on it?'

'I don't have one, or not one that I can make fit. I've got a feeling she should be watched, though. She either knows something, or is up to something that could prove . . . let's say useful. Do you have anyone out there who can check on her?'

'Sure. No problem. I just need the name of the company making the film, we'll track her down that way.'

'I can do better. Ashby's lawyer will have her address. I'll get it from him.'

Maykin said, 'So who's spoken to Ashby if you haven't?'

'Laurie Forbes. She's a staff writer on one of the broadsheets, but she's kind of on the team too.'

Maykin grimaced. 'Never heard of her.'

'She's new.'

Maykin shrugged. If someone new was OK with Elliot, they were OK with him. 'So which angle are you pursuing first?' he said, moving on. 'Financial or political?'

As an answer Elliot explained about the trends in exchange and interest rates that were seeing a gradual weakening of the euro and corresponding strengthening of the pound and dollar. 'There's also a lot of resistance from the British Government to joining the ERM that just doesn't add up,' he said. 'We've got industry giants such as Nissan, Mitsubishi, you name it, threatening to pull out of the UK if it doesn't happen soon, which is going to be disastrous for the economy if they do, and the right sort of questions aren't being asked in the House. Or if they are, the askers are being fobbed off with inconsequential, and even insupportable reasons for the delay. Or they're told the people don't want it, which appears to be true, though polls are easily rigged. My guess is the Opposition is being manipulated too. They have to be, or there would be all hell to pay over the deliberate fudging of crucial issues; and the effects of rising interest rates make for some lethal ammunition for any opposing party. So why aren't they using it?'

'Some are,' Maykin told him.

'Of course, but they're in a minority and it's turning into a lot of hot air.'

'Do you think this minority is aware of what's happening?'

'They're sure to have suspicions, but frankly, all *we've* got is suspicions. There's no real evidence to say we're right about the way it's going to go.'

Maykin gazed thoughtfully down at his beer. Then, finishing it, he signalled to the barman for another round. 'OK,' he said, when their glasses had been cleared, 'the guy you need to talk to here is Wheeler Nash. He knows everything there is to know about foreign exchange. He was with Merrill Lynch for years, ran everything from currencies to commodities. He's at Jarret-Loring now, you know, the wet-dream hedge fund, heading up the whole shebang. If anyone can tell you where this is going, he can – unless he's a part of it, of course. But we're always going to be up against that, and as soon as any of them get wind of these enquiries . . . well, who knows, we might get invited to the party?'

'Anyone else?' Elliot said, jotting down the name of Nash's company.

Maykin shook his head. 'Not right now. Most of my regulars have been struck with a mysterious speech disorder since we first discussed this on the phone.'

'Speech disorder?'

'They don't talk any more. Not about this, not about anything. Frankly, with some of them, it's as if they stopped knowing me. Now, doesn't that tell you something?'

Elliot's eyebrows rose. 'So how do I get hold of Wheeler Nash?' he said.

Maykin took the notebook and scribbled down a couple of numbers and an address. 'That's his home,' he said, tapping the pencil against the address. 'I'll speak to him when I leave here, tell him to expect your call. In the meantime, I say we keep watching the dollar. Look at who gains when it rises, look at who gains when it falls – then try to find who never loses.'

Elliot regarded him closely. They already had a pretty good idea of who never lost; it was just a question of how to prove it. 'I get a feeling a lot of this is going to turn out to be just this side of legal,' he said.

'Sure, they'll know how to use the law. But there'll be some discrepancies in there somewhere, and if we can get a handle on it, believe you me, legal or not, the whole thing'll go sky high. Shit, how can it not? Some greedy-bastard oligarchy playing twenty-first-century Monopoly with entire nations and their economies . . .' He threw out his hands to rest his case.

On returning to the apartment he kept on the Upper West Side, Elliot immediately stripped off his clothes and went to stand under a cooling shower. New York was one of his favourite cities, but not in August, when humidity curdled the air like soup. After standing under the refreshing jets for at least five minutes, he wrapped a towel round his waist, padded out to the kitchenette, and took a cold beer from the fridge. Whilst drinking it he dialled the first number Maykin had given him for Wheeler Nash. No reply. He tried the next and left a message on the voice mail, asking for a call back. Lastly he tried the main Jarret-Loring number.

'I'm sorry, Mr Nash isn't in the office today,' the voice at the other end informed him. 'Can I put you on to his assistant?'

Elliot picked up his watch. 'No, I'll call again,' he said and cut the line. It was nine at night in London, he'd try Laurie next. But he got only halfway through dialling when his mobile rang.

'Elliot Russell,' he said into it, but whoever it was didn't make a good enough connection, and after listening to several seconds of hissing and static, he rang off. They'd call again.

Going back to the land line he redialled Laurie's number at Andrew and Stephen's. While listening to the ringing tone he carried his beer to the window and stared down at the small Victorian park behind his apartment block, where the locals walked their dogs, and joggers cut out of the mainstream to run through paths of colourful flowers and well-tended trees. They'd been shooting some kind of TV drama or movie down there the day he arrived, but there was no sign of the unit now.

After leaving a message on the answerphone, he tried Laurie's mobile and waited again for a connection: another recorded message telling him the phone was either turned off or out of range. Surprised at that, he decided to give her office a go.

'Haven't seen her today,' Gino told him, 'but I've only just got back from Wales. Have you tried her home? She's at Andrew and –'

'I left a message,' Elliot cut in. 'Is Wilbur there?'

'Left about five minutes ago.'

Has anyone seen her today?'

'Hang on, I'll ask.'

As he waited Elliot tried not to let his unease take hold. OK, she'd said she was going to the office today, and if Gino hadn't been there . . .

'No, no one's seen her,' Gino said, coming back on the line. 'Oh, wait, here's Wilbur. I thought he'd gone. I'll pass you over.'

'You're looking for Laurie,' Wilbur's voice snapped down the line.

'She said she was coming in today. Didn't she make it?'

'No. So what's going on? Should I be worried?'

'I don't know,' Elliot responded truthfully. 'I'll get back to you if you do. Meantime, if she does get in touch, tell her to call me. If you need me I'm on my mobile.'

After ringing off he called Stan. To his annoyance, and mounting concern, Stan's mobile asked him to leave a message too, which he did, angrily, telling him to call back the instant he heard Elliot's voice with an update on Laurie Forbes's whereabouts. Next he tried his own office.

Gail answered.

'Have you seen Laurie today?' Elliot demanded.

'No,' Gail answered. 'But Liam spoke to her earlier. She's coming here in the morning for a meeting.'

'What time did he speak to her?'

Gail relayed the question.

'About ten thirty this morning,' Liam's voice called from the distance.

'Has anyone spoken to her since?'

Again Gail relayed the question.

'No,' came the answer.

'Then try to get hold of her. Or Stan,' Elliot barked, 'and don't stop until you do.'

Putting down the phone, he returned to the bedroom, tugged on a fresh polo shirt and faded jeans, pocketed his mobile and went back down to the street. He was in a cab crossing Fifty-fourth on Sixth, when his phone rang again. Hoping it was Laurie he snatched it up, but it was another bad connection, until whoever it was gave up and ended the call.

At last, after dragging through dense afternoon traffic, the cab pulled up outside the address Maykin had given him for Wheeler Nash. It was a smart neighbourhood, just off Washington Square. Telling the driver to wait, he ran up the few steps, checked the nameplates next to the bells and rang Wheeler Nash's. After three more tries he had to accept the man wasn't in.

'Shit!' he muttered, standing back to look up at the building. Where the hell was everyone today?

Returning to the cab, he told the driver to take him to the Twenty-One Club where he was due to meet another contact. Then, intending to try Laurie again, he'd just flicked open his mobile when it rang.

'Elliot Russell,' he barked.

'Tom Maykin,' the voice at the other end told him. 'Where are you?'

'Trying to track down your guy Nash.'

'I thought so. You can stop wasting your time. I just got a call from the West Coast. Wheeler Nash was at the party, but apparently his car went off the freeway last night on the way back to LA airport. He didn't make it.'

300

Elliot was so unprepared for that that it was a moment before he could take it in. 'Was it an accident?' he finally asked.

'It certainly looked like one.'

'What did your guy on the West Coast think?'

'That it was an accident. Of course, if he'd been at the party, he might have another opinion. Who can tell?'

'Is Nash the first to go like this?' Elliot asked after a pause.

'I can give you the names of two others, but there's nothing to tie them together. Or to this one.'

'Who were they?'

'The first was a freelancer. The second worked at the Pentagon.'

Elliot thought of the Nuclear Missile Defence programme – Son of Star Wars. 'When?' he asked.

'Six, seven weeks ago. Five days apart.'

'The government defence guy was a source?'

'So I'm told.'

'We need to meet again,' Elliot said.

'Sure. In London. I'll be there in a couple of weeks. I'll keep at it here and deliver then.'

Elliot rang off and tried Laurie's numbers again. Still no answer.

'Stan!' he cried, when finally he reached the detective. 'Where the hell are you?'

'Driving round in circles in the back of beyond,' Stan answered. 'I've been trying to get hold of you, but this is a hell of a place –'

'Where's Laurie?' Elliot interrupted.

'I don't know. I –'

'What the hell do you mean, you don't know?'

Stan quickly explained what had happened that morning.

'And you're only telling me now?' Elliot stormed. 'Have you got any leads?'

'No trace on the car. All she could tell me was she'd gone sort of north-east out of London. I contacted the police, but she got into the car willingly, so there's nothing they can do. I've been trying to call her since eleven o'clock. Nothing doing.'

'Where are you?'

'Suffolk. Near Long Melford. But I've got to tell you, she could be anywhere by now.'

Elliot was thinking fast. North-east of London . . . the Gatlings' country estate . . . a code that couldn't be broken. 'Get hold of Murray,' he said. 'Tell him you need the Gatlings' address in Suffolk, but *don't* attempt to go in. It'll be heavily guarded and they're likely to shoot before they ask. Just try to get a look, see if you can spot the car.'

'Right, I'll call Murray now.'

Elliot's expression was thunderous as he looked at his watch. He wasn't sure who he was angriest at – himself, Stan or Laurie, or probably the Gatlings for being out of the dammed country while the dirty work was being done. Well, if anything happened to her, if those bastards tried to force that code out of her just to save the corrupt no-good necks of a few billionaires, then there was going to be more merry fucking hell to pay than any syndicate could ever afford. 'If there's a Concorde flight available I'll be back before midnight,' he barked at Stan. 'If not I'll catch the red-eye and be with you by nine in the morning, ten at the latest.'

Chapter 18

The room was hot, airless and smelt faintly, mustily, of the centuries it had passed through. The floor was gnarled, polished wood, the furnishings exquisitely restored antiques, the gloomy collection of art, presumably real. It was an old-fashioned salon, part of a large country house that had a grey Jacobean frontage and a patchily light interior, blending early European baroque with a vaguely frivolous Georgian dressing. When they'd pulled up outside and allowed her to remove the blindfold Laurie had seen only that they were within the elaborate grounds of what appeared to be a large walled estate. It had occurred to her then that it might be where Sophie Long's parents had been brought immediately after Sophie's murder.

As they'd escorted her across the threshold, one of the men, the one with horn-rimmed glasses and a silver-grey crew cut, had removed his jacket exposing a small firearm in a sling over his shirt. If it had been meant to intimidate it had worked, though Laurie was already more afraid than she'd ever been in her life.

Now she'd been here for five, six, maybe even ten hours, with fear merging into every moment, sometimes worsening, sometimes lessening, but always there, pumping her system with adrenalin, firing her to the point of panic, then subsiding slowly, leaving her shaken and depleted, until the next rush began with a renewed round of questions. Her whole body ached with the tension, and from sitting so long in the same chair. She felt grubby and hot, her mouth was stale and her mettle had long since started yielding to the exhaustion that was creeping slowly, inexorably all the way through her.

It was some time now since anyone had spoken, except to ask if she was hungry. She was, but knew she'd be unable to eat, so she'd merely shaken her head. There was a glass of water on the tripod table beside her, which the woman had just replenished, and each time she needed to go to the bathroom the woman escorted her, and waited outside. Mainly, though, they'd maintained their positions throughout the day, Laurie in a wing-backed chair next to the hearth, which had been turned slightly to face the two men who occupied a sofa each. With their loosened ties and casual poses they appeared as relaxed as if they were enjoying a lazy evening at home. The woman was in a chair opposite, watching, listening and occasionally leaving the room to go Laurie didn't know where, though she suspected from the mumbled communication that passed between them on her return, that she was either speaking to someone elsewhere in the house, or making phone calls.

The interrogation had been endless, and though no one had attempted any kind of physical persuasion, the mental anguish, as well as the almost deadening fatigue she was enduring now, could be a torture in itself. So was the confusing repetition of questions. What did Ashby tell her at the prison? Why did she want to see Sandra Chettle? What did she know about Sophie Long? Why didn't she believe Ashby had done it? How much did she know about Ashby's private life? What had Beth Ashby told her when they'd been alone, during those minutes after Ashby's arrest? Had she spoken to Beth Ashby since then? What did she know about Beth Ashby's book? How well did she know Heather Dance? What stories was she working on now? How long had she known Elliot Russell? What was Russell working on now? Was she involved in what he was working on now? They were going round and round in circles, so many questions, so many different answers that she could barely remember now which ones she'd given.

Picking up the water beside her, she drank half of it, then put the glass down again. It tasted sweet, yet citrussy, and the ice had almost melted.

'I don't imagine you want to stay here all night,' the man with the crew cut and glasses eventually said.

Laurie looked at him. The light outside had faded completely into darkness. The lamps in the room might, at any other time, make it homely, a haven from the night. Her thoughts were becoming strange, tinted with delirium, or maybe it was fatigue. Sometimes it seemed as though there were small pockets in time that she was falling into, leaving her uncertain of how many seconds or minutes had passed since the last person spoke. She might even have missed whole chunks of what her captors had said.

'Your parents live in Windsor, don't they?' the man with the crew cut said.

A small, warning chill stole into her blood. Had they mentioned her parents before? Why were they mentioning them now?

'Didn't you have a sister who committed suicide?' he continued.

Her heart contracted. Was this an oblique way of reminding her that her parents wouldn't want to lose another child? Oh God, if only she weren't so tired. She could barely think straight now, and this about her family was disorienting her even more.

'Why is Elliot Russell in New York?' the other man asked.

Her voice sounded cracked and dry as she said, 'I don't know.' How many times had she thought of him today, wondering how he would handle this, what he would or wouldn't tell them, how he would make them give up.

'You said earlier he was meeting someone. So who is he meeting?' the man barked.

Had she said that? She didn't remember saying that. 'I don't know,' she responded.

'Why was Liam Woods in Paris?'

'I don't know. I don't work with them.'

'You said he was there because of the ex-foreign minister's trial. What's Elliot Russell's interest in that?'

Had she told them that about Liam? When had they talked about Paris? 'I don't know why he was in Paris,' she said.

'What other names did Ashby give you when you saw him?'

'Just Sandra Chettle.'

'Why her?'

'He said she might help prove his innocence.'

'How could she do that?'

'He didn't tell me.'

'Where's the transcript of your meeting with Ashby?'

'On my computer. The one that was stolen.'

'Who stole it?'

'I don't know.'

The two men looked at each other. Time after time they came back to the transcript, and the computer, but no one had admitted either to taking it, or being unable to decipher the code. Their knowledge of it was there though, hanging almost palpably in the air, and now she couldn't remember if they'd told her they had it or not.

'When did you last speak to Beth Ashby?' the silver-haired man demanded.

'I told you, I bumped into her a few weeks ago, but she didn't want to talk to me, and I haven't seen her since.'

'You have a friend who works at Buchmanns.'

'Yes.' A sudden throb of unease. Buchmanns? Was this the first mention of Rhona?

'Has she given you a copy of the manuscript?'

Manuscript? Oh yes, that manuscript. 'No. I've never seen it. Nor has she.'

'But you know what the book's about?'

'No.'

'You know what it's based on?'

'No.'

'You said earlier you knew what it was about.'

'No. I didn't say that.'

'Then what did you say?'

'I don't know.' This was becoming too difficult now. Tiredness was moving over her mind like a blanket, even though she felt panicky and upset. If only they would let her sleep . . .

The man with the crew cut exchanged glances with the woman, then the other man said, 'Mrs Ashby made certain remarks recently that suggested you knew what was in the book.'

'No. Why would she say that? I told you, I've never seen the book.'

The friezes around the ceiling seemed to undulate and grow. The cherubs quivered and floated, while the grapes appeared to fall. After a while her head lolled on to the wing of the chair as she started to sink into sleep.

'Miss Forbes,' the silver-haired man suddenly barked.

She was jolted out of sleep, feeling more desperate than ever. She forced her eyes open. They were sore, her vision was blurred; the room seemed hazy and distant.

'Exactly what is it that intrigues you about the Colin Ashby case?'

Everything was still swimming. Her throat was parched, and as she answered her tongue felt too big for her mouth. 'The fact that he might not have done it,' she said.

'Then who do you think did?'

'I don't know.'

'Who does Colin Ashby think it was?' The voice was an echo at the end of a cave.

Who does Colin Ashby think it was? 'He says he doesn't know.'

'You said he had a theory.'

'I don't know what it is,' she mumbled, hardly able to form the sentence.

Minute after minute ticked by until the clock on the mantelshelf struck midnight, and the woman turned the lamps down low. Laurie's eyelids were too heavy to hold up any longer, so she let them fall and listened to the drone of their murmurs, fading and lifting, burring and burbling, soothing, almost like a song. Dimly she wondered if she'd been drugged. She didn't care. She needed more water, and sleep.

'What did Colin Ashby tell you about Sophie Long?' someone suddenly demanded.

Startled, she struggled awake and tried to refocus. 'That he didn't kill her.'

'So who did?'

'I don't know.'

'Why haven't you submitted a story?'

'No one will run it.'

'Do you understand that withholding evidence of a crime is a crime in itself?'

Her head was spinning. This was all just a dream, drifting in and out of focus and eluding reality. 'I'm not withholding evidence,' she said in a voice that belonged to somebody else.

'Are you sure?'

'Yes, I'm sure.'

'That's not what you said earlier.'

Confused, she tried to recall what he meant. But she couldn't, so she stayed silent, swirling in a strange, vaporous cloud of grey.

She had no idea if seconds or minutes passed before she came to again and heard them talking.

'. . . father had a massive heart attack about six months ago,' the woman was saying. 'He's still in fragile health. The mother is a part-time volunteer at the local hospital. The whole family is still recovering from the sister's suicide . . .'

'Stop,' she said, struggling to sit up. Adrenalin was trying to pump into her system, but couldn't quite get there. These mentions of her parents were scaring her more than anything. She *had* to make herself think. 'This has got nothing to do with my family,' she mumbled.

'Of course not,' the silver-haired man assured her.

'They've been through enough,' the woman said.

'So why are you worrying them again?' the crew cut man asked.

'You could go home now,' the woman said.

'If you'd just answer the questions.'

Laurie raised her hands to stop them. 'I am,' she croaked weakly.

'Are you?'

'What did Ashby say at the prison?'

'Why do you want to talk to Sandra Chettle?'

'What's Elliot Russell working on?'

Round and round and round.

'Why are you engaged in foreign exchange research?' the silver-haired man suddenly asked.

The question seemed to jump like a peak on a graph. Had she told them that? How did they know? Was it her voice saying, 'There are certain trends.'

Slowly she became aware that the atmosphere in the room

308

had changed. In her exhausted, or drugged state she thought she must have told them something they hadn't heard before. 'What kind of trends?' someone demanded.

Her mind was rotating like a slow-moving top. Whirrr-rruh Whirrr-rruh. 'I don't know,' she groaned.

'Then how do you know they're trends?'

Her head fell to one side and hit the wing of the chair. Waking with a start, she tried to focus again.

'Is that why Russell's in New York?'

'I don't know where he is.' It was so difficult to marshal her thoughts that she no longer knew what she'd said, or why she was holding anything back. None of it seemed important now. All that mattered was sleep.

'Do you want to go home?'

The thought of home brought tears to her eyes. 'I want to sleep,' she murmured.

But they wouldn't let her. They just kept on going, questioning her, confusing her, misleading and disorienting her. The woman came and went. She smelt food, but couldn't eat. They talked about Elliot and Lysette, and her computer, and Beth Ashby and Rhona . . . Over and over, back and forth, hour after endless hour, until finally unable to take a single moment more, she collapsed into oblivion.

When Laurie finally woke up again she didn't know where she was. The room was dark, the curtains were drawn, and a single sheet was covering her up to the chin. Only her eyes moved as she looked around. Somewhere, at an elusive distance, she could feel fear, but wasn't sure why. Her head seemed thick and heavy, making her think of the attack at the foot of the stairs. Yet she knew it wasn't that. Something else had happened since, something to do with . . . Suddenly it all came rushing back, and as horror engulfed her, her chest heaved in panic.

But no, it was OK. This was Andrew and Stephen's house. This was their bed and the person moving around upstairs, opening and closing cupboard doors, banging pots, was only Rhona. There was nothing to be afraid of now. She was home and safe. The woman had driven her back during the dawn hours, she remembered that now. She'd let herself in the door, then waited to hear the car drive away before coming in here and collapsing on the bed. So there was nothing to be afraid of now.

Though stiff, she forced herself up off the bed and waited for the dizziness to pass. Her flip-flops, she noticed, were under the sheet, telling her she'd gone to bed with them on. The digital clock said eighteen fifteen.

Feeling her senses respond to the smell of sizzling garlic and onions that was drifting down the stairs, she took heart again, for no one but Rhona would be up there cooking, so the irrational dread that they might now be holding her prisoner in her own home was momentarily quelled. Going over to the bathroom she turned on the light and looked in the mirror. The fear she'd experienced, and still couldn't quite shake, had left its mark, for her face was horribly pale, and the purplish shadows round her eyes made them seem haunted and hollow. She took a step forward then gasped and jumped as something upstairs clattered to the floor. Her heart was suddenly thudding wildly, and for one panicked moment she almost rushed upstairs to be with Rhona so she no longer had to be alone. But her clothes felt as though they were stuck to her body; she had to take them off and get in the shower.

Once naked she turned to look at herself in the full-length mirror and felt vaguely surprised to see no evidence of the discomfort she was feeling. Her legs, though sore, were as unblemished as her narrow hips and waist; and her ample breasts, though tender, were as smooth to the touch as her shoulders and arms. No injuries, no below-the-surface bruising, just a stiffness that hopefully the Jacuzzi shower would massage from her limbs.

Ten minutes later she emerged from the shower, her eyes red from crying tears she could hardly explain, and her nerves still horribly on edge. But at least she was fresher now, and hungry beyond endurance, so tugging a short pink T-shirt over her breasts, she stepped into a pair of yellow hipster capris, and after combing out her wet hair, she left in pursuit of the mouth-watering aroma.

'Rhona,' she called out, as she reached the top of the stairs, not wanting to startle her, and still more than half afraid that it wasn't going to be Rhona. 'It's only me,' she said

310

tentatively, 'and whatever you're making I want all of –' She stopped dead. It wasn't Rhona, it was Elliot. She wasn't sure why she was so thrown, but it took a few seconds to assimilate, during which she suddenly and stupidly wanted to cry, then run to him, then run away. Then all she could think of was the fact that she was hardly decently dressed – in fact, so indecently that her midriff was totally bare, and in this skimpy top her breasts might as well be. She never dressed like this in front of a man for fear he'd stop seeing her as a professional. And they did, because it had happened in the past. She'd heard them talking about her as the greatest pair of tits that ever owned a brain, or the knockers they thought of when they needed to come, or other things that were equally, if not *more* sexist and crude, the way men did. And this wasn't just any man, either. This was Elliot.

As he registered her confusion his eyes showed only irony and never dropped from her own. 'You're awake,' he said, lifting a glass of red wine and taking a sip.

'I thought you were Rhona,' she said, feeling the tightness in her nipples, and knowing he could see it, despite not looking.

He shook his head.

She knew she was blushing. 'Uh, I'd better go back . . .' She pointed downstairs.

He only looked at her, and she didn't move. This was so unexpected she wasn't sure what she wanted to do. She felt brazen and shy and confounded by the conflict. In the end she went downstairs to find a shirt to put over the T-shirt, which she left unbuttoned but tied at the waist.

'How are you feeling?' he said when she reappeared a few minutes later. He was standing at the stove now, sprinkling *herbes de Provence* over a thick tomato and olive sauce. The fact that he was here, behaving as though he was always here, combined with the smell that was almost making her drool, and then his question – which had started her heart pounding, for it reminded her of how traumatized she still was – were making it virtually impossible for her to think straight.

'Aren't you supposed to be in New York?' she managed, trying not to wince at the protest in her muscles as she sat on one of the bar stools.

311

He glanced over at her. 'Are you up to some wine?' he said, nodding towards the bottle.

She looked at it. 'Maybe, just a little,' she answered, knowing she probably wasn't.

Taking down a glass he half filled it and passed it over. 'Rhona checked you over while you were sleeping,' he said. 'No untoward measures seem to have been taken, and nothing seems to be broken.'

They both sipped some wine, watching each other over the rims of the glasses. She was so glad he was here. She didn't need to feel afraid while he was here, yet somehow she had to get herself out of this emotional state, for the way it was locking her into him was likely to push her into doing something she'd be horribly embarrassed about later.

'Do you know who they were?' he asked.

She shook her head and looked down at her glass. 'Not really,' she answered. 'There was a woman, and two men. I think they might have drugged me.' The words sent her spinning back into the nightmare, but she kept her head down so the fear wouldn't show.

'They might have given you some form of sodium amytal,' he said. 'It puts you into a kind of twilight zone. Combined with sleep deprivation it can be quite effective.'

She sat quietly for a few minutes, trying to reconstruct the events in a coherent and detailed fashion. It was hard to remain detached from all she was feeling, but the last thing she wanted was for him to know how afraid she still was. 'Do you have any idea who they might have been?' she said. 'I know they weren't the Gatlings . . .'

'No. The Gatlings are in America. The people who questioned you obviously work for them, and are quite possibly affiliated to the secret service. Did you hear them call each other by name at all?'

She was still thinking hard as she shook her head, then her eyes went to his as she said, 'They asked me about Liam. They knew he was in Paris, but I don't know whether *I* told them why, or if they knew anyway.'

'It's OK,' he said. 'None of us really knows anything yet to be in any serious danger, but it's going to come.'

Her eyes widened, as her heart gave a new thump of

unease. 'Why do you say that? I mean, we always knew . . .' She didn't want him to think she couldn't cope with the danger, and she was on the verge of sounding that way. 'Did something happen in New York?' she said. 'Actually, why are you back already?'

His eyes narrowed as he regarded her.

She felt foolish then. He'd come back because of her, of course. Knowing that made her feel strangely weak, then unbalanced inside. She took a sip of wine, which didn't make her feel any better. Then attempting a joke she laughed and said, 'So you came rushing back like a B-movie hero? Nice one.' As the words left her mouth she wished she could just shove them right back in again, and the way he cocked an eyebrow didn't help one bit.

'So how did you find out where I was?' she asked, as he went to drop spaghetti into a pan of boiling water.

'You told Stan north-east out of London and, knowing the Gatlings have a home in Suffolk, it was just a matter of finding out where. Not that Stan could get in when he got there, but by letting them know he was there, they might have let you go sooner rather than later.'

She watched him lower the gas, and found, to her surprise, that she was feeling a little stronger now. However, she was only too aware that there was no emotional safe ground here, for whichever way her mind went, whether to her inter-rogation, or to him, she was likely to become overwhelmed at any moment.

'Where do you keep the placemats and napkins?' he asked, checking the pasta.

Sliding down from the stool she went to the dining-room sideboard and took them out. 'Where's Rhona, by the way?' she asked.

'With somebody called Angelo. He flew in from Athens at five this afternoon and is going to be here for a few days, so, to quote her, she's "making the most of it".'

'In my hour of need,' Laurie commented drily. 'But her men's is always greater. Where shall we eat? At the table or the counter?'

'You choose.'

Wondering if the table might seem a little too intimate she

started back to the counter. When she got there she performed a mental glance back at the table. With the rain streaming down outside, and the wind howling up a nice summer gale, it would be more cosy over there, and maybe she'd light a couple of candles. But no, candles were going too far; she didn't want to give the wrong impression. However, it might create a warm, friendly sort of glow . . . Her promise to Rhona suddenly rose to the front of her mind and, returning to the counter, she set down the mats. There just wasn't any way she could talk about Lysette tonight, not when she was already in such a confused and vulnerable state.

Suddenly feeling the need to sit down, she pulled a chair from the dining table and dropped her head between her knees.

'Are you OK?' he asked.

'I think so,' she answered, coming up slowly. 'Probably just hunger. I haven't eaten for what feels like a week, and that smells so good.'

He said no more, merely carried on preparing the meal, while she sat watching him, remembering how often she'd sat with him like this in the past, either waiting for Lysette to return from one of her rescue missions, or removing herself from the crowd to come and chat as he cooked. They'd spent a lot of time back then, just the two of them, in corners at parties, or apart from the throng in pubs. She wondered if he'd ever noticed it too; or what he'd thought about the frequency with which she'd visited Lysette. He'd never seemed to mind, but she couldn't say he'd ever seemed to welcome it either. He'd just been, as he was now, polite, interested in a professional sense, concerned in a chivalrous male sense, but never anything deeper than that. Which was why she wasn't going to attach any other kind of meaning to his early return from New York. He'd merely done what he felt was right, and being here now, cooking, was no more than an extension of that.

'You've gone quiet,' he commented, while draining the pasta.

'I was wondering about your trip to New York,' she told him, averting her head so he wouldn't see the tears that had suddenly risen in her eyes. 'You said something just now that intimated it hadn't been an entire waste of time.'

'Far from it,' he responded. 'Tom Maykin's joining the team, which is going to be invaluable considering the number of American players there are sure to be. Liam's got a couple of French reporters on it too, and Jerome and Jed are flying to Hong Kong to see who they can pull in from that end. Would you like bread with this?'

She nodded. 'Stacks of it.' She'd be better once she'd eaten.

'Maykin put me in touch with a foreign exchange expert,' he was saying.

'Oh God,' she groaned, suddenly remembering. 'They know we're looking into it. They brought it up last night. They wanted to know why we're interested.'

'What did you tell them?'

'That there were certain trends. I might even have said between the dollar and euro, I don't recall. But it was definitely mentioned.'

He considered her answer while ladling two piles of spaghetti on to their plates.

'Maybe I should back out of this now,' she said. 'I can see I'm becoming more of a hindrance than a help. First the break-in, now this . . .'

'Do you want to back out?' he asked, reaching for the sauce.

'No, of course not, but –'

'Then let's end that conversation. Can you get the bread from the oven?'

Surprised that he hadn't jumped at her offer, she lined a basket with a napkin and dropped in the warm bread, while he finished dishing up. This easy domesticity, his nearness, the response of her body were all becoming a bit too hard to manage again.

'Actually,' she said, putting the counter-bar between them, 'there's another reason I should back out.'

His eyes met hers.

She wished they weren't so intense, for they affected her train of thought and there was a good chance now that her voice was going to sound quavery or strained when she spoke. 'Well, uh, it's just, well . . . actually there are two reasons,' she said, mercifully finding her mettle at the end. 'They talked about my parents last night.'

His face darkened. 'Go on.'

'They talked about my father's heart and Lysette's death . . .' She took a breath. 'If anything were to happen to them because of my involvement in this –'

'It won't,' he assured her. 'They were using it as a means of persuasion or, more accurately, intimidation.'

She nodded. 'I thought as much, I just needed to hear you say it too.' She looked down at her plate, hesitated for a moment, then twisted her fork into the spaghetti. Thank God for this monstrous hunger, for not even all the emotional turmoil could get the better of it. 'Mmm,' she murmured, as the rich tangy flavour of the sauce sank into her taste buds, momentarily obliterating all other sensory confusions.

He was still watching her, eating, taking a sip of wine and waiting for her to speak again. In the end he said, 'You mentioned two reasons.'

She stopped chewing and her eyes remained on her plate, as her appetite abruptly fled. But no, she'd already decided she wasn't going to do it, because now had to be just about the worst time to tell him how she'd let him take the blame for Lysette's death. She simply wasn't up to dealing with his anger or contempt on top of everything else. She'd have to confess at some point, she accepted that, but only when she'd found a way that wouldn't force her to admit how she felt about him too. So refilling her fork, she tried infusing her smile with levity as she said, 'The other doesn't really matter, and this is so delicious you're going to have to excuse me from speaking for a while.'

His eyes were knowing as he watched her, telling her that he wasn't fooled by her lightness. However, he didn't push it, just carried on eating and drinking.

She was first to break the silence, saying, 'They mentioned Beth Ashby's book quite a lot. They seemed to think I knew what it was about, or that it contained something . . . well, I don't know, sensitive, or revelatory, I suppose.'

He appeared more entertained than intrigued. 'As we're pretty certain it was them who stole it, it would be my guess that they're not sure whether they need to worry about what's in it or not,' he said. 'Which means it probably contains something that could be construed or misconstrued in a number of different ways, one or more of which might throw a light on them that they'd rather avoid.' He laughed. 'If I'm right, then coupled with your code, they must be going out of their minds. As a matter of fact, what is your code?'

Laurie rolled her eyes, and didn't speak until she'd finished chewing and swallowed. 'It's too childish to admit,' she said, 'and to be honest, you'd have to be me or Lysette to really understand it.'

'Then give me an example.'

Grimacing, she said, 'OK. Take the name Gatling. Instead of that I used Jermyn. Why? Because when we were at school there were two Annas in our class, one was Gatling, the other was Jermyn. And instead of Ashby, I used Gregory, because there was someone who lived near us for a while, whose name was Gregory Ash. For dollar I used snake, the S is like a snake, for pound I used weight, and for euro I used target.'

He was looking mildly perplexed, though amused. 'Ingenious,' he remarked. 'No wonder they didn't decipher a word.'

'Lysette would have got it, eventually,' she said. 'It was a mind-reading exercise really, and there's more to it than that, but it's too complicated to go into. I suppose it's part of being a twin.'

He nodded, and again his eyes were on hers in a way she found almost too pervasive.

'So do you think we should put some pressure on Rhona to get us the book?' she said, going back to her meal.

'Leave it with me,' he answered. 'I'm going to see if there's another way. Her contact with you is too well known for her to take the risk.' As he finished speaking the phone began ringing. Since he was the closest he picked it up.

'Yes, Wilbur, she's awake now,' he said. 'No, she's fine. I guess she's just bought herself a few more days off, though.' He looked at Laurie and winked. 'Why don't I get her to call you when she's finished eating?' He paused, frowned, then said, 'I know it's not you asking, Wilbur, so you can tell whoever is that she doesn't remember a thing.'

As he hung up Laurie said, 'Have you checked the

317

messages? I've just remembered, when I was getting out of the car this morning in my near comatose state, they said there'd be a phone number for me to call if I had any information to pass on. As if I would.'

Leaning back he hit the play button on the machine and together they listened to the calls. Sure enough, the fourth was an unknown voice repeating the same number twice.

She felt suddenly angry. 'Do they seriously believe I'm going to tell them anything?' she demanded.

He shrugged. 'It's hard to know. I suppose they think it's worth a shot.'

'I could sell my abduction to half the editors in town, didn't they think of that?'

'Probably, but after weighing it all up they obviously decided to take the risk. You might be a reporter, but an ego the size of Marcus Gatling's probably wouldn't consider you an enormous threat.'

Her eyes narrowed at that. 'So he throws back the minnow in the hope of reeling in the shark?' she retorted.

He laughed. 'Would that be a reference to me?'

'Well, if I were them I wouldn't put money on *me* finding out what's really going on either. After all, I'm Miss Insignificant compared to you, with your killer reputation for getting to the truth, not to mention all those contacts in places so high you get vertigo just thinking of them. So the prospect of you being on the case has got to be making them nervous, at the very least. And they're not going to grab *you* off the street, are they? So I suppose their plan is to frighten the living daylights out of me, then send me back to you to get details on just how widely and powerfully your contacts are spread, and to give them regular updates on everything you're finding out regarding Ashby, Sophie Long and the currency scam.'

He continued to look at her, mulling it all over until finally he said, 'It's a touch dramatic, and you're giving me far too much credit for the kind of contacts I might have, but there's a chance you're on the right track.' He picked up his wine, but didn't drink. 'What I'd really like to know at this point, though,' he said, 'is what's upsetting them most? The fact that we might be on to their finance skulduggery; or that we won't let go of Sophie Long's murder.'

'Well, as the two are obviously totally interlinked,' she responded, 'I'd say it has to be both. The question is, how many connections are there between the two that we don't yet know about?'

They sat with that for a moment, considering the labyrinthine routes they were taking towards an end that still felt a long way from sight. Finally she said, 'No word from Bruce Cottle on whether his wife'll talk to me, I suppose?'

'We'll try him tomorrow,' he answered. 'He's also finding out if Ashby will see you again. I thought it might be a good idea,' he added, when he saw her surprise. 'And I'm sending Gail down to Devon to have another chat with Heather Dance. Since she's in regular contact with Ashby, there might be something new on that front.'

'Are you going back to New York?'

He shook his head. 'Not immediately. Tom Maykin's taking over that end. He's going to be here in a couple of weeks; he can fill us in then. But something happened while I was there that was . . . how should I put it? Dubious? Worrisome?'

'Oh?'

He explained about Wheeler Nash's accident on a Los Angeles freeway, adding, 'Of course, there's a good chance it was just that, an accident, but I'm told he's not the first to make an abrupt departure for the Elysian Fields in the past six weeks. Apparently there are two others, and that doesn't include Sophie Long.'

'Who were the other two?'

'A journalist and a Pentagon insider. They're probably going to be as hard to link to the syndicate as Sophie Long is, in that the connection's there, in her case through Ashby, but that's where we draw a blank, because we still don't know for certain if he was part of it. Tom Maykin's coming up with much the same kind of results for the other two – a connection of sorts, but nothing conclusive.'

'What does he think about the dollar/euro situation?'

'That's turning out particularly interesting from his end,' he answered. 'It seems just about every reporter he's spoken to has, at some stage or another, been bothered by, or is suspicious of the trends, but so far he hasn't found anyone who's actually doing anything about it. As he put it, it's like the niggling ache that never seems serious enough to take to the doctor, then when you finally do, it turns out to be a full-blown terminal cancer.'

'Nice analogy,' she commented.

His expression was wry. 'So no definitive answers,' he continued. 'We can all expound a theory, of course, but frankly I'd rather leave it to the experts, because the scenario I'm coming up with right now is so fantastic it's off the scale of possible, never mind probable.'

'And that is?' she prompted, when he went no further.

He shook his head.

'Well, I'm nowhere near so coy,' she stated rashly. 'Here's my theory for what it's worth. I think they're trying to kill the euro outright. Not just devalue it to make millions the way they do when they stage a run on a currency, but to annihilate it completely.'

Though his eyebrows went up, his expression showed more interest than surprise. 'How would that serve them?' he asked.

'I don't know. That part's still eluding me, but if I'm right we could find that the motive is more political than financial and for the possible ramifications of that I'll have to upgrade my crystal ball, not to mention my fall-out shelter.'

He nodded thoughtfully, took another sip of wine, then with a twinkle in his eye he said, 'I thought you had to be a twin to think the same way.'

She frowned, then understanding she smiled. 'So do I take it we're not a million miles apart on this?'

He looked at her hard. 'I'd say we're a lot closer than that,' he responded.

The undertone was changing again, but this time instead of trying to avoid it, she found herself attempting to go with it.

'Would you like some more to eat?' he offered, his eyes still on hers.

Not breaking the gaze, she pushed her plate towards him.

He didn't move and her heart began pounding so hard she felt sure he could hear it. His expression was impossible to read, but still she willed him to do or say something that would take this moment at least one step closer to the promise it was exuding. In the end he merely picked up the plates and carried them to the stove.

Crushed, but strangely elated too, she watched him and listened to the rain outside. It sounded harder than before, and the smell of wet earth, coming in through the open window, was flowing into her senses in a way that almost seemed to keep the moment going. It was suiting her now to remember how Rhona had insisted he felt the same way she did. If she could make herself believe that, then she might make herself accept that he was waiting for her to speak first. She wanted to, more than anything, but his next words told her that his mind simply wasn't in the same place as hers.

'I keep asking myself about that book,' he said, returning with two smaller helpings than before. 'It was obviously written before Sophie Long's murder . . . Has Ashby read it, did he tell you?'

'Yes. But he only said it was good, and that she's got talent. He didn't tell me what it was about.'

'Mm, we definitely need to get our hands on it,' he stated. 'Remind me of the title again.'

'*Carlotta's Symphony of Love and Death.* And it shouldn't be so hard to get a copy now that the film company has it,' she suddenly realized. 'Or at least something that'll tell us what it's about. Don't the trade papers in Hollywood announce that sort of thing when a project goes into development?'

'Mm,' he responded. 'Usually, yes, they do. We'll probably need more than a synopsis, but it'll do for a start.'

'I'll get on the Internet tomorrow, see what I can turn up.'

They ate in silence then, immersed in their own thoughts, until they'd finished and he got up to clear away the plates.

'I don't think I've given this enough consideration before,' he said finally, 'but if that book does contain something they're not comfortable with, or has some kind of obscurity that's bothering them, they're not going to let it rest.'

Laurie was watching him closely.

'My guess is,' he continued, 'that it'll get pulled before it ever hits the shelves.'

'But even if they do that,' she stated, 'it's still not dealing with Beth Ashby herself.'

'Precisely.' He was very still, his eyes like steel. Then

looking at his watch, he picked up his keys and said, 'Get some more sleep. Stan's outside. I'll call you in the morning.'

He was gone almost before she could catch her breath – a quick brush past her, footsteps on the stairs, and the front door banging behind him. She considered calling his mobile to ask where he was going, but then decided just to leave it and carry on clearing up, stacking the plates in the dishwasher, wiping down surfaces and putting the leftovers in the fridge. The place felt depressingly empty now, as though the life had gone from it, and the splash of the rain outside seemed lonely, and sad. She thought of the moments during the past hour that had felt so intense, and knew with a growing dismay that none of the mildly flirtatious exchanges reached him the way they did her. In fact, if he noticed them at all they seemed simply to amuse him, as they had when Lysette was alive. So nothing had changed. Rhona was wrong. He still considered himself to be some kind of older brother, or good friend, or a mentor even. The part that had changed, though, was knowing now how desperately he'd wanted to end his relationship with Lysette. So what must it be like for him spending time with her, who looked and sounded so like the woman he'd wanted to get out of his life, who had resorted to suicide rather than go on without him? Was she some kind of penance, maybe? A way of purging his guilt?

Chapter 19

Being an airhead was absolutely the way to go. Ava's sophistication and subtlety might work in England, but in LA it was about as effective as a whisper in an uproar. Here, everything was totally out there, in your face, brazen, wicked, glittering and sensationally overdone – the perfect backdrop for the showy world of make-believe and megabucks. It was OK to be anyone or anything you wanted in LA, because here, amongst all the millionaires' mansions, up-thrusting palms, and dazzling beaches, the arcane and outrageous weren't only expected they were demanded. And pretending not to have a brain, when she'd fenced for so many years with all those insufferable pseudo-intellectual friends of Colin's, made life so wonderfully easy and fun. She didn't have to think about anything she didn't want to. Life before LA was over, all hail the great culture of soundbites and silicone.

She'd been here for almost a month now, sharing a chic, art deco-style house in the Hollywood Hills with Mitzi Bower, whose big, fluffy blonde hair seemed to float like a cloud around her head, with two little Heidi plaits poking out underneath. Her legs were long and skinny, her breasts were like melons, and her regularly peeled face was as exquisitely smooth as her lips were spongy and plump. Though she might look, and occasionally behave, like a Barbie doll, between the hours of ten and three she was a serious, disciplined and extremely talented writer, whose face, without all the paint, was actually more beautiful than with it. There was no doubting how much she adored her work, for her attention to detail and dedication to character dominated her mind, even outside of her scheduled hours. So even when being a serious party animal, schmoozing and grooving, dancing and romancing, for Mitzi it was all about reaction and relations, pushing limits, breaking barriers, raising money, generating buzz and being prepared to try just about anything once for the sake of her art.

Ava was getting that way too. The freedom to be this whole other person who didn't have to worry about morals, or money – or much of anything, actually – was so exhilarating that she never wanted to come down from the high. There were certain substances guaranteed to keep her there, of course, and for a while now she'd been psyching herself up to try them, but for some reason she couldn't quite bring herself to yet. Of course, it was Beth holding her back, for handing her look and lifestyle over to Ava was one thing, losing control of her mind was another altogether.

'But that's OK,' Mitzi told her, sitting up on her lounger to rearrange her towel. 'You see, you got to know your limitations, and it sounds like you do. That's good.' Her tight, tanned limbs, hand-span hips and huge breasts were all bared to the sun, though her cotton candy hair was currently undergoing a touch-up inside a clipped-on plastic bag, while her forty-two-year-old face was fighting off the ageing process under a creamy white goo.

On the bed next to her Ava was massaging sun cream into her legs. 'I'm not saying I don't want to try it ever,' she assured her, 'and don't think I've got a problem with you taking it –'

'I don't,' Mitzi interrupted. 'Now, how're you feeling? Still sore?'

Ava looked down at her new D cup breasts and felt almost light-headed, even slightly nauseous at what she'd done. Not that she regretted it for a minute, for already, even though they'd only been out of bandages a week, they looked and felt fantastic. 'I just wish I'd done it years ago,' she confessed. 'They'd have changed my life.'

Mitzi laughed. 'They still will, girl, believe me,' she responded, reaching over to answer her cellphone.

As she talked, Ava stared across the pool towards the beautiful golden mountains way out on the horizon. No matter what else was going on in this house, how many visitors they might have, how loud and raucous the parties or intense the writing, it was impossible to be unaware of the sheer loveliness of the scenery the place overlooked. It was so soothing and entrancing, it was almost transcendent. She recalled the day Theo had first brought them here, having collected her from the Beverly Hills Hotel to drive her up through the canyons to a place she'd never have dreamt existed, right in the heart of LA. And that was where they were, for just along the road, almost hidden in the wilds of Franklin Canyon Park, was a small concrete plaque marking the geographical centre of Los Angeles. Theo had seemed to take great pride in showing them that.

She wondered where he was now, New York or Memphis. He hadn't called for a few days, so she'd lost track of his movements, though the last time they'd spoken he was at his office in Manhattan. He took his work even more seriously than he took himself, she'd discovered, and with so many projects, at so many different stages of development, he almost literally never stopped. Which meant she'd hardly seen him since arriving – just the odd day here and there, and a few hurried phone calls as he moved from one city to the next, on a perpetual quest for investment, talent or just the need to expand his contacts. It was funny how she seemed to miss him, when she hardly even knew him. She couldn't even say they'd connected particularly, though she guessed the warmth she felt towards him was because he was a kind of connection with home. A very nebulous one, it was true, but actually that was all she wanted – a virtually transparent thread to link her to where she had come from, but that didn't make any demands or inspire any guilt.

'So what were we saying?' Mitzi said, dropping the phone back in the basket beside her.

Ava screwed up her nose. 'Can't remember,' she responded. 'But I was just thinking about Theo. Have you heard from him lately? Do you know where he is?'

'Still in New York, I think, and no contact suits me just fine, because the last thing I need is a producer breathing down my neck while I'm trying to create. Did you take a look at the scenes I did yesterday, by the way?'

'Not yet. Where are they?'

'Probably still on the printer.'

Ava stood up, stretched out her long, sun-bronzed limbs, then stalked over to the edge of the pool. The sun was so dazzling it was hard to look at the water as it rippled and shimmered and reflected the sheer blue of the sky above. She was wearing nothing more than a glistening gold thong and a pair of designer shades. The hot, arid air was like a fire on her skin, embracing every part of her with an intensity that was almost erotic. She adored the sense of freedom that this near-nudity gave her, as though shedding her clothes, in a way Beth had never even dreamt of, was somehow shedding her past. A slow smile started to curve her lips as she realized Mitzi was watching her and, putting her hands on her hips, she pivoted to treat her to a full-frontal view.

Mitzi's eyebrows arched with amusement. 'Gorgeous,' she assured her. 'I can't even see any scars already.'

'You know, one of the best things about them,' Ava said, cupping her new breasts in her hands, 'is how sexy they make you *feel*, never mind look. It's a whole other world, having boobs like this.' She smiled warmly to herself, wanting to add how Colin would love them. But they never spoke about him, so the thought stayed with her.

'Did you tell Theo yet?' Mitzi asked.

Ava looked surprised. 'No. Why would I? I can't imagine he'd be interested.'

Mitzi shrugged. 'He's a strange guy, isn't he? I've known him for a couple of years, but I still can't say I *know* him. I thought he might be gay until I found out he had a wife and kid. Not that that means anything, I suppose, and they're not together any more anyhow, so maybe he is.'

Wading down to the first wide shallow step of the pool, Ava sat on the edge and began splashing water on to her skin. 'So what have we got going on tonight?' she said.

Mitzi yawned and stretched. 'Couple of parties,' she answered. 'A few of the guys are dropping in to watch the sun set. I guess we need to mix a pitcher of margatinis for that.'

Ava slipped into the water and started to swim, carving a slow, smooth path through the water, feeling its coolness glide over her like a loving caress. This was truly paradise, and right now she could feel in love with Theo just for bringing her here.

Mitzi sat on the lounger watching her, and wondering what was really going through her mind. It was hard to tell with Ava, for she'd never met such an unusual woman, and rarely taken to one so warmly. As a writer Mitzi was fascinated by the contradictions of her character, which went way beyond her change of name and altered look, for she was an introvert who was an exhibitionist, a chameleon who seemed to thrive on being noticed. She almost never talked about her life in England; it was as though the husband who was in prison for murder had ceased to exist. There were no letters, no phone calls, no pining or longing, or none that she ever confessed to. As far as Mitzi was aware she hadn't spoken to her parents since being here either, though she had some, because Mitzi had read about them in one of the articles she'd dug out during her research. She hadn't even returned the calls from her agent – or her closest friend, Georgie, whose messages were starting to sound so worried that Mitzi was considering ringing back herself, just to reassure the poor woman that Beth, as she called her, was alive and well and having a ball.

And she was having a ball. She was like a spirit that had been trapped in the wrong body, the wrong time, for so long that now she was free everything had to be experienced to the extreme. She was Carlotta in her book, Mitzi was certain of that, though how similarly the fiction resembled reality she had no way of knowing. She hadn't asked, because Ava had made it clear from the start that she wasn't Carlotta, that the book had nothing to do with her life, it was just a story.

'I know I've said this before, but you've got a really cool way of describing Carlotta's feelings,' Mitzi said, after Ava had finished her swim, and gone into the house to retrieve the new scenes.

Ava's pleasure showed as she lay down on her lounger. 'Thank you,' she said.

'All that stuff she's thinking,' Mitzi continued, 'you know, about who she is, and what she's doing in a place she doesn't understand. It really gets to me every time I read it. It goes right to the heart of loneliness, in a way that's so raw and uncompromising . . . I'll have to put it in narration, because I sure don't want to leave it out. Did you ever try any of that regression stuff yourself? You know, going back to a past life? Was that how you got the idea?'

Ava shook her head. 'No,' she answered. 'I just found while I was writing it that Carlotta needed to become someone else – someone who was her, but not her, if you know what I mean. Then one morning I was listening to a programme on the radio about past lives, and their effect on the present, and I thought, that's it! That's what's happening to Carlotta. All the marital abuse, and emotional repression she's suffering in the eighteenth century, the way all those corrupt and power- ful men in her husband's circle turn him into a monster, is setting the scene for her eventual breakdown in the twenty- first century.'

'Wow,' Mitzi murmured. 'That's so cool. And it really works. And I just love how the husband comes good second time around, the way he wakes up to who she really is.' She chuckled. 'I've got to admit, if you hadn't told me yourself, I'd still be in the dark over some of that. All those men, that poor, wretched girl, the one who died, so innocent in it all . . . the sacrificial lamb.' She hesitated, wondering if she'd gone too far, but Ava's expression was benign, so she said, 'I'd love to know what gave you the inspiration for Carlotta in the first place.'

Ava inhaled deeply, writhed a little, then, sitting up, she gazed out at the mountains, seeing them as though they were the hills surrounding a far distant place that she loved. 'I was in Italy, on holiday,' she said. 'Do you know the lakes?'

Mitzi shook her head. 'Never been to Europe.'

'Well, the lakes in Northern Italy are a very special kind of place. They're not just steeped in natural beauty, the mountains, the trees, the lakes themselves, of course, they seem to hold a sense of mystery, and an enticement, or maybe it's a challenge, to find out their secrets. One day I was visiting an old house, on the south-eastern shore of Lake Maggiore, and I came across a small painting of a woman sitting at a piano with a half-written musical score on the stand. She was looking out, towards the artist in a mournful, yet slightly surprised sort of way. The only words on the unfinished score were Carlotta Gaspari. I couldn't find out anything about her, if the name was even hers, but the longer I stared into her eyes the more I realized I was seeing, even feeling, things about her life that felt as though they were a part of my life too. There was this kind of synergy that went beyond anything I'd ever experienced before. I could almost hear her speaking to me, which I know sounds crazy, but I swear that was what it was like. I even felt tears on my cheeks when I sensed she'd lost a child, because I'd recently lost one too. I stood there absorbing terrible details of her pain, not only about the child, but about the husband she adored, who loved her, yet beat and humiliated her, and the dreadful loneliness she felt at having no one to turn to. Have you ever been beaten by a man?'

'Once,' Mitzi confessed. 'What about you?'

Ava shook her head. 'Never,' she answered. 'Yet, when I was looking at that woman, Carlotta, I truly felt as though I had been. I honestly don't know what happened to make me connect with her like that, but by the time I left I knew that I had to write something about her. Even if I had to fictionalize most of the story, I just had to tell it.'

'Have you ever been back to see the portrait?' Mitzi asked.

'No. To be honest, I'm almost afraid to, in case she's gone, or doesn't speak to me again. I'd feel as though I'd lost a part of myself if that happened.' Then smiling, she said, 'If she is still there you'll meet her when we go to film.'

'Sure,' Mitzi responded, drawing out the word. 'And what a privilege having you make the introduction. After all, whoever she was once, she's your creation now.'

Ava nodded slowly, but said nothing.

'What about the husband, did you kind of, like, *see* him at all?' Mitzi asked. 'You know, while Carlotta was talking to you?'

'Not really,' Ava answered. 'Images of my own kept getting in the way.'

'Is there any similarity between the two men?'

'Maybe. In certain ways. But not all.'

Mitzi waited, hoping she'd say more, but she didn't. So Mitzi said, 'You know, I'm going to talk to Theo, because I reckon we should be over there now, writing this in the place that inspired it, and where we're going to shoot. I could experience all the atmosphere and stuff for myself. It's got to help.'

Ava smiled and nodded, then picked up the script as the phone inside started to ring.

Mitzi was intrigued by the way Ava seemed to tune out the sound, as though it either wasn't happening, or couldn't be anything to do with her. 'You know what, that could be your friend Georgie,' she said. 'She generally calls around this time.'

Ava's eyes remained on the script.

'Why don't you go talk to her?' Mitzi pressed gently. 'She sounds really worried about you. Just tell her you're OK.'

Ava continued staring at the script, but Mitzi could see her eyes filling with tears.

'What is it, babe?' she said softly. 'Why won't you talk to her?'

'Actually, I'm afraid to,' Ava answered, not sounding like Ava at all.

'Why?'

'Because of what she might tell me.'

Inside the answerphone clicked on. Mitzi sat very still, as though any slight movement would chase away the confidence that, like a frightened mouse, was hardly out of hiding.

'I want to talk to her,' Ava said. 'I miss her so much, and I know she's worried . . .'

'What are you so afraid of?' Mitzi prompted. 'What do you think she's going to tell you that can be so bad?'

'I don't know. I've given up guessing, because it's never what I'm expecting.' Her eyes were on an unfocused place ahead of her, seeing only she knew what. 'And what if he's changed his mind about seeing me?' she said. 'Should I go? Or should I stay here, and let him pay for what he's done? All the hurt he's caused, the pain and anguish . . . that poor innocent girl, the sacrificial lamb.'

On hearing her own words Mitzi again went very still, for this was as clear an admission as any that the book in some way did reflect real life. 'So are you saying he killed her because he was made to?' she said.

At that Ava seemed to break out of the hush and turned to look at her. 'You're talking about the book,' she said.

'Isn't it one and the same thing?'

'No. But they think it is.'

'Who's they?'

She shook her head. 'Never mind. You're right. I should talk to Georgie. I need to. There might be a message.'

Not sure whether she meant on the machine or from her husband, Mitzi watched her get up and walk into the house. For some reason she wasn't surprised when Ava wrapped herself in a thin cotton robe before picking up the phone.

'Georgie? It's me. How are you?' she said when Georgie's voice came down the line.

'Beth! For heaven's sake. How are *you*? I've been going out of my mind over here. The only reason I know you're still alive is because I managed to track down your producer, what's his name? Theo. Are you all right? Oh my God, I think I'm going to cry with relief. Just tell me, are you all right?'

'I'm better than that,' Ava laughed. 'So much better I hardly know where to start. I'm really sorry you've been so worried. I kept meaning to call, but the time was always wrong – the middle of the night for you, or during working hours for me and Mitzi. But here I am now, and guess what.'

'I don't know, tell me? Have you fallen in love?'

Ava gave a shout of laughter. 'You're such a romantic! No, I haven't fallen in love, except with myself. I'm Ava all the time now. You're the only one who calls me Beth, and you should see me, Georgie. Even if I say it myself, I look fantastic.'

'So what's new? Ava always did. It was only Beth who insisted on making herself dowdy.'

'Yes, but even Ava's never been this gorgeous before. She has – *I* have . . . Georgie, I have *breasts*. You should see them. They're like . . . What are they like? A *Playboy* centrefold and some. They're out of this world.'

'What do you mean?' Georgie said, sounding confused and not entirely thrilled. 'Are you saying you've had some kind of surgery?'

Ava laughed. 'Well, they didn't grow overnight on their own,' she said. 'Of course I've had surgery. Everyone does out here. I'm starting to live now, and I love it.'

'Big breasts and you get a life,' Georgie said cynically. 'You'd have hated that once.'

'Because I didn't have them,' Ava laughed. 'I was jealous, and now I don't need to be. I've also got fuller lips. Not that big, but enough to make me look ten years younger, and all kind of pouty and sexy. It's amazing the difference it makes. I could –'

'Beth, I have to tell you,' Georgie interrupted, 'I'm not sure I approve of this. I mean colouring your hair and changing the way you dress is one thing, having actual surgery –'

'Georgie, it's fine. Honestly. It's just the way things are out here. It's another world. It's hot so people naturally don't wear many clothes. That means they want their bodies to look good, and this is a way of doing it.'

'But you're not one of them.'

'I am while I'm here. Now, let's change the subject. How's little Blake?'

There was a brief pause before Georgie said, 'He's great. Four new teeth and he's got a girlfriend called Miranda.' Then reverting straight back to Beth, she said, 'How's the script going? Do you think you'll be there much longer?'

'It's hard to say. But there's a chance we might relocate to Italy. If we do, I hope you'll join us for a long weekend, at the very least.'

The smile was audible in Georgie's voice as she said, 'Try to keep me away. When's it likely to be?'

'I don't know. We've got to talk to Theo about it first.'

'By we, I take it you mean you and Mitzi. So what's she like?'

'Not you, but great. We party a lot, which is a kind of subculture here, because most people are in bed by ten. The rest of us keep it going through the early hours . . .'

'*Through* the early hours? You're sounding like an American.'

'I hope so. Honestly, I can't stress how much I love it here. The people are so warm and friendly. They all belong to spiritual groups and say happy and positive things to each other. Whether or not they mean them, God only knows, the fact is they say them with a passion and frequency that's supposed to make it true.'

332

'Your agent's rung here a few times, by the way,' Georgie said. 'Apparently you haven't had time to call him either.'

'I keep meaning to, but it's just been so hectic.'

'I think you should call him.'

'OK. I will.'

Georgie waited, giving her the chance to say more about that, or to ask about Colin, but once again Ava was gushing about the superior qualities of the LA scene. In the end, Georgie plunged right in and said, 'What about Colin? Are you interested to hear what's happening to him?'

There was a beat before Ava said, 'You don't have to say it like that. You know I am. You should also know that I'm afraid of it too. I mean, how would you feel if every time something happened a woman was dead, or some bastard child –'

'All right, point taken and I'm sorry. I suppose I just find it odd that you haven't bothered to find out anything about him at all.'

'What has he bothered to find out about me?' Ava cried.

'He asks about you every time Bruce sees him. He wants to know if you're all right. If you're happy. What's happening in LA. So what are we supposed to tell him?'

'That I've got big tits, a great house and a fantastic social life.'

Georgie was silent.

'Well, what do you want me to say?' Ava implored. 'He doesn't want to see me. He won't write; he doesn't send any messages. All I get is a letter telling me if he gets out he's going to live with another woman.'

'That might be true, but it doesn't mean he doesn't care about you any more.'

'I don't want him to care about me. I don't need his pity. I've got my own life now.'

'Beth . . .'

'For God's sake, Georgie, how much more of this do you think I can take? It's hard enough having a husband where he is for the murder of a poor young girl, who was some kind of sacrificial lamb –'

'Some kind of *what*?' Georgie said.

'Sacrificial lamb. It's the way Mitzi described her, and she's right. That's what Sophie Long was, a sacrificial lamb.'

'What are you saying?' Georgie said. 'What's that supposed to mean exactly?'

'Ask Colin. He'll be able to explain it.'

'I'd like to hear it from you.'

'No. Ask him. Or read the book, then ask Marcus Gatling.' She laughed brittly. 'I didn't tell you about that, did I?' she said. 'Would you believe I bumped into dear Marcus and Leonora on the plane coming over here? We had a bit of a scene, actually. The old cod almost had an apoplexy when I told him there was new evidence to say Colin didn't do it. You should have seen his face. And when I told him his secrets might not be safe with me I thought he was going to explode.'

There was a beat before Georgie said, 'What secrets?'

Ava laughed. 'That's what he's wondering,' she responded.

'Beth, he's not someone to mess with,' Georgie warned. 'You know that, so just steer clear of him, is my advice.'

'Which I'll happily take.'

There was another short silence before Georgie said, 'So *do* you know things about him?'

'Well, let's just say I'm pretty certain it was him who had my book stolen from the publisher.'

'How do you know?'

'Who else would it be? Certainly not anyone from the press, because what could they do with it? They'd be sued if they printed without permission and I was hardly going to give it, was I?'

'But why do you say it was Marcus Gatling?'

'Because men in his position are always paranoid about the things they've got to hide.'

'So what's he got to hide?'

'You'd best ask him.'

'But he thinks, or thought, there might be something in your book that's likely to what? Expose him in some way?'

'Evidently.'

'Is there?'

Ava laughed. 'Why would I write about him? He hardly cuts a romantic figure, does he? In fact, the only reason his wife's with him is because of all that power and money. Everyone knows that.'

'So there's nothing about him in the book? Nothing that could even be construed as being about him?'

Ava frowned. 'Why are you asking?'

Georgie took a breath.

Ava's heart gave a beat of unease. 'Georgie. What's going on? Why are you asking all these questions about the book?'

Georgie braced herself, and said, 'Your agent should be telling you this really, but apparently they're not going to publish it.'

Ava froze. Then her mind spun into turmoil. They couldn't do this. They just couldn't, because without a book there would be no Ava, and without Ava there would be only Beth, and Beth couldn't cope with all this. 'But we had a deal!' she cried. 'I signed a contract!'

'Which apparently stipulates that you have to comply with certain editorial demands, and you've refused to do so. So on that basis, they've cancelled the book.'

Ava could hardly think. The sun was so dazzling she could no longer see.

'It's why your agent's been trying to call,' Georgie told her.

'What about the film? They can't cancel that too. Can they?'

'I don't know.'

'But Theo loves this book. He really wants to make it.'

Georgie was silent.

'What if I agree to the changes? Will they publish it then?'

'I don't know,' Georgie said again.

Ava was trying not to panic. She'd known she'd be made to pay for that incident on the plane, she knew too that it wasn't going to end here, but like a fool she'd been trying to convince herself it would. Oh God, if only she hadn't been drunk she'd never have approached him; he might not even have known she was there. But it was too late now, she'd taunted him with his own nightmares, and here they were coming to haunt her.

'Does Colin know any of this?' she demanded suddenly.

'I'm sure Bruce has told him.'

'Doesn't he have any advice? He knows the man better than anyone. What does he say I should do?'

'I don't know. Bruce hasn't told me.'

335

'Is he there?'

'No. He's in London tonight. But listen, before you call him I think you should know that Colin's instructed him to proceed with a divorce.'

Ava reeled under the blow. 'No! He can't!' she cried. 'He doesn't understand. It's not supposed to happen like that . . .'

'What isn't?' Georgie said.

'Nothing. None of it. Georgie, this is why I didn't want to talk to you – because every time there's something else, something that totally devastates me, and I can't take any more. I want to help him. I need to be there for him.'

'If you really mean that, then you still can be.'

'How? Just tell me how. He won't see me –'

'Talk to Laurie Forbes, or Elliot Russell.'

'No! I'm not talking to anyone from the press.'

'Why?'

'You know why. I don't trust them.'

'They really want to help you. In fact, they're worried about you.'

'What do you mean? Have you been talking to them about me? Georgie, you can't do that. As my friend –'

'No, I haven't spoken to them at all. But Bruce has, and he tells me what they're saying. They're really keen to talk to you, and if not to you then to me, but I won't do anything unless you say it's all right.'

'It's not,' Ava said without hesitation. 'It's really not. Just stay clear of them, Georgie. Don't talk to any one of them.'

'But if Colin's prepared to trust them, why won't you?'

'You just don't understand, Georgie. He's using them . . .'

'What do you mean? How is he using them?'

Not wanting to get into it any more than that, Ava suddenly banged down the phone. Then throwing off her wrap she stalked back out to the pool. 'I knew I should never have made that call,' she said shrilly. '*I knew it!*'

Mitzi only looked at her, not sure what to say.

Suddenly Ava swung round, eyes glittering, mouth trembling. 'Where's Fabio and his star dust?' she demanded angrily. 'I'm ready to give it a go.'

Chapter 20

Elliot's Porsche was speeding through the rosy early morning sunlight, like a pinball following the winding grey ribbon of road that carved through the dewy fields of Kent. The sun was rising in a vast, golden orb over the horizon, creating one of those magical, invigorating mornings that never failed to instil exuberance, though Laurie was still stifling the occasional yawn after getting up so early.

The anticipation she was feeling, as they drew closer to the south coast, wasn't unlike how she'd felt as a child on a day trip to the sea, though the seriousness of their purpose today tempered the edges of her excitement and kept her focused. They were heading for a rendezvous with one of Elliot's most infiltrated government sources, who'd made contact a few days ago from his holiday home in Brittany. As Elliot had been trying to reach him virtually since the day of Ashby's arrest, the man's call had created quite a stir in the office, not to mention some high expectation in Elliot. Their meeting point was a café just outside of Le Touquet, on the northern coast of France. For the occasion Laurie had dressed in a pair of straight black jeans, a white sleeveless sweater and a boxy dog-toothed jacket, which was one of the smartest outfits she owned. She'd also thickened her lashes with mascara, highlighted her cheeks and coated her lips with a subtle caramel frosting. And just to finish it off, she'd replaced her perpetually scruffy topknot with a demure, low-lying pony-tail that was trapped into obedience by an extremely sophisticated slide. She didn't actually want to admit that it was all for Elliot, who'd risen admirably to the occasion when he'd come to pick her up by making no comment at all, so she couldn't actually allow herself to feel miffed by his neglect, even though she was.

They'd been working on this story for over a month now, seeing each other virtually every day, as they and the rest of the team co-ordinated the information that was coming in with increasing regularity from all over the world. The potential scale of the syndicate's operations was now growing to such an extent that Elliot's team was on it full time, as was Tom Maykin and at least a dozen other reporters from Australia to Asia, Brussels to the Bahamas and London to Washington. Neither Elliot nor Laurie had mentioned the fact that she hadn't returned to the office since her short stay at the Gatlings' home, but she knew very well that there was no way she could go back now, when the paper's behaviour towards her and the story would necessarily be included in her and Elliot's final report. So effectively she was out of a job, but since it had yet to be made official, and her salary had yet to cease, she'd decided to put it to the back of her mind as something that needed to be dealt with when she had time.

What her mind wasn't managing to escape quite so easily was the possibility that Gatling's people might try abducting her again. She hadn't heard from them, nor had Stan spotted anyone keeping tabs on her, but for some reason she couldn't shake the feeling of foreboding. She hadn't told anyone about it, especially not Elliot, though she occasionally wondered if he sensed it. But that was probably just her being fanciful, wanting him to care when no doubt he'd all but forgotten the entire incident.

Taking her mobile out of her bag she clicked on to answer.

'Laurie? It's Bruce Cottle. I hope I'm not too early.'

'Oh hi, Bruce,' she said, glancing at Elliot. 'Not at all. What gets you up at this hour?'

'I went down to the country last night,' he said, 'so I'm trying to beat the traffic into London. Giles and I are seeing Colin later. We're hoping we might have more luck persuading him to meet you again.'

'Good. If you can't then at least try to find out why he's being so reticent. And ask him if he knows where Heather Dance is. Apart from an email telling us she's all right, she and her mother might have vanished off the face of the earth.'

338

'OK,' Bruce said. 'We've been through it with him before, but I'm prepared to do it again. Where are you now?'

'Actually, we're heading towards the Channel Tunnel, and if we go much faster we might gain enough momentum to fly off the edge of England and land in France without the aid of a train.'

Elliot slanted her a look, as Bruce said 'Oh, that's a shame, I was hoping to see you later, but if you're not around –'

'We'll be back by late afternoon. What is it?'

'Georgie's spoken to Beth on the phone. She only told me about it last night. It happened a few days ago.'

'You sound worried,' Laurie commented, starting to feel the same way. 'What happened?'

'Well, Georgie wasn't at all happy with the conversation. She's got herself quite worked up about it. Beth's . . .' He seemed at a loss for a moment, then more firmly, he said, 'Well, to begin with she claims there was some kind of encounter with Marcus Gatling and his wife on the plane going out there.'

Immediately Laurie said, 'Bruce, I need to put you on the speaker for this, so I'll have to call you back with Elliot's phone. You're in your car, yes?'

Bruce confirmed it, and a couple of minutes later his voice was coming from the tiny overhead speaker.

'I don't know the details,' he was saying, 'only what Georgie told me, but I think it would be a good idea for you to talk to her.'

Laurie gave a laugh of surprise. 'I've been trying, Bruce,' she reminded him.

'I know, and she still won't agree without Beth's permission, but I think, if you go down there, if you just turn up unannounced, she might change her mind.'

Laurie looked at Elliot as he said, 'Tell us more about this encounter with Gatling.'

'All I know is that she told him there was new evidence to say Colin didn't do it, which apparently he didn't take too well. And she also said something about his secrets not being safe with her.'

Elliot's expression was dark. 'What does that mean?' he said. 'What secrets?'

'Georgie didn't know, but when she asked Beth she more or less said she was winding him up.'

Laurie and Elliot exchanged glances.

'Has there been any contact since?' Elliot asked.

'I don't think so.'

'Did she give any indication of being afraid of Gatling?'

'Not that Georgie mentioned. She's never liked the man, though, or his wife, but winding him up like that . . . She'd never have done it before. She was always too unsure of herself. She seems to have lost some of that now, though.'

'How did she take the news of the book being pulled?' Laurie asked. 'Did she already know? Did Georgie mention it?'

'She was upset, angry, all the things you'd expect.'

'Surprised?'

'I don't know. But apparently she's convinced it was Gatling who had her book stolen from the publishers. She didn't say why, but she did say something that both Georgie and I find very strange indeed. She referred to Sophie Long as being a sacrificial lamb, and when Georgie asked her what she meant she said Georgie should either ask Colin, or read the book, then ask Marcus Gatling.'

'Confirmation,' Laurie said in an undertone to Elliot, 'that even her best friend hasn't read the book.'

'What was that?' Bruce said.

'Nothing,' Laurie replied, braking with Elliot as he slowed for the tunnel approach. 'When's a good time for me to go down there?'

'Probably during the late afternoons,' he answered. 'She won't be there for the next few days. She's going to a health farm with my sister . . .'

'OK, I'll wait to hear from you.'

'There's just one other thing,' he said, before she broke the connection. 'Apparently she's had some plastic surgery. Beth, I mean, not Georgie.'

Laurie looked at Elliot. 'What kind of plastic surgery?' she asked.

'Breast enlargement and something to do with her lips.'

At that Laurie's eyes started to dance, for she knew that

Elliot, like her, had imagined something much more sinister than bulging breasts and rubbery lips.

'It's out of character for her to do something like that,' Bruce said. 'Or it always was in the past. Lately we haven't been quite sure what to expect.'

'OK,' Laurie said as a blast of static interrupted the line, 'we're about to board the train now, so we'll speak to you later.'

As she rang off, and they pulled alongside a toll booth to buy a ticket, Elliot said, 'Tom Maykin told me last night that the Gatlings were back in California, so I'd say, given the way things seem to happen in places where they're not, that for the moment at least Beth Ashby's got no more to worry about than the writing of a screenplay that doesn't appear to have been cancelled, and what she's going to do with her old bras.'

Though Laurie smiled at the joke, she was deep in thought, trying to imagine what Beth Ashby looked like now, where she lived, what her life was really like over there in LA.

'That was interesting, what she said about Sophie Long being a sacrificial lamb, don't you think?' she said as they inched on to the train behind a new Vauxhall Zafira.

'Very. But since all trace of every copy of the manuscript seems to have vanished since the book was cancelled, we're left with a scant synopsis from the *Hollywood Reporter* that tells us . . . What did it say again?'

'Something about a journey of love through time, and an existential righting of old wrongs.'

'Sounds more like a clue from *The Times* crossword than the plot for a feature film,' he commented, 'but as we've already been through it a hundred times, we won't go there again.' And bringing the car to a stop, he turned off the engine, unfastened his seat belt and turned on the CD.

'Opera?' she said, as the opening strains of *La Traviata* began drifting into the car. 'You like opera?'

He briefly opened one eye. 'Yes. Do you?'

'Yes,' she answered.

'Then relax and listen.'

She nodded and looked out of the window as the train doors started to close. Her heartbeat was increasing, as the music filled up the car and swamped her with a longing to groan and laugh, for she knew very well he loved opera, she even knew which were his favourites, and though they might not be her favourites too, the passion, the drama, the sheer power and visceral energy were, for her, just about the greatest aphrodisiac imaginable. So exactly how she was going to relax when every chord and cadenza, aria and bravura was inciting such eroticism in her mind that her body might just lose control, was a feat she was going to find it impossible to perform, unless, by some God-saving miracle, she could manage to fall asleep.

It was around ten when Laurie was woken by the sound of the Porsche engine dying. Stiff and bleary-eyed she struggled to sit up, remembering just in time not to rub her eyes. To her surprise, they seemed to be there, for they were on the outskirts of what might be called a village, though it appeared to consist of no more than a few dreary rain-soaked houses either side of the road, a closed *boulangerie* next door to a single-pump garage, also closed, and an almost derelict-looking café called Emile's.

Elliot was already getting out of the car so, following suit, she picked up her bag and thanked him as he came to hold the door open. The promise of sun later was glinting through breaks in the thick wedges of cloud, but by the time they'd crossed to the café, a few fat blobs of rain were starting to fall.

An old-fashioned bell jangled overhead as they entered, and immediately, through the smoky darkness, they were assailed by the smell of cheap red wine, tobacco and strong coffee. Relics of past Christmases hung dejectedly from a couple of the overhead beams, and a small TV on the bar was showing an episode of *Murder She Wrote*, dubbed into French. Two elderly men, dressed in blue serge, with unfiltered cigarettes dangling from their lips, were so engrossed in the programme that they didn't even look up when the door opened. Another, younger, man, whose elbows were resting on the bar as he too absorbed Jessica Fletcher's story, glanced their way and greeted them with a gruff, 'Bonjour.'

'Are you sure we're in the right place?' Laurie whispered, looking round at the vinyl-topped table where ashtrays had been left overflowing, and a few smeary glasses awaited collection. The windows had brass poles across their centres, supporting dingy nets, and the cheap plastic chairs were scattered haphazardly, as though a crowd had taken off in a hurry.

'You surely can't be doubting me,' Elliot responded.

'*Qu'est-ce que vous voulez?*' the younger man growled.

'Do you speak French?' Elliot said from the corner of his mouth.

'Yes, so do you,' she answered from the corner of hers. 'I'll have a beer.'

Laughing, Elliot ordered two then pulled a couple of chairs up to the cleanest-looking table.

Laurie sat down, praying she wouldn't need the loo, and was about to speak when his mobile rang. He was quiet as he listened to the caller. Then, looking at her with comically raised eyebrows, he said, 'Great news, my friend. Call me when you get here.'

'Was that Eaton?' Laurie said, referring to the man they were supposed to be meeting.

'No. It was Karl, calling from Frankfurt. He's arriving in London tonight.'

Laurie nodded. There was so much coming and going now that she'd almost lost track of who was due in when, and where she was supposed to be next. Just thank God for Murray, was all she could say, whose powers of co-ordination were in a science fiction league of their own.

'By the way, did you know you talk in your sleep?' Elliot commented, leaning back in his chair and stretching out his legs.

Laurie's eyes flew open as colour flooded her cheeks. 'That's not true,' she declared. 'I never talk in my sleep.'

'I don't know about never,' he responded, 'but you did on the way here.'

'What did I say?'

His eyes were shining with mirth. 'I don't know that I can repeat it,' he teased.

'Elliot! Don't do this,' she warned. 'I want to know what I said.'

'And I want to know what you were dreaming.'

'No! I can't remember. Nothing.' In fact, it was true, she

couldn't remember dreaming, but she knew very well what she'd been thinking before she'd dropped off to sleep. Then, realizing the more she reacted the more he was going to tease her, she said, 'Well, actually, now I come to think of it . . . Whatever I said couldn't possibly have measured up to what was actually going on.'

He looked surprised. 'Now I'm really interested,' he said.

'Mm, shame I'm not going to tell you,' she responded, as their drinks arrived.

Picking up his beer he looked at her over the glass as he drank, then the moment passed, as these flirtatious moments always did, leaving her wondering if she'd gone too far, or read more into it than was actually there.

'There was a Frenchman and an Englishman,' he said, putting his glass down as he launched into the joke. 'Jean-Claude and Bert. Jean-Claude says: "You know, Bert, I am very proud to be a Frenchman, it is the best thing to be, but if I weren't a Frenchman I would want to be an Englishman." And Bert says: "You know Jean-Claude, I am very proud to be an Englishman, it is the best thing to be, but if I weren't an Englishman I would want to be . . ."'

It took her a moment, then laughing she said, 'That's terrible.'

'I know,' he responded, getting to his feet as the door opened. 'David, it's good to see you,' he said to the extremely elegant, immaculately groomed man who'd just arrived.

'Elliot, my friend. Glad you found it all right.' Eaton closed the door, and his eyes moved to Laurie as he came to shake Elliot's hand.

Elliot immediately introduced her.

Eaton frowned. 'If I didn't know you, Elliot, I'd have a problem with this,' he said frankly.

'If you didn't know me you wouldn't be here,' Elliot responded lightly. 'What'll you have to drink?'

'*Encore une bière*,' Eaton replied, speaking to the barman.

Elliot gestured for him to sit, saying, 'I was wondering if we were ever going to hear from you.'

'This is the first opportunity I've had,' Eaton replied. 'Everyone's being watched every minute now. You just don't know what it's like. All hell broke loose after Ashby killed that

344

girl. They're running so damned scared, the lot of them, they'd be laughable if it weren't so bloody dangerous. Anyway, they know you're on to them, I hope you're aware of that.'

'Of course. Who's "they" exactly?'

'Everyone from the PM down. They just can't work out how much you know.'

'So am I supposed to tell you? Is that what this is about?'

'You know me better than that.'

The barman set down Eaton's drink, and after taking a sip, he said to Laurie, 'You must be the one who visited Ashby.'

She nodded.

His shrewd grey eyes clung to hers for a moment; then he turned back to Elliot. 'So how much do you know?' he said.

Elliot smirked. 'I'll tell you this,' he replied. 'We've got a lot more people working on it than you might imagine, and we're getting a pretty good idea of what's involved. Frankly, it's too big for one story, so we're structuring it to unfold in ten or more. So just when they think it's all dying down . . .' His fingers mimicked an explosion.

Eaton looked down at his drink. 'What kind of themes are you looking at?' he said.

'You name it. Everything from presidential pardons, to ministerial witch-hunts, to the contentious little Son of Star Wars, to highly suspect currency dealings. There's a lot of crossover, but every link is tainted with gold, or maybe that should be green, as in greenback.'

Eaton's eyebrows flickered.

'Why don't we make a start on the dollar versus the euro?' Elliot suggested.

Eaton nodded, as though confirming his approval.

'I need names.'

Eaton gave a dry laugh. 'Just pick one and say bingo,' he responded. 'Sabilio. Gatling times two. Wingate. Chiselhurst. Kleinstein. Fulmer. They're spread out all over the place, from London to Washington, Sydney to Hong Kong. They're standing to make billions out of this – pounds not dollars – and no one can back out even if they wanted to. They're all in too deep. The entire wealth of some vast corporations is behind it – insurance, international banking, petrochemicals, telecommunications, you name it.'

'So what's their goal? How are they doing it?'

'How? In more ways than you and I even know exist,' Eaton responded, glancing at Laurie. 'They've got some of the best financial brains behind it. But I can tell you this, Britain's not going to give up sterling for the euro, it's going to give it up for the US dollar.'

Laurie's shock came out in a gasp of laughter. She looked at Elliot, but he was registering neither surprise nor disbelief. 'This has to go back a long way if it's serious,' he said.

'It does.'

'But what about Britain's relationship with the rest of Europe?' Laurie interjected.

Eaton merely looked at her.

'I don't see how they can just thrust this on the people,' she protested. 'I mean you surely can't just announce one day that Britain's currency is now the dollar, as though nothing else has ever gone before, and no one's opinion except those making the decision counts. Referendums, even elections, are held based on this sort of thing.'

Eaton nodded agreement.

Her frustration was mounting. 'OK, let's say they do pull it off, what's it going to mean for the country?' she demanded.

'It's hard to predict exactly,' Eaton answered, 'but the Community's retaliation is sure to be swift, so trade will probably be the worst hit, at least initially. The economy's going to be all over the place for years . . .'

'Where are they operating from?' Elliot said.

'Companies in the Bahamas, Guernsey and Hong Kong. You'll find most of the banks are Swiss.'

Elliot nodded. That at least confirmed what he already knew.

Laurie said, 'Is Colin Ashby part of it?'

Eaton's grey eyes focused on hers. 'I don't know how far into it he was, but there's a good chance he was in, yes.'

'What about Sophie Long? Why would he kill her?'

'I'm afraid you'll have to ask him.'

'He says he didn't do it.'

'Which has thrown a lot of people into a panic,' Eaton replied. 'Believe me, there have been some nasty exchanges going on behind the scenes since that murder, because if Ashby's telling the truth, it means there's a chance someone amongst them has ordered a killing without the others' agreement. No one knows for sure who did it, or why, so everyone's a suspect. Trust, or the lack of it, has become a big issue, and paranoia is making them more dangerous than ever. From what you've told me it's clear you've already uncovered enough information to cause an international scandal, if not disaster, so I want to drive it home to you, if someone can give the order to kill once, then, in this kind of climate, they're more likely to do it again.'

Elliot's eyes remained firmly on his.

Laurie said, 'Do you personally have any theories on the killing?'

'Truthfully, I think Ashby did it,' Eaton answered. 'The evidence is all there, and who in his right mind, if he finds a dead body, is going to take off his trousers and go and sit on the bed next to the corpse? It doesn't make any sense, unless he has a pretty sick sex life.'

Her eyes didn't waver from his.

He shrugged. 'OK. Select a name from those I've already given you,' he said, 'it could be any one of them.'

'Including Marcus Gatling?'

'Yes, but I should tell you he's been the most vigorous in trying to find out who it might have been.'

'Could be a bluff,' Elliot stated.

Eaton conceded with a nod. Then glancing at his watch he said, 'I promised my wife I'd be back by one. Friends are joining us from the Isle of Wight.'

Elliot got to his feet, gestured to the barman for a bill, and minutes later he and Laurie were in the Porsche heading back to Boulogne.

'So what do you make of all that?' she asked, as he put his foot down to pass a slow-moving cattle truck.

'It's hard to tell how much was bullshit, and how much wasn't.' He sounded frustrated, angry even. 'There's definitely something going on with the euro, we know that, but rejecting it in favour of the dollar . . . You know what I think? I think Gatling's just used Eaton to keep us busy with wild-goose chases all over the world, while they take their plans to the finish. At the same time, I think Eaton's trying to let us know that we're on the right track, we've got the right

347

names in the frame, and we should stay with it.'

'But stay with what?' she said.

'The probability that they're planning some kind of run on the euro that's going to help them clean up the day Britain joins. They can buy in dollars or pounds – both currencies are strong – so it'll make them a fortune either way.'

All the way back to the terminal they discussed the possible ramifications of what Eaton had told them, many of which were so fantastic they were hard to voice. In the end, as they joined a short queue to board the train Elliot said, 'No. I tell you, it's just not going to happen, because the worst-case scenario of Continental Europe declaring war on the US, with Britain floundering about somewhere in the middle, is the only logical place for this to go. So no. I'm not buying it, and Gatling's out of his tiny mind if he thinks I will.'

She waited for him to hand over the ticket, then said, 'What did you think of Gatling shouting the loudest about Sophie Long?'

'What I said at the time, I think it's a bluff. Why else is he interfering with police investigations and getting his own people in on the act? *Fuck the man!*' he suddenly swore, banging a fist against the wheel. 'Eaton was always a damned good source, but he's staying on the fence over this. I take it you picked up on the threat disguised as a warning?'

Laurie frowned.

'"If someone can give the order to kill once . . . they're more than likely to do it again,"' he quoted.

Fear blossomed in Laurie's head as she turned to look at him. He looked at her too, then someone behind tooted and he inched forward towards the train.

Neither of them spoke again until they were nose to tail inside the carriage with the engine turned off. As he selected another CD, and the haunting voice of Renata Scotto stole movingly into the car, Laurie was reminded of the journey over and how he'd teased her about talking in her sleep after. But she was too sobered by the words he'd just uttered to return to those light-hearted moments now.

He turned to look at her and the tension in his face lessened when he saw how anxious she was. Reaching for her hand he squeezed it, then held on to it as her eyes came up to his.

348

'It'll be all right,' he said softly.

She nodded. 'I know.'

He continued to watch her in a way that seemed to ease her from the threat of danger towards a place of safety just for being with him. His hand was still on hers; the air in the car was changing, becoming dense, as though charging with feeling. Her heart was starting to thud, and her lips parted as she took a breath.

He moved towards her, slowly, carefully, and a wealth of emotion began rising in her like a slow-motion rush of champagne. She stopped breathing, and lowered her eyes as his fingers came to her face. She could feel him so close; the male scent of him was moving all the way through her. There was a moment in which everything seemed to stop, then the feel of his lips on her forehead turned her heart inside out, and her hope into crushing disappointment. She didn't want this kind of kiss! Didn't he understand that? It wasn't enough. It made him a friend, or a brother and from him she wanted neither.

She turned her head away, not wanting him to see her frustration. It was on the tip of her tongue to tell him how she felt, to shout it at him even, but pride made her hold back. Apart from anything else they had the rest of this journey to get through, and the last thing she wanted was to be trapped in a car with him while he tried to deal with the embarrassment of her confession.

Then almost without thinking she turned to him and said, 'We have to talk.'

His expression gave nothing away, as he said, 'OK.'

'Not now. Not here. I'm just saying, we need to talk.'

He nodded.

She turned away again, still angry, with herself now as much as with him. But at least she'd admitted there was something to discuss. It would be much harder to draw back from it after that, and she didn't have to feel quite so cowardly for continuing to avoid it. Just, please God, he didn't try to take the initiative from here, because she really did need to be in control when she told him, *and* in a place from which she could escape with some dignity and ease.

*

Ava was alone in the house. Mitzi had returned to her own home in Laguna Beach and wouldn't be back until tomorrow. Ava could have gone too, but she'd stayed here because she'd wanted to sleep off the aftereffects of last night, which had begun with a movie première celebration at the Playboy Mansion, but though it had been star-studded and glamorous beyond belief, she couldn't remember anything especially outrageous happening. It had just been fun to be there, though maybe not as much as the party they'd gone on to, where Fabio sprinkled them in yet more star dust and they'd danced and danced until they couldn't stay upright any more. After that, the rest of the night and all of this morning had faded into more of a blur than a memory, and she didn't have much inclination to try to pull it into focus.

Now it was three in the afternoon and she couldn't stop crying. She didn't remember ever, even in the very worst moments of the past few months, feeling this bleak or alone. It was welling up around her like a sinister, smothering force; sucking her into an abyss of total darkness and despair. She needed Fabio and his star dust so badly it might actually be killing her. Or maybe she'd end up killing herself if she had to go on living with her own thoughts and the conversation she'd had with Georgie. A week had passed since, a week in which Fabio and his magic had been there constantly, setting her free from the fear, removing her from the need to act, even to think. Thank God for Fabio, because she might not be making it without him. But these in-between times, when she couldn't find him, were a torment she could hardly stand. It was as though opening that phone line to Georgie had unblocked some kind of channel and now all the hell of there was spewing all over the Utopia of here. They'd cancelled her book, Colin was divorcing her, and she still had no idea if the publisher was going to pay her. How was she going to pay Fabio if she didn't have any money? But it was OK. Theo had vowed to make the film, come what may, and though he wasn't offering much, the little he'd deposited into her account would help for a while. Theo. Theo. If only she'd kept it so that he was her sole link to England.

He said he'd be back in LA soon, and for her it couldn't be soon enough. He and Mitzi were everything to her now, and

350

she wanted them where she could see them, and touch them, and know that they were there for her too. But they weren't here now, and Fabio wasn't answering his phone. If he would she wouldn't be sitting here, on the edge of her unmade bed, clad only in a T-shirt, blinds drawn against the sun, address book open on the squashed pillow where a stranger's head had lain the previous night.

She listened to the ringing at the other end of the line – ringing and ringing. She tried to picture Heather Dance's house, and the phone, shrilling through the bedroom, the hall and the kitchen. She counted fourteen times then pushed down the connectors. She tried again and again, but there was still no reply. There was no answer from Heather's mother either. Tears streamed down her face, her hands shook as she turned over the pages in her book. There was another number; one she'd almost forgotten she had. She'd try that, because now, today, this minute, it was vital that she spoke to Heather Dance.

She dialled the other number. It was a different ringing sound this time, a friendly burble in contrast to the cold harshness of before. It burbled four times then Heather's Welsh voice said, 'Hello?'

Ava held her breath. Her hand was gripping the receiver so hard it hurt. She didn't know what to say. She shouldn't be doing this. It was madness, guaranteed to bring her even more pain – but who else could she talk to?

'Hello?' Heather said again. 'Is anyone there?'

A small sob escaped Ava's lips.

'Beth, is that you?' Heather said softly.

She nodded and more tears flowed down her cheeks. 'Yes,' she answered, hardly able to push her voice through the anguish. 'Yes, it is.'

Heather was quiet for a moment, then in her warm, mellifluous tones she said, 'I won't ask how you managed to find me, just tell me how you are.'

'I'm fine.' She clutched more tissues from the box beside her and dabbed her face. 'Have you . . . Have you seen Colin?' she asked through her tears.

'Only once.'

'Me too. Only once. Do you speak to him much?'

351

'Not now. More in the first few weeks. He's very worried about you. We all are.'

'I'm fine.' Grief was swelling so hard inside her it was as though it might break through her skin. 'Heather, I . . . I don't know how much more I can take.'

'Beth, you'll be all right,' Heather told her. 'You're stronger than you think.'

'Yes. Yes,' she choked, and pressed a hand to her mouth to stop herself howling. 'Colin's divorcing me, did he tell you?'

There was a pause before Heather said, 'Yes.'

Beth sobbed and her voice relayed her torment as she said, 'Did he have to do it this way?'

'He hasn't handled it well,' Heather agreed. 'He knows that. It's often those we love that we end up hurting the most.'

'If he loves me, then why's he doing this?'

Heather didn't answer.

'Because he loves you and Jessica more.' Beth's heart was exploding, her mouth opened wide in a silent scream of pain.

'Maybe he'll change his mind,' Heather said.

Please God, oh, please, please God, she cried inside.

Several minutes ticked by, until finally Heather said, 'Are you still there?'

'Yes,' Beth answered brokenly.

'How are you enjoying LA?'

Beth sniffed and wiped her nose. 'I love it, and I hate it,' she answered. 'It's not home; it's just a place to be until . . . until it's all over. People from the press keep wanting to talk to me.'

'I know. Me too.'

'I wish they'd leave me alone.'

'They will, eventually.' Heather paused, then said, 'The important thing for you to remember, Beth, is that you haven't done anything wrong. You've got to stop blaming yourself. There was nothing you could have done to prevent what happened.'

Beth was suddenly sobbing so hard it was a while before she could speak. 'Is that what Colin thinks too?' she said. 'That I'm blaming myself?'

'Yes. He knows you. He says it's what you would do, but we all know who's behind it.'

352

Beth nodded and pressed a fist to her burning cheek. 'I saw him, on the plane coming over here. He frightens me, Heather. I said things . . . things I shouldn't have said. I'm afraid he'll come after me now.'

'What did you say?'

'Nothing. It doesn't matter now. I have to go.' And abruptly she put down the phone.

Minutes later she was dressed and in the car, speeding along Mulholland Drive towards Beverly Glen. She knew where Fabio lived, in a smart little villa off Tulepo, so she'd go to his home, and if he wasn't there she'd just keep driving till she found him.

Chapter 21

As the tall iron gates to Georgie Cottle's home swung slowly open, Laurie peered out from under her umbrella, trying to spot the security camera. It had to be there somewhere, because she hadn't even rung the bell. However, the rain was so dense it was hard to see anything, so she quickly ran back to the taxi, handed over two twenty-pound notes, then started up the drive, battling a belligerent wind for possession of her umbrella.

By the time she got to the front door it was already open and an anxious Georgie Cottle, with an enormous biscuit-coloured dog, was waiting to greet her.

'You must be Laurie Forbes,' she said, struggling to hang on to the overexcited beast. 'Bruce told me you were coming. Dillon, will you be*have!*'

But Dillon didn't want to, and as Laurie shook out her umbrella and stooped to prop it in a corner of the porch, he landed his huge front paws square on her back, almost knocking her over.

'Dillon!' Georgie gasped. 'You bad boy.'

'It's OK,' Laurie laughed, tousling his ears. 'I'll just make a note that this place is OK to burgle while this old dafty's in charge.'

'You don't know how right you are,' Georgie groaned and, grabbing his collar again, she hauled him inside. 'He'll calm down in a minute,' she promised, as Laurie stepped over the threshold too. 'He just loves meeting new people. He's better once he knows you.'

'Well, I have to confess,' Laurie said, 'it's a much warmer welcome than I'd expected.'

Georgie immediately looked worried. 'Oh dear, I hope you haven't taken it personally, me not wanting to see you,' she said hurriedly. 'It was simply that I didn't want to upset Beth.'

'I understand,' Laurie assured her. 'So what changed your mind?' she asked, following her along the hall. 'Or is it Beth who's had a change of heart?' she added hopefully.

Seeming not to hear, Georgie said, 'I hope the kitchen's OK. My mother and Blake are in the sitting room, and the drawing room's a bit chilly today.' At which point both she and Dillon made a flying entry into the kitchen, which ended in a skidding halt at the table.

'This is fine,' Laurie said, trying not to laugh, though her stomach wasn't making quite the same effort with its rumbling, for the smell of freshly brewed coffee had just reached her, and the plate of shortbread biscuits and huge macaroons at the centre of the table, which Dillon obviously already knew about, had just caught her eye. She really must learn to eat breakfast and/or lunch before she came out, otherwise hunger was too distracting.

'Dillon, go to your basket,' Georgie commanded. Dillon stayed right where he was. 'Please, sit down and help yourself to biscuits,' she said to Laurie. 'My mother makes the macaroons. They're jolly good.'

'Thank you,' Laurie responded, shrugging off her backpack. 'You have a beautiful home,' she commented, sinking into a downy seat pad on one of the farmhouse chairs and sliding a macaroon on to a leaf-patterned china plate.

'It's been in Bruce's family for five generations,' Georgie responded, bringing two mugs of coffee to the table. 'His parents live at their farm in Kenya now, so he's acquired part of his inheritance early.'

'Mm, mm, mm,' Laurie muttered in response to the macaroon. '*This* is to die for.'

Georgie smiled. Then, tossing a biscuit into Dillon's basket and telling him again to lie down, she said, 'I hope you don't mind me saying, but you're younger than I expected. I'd managed to create this image of you being much older and rather ferocious, though I can't think why when I already knew what you looked like.'

Remembering their brief meeting at Beth Ashby's house, the day Ashby was arrested, Laurie said, 'You could be excused for thinking I'd grown horns since our first encounter, but I promise it was never my intention to upset or alienate Beth Ashby the way I seem to have. Quite the reverse, actually.'

Georgie looked down at her coffee. 'I'm sure,' she responded. 'But Beth has never had much liking for reporters.'

'Really? I'd have thought, with her husband being who he is, that some of her best friends would be reporters.'

Since Laurie's tone was ironic, Georgie smiled politely. 'I probably shouldn't tell you this,' she said, 'but she's always had a bit of an inferiority complex where his colleagues are concerned, and to be frank, they haven't always treated her well. They can be extremely condescending; I've even been there sometimes when it happens.'

Laurie's eyes rolled. 'Believe me, I know how she feels,' she replied. 'There's a group on the paper I work for who've done their level best to make my life a misery ever since I started. Any opportunity they get to treat me like an idiot, or shut me out, they take it.'

'So how do you handle it?'

'Not unlike the way Beth does, I try to pretend they're not there.'

Georgie looked down at her coffee. 'The problem is,' she said, 'as far as Beth's concerned you're one of them, which is why I feel so dreadful about doing this. She'd go berserk if she knew.'

'So what's happened to change your mind?'

Georgie's expression showed her unease, as she blinked a few times and avoided meeting Laurie's eyes. 'I had a message, on the answerphone,' she said finally. 'It was waiting last night when I got back from the health farm. It's terrible. So awful I can hardly bear to listen to it again.'

'I presume it was from Beth.'

Georgie nodded. 'I played it to Bruce over the phone, and he said I should let you listen to it, when you got here. So I'm trusting you because he does. I don't know if he's right, I just know I have to do something.' She got to her feet and went to the kitchen counter. 'I won't tell you anything before I play it,' she said. 'I just want you to listen, then tell me what you think.'

She pushed the button, there was a long beep followed by the sound of muffled laughing and music, then a loud, ecstatic female voice saying, 'Georgieeeeee! My darling, how are you? I love you. I love you. I love you. Where are you? You have to get yourself over here. You're missing all the fun. It's so wonderful, Georgie. Everything happens here. You'd absolutely adore Mitzi. She's so fantastic and she's dying to meet you. Oh, by the way, Italy's not happening yet. Theo wants us to stay in LA, do some more networking, so you've got to come over.' She hiccupped, then laughed. 'I want you to tell them all to fuck off about my book. Theo's making the movie anyway, so they can just go screw themselves. They're not getting to me that way. I know Marcus is going to come after me anyway, but do you know *what*? I couldn't care *less*. I know he's afraid of what I might know, and so he should be, because if he doesn't leave me alone I'll tell everyone. You can pass that on, Georgie. Tell him to leave me alone or he'll be sorry. And you can tell Colin I said that too. He can have his divorce, because I have got so many men here, just begging for it . . .' She shrieked and giggled, as though to confirm it. Then Georgie's eyes went down as Beth said, 'All the way, babe. Ooooh yes. I just love it. I love you too, Georgie. Honestly, you've got to come over. It's all sex and drugs and rock and roll . . . Tell my mother she's a bitch. Hah! Hah! I'm never coming back. I'm staying here for ever and ever and ever . . . Amen. Bye, my darling, call as soon as you can. I love you. If I were a man I'd want to be Bruce.'

Georgie turned off the machine and kept her eyes averted. Laurie could see how upset she was, confused and even angry. In the end she threw out her question like a challenge: 'She was more than just drunk, wasn't she?'

Laurie nodded. 'It certainly sounded like it,' she said.

'She's never taken drugs in her life,' Georgie snapped, coming back to the table. 'This is all so unlike her. She's changed so much since Colin's arrest – not that I blame her, it's a terrible thing to have to go through, but the way she is now . . .' She stopped, took a quick, nervous sip of coffee, then said, 'The name she wrote the book under, Ava Montgomery, that's who you were just listening to. It's as though she's taken Beth over. At first it really seemed to do her good, being someone who wasn't dependent on Colin. It was like an escape . . . But now it's like she's an impostor inside her own skin.' She put a hand to her head, as though unable to believe she'd just uttered such words. 'You know about the divorce, I take it?' she suddenly said.

Laurie nodded.

'Yes, well, she just mentioned it, didn't she? Dear God, I don't know why he's doing this. It doesn't make any sense when he's always been so protective of her, as though he couldn't bear anything to hurt her, even though there was no greater culprit than him. But he always used to try and hide it. He never rubbed her face in his affairs, or certainly not the way he did with Heather Dance.' She drank some more coffee. 'I don't understand why he did that. Bruce said it was to protect Heather Dance. But what about Beth? Why didn't he tell her himself, rather than let her find out like that? It was so cruel. If you saw what it did to her . . .'

'Why do you think he didn't tell her?' Laurie asked gently.

Georgie sighed and shook her head. 'Probably because like so many men he's a coward,' she answered. 'He didn't want to have to deal with her pain, so doing it this way he was off the hook. He knew, if he had to face her, he'd never be able to go through with it.' She looked at Laurie. 'It's possible to love someone yet not want to be married to them any more,' she said, 'especially when you have a child by somebody else. It was that that hurt the most, of course.'

'Of course,' Laurie echoed, wishing she could take out her notebook, but Bruce had advised her not to turn her visit into an interview, so it had to stay where it was. 'What about you and Bruce?' she asked. 'Did you know about Heather Dance before all this?'

'No, thank God. I'd have hated knowing something like that without Beth knowing too. I'd have had to tell her. As a matter of fact it was me who told her in the end, because Bruce called to warn me that it was about to come out in the paper.'

Laurie watched the concern in Georgie's face and thought how fortunate Beth Ashby was to have a friend who cared this much. Obviously it said something about Beth too, that she could inspire this kind of love and loyalty. 'On the tape,' she said, picking up her coffee, 'when Beth claimed to know something about Marcus Gatling . . . do you have any idea what that might be?'

Georgie shook her head. 'When she first told me about it she said she was just winding him up. Now she's saying she does know something. To be honest – well, I've been wondering for a while now if she was holding something back.'

Laurie's heartbeat quickened. 'Why do you say that?' she prompted.

'I'm not sure. It's hard to put into words. It's just a feeling really. The way she's been behaving . . . There were times, even before she left, when the change in her was so noticeable it was like having a stranger in the house. Of course, I never said anything. I suppose I was encouraging the Ava thing, because it made her seem so much happier and on top of things. The blonde hair really suited her, and the male attention she was getting . . .' She laughed without humour. 'You'd have thought no one had ever looked at her before, but that's not true. She's always been attractive, she just never seemed to know it. Or use it. She was married to Colin and to my certain knowledge she never looked at another man. Until she became Ava.'

'What about the book? Have you ever read it?'

Georgie shook her head. 'She's always said that it's not based on her, or Colin, or their lives, but then there was that strange remark she made about Sophie Long being a sacrificial lamb, like someone in the book. Did Bruce tell you about that?'

Laurie nodded. 'She didn't expand on it at all?'

'Only to say that Colin, or Marcus Gatling, could explain it. But Colin's pleading ignorance, and who on earth's going to ask Marcus Gatling?'

Knowing Elliot would, given half a chance, Laurie said, 'Has she ever talked about what happened to Sophie Long?'

'Yes, of course. For weeks we hardly talked about anything else.'

'She was at home writing when it happened, wasn't she?'

Georgie nodded. 'You know that. You were the first to arrive after it happened.'

359

'What was she writing, if the book had already been submitted?'

'Another book, I suppose. I'm not really sure.'

'Did she know where her husband was that day?'

'It came out at the time,' Georgie reminded her, 'that they'd had a bit of a tiff, so he wasn't staying at home.'

'So she wouldn't have known where he was, or what he was doing?'

'I wouldn't imagine so. I mean, she certainly wouldn't have known he was planning to kill someone.'

Laurie dropped her eyes. 'No, of course not,' she responded quietly. 'I'm sorry.' Then after a pause: 'Do you know if she saw anyone else that morning? Someone say, from her husband's office?'

'That's not very likely. I've just told you how much she dislikes his colleagues, so she's never really mixed with them unless he was there too.'

'But someone could have dropped in to see her. Or asked her to meet them somewhere?'

'As I said, it's not very likely.'

'She did go out though, didn't she?'

'Just to the end of the road to get some more paper for her printer. The police have got the receipt.'

She was becoming defensive again, which made Laurie wonder if she was as reassured by the paper shop alibi as she'd like to be. Certainly Beth had gone there, for the date and time on the receipt proved it, and the shop assistant recalled her. However, the very fact that those details coincided so neatly with the estimated time of the murder could, to some people's minds, suggest that the alibi was deliberate, rather than chance. And how long had Beth Ashby gone out for? The receipt certainly didn't tell anyone that, or if she'd met someone while she was out – though if she'd been gone for more than a few minutes the cleaner would obviously have noticed. All kinds of scenarios were buzzing around in Laurie's mind now, though, for the moment at least, she was unable to find one that offered any kind of explanation for what Beth had said about Marcus Gatling on the tape.

'Do you mind if I ask you a very blunt question?' she said.

'You can try,' Georgie answered.

'Do you believe Colin Ashby killed Sophie Long?'

Georgie flushed and looked awkwardly off towards the dog, who was now snoring loudly. 'I don't know,' she replied. 'Sometimes yes, sometimes no. I think that's how it is for Beth too. It's what's driving her into the kind of state she was in when she left that message. The not knowing, having it go round and round in her head, until it must be driving her crazy.'

Laurie nodded. That was certainly one possible reason for Beth's strange state of mind. 'Has Bruce told you anything about the syndicate that Marcus Gatling's involved with?' she asked.

Georgie nodded.

'Has Beth ever mentioned it?'

'Never.'

'Which doesn't necessarily mean she doesn't know about it?'

'No, I suppose not, but we usually tell each other everything.'

Laurie noted the echo of Sophie Long's mother. 'Do you think you could ask her about it?' she said.

Georgie looked doubtful. 'I can try,' she said, 'but I'm pretty sure she doesn't know . . .' She stopped, looked down at her empty cup, then said, 'You think it's what she might be hiding?'

'It could be,' Laurie answered.

'So do you think they will go after her? Do they mean her some harm?'

'It's possible,' Laurie responded.

'Oh God, it's all so sinister and horrible,' Georgie groaned, burying her face in her hands. 'To think of anyone hurting her . . .'

'That's what we're trying to avoid,' Laurie reminded her. 'So please try to get her to tell you what she knows.'

Georgie nodded. 'If she's taking drugs . . . Do you think she's more likely to talk when she's high? Should I try asking then?'

'It might be an idea,' Laurie agreed. 'And while you're at it, you should probably try to persuade her to come home.'

'I'd love to,' Georgie responded. 'But you heard what she

said, so I wouldn't hold out much hope on that front – at least not until after that film's been made.'

'But it's worth a try.'

'Of course.'

Laurie picked up her bag.

Georgie got to her feet and stood behind her chair. 'Bruce said you wouldn't splash details of the tape all over the front page,' she said. 'You won't, will you?'

Laurie shook her head. 'Not at all,' she answered. 'But it would be very helpful if you'd let me take it so I can make a copy.'

Georgie looked uncertain, then, turning to the machine, she clicked it open. 'Here,' she said. 'I'm trusting you because I really do believe you want to help her. Please don't prove me wrong.'

'I won't,' Laurie assured her. 'I promise.'

As she boarded the train back to London Laurie was on the phone to Elliot. 'Something that's really bothering me,' she said, keeping her voice low as she turned into a first-class carriage and began edging down the aisle, 'is if they suspect Beth of knowing more than she should, why haven't they just got rid of her the way they did with Sophie? They, by the way, could include Colin, so that's not me writing him off as a suspect.'

'I'd say,' he responded, 'that Mrs Ashby suddenly dead at this time would create a great deal more problems than Mrs Ashby alive, whatever she might know.'

'Because,' Laurie responded, moving into a window seat, 'coming so soon after Sophie's sudden departure, it would inevitably spark off all kinds of enquiries that they wouldn't be able to avoid with as much ease as they are now. Yes, I see what you mean.'

'It could also,' he continued, 'weaken the case against Ashby, because if his wife vanished now his alibi couldn't be more cast iron, and if he didn't kill her, then maybe he didn't kill Sophie Long either.'

'Mmm, good point,' Laurie responded, as the stationmaster blew his whistle and waved to the driver. 'Which gets us where?'

'To the reason why Beth Ashby is still breathing, and an increased reason to believe that Ashby might well have been framed.'

'Mm,' she said again. Then scowling discouragement at a woman who looked about to plonk herself down opposite, she said, 'OK. Next. I know we've been over this a hundred times already, but once again, Beth Ashby going out to get paper at more or less the same time as the murder . . . The alibi's just so convenient.'

'But if science has failed to put her at the scene of the crime, suspicions certainly won't.'

'And then there's the cleaner who says she was there the whole time, except those few minutes, of course. What about the fibres that remain a mystery? Obviously they've ruled out Beth Ashby, but do we know about Heather Dance?'

'She has a rock-solid alibi,' he reminded her.

Laurie sighed. 'On duty at the play group,' she muttered. 'OK, this is right out there now, probably completely off the wall, but you don't suppose the two of them got together and paid someone to kill Sophie and make it look as though Colin did it? And maybe that's why Beth popped out at that time, to make the pay-off?'

Elliot was quiet for a moment. 'I guess it's possible,' he said, sounding as doubtful as Laurie felt. 'But first of all, *why* would they want to frame Colin like that? And secondly, where would Gatling and the syndicate fit in?'

'I've got no idea on either count,' she responded. 'I'm just struggling to come up with something more than the flimsy suspicions we've currently got. Where are you?'

'On my way to a meeting in the City.'

'Something big?'

'Promising.'

'Good. Are we all getting together later?'

'Seven. At The Grapes,' and the line went dead.

Rolling her eyes, she clicked off her own phone, then took out her notebook and headset. Now was as good a time as any to start jotting down details of what was on the tape, as well as what she'd discussed with Georgie Cottle. It was a shame she wouldn't be able to quote directly from the tape, but there were ways round it that would still paint the same picture, so she wasn't unduly concerned.

She was still making notes when several more people got on the train at Didcot. She watched them absently as they moved down the carriage, breaking off into various seats, jamming luggage between the seat backs, unclipping briefcases or unfolding papers. Her mind was so full of imagined goings on in Sophie Long's flat, on a street near Beth Ashby's old Fulham home, in the offices of Marcus Gatling, and even in Ava Montgomery's new LA life, that she barely noticed the man who slipped into the seat opposite. She merely returned to her notes and jotted down a reminder to try interviewing Mitzi Bower or Theo Kennedy about Beth Ashby's book, since they were probably the only source now of finding out what it was about.

Yawning as the train pulled out of the station, she was just taking off her headset when the man opposite her said, 'Hello, Laurie.'

Her eyes had yet to move to his face, but she instinctively knew who it was, and already she was reacting.

'How are you?' he asked, adjusting his horn-rimmed glasses.

As fear erupted in her heart she looked wildly round at the other passengers. They were all behind papers or attached to phones, oblivious to her, but at least they were there.

'How was Mrs Cottle?' he said, smiling.

She turned back to him. Her mind was in turmoil; she couldn't make herself think.

He continued to smile. 'What did the two of you discuss?' he enquired.

She didn't answer. She didn't know what to say.

'What did you discuss?' he asked again, his tone transporting her back to the relentless questioning she'd undergone at the house in Suffolk.

She looked at him, and reminded herself that they were in a public place. There was nothing he could do with all these people around. 'That's between me and Georgie,' she responded, sounding far more composed than she felt.

The smile never wavered. 'Believe me, that's not a clever reply,' he told her.

Her hands were shaking, her whole body felt weak. She

wanted to scream at him to get away from her, but she was too afraid of what he might do. 'We talked about a lot of things,' she said.

He pushed up his glasses again. 'Please don't think, because we're on a train, that pressure can't be exerted,' he said in his chillingly benign tone.

Anger made a sudden break through the fear. 'Are you threatening me?' she challenged, hoping to catch someone's attention. 'Did you just threaten me?' She was shocked by how forceful she sounded when inside she was like jelly.

'I merely stated a fact,' he replied, and reaching into his inside pocket he took out a mobile phone.

For one horrifying moment she'd thought it was going to be a gun, and as he laid it on the table, just a few inches from hers, she could still feel the frenzied pounding of her heart.

Her eyes moved between the phone and him, trying to work out its significance. He merely watched her, then after a while he picked it up, pushed two buttons and put it to his ear. 'OK,' he said into it, and rang off.

As alarm smothered her confusion she looked round again, trying to think what to do. Who had he been talking to? What was OK? Was there someone else here on the train? Were they planning to do something to her? Oh God, how was she going to get out of here?

'Did you make a tape of your interview with Mrs Cottle?' he asked.

Her eyes moved back to his.

He waited.

'It wasn't an interview,' she replied.

'Is that what you're writing?' he said, nodding towards her notebook.

She looked down at it.

'Were you listening to the tape? Is that why you're wearing a headset?'

Her eyes went back to his face. 'I don't believe this,' she cried. 'Just who the hell do you think you are, accosting me on a train, harassing me, bullying me –'

'Why don't you just hand over the tape and I'll be gone.' His hand came out, waiting to receive it.

She glared at him, disguising her fear with fury. 'Maybe

you'd like me to pull the emergency cord,' she said through her teeth.

'By all means. But it won't help you keep the notebook and tape.'

His certainty was unnerving her badly.

'The tape,' he repeated.

His hand remained cupped on the table. She looked at it and felt a horrible welling of impotence. Hardly an hour had passed since she'd promised Georgie that the tape would be safe with her, and already it wasn't. She glanced up at the red emergency handle.

He looked up too, then gestured towards it, as though inviting her to continue.

More fear crowded into her heart. She didn't understand it. Pulling the cord couldn't help him, yet the threat didn't bother him. For one wildly paranoid moment she wondered if everyone in the carriage was with him, but that was absurd. This was a public train for God's sake. So he was bluffing. He was pretending to be unconcerned about the cord, so why not call the bluff?

She was about to get to her feet when her mobile suddenly rang. She looked at it, hesitated, then grabbed it before he could. 'Laurie Forbes,' she barked.

'Laurie. It's Dad.'

'Dad!' She glared at the man, as though mention of her father would make him back off.

'Darling, there's a gentleman here claiming that you're withholding important information regarding a murder case.'

She blinked as her own weapon came back to hit her between the eyes.

'Is it true, darling?'

'Dad, listen . . .' But she didn't know what to say. The horror of what was happening was closing around her like a siege.

'Laurie, I know you're very dedicated to your job, but if you can help solve a murder, darling –'

'I know, Dad. I know. It's just . . . Who is the man? Did he give you his name?'

'He's Chief Inspector Cormand, from Scotland Yard.'

Suddenly she wanted to scream at her father, tell him to wake up and realize that it was hardly normal for someone to come to him if they wanted information from her. Didn't he realize he was being used? That even as he spoke he was being held hostage in his own home? In truth she hoped to God he didn't, for it would scare him half to death.

She looked at the man facing her and felt a near murderous rage sweep right the way through her. 'Tell the inspector,' she said through clenched teeth to her father, 'that his colleague has the information he's looking for.'

She heard her father relay the message, then another voice came on to the line saying, 'Perhaps I could speak to my colleague.'

As Laurie handed over the phone, she dug into her bag and extracted the tape from the machine. She had no choice but to hand it over now. She just hoped to God it was enough to make them leave her parents alone.

'Everything's satisfactory,' the man said into the phone as he took the tape and scooped up the notebook too.

Laurie snatched the phone as he passed it back. 'Hello? Dad? Are you there?' she said tersely, but the line was dead. She looked at the man. 'If anything happens to him –'

'It won't,' he assured her. 'Unless we find you've cheated us in some way.'

Frustration was roiling around inside her, making her want to rant and rage and tear at his face, but fear held her back.

'Tell Elliot Russell,' he said, getting to his feet, 'that he's doing himself no favours going down the road he's on.'

'Why don't you tell him yourself?' she spat. 'Or is it only women you terrorize?'

His smile was chilling as he said, 'Let me assure you, Laurie, you have no exclusivity on our attention.' And slipping the tape and notebook into his pocket he turned and walked off down the carriage.

The instant he'd vanished she speed-dialled her father. 'Dad? Are you OK?' she demanded breathlessly. 'Is he gone?'

'Mum's just seeing him out. Are you all right? You sound flustered.'

'No. I'm fine. I'm fine. I just don't like the idea of people coming to bother you, when they should be coming straight to me.'

'Yes, well, I must say I found it a bit odd, but I expect they didn't realize you're not living at home any more. So you've given them what they wanted?'

'I have. Did he say anything else? He didn't threaten you or anything, did he?'

'No, of course not. He's a policeman, Laurie. Policemen don't go into people's homes and start threatening them for no reason.'

'No. No. You're right,' she said, forcing herself to calm down. 'I'm just . . . Well, maybe I should come home, make sure you're all right.'

'What on earth for? I told you, we're fine. Just you avoid getting on the wrong side of the law again. It never pays.'

'OK. I'm sorry. I didn't mean to get you involved. It was such a little thing.'

'Obviously not to them. So next time, let them be the judge and spare yourself this kind of upset. Mum's back now, do you want to say hello?'

After a quick, reassuring exchange with her mother, she rang off and called Elliot.

'What time's the train due in?' he asked, when she'd finished telling him what had happened.

'Five forty.'

'I'll be at the station to meet you.'

When she got there, right on time, he was waiting at the end of the platform.

'Are you all right?' he said, as she reached him.

Feeling the way she did, she wished she could just throw herself into his arms. 'Yes. I'm fine,' she said, tears suddenly welling up in her eyes and choking her voice. 'Sorry, I'm not crying really. It's just a reflex action. It's because it was my parents.'

'Of course,' he said. 'Are you sure they're all right?'

'They said they were. I think I should go and make certain.'

'Leave it for a day or two,' he advised. 'You'll only worry them if you go rushing over there now. Stan's dispatched one of his colleagues to watch the place for a while.' He was looking around the crowded station. 'Did you see him get off the train?'

Looking around too, she shook her head.

His eyes were waiting for hers as she turned back, making her have to fight another longing for his embrace.

'Do you think it was a genuine policeman who went to see them?' she asked, as he took her arm and began steering her through the crowd.

'Certainly I know Cormand's name,' he answered. 'And technically speaking they're right, it could be said that you were withholding information.'

Her head came up in surprise. 'Whose side are you on?' she demanded.

Laughing he opened the car door and waited for her to get in.

'God, I *hate* it that someone can do that,' she seethed as he started the engine, 'and on a train of all places. I felt so . . . powerless!'

'You did the right thing handing the tape over,' he assured her. 'You presumably remember what was on it?'

'Yes, I do,' she answered, her heart sinking like lead. 'That's the worst part of it. It wasn't one of my tapes, it was Georgie Cottle's, with a phone message from Beth Ashby outright admitting, even threatening, to go public with what she knows about Gatling if he doesn't leave her alone.'

Elliot's alarm showed. 'Did she say what it was?' he asked.

'No.'

'Then that could be a problem.'

'Don't, I feel terrible enough,' she groaned. 'Absolutely dreadful in fact.'

'But you didn't have a choice,' he reminded her forcefully. 'There's no knowing how far they're prepared to go with this, and there's no point running the risk of your father's health to find out.'

As the absolute dread of that prospect shuddered through her she fell silent, for she didn't want even to think about it, never mind discuss it. 'I shouldn't have gone without Stan,' she mumbled after a while.

'Yes, why did you?' he challenged.

Her eyes slid sideways towards the passing traffic. Should

she tell him it was to prove to herself that she wasn't afraid to go somewhere alone? But no, she couldn't, because if he knew how badly this was all getting to her he'd make her give it up and that was the last thing she wanted.

Fortunately his phone rang then, and by the time he finished the call he seemed to have forgotten the question.

'You know, I don't think I'm feeling up to The Grapes tonight,' she said pressing her fingers to her temples.

'That's good, because it's not where we're going.'

She turned to him in surprise.

'There's a new place, just opened near the Opera House,' he said. 'I thought we'd go there instead.'

'What do you mean? Is everyone going?'

'No, just us.'

She had an immediate physical reaction to that, which, thank God, he couldn't see. 'What is it? A pub?'

'No. A restaurant.'

She frowned. 'So we're going for dinner?'

'That's the general idea in a restaurant.'

'Why?'

'Because we both need to eat? Don't we?'

She nodded. 'Yes. I suppose so.'

'And we also,' he added, 'need to talk.'

Her heart immediately turned over, for though she might like to tell herself it was about the story, she knew it was a follow-up to what she'd said on the way back from France. She was thinking fast, trying to come up with a way out of it. She'd never dreamt he'd bring it up again this soon; had even dared to hope he might have forgotten it altogether, but obviously he hadn't and now all reasonable excuses were eluding her. Unless she claimed to be too shaken up by what had happened on the train. Which she was. It had been horrible – so bad, in fact, it had completely stolen her appetite. Not only that, it had actually made her nauseous. So no, what she needed to do was go home and have a quiet evening alone, burn some essential oils, listen to soft music, soak in the bath, slide into bed early . . .

But just over an hour later she was in a discreet, candlelit corner thanking a waiter as he passed her a menu, and agreeing they should go straight to wine.

As it turned out there was no opportunity to talk over dinner. His phone hardly stopped ringing and, thanks to the rowdy group that took over the next table, he had to keep going outside to take the calls. It also meant that what small snatches they did spend together, they could hardly hear each other above the din, so in the end they passed on dessert and coffee and ran back through the rain to the car.

'Sorry it didn't quite work out,' he said, as they drove down through Covent Garden and turned on to the Strand.

'The food was good,' she responded. 'And the wine. I take it from all those phone calls that something's happening.'

'Quite a lot actually,' he confirmed. 'But the details are changing by the minute.'

'It's moving forward, though?'

'I'd say so. Still no paper trail of any substance, but the targeting of the euro is emerging as a five- possibly six-year strategy that's due for completion around January or February 2003.'

'Meaning?'

'Tens of billions for those who stage the run, and that's just on the currency play.'

'What about introducing the US dollar into Britain?'

'Still no evidence of that, but we won't rule it out. One way or another it'll be part of the story, either as a red herring we were thrown, or as a fact.'

'So what's stopping us going to print right away?' she said.

'Same as always. We're still hoping to root out evidence to prove that the syndicate actually exists, *and* who's operating it. If we don't get that evidence by December, we'll go anyway, because the speculation alone will kill the strategy. If we can tie in the real truth of why Sophie Long was murdered, and even confirm who did, or didn't do it, all the better.'

She nodded, and turned to look out of the window. This conversation was merely a variation on one they'd had several times this past week, and though she'd stepped back from the financial investigation herself, concentrating more on the Colin Ashby/Sophie Long side of the story, she was naturally interested to know how his side of things was progressing. Tonight, though, she was preoccupied with the confession she was working up to, for despite the evening's distractions, she knew it was unlikely he'd forgotten their decision to talk, and though she wasn't looking forward to it one bit, she wasn't going to put it off any longer either. The problem now, though, was knowing how to begin.

They drove on in silence, through the dark, almost deserted City streets, where pools of white streetlight shone out of wet roads, and the wind carried stray litter along the pavements and gutter. The radio was tuned to a classical station, but the music was turned down low, so she could hear the hum of the heater above it. From the corner of her eye she could see his hands on the wheel. She'd always loved his hands, for the way they were both elegant and masculine, seeming to exude strength and ruggedness as well as tenderness and care. They could almost be a metaphor for the man himself, she thought, then averted her eyes as shame swept through her for the way she'd tried to turn him into a monster. Headstrong, arrogant, impatient and occasionally ruthless he might be, but his sense of what was right would never have allowed him to do to anyone what she'd done to him. It was what made her transference of guilt so unacceptable, because she'd known he'd take it, and even now, no matter what she said, he'd probably still want to shoulder it, because he'd never agree that her role in Lysette's death could negate his. Maybe it couldn't, but that wouldn't change how deeply he was going to resent, or even despise her when he discovered how, in her guilty and cowardly heart, she'd hidden the truth of that last phone call, and encouraged the world to believe that it was his cruelty and neglect that had finally pushed Lysette over the edge, when there was no doubt in her mind, if she'd let Lysette come to her that night, she'd be alive today.

Suddenly pushing aside the dread of his reaction, she took a breath and said, 'You should know that it wasn't your fault Lysette killed herself. It was mine, because she called me after you threw her out that night and I wouldn't see her. She begged me to let her come over, but I just kept on refusing. I was terrible to her, cruel and unfeeling. She couldn't bear to be alone while you were with another woman, and I couldn't bear her to be with me.'

She stopped, tense and fearful, eyes fixed on an unfocused place ahead. 'After,' she said, pushing her voice over the strain in her heart, 'when they told me she was dead, I wanted to die too. All I could hear was her pleading with me to listen, and me saying no. Now I'd never be able to hear her again, never be able to say yes. I can't tell you how terrible it was. Nothing had ever felt like that before, and I know it never will again. I wanted to punish myself in the worst possible way, but I didn't know how. I couldn't do to my parents what she'd done, though God knows I wanted to. I was so angry, and desperate. I needed someone else to blame, or something that would allow me to hide from the truth, and pretend that last call had never happened. I never told anyone about it. Not until the police traced it to me, did I ever even admit she'd made it, and then all I said was that she'd told me you'd thrown her out because you had another woman. But it didn't stop there, because once I realized that people were angry with you, I saw how I could avoid the blame if I told them you'd actually said she should go ahead and kill herself, because if that was what she wanted at least it would get her out of your life. So I told them. I was suffering so much, and I wanted you to suffer too. I wanted everyone to blame you, because I hated you . . . My sister was dead because of you. You'd found another woman and Lysette and I . . . We didn't matter any more. We were history for you, so I wanted everyone to despise you for what you'd done to us.'

She stopped again. A few minutes ago they'd pulled up outside Andrew and Stephen's house, but he hadn't turned off the engine, or even released it from the gears. She turned to look at him. His face was lost in shadow, so there was no way of knowing what he was thinking, but though she longed to know, she dreaded it too. If only he'd turn off the engine, at least it would be a sign he wanted her to continue.

In the end she said, 'I felt so many things back then that I'm ashamed of now. I used them to make myself hate you, and punish you, for things that just weren't your fault. I told myself that if you hadn't come into our lives none of it would have happened. I was so torn apart by my own guilt, and loss, that no one else mattered, and as long as I blamed you I could avoid blaming myself –' She broke off abruptly and felt the tension press harder into her head. 'I did, and thought, some terrible things,' she said. 'I can't change them now, but I need to tell you about them, so that you don't have to go on living with a guilt that's not yours.'

In the silence that followed she could hear her heart pounding above the patter of rain on the roof, and the low purr of the engine. The windows were steaming; the music was a thin haunting wail of viola. She couldn't say any more. She needed him to respond now, even if it was to tell her to get out. Then realizing that his silence was probably saying just that, she pushed open the door and stepped out into the drizzling rain. She looked down at him, but he didn't look back.

'I'm sorry,' she whispered brokenly.

Her heart was so heavy, and her throat so tight, that she didn't even try to say more. She simply closed the door, walked down the short front path, and took out her keys. She expected to hear the engine rev up as he drove away, but he was still there, sitting alone with the terrible feelings she'd just left him with. She desperately wanted to go back, but she forced herself not to look round. It was up to him now. There was no more she could do, so she let herself into the house, closed the door and leaned back against it, waiting for the sound of his car, as it drove off down the street. When it came, she sank to the floor, hugging her knees to her chest, and burying her face to stifle the sound of her pain. But no matter how much he despised her now, it was never going to compare with how much she despised herself.

Feeling the cat rub against her, she scooped it up and drew it in close. Despair and anguish wrenched at her heart, as she remembered all her jealousy and self-torment, and relived those terrible early days of grief and shock. This never-ending guilt, combined with his rejection, was no less than she deserved, and who could blame him for driving away when she'd just told him how hard she'd tried to make people hate him? She hadn't succeeded, but it was enough that she'd been malicious and dishonest enough to try. How disgusted he must be by her now, knowing how cowardly and cruel she really was.

Letting the cat go, she wrapped her arms round her head and tried to imagine what it was going to be like from here.

Could they continue working together? They were so embroiled in this story now, that neither one of them would want to let go, and in truth she was glad, for it meant that on one level it would keep them together. On all others, she had no idea what would happen. She'd hoped they would talk, that somehow they'd clear the air in a way that would help them eventually to forgive and forget, then finally move on. But now they were in this limbo, with only half the truth spoken, no anger or recriminations aired, no explanations given, nor apologies or forgiveness offered. It was all so unfinished, yet he'd given her no encouragement to go further, had shown no willingness to keep her in the car, or come into the house with her.

Getting to her feet, she was about to go into the bedroom when she heard a car coming down the street. She stood very still, hoping and praying, fearing and dreading. But it was him, she knew it; she just didn't know what this might mean.

The night fell into silence as the engine died. Then she heard the car door closing and his footsteps on the path. She walked to the door and opened it before he could knock.

For a moment he only looked at her. Then, reaching for her, he pulled her into his arms. 'I'm sorry,' he whispered, holding her tight. 'I'm sorry I drove away. Sorry that you've had to go through what you have. It's been harder for you than anyone. I know that.'

'No, it's me who should be sorry,' she said, clinging to him as he tightened his embrace. 'What I did to you, the way I let you take the blame –'

'Was understandable. You were in pain and grief, you needed to lash out, and I should have realized it sooner.'

He took her inside and closed the door. Then leading her through to the bedroom, he lay down on the bed with her, and continued to hold her. 'We needed to do this a long time ago,' he said into the darkness.

'Yes,' she whispered, her voice muffled by his shoulder, her senses swimming in so many emotions it wasn't possible for one to dominate the others.

They lay quietly for a long, long time, feeling the strength and comfort of each other, as the pain and need of the past year surfaced in their hearts.

In the end, she said, 'Can you forgive me?'

'Of course. Why do you think I'm here?' Then drawing back to look at her in the soft shades of moonlight, he said, 'Have you never discussed any of this with your parents?'

'No. But I should. They're ready to forgive you, and I want them to know that you weren't to blame. It's me –'

'Sssh,' he said, lifting a hand to her face. 'No one's to blame. I know it's hard, and I haven't done too well with it myself, but hearing you blame yourself makes me realize that what's really important is understanding and forgiving, and that includes forgiving Lysette.'

She nodded and closed her eyes. 'You're right, I do need to forgive her, because I've been so angry with her. But I loved her so much, and I didn't feel I had the right to be angry when I'd let her down so badly, and when I knew she'd forgive me anything.' She took a breath, then covered his hand with her own. 'She was so precious to me, to us all, and she loved us so much that I still can't believe she'd hurt us like that.'

'Stop,' he said gently. 'We've survived it, and we're here. As your father said at the funeral, the only way past this is through it. And now we're coming through. There are always going to be things we regret, but knowing her as you did, can you honestly believe she'd want you to go on suffering the way you are? She didn't kill herself to hurt you, or me, or anyone, she did it to end the torment of being here at all. She couldn't cope with the world's tragedies, or the cold brutality of people. It confused her. You know that. All she ever wanted was everyone to be happy, and love one another.'

'She wasn't capable of wishing anyone anything else. Even if it caused her pain, she'd still want someone to be happy.'

'Especially you,' he said.

Swallowing hard, she turned to sit up and hugged her knees. She felt dazed by what was happening; caught up in grief, yet so weakened by other emotions that she hardly knew what she was feeling. 'Did you ever love her?' she asked, resting her cheek on her arms and staring at the wall.

'Of course. It was impossible not to.'

When she tilted her head down, she could see him. 'She adored you.'

376

'Which was why it was so hard living with her. She refused to see my faults, just blinded herself to everything that wasn't good, as though it would make me as pure in spirit as she was.'

She smiled mistily. 'She used to say the same about you, that you were hard to live with.'

'I'm sure that's true, but probably worse with her, because when the time came, which it did long before she died, I just couldn't make her let go. God knows I tried, but I just couldn't make her understand that there was no future for us.'

'The other woman –'

'There was no other woman. It was all I could think of to make her accept it was over.'

Laurie's eyes closed as her heart burned with all that had resulted from the lie. But, of course, there was no way he could have known it would end the way it had, even though Lysette had threatened it. After all, she'd made the same threat during that last phone call to her sister, and Laurie hadn't believed her either. So had she done it to show them both? No. It simply wasn't in Lysette's nature to do something so cruel, or certainly not consciously.

Lying back down beside him she looked into his face and felt the enormity of her feelings swelling inside her. She wanted to touch him, yet was afraid to. She was so raw and fragile, as though she might break apart. 'What do you think about, when you think about her?' she asked.

He smiled and looked past her as though able to see his own thoughts. 'Dandelions,' he said. 'She was so delicate, and ethereal, that sometimes I used to think that, like a dandelion, she might just float away.'

Laurie smiled shakily. 'We always used to call her the fairy when we were young. Mum even made her some wings once.'

'I've seen the photos,' he reminded her. 'And I've seen them of you too. The little tomboy in her tree house, or helping Dad under the car, riding a bike that was too big, and showing off a trout she'd landed all by herself.'

She laughed and rolled her eyes.

He touched her face, smoothing her jaw with his thumb.

'Yes, I loved Lysette,' he said, 'but in many ways it was like loving a child whose expectations you could never live up to.'

She continued to look at him, wondering if he was going to say more, longing for him to, and allowing her eyes to show the needs of her heart and her body. She could feel his breath on her face, his fingers touching her, moving into her hair. His eyes were searching her face, and her lips parted as she took a breath. Then her heart seemed to stop as, pulling her to him, he covered her mouth with his own and kissed her with more tenderness, more feeling than she'd ever known. There was nothing else in the world beyond the sheer beauty and intimacy that was embracing them; nothing stronger than the need for more as it flowed through her in silent currents of desire. She heard the moan of her own voice echo in his throat as he pulled her closer, and his mouth increased its pressure. The longing inside her was so pure, yet febrile, she could hardly contain it.

When finally he let her go it was as though she'd just been released from a fast-flowing current. Their eyes remained on each other's, seeming to drink in the moment until, smiling, she said, 'What are you thinking?'

A few seconds ticked by as he continued to look at her. 'I'm thinking,' he responded, 'that I should go now.'

Shock and disappointment seared through her. 'You don't have to,' she said before she could stop herself.

He smiled, pressed his lips to her forehead and got up from the bed.

She got up too, desperate to hide her confusion, stunned by the unexpectedness of this when he'd just kissed her the way he had.

'Don't blame yourself any more,' he said gently. 'Let it go now. It's time to live your life.'

His words were like bludgeons on her heart that only moments ago had been so full of hope. She nodded, and somehow forced herself to smile. 'Thanks,' she said, and immediately wished she hadn't. She just wanted him to go now; to leave her alone with this excruciating shame before she did something to compound it even further.

When they reached the door he tried to tilt her face up so he could see it, but she moved her head aside.

'We've both got a lot of thinking to do,' he said.

Inside she was screaming. *Just go! Don't keep standing there giving me even more false hope that you already have.*

When at last she closed the door behind him, she took herself back into the bedroom and stared down at the tousled bed. She could hardly believe what had happened. What a fool! What a pathetic, self-deluding idiot! How was she ever going to face him again? She didn't even want to think about what must be going through his mind now; it was all just too humiliating to bear. She covered her face with her hands. This was unthinkable, insufferable, and the fact that Rhona had made the mistake too was no comfort at all.

Going into the bathroom she looked at her face in the mirror. It was pale and drawn, and dampened by tears. She shook her head in despair. Had she really been so stupid? Had she honestly believed they'd just fall into each other's arms declaring love and forgiveness, then start out for the sunset, as though some sudden and miraculous healing had taken place? She had to get a grip on reality here; force herself to be rational and do what she could to rescue some dignity from the shame. If she didn't, there was just no way she could continue with the story, and hard as it might be to carry on seeing him now, she just wasn't prepared to give it up. And besides, she didn't really have to feel quite so bad, for she hadn't actually come right out and told him how she felt. OK, he probably sensed it, but it had taken two to make that kiss happen, and he was the one who'd initiated it, not her. So what was she supposed to be thinking now?

Chapter 22

Marcus Gatling was standing at a wide, mesh-covered window, looking out over the undulating splendour of the vast green veldt that formed part of the highly exclusive, and privately owned game reserve, whose sprawling acreage curled itself around the far south-western borders of the Kruger National Park. On the near shore of the watering hole below, a small herd of impala was drinking from the murky waters, while the interested eyes and snout of a hippopotamus broke the surface nearby, like smooth wet rocks glistening in the evening light. The sun, way in the distance, was descending rapidly towards the horizon, where stark, jagged tree limbs and the dark, tilting shapes of giraffes and other animals, created a remote kind of theatre against a flame-orange backdrop that was slowly fading into night.

Behind Gatling, in the lavishly furnished lounge of the reserve's main lodge, where the trophy heads of lions and buffalo gazed ferociously down on the leopard- and cheetah-skin rugs, were his wife, Leonora, Nicholas Sabilio, the reserve's South African owner; Abe Kleinstein, Hank Wingate, Hans Brunner and Marion le Grecque. They comprised seven out of the twenty-two premier syndicate members, all other participators being at varying levels below, and spreading out through the globe with the same power and complexity as the dominant beasts out there stalked, exploited and conquered the fertile plains of the bush.

Everyone was silent as the tape played, filling the room with the slurring, yet defiant tones of Beth Ashby, as she left the damning message on her best friend's answering machine. It wasn't the first time any of them had heard it – copies had been made and dispatched to each of them to alert them to the urgency of this meeting – this was simply a rerun to refresh their memories and focus their minds. However, it wasn't by any means the only item on the agenda, for equal priority was being given to Elliot Russell and Tom Maykin's investigation, which had lately started gaining some potentially catastrophic momentum.

When the tape finished and Leonora turned off the machine, all eyes went to Gatling who continued his observation of a small flock of black and white wading birds, that he decided were probably avocets, until, in perfect unison, they rose up from the waters, and he saw they were black-winged stilts. As they vanished overhead he turned to survey the gathering. The tension was almost palpable. There was tremendous pressure on him over this, and they were all waiting to hear what he had to say.

Leonora's eyes were slanted towards the flickering hearth fire. She too was intrigued to learn of his plans, since their repeated, and frequently angry, discussions of the Beth Ashby matter had not yet brought them to a satisfactory proposal on how it should be dealt with. Which was presumably why he sidestepped it for the moment, and began by addressing the syndicate's more universal problem.

'We none of us need reminding,' he said, 'just how many billions we've already invested in our various projects, so I would suggest we start by discussing how we are going to address the troublesome penetration of Russell and Maykin's investigation and what, potentially, it could mean.'

There was some shuffling and grunting at this typical British understatement, until Brunner said, 'What we need to know first is just how far into us they actually are.'

Abe Kleinstein removed a smoking cigar from his mouth and placed it in an oyster-shell ashtray. 'I've already got a team working on that,' he informed him. 'Max Erwin's heading it and reporting direct to me.'

As Max Erwin was a name known to them all, there were general murmurs of approval, backed up by Gatling saying, 'I'm sure Max, with his background and skills, is the best man for this job, and I'm grateful to you, Abe, for setting his inquiries in motion.' He returned his steely gaze to the others. 'However, we need to face the fact that if this investigation delays our schedule, we could be forced to roll over our positions. In the light of that possibility, we should decide now, gentlemen, just how many more billions we are prepared to commit under such circumstances. Or do we risk losing everything we've put in to date?'

The room remained silent as everyone contemplated the unthinkable loss of two billion dollars.

Gatling pressed on. 'Let's not forget that our put options on the euro expire in January. This means our five-year strategy is very possibly already in jeopardy, so we need to reaffirm our commitment to our goals *now*, each and every one of us.'

Marion le Grecque, a tall, reedy Frenchman with deep-set owlish eyes and a crooked beaked nose, was the first to speak, in an accent that was a jarring blend of upper-crust Parisian and East Coast American. 'I would say, Marcus, *my friend*,' he began, 'that before any of us makes such a commitment, that we should wait for Max's initial reports, and in the meantime take whatever steps are necessary to find out what Beth Ashby knows about you.'

Leonora's dark eyes flashed. 'There is a very strong possibility,' she responded, keeping the edge from her voice, 'that what Beth Ashby knows concerns the entire syndicate, not just Marcus.'

Le Grecque made a smooth, though supercilious nod of concession.

'Do we actually need to find out what it is?' Nicholas Sabilio demanded. 'If we simply ensure she can never tell anyone, the problem will be solved.'

Gatling shook his head. 'You're forgetting, Nicholas, that Colin Ashby is currently awaiting trial for the murder of his girlfriend. If his wife were to disappear so soon after, the entire case would erupt into a media frenzy. As you know, we cannot afford such publicity.'

Abe Kleinstein spoke again, his marked Brooklyn accent carrying the tone of the Americans coming to the rescue again. 'Hank and I were discussing this on the jet coming over,' he said, 'and we've come up with what we reckon could be the best way to go.'

382

All eyes were on him.

'We know,' he said, looking at them all in turn, 'that Theo Kennedy, who's producing the film of Beth Ashby's book, has been trying to get Eric Weston to direct it. Well, it just so happens that one of my companies was responsible for sixty per cent of the funding of Weston's last film, which means we're in a position to acquire Mr Weston's services on Mr Kennedy's behalf.'

He paused a moment for that to register, while next to him Hank Wingate, the Texan oil magnate, looking as smug as a Republican who'd just stolen an election, spread his beefy arms across the back of the wooden-framed sofa, and raised a colossal hand-tooled, lizardskin boot to rest on one knee.

'Once Theo Kennedy has his director of choice,' Kleinstein continued, 'all he's going to need are the stars and the finance. Since the film's never going to happen, the stars aren't an issue, but the raising of finance, as we know, is something Beth Ashby – or Ava Montgomery, as she's now calling herself – and her writer friend, Mitzi Bower, have been involving themselves in. So we get Weston on board, then have him invite Ava and her friend to a party at my place in LA, where he's going to introduce them to some serious money.'

Leonora's sharp eyes slid back to Wingate. She could already guess where this was going, but could see that the others needed it spelt out, so she merely listened as Kleinstein unveiled the remaining details of the simple, yet ingenious plan he and Wingate had devised, which wouldn't only get the syndicate what it wanted, but would, from the look of Wingate, afford him some personal pleasure in the acquiring.

'This is, like, absolutely major,' Mitzi declared, as she nudged past Ava in the bathroom, and tugged a fresh towel from the overhead rack. 'I mean, like so major I can't describe it. Do you mind if I take this? Mine are all used up.'

'Be my guest,' Ava responded, leaning towards the mirror as she carefully circled her eyes with a sparkly blue liquid the way Mitzi had taught her. It not only covered the dark shadows of sleeplessness and hunger, it helped enliven her whole face, particularly after she'd squeezed in the drops that made the whites of her eyes glow. Standing back to survey the results, she gave a sigh of rapture. 'Ravishing. Simply ravishing.' She sniffed hard, waited for the sting to subside, then dabbed her nose with a tissue. 'What are you wearing, by the way?'

'The red Hervé Léger,' Mitzi shouted from her adjoining bathroom. 'What about you?'

'I'm torn between the Betsy Johnson pink silk chiffon and the white leather front zip-up. Have you ever met Eric Weston before?'

'Yep. A couple of times. He looks like your archetypal nerd – you know, skinny, loud shirts, thick glasses with black frames, knock knees, but he's like a genius when it comes to making movies. Ah, that'll be Fabio come to stock us up for the evening,' and tucking her towel in tighter, she trotted off to answer the door, while Ava fished in her make-up bag for the small supply she had left over from earlier.

After razoring it into two short, thin lines on the mirrored tile she kept specially, she plucked a straw from the selection that was arranged like flowers in her tooth mug, made two lung-deep inhalations, then used a finger to dab up the remaining evidence, which she rubbed into her gums. Seconds later the renewed rush erupted so fast through her system that she swore she saw her pupils dilate. A beat later she was flooded with such euphoria that when Fabio came into the bathroom she threw her arms around him, overcome by the sheer depth of her love.

'Good job I'm gay, ducky,' he said patting her bottom. Then pocketing the wad of dollar bills Mitzi was handing over, he bade them a fond farewell and left.

An hour later they were just about ready to go when Theo rang. 'Ava?' he said.

'That'll be me,' she replied. 'Am I talking to the most gorgeous man on the planet?'

'That'll be me,' he responded, surprising her with this rare show of humour. 'I was just calling to wish you luck.'

'That is *so* sweet,' she gushed. 'Mitz. It's Theo, ringing to wish us luck. Isn't that incredibly sweet? Theo, you are just the most thoughtful, wonderful man on earth. And don't you worry. You can leave all this to us. We are going to show those guys such a good time they'll be financing every movie you make for the next ten years.'

Theo sounded happy. 'Great,' he chuckled. 'Just don't get too carried away, because Kleinstein's parties can be pretty wild, from what I hear.'

Ava sighed. 'You know, it's so hard working for you,' she complained, winking at Mitzi.

'Why? I'm sorry. What's happened?'

'I mean all this fun we're being forced to have to help you raise money . . . It's wearing us out, Theo.'

'I get it. You're joking, right?'

'Right. Where are you?'

'New York.'

'Ready for bed?'

'Actually, yes.'

'Such a waste,' she purred, turning to the full-length mirror at the end of the hall. 'Incidentally, how much more do we need to raise?' she asked, allowing Mitzi to sprinkle glitter over her bare shoulders and arms.

'Well, we've got promises amounting to around five million now,' he answered. 'If we could get another five we'd be in a position to make some serious offers to the talent, which, in turn, might get us into pre-production this side of Christmas. Are you taking the script with you?'

'You mean Mitzi's outline?' she responded, lowering the front zip of her white leather dress to the waist so that Mitzi could put glitter on her breasts. 'No. Mitz thinks it's best to send it over there tomorrow.'

'It looks too set up otherwise,' Mitzi shouted down the receiver.

'OK. Your call. But this could be it, ladies, so I want you to know, I'm right there with you.'

'We wish,' Ava responded.

After ringing off, she rearranged her zip so that the top four inches of the sleeveless, strapless bodice parted in a V over her cleavage. Then, tilting her head to one side, she said, 'You know, I think I'm in love with Theo.'

'That's because he's not here, giving you grief,' Mitzi laughed, shoving her towards the door. 'Oh God, who's that now?' she grumbled as the phone rang again.

They paused, waiting for the machine to pick up. A moment later Georgie's voice said, 'Hi, it's Georgie again. I'm trying to get hold of Beth. I've called a few times now. I just need to know if she's all right, if she's getting my messages . . .'

'It's five o'clock in the morning her time,' Ava whispered.

'Take it. Just tell her you're on your way out, but you're OK.'

'. . . Please call me if you get this message, Beth,' Georgie was saying. 'I'd just like to know what's happening over there . . .'

'Georgieeee!' Ava gushed into the receiver. 'How are you? I'm so sorry I haven't called you back. It's been so hectic over here. I'm even on my way out now. But I'm fine. Stop worrying. I'm having a fab and groovy time.'

'I got your last message,' Georgie said. 'The one where you mentioned Marcus Gatling and –'

'Oh God, I didn't answer the phone to talk about him!' Ava broke in abruptly.

'But you said you thought he'd come after you. What do you mean by that Beth? What do you think?'

'Georgie! For God's sake. I'm about to go out to a party, and you're putting me in a really bad mood.'

'But if you think –'

'Just ignore that message, will you?' Ava snapped, putting a hand to her head as a sudden rush of blood dizzied her. 'Pretend it never happened. Now I've got to go. Mitzi's already in the car. I'll try and call tomorrow. OK?'

Georgie was silent.

'OK?' Ava pressed.

'I suppose it'll have to be,' Georgie responded.

'Yes, it will. Now I'm going,' and banging the receiver down she snatched up her purse and stalked off to the front door. As she tried to lock it the keys slipped out of her fingers and hit her foot. *'For God's sake,'* she seethed, stooping to pick them up. 'This sort of thing makes me so damned angry. What's the matter with it? Why won't it go in? Go in, you stupid bastard.'

'Hey!' Mitzi cried, laughing as she came to the rescue. 'Just calm down, will you? It'll go in,' and taking the key, she inserted it, turned it, then dropped it into her bag. 'Are you OK?' she said, putting a hand on Ava's shoulder.

Ava nodded, but her head was swimming in a horrible numbing sort of way and her heart was pounding so hard it was like a hammer inside her.

'Breathe deep,' Mitzi instructed. 'In slow. Hold. Let it out. In slow. Hold. Let it out.'

Ava took the breaths, leaning a hand against the wall and watching the ground billowing up around her. The sound of a car passing was like a saw through her brain.

'Keep going,' Mitzi said, breathing with her. 'It's OK. Everything's beautiful and funky, and so, so cool. You're gorgeous and I love you, and you love me, and we love the world. Look at the pretty flowers, and the lemons on the tree. Look at your beautiful body, and think of the freedom you have. Think about the movie, and Italy, and Carlotta, and how we're going to that party to make all our dreams come true.'

By the time she stopped Ava was laughing through the mayhem inside her. But it was subsiding now, settling back into a bubbling river of euphoria that gushed into an ocean of bliss when Mitzi added a sprinkle of the magic ingredient.

'We ready to go now?' Mitzi asked.

'Take me to it,' Ava commanded, sniffing again, and holding her breath for a count of ten. Then strutting over to the open-topped Mercedes Kompressor, she threw open the door and stepped inside. 'So where were we, before that little black spot erupted on to the landscape?' she demanded.

'In heaven,' Mitzi answered, reversing up the short drive on to Mulholland. 'Absolute heaven. Weren't you saying you were in love with Theo?'

'Was I?' Ava frowned, then shrieked with laughter. 'Imagine being in love with Theo. But I adore him, don't you? He's so wonderful, and thoughtful, and wasn't that just so sweet of him to call? How many men do you know would bother to do that?'

'All of them, if they thought they were getting something out of it,' Mitzi responded, putting the car into drive, and speeding off towards the cross with Beverly Glen.

'You're so cynical,' Ava laughed, poking her in the ribs. 'But we're the ones who really stand to gain from this, in every way. God, I feel so horny tonight. Don't you?'

'Rampant, darling,' Mitzi grinned, affecting an English accent.

'I wonder if Theo ever has sex,' Ava said, letting her head fall back. 'One thing we know for certain, he'll have read all the books.' And they burst into hysterical laughter.

'Tell me about his wife again,' Ava demanded when she'd managed to get her breath back.

'Oh God, didn't I tell you?' Mitzi cried, having to shout above the wind. 'I just heard the other day, that she's trying to take him for every penny now. You've just got to hate the woman, because he's such a regular guy. You know – great dad, model son, more scruples than a Sunday school, he's even a great husband. He's just not the type to play around, is he? I mean, can you imagine it? But she's trying to make out he's had orgies in front of the kid, drug-taking, you name it, and to the best of my knowledge the man's never even smoked pot, never mind the rest of it.' After slowing up behind a truck, she put her foot down, whizzed round it and they both cheered and waved as the driver honked them. 'What were we saying?' Mitzi laughed. 'Oh yeah. Mrs Theo Kennedy is what we refer to here as a Valley girl. Zero brains, laughable talent – she calls herself an actress – giant jugs, that are real by the way, so are going to start looking pretty gross any time now, and two ex-husbands who she's already managed to fleece. What was he thinking when he married her? But we all know men are suckers for tits, which is why we've got them, babe.' She performed a lewd, masculine growl as she chucked a hand under one of her own. 'Just thank God we've got brains and talent too. Now, enough of all these worthy cerebral insights, let's get down to the wonderful Carlotta and the way we're going to handle tonight's investors.'

'Remind me who they are again.'

'OK. There's Abe Kleinstein, he's the one giving the party. Apparently he put up the money for Eric's last film, which is the real hot talk of the town, expected to win a handful of Oscars next March, and to gross over a hundred mill, so he's a definite contender for a second time around. And then there's going to be some rich Texan oil guy who's considering getting into the entertainment business, and it's going to be our job to make sure he does.'

Ava threw out her arms to the rushing wind. 'Stand by, roll camera, action!' she cried.

'Wrong order,' Mitzi laughed, 'but it'll do. Did you bring some with you, by the way? I'm not sure how much I've got left.'

Ava waggled her tiny heart-shaped purse.

Mitzi blew her a kiss, then drove recklessly on along the twisting mountain-top road where millionaires' mansions nestled way back in the seclusion of their tree-lined estates, and glimpses of the canyons and valleys below glittered like fallen skies full of stars.

'Are we there already?' Ava frowned, looking around as Mitzi steered the car in through an enormous set of gates, and accelerated up the steeply winding drive.

'I told you, it was just past Beverly Ranch,' Mitzi answered.

'We could have walked.'

Mitzi shrieked in horror. 'Did you hear her? Did the girl say *walk*? Did no one ever tell her, you *don't walk in LA*?'

Rolling her eyes, Ava gazed out at the dense oaks whose giant trunks stood like sentries along the way, while their branches entwined overhead like wild hairstyles tangled in the wind. In her mind she was composing a sonnet to its splendour, effusing gratitude to God for this perfection, and hugging her hands to her shoulders as though embracing its charm.

'Anyone for tennis?' she suddenly cried, as they reached a fork that directed them right for the tennis courts and left for the residence. Mitzi spun them off to the left, steered them round several more bends, until the trees ended and a full-scale, perfect copy of a seventeenth-century French chateau appeared at the other end of a vast circular lawn that was lit up like a football field.

'Unbelievable,' Ava declared, slightly stunned by the sheer size and magnificence of the place. 'It doesn't look so big from the road.'

'Because you can only see the turrets from the road,' Mitzi reminded her, looking up at the clusters of tall grey steeples that might have appeared more authentic without the American flag flapping about in front of them. 'Awesome, isn't it?' she stated. 'Apparently it's a copy of one in the Loire Valley. Chinon, I think.'

'Chinon's a ruin,' Ava told her.

'Oh well, it can't be that one then, can it?' and they dissolved into more uncontrollable laughter.

'I read somewhere that most of the ceilings and fireplaces and stuff are originals from other chateaux, which he's had shipped over,' Mitzi said, dabbing the tears from under her eyes. They were driving around the lawn now, crunching slowly along the gravel, with several other cars behind and a few in front. 'Oh, wow! Will you just check out all those limos,' she suddenly cried, as they passed a small turning that led into some kind of parking zone. 'There've got to be at least a dozen.'

'We need to have sex in the back of one of those,' Ava decided, reaching inside the bustier top of her dress to plump up her cleavage. Just to look at it made her heart skip with pleasure. How did women with small ones ever have fun?

'You are *so* high!' Mitzi laughed, as they abandoned the car to a valet and Ava slipped him a twenty-dollar bill. 'You're supposed to tip when we pick it up, not before.'

'But he was so cute,' Ava cried, twirling and skipping towards the open front doors.

'You wearing panties?' Mitzi whispered, smoothing her hands down over the clinging spandex of her own dress.

'Yes. Are you?'

'What in this?' Mitzi laughed.

Laughing too, Ava tossed her little purse over one shoulder and followed Mitzi to where a uniformed butler, with a clipboard and small round spectacles, was waiting to greet the guests.

'Can I have your names, please?' he politely enquired. Mitzi gave them and, after searching the list, he said, 'Ah yes. Mr Kleinstein is expecting you. Ezra here will show you the way.'

Ezra was a liveried footman who gestured for them to go ahead of him, across the dark maple wood hallway with all its dour portraits and antique furnishings, towards an open door where several people were already gathered, and loud music was making the place throb. As they passed a mirror in a pillar Mitzi stopped for a quick check over. Ava came to stand beside her, and as they caught each other's eye in the reflection they started to laugh. Hollywood might be full of blonde bombshells, but they had to be two of the most explosive.

'OK, baby, let's go tear up that dance floor,' Mitzi growled.

They were already jigging in time to the beat, but as they headed for the bar Ezra stopped them. 'Mr Kleinstein has requested you be shown straight through to the conservatory,' he explained. 'It's this way.'

Mitzi's eyebrows arched. Then, beckoning for Ava to follow, she wiggled along after him, out to the pool, where another bar had been set up, different music was playing, and nude swimming had already begun.

'Check out the blond guy next to the fountain,' Mitzi whispered over her shoulder. 'Got to get those shorts off, what do you say?'

'Consider it done,' Ava responded, giving a little wave to the Matthew McConaughey lookalike who'd just spotted them too.

Head in the clouds, Mitzi stalked on behind Ezra, passing lushly cushioned loungers where clothes and drinks had been abandoned, until they reached a set of giant glass doors at the far end of the pool. A dark tint made it impossible to see in, but all was revealed as the footman slid one of them open and gestured for them to step into the stark, white interior, with all its moist green ferns and exotic palms, thickly padded bamboo furniture and exquisite marble statues that had to be copies because the originals were known to be in museums.

'Now this is what you call style,' Mitzi murmured, as a tall, carefully groomed man in his early sixties got up to greet them.

'You've got to be Ava and Mitzi,' he said, showing his perfectly aligned and overbleached teeth in a twinkling, paternal smile.

'She's Ava, I'm Mitzi,' Mitzi informed him, taking his outstretched hand.

'Good to meet you, ladies,' he said warmly. 'I'm Abe Kleinstein, your host for this evening.'

As he shook Ava's hand she treated him to one of her more seductive appraisals. 'You have a beautiful home,' she told him, holding on to his eyes.

'Aaah,' he sighed, putting a hand to his heart. 'An English accent.' He turned to the group of five or six men who were smoking long, fat cigars and drinking malt whisky. 'She's from England,' he told them. 'London's one of my favourite cities. I get there as often as I can.' As he spoke his eyes were sweeping the length of her, and it was obvious he liked what he saw, while Ava was overflowing with affection for his kind, lived-in face, and the way he dressed in such elegantly tailored clothes, that suggested he wasn't only rich, but had class. She suddenly wanted to put her arms around him and tell him how happy and honoured she was to be here, that she would do anything to show her appreciation, just anything.

'Gentlemen,' Kleinstein said, taking her and Mitzi by the elbows, 'let me introduce two very special ladies. Ava here wrote the book that Theo Kennedy's bought an option on, and that Eric here's in line to direct.'

'Hey!' Eric said, raising his glass towards them.

'Hey,' Mitzi responded. 'Cool shirt.'

Eric glanced down at the vibrant colours of his Hawaiian vacation purchase that was at least one size too big and so wrong for his newly dyed orange hair. 'Glad you like it,' he said. 'Cool dress. Mitzi's doing the screenplay,' he informed everyone.

Kleinstein was beaming. 'Did you ever see a couple of writers who looked like this?' he demanded.

There was a general murmur of approval, which everyone seemed to enjoy, then Kleinstein said, 'Ava, I want to introduce you to Hank Wingate. He's an old buddy of mine from Texas, and we're trying to get him interested in the movie world. Maybe you can help us out here.'

'I'd be delighted,' she responded, taking Wingate's hand as he heaved his bulk out of the chair and doffed his ten-gallon hat. Though large, he was almost aggressively handsome, and his fist, as it closed around hers, was like a five-pronged steel vice.

'Sure am glad to meet y'all,' he told her, his blue eyes boring hard into hers.

Ava laughed at his accent, then told him earnestly and soulfully how much she admired it, and him, and everyone from Texas, which was a place she longed to visit.

'OK, so what'll you ladies have to drink?' Kleinstein offered, breaking into her eulogy. Then to the barman who was behind an all-glass oval bar, 'Fix the ladies whatever they want, Manny. Manny'll take care of you,' he told them. 'We got some business to finish up here, then we'll move on to your project. Is that OK with you? I thought it'd be a good idea to get all the serious stuff out of the way before we get down to some partying.' He grinned. 'And I hear you two ladies know how to party.'

'You better believe it,' Mitzi responded, and with a quick shake of her shoulders she made for the bar.

Ava's hand was still in Wingate's, so looking up at him from under her lashes, she blew him a Marilyn kiss, and went to join Mitzi, peering back over her shoulder as she heard his rumble of laughter.

'I'll have a vodka martini,' she told the barman, climbing on to one of the stools.

'That'll be two vodka martinis,' the barman responded.

Behind them Kleinstein and his cronies returned to their meeting.

'Are you OK with this?' Mitzi whispered. 'It seems they've already got it all set up for you and Wingate.'

'If he can make the movie happen, then he's my man,' Ava trilled happily. 'Actually, he's quite cute, in a grisly bear sort of way.' She glanced over in his direction, but he was engrossed in whatever they were discussing.

'Look out, here comes Eric,' Mitzi warned, so he could hear too.

'You girls are just dynamite,' he told them in a quiet voice. 'I'm telling you, Wingate's going to come through on this. Kleinstein's put him in the frame for the full five million, and provided we treat him right –'

'Where's the "we"?' Mitzi demanded, picking up her martini.

He had the grace to look chastened as he said, 'If I had your talents, believe me, I'd be sitting here dressed like that right now. But you're cool about this, right? These guys are the make or break –'

'Yeah, we know,' Mitzi told him. 'You just joined the project, remember? We know where it's at.'

'Do you? Did Theo tell you he's paying you out of his own pocket now? The five million promised amounts to zip until it turns into cash. And there's none of that yet, so right now he's financing everything himself, which is how come he can't pay me.'

Ava was frowning. 'I didn't realize he was doing that, did you?' she said to Mitzi.

Mitzi shook her head. 'But hey, it happens. Producers are doing it all the time. He'll more than make his money back once we get these guys to green-light us.'

'We need the right distributors for that,' Weston reminded her. 'Which is where Kleinstein comes in. He's got more connections in this town than Pac Bell.'

'Hey, what do we have here?' Ava demanded, as the barman slid a silver filigree bowl, lined with blue glass and filled with white powder in front of them. 'Is this what I think it is?' She looked at Mitzi.

'It'll be the best,' Eric assured them.

'Help yourselves, ladies,' Kleinstein called from where he was sitting.

Ava blew him a kiss, then watched as Mitzi filled the tiny silver scoop and lifted it to each nostril. 'Bliss,' she declared, when finally she exhaled. 'Oh God, I think I'm going to come.'

Ava went next, inhaling deep and long, then dipping a finger into the bowl to rub more powder into her gums.

'She was already high as a kite before we came in here,' Mitzi confided to Eric. 'There'll be no holding her back now.'

'That's what I want to hear,' he responded, reaching for the scoop.

Ten minutes later they were euphorically engaged in high praise of each other's talents, talking loudly and forcefully about Mitzi's brilliance, Ava's subtlety and Eric's movies, that were right up there in the realms of serious art. 'And what about Theo?' Ava demanded. 'Isn't he something else, putting his own money into the project? He really deserves to see it made. We've got to get this made!'

By the time Wingate and Kleinstein joined them, they were attempting to outdo each other in expressing their stupendous good fortune of actually being right here, in this room, the very heartbeat of Hollywood, where most people wouldn't even get past the mailbox, never mind into the C dip.

Listening with some amusement, Kleinstein helped himself to C dip from the silver bowl, then handed it to Mitzi with the suggestion they go pass it around the other men. Taking Eric with them, he left Wingate to perch on the stool Mitzi had just vacated, while the barman fixed him another large malt.

'So, young lady,' he said, looking right into Ava's eyes, 'I guess you better tell me about this book of yours, and why it'll make a great movie.'

Tilting her head playfully to one side, she said, 'How long have I got?'

'I'd say as long as it takes,' he told her. 'But I'm going to let you into a secret. It's going to help your case a lot if I can look at those there puppies while you're a-telling me.'

It was a moment before she realized he meant her breasts and, smouldering at the vulgarity of his expression, she hooked a finger into the zipper ring and, keeping her eyes fixed on his face, pulled it slowly down to her waist.

'Now that's what I call puppies,' he declared, as the top of the dress descended on to her hips like wings.

'I'm glad you like them,' she responded.

'How about you take the whole thing off?' he suggested, sweeping a hand down over the rest of the dress.

Her eyebrows went up, but obediently she got to her feet, drew the zip down to the hem, then let the dress fall to the floor. The silver monograms on her thong matched those on the toes of her shoes. Then, laughing as the others whistled and cheered, she made a graceful curtsy, spun round a couple of times, curtsied again then climbed back on to the stool.

'The book,' he reminded her as she picked up her drink.

As she talked he began fondling her, rotating her nipples with his fingers and cupping each heavy breast with his massive hands. She kept on with the story, sipping her martini and feeling the overwhelming love she had for Carlotta infusing her heart more deeply than ever with every word she spoke. Now and again, above her own voice, she heard Mitzi or someone else laughing, then she was vaguely aware of the doors sliding open and the room filling with noise from the pool as the others left. She was still talking, passionately, brilliantly, persuasively about Carlotta and Rodrigo and the terrible fate they had suffered, then finally overcome. And all the time she talked, he stroked and squeezed, pressed and tugged, while Manny, the barman, refilled their drinks and kept the white stuff handy.

When at last she finished his hands were on her thighs, and his mouth was clamped greedily to one nipple. She ran her fingers through his thick, greying hair and pulled him in tighter. 'God, I love you,' she seethed. 'You're such an animal, you make me feel sexier than sex itself. I want you to do everything to me that you ever dreamt of.'

'That's where I'm a-going baby,' he told her, raising his head and wiping the back of a hand across his mouth.

'I want you to come to Italy with us when we go,' she said, fumbling with his belt. 'I want you to know that I'm going to be there for you. Whatever you want –'

He put a hand gently on her lips, as Manny coughed discreetly and said, 'Sir, Mr Kleinstein asked me to remind you about the phone call, sir.'

Wingate groaned, then laughingly shook his head. 'What can I say? You go join the party, girl. I'll come find you when I'm through.'

After he'd gone Ava picked up her drink and sauntered out to the pool. There was no point wearing anything now, since no one else was. In fact, in her thong and high-heels she was decidedly overdressed. A lot more people had arrived since she and Mitzi had gone into the conservatory, so most of the loungers were now occupied, and the pool was as busy as a Sunset disco.

She began looking for Mitzi, then turned round as a voice nearby said, 'Care to dance?'

It was the McConaughey lookalike Mitzi had admired earlier, stark naked now, except for a gold star of David lying amongst the curling blond hairs on his chest.

'I'd love to,' she responded and gliding into his arms she began moving with him to the music.

'So how do you know Abe?' he asked.

'Through friends. What about you?'

'He's my dad.'

'Oh.' She giggled, then finished her drink. 'So are you in the movie business too?' she asked, putting her glass on a passing tray.

'No. I drive cars. The Indie type. How about you? What do you do?'

'I'm a writer.'

'That's cool.'

They carried on dancing, hardly in rhythm, but it was the feel of each other's bodies rubbing in the right places that was guiding their movements. He was gazing down into her eyes, then laughed as a rush of unadulterated happiness made her throw back her head and start reciting poetry to the moon. He held her waist and watched her as she finally came back to earth, and gazed wondrously around her.

'Look at everyone,' she cried passionately. 'They're all so beautiful and real and vital. They're not ashamed of their bodies, and I love them for it. Don't you love them for it?'

'Sure,' he agreed.

As another swell of ecstasy engulfed her, she felt hands on her breasts and leaning back into the man behind her she said, 'I don't know who you are, but I love you.'

'I love you too, babe,' he responded, kissing her neck.

Abe's son melted into the crowd, then the man behind disappeared too after a while, leaving her to dance with someone she thought was Yuri, her first black lover, but who turned out not to be. Later she went to stand at the edge of the terrace, leaned against the railings and gazed down into the inky black canyon below. Someone lowered her thong, so she stepped out of it, then walked on round the pool, stopping in front of a cabana where six or more people were writhing in mutual pleasure.

She was about to go in search of another drink when she noticed a man watching her from over by the conservatory. He was one of the few people present who was dressed, and she couldn't help but smile at his apparent embarrassment. Deciding to help him over it she picked up the nearest full glass and headed his way.

'This is a crazy, wild party,' she told him as she sauntered up to join him, 'and I'm here to help you get into it.'

'I'm OK,' he responded.

Laughing, she turned her back and looked at him over one shoulder. He wasn't particularly tall, or good-looking, or even encouraging, but tonight she was in love with the whole world, so the whole world must be in love with her. 'I noticed you watching me,' she said teasingly.

'You're hard to miss,' he responded.

Her eyes narrowed mischievously. Then, spinning round to face him, she stretched out her arms. 'Which part of me do you like best?' she challenged.

'It's all pretty good,' he told her.

Putting her drink down, she took his hands and placed them over her breasts. 'There, doesn't that feel good?' she purred, starting to unbutton his shirt.

For a moment he looked at her, then his eyes moved past her, and releasing her breasts, he removed her hands from his shirt. 'Abe,' he said, as Kleinstein joined them.

'Max,' Kleinstein responded. 'I didn't expect to see you tonight.'

'I got back early,' Max answered. 'I was hoping we could talk.'

Kleinstein smiled. 'We've got a lot to discuss, my friend,' he said. 'Come back tomorrow. Around ten.'

Max nodded. Then, after a quick glance at Ava, who was swaying dreamily to the music, he walked back into the house.

'Who is he?' she asked Kleinstein as he coasted a hand over the rise and dip of her waist and gazed appreciatively at her nudity.

'Max? Oh, just an old friend,' he replied. Squeezing her bottom, he said, 'So, what are we going to do to persuade Mr Wingate to help you with your movie?'

'I don't know,' she pouted. 'He disappeared to make a phone call, and I haven't seen him since.'

He laughed. 'Does it turn you on to play the hooker?' he said roughly in her ear.

'Mmm,' she replied, resting her head on his shoulder.

'Well, tonight you can be Mr Wingate's very own,' he told her, walking her gently back towards the house. 'He's waiting for you, right now, in a room we got set up specially.'

'Is there something to drink there?'

'Oh sure. There's everything there.'

'Even star dust?'

'More star dust than you ever dreamt about.'

He steered her in through the crowded drawing room where most were dressed, but some weren't, on out through the hall, then up the stairs and along a brightly lit corridor that led to the east wing. His arm was round her, holding her steady as she staggered and swayed and extolled true love for everyone in her life she could think of, especially Georgie.

'Where are we going?' she said as they started up another staircase.

'To see Mr Wingate,' he reminded her.

'Oh yes.' She gave a sigh of pleasure. 'I told him about my book.'

'I know. And he was very impressed.'

'He's a wonderful man.'

'He thinks you're wonderful too.'

'I love him,' she said.

'That's good. That's very good, because he's right in here, and now you can tell him yourself.'

As he pushed open a door he held on to her, then led her into a large, circular room where Wingate was standing next to a *faux* Louis XV bed, wearing a dark silk robe, which was belted over his stomach and showed his bare legs from the knees down. In one hand was a full glass of Scotch and fat Cuban cigar, the other was tucked into a front patch pocket. 'Ava,' he boomed. 'Y'all are here at last, and now I reckon it's about time you and me had ourselves some fun. What d'you say, girl?'

Throwing out her arms, she spun round in circles, moving towards him, saying, 'I love fun. There's nothing more fun than fun,' and laughing, she kicked off her shoes and threw herself on to the bed, while behind her Kleinstein discreetly withdrew from the room.

It was right on ten when Max Erwin arrived at the chateau the following morning, to find the gates wide open and no sign of the normally ubiquitous security. Driving into this place always unnerved him, even when things were in order, for the double game he was playing with the syndicate was the most dangerous of his entire career. If they ever found out he was working against them, rather than for them, he'd be dead. He was under no illusion about that, which was why he so often wondered if he'd ever truly have the guts to expose them. He wondered too if their trust in him was as genuine as it appeared, for knowing he was a reporter surely had to make them leery, despite the colossal sums they were paying him to keep them informed of any kind of journalistic inquiries that might jeopardize their existence. And Tom Maykin's hook-up with the Brit Elliot Russell was causing them a lot of problems right now, which was why he was here, to feed them information that he and Maykin had prepared.

He took the Audi slowly along the drive for fear of running into any stray partygoers, who might come staggering blindly – and even nakedly – out of the bushes. However, there was remarkably little evidence of the previous night's Bacchanalia, at least on this side of the house. He wouldn't want to vouch for the pool and its environs.

As he reached the sign directing him to the residence he took out his mobile and hit the speed dial. 'OK, I'm just driving up to the chateau now,' he said when he made the connection to Maykin.

'Got you,' Maykin responded.

As he clicked off the line, he came into view of the house, and was surprised to see a paramedic unit, red light flashing, parked right outside. His curiosity increased when he noticed the front door was wide open, yet no sign of anyone around.

Leaving his car at a considerate distance, he trotted over to the house and went into the hall. Still no one in sight, nor could he hear anything, until he finally made out the mumble of distant voices. Not sure where it was coming from, he was about to head round to the pool when the sound of running footsteps made him turn back. Seconds later a medical unit burst on to the upstairs landing, carrying a stretcher, and began running down the stairs.

Immediately Erwin stepped aside, half expecting their patient to be Kleinstein, until he noticed Kleinstein bringing up the rear. As the unit rushed by, Erwin's glimpse of the victim was brief, but despite the rolling eyes and oxygen mask, he could see that it was the blonde he'd met last night out by the pool.

'What happened?' he murmured as Kleinstein joined him.

'Overdose, I'm afraid,' Kleinstein answered. 'It happens. I'd just rather it didn't happen here.'

Erwin's expression showed only a grim understanding. 'Is she going to be OK?' he asked.

'Sure. They'll fix her up. I guess there'll be a few questions to answer, but we already cleaned the place up before we called in the medics.' And, treating Erwin to a chummy slap on the back, he led him through to the den. 'We've got a lot to discuss, my friend,' he said, opening the door for Erwin to go ahead. 'And I hope you've got a lot to report.'

An hour later Erwin left the house, drove out of the gates, and sped along Mulholland Drive towards Benedict Canyon. From there he drove all the way down to Sunset, where he pulled into the Beverly Hills Hotel and booked himself a room. As soon as the door was closed he picked up the phone and told the operator to connect him to Cedars Sinai Medical Center. It took a few minutes to find out what he needed to know.

Taking out his mobile, he hit the speed dial again and said to Maykin, 'Beth Ashby's in the hospital. The official story's an overdose, but there are severe bodily injuries. I'll know how severe once I've been over there to check for myself.'

CHAPTER 23

An Indian summer had blazed so gloriously through the day that enough heat was left behind to warm the evening, and make it possible to sit out on the small, wooden deck at the back of The Grapes. Elliot's entire team was there, having put in a full ten-hour Sunday yesterday, so the drinks tonight were all on him, though the handsome knighted thespian, who lived a couple of doors down, had just spotted them from his own riverview balcony and, after lamenting the fact that he was due at the theatre in half an hour so couldn't join them, had promptly got on the phone to the landlord, and instructed him to deliver a round to the darling girl and her friends.

Laurie knew it was going to be a while before she lived that one down, so she was just rolling with it as Jed said, 'Now what shall we do, darling girl? Should we eat here, or should we repair to the theatah to watch darling boy's performance?'

'He's had great reviews,' Gail told them.

'What's he in?' Liam asked.

'Darling girl will know,' Jed replied.

Slanting him a look, Laurie said, 'Actually, it's a Jane Austen, isn't it?'

Gail nodded. '*Emma*. One of my favourites.'

'Mine too,' Murray agreed. 'Or no, maybe I prefer *Mansfield Park*.'

'Oh no,' Laurie protested. 'Fanny Price is much too feisty and gutsy for that wimp Edmund. Ugh, as heroes go he's about as dashing as a cod.'

Elliot's eyes were simmering with amusement as he picked up his drink. She was laughing too, doing, she thought, a very

402

good job of hiding her feelings. But when he looked at her the way he was looking at her now, she was certain he had some too.

He broke the gaze as his mobile rang, and held up a hand to block the chorus of disapproval that he hadn't turned it off.

'Elliot Russell,' he said.

'Tom Maykin,' the voice at the other end told him. 'I've just heard from my guy in LA. Beth Ashby's in the hospital. I don't think it's life-threatening, but it sounds pretty serious.'

Aware of Laurie sitting so close, Elliot said, 'Hang on, I'm going to take this out by the car. The reception's better there.' When he got out to Narrow Street he put the phone back to his ear. 'What happened?' he asked.

Maykin gave him what details he had. 'My guy's calling back once he's been over to see her,' he finished, 'but from what he told me it wasn't the OD that was the problem, so much as the injuries to her back and legs.'

Elliot frowned. 'What sort of injuries?'

'Wait for this. The sort caused by a whip. The goddammed bastards have whipped the information out of her, and right now a couple of surgeons are having to sew up the mess.'

Elliot's revulsion showed on his face. In his mind's eye he could see much more than he wanted to, could almost even feel it too, so God knew what it had been like for Beth Ashby actually having to suffer it. Forcing his mind past it, he said, 'Do you know that for certain? That they got the information?'

'Yeah, apparently they did. But as of now we still don't know what it was. Kleinstein wasn't forthcoming on the detail.'

Elliot frowned. 'You got this from Kleinstein?'

'My guy's right in there, working with him. It's where we're getting most of our information.'

'Can I talk to him?'

'I'd have to check with him first. He's in a pretty sensitive position, you've got to understand that.'

'Sure. But I'd appreciate it, if he's willing.'

'There goes my other line. I'll get back to you as soon as I have more.'

Elliot flipped closed his phone and stood staring across the street towards the end of the modern terrace. Though his eyes were on Andrew and Stephen's house he was thinking of what had been done to Beth Ashby, and that Gatling, in typical absentia fashion, had been in London last night.

'Are you OK?' Laurie said, coming up behind him.

Turning to her, he looked down into her lovely, quizzical face. This was going to be hard for her to hear, and he knew already that she was going to blame herself, for there was a very good chance this had happened as a result of the message tape from Georgie Cottle's machine.

'You're not, are you?' she said. 'Something's happened. Who was on the phone?'

'Tom Maykin.'

'And?'

As he told her what had happened he watched her eyes fill with horror, then anguish as, pressing her hands to her head, she said, 'It was the tape, wasn't it?'

'We don't know that for certain.'

'But the timing . . . It had to be the tape. If I hadn't handed it over . . .'

'I'm still not agreeing it was the tape,' he responded. 'But even if it was you had no idea this would happen so –'

'But we did, didn't we?' she cried. 'We both knew that it was likely to be serious for her, and neither one of us tried to warn her.'

'Laurie, she won't even speak to Georgie half the time, so just stop this, OK? I know you feel responsible, I do too, but rather than stand around here blaming ourselves, we've got to decide what we're going to do.'

She nodded, and looked away. 'OK. You're right,' she said. 'I guess one of the first things is finding out what the information was.'

'Maykin's chap is the best placed for that right now.'

Her mind was working fast. 'What's it telling us, that she's still alive?' she asked, starting to pace. 'What does it mean?'

'That what she knew wasn't as damning as they thought? Or . . .'

Her blue eyes came up to his. 'Or?'

'She's worked out a way of keeping herself alive by

404

arranging for certain evidence, or information, to be revealed should she meet an untimely death?'

Her eyes remained on his as she digested that. 'If that is the case,' she said, 'should we assume Colin knows about it too?'

'We shouldn't rule it out. Generally that kind of information is left with a lawyer. I'll speak to Bruce, find out what, if anything, he's got locked up in his safe belonging to the Ashbys. Of course, it's unlikely to be with him, but we need to speak to him anyway, to get him to relay the news about Beth to Colin – and to get you back in there for a visit, if he can.'

'In the meantime,' she said, 'someone's going to have to tell Georgie Cottle what's happened.' Her eyes closed at the dread of it. 'It'll have to be me. I'll have to explain why we think it happened now, and why I handed the tape over.'

'She'll understand,' Elliot assured her.

'Will she? And what about Beth? Oh my God, I don't even want to think about what they did.'

Taking out his phone as it rang, he reached for her hand and held it tight.

'Tom Maykin again,' the voice at the other end told him. 'My guy's just called from outside the hospital. They're keeping her in for a couple of days, should be sending her home on Wednesday. Apparently the producer's on his way over from New York, and the writer's at the hospital now. Kleinstein's people have taken care of the cops. As far as we know nothing's leaked out to the press yet, apart from ourselves.'

'How is she?'

'Still out. But the surgery's over. More than twenty lashes using some heavy-duty son-of-a-bitch. They had her tied up, hands and feet, so she couldn't escape it.'

Elliot stiffened. This was the kind of detail Laurie didn't need to hear. 'Can I speak to your guy?' he asked.

'He's not ready yet. But he's not ruling it out. Listen, I've got to go. It's a holiday here and we've got a big family thing going on. But I need to speak to you again. There's more on the currency scam, details that might just get us a whole lot closer to where we need to go.'

As Elliot rang off Laurie looked at him, waiting for him to fill her in.

405

'The writer's with her, the producer's on his way,' he told her.

'So she won't be alone, that's good. How is she?'

'Out of surgery. Pulling through.'

Looking up at him, she said, 'Elliot, I want to go over there. No listen, I have to do something to make her understand that we're on her side. I could talk to the writer and producer as well, get them to tell me what's in that damned book at least.'

'I hear what you're saying, but don't let's rush into anything now,' he responded. 'Wait for her to leave the hospital, see what ripples out of this regarding the syndicate, then we'll decide from there.'

She nodded. Then, becoming too aware of her hand in his, she freed it and, attempting a smile, said, 'As always, you're right.'

His eyes were ironic, 'I'm glad you think so,' he commented.

She pulled a face, then looked off down the street.

Neither of them moved, though she knew he was still watching her, and her heart was thudding hard with the longing for him to say or do something that would at least acknowledge that anything was going on between them.

'We need to talk again,' he said finally.

Relief almost made her laugh, but she only nodded, and glanced briefly up at him. 'Not now though,' she said.

'No.'

For a moment neither seemed to know what to do. Then a horrible sensation swept through her as he said, 'I don't want to hurt you.'

Dizzied, and feeling herself recoiling from any more, she started to turn back to the pub.

'Laurie,' he said.

'It's OK. I can handle it,' she responded.

'Listen . . .'

But she was already gone.

Dashing a hand through his hair he swore under his breath, for he knew very well that he'd just done exactly what he'd tried not to. But which was worse, he asked himself, hurting her or lying to them both?

*

406

Though the sun was dazzlingly bright outside, the room where Ava lay was shady and cool, and safe from the world beyond. The blue and cream silk-canopied bed made a plush, feathery haven in the midst of all the white lacquer chests and cupboards that contained her belongings. Rhinestone chain belts and floaty chiffon scarves were draped over an exquisite hand-painted screen; red kidskin mules, jewelled ankle straps and four-inch black heels were amongst the shoes that were tumbling from the door of a closet that wouldn't stay shut. A photograph of her and Colin was on the bedside table; another of Georgie and Blake was on top of the large-screen TV at the foot of the bed.

Since bringing her back here, to the house on Mulholland, Theo had hardly left her side. He was taking care of her himself, because he believed that no one was more responsible than he for what had happened. In his heart, he'd known how she and Mitzi were helping to raise the finance, but if they were OK with it, and it was going to get the movie funded, why interfere? Why even own up to knowing, when so much of it went on – don't discuss it; just let it happen. Or in this case, set it up and let it happen, because that was what he'd done. Even that night, when he'd called to wish them luck, he'd known what he was wishing them luck for, and his advice, not to get carried away, was all the more despicable for its intention to purify his involvement. But God knew how many movies got backing that way, and half the careers in Hollywood would never have been launched if those kinds of favours hadn't been put out at the start.

So Ava had only been keeping up the age-old tradition of putting out for putting up – she puts out the favours, the guy puts up the cash. Parties went on in Hollywood every night of the week to accommodate the system, and though Theo had never actually articulated it to himself, he'd pretty much known she'd get into it, because he'd been aware when he brought her out here of how vulnerable she was after what had happened to her husband; just like he'd known how persuasive, and even irresistible, Mitzi's kind of lifestyle could be to someone who was in such dire need of escape.

Well, it was over now. Mitzi had gone back to her house in Laguna, too uncomfortable to stay and witness the results of her little Svengali trip; and Eric Weston, goddamn him, had vanished off the face of the planet since the bitter encounter they'd had just after Theo had flown in.

'Honest to God, man,' Weston had cried, 'I swear I had no idea the guy was into all that S&M crap. Fuck, he's got to be some kind of psycho, doing something like that . . .'

'Which one was it?' Theo demanded. 'Who did that to her?'

'It had to be Wingate,' Weston answered. 'But if you're thinking of going to the cops, Kleinstein's already dealt with them. They take care of their own, those bastards.'

Knowing how true that was, Theo moved on to the next. 'Who gave her the drugs?' he growled.

'I got no idea who her supplier was, but Mitzi told me she was high before she got there that night. And there was a shitload of it going round the party. She couldn't get enough of it. Nor the dudes. But hell, she's a game chick. You got to know that. Why else would you send her there? You know what Kleinstein's parties are like?'

'I've never heard of anyone coming out in that state,' Theo snarled.

'For Christ's sake, no one forced her.'

'Have you seen her wrists and ankles?' Theo raged. 'Go take a look, then come back and tell me no one forced her.'

'Hey, come on, give me a break man,' Weston groaned. 'I'm a director who was just trying to help you get your shit together, right? And who knows, we could find ourselves with a whole lot more than five mill after she put out like that.'

At that Theo grabbed him by the throat, hauled him physically out of the house and dumped him across the hood of his car, leaving him to decide how he was going to get in without the keys he'd dropped in the scuffle.

Now, the only one left to tell him what had really happened was Ava herself, and so far she hadn't spoken a word. She simply lay there, staring up at the ceiling, hardly moving, except while she slept, when she'd writhe a little and mumble and moan, and call her husband's name in a voice of such anguish it was almost as hard to listen as it was to look at her wounds. But as her self-appointed nurse Theo made himself, regularly, checking to make sure none of the swollen, livid

408

weals across her back and thighs was doing anything but healing. There was still a long way to go, but at the end of next week he was taking her to have the eighteen stitches removed. Three were in the two weals across her breasts, two more were in her lips from where she'd been slapped or punched; the rest were across her shoulders and back. The bruises from the bonds that had held her wrists and ankles would no doubt clear up the fastest, while what would undoubtedly take the longest was whatever damage had been done to her mind, not only by the physical experience, but by the cocktail of drugs they'd had to pump from her system.

Since coming back from the hospital he'd been sleeping in the room Mitzi had vacated and working in the study overlooking the pool. Occasionally people dropped in, or called on the phone, mainly friends of Mitzi's whom he redirected, and if anyone but Georgie asked for Ava he told them she'd returned to England, though Georgie actually asked for Beth not Ava. He'd spoken to her a couple of times, keeping her posted on progress, and assuring her that as soon as Beth was up to it he'd have her call. He could hear how concerned she was, but he had no more to offer right now, though he'd have encouraged her to come over had she not confessed that her husband was refusing to allow it. He didn't get into why; he had too much else going on to spend time on anyone else's problems right now, like trying to keep this movie alive with no director, no writer, and no goddamn book to back it up. He had to confess that a part of him was almost prepared to try to get Kleinstein on the line to find out if there were any funds forthcoming, because, God knew, the man owed big time after this.

Now, having exhausted all the contacts he could think of for today, he was sitting in a deep armchair that he'd positioned in front of the window in Ava's room. His thick blond hair flopped across his forehead, while his handsome, clean-cut features were set in a frown of concentration, as he read a script by a new writer, that was supposed to be a comedy, but had so far failed to elicit so much as a smile, though he had to admit he was hardly in the mood.

Hearing Ava moan he glanced up, expecting to find her still

409

asleep, but, seeing her eyes open, he put down the script and went to sit on the edge of the bed. 'OK?' he said softly, looking down at her pale, battered face.

She gazed back at him with eyes that didn't appear fully focused. 'Colin,' she murmured.

'You're going to be OK,' he told her. 'You're pulling through.'

Her head moved from side to side in sluggish agitation. 'Colin,' she said again, then her face crumpled as she started to cry. 'I'm sorry,' she wailed. 'Oh God, I'm sorry.'

It wasn't the first time she'd woken disoriented and distressed like this, so he took her hands and held them between his own, hoping that somehow the contact would steady her.

'Please forgive me,' she gasped. 'I didn't mean to . . .'

'Hey, come on, none of this is your fault,' he told her. 'Let's just get you well and put it behind us, huh?'

'Colin,' she said brokenly. 'I want to see Colin.' Her grip tightened on his hands as desperation came into her eyes.

Not wanting to remind her of how impossible that was, he said, 'How about we get you something to eat?'

'*Colin!*' she cried. 'I have to see Colin.'

'Sssh,' he soothed, pushing her down gently as she tried to get up. 'It'll be all right.'

'No. It won't. It can't,' she protested. 'Oh God, help me. *Please*. What have I done?'

'You didn't do anything,' he told her. 'You've just got to get yourself well.'

Her eyes came to his, and as their gaze held he willed her to stay with him, to understand who he was and what he was saying. 'Why are you here?' she asked, still seeming bewildered, though this was the first coherent utterance she'd made in four days.

'Someone had to take care of you,' he answered.

'You came all the way from New York?'

'It's not so far. And I live here, remember?'

'Where?'

'Actually, right here at the moment.'

She looked around, frowning as though unsure where she was. 'Where's Mitzi?' she finally asked.

'At her own place in Laguna.'

Slowly her eyes began to dilate, then, noticing their joined hands, she snatched hers away. 'No!' she cried. 'No! No!'

'What? What is it?' he said, his eyes filling with alarm as she began cowering away.

'It was you who told them, wasn't it?' she wept. 'No, don't touch me,' she gasped as he tried to capture her hands.

'OK, OK,' he said, backing off. 'I'm not going to hurt you.'

Her breath was becoming laboured; her eyes seemed to be hunting for escape. 'You told them, didn't you?' she accused. 'You know who I am, so you told them.'

'I don't know what you're talking about,' he said. 'I didn't tell anyone anything.'

'Then how did they know who I was?'

'Who? How did who know?'

'Them! The ones who did this to me. Did you know they were going to do it?'

'Of course not. Hell, I'm the one who's been taking care of you here –'

'Because you're one of them! You've sent Mitzi away and you've got me here like a prisoner.'

'Ava, that's not true.'

'I'm not Ava. I'm Beth. You know I'm Beth, and you told them.' She was sobbing now, as tears streamed down her cheeks. 'I want to see Colin,' she cried, throwing back the sheets. 'I have to see him.'

'You're going to hurt yourself. Ava. Beth, for God's sake –'

'No! Don't touch me,' she shrieked, backing into a corner as he tried to get hold of her. 'I'll kill you if you come near me.'

'Please, I swear I only want to help you,' he said.

She was still glaring at him, her eyes as wild as a cat's, her hands crooked ready to claw. He saw that blood was seeping from her wounds, staining her nightdress, while her breath was coming in short, frightened gasps.

The stand-off continued, with neither of them moving, or breaking the stare, until very slowly and cautiously he took a step towards her. 'I'm really not going to hurt you,' he said, holding it there. 'You've been through a bad time, I know that, but honest to God I had no idea anything like this was going to happen.'

Somewhere, behind the paranoia, he thought he could sense a longing to believe him, a desperation to be helped, even rescued from her fear. He moved a little closer. 'Come on,' he said gently. His hand was only inches from hers now, but there was still a panic about her eyes, and he was afraid, if she attacked, that he'd open her wounds trying to hold her off. He tried another step, then caught her as she fell sobbing against him.

'I didn't tell them anything,' she gasped. 'I swear I didn't tell them anything.'

'That's good,' he said, stroking her hair. 'It's good you didn't tell them.' He didn't know what she was talking about; it just seemed the right thing to say. 'Come on, let's get you back to bed,' he said after a while. To his relief she didn't resist, nor did she object to him checking her wounds. She merely lay there, staring at the blinds as though disconnecting from what was happening to her body, maybe even disconnecting from her mind too. But at least she'd spoken, he told himself. Maybe next he could persuade her to eat.

That night Beth lay alone in the darkness, watching the shadow of a giant yucca swaying and swooping across the blinds, as a Santa Ana wind hurled its might through the valley below. It was reminding her of the Punch and Judy shows she'd watched as a child – alone, at the back of the crowd, too shy to make friends though longing to. Once, she'd turned round, looking for her mother, and had cried when she couldn't find her. She'd cried for her again the other night: *'Mummy! Mummy! Mummy!'* she'd sobbed, hardly able to get her breath, trapped with her arms and legs spreadeagled, tears, saliva, mucus and blood streaming over her face. *'No! Please, no more! MUMMY!'* she'd screamed as the whip tore into her flesh and terror scrambled her brain. It must have been an instinctive, primal response, because her mother would never come to save her. It was her father who'd found her as a child, then Joyce had slapped her for wandering off. As far as her mother was concerned the whipping would be her just deserts for behaving like a tart. Colin and Georgie were the only ones who'd ever cared. She wondered why Georgie wasn't here now, but maybe she didn't know. She hoped not, because she didn't want anyone to know.

She felt calm at the moment, though still nervous of any movement outside, and afraid of the way her memory kept trying to lead her back into that black, terrifying hell of screaming and begging and pain so intense she'd wanted to die. She forced herself to think of Theo and how he'd fed her earlier, like a child, one spoonful of gazpacho soup at a time, arm around her, napkin ready to dab her chin. He hadn't made hot soup, he'd told her, because he was afraid it might burn her lips. She hadn't looked in the mirror, but knew, because she could feel it, that her lips were cut and bruised and maybe even stitched. That was how it had all started, when the Texan had punched her in the face. At least she thought it was, it was hard to remember now, and she didn't want to anyway. It was harder to avoid when Theo had taken off her nightdress and lowered her into the bath, but he'd put a clotheshorse in front of the mirror so she couldn't see her reflection. He was so gentle and careful as he sponged her, but she'd cried anyway because the pain had torn through the gashes like knives. After he'd dried her he gently rubbed in the cream that would help to numb and heal and cleanse. She wondered what it was like for him, having to touch the bloated edges of the welts and red raw tissue of the wounds.

As he'd dressed her in a clean, cotton nightdress she'd never seen before, she'd started to become aware of his voice, lilting musically upwards, descending dramatically down, until she realized he was telling her the story of Goldilocks and the Three Bears. She was surprised and touched; it made her want to cry. He'd finished when she was lying in bed, tucked up with the lights out. 'And they all lived happily ever after,' he'd whispered, before kissing her on the forehead and quietly leaving the room.

Now, minute after minute was ticking by, taking her further and deeper into the night. She was listening, almost breathlessly, to the gusting wind outside, imagining an insect clinging to the false sanctuary of an autumn leaf that was, any minute, going to be wrenched from the tree, and swept into the chaos of the storm. The insect was her. Sleep was stalking the shadows, waiting to carry her to a place she was too terrified to go, but her eyelids were heavy and her mind was drifting towards the edge. She reached it and began to stumble over. She was falling, falling, but before she hit the bottom she came awake with a start. Her heart was pounding and a film of sweat was damp on her skin. Her wounds throbbed and burned; it was as though her entire body was on fire with the pain.

She had to escape it. She couldn't bear it. The torment just went on and on and on. She had to go, find somewhere else to hide, because she couldn't stay here and she couldn't go back. It didn't matter whether she was Beth or Ava, she wasn't safe anywhere now, not even inside her own head.

She needed some star dust. She couldn't stand herself or life without it. It was the only way she could survive this.

Pushing aside the sheet, she eased herself carefully from the bed and padded out to the hall. There were no lights on anywhere, so she stole steadily, gingerly through the darkness, her hands lightly touching the walls to guide her, her bare feet treading soundlessly on the limestone floor, then tapping ahead like a blind man's stick to find the two steps that led down to the kitchen. As though to assist her, the moon appeared through the clouds, throwing a misty grey light over the counter-tops and cupboards. Through the large glass doors she could see the pool undulating in the wind, debris skimming its surface. It was as though the world had ceased to exist in colour, only in shades of grey. It was eerie, like a dream.

She crossed to the sink, opened the cupboard beneath it, and found that the Oriental pots, where she and Mitzi had kept their supplies, were gone. She started to shake as panic welled up inside her. She had to have it. She needed it now or the fear would drive her mad. She began searching, opening drawers and cupboards, boxes and even books, to see where he might have hidden it.

'You won't find any,' Theo told her from the doorway.

She spun round, furious and desperate. 'Where did you put it?' she hissed. 'I need it.'

He turned on the light and the world returned to colour. 'No you don't,' he said calmly.

'Don't treat me like a child,' she seethed. 'Now where is it?'

Her eyes were wild; her shoulders were heaving up and down, cutting her through with pain.

'Mitzi took it,' he answered.

'I have to call her.' She made to grab the phone, but he was too fast, and snatched it away.

'I'm trying to help you here, and you're not making it easy,' he told her.

'No one's asking you to. I can take care of myself.'

'When that's true, I'll go and you can do as you like. Until then, you can learn to live without it.'

She glared at him, eyes full of hate. She wanted to rip the phone from his hands and smash his head against the wall. She wanted to kill him and everyone that was doing this to her – Mitzi, Wingate, Fabio, Colin . . . She loathed and despised them for taking her life and making it theirs. She needed it back. She had to be in control so she could make it all right. The coke made it all right, but he wouldn't let her have it. So she had to make him. Somehow she had to find a way of forcing him to give her what she craved, but she didn't have the strength, and her back hurt so much she had to stop sobbing because it only made it hurt more.

'You don't understand,' she choked. 'It's the nightmares. I can't stand them. I'm afraid to go to sleep.'

'They're just nightmares,' he told her. 'They're not real.'

'But that's how they feel. If you knew what they were like . . .'

'So tell me.'

She shook her head. 'I can't. I can't tell anyone.'

Going to take some water from the fridge, he poured two glasses and handed one to her. 'What are you so afraid of?' he asked bluntly. 'I mean, *really*. What are you running away from?'

She took a sip of water, then pressed a hand to her head, as though that might stop it throbbing. 'It has to do with my husband,' she said, still sobbing, though no longer crying. 'I think he must have been involved in something, and now they want to know how much he told me.'

'They being Kleinstein and Wingate?'

She nodded.

'So what do they want to know?'

'I can't tell you,' she said.

'Is it to do with the girl who was killed?'

'Yes. I think so. Partly, anyway.'

'Did your husband do it?'

She nodded then turned away. 'I think so, but I don't want to discuss it,' she said.

He looked down at her, wishing there was a way of knowing what was really going on in her head. 'Did anyone ever hurt you like this before?' he said. 'When you were in the UK?'

'No.'

'So why now?'

'I think they're afraid.'

'What of?'

'I'm not sure. It's hard to remember what was said. I just know that they were expecting me to tell them more than I could.'

'So what did you tell them?'

Her eyes came back to his, and he felt a chill run down his spine as she said, 'I told them the truth. But it wasn't enough, because the man Wingate said: "Don't go thinking we're finished with you yet, lady, because we're not." ' She started to shake again as the memory of those words pushed her fear back to the surface. It wasn't over; they'd be back for her. That was what he'd said and she knew it was true. So she had to run and hide. She needed somewhere else to go. Her head was swimming again; her limbs felt like sharpened knives.

'Here, sit down,' he said, helping her to a chair.

Her hands were bunched together in her lap; evidence of the torture circled her wrists like bangles. Her tears fell on to them, trickling over the tender skin and dripping on to her nightdress. 'So now do you understand why I'm afraid to go to sleep?' she said, looking up at him. 'It's not only the nightmares, it's them. I'm terrified they're going to come after me and it'll happen all over again. I don't think I could live through it again.' The terror in her eyes was so real that he reached for her hands. 'I've got to go somewhere else,' she choked. 'I can't stay here.'

'You'll be all right,' he soothed. 'You're not strong enough to go anywhere yet, and I'll be here.'

'But not all the time. You have to go out, and I don't want to be here alone.'

'We'll work something out,' he assured her, looking at the blood seeping through her nightgown. 'You shouldn't be out of bed. Come on, I'll give you a couple more painkillers, then we'll take you back.'

When he'd settled her down under the sheets, she said, 'Will you lie down next to me? I'd feel safer then. They might come in through the window.'

For a while they flicked through the TV channels, until finding *Mrs Miniver* on Movie Classics she said, 'This is one of my favourites. The last time I watched it was with my granddad. He loved it too.'

'So you want to watch it again?'

'Yes. I think so. It might make me cry, though. I expect you're fed up of me crying.'

'I'll get some Kleenex,' he said, 'because I'm damned sure it's going to make me cry too.'

As it turned out she fell asleep well before the end of the film, a hand curled into the crook of his arm, and her head resting against him. A tide of affection swelled through him as he gazed down at her. She seemed so lost, and afraid, and so obviously in need of protection, that he knew he had to do what any other man in his shoes would do. He'd make enquiries tomorrow on where to get a gun, then he'd find someone to teach them both how to use it, because, God knew, if any of those bastards who'd done that to her ever came calling here, he wasn't going to think twice about using the damned thing himself.

CHAPTER 24

Dear Elliot,

In light of what's recently happened to Beth and the fact that you have managed to track me down, I am moving away from here to a place that even Colin knows nothing about. I should have known you'd find me eventually – was it through the bank and the mortgage Colin took on our little place in Cornwall? Or did you employ some other means? I don't suppose you'll tell, and it doesn't really matter now. I just beg you, for Jessica's sake even more than mine, please don't try to find me again. What they did to Beth has shown us how right Colin was to fear them, and I know the last thing you'd want is to inadvertently lead them to us. Maybe they'll find me without your help, or maybe, if I can demonstrate that I no longer have any contact with the press, they'll feel less threatened and leave me alone. For the moment at least, I'm banking on the latter. I want you to know that I truly appreciate your concern for my and Jess's wellbeing, but I hope you'll understand and respect my wishes not to pursue us.

With sincere affection,

Heather

As she finished reading the email Laurie looked across the desk at Elliot. 'Is Gail still down there?' she said, turning his laptop round and pushing it back towards him.

He nodded. 'But not for much longer. I have to do as the woman asks.' He picked up the phone as Murray alerted him to a Priority Two. 'She's clearly terrified, and not without reason. Elliot Russell.'

Laurie returned to her own computer, inwardly wincing as she recalled the graphic shots of Beth's injuries that Tom Maykin's contact had somehow obtained. They'd arrived as an email attachment a week ago, along with a forty-page dossier detailing over a hundred different US policies and financial strategies – both short and long term, national and international – that the syndicate had almost certainly already reaped the benefits of, or were currently designing. The run on the euro was in the latter category, featuring large.

Having spent the past hour poring over the latest reports, Laurie returned to her own files and the reconstruction of all she could remember from the computer that had been stolen. It was a laborious task, and frustrating, for without the original transcripts it was virtually impossible to know the accuracy of what she was recalling. Most irritating at that moment was the loss of the interviews with Sophie Long's neighbours, for so much had happened since those early days that she could hardly remember anything they'd said.

'That was Liam,' Elliot remarked, putting the phone down. 'He and Jed are flying to Sydney tomorrow, in case anyone's interested.'

'Where are they now?' Laurie asked, eyes still on her screen.

'Tokyo. A couple of reporters have backed out over there, which was what the call was about.'

'Too much heat?' Murray enquired.

Elliot nodded. 'It's not a disaster,' he said. 'There are others who can take their places,' and he turned back to his own screen.

A while later, noticing it was dark outside, Murray said, 'Who's for sushi?'

Both Elliot and Laurie raised their hands, as Jerome said, 'I'll come with you. If I keep going round the cyber globe at this rate I'll end up as some kind of weird Orwellian prophecy with air miles.'

Just as the door closed behind them, Laurie's mobile rang. As it was closest to Elliot he picked it up and handed it to her. For a brief moment their eyes met, then turning away, she tucked it into her shoulder and resumed typing. 'Laurie Forbes,' she said.

'It's Bruce. Are you sitting down?'

Her fingers immediately stopped. 'Yes,' she answered, looking at Elliot.

'Colin's agreed to see you next Thursday.'

'You're kidding! That's fantastic. What changed his mind?' To Elliot she said: 'Ashby's agreed to see me.'

Elliot's eyebrows rose.

'Maybe what happened to Beth,' Bruce answered. 'I don't know. He just said he'd do it.'

'Great. What time?'

'Two thirty. You should get the VO by the beginning of next week.'

'Great. Thanks, Bruce. Before you go, has Georgie heard from Beth yet?'

'No, not yet. But she's in regular touch with the producer chap, Theo.'

'So how is she?'

'Making progress.'

'Is Georgie going out there?'

'My mind's made up on that,' he said shortly. 'I don't want her any more involved in this than she already is.'

Thinking of how awful that would make Beth feel were she to hear it, Laurie said, 'I'm still not having any luck getting hold of Theo Kennedy.'

'Believe me, if I had the number of that house I'd give it to you,' he replied. 'But it would mean snooping through my wife's address book and that I won't do.'

'But Georgie can't be the only one who has it?' she said, thinking how misplaced integrity could sometimes be.

'She's the only one I know who has it,' he responded.

'And after what happened when she gave me the tape, there's no way she's going to part with the number now,' Laurie said dismally. 'I hear you. But if anything changes . . .'

'I'll let you know. And listen, don't give yourself such a hard time over that tape. Georgie understands, now you've explained about your parents. She's just not sure what to do for the best at the moment.'

After ringing off Laurie checked the bottom corner of her computer screen for the time, made a quick calculation and was about to start dialling when Elliot said, 'Laurie, now probably isn't the time, but –'

'No, it isn't,' she interrupted.

'You don't know what I was going to say.'

'I can guess, and I told you before, I can handle it.'

'You're talking about us, I was talking about your state of employment.'

Flushing, she put the phone down and looked at him. 'I'm sorry,' she said, feeling so excruciatingly embarrassed she wanted to vanish into thin air. 'So what about my state of employment? Don't tell me, you want to fire me?' Though she was joking, it suddenly occurred to her that she might be right, and already she was starting to panic.

'The reverse actually,' he responded. 'I'd like you to join the team. I mean, officially.'

Though relief and even joy flooded her heart to know he wanted to keep her in his life, she was already shaking her head. 'You know I can't do that,' she told him. 'Once this is over, well,' she looked away, 'it'll be over.'

He allowed a few seconds to tick by before saying, 'It doesn't have to be.'

Her eyes remained averted. Did she want to know what that meant? Did she want to grasp at a hope that probably wasn't even there to be grasped? God knew, it was hard enough being around him every day, with him knowing how she felt – was she really going to make it worse by getting into this any deeper now?

'I want you to know that this isn't easy for me either,' he said softly.

Her head immediately came up, but before she could speak he cut her off.

'For a good deal of the time I was with Lysette I wanted you,' he told her. 'That didn't change after she died, but I didn't think it would ever happen. I resigned myself to it, told myself I had to move on. Then all this came up with the story, and we were thrown together . . . OK, I know I went out of my way to make it happen too, but –'

'But now you've found out you were wrong,' she provided. 'That you don't have feelings for me after all.'

'Don't put words in my mouth,' he growled. 'What I'm trying to say is since the night we talked . . .' He stopped, uncharacteristically at a loss. 'Well, frankly, I look at you and

I don't know who the hell I'm seeing any more,' he said bluntly.

Her eyes were steeped in frustration and despair, though somewhere deep in her heart, hope was daring to stir. 'I don't know what I'm supposed to say to that,' she responded.

'I'm just trying to tell you . . . What I'm saying is, I don't know how to get past this. I want to make it up to you . . .'

Anger flared. 'I don't need your pity!' she snapped. 'You don't have to make anything up to me.'

'I'm sorry, that came out wrong. What I meant was, my feelings for you haven't changed. They've just become well, I don't know what they've become . . .'

'Brotherly?' she suggested sarcastically.

'Don't be ridiculous.'

'I'm sorry, I thought you were expecting me to tell you what they are.'

'No. I'm just trying to be straight with you.'

'And you think I want to hear all this?'

'Obviously not.'

'Got it,' she said. 'Now if you don't mind I need to make this phone call.'

As she dialled Mitzi Bower's agent in LA her heart was pounding with misery, for she hadn't meant to say any of that, it had just come out and now there was no way of taking it back. Worse was knowing how much she'd just hurt him when all he'd been trying to do was explain how he felt.

By the time Murray and Jerome returned she'd failed once again to get hold of Mitzi Bower's agent, and was back at her computer, still feeling totally wretched and torn apart by the longing to go and put her arms around Elliot. But of course she wouldn't. Pride would never let her run the risk of being pushed away.

'Look who we found at the sushi bar,' Murray declared, plonking a pile of cartons on Liam's empty desk.

Both Laurie and Elliot looked up, and registered the same surprise when they saw who was coming in with Jerome.

'I hope you don't mind,' Wilbur said, setting down the cartons he'd been seconded to carry.

'Of course not,' Elliot assured him.

'We met him at the sushi bar,' Jerome said, not having

422

heard Murray say the same thing. 'In fact, dinner's on Wilbur.'

'How generous,' Elliot remarked, watching him closely.

Wilbur's birdlike eyes were hunting from side to side in their normal fashion, though his awkwardness was clear. 'I just wanted to check you were all right,' he said, not quite looking at Laurie.

'Of course I am,' she responded. 'Why wouldn't I be?'

'Well, with all that's been happening . . .'

Laurie and Elliot exchanged glances. 'All what?' Elliot asked.

Wilbur was looking more uncomfortable by the minute.

'It's all right to talk,' Laurie told him. 'Sam deBugger was in this morning.'

Wilbur frowned.

'Never mind,' she said. 'They all know what we're doing now, so we don't really try to hide it any more.'

'Is that wise?' he asked.

'Probably, because it's the avenues they try to block that we know we have to really push. In other words, they keep giving themselves away. Am I right, Jerome?'

Jerome nodded, his mouth was too full of yellow tail to speak.

'So to what do we really owe this pleasure?' Elliot enquired. 'Or would you prefer to eat first?'

Wilbur waved a hand. 'I've just come . . .' He glanced briefly at Laurie, 'I need to take back the computer,' he said.

'What now!' she cried, thinking of all the information she'd so painstakingly re-created and hadn't yet backed up.

'Actually, I was supposed to have done it a week ago,' he told her.

'But you're surely not going to take it right now, this minute.'

He looked at his watch.

'I'm afraid a few sushi dinners doesn't buy back the computer just like that,' Elliot informed him. 'She needs time to copy and erase. You'll get it when she's done.'

Wilbur nodded. It was clear to them all that he'd been told to give no notice of the retrieval, for the very purpose of acquiring whatever information she had stored. In the end, he said, 'Have it in my office by ten in the morning.'

Laurie looked at him, wondering what that might cost him, and praying it wouldn't be too much.

'You'll need to clear out your desk at the same time,' he said quietly.

Since she was surprised not to have received that instruction long before now she said nothing until he reached the door. 'If you can wait half an hour,' she said, 'I can let you take it tonight with certain selected documents still on it.'

He looked at her, obviously embarrassed, then came back into the room.

Her eyes went to Elliot, who winked, telling her she'd done the right thing.

Her smile was small as her chest grew tight with emotion. It was so like Elliot not to bear a grudge, to carry on as though her earlier insensitivity hadn't even happened. It was, perversely, what made it so hard to be around him like this, for it only made her want him all the more. And now he'd admitted that he'd once had feelings, there was going to be no controlling the urge to do whatever she could to make him overcome the confusion he'd developed between her and Lysette.

Theo was in his car, crawling through West Hollywood towards Beverly Hills. He'd just come from a meeting with a writer he'd hoped might take on *Carlotta*, but it hadn't worked out. The man didn't have the right attitude. It needed sensitivity, subtlety, qualities the guy was so short on it was no wonder he was offering to do a first draft on spec – no one in their right mind would pay him to write.

'It was a waste of time,' he said to his agent, when Kurt's voice finally came down the line. 'Did you get anywhere with the other names I gave you?'

'No one's taking any calls,' Kurt told him bluntly.

Theo's heart sank, though he couldn't say he was surprised. It wouldn't take long for Kleinstein to put out the word, and it sure seemed to be out there from the way his phone had stopped ringing.

'I've had Mitzi's lawyer on,' Kurt said. 'She wants paying for the work she did.'

'I know.'

424

'I've had some reporter on from London too. She wants to talk about the story.'

'What about it?'

'Dunno. She left a number, said to call any time.'

'OK. I'll get it from you later. I'm in the car right now.'

There was a pause, then Kurt said, 'I'm sorry, man.'

Theo clicked off the line, then turned off Santa Monica where the road was torn up, and headed up Sweetzer to Sunset, though the traffic wasn't much better there. He stopped at Starbucks, got himself a coffee, then returned to the car and called Beth.

'Hi, honey. It's me. Are you going to pick up . . .?'

'I'm here,' she said breathlessly. 'I was waiting for your call. Are you on your way home?'

'In about thirty minutes,' he answered. 'The traffic's pretty snarled up. Did anyone call? Any messages?'

'No. No one. Just Georgie.'

'Did you talk to her?'

'Yes.'

'That's good.' He smiled. 'You must have put her mind at rest.'

'I think so. How did it go with the writer?'

'Pah, forget it. The guy's a moron. We could make a better job of it on our own.'

'Shall we try?' she said. 'If you bring home lots of screen-plays I can read them, get some idea of how they're set out, and whatever else I need to know.'

'It's an idea,' he said. 'We'll talk about it. Did you take your medication?'

'Yes.' Then, after a pause, 'I missed you. I don't like being here alone.'

'I know. I'll be home soon.'

'I'm sorry,' she said. 'I'm putting too much pressure on you.'

'It's OK. You're doing great. This is the first time you've been on your own since, so you were bound to be nervous.'

'It helps having the gun,' she assured him.

'Good. Just go careful with it. Now, I've got another call coming in, so I'll see you when I get home.' After switching lines he said, 'This is Theo.'

'Theo, it's Georgie. I've just spoken to Beth.'

'She told me. What did you think?'

'She sounds sad, and afraid, but it was a relief not to hear her stoned out of her mind. She didn't like you being out of the house.'

'If you saw what they did to her, you wouldn't blame her,' he responded, slowing for a red light at Doheny, where a producer and director he knew were waiting to cross the street. He didn't bother to alert them to his presence, merely watched their animated exchange and wondered what their project was as they passed right in front of him.

'Do you think they'll be back?' Georgie said.

'God knows. But more importantly, she thinks they will.'

Georgie sounded emotional as she said, 'I'm sorry I can't come over there. I really want to, but –'

'It's OK. I don't blame your husband. There's something nasty going on with all this. You're better out of it.'

'Has she told you any more?'

'No. I don't want to push her. If we can, I'd rather just let it go.'

Georgie hesitated, but then seeming to think better of cautioning him, which was what he'd expected, she said, 'I really appreciate the way you're taking care of her. Especially when you hardly know her.'

He thought of how he dressed and undressed her, bathed her, assisted her with the toilet, and had even, for the last two days, helped her deal with her time of the month. She so hated having to rely on him for that too, that he was going to stop by the market on the way home to get her some towels. They'd be easier to manage than tampons, so she should be able to do it herself.

'She says you're a very special man,' Georgie told him.

'She's special too.'

'I'm glad you think so,' Georgie said, the affection audible in her voice. 'How's it going with the script? Have you found anyone to replace Mitzi?'

'I'm still working on it. Listen, I've got to go, I'm heading into the canyon now, so I'll probably lose you.'

'OK. But just quickly before you go, there's a reporter here who's keen to talk to you. Her name's Laurie Forbes.'

'I think she's already spoken to my agent.'

'Probably. She wants to talk to you about the book, or script, so I was thinking, maybe the publicity will help generate some more interest.'

'It could,' he confirmed.

'So can I give her the number of your mobile?'

'Sure. Tell her to call the house as well, if you like.'

'Well, actually, it might be best if you don't tell Beth about it because I'm not sure she'd welcome the idea.'

'No secrets, Georgie,' he said. 'I'll discuss it with her, and if we think it'll work out, we'll do it. If not we won't.'

When he pulled into the drive twenty minutes later, Beth was waiting to greet him.

'Hi,' she said, holding the front door wide for him to enter. 'It's a lovely evening, I thought we could barbecue some steaks.'

'Sounds good,' he responded, looking down into her eyes. 'Are you OK?'

If she guessed he was checking for the telltale signs she didn't mention it, merely held his gaze as though to show him she was clean. Then blushing slightly, she said, 'I wanted to put on something nice, but this was all I could manage.'

'You look great,' he told her, smiling at the way his big white shirt engulfed her. 'There's a gift for you in the bag.'

When she opened it and saw the towels she started to laugh, then cry. 'Can you imagine, getting so emotional over something that doesn't even sparkle,' she laughed.

'Who says there's no sparkle?' he challenged.

Surprised and curious, she looked in the bag again, then pulled out a card. Hanging from the front was a tiny fake diamond. The message inside read: 'This is what you get for being an independent woman.'

'Oh God,' she spluttered, 'I don't think anyone's ever . . .' She caught her breath and looked up at him. 'Thank you,' she said, laughing again. 'It's beautiful.'

'I'm glad you like it,' he said softly. 'So how about we go do something about those steaks?'

Though bending was still difficult, and the acts of sitting down and standing up had to be undertaken slowly, her movements were becoming more fluid now, so she insisted on preparing the salad while he supervised the steaks. And though it hurt like hell she managed to pull a cork from a bottle of red wine, which she set tentatively on the table next to the pool, not sure if he would drink it.

But he did, and much later, after they'd finished eating and were sitting side by side, watching the fading orange rays of a sunset that was still washing the mountains in a warm, golden glow, he said, 'I've got to tell you I'm real proud of the way you're pulling this together.'

'I wouldn't have been able to do it without you,' she whispered, looking down at her half-glass of wine. Then as he reached for her hand and held it loosely on his knee, she said, 'Before, I thought . . . I don't know what I thought, but you're different to the way I imagined.'

Smiling, he squeezed her hand.

'I don't think I've felt this calm since . . . well, since the day my husband was arrested.'

'It's been a rough road,' he said.

'If I'd known you were at the end of it I might have handled it better.'

Raising her fingers to his mouth he kissed them gently, then picked up his wine and drank.

'Theo,' she said after a while.

'Mm?' he responded, watching the lights of the planes as they glided steadily in and out of the Burbank airport.

'I'd like to ask you something. Well, two things, actually.'

Realizing she wanted his full attention, he turned his chair so he was facing her, and took both her hands. 'Shoot,' he said gently.

'The first is . . .' She laughed self-consciously. 'Well, ever since that night at Kleinstein's I've been terrified of a lot of things, and one of them was of being pregnant. It would have been too cruel of God if I had been, because I've had such trouble in the past . . . But I know I'm not now, and . . . I don't really know how to say this . . .'

'Just say it,' he whispered.

'Well, I was wondering if, when my time is over in a couple of days . . . I know with all these scars and things I don't look very good, and you probably don't want to anyway, I was just hoping . . . You see, I don't want that monster to be the last person to . . . but it's more than that –' She stopped as he put his fingers over her lips.

'If you're asking me will I make love to you, the answer's yes,' he said.

Her eyes gazed deeply into his, and though the swelling emotion in her heart was pushing her to the verge of tears she managed to hold back, as he touched his mouth tenderly, lovingly to hers.

'Second question,' he prompted as she looked down at their joined hands.

Her mouth trembled with laughter, as tears filled her eyes. 'Will you call me Beth?'

Lifting her chin, he kissed her again, gently because of her injured mouth, but with such feeling she could feel it tightening in her chest like a fist. 'My darling Beth,' he whispered.

Laurie raced down over the thinly carpeted stairs, across the tiled hall where a resident was checking his mailbox, threw open the heavy front door and dashed across the street to where Stan, her very own bodyguard-cum-chauffeur, was waiting. Leaping into the car she told him to drive while taking out her mobile to speed-dial Elliot.

'It's me!' she cried, looking back at the white stucco house, with its deep bay windows and black iron railings. 'Where are you? Can you talk?'

'On my way to a café in Montmartre,' he responded. 'What's all the excitement?'

'I've just made the most amazing discovery,' she said breathlessly. 'God, you aren't going to believe this.'

'Where are we going?' Stan broke in.

'Wandsworth Prison, and we're already late. Elliot?'

'I'm still here.'

'I've just left Sophie Long's building,' she told him. 'Remember, I was coming back to talk to the neighbours again? Well, it turns out that the old Czech who lives upstairs, Mr Karowski – the one who's partially deaf and hardly speaks English? – has a wife.'

'Good for him. Did he just get married?'

'No! They've been married for years and his wife – who

speaks perfect English – has not, until today, ever been interviewed by anyone, either from the press or the police, regarding Sophie Long's murder.'

'That's not possible,' he stated.

'You might think so, but it happens to be true, because the day before Sophie was killed Mrs Karowski got a call to tell her that her sister in Prague was very ill, possibly dying. So she immediately booked a flight for the following day, leaving at five in the afternoon, by which time all hell had broken loose in the flat below. So, knowing she wouldn't be allowed to go if she came forward with what she'd seen, she slipped off before anyone could talk to her, and only came back a week ago. Honest to God, she had her coat on ready to go to the police when I turned up.'

'I've got a feeling I'm going to like this,' Elliot responded.

'You are,' Laurie promised. 'Apparently about an hour before all the uproar started she saw a man coming out of Sophie's flat who fits Marcus Gatling's description to a T. And, wait for this, there was a woman waiting in a car outside who sounds like none other than Mrs Marcus.'

'I knew it,' he said. 'I damned well knew it.'

'Hang on. We've got no proof, and I need to talk to my contact at the Yard to find out if anyone else saw the mystery man and woman, and if they did, whether or not they've been identified. I don't think they will have, though, because it would have surely come out by now. Stay on the Fulham Road,' she advised Stan, 'King's Road's always a nightmare.'

'Of course, just because he was there, doesn't actually mean he did it,' Elliot said reasonably.

'I know, but think what a difference this is going to make to Ashby's defence. And imagine the *scandal*. Oh, thank God for stolen computers. I might never have gone back there otherwise.'

Elliot was laughing. 'This is a major breakthrough,' he told her. 'Well done.'

'Thank you,' she responded. 'When are you back?'

'Tomorrow night. Tom Maykin flies in on Saturday so we should be in for a heavy weekend.'

'OK. I'm going to ring off now. I've got more calls to make before I go into the prison.'

430

Hearing the line go dead she looked at her phone and said, 'Why did I even bother to tell him? I should have rung off first.'

'Do you want me to get you something to eat while you're on the inside?' Stan asked, as they sped along Wandsworth Bridge Road. 'I only mention it because I'm starving.'

'Get me whatever you have,' she answered, dialling Bruce's number. To her frustration he was in a meeting, so she left a message and tried Giles Parker. He was in court, so she called Chilton at the Yard. After divulging her new information, and extracting a promise that he'd get back to her by the end of the day no matter what, she tracked down Rhona, who'd offered to go and pick up her new laptop from a shop on Tottenham Court Road.

'You owe me two thousand four hundred pounds,' Rhona told her. 'Half my life savings.'

'You'll get a cheque tonight,' Laurie assured her, 'for my entire life savings. *And* I'm unemployed, remember?'

'OK. You win that one, but I'm withholding the sympathy since Elliot offered you a job and you turned it down. Just tell me this, if things were working out between you, I mean in a romantic sense, would you have accepted him then?'

'No,' Laurie answered.

'Very wise, it would only ruin it in the end. So how are things progressing on that front?'

Laurie's heart contracted. 'They're not. Nothing's been mentioned since the night I told you about.'

'You mean you're managing to play it cool?' Rhona cried incredulously.

Laurie had to laugh. 'Only because I haven't worked up the guts to confront it again,' she confessed.

'Then don't. Let him come to terms with Lysette, or whatever's bothering him in his own sweet time, because if you go trying to force the issue you'll just complicate it further.'

Laurie sighed. 'But what if he ends up discovering he's over us both?' she said.

Rhona laughed.

'I'm glad one of us can see the funny side,' Laurie commented sourly. 'Anyway, I have to go now, I'm at the prison. See you around seven at The Grapes. Gino and Flaxie are joining us, so are Murray and Gail, and Stan, of course. Do you want to stay the night?'

'If Stan's going to be there how can I resist?' she drawled.

Laughing, Laurie flipped off the phone, stashed it in the glove box then, checking she had the phone cards and cigarettes Bruce had advised her to bring, she left Stan to go and feed himself while she hurried to join the small, ragged group that was just being ushered through to the visiting room.

When she got there she spotted Ashby right away, seated at the same table as before, though his head remained down as the visitors spread out to sit with their various friends or relatives.

'Hello,' she said, pulling out the chair opposite him and sitting down.

He lifted his head and her heart gave an unsteady beat of shock, for the deterioration of his appearance was so marked she could almost be staring at the ghost of the man she'd met before. Nothing Bruce had said had prepared her for the shadowy, sunken eyes that were watching her now, languid and dull, red-rimmed and conveying such gloom it was as though there was no light in him at all.

Realizing it wouldn't be appropriate to ask how he was, she glanced briefly at the couple next to them, who seemed interested only in each other. Then, pulling her chair in closer, she said, 'I have some news.'

For a while, as she updated him on their investigation into the syndicate and its run on the euro, then told him about her visit to Sophie Long's neighbour, he seemed to scrutinize her face, but then his eyes fell away, and by the time she'd finished she wasn't entirely sure if he'd actually registered the fact that Marcus Gatling might have been at Sophie's flat only an hour before he had.

'Are you OK?' she asked, lowering her head to peer into his thin, haggard face.

When he raised his eyes they seemed almost desolate, and not entirely connected to his surroundings. 'How did you get on with the contacts I gave you?' he said.

'I'm afraid they wouldn't speak to me,' she told him.

As though expecting the answer he said, 'Then you've done well to get as far as you have.'

His eyes drifted for a moment, then, realizing he was looking at someone across the room, she turned to see who it was. An attractive, well-groomed woman in her late thirties appeared to be watching them, but as Laurie turned round she returned her attention to the man she was visiting. Surprised, Laurie looked at Colin, but he was staring vacantly in another direction.

'You know, even if Marcus was there,' he said, 'he wouldn't have done it. That's not his style.'

'But the very fact he *was* there, if it was him, means something,' she reminded him.

He nodded. Then bringing his gaze to hers, 'How's Beth?'

Going with the change of subject again, she said, 'I hear she's getting better.'

His expression remained solemn, almost morose. 'I don't hear from Heather any more,' he said. 'Maybe she's writing and they're not passing the letters on.'

'Elliot had an email from her. After what happened to Beth, I think, for Jessica's sake she needs to distance herself for a while.'

'Of course. She has to put Jessica first.'

His depression and resignation to what was happening to him were in such contrast to the energetic and charismatic man he'd once been, that Laurie could only wonder why Bruce and Giles hadn't managed to get him transferred from here by now. She looked down at his bony fingers, linked loosely on the table, only inches from her own, and on impulse covered them, as though trying to squeeze in some life and affection. For a moment it seemed to work as he nodded and attempted a smile. Then she sensed him retreat back into himself again.

'Colin?' she said softly.

He looked up, a vaguely quizzical expression in his eyes as though surprised someone knew his name.

'Why did you want me to come today?'

'I wanted to know about Beth,' he answered. 'It's my fault, all that's happening to her. Bruce tells me how she is, but I thought maybe you might know more.'

She kept her eyes and hands on his. Clearly, despite wanting to divorce her, he still cared about his wife a great deal. 'We only know as much as you do,' she said.

'Have you seen her?'

'Only pictures, of what they did.'

His eyes dropped for a moment. 'Do you know what she told them?'

'No. It's one of the things we're trying to find out. Do you know what she might have told them? Could it have been anything that might help get you out of here?'

His sigh was dismal, his expression falling into despair, as he said, 'Believe me, if she knew something that would put them here instead of me, she wouldn't keep it to herself.' Then, sliding his hands out from under hers, he started rubbing his face.

She waited, noticing the frayed cuffs of his shirt, and jaundiced pallor of his skin. Finally he said, 'She should know better than to mess with Gatling. She taunted him, on the plane, Bruce told me about that . . .' Then, looking into her eyes, he said, 'I hear some producer's taking care of her now.'

'Theo Kennedy,' she confirmed.

It was a while before he spoke again, saying, 'So Marcus and Leonora were at the flat before me.'

She watched him, wondering what he really thought about his wife being looked after by another man, why he'd just let the subject go, and returned to the Gatlings as though they'd never stopped discussing them. 'Like I said, I only found out this morning,' she answered.

'Have you told anyone else yet?'

'Only Elliot. We still don't know for certain it was them,' she added, hating the idea of getting his hopes up only for them to be dashed again if it turned out the couple the neighbour had seen had already been identified as someone completely different. 'Was it likely to be them?' she asked.

'I don't know. Maybe Marcus was seeing Sophie the same way I was.'

'But his wife was there too,' she reminded him.

He shrugged. 'They have their own kind of marriage.'

'What does that mean?'

434

'That they don't do much without the other knowing about it. It helps eliminate the risk of blackmail.'

'So you think Gatling was one of Sophie's clients?'

'It's possible. I don't think he killed her, though.'

'What about his wife? Could she have done it?'

His laugh was mirthless. 'Leonora would do anything if it was in the best interests of Leonora,' he responded.

'So how would killing Sophie Long be in her interests?'

'I'm afraid that's a question you'll have to ask her.'

Though her overriding feeling was compassion for someone so broken, Laurie forced herself to put it aside and remember who this seemingly hollow wreck of a man really was, how expertly he had manipulated interviews in the past, and wondered if in some bizarre Machiavellian way he was drawing on that skill now in order to gain information rather than give it.

'Did you ever have an affair with Leonora Gatling?' she asked bluntly.

'Yes,' he answered.

'Did her husband know about it?'

'Of course.'

'Could that have had any bearing on what happened to Sophie Long?'

'Leonora and I stopped sleeping together over ten years ago,' he answered.

'That's neither a yes or a no,' she pointed out.

'It was a no,' he said.

'Are you certain about that?'

'As certain as I can be.'

'Has either of them made any contact with you since you've been in here?'

'Not directly.'

'But indirectly?'

'Look at me,' he said.

Feeling herself flush at the reference to his appearance, she glanced down at her hands.

'They want me to plead guilty,' he said. 'They want this case cut and dried. Over.'

'Which suggests they're involved,' she pointed out.

He didn't say anything, so, tightening her hold on his

435

hands again, she said, 'How well does your wife know them?'

'Not well.'

'Are you certain about that?'

'As certain as I can be.'

'Does Heather Dance know them?'

'No.' And before she could ask: 'As certain as I can be.'

The way his eyes connected with hers, fell away, then connected again was making it impossible to tell whether or not he was lying, and for once her instincts were failing her. 'When I was last here,' she said, 'you told me it wasn't possible for your wife to know anything about the syndicate. I think those were the words you used.'

'Then maybe what I should have said was that she'd never heard about it from me,' he responded.

'So now you think there's a chance she does know?'

'They obviously did what they did for a reason,' he replied.

Her blue eyes were steady on his. 'And you know that reason, don't you?' she challenged.

He didn't flinch from the gaze, but he didn't answer either.

'What was it?' she demanded. 'Why did they do that to her?'

'You know why they did it. To get information.'

'What information?'

'I was hoping you'd tell me that,' he replied. 'It was why I wanted you to come.'

Covering her exasperation with a deep intake of air, she said, 'Tell me, do you want to get out of here?'

'You have to ask?' he responded.

'Then I can only wonder why you're not telling the truth,' she said. 'Or is it that the truth will keep you here?'

At that, what little spark she'd drawn earlier seemed to die, and as he almost physically sank back inside himself she could feel herself being torn by equal amounts of frustration and pity.

To Elliot on the phone later she said, 'I don't know what's going on with him. I truly don't. One minute I'm convinced he didn't do it, the next I think he's playing games with me, and then I've got no idea what to think.'

'But at least it wasn't a waste of time,' he reminded her. 'We now know that he had an affair with Leonora, for what it's worth. That Gatling was probably a client of Sophie's, which apparently his wife was party to, though, interestingly, it didn't come out in the police investigation, nor was it mentioned by Brad Pinkton. And we also know that he's in some way concerned about what Beth might have divulged during her ordeal.'

'Is there any news on that yet?' she asked.

'I spoke to Tom Maykin earlier, nothing then,' he answered. 'His contact in LA's gone to ground for a while, but there's a chance we might meet up with him over the weekend.'

'He's coming here?'

'No. Change of plan. Jerome and I are going to New York. Liam and Jed are meeting us there.'

'So when will you be back in London?'

'Monday. Tuesday at the latest. Rewind to the Gatlings. If it turns out to be them, the mystery of the fibres is probably solved. Actually, even if it's not them.'

'Of course.'

'Not only that,' he continued, 'it has to have crossed your mind that maybe this is what Beth Ashby's hiding. The knowledge that the Gatlings were there.'

'Yes, it has crossed my mind,' she said. 'But how would she know, unless she was there herself, and we know she wasn't?'

'That's a question for Beth Ashby.'

'OK. Here's one for you, two actually: let's suppose she did know the Gatlings were there, and they've now managed to beat it out of her, is it likely they'd have let her go? And if she did know, why not tell the police right at the beginning?'

'Curiouser and curiouser,' he responded. 'I'll let you ponder that while I'm in New York. Where are you now?'

'In the car with Stan, on the way back to the house. Oh, listen, someone's beeping. I'm hoping it might be Chilton. I'll call you back.' Switching lines, she said, 'Laurie Forbes.'

'OK,' Chilton said with no preamble. 'There are no reports of any unidentified persons coming out of the house at the time in question. Male or female.'

'What about identified persons?'

'None of those either.'

'So Mrs Karowski was the only one who spotted the rotund

man with a squashed angry face and good-looking older woman with dark hair worn in a French pleat?'

'It would seem so. You can't withhold this evidence, you know?'

'I'm not intending to. Nor is Mrs Karowski.'

'So do you have any idea who this couple might be?'

'I have a theory, yes. And if I'm right, I'm going to be fascinated to see how the police handle it.'

As she rang off Stan was pulling up outside the house, so leaving him in the car with his radio poker – *radio poker!* – she went inside to shower and change before popping across the road to the pub. By the time she was ready to leave she was back on the phone to Elliot.

'I keep going over and over this,' she told him, 'and no matter how illogical or even impossible it might seem, I can't help wondering if, in some way, shape or form, Heather Dance is playing a role in this that we haven't yet fathomed.'

'I suppose anything's possible,' he responded, 'but I can't offer you any answers.'

'And I don't suppose she's going to spill it all in response to a polite little email enquiry, is she? Or even to a walloping great threatening one?'

'We could probably find her again if we put our minds to it,' he said, 'but I'd say the better way to go right now is for me to exert some pressure on Tom Maykin this weekend to get his contact either to find out, or reveal, what Beth Ashby said to end her ordeal.'

'Presuming it is at an end.'

'Nothing's happened since.'

'So why are phrases like "lull before the storm", and "autumn hiatus" coming to mind?'

'Funny, but I was just thinking the same thing.'

Chapter 25

'Georgie! It's me!'

'Beth? How are you?'

Beth smiled and reached across the table for Theo's hand. 'I'm great,' she responded, gazing into his eyes. 'Theo and I . . . He's so wonderful, Georgie. I really want you to meet him.'

Theo lifted her hand to his lips and kissed it.

'Does that mean you're coming over?' Georgie asked, sounding hopeful.

'Not yet. We're working really hard on trying to get this screenplay together. It's such a wonderful experience, collaborating like this. He's so patient and kind and clever . . . She laughed as he bit gently into her hand. 'I'm learning so much about so many things. I'm starting to understand what sharing and togetherness is really about.'

'That's good,' Georgie responded. 'I'm happy for you.'

Beth laughed softly. 'Thank you,' she said. 'But actually, that's not the real reason for calling. I just wanted you to know the way things are between us. How special he is.'

'Come to the point,' Theo chided.

'OK. Well, Georgie, we've had a really good idea. One that could make all the difference to our screenplay and our lives together.'

'Oh?' Georgie replied.

Beth's eyes remained on Theo's as she related the details of the plan. It was as though she was seeking reassurance, needing to know she was explaining it correctly, wasn't missing anything out, or giving it the wrong slant. His occasional nod and squeeze of her hand told her she was doing just fine, and by the time she'd finished her heart was warm with the joy of doing this for him – for them both.

At her end Georgie remained silent.

'So what do you think?' Beth prompted. 'It could make all the difference in the world if I do this.'

'Is Theo there? Can I speak to him?' Georgie said.

Getting up, Beth went to sit on his lap. 'She wants to speak to you,' she told him, but before handing the phone over she kissed him lingeringly on the mouth. 'Oh, by the way,' she said down the line to Georgie, 'he calls me Beth now so you don't have to worry about the Ava thing.'

At her end Georgie waited as they murmured and laughed some more, then Theo's voice said, 'Hey, Georgie. How are you doing?'

'I'm fine,' she lied. 'Is she serious about this?'

'We've discussed it a lot, and she sure seems to be,' he answered, watching Beth as she strolled out to the pool, wearing a plain navy swimsuit and low-heeled mules. Her scars, though still horribly noticeable, were healing well, and the way they were getting it together with the script, and their relationship, had to be helping the process.

'So you're happy to go along with it?' Georgie asked.

'Whatever makes her happy,' he responded.

'But she's doing it for you.'

'I know. But I think it's going to be good for her. She wants to do it.'

'Is she physically up to it?'

'I think so.'

'What about mentally?'

'You just spoke to her. How does she sound to you?'

'To be frank, I'm not sure. Maybe I need to see her.'

'She's doing great,' he assured her. 'No drugs. No alcohol, except wine with dinner. No parties. It's just the two of us, and the nightmares seem to be easing off since we got into this project. It's giving her something else to focus on.'

Georgie was struggling for more objections, more reasons to say why this wasn't a good idea. But in the end she had to accept that maybe she was just being overprotective, that if Beth really wanted to do it, then why not let her. After all, Theo could be right, it might help in the end.

'OK,' she said finally. 'I'll call you back after I've spoken to Laurie Forbes.'

Laurie had just finished talking to an extremely helpful reporter from the *LA Times*, who'd managed to get her Mitzi Bower's private number, when her phone rang again.

'This is Laurie,' she answered chirpily, mimicking the response of the *Times* reporter.

'It's Georgie Cottle. I hope it's all right to call. Bruce gave me the number of your mobile.'

'Of course it is,' Laurie responded warmly. 'How are you?'

'Confused,' Georgie confessed. 'I've just spoken to Beth and she's come up with an idea that's stunned me a bit.'

Laurie could hardly contain her eagerness to know more, though her voice was perfectly controlled as she said, 'What was it?'

'Well, I don't see why there should be a problem, if you're willing to do it her way,' Georgie said.

'Do what?' Laurie prompted.

'An interview.'

Laurie's eyes closed as triumph flooded through her like a giant rush of speed. 'She's willing to do an interview?' she said, wanting to make absolutely certain she had this right.

'Actually, I think it's more Theo's idea than hers, but yes, she says she's willing to do it. However, there are conditions,' she cautioned.

'Such as.'

'Well, to begin with she'll only talk to you if Theo's there, and it has to be in the LA house.'

'No problem,' Laurie assured her.

'She doesn't want to discuss Colin at all. You're not even to bring his name up.'

'If that's what she wants,' Laurie responded, deciding to worry about that *after* she'd got a foot in the door.

'What she wants you to do,' Georgie continued, 'is a kind of glamour spread with lots of photos showing how happy she is in Hollywood, and what a wonderful man she's found, how they're working together on the screenplay of her book. She wants you to write a lot about that, make it the main focus really, because I think she's hoping to find another publisher.'

'Then I'll need to read it,' Laurie pointed out.

'They're prepared to send you a floppy disk of the manuscript,' Georgie answered.

Laurie was almost reeling with how well today was progressing.

'She wants it to be your paper because it's got class,' Georgie told her. 'No tabloids, no cheap publicity magazines. A serious broadsheet, she says, though she's happy for it to go in the weekend colour supplement. She also wants full copy approval and to retain all rights to the photographs.'

Deciding that now was obviously not the time to reveal her true status with the paper, Laurie said, 'It sounds as though she's got it all worked out.'

'I think we can safely assume that Theo's advising her,' Georgie said. 'But don't forget who her husband is. She's far from naïve in these matters.'

Laurie hurriedly scribbled a note to Murray and shoved it in front of him as he passed: *Got interview with Beth Ashby!!* Reading it, Murray punched the air in victory.

'How is she?' Laurie asked Georgie, grinning.

'Theo insists she's doing well, but without seeing her myself it's hard to say. Certainly she sounded more like her old self, but there's still something there – or should I say, Ava's still there – because a spread of this nature just isn't Beth's style. She's normally terribly private, and the idea of this sort of exposure would have been complete anathema to her once.'

'Maybe there were things about the Ava experience that are worth hanging on to,' Laurie suggested.

'Maybe,' Georgie conceded with a sigh. 'But do you know what I think this is really about? Or at least partly about? Colin. I think she's going to use this to send him some kind of message.'

Laurie was instantly curious. 'Really?' she said.

'Well, he's saying he wants a divorce, so now she's saying, "I don't need you, look how well I'm doing without you. In fact, I'm shouting it from the rooftops how well I'm doing with my glamorous house and pool in Hollywood, with my new-look hair, improved bust-line and handsome producer boyfriend. How are you getting on in your little cell, dear?"

442

Or something like that. That's not Beth, but she's changed a lot since Colin's arrest, and after the way he's treated her, if that is what she's doing, I'm not really sure I blame her.'

'No,' Laurie murmured. She mulled that over for a moment, then said, 'So when does she want to do it?'

'Provided you agree to her terms, as soon as you like.'

Still not quite able to believe that she was about to scoop the most coveted interview in the entire Ashby affair, Laurie grinned again. 'OK. I'll call you when I've got my flight details and hotel sorted out,' she said. 'And, Georgie? Thanks.'

'I hope you're still saying that once this is all over,' Georgie responded, 'though I'm beginning to wonder if it ever will be.'

After ringing off Laurie danced around the office with Murray, then got him to rustle up a couple of his legendary martinis while she called Rhona to make sure she could look after the house and cat while she was away.

'What time does Elliot arrive in New York?' she demanded, laughing as Murray performed his very own martini tribal dance with the shaker.

'Twenty-three hundred hours our time,' he responded. 'Then he's going straight to a meeting.'

'Damn! I really want to talk to him. This is going to blow his mind.'

'Well, we can go ahead and book your flights and everything,' Murray suggested.

Laurie winced as she thought of her empty savings account. However, she had credit cards, and though LA was expensive it didn't even come close to London, so she should be able to get by.

'Have you been there before? Do you know where you want to stay?' Murray asked, presenting her with a clear, conical glass then pouring in the martini.

'Yes, I have been there before,' she answered. 'But I was reading the other day about a new hotel called W in the Westwood area. Do you know about it?'

'Oh yes. Very chic. Absolutely the place to be seen,' he assured her.

'I wonder how much it is? It looked very stylish and Zen, which probably means it's way out of my budget.'

'Leave it to me. By the time I've finished you'll probably be in for free.'

Laughing, she picked up the martini, then moaned with pleasure as the smooth, fiery vodka snaked through her like a lit fuse. 'You're a genius,' she told him. 'Where's Gail, by the way?'

'Out earning us a crust. Elliot's put her on other duties while the rest of you concentrate on this, with occasional back-up when any of you need it. Now, what about the flight?' he said, getting busy with his computer. 'We've got our deals with Virgin and American, which would you prefer?'

'Stop! Stop!' she laughed. 'I want to speak to Elliot first, see if there's a chance of him meeting me out there.'

All that weekend Laurie worked on preparing for the interview, searching out as much information as she could find on Theo Kennedy, from his place of birth – Oxnard, California; to his college education – UCLA; to his invalid mother – died when he was fifteen; to his two divorces, third in the works; to his not unimpressive feature film record. This she added to the substantial amount she already had on Beth Ashby, which ran the full gamut of birthplace, boarding school education, her career as a kindergarten teacher and, of course, her marriage to the famed Colin Ashby. She then wrote an extensive piece covering what she knew of Beth's movements and career since her husband's arrest. It proved an extremely valuable exercise, for it helped focus her mind on the vital task of getting to the heart of the woman.

'Of course what I really need to ask about is Colin,' she grumbled to Elliot when he called on Sunday night. 'But I'm hoping once I'm in there and we get talking she'll open up anyway.'

'People almost always say more than they mean to,' he reminded her.

'Which is why I'm preparing for all eventualities.'

'What time's your flight tomorrow?'

'Eleven.'

'Stan's going with you?'

'Yes. And guess what I've got to read on the plane?

444

Carlotta's Symphony of Love and Death by Ava Montgomery. It arrived by courier about three hours ago.'

'So have you looked at it yet?'

'No. I'm saving it.' Then hoping her next question was going to sound totally professional, with no undertones of personal interest, she said, 'Has Tom Maykin managed to set it up for you to meet his LA contact?'

'Actually, he has,' he confirmed. 'But I won't be there until Wednesday. Something's come up in London that's got even greater priority.'

'Oh?' she said, intrigued.

'I've just had a call from Marcus Gatling. He wants to meet on Tuesday night.'

This news was so unexpected, so earth-shattering, in fact, that for several moments it stunned her into silence, and even then all she managed was, 'Oh my God.'

'We're making some serious inroads over here,' he told her.

'You must be to get a call from the man himself. So what have you got that's winkled him out of his shell?'

'Possibly the real motivation behind trying to destroy the euro. It's got nothing to do with introducing the US dollar, and everything to do with installing their own choice of leaders into key European nations. There's not really any doubt now that they've already got their people in power in the US, so if they can wipe out the euro they'll create the kind of economic downturns and political insecurity that'll enable them to do the same in Europe. In some cases we can even identify the men and women they've got in line for the new positions.'

'That's unbelievable,' she murmured. 'I mean, what you're saying is that they're operating as some kind of exclusive world government.'

'I suppose that's one way of putting it,' he responded. 'It's still hard to prove anything, or actually hook up the connections, but we're working on it. And this invitation from Gatling tells me we could very well be a lot closer than we realize.'

'Mm . . . So where are you meeting? Who else is going to be there?'

'Just him and me. He's picking me up at the office.'

'You're going somewhere with him in a car, and you don't know where?' she cried.

'Calm down,' he laughed. 'The man's not stupid. There are just too many of us involved in this now for him to be planning my dispatch from the mortal coil. Besides, one of Stan's colleagues will be following on behind.'

'With a gun?'

'I don't know about that,' he laughed. 'But I'm telling you, nothing's going to happen. At least not the way you're thinking. Incidentally, I'm arranging to meet Rose Newman earlier in the day, the independent documentary producer. Do you know her?'

'Not personally, but I know her name, obviously. She's TV's answer to you.'

'I'm not sure how to respond to that, but we've been discussing coverage deals with one or two cable stations here in the States, and Rose is probably the best person to talk to in Britain. She does a lot for French and German TV stations too, so she'll probably bring them into the deal. You should meet her when this is over; I think you'll like each other. Her daughter's about my age, not interested in the business at all, and her son's just taking over from his father as Rose's cameraman.'

'I'd love to,' Laurie responded. 'Which newspapers are you talking to?'

'Obviously not your old employer,' he answered wryly. 'We're still working on it, but it's looking like the *Guardian* or *Express* in London; the *Wall Street Journal, Boston Globe, Times Picayune* and *Dallas Morning Herald* in the States. *Le Monde, Berliner Zeitung, La Repubblica, El Mundo, Far East Economic Review*, the *Australian*, South Africa's *Mail* and *Guardian* . . .'

'That is quite a line-up,' she declared.

'If all goes well we could retire on this,' he told her wryly. 'But coming back to earth, I want to be in LA before you go to see Beth Ashby. When is it again?'

'Thursday at twelve. Mitzi Bower's agreed to see me on Wednesday.'

'Great. This really is coming together from all angles now. Where are you staying?'

'W Hotel in Westwood. All the rooms are suites,

446

apparently. Murray's booked you in too. I'll get him to alter the dates.'

'OK.'

He fell silent then, but she knew he was still there.

'So I guess that's about it,' he said finally.

'I guess so,' she confirmed.

'You ready for bed?'

'More or less.'

He paused again, then said, 'Am I allowed to say I miss you?'

His words reached her like an embrace. 'I'm not sure,' she answered, trying hard to stay detached, but failing miserably.

'Then perhaps I should just say goodnight.'

'Perhaps you should.'

Several seconds ticked by.

'Haven't you hung up on me yet?' she asked.

'No.'

'You usually do.'

'I miss you,' he said softly.

Her heart was in her throat. 'Elliot, don't say things unless you mean them,' she said.

'I mean it,' he said.

There was so much she wanted to say, too much, but she only let quiet seconds tick by before whispering, 'Goodnight,' and putting the phone down.

The following morning she boarded the American Airlines non-stop flight to Los Angeles. Stan was with her, tickled pink that he was travelling in business class, which Elliot had insisted on because of the length of the journey. After they'd drunk their welcome champagne, checked out the movies on offer, listened to the flight safety procedures, then made their meal selection from the small *à la carte* menu, Laurie took out her computer and called up *Carlotta's Symphony of Love and Death*.

Because the flight was ten and a half hours long she only made it halfway through the book before her computer's battery gave out. Never, she thought, as she lowered the lid, had a battery been so cursed, for by then she was so entranced by the story and emotionally involved with the characters

447

that it was like wrenching herself away from intense desire. It simply wouldn't leave her, she had to know more, because Beth Ashby's stunning gift for prose, the way in which she wove reality into dream and dream into reality, moved so fluidly through time and back again, plundered emotions and entwined cruelty with love and weakness with obsession so that it was impossible for each to exist without the other, was breathtaking, brilliant, beautiful and intensely harrowing. And what made the battery failure even more unacceptable – before the stewardess showed her where to plug in – was that she was just starting to see how, or at least why, this book had caused Marcus Gatling so much concern.

On Tuesday evening, after Murray and Gail had gone, Elliot remained at his desk, a single lamp funnelling a glow over the paperwork in front of him, while the window behind was like a vast, black canvas portraying a few scattered stars, and the small sprinkles of light from planes flying soundlessly by. The street below was silent, except for the occasional passing car, while the river undulated its shapeless reflections like quivering sheets of vellum. His computer, along with the rest of the high-tech machinery that had a solid hold on the place, was quiet for once, though a five-page fax had just come through from Tom Maykin in New York. He cast an eye over it, then returned to the documents he'd been studying for the past few hours.

It was all tying together: the billions invested in put options, futures speculations on commodity exchanges; the slide of the euro versus the dollar and pound; the fluctuation of global interest rates that chimed with certain international and economic policies – and most importantly of all, from his perspective – examples of what it could all mean for the British public.

Sighing, he sat back in his chair and rubbed a thumb and forefinger across his eyes. The biggest problem they were facing was linking it all to the syndicate members themselves. There was simply no evidence to show that any one of the names they had, such as Gatling, Kleinstein, Brunner, Wingate and Sabilio, would be the personal beneficiaries of the strategy, though certainly there were links to the

448

corporations, banks and big industries in which they were involved. However, the idea of exposing those companies, watching their stocks plummet, their employees getting laid off and customers suffering, while those responsible not only remained anonymous and unaccountable, but rich, wasn't one either he or the rest of the investigative team were prepared to tolerate.

Getting to his feet, he was on the point of going to recharge his coffee when the phone rang.

'Mr Gatling is waiting downstairs,' a voice told him.

Elliot glanced at his watch: ten minutes before the appointed time, but that was OK, he was as ready for this as he'd ever be considering he was only guessing at its purpose. Putting the phone down, he picked up his coat and tucked Maykin's fax into an inside pocket. There were plenty more copies between here and New York, so he had no fear of Gatling seizing them. To the contrary, he might find it worthwhile revealing what they'd found so far.

As he stepped out into the street a brisk wind tore at his coat, while a passing river barge hooted into the night. A sleek black saloon car with tinted windows and personalized plates was parked at the kerb, a uniformed chauffeur standing beside it. Elliot glanced up the street to where one of Stan's colleagues was parked in a dark Toyota Corolla. Neither man gave any indication of seeing the other, but both knew the other was there.

The chauffeur came forward. Gatling had warned him he'd be frisked, so Elliot allowed it to happen then waited as the man opened a back door of the car and gestured for him to get in. As he did so Elliot felt a thud of unease. These past months had more than proved how deeply Gatling's power had infiltrated not only governments, media and financial institutions, but the very laws that controlled them, so by getting into this car now he wasn't just stepping into the lion's den, he was doing so knowing that his only protection was his wits – and the man in the Toyota Corolla who wouldn't be able to save his life, but might at least witness its end.

Gatling was alone in the back compartment, where a single light burned overhead and Mozart played quietly on the sound system. He directed Elliot to a backward-facing seat opposite his own. He was wearing a light-coloured raincoat over a smart, pinstriped suit, and a heavy Gladstone briefcase was beside his feet. His fleshy jowls were quivering slightly, though Elliot knew they always did, just as his jutting lower lip was constantly moist.

The chauffeur closed the door and to Elliot's surprise and relief, resumed his sentry position beside it.

'It was good of you to spare the time,' Gatling said, his gravelly voice expressing no pleasure.

Elliot said nothing, only looked at the sharp, watery eyes, with their bristly brows that met on the bridge of his nose and divided in a large V towards his hairline.

'You've gone far enough with your investigation to know that we cannot allow it to continue,' Gatling stated, coming straight to the point. 'You'll never get the evidence you're looking for, so the wisest course you could follow now is to stop trying and let this go.'

Elliot merely looked at him.

'It would be in your own best interests,' Gatling advised.

A few seconds ticked by, then Elliot said, 'Or you'll do to me what you're doing to Colin Ashby?'

Gatling's eyes were like flint.

'Or what you had done to Beth Ashby?' Elliot suggested.

Still Gatling didn't answer.

'Or maybe you'll go as far as to repeat what you did to Sophie Long?' Elliot said.

Not by even the flicker of a muscle did Gatling show any response to the accusations. He merely continued as if Elliot hadn't spoken. 'Your speculations could lead to serious disruption, not only here in this country, but around the world,' he said. 'And that's all it is, speculation. So are you really prepared to face the consequences of going public with your findings, when you have no means of acquiring the proof you're seeking? Can you afford the considerable legal problems you'll incur, and that'll tie you up for years?'

Elliot's eyebrows went up. Threatening to sue him was not an eventuality he'd expected, though in retrospect he probably should have. 'So what would you suggest I do with my findings?' he enquired.

'Burn them.'

'Well, we both know I'm not going to do that, so shall we move on?'

Gatling's face twitched, and for the first time, as he loosened his collar, Elliot got a glimpse of just how pressured he was. He had a mental image of the syndicate's élite sitting around a table ordering Gatling to go and sort this out. If it weren't for that silly little hooker, none of this would be happening, and since this was Gatling's territory, it was Gatling's problem, therefore Gatling's neck was on the line. And what was the penalty if Gatling didn't succeed, Elliot wondered. Just what were they planning to do in the event that Elliot Russell and the two dozen or more reporters already involved in this didn't play ball? They clearly had to be insane if they thought anything anyone did could alter the course now, and insane they weren't, so he was more than intrigued to find out where this was going.

'I know you to be a man of common sense and integrity,' Gatling said, 'so I don't believe you'd act irresponsibly over this.'

Elliot blinked, not entirely sure he'd heard right. 'Just a minute,' he said. 'Are you telling me you believe it would be more honourable for me to save *you* from a multibillion-dollar loss on put options, than to alert the European public to how you, in the guise of Britain and America, are intending to cripple their economies? Is that what you're saying? You think I would put your corrupt little power-broking empire before the integrity of this nation? You think I really give a fuck about your assets compared to those of the people you're trying to cheat out of everything, from their democratically elected governments, to their entire life's savings? Let me tell you this, I care as much about your syndicate and its diabolical strategies as you and your wife cared about Sophie Long's life. Now, does that paint the picture of my integrity clearly enough for you? Is there anything about it you don't understand, because I'll be happy to explain further, if there's something you didn't quite catch.'

The way Gatling had flinched at the mention of Sophie Long's name should have told Elliot to stop there, but disgust and anger had carried him away, giving Gatling a chance to recover and behave as though it hadn't happened.

451

'I was afraid, or maybe I hoped, that would be your response,' Gatling said. And leaning forward he opened his briefcase. For one appalling moment Elliot truly believed he was going to bring out a gun, but all that emerged was a single sheet of paper.

Elliot read it quickly. This time there were no surprises, for this proposal, these figures were actually what he'd expected – indeed, they had to know that, apart from murder, inviting him in was the only way they were going to stop him. And certainly the number of zeros on the bottom line was enough to stop most, even if there were thirty or more who needed paying off too. He looked at Gatling and in the dim light saw the beads of sweat on his face. If he played this out long enough he'd either double the figure in front of the zeros or give Gatling a heart attack.

'You can become a multimillionaire overnight,' Gatling told him, perspiring profusely now, 'and it will all be legal. You won't even have to make an investment. That's already been done. All you have to do is collect.' His hand went up as Elliot started to speak. 'No, don't give me an answer now. Think about it first. Think of what it'll mean to your life, the freedom it'll buy you, the . . . That's it. That's right,' he said as Elliot folded the sheet of paper and pocketed it. 'Think about it, then call me and we can talk again.'

'You know what I can't quite believe,' Elliot said, 'is that you thought, even for a minute, that I'd go for it.'

'It's a lot of money, for Christ's sake!' Gatling spluttered. 'Five million pounds. And that's just to start. No man in his right mind walks away from that.'

'Then I guess that puts me in the same league as Colin Ashby.'

There was a moment's silence, before Elliot crooked an eyebrow, as though expecting an answer. 'He did walk away from it, didn't he?' he prompted.

'Ashby was a fool,' Gatling snapped. 'I never believed he would take it. It was Leonora's idea. She was always soft on the man.'

'Until she set up Sophie Long's murder to make it look as though Ashby did it?' Elliot suggested. 'Was that her way of paying him back for turning you down? You were seen

452

coming out of there, you know? A neighbour described you both.'

Gatling's eyes were bulging. His face was trembling so hard that saliva was sprinkling from his lips. 'We didn't kill her,' he rasped. 'We were there, it's true, but Leonora didn't come in, and that girl was alive when I left. I swear it. She was alive when I left.'

'So who killed her?'

'Ashby. Who do you think?'

'Who do *I* think?' Elliot said incredulously. 'I think it was you. And Beth Ashby knows it was you, doesn't she?'

It was another bluff that paid off, for Gatling's face looked as though it couldn't decide whether to explode or deflate. 'I don't know what she's told you,' he growled, 'but I suggest you speak to her again and this time *make* her tell you the truth.'

'Would that entail using a whip?' Elliot challenged smoothly.

'Yes, it probably would,' Gatling responded frankly. 'And if you do then you too will find out that there's not a single damned thing any of us can do about it. Not a single damned thing.'

Chapter 26

Theo was in his small, one-bedroom apartment, just north of Ventura Boulevard in Sherman Oaks. It was on what realtors termed the 'wrong' side of the boulevard, since those with money lived on the south side, and in the hills above, enjoying spectacular views of the San Fernando Valley and San Gabriel mountains beyond. Much like the house he was renting for Ava. In his mind, he still thought of her as Ava, even though he'd started calling her Beth.

She'd be expecting him back any minute, and he wondered what she'd do when he didn't come. His cellphone was turned off, and no one she knew could tell her where he lived. Not many people knew anyway, just the utility companies, the landlord, his agent and his wife, Jolynne. She had to know in case there was any kind of emergency with their son, Dwayne. There never had been, not in the eighteen months since he'd left their palatial home in Brentwood, though he doubted she'd call even if there were – unless it required money.

He didn't feel good about this. In fact he felt so bad he couldn't even make himself sit down, for fear the guilt would close around him like a trap and never let go. But he wasn't going back there, so he'd just have to learn to live with it. It wasn't that he didn't care for her, because he did. She was beautiful, loving, responsive, so eager to please and to learn, that it filled his heart with pride every time she produced another scene for him to read. She really was making a great job of the script. Getting her involved like that was doing more to heal her than anything else, but what was the point in continuing when he knew it was never going to be made? The doors were as closed on that as they were on a plague. No one was ever going to touch it – and if he stayed attached no one was ever going to touch him either. That was how his agent had put it that morning. 'Get out of there, man,' he'd growled. 'The project's poison and you're going to kill yourself if you stay with it.'

So here he was, distancing himself and protecting his future for the sake of his son. It wasn't that he wanted to let Ava down, he just had to. God knew, he hated thinking of her up there on that hill all alone, scared because he hadn't come back, terrified in case Wingate or Kleinstein turned up. But she had a gun now. It wasn't as if he'd left her unprotected. He just wished he'd been able to pay the rent too, at least to the end of the month. He didn't know how much cash she had, but her friends in Britain would take care of her. Georgie would come get her, or pay to fly her back. She'd be all right. It wasn't as if she had no one. She could survive without him, he'd just made it easier for a while, nursing her, the way he'd nursed his mother. He had a gift for that, but he had a terror of it too, because his mother had died and left him. He didn't want to be left again after he'd put in so much care and love. He didn't want to get that close again, which was why none of his marriages had worked; he had to leave them before they left him.

Walking through to the kitchen he took a beer from the icebox and popped the tab. The session with his therapist that morning had been the toughest yet. He was still shaken by the admissions he'd made, about his mother, his wives, his girlfriends, even his son. He hated to love. He could do it, but he couldn't sustain it. He was a failure at love. In a way he was like Carlotta, who was driven by her weaknesses and eaten up by her obsessions, though perhaps not as extreme.

He'd cried during the session and he was crying again now. Beth's novel was a beautiful story, it deserved to be published, and the movie ought to be made. He wanted to make it. He wanted to go back. He wanted to love. But he didn't have what it took to fight Kleinstein, nor his own demons. She was a special woman, worthy of someone far nobler than he, so he'd just stay right here and wait until someone told him she'd gone.

455

'Mitzi? It's Ava.'

'Ava? This is a surprise. How are you?'

'Is Theo with you?'

Mitzi laughed. 'Are you kidding? He won't talk to me after what happened. You know that.'

Beth looked around the wide, familiar sitting room with its sprawling sofas and chairs, strange abstract paintings, and eclectic cabinets and tables. It was all so silent and still, hushed as though listening to her speak. She didn't like it. She was trapped in here by the darkness outside. She wanted to cower away and hide. 'I don't know where he is,' she said brokenly. 'He went out this morning and he hasn't come back.'

'Did he say where he was going?'

'He had a couple of appointments. I don't know where. I tried his agent, but he says he hasn't seen him.'

'What about the office on Wilshire?'

'He closed it down a couple of weeks ago.'

'Well, he's probably just got caught up in a meeting.'

Beth started and gasped as an old chest suddenly creaked. Trembling she turned to stare at it, willing herself to stay calm. Old pieces of furniture did that. There was no one else here. No one hiding, or watching. The blinds were all drawn. The doors were locked. There was nothing to be afraid of. She had a gun. 'He said he'd be back for lunch,' she told Mitzi. 'So why hasn't he called? Something's happened to him. I know it. I've called the hospitals, but no one's heard of him, so where else can he be?' Her hand was full of tissues. She dragged them over her tear-stained face, then reached for the Valium they'd given her when she'd left the hospital. 'Do you think they've got him?' she whispered to Mitzi, hugging the bottle to her.

'Who?' Mitzi responded.

'Kleinstein and Wingate. Do you think they've got him?'

There was a pause before Mitzi said, 'Listen, honey, he's going to be back any minute, you'll see. So you just hang on in there. OK?'

'I'm so afraid, Mitzi.'

'I know. But nothing bad's going to happen. Theo won't let

it. Now you just hang up the line, and I'll make some calls, see if I can find out where he is.'

'You'll ring me back, won't you?'

'Sure I will. You just relax now. Everything's going to be OK.'

Leonora Gatling was sitting very still; her beautiful face, though deathly pale, registered little emotion as her husband related the details of his short meeting with Elliot Russell. It was late, she'd just returned from an intense three days in Zurich and Liechtenstein, going through all the stress of relocating funds, checking and double-checking multimillion-dollar accounts, reporting constantly to Kleinstein, Wingate and Brunner, while keeping an open line to the Far East, where more bad news was coming in by the minute. And now this.

'Have you checked to find out if this neighbour exists?' she said tightly when he'd finished.

He nodded. 'She's been to the police and given them a description.'

'So what's to lead them to us? We have no connection to Sophie Long. We made sure of that.'

'Russell's convinced it was us.'

Her dark eyes flashed with fury. 'Then we need to convince him otherwise, don't we?' she said through her teeth.

'And just how do you propose to do that?' he responded in equal tone.

Getting up from her chair she walked to the drinks trolley and poured herself a large Scotch. 'You have to get those fibres out of police hands,' she declared. 'That's all that can tie us to that place. The rest will be surmise.'

'You're surely not forgetting Beth Ashby,' he sneered.

'For Christ's sake, she's not going to tell them anything.'

'Are you sure about that? Laurie Forbes is already out there in LA and Russell's on his way. They're going to talk to her . . .'

Leonora dashed her glass back on the trolley and spun round. 'Then we'd better make sure they don't, hadn't we?' she seethed. And picking up the phone she thrust it in his face. 'You know Kleinstein's number. Call it.'

Laurie was sitting in one of the chic, tented cabanas poolside at W Hotel in Westwood, the trendy, villagey enclave of central LA. The front drapes were scooped lavishly aside, allowing her to watch the comings and goings of the young, rich and famous, as well as the wannabes and star gazers as they lolled on the low-lying double beds that were spread about the harem-style, Zen-like terraces of the gardens and pool. Others were schmoozing their way through late hot-deal lunches, or parading the flowered walkways to be seen, or simply swimming in the crystal-blue water, while catching those vital rays in order to enhance the masterful work that their surgeons and trainers had put into creating those gorgeous bodies.

Though still bedazzled by the glamour – fake and real – and blown away by how many film and rock stars she'd recognized gliding in and out of the hotel, right now none of it was holding Laurie's fascination more than the woman who was sharing the cabana with her, whose nest of dyed-blonde hair, cutesy little plaits, pluscious lips – to borrow a phrase she'd overheard in the bar last night – and startlingly large blue eyes, made her so like Barbie that it might have been hard to take her seriously were it not for the throaty timbre of her voice that made her words quite compelling to listen to.

'In my opinion,' Mitzi was saying, checking the top of her strapless Lycra top to make sure it hadn't slipped down *too* far, 'the book's a literary ballet, with all the grace and style, drama, tragedy, fantasy and reality that goes with it, and some. She's not only an accomplished writer, she's out-and-out gifted. It's a crime they're not publishing it, and it breaks my heart to think of the movie not being made.' Her languid, though intensely perceptive eyes moved to Laurie. 'This is off the record, right?' she said.

Laurie nodded.

'OK. Well, Abe Kleinstein's people have put the word out, and now no one in their right mind's going to touch that project.'

'When did that happen?' Laurie asked, shifting on her pile of downy cushions to tuck her feet in under her.

'A couple of weeks ago. After the incident at the house.'

'Kleinstein's house?'

Mitzi nodded.

'Were you there?'

'At the party? Sure, but not while they were doing that to her. No way was I there during that. I didn't even know it had happened until after they'd taken her to the hospital. Someone called me, don't ask me who, he didn't give his name, to tell me where she was. So I called Theo and went straight down to Cedars.' She was unscrewing the cap of an expensive tube of sun block, which she rubbed into her neck as she continued. 'I thought she'd stayed the night at Kleinstein's because she wanted to, not because they had her as some kind of prisoner,' she said. 'Believe me, if I'd known what they were doing I'd have called the police. It's sick, that kind of stuff. I mean *sick*.'

'Have you seen her since?'

'No. Theo's kept her under wraps, won't let anyone near her. She called, though, last night. Didn't know where he was. She seemed to think Kleinstein might have him, so that'll tell you what a bad way she's in since they half killed her. She's paranoid they're going to do something like it again. To her. To Theo. To anyone, I guess.'

Laurie watched Mitzi's square-topped acrylic nails as she put the sun cream down on the polished wooden block that was centred in the slew of cushions they were sitting on, then pick up her glass of iced tea, which she sucked in through a straw. 'I'll guarantee you Theo was back there before she had a chance to ring anyone else,' she said. 'She's just all worked up since it happened. Shame, because she could do with a break after all that stuff with her husband.'

Laurie nodded agreement. 'Did she ever talk about him?' she asked, taking a sip of her own iced tea.

'Not really. It was like she was trying to forget. You know, put it behind her and move on.' Mitzi's eyes were tracking the progress of a statuesque brunette who was sashaying up to the edge of the pool. 'Do you recognize her?' she said to Laurie.

Laurie shook her head.

'She's in one of the afternoon soaps. Maybe it doesn't go

459

out in Britain. If not you're lucky. And if she could act as good as she looks she'd get lucky too, but, boy, does she suck when it comes to speaking and moving at the same time.'

Laurie watched the woman kick gently at the water, thinking that this was probably the only place on earth where so many varying degrees of perfection were visible in the form of the human body. Stan, who didn't quite make any of those varying degrees, and who was currently reclining in all his pinked-up splendour on a smart wooden chaise, was firmly convinced he'd died and gone to heaven.

'So no,' Mitzi said, 'she never really talked about her husband, though I always got the impression she wanted to.'

'Is the book based on her and Colin, do you know?'

'Initially she used to say it wasn't,' Mitzi answered. 'She told me it was inspired by a painting she'd seen in Italy, of a woman sitting at a piano – hence *Carlotta's Symphony*. She felt a kind of affinity with her she said, but then certain things she said, or the way she sometimes looked, you could tell there was more to it, that it was probably coming from her own life too.'

'What sort of things?'

'Well, let me see . . . OK. You know the scene where Rodrigo's just died and Carlotta's holding his body in her arms?'

Laurie nodded. 'So how does it connect with her and Colin?' she prompted.

Mitzi drank more tea, then smiled as the relaxing tones of a blues sax began drifting from hidden speakers. 'Well, what she said about it – this is Ava speaking now, or Beth as you call her – she said, "Carlotta had to do what she did to free Rodrigo from the men who were controlling him. I just wish I could have done the same."' Her eyebrows made a lazy arch. 'Now, do you think that was weird, because I sure do.'

'It's certainly interesting,' Laurie responded, frowning as she thought about it.

'And what actually prompts her to do it,' Mitzi continued, 'is the fact that the aristocrats have murdered a young girl to make it look as though Rodrigo did it. Or that's the way it's told in the first part of the book.'

'So did they murder her?' Laurie asked.

Mitzi nodded. 'You read it, so you know they did,' she said.

'It wasn't that straightforward,' Laurie responded.

'No, I guess not,' Mitzi conceded. 'But then she kills herself, leaving us with both Carlotta and Rodrigo dead, and if we're supposed to be linking it to Ava, or Beth, and Colin, they're still very much alive.'

'Mm,' Laurie responded. 'Let's go back to the young girl.'

'You know who she was, don't you? I mean in real life.'

'I presume Sophie Long.'

Mitzi smiled and shook her head. 'That's what I thought. But no, it was her, Ava. Beth. Carlotta.'

Laurie blinked in surprise.

Mitzi watched her for a moment. 'Takes some getting used to, doesn't it?' she said.

It certainly did.

'When the Italian aristocrats murdered the young girl,' Mitzi explained, 'they were actually murdering a *part* of Carlotta. They killed her innocence and beauty.'

'Which would be why,' Laurie continued, starting to see it now, 'she had no qualms about killing Rodrigo, because she knew that her real heart and soul were already there, waiting for him.'

'Precisely,' Mitzi responded. 'But it doesn't help with the girl, does it? Because the only real murder in the book was actually Carlotta killing Rodrigo – and we know very well that Beth hasn't killed Colin, so there's no symmetry there.'

'And what the aristocrats did was destroy a human spirit,' Laurie said, 'which should be a crime, but isn't.'

Mitzi nodded.

Laurie turned to gaze up at a slender, towering palm, so vivid against the pristine blue of the sky, and supple in the eddying currents of air that were swaying it. She was thinking about Colin Ashby, far away in the darkness of his prison cell, trying to deal with his guilt, or maybe the injustice of his confinement, and Beth Ashby somewhere up there in the hills, trying to heal the wounds of her body and steady the anguish of her mind. The story and its extraordinary complexity was, in some ways, easy to understand in the context of today, yet in others was simply too allusive, metaphoric

461

and obscure. For instance she could see that the Italian aristocrats were today's syndicate. But Sophie Long, the sacrificial lamb, though a part of Carlotta's psyche in the book, had been a wholly separate person in life. There was nothing allegorical or ambiguous about her murder. And what Laurie had to keep remembering was that the book had been written *before* Beth had even known of Sophie Long's existence.

Her mind went back to the day she'd broken the news to Beth of Colin's arrest. She could see her face now as they stood together in the kitchen, the press banging on the door, the phone ringing non-stop. She was deathly pale, and barely registering what she was saying as she asked who he'd killed. No, Laurie was certain Beth had never heard of Sophie Long until that day, so it wasn't possible to make the connection between a dimension of Carlotta's psyche and Sophie Long's reality. However, there was no doubt in her mind that it was the book's early claim, that the aristocrats had killed the girl to make it look as though Rodrigo had done it, that had forced the Gatlings to stop it from being published. In truth, they probably weren't any closer to understanding the symbolism that came later than she was, but they obviously weren't taking any chances. Ashby was still swearing he hadn't done it, and once the case went to trial, if the book was out then, God only knew what the press would make of the similarities. So the question now was the same one that had been haunting them all along: what did Beth Ashby know about Sophie Long's murder?

Looking at Mitzi Laurie said, 'You know the book better than anyone except Beth – how close to reality do you think it is?'

Mitzi shrugged. 'I think it comes and goes,' she answered. 'Sometimes it's so obviously real it hurts, and others it's pure fantasy and dream. I'll tell you this though: the character that really fascinated me was Ava herself. I didn't know Beth, but I get the sense she was like Carlotta. Her innocence, beauty, courage, all that had gone – stamped or beaten out of her by her husband and his friends, or "the aristocrats" as they're called in the book. Then when the girl was killed, I mean Sophie Long now, I think that for Beth it was so traumatic, so shocking, to have something that was so close to her book actually happen like that, that it was like she was responsible.'

Laurie was watching her intently.

'I'm a writer myself, so I know how freaked out you can get when you write something, and then it happens,' Mitzi said.

Laurie took a breath and let it out slowly. 'You presumably know that her husband was involved with, or certainly associated with, a group of very powerful men?'

'I didn't know it, but considering who he is, and having read about the aristocrats, it wasn't hard to guess.'

'One of them's Abe Kleinstein, whose party you were at –' She stopped as Mitzi's hands went up.

'Don't tell me any more than that,' Mitzi implored. 'I can guess where you're going with it, so don't let's put it out there, huh? I've got to live and work in this town and the less I know about men like that, the more chance I've got of surviving. Already, I don't know how my association with the screenplay's going to affect me. I haven't been offered another job yet, so I'm already nervous.' She pronounced it 'noyvuss', like a New Yorker. 'I tell you, it saddens me to say it, but she's not good news. Word's out, and anyone fool enough to ignore it is history.'

'That's terrible,' Laurie remarked.

Mitzi's right eyebrow went up as she waved a hand to indicate their surroundings. 'It might look like Never-Never-Land round here,' she said, 'but believe me, it's one of the cruellest places on earth.'

Laurie looked out at the glossy, shimmery beauty, with its ambient tranquillity and sybarite's lures, and found herself thinking of an exquisite, placid landscape that existed only on a canvas, while reality seethed and raged and roiled beyond the viewer's eye.

'But why does she need to worry?' Mitzi said. 'This isn't her home. She's not planning to stay, even if she and Theo do get it together, because he's not going to work here again – at least not according to the grapes on my patch of the vine, so why would they hang around?'

Laurie turned back to look at her. 'Where would they go?' she said.

Mitzi shrugged. 'You'd have to ask them. In her case, hopefully to a shrink, someone who can help straighten her out.'

Laurie tried to picture the woman she'd last seen in the doorway of her publishers – another entity, or group of people who'd ultimately let her down – and wondered what she was like now, after the surgery, the promiscuity, the beating and the unimaginable mental torment. Returning her eyes to Mitzi she said, 'So based on the book, and how it ends, who would *you* say killed Sophie Long?'

'Oh no,' Mitzi responded, shaking her head and wagging a finger. 'I'm not getting into it. I just told you already, I've got to work in this town, and those two Brits who are a part of all this are way too connected here for me to get into naming any names.'

Laurie smiled. 'Thank you,' she said. 'It's what I think too. It's just a case of proving it, but we're getting there.'

Mitzi winked and picked up her purse. 'Hey, listen,' she said, getting to her feet, 'when you see Ava, send her my love, will you, and tell her I'm sorry it worked out this way? She's a good person. I really like her and I miss having her as a friend.'

'I'm sure she'd rather hear it from you.'

'Yeah, well. You know how it is.' She ran a finger under the belt of her psychedelic, sprayed-on hipsters, then, looking at Laurie's one-piece swimsuit and modest sarong, she said, 'You know you're not making the best of yourself, girl. You got a great figure there. You should use it, because you can sure do a lot better than the whale that's got himself beached over there, who can't keep his eyes off you.'

Laughing, Laurie looked across at Stan and waved. 'But he's got a good heart,' she said.

After Mitzi had gone she sat back down, plugged in her computer and set it up on a cushion. Before using the Internet connection that came right into each cabana – was there anything they hadn't thought of at this hotel? – she wanted to write up this past hour with Mitzi, because she was certain it had been more informative than she was currently getting her mind round. In fact, the startling synchronicity between fact and fiction was so fascinating she could hardly wait to discuss it with Elliot. However, he'd need to read the book first, and she could tell, from the distracted tone of his emails, that he was so engrossed in the syndicate's financial convolutions that he'd want to concentrate on that during the flight out – and once here he'd probably be constantly holed up with Tom Maykin's contact.

Her heart skipped several beats at the thought of him coming, and the nerves that followed almost made her feel sick. She knew she shouldn't be reading too much into him saying he missed her, but it was almost impossible not to, and the scenarios she'd created since were so romantic, not to mention erotic, that she just knew she was setting herself up to be disappointed. The trouble was, there was no stopping them, and the only respite she got was when she managed to immerse herself in the story.

A frisson of excitement coursed through her then at the prospect of finally meeting and talking to Beth Ashby at noon on Thursday. Of course she could be setting herself up for disappointment there too, but somehow she just knew that this was going to be one of the most important interviews of her career.

'Georgie? Georgie, I'm sorry if I woke you.'

Glancing at the clock as she came awake Georgie said, 'Beth? Are you all right? It's ten past five in the morning here.'

'I know. I'm sorry. I just had to talk to you.'

'What is it? Has something happened?'

'Yes. No. I've just had a call from the reporter, Laurie Forbes, confirming our arrangement for tomorrow. I can't do it, Georgie. Theo's not here. I still don't know where he is, and I can't see her on my own.'

Georgie looked round as Bruce reached out to turn on the light. 'Beth?' he said.

She nodded.

'You've got to call her, Georgie. Please tell her it can't happen.'

'But, Beth –'

'No, Georgie. I don't want her here. Tell her I've changed my mind. Please. *Please*, Georgie . . .'

'Beth, listen. If you'll just calm down a minute –'

'I can't. I don't have any more Valium. It's run out and I'm so afraid, Georgie . . .'

'Oh Beth,' Georgie cried, sitting up. 'Please, just get on a plane and come home.'

'I can't leave Theo. We're doing the script together . . .'

'But you don't know where he is. Have you spoken to Mitzi again?'

'No. She never called back.'

'Oh, Beth, you're all on your own. Please, let me book you a flight.'

'I can't come back there, Georgie. I just can't.'

'Why? We love you, Beth. You should be with people who –'

'Stop it! Please! I can't bear it,' Beth sobbed. 'Just call Laurie Forbes and tell her not to come. I won't let her in. I don't want to see her. She's one of them and I hate them all.'

Georgie flinched as the line went dead. Then, replacing the receiver, she turned to look at Bruce. 'Did you hear any of it?' she asked.

He nodded. 'Enough.'

'So what shall I do?'

He glanced at the clock. 'What time is it in LA?' he said.

'Quarter past nine at night.'

'OK. Laurie's not due to go there until noon their time tomorrow, so let's think about this.'

'No,' Georgie said suddenly throwing back the covers. 'I don't need to think about it. I know what I want to do, what I *have* to do.'

'Where are you going?' Bruce demanded.

'To get Laurie Forbes's number.'

She was in the kitchen, waiting for Laurie to answer her mobile when Bruce came in and put a dressing gown round her. 'Hello, Laurie!' she cried making the connection.

'. . . not able to take your call at the moment,' Laurie's recorded voice was saying, 'but please leave a message and I'll get right back to you.'

'Laurie. It's Georgie. Please call me the instant you get this message. It's very important. I need to talk to you before you see Beth. *Please* call me.'

*

Laurie was laughing at the twinkle in Elliot's eye as they sat facing each other in one of the intimate, candlelit niches of W Hotel's *Nuevo Latino* restaurant, Mojo – pronounced Moe-hoe – which was set back from the long, polished granite bar, where many of the town's élite were currently gathered. She'd have quite liked Stan to go and join them, but she could hardly say so, and besides, she could see how very tired Elliot was after three transatlantic flights in the past five days, and two virtually sleepless nights. So actually, Stan's hilarious accounts of his apparently disastrous seduction technique weren't as unwelcome as her churlish mind was making out, for it was insane to expect anything to happen tonight.

Stan had just got to the punchline of a toe-curling encounter with a babe he'd offered to cast in his movie, only to find out she was an undercover detective trying to infiltrate a drug cartel, when the waiter arrived with their main courses, and abruptly drew back, as though the sudden eruption of laughter might shatter the plates.

'Of course, there's every chance she was spinning you a line too,' Elliot remarked, as the waiter tried to sort out what was for whom.

'No, mine's the Chilean seabass,' Laurie told him, as he put it in front of Elliot.

'Mine's the chicken rostizado,' Elliot said.

'So, señor,' the waiter declared happily to Stan, 'must be the ribeye steak.'

'That's me,' Stan confirmed, tucking his napkin under his chin. 'Got any ketchup, mate?'

'Of course. I bring right away.'

Elliot's eyes were alive with laughter as he added, 'And another bottle of the Far Niente. Good choice,' he told Laurie. 'Who told you about it?'

'Stan,' she responded. 'He read up about California wines on the plane coming over, so he's our expert.'

Stan mumbled something in response, but his mouth was already bulging with steak, so it was impossible to decipher.

'What time are you meeting Tom Maykin's contact tomorrow?' Laurie asked Elliot, as they started to eat.

'Eight. And you? What time are you seeing Beth Ashby?'

'Noon.'

He looked at Stan. 'Have you been up there to check the house out?' he asked.

'Mm,' Stan answered, picking up his wine and glugging it back. 'Didn't see her, though. Just a weird Hispanic-looking geezer who went in at one point then came out again about ten minutes later.'

'Did you speak to him?'

'No. Just noted down his number plate.'

'A supplier?' Elliot commented looking at Laurie.

'That's what we're assuming.'

His eyes were intent on hers, and she was glad he had no way of reading her mind, for the thoughts going through it weren't particularly connected to what they were discussing. In fact, right at that moment, they were so explicitly sexual that it wasn't only her cheeks that were burning.

'I don't have a good feeling about you going up there,' he suddenly stated. His voice was surprisingly harsh, and his eyes were no longer on hers. 'Is there any chance you can get her to come here?' he added.

Shame was twisting Laurie's heart. Had he somehow managed to sense her thoughts, was that what had changed his tone? Certainly he seemed to have withdrawn from her now, in a way that was almost as physical as it was abrupt. 'You know I can't,' she answered shortly. 'But there's nothing to worry about. Stan'll be with me, and even if she's high, what's she going to do, apart from make me her best friend?'

The small attempt at humour fell on stony ground. 'It's not her I'm worried about,' he responded. 'It's the Wingates and Kleinsteins of the world.'

'Why? They got what they wanted didn't they?'

'Did they? I don't know.' Sitting back he picked up his wine. 'What's your instinct telling you, Stan?' he asked.

Stan shrugged. 'I'm going to be right there,' he said. 'She'll be OK.'

Laurie's emotions were struggling for direction, for though his concern was pleasing, his abruptness was really making her angry. However, she didn't want to cause a scene in front of Stan, and would she know what to say anyway?

'OK,' he said finally. 'Just make sure that if anything

doesn't feel right, or if anyone turns up looking out of place, that you get out of there straight away.'

'And take Beth Ashby with me?'

'Of course. But don't try playing the hero. Make yourself a priority.'

By the time coffee was served and they'd finished the second bottle of wine Elliot was past pretending he could stay awake any longer. 'If I'm up in time I'll meet you for breakfast,' he told them, picking up his room key. 'If not I'll go straight to the meeting and catch up with you later.'

He looked at Laurie who was staring down at her glass. 'If I don't see you before, good luck tomorrow,' he said.

She nodded, and detested herself for feeling so crushed that he was leaving now, with the air between them still so tense. 'Thank you,' she said, only half glancing up.

After clapping Stan on the shoulder he walked away, leaving her suppressing the urge to shout after him that not three days ago he'd told her he missed her. Didn't it mean anything now? Was it just something he'd said that she was supposed to forget? The dread of it lodged in her heart, making it suddenly hard to listen to Stan as he continued chuntering on after Elliot had gone. What if he really did regret saying it; was angry with himself for having even gone there? He was probably, even now, desperately trying to think how to back off from it. In fact, his insistence that Stan join them for dinner was very likely to avoid being alone with her. And he'd already set the scene for not turning up to breakfast, so this probably wasn't paranoia, or insecurity, she was dealing with now, but harsh reality.

Of course, she'd been a complete fool to read so much into so little, so it was her own fault that she was feeling so upset she was almost crying with frustration. It didn't help that he was in the very next room to her either, because when she went up, some twenty minutes later, and saw that his light was still on, she could only presume that he hadn't been that tired after all, but had wanted to escape the awkwardness of them going to bed at the same time.

Pushing open her own door she bit down hard on the urge to scream, or go back there and kick his door. She almost wished she'd never come here now, and the fact that she

469

knew very well that she was completely overreacting wasn't making her feel any better.

Noticing the red flashing light on her mobile, and despairing of her ludicrous hope that it would be a message from him, she picked the phone up and carried it into the bedroom.

The instant she heard the urgency in Georgie's voice she searched out the number and called her back. 'It's Laurie, what is it?' she said when Georgie answered on the second ring.

'I've had a call from Beth,' Georgie told her. 'She doesn't want to do the interview.'

'Oh no! She can't –'

'But listen, I want you to go anyway. She's on her own. I don't know where Theo is; he disappeared three days ago and she's terrified. I just want you to know how the land lies before you go round there. She'll try to resist you but, please, do whatever it takes to make her see you. If I could get there in time to come with you I would, but it's not possible now. So, please, Laurie, make sure she's all right and try to make her understand that this is where she should be. This is where people love her, so she doesn't need to be on her own out there.'

'OK,' Laurie responded. 'Thanks for the warning. I'll call as soon as I have some news.'

Relieved that the interview hadn't been cancelled, and glad of the distraction, she wandered into the bathroom and turned on the shower. Of course Elliot could always have fallen asleep with the light on. And where else was Stan supposed to go for dinner? In fact, there was still a chance he would make it for breakfast, but even if he didn't, they were here for at least six more days so there was plenty of time for something to happen, and something would, she was sure of it.

Kleinstein was on board his Gulfstream jet, mid-flight from New York to Los Angeles. The aircraft had been equipped to meet all his business needs whilst travelling, and currently there was pandemonium going on as his three senior aides screamed at traders and bankers from London to Hong Kong, trying to avert the disaster they were heading right into. Everyone knew it was only a matter of time now before Russell and Maykin blew the whistle. Already rumours were flying, causing the markets to react and getting just about every news bulletin and respectable paper on the planet commenting, or even leading, with the curious and potentially serious stock fluctuations. However, as yet, not even the most informed or canny of pundits had mentioned the existence of any kind of syndicate.

At that moment Kleinstein was on the telephone with Gatling, his back turned to the rest of the cabin, a finger plugged in one ear. 'I hear what you're saying,' he growled into the receiver, 'I hear you every time, so I'll tell you again, if you'd let us deal with the problem right up front we wouldn't be in this fucking mess.'

'If you'd just listen,' Gatling seethed, 'I'm trying to tell you there's still a chance we can salvage something.'

'Impress me,' Kleinstein snarled.

'Elliot Russell's just arrived in LA,' Gatling told him. 'His girlfriend's there too, the one who interviewed Ashby in the prison. Apparently she's due to see Beth Ashby tomorrow. If you send someone in there we can use her to make Russell and Maykin drop the investigation.'

Kleinstein was grinding his teeth as he rapidly thought it through. 'It could buy us some more time at the very least,' he conceded. 'OK. Leave it with me.'

After banging down the phone he returned to the bedlam, until, having gained a good enough picture of just how bad it was getting, he walked over to where Croner, his bodyguard, was watching a game.

Croner listened attentively as his boss explained what he wanted him to do. It wasn't difficult, nothing complicated, he could be in and out of there in a couple of minutes. 'Where do I take her?' he asked.

'To the house. We'll work something out after that.'

'And the other one? What do I do about her?'

'Who, Ava?' Kleinstein smirked. 'What we should have done at the beginning,' and, forming his hand into a gun, he pointed it at his head and fired.

Chapter 27

Beth was removing wilted hibiscus blooms from their stems –
plucking exhausted little trumpets from puckered little
mouths – and dropping them into her basket where dead
geraniums and dried-up nasturtiums were already covering
the bottom. As she moved around the terrace she carried a
watering can, and wore a large straw hat to protect her head
from the blistering sun. The temperature had suddenly
soared again, scorching her back through her thin rose-pink
dress, but she hardly noticed, as she snipped and pulled and
watered, wanting urgently to get this done before she left.

Her hands were scratched and soiled, her face wholly
intent as she carried out her task, blinking at the bright, blurry
colours and delicately perfumed wafts that brushed past on
the breeze. She hadn't packed, because she wouldn't be
taking anything with her. She couldn't, and anyway she
didn't need to. She'd made all the arrangements. It was all
very simple, sliding towards the end the only way she could
now. There were envelopes, with names on, saying goodbye
to those who mattered. They wouldn't be able to reach her
after, so she'd been kind and loving where she could.

Inside, the phone rang, but she didn't look up. The machine
recorded a voice, but she didn't listen. Sweat trickled down
her face and neck; butterflies flitted round her arms, while
hummingbirds hovered over the feeder, drinking nectar from
the pin-sized holes, their tiny wings vibrating in a blur.
Yesterday she'd seen an eagle, suspended in the air a
hundred feet above, its colossal wings spread wide to reveal
the golden hue of its torso, while its black, beady eyes probed
the fertile valley below. Its cry was ugly, but not as chilling as

472

the screams of the coyotes that pierced the night like the ghoulish, wounded cries of children. She wondered if Colin had ever seen a hummingbird in the wild, or an eagle, or a coyote. If he had, she couldn't remember him telling her.

Her heartbeat thickened as the sun's rays became fiercer and the inevitable hour drew close. She just had a few more flowers to tend, then she'd take a shower and prepare herself. She wanted everything to be as pristine and beautiful as she could make it. Then she cried because she was afraid, and she couldn't stop thinking about how wrong it had all gone.

Hearing the doorbell she paused and dabbed her eyes. It couldn't be them. She wasn't ready. No one would come yet. Or would they? She turned to look at the house, then flinched as the bell rang again. If it was Wingate, and he forced his way in, she'd shoot him dead. If it was anyone else, and they'd come too early she'd . . . What would she do? She felt in her pocket for the Valium that had been delivered by the boy at the pharmacy. It couldn't be anyone she was expecting, so there was no need to answer. Whoever it was would go away if she just pretended there was nobody in.

Laurie was standing in the meagre shade of an orange tree, swearing under her breath as she failed to get a reception for her mobile phone. Closing it down, she returned to the door and pressed the bell again. As she waited, she stood back to get a good look at the front of the single-storey house, with its steeply sloping roofs and dazzling white walls that were partially covered by vines. Not a sound, nor a sign of anyone.

The gravel crunched underfoot as she walked back up the drive to where Stan was parked at the other side of the hedge. The sun was so hot and dry, it was almost like passing through fire. The car engine was idling to keep the air-con going, but the leather seat still burnt her legs as she sank into it, and closed the door.

'Can you get a reception on your phone?' she said, taking a bottle of warm water from the beverage-holder.

He tried. 'Nope, nothing,' he said.

Wiping her mouth with her hand, she looked back at the house. It was barely visible through the density of the hedge, merely patches of white stucco and a few colourful blooms.

'She's in there, I'm certain of it,' she said. 'Where else could she be?'

'Is there a back way in?'

'There's a gate at the side of the garage, but it's locked.'

'So what do you want to do?'

She was thinking about that. 'Actually, the phones have given me an idea,' she said, opening the door to get out again. 'Maybe it'll work.'

'Want me to come?'

'No. You stay here. I don't want her to see you. In fact, pull forward a bit so there's no sign of the car from the house.'

After she got out he eased the car forward, just managing to stay out of the ditch, then stopped on a small grassy verge in front of next door's wall.

Laurie looked around. The narrow, winding road that snaked along the crest of the mountains was overhung with drooping eucalyptus trees and fringed by high, impenetrable hedges. Beyond, hidden from view, were vast private estates whose gardens descended into the canyons below. There were smaller houses too, like this one, set back from the road, yet seeming just as uninhabited, equally as remote. It was all so quiet and still – merely the occasional whisper of air that stirred the trees, the ubiquitous insect life, and the distant hum of a strimmer.

Going back down the drive she took a wet-wipe from her bag to cool her neck. She'd put sun block on before coming out, but the heat was so intense she could feel it blazing into her skin like flames. How did anyone survive in this climate? But, of course, it was why no one was about.

When she reached the door she tried the bell again, waited a moment, then walked along to peer into the closest window. Reflections of the sky and treetops made it hard to see, but she could tell it was a bedroom, with an unmade bed and an open wardrobe door. The next window was frosted, so presumably a bathroom; the one after was too high for her to reach, though from the cupboards that were visible she deduced it was the kitchen.

The sun was merciless. She had to get out of it soon. 'Beth!' she called. 'Beth, are you in there?'

The only answer was the monotonous buzz of cicadas.

She went back to the front door, rang the bell then rapped on the highly polished cedar wood. 'Beth. It's Laurie Forbes. We're supposed to meet today.' She listened with an ear to the doorjamb. 'Beth, I know you're there,' she cried, actually starting to wonder if she was. 'Please, I just want to make sure you're all right. Georgie's worried about you. We all are.'

'Go away!'

Laurie started. The voice had come from the other side of the door – a mere two feet away. She pictured Beth standing there, eye pressed to the optic watching the contorted image of the woman outside. 'Beth, please let me in,' she implored. 'I just want –'

'I said, go away.'

'I won't keep you a moment. Georgie asked –'

'Tell Georgie I'm fine. She shouldn't worry, everything's working out.'

Laurie wondered what that meant, but this wasn't the time to ask. 'OK, I'll tell her. But if you could just open the door –'

'I can't.'

'Just for a moment.'

'I told you, I *can't*.'

'There's no need to be afraid,' Laurie assured her. 'You don't even have to talk to me if you don't want to. I just promised Georgie that I'd see for myself that you're all right.'

Beth was silent.

Laurie waited, almost daring to hope. She heard no movement inside, but sensed she was still there, the other side of the door. 'All right,' she said finally. 'I'll leave, but I let my taxi go, so I don't have a way of getting back. My mobile doesn't work up here. If I could use your phone for a moment . . .'

Long seconds ticked by. Nothing stirred; the only sound was the continuing drone of cicadas. Then it stopped, leaving an eerie silence, as though life everywhere had abruptly ceased.

'Beth, it's very hot out here,' she said, 'and you know how far it is to a phone. Please, it won't take a minute.'

There was another interminable silence. Praying that Beth hadn't gone to ring a taxi for her, she was about to call out again when, to her amazement, the sound of a bolt sliding back was followed by the clank of a security chain. The large brass handle dipped and the door began to open.

With the sun's glare still in her eyes Laurie couldn't make out the interior, just a dark, indefinable mass beyond the first few feet of light. 'Thank you,' she said, experiencing a pulse of unease as she stepped up to the threshold.

'The phone's through there,' Beth said, coming out from behind the door and pointing down the hall.

Laurie turned to look at her and had to fight not to gasp, for the sight of her was not at all what she'd expected. Her hair was lank, uncombed and showing an inch of dark roots, her face was smeared with dirt, her eyes were puffy and red, and she seemed so fragile and thin that the collagen in her lips and implants in her breasts made her seem almost cartoonish.

'Thank you,' she said again, and turned in the direction Beth had pointed.

Behind her Beth closed and locked the door, then followed. 'Georgie should have told you, I don't want to be interviewed,' she said as they reached the kitchen. 'I asked her to give you the message.' Her voice sounded raspy and dry, as though she hadn't drunk anything in days.

'She did, but she was worried, and as I was in LA anyway –'

'There's nothing to worry about,' Beth said. 'Everything's OK.' She shrugged self-consciously. 'It might not look it, but it is.' For a moment her eyes met Laurie's, then they darted away. 'I look terrible. I know,' she said going to the fridge. 'But I wasn't expecting you. I'd have had a shower, washed my hair. It wasn't worth doing until I'd finished the garden. Would you like some water?'

Laurie nodded. 'Yes, please.'

She took out a bottle of Evian then let the door swing closed on its own. 'I was thinking, a couple of days ago,' she said, as she unscrewed the top, 'about the first time we met, you and I. Do you remember, when you came to my house and told me Colin had been arrested?'

'Yes, of course.'

Beth shrugged. 'I was just thinking about it,' she said. 'It seems so long ago now, but what was it, four, five months?'

'More or less,' Laurie answered.

She took two glasses from a cupboard, pushed them under the ice-shoot, then filled them with water. 'The phone's over there,' she said, nodding towards it. 'There's a taxi number on the board next to it.'

Laurie went to pick it up. The number she dialled put her straight through to the voice mail at the hotel. She keyed in her own password then ordered a taxi to come as soon as possible.

When she'd finished she turned round to find Beth staring right at her.

Startled, she felt herself colour as she said, 'Shouldn't be long.'

Beth passed her a glass of water.

Laurie swallowed some, watching her over the rim of the glass. Though on one level she seemed quite normal, there was something about her that was making Laurie edgy.

Suddenly the phone rang.

Laurie gasped, then laughed. Then they both stood there listening as Mitzi's voice announced that there was no one in, so please leave a message. The tone sounded, then the line went dead.

Beth carried her drink over to the sliding French windows and gazed out to where she'd left her watering can and basket, next to the gazebo. After a while she said, 'I really wasn't going to let you in, you know. But then I thought, why not? I don't like being alone.'

'Georgie wants you to go home.'

'Home? With her and Bruce?' She shook her head. 'My home is with Colin and that's over now, isn't it? There's no home for us any more.'

Not sure whether she meant because he was in prison, or because he was divorcing her, Laurie said softly, 'You could make another. Start a new life.'

'What do you think I've been doing here?' She laughed drily. 'I haven't made much of a success of it, though, have I? But it's OK. It'll all be over soon, and it's good that you'll be here when it happens. You can be a witness.'

'When what happens?' Laurie said, experiencing another beat of unease.

'Actually, you could probably make the call,' Beth

continued. 'If it works out that way. But it might not. We'll see.'

Laurie frowned. 'I don't understand. What call?' she asked.

Beth turned away from the window and smiled. 'It won't work out that way,' she assured her, 'so don't worry. Shall we go and sit down? It's prettier outside, but cooler in the sitting room.'

Laurie followed her back along the hall, then down the three steps that descended from the square entrance hall into the sitting room. There were several armchairs and two sofas grouped around a large glass coffee table in front of the fireplace. Magazines were scattered about the rugs and limestone floor, some open, some not. A few cigarette ends littered an ashtray, and the TV cabinet had been moved out of its corner, bringing it closer to the nearest chair. Beth turned the chair to face into the room and sat down. Laurie chose one of the sofas, avoiding the thin shafts of sunlight that cut through the closed slats of the shutters.

Beth smiled warmly and raised her glass.

Laurie returned the salute and they both drank. She had no idea what was going to happen now, whether someone was going to arrive as Beth had intimated, whether she'd guess the taxi was a hoax and make her leave, or even if she might suddenly open up and talk. Her expression was so benign, there was simply no knowing what was going on in her mind, though surely, if there was a chance someone might come, and that it might be Kleinstein, or Wingate, she wouldn't be this calm.

Taking small heart from that, Laurie sipped her water again and was about to speak when Beth suddenly said, 'You heard about what they did to me, didn't you? I know, because you told Georgie. I just wondered who told you.'

Surprised by the frankness, Laurie said, 'Actually, someone told Elliot Russell and he told me.'

Beth nodded. 'Someone,' she repeated. 'Always protecting your sources. Colin was very particular about that too.' She looked towards the fireplace, tilting her glass back and forth to make the ice clink, then her eyes slanted back to Laurie. 'How is he?' she asked. 'You've seen him, haven't you?'

'I'm afraid he doesn't look very good,' Laurie answered. 'I think he's finding it hard in prison.'

The corners of Beth's mouth went down as she acknowledged that. Then gazing off towards the hearth again she said, 'He wouldn't see me. Except once.' She paused, then attempted a laugh. 'That hurt a lot,' she confessed. 'Almost as much as Heather Dance and her child. But he was always hurting me, one way or another, so I shouldn't have been surprised when he did it again.'

'Was he ever physical?' Laurie dared to ask. 'I mean in the way he hurt you?'

Unfazed by the presumption, Beth merely shook her head. 'No, but sometimes I almost wished he would be. At least that kind of pain goes away. The other just stays and stays and . . .' She smiled, brightly. 'But it wasn't all pain. We loved each other too, and . . .'

'And?' Laurie prompted.

'Nothing. We just loved each other. As a matter of fact we still do, but he's got a child by someone else now, so he has to go to her, if they free him.'

'Do you think they will?'

Beth nodded, then drank some water. The mouthful was too large. 'Yes, if he can prove he didn't do it,' she said, wiping the excess liquid from her chin.

'Did he do it?'

'He keeps saying he didn't, so maybe we should believe him. Georgie says you already do.'

Laurie was watching her closely. 'I think there's a chance he's telling the truth, yes,' she admitted. 'Don't you?'

Beth's eyes widened with surprise. 'Does it matter what I think?' she said.

'I'm sure it does to him.'

She seemed to find that amusing. Then, after drinking some more, she leant forward to put her glass on the table. 'Of course, it's all much more complicated than it appears, you do realize that, don't you?' she said.

'I think so,' Laurie answered. 'I'm just not sure how.'

'You've read my book? We sent it to you.'

Laurie nodded.

'So you've been trying to work it all out from that?'

Again Laurie nodded.

'That's why you asked if he'd ever hurt me physically, of course. But no, Colin wasn't like Rodrigo in that respect.'

'But he was in others?'

Beth nodded. 'Oh yes. Very much so.'

'Did he help you write it?'

Her eyes flashed angrily. 'No! Did he tell you that? He's a liar if he told you that.'

'No, no,' Laurie assured her. 'He didn't say that at all. It was just me asking.'

'Why?' she spat. 'Do you think I'm incapable of creating something like that alone? Yes, of course you do. You're one of them. You all think I'm nothing –'

'That's not true,' Laurie cried. 'No one thinks that about you, least of all me. The book is brilliant. I honestly didn't mean any offence. It was stupid and insensitive. I'm sorry.'

Beth eyed her suspiciously, like a mouse watching a cat, or maybe it was the other way round.

'I'm sorry,' Laurie said again.

The hostility slowly retreated, then a smile began to play on her lips. 'So tell me what you liked best about the book,' she challenged.

Relieved that the small storm was over, Laurie seized the firmer ground, saying, 'Probably the way you ended it, in modern times. It had such a wonderful pathos. I actually cried and laughed at the same time. I was so afraid it would be tragic, like her previous life.'

Beth almost glowed. 'Life should be more like fiction, don't you agree?' she said, pressing her hands together and pushing them between her knees. 'Think how happy we'd all be if we could write our own lives. I've never seen the point in misery, have you?'

Laurie smiled. 'Not really,' she replied.

Beth laughed. 'Who'd write themselves a life of misery?' she said. 'Not me, that's for sure. I've got God to thank for mine. Have you ever known misery? You don't look as though you have.'

'My sister died a year ago,' Laurie answered. 'That was very hard. She was my twin.'

'Oh dear, yes, I can imagine that would be hard. How did she die?'

'She committed suicide.'

Beth's eyes rounded. 'Really?' she said. 'Why?'

'She . . . It's not easy to talk about . . .'

'Was it to do with a man?'

'Partly.'

Beth nodded, her eyes full of knowing. 'So she understood what misery was. How did she do it?'

'You mean kill herself? She drove her car into a wall.'

Beth drew back in horror. 'That's terrible,' she exclaimed. 'Poor girl. Poor, poor girl. Death can be so violent.'

Wanting to get off the subject Laurie said, 'How long did it take you to write the book?'

Beth rolled her eyes. 'All my life,' she smiled. 'Or that's how it feels.' Gazing off at nothing, she said, 'We are the sum total of our life's experiences, are we not? No, don't agree with me, because we're not. We're all of us more than life gives us – much, much more. You are more than just the person sitting there on that sofa, prying into my life. This is only one aspect of you. There are others, so many you probably don't even know the half, and never will, unless you're brave enough to explore them.'

'Have you been able to?' Laurie asked.

'Explore my other dimensions? Of course. Writers have to. You see, every character I create has come from inside of me.'

'Even the aristocrats?'

She nodded. 'Correct.'

'What about inspiration? Doesn't that come from outside of you?'

'Of course. It can't be otherwise.' Her eyes seemed to drift off for a moment. Then, as though addressing an imagined dilemma, she said, 'I've never wanted to hurt anyone, the way they hurt me.' She looked at Laurie. 'Do you know the reason they beat me with a whip? Would you like to see the scars?' She was already lowering the zip of her dress and standing up to show her back.

One glimpse of the still-livid welts, cutting through the soft bronze skin of her back like angry red tongues, was enough to make Laurie wince and look away.

'Not pretty, is it?' Beth said, pulling her dress back up and sitting down. 'Do you know why they did it?'

Laurie shook her head.

'They did it,' she said, 'because they didn't understand my book. They thought I was accusing them of murder, but how could I when I wrote it before Sophie Long died?'

Laurie's heartbeat was slowing, but she said nothing, only waited for her to go on.

She laughed suddenly, almost bitterly. 'What a comedy of errors it turned out to be,' she said. 'Them beating me for something they didn't understand, me telling them the very last thing they expected to hear.'

'Which was what?' Laurie asked.

Beth's eyes narrowed as she looked at her. 'You're not asking the right questions,' she told her. 'You should be asking why they were so concerned about an accusation of murder.'

'OK,' Laurie responded. 'So why were they?'

Beth's head went to one side, as though considering the answer. Finally she said, 'They thought I knew about some approach they'd made to Colin, something that was going to make him fantastically rich. But I didn't, not until that night. All I knew was that Marcus Gatling had far too much power over my husband, and I hated him for it. Colin would never admit it, of course, but it was true. He was a victim of his own ego. He wouldn't allow himself to see how deeply he was in the pockets of men who wanted to control him for their own purposes, first as a reporter, then as an editor, then as a government puppet. They didn't put him there because he was good; they put him there to serve them. Of course you're recognizing all this from the book, aren't you?'

Laurie nodded.

'Well, obviously, I was drawing on Marcus Gatling and his cronies when I devised the aristocrats – cronies who were faceless to me until the night they did this.' She was pointing over her shoulder at her back. 'But they weren't the only source I had to draw on because there were Colin's colleagues too, the ones who'd ridiculed and ignored me for years. Those who talked across me as if I weren't there; never asking my opinion on anything, or just dismissing it if I gave one. They knew Colin was having affairs all over the place, so if he had no respect for me, why should they? And if I had no respect for myself, which obviously I didn't because of the way I kept taking him back, then I wasn't really worth bothering with at all. So the aristocrats comprise every one of them, his colleagues, his friends, his mentors, even his mistresses. But Marcus Gatling presumed I was referring only to him, that like the Hydra I'd given him many heads, but the body, the muse, was no one but him. That's what guilt does, you see. It makes you lose perspective, confuses rationale. It's an extremely uneasy bedfellow, and when you can't sleep at night paranoia soon comes calling.' She smiled and picked up her water. 'Am I going too fast for you?' she said. 'Is it all making sense?'

Laurie nodded. 'I think so,' she answered, judging it best to hold back her questions for now.

'So the killing of Carlotta's spirit in the book,' Beth continued, 'symbolises the killing of mine in life, because that's what they've done to me: they've killed who I really am. They've treated me as though I don't exist, so I've stopped existing. Beth Ashby died the day of Sophie Long's murder, and Ava Montgomery was born, which sounds insane because it is. But that was how it felt, because, you see, the timing was so propitious. My husband was arrested for murder, and only a few hours later I received a call telling me my book was going to be published. So on the one hand my nightmares were just beginning, while on the other a dream was coming true. Which would you have chosen? The disgrace of the man you love? Or the glory of the woman you've created? I wanted both, of course. I wasn't just going to walk away and leave him. He needed me now in a way he never had before, and because I love him, the way Carlotta loves Rodrigo – with all my heart and soul – I wanted to be there for him. But he wouldn't let me. He told me to go and make a new life, that he was divorcing me and didn't want to see me again. The killing of my spirit wasn't over. It was just going to go on and on. That was how it felt. No one loved Beth; no one wanted her, not even Colin any more. So why should I want her? Why should I struggle to keep her alive when Ava was so full of promise, had already received her first recognition that was in no way dependent on him, or because of him. I'd done it alone, and no one could ever say I was being published because I was his wife, because no one knew until after. They thought Ava Montgomery was a real person, which she was, because she's a part of me, the part that had the courage and confidence to write the book, and believe in it enough to submit it. Beth couldn't have done that. She was too timid, too insecure and dulled by Colin's shadow. So it really was as though Beth started to die that day, as Ava came alive. Along with Carlotta and Sophie, Beth became the victim of the aristocrats.' She used her fingers to mark quotes around aristocrats. 'But of course I'm still here, you're looking at me, listening to me, you're probably even slightly nervous of me. I don't blame you. I'm afraid too, because I can't sleep, and now paranoia has come calling on me.'

'Is your paranoia driven by guilt?' Laurie asked.

Beth nodded. 'Yes. Essentially, yes.'

'What kind of guilt?'

She sighed and seemed to think about that for a while. 'The guilt of my husband,' she answered, 'the guilt of my own thoughts, my actions.'

'Of writing something that then proved itself in reality?'

Beth stared at her hard. 'Now you're going to say that it was a fluke, that I couldn't possibly have known, so it doesn't make me responsible,' she said.

'The responsibility lies with the person who did it,' Laurie responded.

'Of course, and I have no intention of taking it away from that person. The girl was a sacrificial lamb, just like in the book.'

'But Sophie Long wasn't a dimension of some fictional character's psyche,' Laurie protested. 'She was real.'

Beth nodded. 'Yes, she was, that's why they were so paranoid.'

'They being Marcus Gatling and his wife?'

'Yes.'

'Did you know,' Laurie said, 'that they were at Sophie's flat the morning she was killed?'

Beth blinked, then frowned and looked at her strangely.

'How do you know that?' she asked. 'No one's ever mentioned it before.' Then after a pause, 'Why were they there?'

'I don't know. Do you?'

'Me?' she laughed. 'Why would I know?'

Laurie's eyes were watching her very closely.

'Why would I know?' she cried, throwing out her arms.

'You may not know *why* they were there, but you do know they were there, don't you?' Laurie challenged.

She didn't answer.

'Why are you protecting them?'

Her eyebrows flew up. 'To protect myself, of course.'

'From what?'

She looked at Laurie incredulously. 'More of this,' she said, indicating her back again.

'What else?' Laurie challenged. 'There is more, isn't there?'

'You really don't know what it is? After all I've just said, you still don't know what it is?'

Laurie shook her head slowly, though in truth she thought she might. 'How do you know they were there?' she said.

Beth only looked at her.

'You saw them, didn't you?'

Her expression didn't change.

'That's what you told them that night when they beat you, wasn't it, that you'd seen them at Sophie Long's the day she was murdered?'

Beth laughed softly. 'A comedy of errors,' she repeated.

Laurie looked at her, praying her fear didn't show. She didn't want to go any further with this now, for she knew absolutely where it was going to end.

'Yes, you're right,' Beth told her. 'I can see in your eyes that you know now. So there you have it. Now you know the truth. Is it what you were expecting?'

Elliot was staring at Max Erwin. They'd been working together since eight that morning, connecting all their findings with those that were coming in from around the world, and only now had Beth Ashby's name come up – and in such a way that Elliot couldn't quite believe what he'd just heard.

'You're telling me she confessed to killing the girl?' he repeated. 'That's what they beat out of her?'

Erwin nodded. 'Kleinstein just told me last night. They thought she knew something about the syndicate, might be planning some kind of blackmail or something, but Gatling was always scared he'd been seen coming out of the hooker's apartment. And it turns out he was, but not by Mr Ashby, who'd then told Mrs Ashby, the way he suspected . . .'

'For Christ's sake,' Elliot muttered, grabbing for his phone. 'Laurie's up there with her now. Are you sure you've got that right?' he demanded as he speed-dialled the number.

'That's what the man said,' Erwin responded. 'She confessed to killing the girl herself.'

'Damn!' Elliot swore as the automated voice told him the unit was out of range. He tried Stan and got the same response. 'I've got to go up there,' he said, and, snatching up his car keys, he ran to the door.

'I'll drive,' Erwin said, coming after him. 'I know the town better.'

As they sped along Lincoln, heading for the 10 Freeway, Elliot tried the number at Beth Ashby's house. The machine picked up so he left a message for Laurie to call him urgently.

'Step on it,' he said to Erwin. 'I've got a really bad feeling about this.'

'*Shit!*' Erwin swore, as the lights turned red on Venice. Swerving sharply to the right, he accelerated fast down a side street, made several more turns, then sped down the ramp on to the freeway.

Elliot was so tense he barely noticed where they were. The fact that Laurie was in a house alone with a killer was all he could think about. But Beth Ashby had no reason to hurt her, provided Laurie didn't know the truth. Just don't let Beth Ashby choose today to make her second confession! A thousand questions began pouring into his head. He had no answers, though he understood now what Gatling had meant when he'd said there wasn't a damned thing they could do about it. Beth Ashby had confessed to the killing, but if Gatling had her arrested there wasn't only how the information had been extracted to consider, there was what she could tell the police about Gatling and his wife being at

486

the flat right before the murder. No matter that they hadn't committed the crime themselves, the scandal and publicity would be anathema to people like them.

'What the fuck was he doing there?' he demanded of Erwin.

Erwin glanced at him. 'The girl was a hooker,' he reminded him.

'So he was there, getting laid?'

'Apparently. His wife dropped him off, then came back for him half an hour later.'

At any other time Elliot might have laughed. 'So Beth Ashby commits a murder that's got nothing at all to do with anything, except the fact that her husband's screwing the girl, and now all this?' he said, hardly believing his own words.

'That's the way I'm reading it,' Erwin answered. 'In fact, that's the way they're all reading it, Kleinstein, Wingate, Brunner, the whole lot of them.'

Elliot was still trying to get his mind round it. 'So if the Gatlings hadn't panicked and interfered with the police investigation –'

'The euro would still be on a slow boat to extinction,' Erwin confirmed, speeding across the flyover from the 10 to the 405, 'and Mrs Ashby would very probably already be toast.'

'And by the time they found out the truth – that she'd done it – it was already too late for them,' Elliot said. 'Why didn't they have her arrested anyway?'

'Were they looking for any more publicity?' Erwin asked incredulously. 'Besides, what the hell did they care who killed the girl, just as long as none of them was in the frame.'

'Does she know anything about the syndicate?'

'She might have pieced something together by now from the questions they asked, but from what Kleinstein tells me, it doesn't seem like she had a clue before.'

'Jesus Christ,' Elliot muttered, shaking his head. 'To think of everything that's happened . . . No one ever even suspected her, or not seriously . . . How the hell did she do it?'

'That I don't know,' Erwin answered. 'But what I do know, from the look of this traffic, is that we're not going to get there any time soon.'

A bolt of fear shot through Elliot's heart. If anything happened to Laurie, anything at all . . .

Laurie and Beth were still in the sitting room. Neither had moved nor spoken since Beth had admitted to killing Sophie, though the air had noticeably altered. Laurie guessed it was her own fear that had changed it, though Beth too seemed more tense, and even afraid.

In the end Beth was the first to speak. 'You know one of the greatest ironies of all this for me,' she said, 'is how, by over-intellectualizing my book, they've turned it into the weapon of their own destruction. Hoist with their own petard, you might say. If they'd just left me alone . . . But they couldn't, could they? Guilty consciences and paranoia wouldn't allow it. They have so much to hide – people like that always do. And all the time they were afraid of what I might know, it never seemed to occur to them that I might have seen them at Sophie's. If it had, then they'd have had to wonder, wouldn't they, how I had seen them? And if they'd asked themselves that . . .' She paused, took a breath then said, 'If they hadn't been at Sophie's that day, they wouldn't have hampered the police investigation, and who knows what the police might have found, given a free rein. Did it surprise you to find that the police could be controlled? You must have noticed during your investigation.'

'No, it didn't surprise me,' Laurie answered.

She nodded. 'Colin used to hate that,' she said, 'the fact that power could be wielded over the law. He knew it was naïve to think it couldn't, but he was honourable, in his way. He liked things to be right. It was only with me that he kept getting it wrong, but whoever cared about me?' She smiled sadly and looked down at her hands. 'They knew they were the aristocrats,' she continued, 'and the fact that they were at Sophie's that day, and were afraid of it coming out, was enough to make them destroy my book and now the film. So they've taken my husband, my spirit and now my dreams. They have so much and I wanted so little.'

'What about what Sophie wanted?' Laurie asked quietly.

Beth looked confused. 'What did she want?' she said.

Her life, Laurie wanted to say, but didn't quite dare. 'Wasn't she an innocent victim?' she said.

Beth nodded sadly. 'Yes, she was,' she answered. 'The sacrificial lamb, as Mitzi called her. That's how it became confused. The murder in the book, which appeared literal at first, turned out only to be symbolic, so they didn't know what to make of it. Was I talking about Sophie Long? It could hardly be likely when the book had obviously been written before, but the questions it might throw up for a discerning reporter . . .' She looked at Laurie and inclined her head, almost graciously.

'But when Georgie asked about the sacrificial lamb you told her to ask Colin, or Gatling,' Laurie said.

Beth smiled. 'Of course.'

Yes, of course, Laurie conceded. It had been a way of keeping the attention focused on them and away from herself. Whatever else Beth Ashby was, she was very far from stupid.

'I expect, what you'd really like me to tell you now,' Beth said, 'is why I killed Sophie. Why she had to be the sacrificial lamb.'

Laurie waited, her eyes reflecting as much unease as intrigue.

Beth's breath shuddered slightly as she inhaled. 'I killed her,' she said, 'because he was going to leave me.' As she spoke her veneer of bravado, the bluster of being a writer whom everyone had praised, seemed to crumble.

'For Sophie?' Laurie said.

'No, for Heather.'

Laurie frowned.

Beth watched her for a moment, then said, 'I knew about Heather long before it was in the paper. And Jessica. And Sophie. I knew about them all. He couldn't keep anything secret from me, not where his women were concerned. Half the time he didn't even bother to try. It was just the way he was, he used to tell me; he couldn't help it. It's like that for some men; they can't resist the opposite sex, but it doesn't really mean anything. I was his wife; he always came home, so I should understand that I was loved above all the others. And I did understand. He did love me, but it still tore me apart every time I knew he was with another woman. I wanted to be enough. I needed to matter so much that he'd never want anyone else. It seemed such a simple thing to want, when so many other women had it, but with Colin it wasn't possible.'

Laurie watched her as the mask fell away some more and she stared down at her empty glass. It was like watching an unhappy child emerge from the sophistication of a woman's defences.

'Of course I should have left him,' she said, still staring at her glass. 'Any normal woman would have. But I'm not normal, am I? I can't be to have put up with what I did.' She looked at Laurie. 'Do you have any idea what it's like to love someone so much that it's as though your whole life depends on it, and then have him treat you as though you're just there to be walked over, on his way out to someone else's bed? I hated him for that. It made me so angry. I'd even attack him physically, but he always managed to win me round in the end. He knew I loved him, and he loved me too, so it was like a game to him. Even after I'd thrown him out and told him I never wanted to see him again, he'd always come back, knowing I wouldn't say no, because I couldn't. How could I when life without him was an even worse hell than life with him? That's what being in love is like, you know? Hell. At least it is for me.'

The phone rang in the kitchen, but she made no attempt to get up and answer it, merely waited for the machine to kick in, then whoever it was to leave a message. Someone did, but from this distance it was impossible to hear who.

Laurie said, 'How did you find out about Heather?'

Beth's eyebrows went up, though she was staring down at the glass again. 'I followed him,' she answered. 'It was last summer, a year ago. He was going to a conference for the weekend, he said. I knew it was in Cornwall because it was written in his diary, "Cornwall". Can you imagine following someone all that way, knowing that you're going to have your heart broken at the end of it? Was I mad for doing it? Yes, of course. Would I have been mad to stay at home and believe his lies? Yes, of course. Whichever way, I was mad because I couldn't stop loving a man who couldn't stop

490

loving other women. What difference was it going to make when I caught him? It wasn't as though he'd never done it before. And I'd forgive him, because I always did. But this time it turned out to be different. This time, when he got to the house that I later found out he owned, with her, there wasn't only a woman sitting outside on the grass, there was a little girl too. I knew, even before she ran into his arms that she was his. I could see the resemblance. They were all so wrapped up in each other they didn't even notice me. Such a happy, loving little family scene.'

Laurie's heart was responding with compassion, for she could easily imagine how devastating it must have been. She could even see it now, in the way Beth was holding herself. 'Did you ever actually meet Heather?' she asked.

'No. Never,' she whispered. Then in a slightly stronger voice, 'We spoke once on the phone, quite recently actually, but we never met.'

Laurie wondered what the call had been about, but didn't ask.

'I kept waiting for him to tell me about her,' she said, 'but he didn't. It was only a matter of time, though. I knew that. He was going to leave, he had to for the child.'

'So did he tell you, in the end, that he was going to?' Laurie said, when she stopped.

'No. I just knew he would.'

'But if you were convinced he was going to leave you for Heather,' Laurie said, 'why did you –' She broke off, not wanting to say the word.

'Kill Sophie? Two reasons: I couldn't deprive little Jessica of her mother; and killing Sophie would make him more mine than he'd ever been.'

Laurie frowned. 'How could it do that?'

'If he went to prison there couldn't be any more women, could there? And I'd always know where he was.'

Oh my God, Laurie was thinking, *she really did plan it. She really knew what she was doing.* 'So how . . .? What happened?' she heard herself ask.

'It wasn't hard,' she answered. 'I mean, arranging it. Doing it was horrible. I hated that.' She put a hand to her head, as though to block out the image. 'She's always there. She never

491

leaves me, no matter how hard I try to tell myself Colin did it, she keeps coming back to remind me he didn't.' Her head came up; her eyes were swimming in tears, seeming to plead for understanding. 'I had to convince myself completely that he was guilty,' she explained. 'I had to tell myself that I'd never heard of Heather, or Jessica, or Sophie, before that day. I couldn't allow even my thoughts to wander into areas of danger, in case I ever said anything to give myself away. I was sure, if I tried hard enough, it would become like the truth – that Colin did it so he deserved to be where he was. And sometimes it worked. Of course, it helped being Ava. She allowed me the freedom of being someone else completely, who didn't care about Colin, or the other women, or what had happened. It was all nothing to her. She didn't consider him, just like he'd never considered me. It's strange how once you've stepped on to the other side of the law the whole world looks different. Nothing is ever the same again. There are no barriers any more, nothing to say how far you can, or can't, go. It's like falling through space, there's nowhere to land. You don't belong anywhere any more, and there's no way to turn back.' Tears were spilling into the dust on her face, while her hands were clenched around the glass in her lap.

Laurie watched her eyes blink sightlessly. It was as though she was in another place, another time, somewhere remote from her conscience, yet still connected to the pain.

'I don't understand how you did it,' Laurie said after a while. 'You had an alibi. The cleaner, the receipt for the paper . . .'

Beth's head came up and as she stared off into the distance she made a dry, sad sound in her throat, like a sob, yet like a laugh too. 'The cleaner was easy,' she said. 'There's a door to the outside from my study, so I often used to go out and come back without her knowing. She hardly ever knew what was going on anyway. And I got the paper just in case anyone else saw me – I could give it as my reason for popping out.'

Laurie thought about the loud, harassed woman she'd interviewed, who had sworn Mrs Ashby 'never leave the house, except for two minutes to buy paper'. Yes, she could imagine the woman being so wrapped up in herself that she might not notice what else was going on around her. 'What about Sophie's flat?' she said. 'There's no evidence to say you were there.'

'I'm sure there is, considering the sophistication of today's techniques,' she responded. 'But everything pointed to Colin, and because the investigation wasn't allowed to go any further, the fact that I wore his tracksuit and trainers, and kept my hair tied up in a scarf, worked. I knew he was seeing her that day, because it was in his diary. "Sophie", it said. Just like it had said "Cornwall". "Sophie" – no attempt even to disguise it. Does that tell you how little respect he had for me? He didn't even care that I knew. I'd told him to get out a few days before, so I knew he was staying with her, or Heather – it didn't really matter which. He had an arrangement to see Sophie at twelve on that particular day. Everyone else's husband eats during their lunch break – but that's what mine does. So I called her in the morning and told her I wanted to surprise him by being there too, ready for a threesome when he arrived. I offered to double her fee, which she agreed to, and then I told her what his real fantasy was, to make sure she had everything to hand. Then, when the time came, I went over there.' She took several breaths, as though she'd been running. Her hands were clamped tightly together now, the glass had slipped to the floor.

'I stayed outside at first. I was across the street, in my car, pretending to sort out paperwork, in case anyone was watching. That was when I saw Marcus come out of the building. Then Leonora pulled up and drove him away. I guessed he was one of Sophie's clients, and I knew that Leonora was tolerant, so I wasn't really surprised. Besides, I was there for my own reasons and they were all I could think of.'

She inhaled deeply, shakily, then continued. 'I went inside and we both got undressed,' she said. 'She was a sweet girl. Pretty. I could see why he liked her. She was very malleable, obliging, but nervous, I suppose because it was me. To make her feel more at ease, I pretended, in my mind, that I was Colin, and kissed her and fondled her. I was intrigued to know what a woman would feel like to him.' She bowed her head, then her shoulders began to shake as she cried.

'She lay down on the bed,' she continued, 'and I handcuffed her to the four little posts. Then I picked up her tights . . .' Her breath was coming in short, harsh bursts, and as she gasped for air, tears began streaming fast down her cheeks. 'It was horrible,' she choked. 'She was so afraid, and her eyes were looking back at me, getting bigger and bigger, so I had to turn away. She didn't deserve to die, but it was the only way I could make him stop.' She dashed a hand over her face. 'It was Colin,' she cried in despair. 'If it weren't for him I'd never have done it. So it was his fault. If he'd been faithful, if he'd loved me enough . . . He deserves to pay. Don't you see that? He killed her as surely as I did, so the guilt is ours to share. I would have stayed faithful to him all the time he was in prison. I would have visited him and written to him. He would have been mine then.'

Though appalled, Laurie's eyes shone with pity too, for the tortured rationale wasn't really that hard to understand. However, the image of the poor, terrified girl who'd lost her life in a struggle she had no way of understanding was turning her heart inside out. 'What did you do after?' she finally asked.

'After?' Beth repeated. 'What did I do? I knew Colin would be arriving any minute, so I got dressed in a hurry, went down to my car and drove back to Fulham, stopping on the way to buy some paper for my printer. Then when I got home I began psyching myself into believing Colin had done it, that I had been at my desk in the study the entire time, except when I went to get paper. I'd never told anyone about Sophie, or Jessica and Heather, not even Georgie. So I worked at convincing myself that I really never had known anything about them, and when you came along to tell me he'd been arrested, that was when I got my first practice of lying even to myself. But it was a terrible shock, you coming like that. I hadn't expected to be told that way. I even wondered if you were another of his mistresses, or if you were a policewoman come to tell me he'd been in an accident. I thought it had all gone horribly wrong, that for some reason he hadn't turned up there. Then the others started arriving, and you pushed me inside and told me. It had all gone to plan. Even better than I'd planned, because I had no idea he'd take his trousers off as soon as he got into the flat. He told me after that it's a game they played. He'd never done that with me. I wish he had. I wish he'd done everything with me, then none of this would have happened.'

She tried to smile through her tears, but her lips twisted and she choked on another breath. 'I need some more water,' she spluttered. 'Would you like some?'

Laurie nodded and handed over her glass. As soon as Beth had disappeared she crossed swiftly to the front door and tried to open it. It wouldn't budge. Trying not to panic she hunted the nearby pots and drawers for keys. Nothing. She looked for a sign of another way out. Only doors to bedrooms or cupboards.

Hearing her moving around in a nearby room, she went back to the fireplace and tried to look interested in the Polaroids that were propped amongst the various candlesticks and books. They were mostly scenes from parties that appeared to have taken place in this house, though there were a couple of Beth alone, one of them topless, with three words written underneath: Great New Boobs. She looked so happy, and carefree and beautiful, it was hard to connect her with the woman who'd just been confessing to the utter devastation of her life.

'Mementoes of some good times,' Beth said behind her. 'I expect you have those too.'

Laurie turned round, smiling. Then her eyes dilated as cold terror wrenched at her heart. 'Oh God, Beth, no,' she murmured, taking a step back.

'Theo gave me this to protect myself,' she said, looking down at the gun. In her other hand was a notepad and pen. 'So that's what I'm doing,' she said. 'I'd already planned to before you came. I was getting ready. Cleaning everything up. Making it all nice. I was going to have a shower and wash my hair too, so that when they came I'd look my best. Of course, I'd be dead, and there would be blood, but . . .' Her eyes and voice drifted for a moment. Then, returning to Laurie, she said, 'I've left notes for everyone. I thought probably you'd like to leave some too.' She held out the notepad and pen.

Laurie's head was pounding, her heart racing with fear. 'What for?' she said, the horror of understanding making her

495

dizzy.

'It's a funny thing,' Beth said, not appearing to have heard the question, 'but as I was talking to you I realized that even though I've told them I killed Sophie Long, there's nothing they can do, is there? Or nothing they'd want to do. I'm no longer a threat, of no interest to them at all. And you're the only other one who knows.'

'Beth, please, I swear I won't tell –'

'Ah, but we both know you will,' she interrupted. 'It's too good a story to pass up, and I don't blame you for wanting it. But you see, if you tell anyone they'll let Colin go free, and he doesn't deserve that.'

'Beth, please,' Laurie begged, 'you don't know what you're saying . . .'

'I want him to stay in prison,' she continued, 'and he will if there's no one here to tell what really happened. He doesn't even know himself.'

'Oh God,' Laurie sobbed, her whole body starting to shake. 'You can't mean what you're saying, Beth. Please, just put the gun down.'

Beth dropped the notepad and pen on to the sofa. 'I'll give you time to write,' she said, using her fingers to wipe away her own tears. 'I'm sure there are people you want to say goodbye to.'

'I can't,' Laurie sobbed. 'Please, Beth. It's my parents. It'll kill them if you do this. My sister, I told you, she took her own life . . . I can't put them through it again. Please, I beg you, put the gun down.'

'My parents won't care,' she responded, the words fractured by her own sobs. 'You're lucky to have parents who do. Are you married?'

'No,' she answered, thinking of Elliot. Oh God, how desperately she wanted to run to him now, to feel the safety of his arms. If anything happened she knew he'd blame himself, but it wasn't his fault. He hadn't wanted her to come.

'Do you have any children?' Beth asked.

'No.'

Beth's voice was submerged in a terrible sadness as she said, 'I had two, but they didn't stay with me either.'

Suddenly thinking of the book Laurie cried, 'You wrote a

happy ending. It all worked out, so why are you doing this?'

Beth blinked in surprise. 'This isn't fiction,' she replied. 'I could only control him in fiction. In reality, he doesn't want me.'

'But it has nothing to do with me,' Laurie gasped. 'I'm really sorry for you, truly I am, and I wish things had been better –'

'I know you do,' Beth cut in, 'and they will be, once I leave here. They'll be better for you too. Just think, your sister will be there. So you already have someone.' She gestured to the notepad. 'You can say what you like. Blame it on me, because it won't be a lie. Just don't tell them about Sophie. I'll check. After.'

After she was dead! Oh God, she had to make herself think. She had somehow to grab the gun, get out of the house, or at least alert Stan. Her chest hurt she was so afraid, her limbs were like lead. She had to distract her, overpower her, do something to save herself.

She edged forward, as though to pick up the pen. She wanted desperately to run, but knew if she did Beth would fire.

'You see, this is what I mean about being the other side of the law,' Beth said. 'Things don't mean the same any more.'

Laurie was reaching for the pen, hardly knowing what she was doing. It was mere reflex that suddenly made her gasp and spin her head towards the door, as though someone had come in.

Beth spun round too.

Laurie threw herself at the sofa and shoved it back with all her might.

Beth cried out in surprise as the sofa hit her, but though she staggered against the wall she didn't let go of the gun.

Laurie stared at her in horror. Beth stared back. Then, righting herself, she lifted the gun and cocked it ready to fire.

Max Erwin swerved hard round the bend, righted the car, then sped along Mulholland Drive. Stan's Camry came into view. Erwin hit the brakes, and screeched to a stop. Elliot was already jumping out.

Stan was opening his door as Elliot ran up.

'Is she still in there?' Elliot demanded, his face taut with fear.

'Yeah. What's happened? Why are you here?'

'Is anyone else in there?' Elliot said, looking back at the house.

'Just Beth Ashby, as far I know.'

Max Erwin joined them. 'Do we knock, or try to find another way in?' he said.

Elliot was already starting down the drive. 'Let's try the windows first,' he answered, 'try to see what's going on.'

Stan was right behind them. Erwin went to press an ear against the front door, as Elliot checked the first window. Stan was about to try the next when a gunshot suddenly reverberated through the house.

'Jesus Christ,' Erwin muttered, his eyes showing horror as he turned to Elliot.

Ashen-faced, Elliot ran past him, yelling, 'Laurie! Laurie, open the door!' He hammered frantically, but no one responded.

Behind them a car pulled in to the drive, a black Lexus with tinted windows and personalized plates. It was difficult to make out anyone inside, but as it reversed at speed, then tore off down the road, Erwin hissed, 'Shit! That was Croner, Kleinstein's man.'

As Elliot looked at him the gun went off again. 'Laurie!' he roared, hammering violently on the door. 'For Christ's sake, let me in.'

There was the sound of smashing glass.

'Here, this way,' Stan yelled, punching out the rest of the window. 'She's in here.' He heaved himself up on to the ledge and was about to go through, when he suddenly froze. 'Oh my God, no,' he choked, putting out a hand. 'Stop. Stay right where you are. You don't want to go in there.'

But Elliot was already grabbing his legs and, tearing him down from the sill, he vaulted up there himself. 'Oh no,' he groaned when he saw inside. 'Oh God, Laurie *no!*'

Chapter 28

A gauzy, white marine layer was rolling in from the Pacific as the plane rose up from the ground, leaving LAX and vanishing into a covering bank of cloud. The ocean below was a marauding swell of white-topped waves; the beaches were deserted.

After the drinks were served and the plane was well established on its southbound journey, Elliot got up from his seat and moved forward three rows to sit beside Max Erwin. For the past week both men had been dealing with so many detectives, phone calls, and emails that neither had managed much sleep, nor did they anticipate any if they remained in LA now that so much press attention was focused their way. Besides, Erwin was in a highly vulnerable position after Kleinstein's man, Croner, had seen him outside Beth's house with Elliot. So now they were headed to the relative seclusion and safety of a Mexican fishing village, just north of Puerto Vallarta, where Max Erwin kept a villa that no one knew anything about. Once there they intended to spend four solid days wrapping up the first of many stories featuring the syndicate, primarily exposing its existence, its major players and its strategy regarding the euro. The follow-up stories were being prepared by other reporters, working around the globe, and were being timed to hit the stands, or the airwaves, just as the shock of the previous story was starting to fade.

Of course, by now the entire syndicate knew they were about to be exposed, so it was anyone's guess what measures were being taken to downplay, or even negate their roles. Meanwhile, markets were responding in unnervingly erratic ways, and several unexpected resignations from major corporations were daily making headlines. Elliot's team, having gained confirmation of Gatling's visit to Sophie Long's apartment, had sold that story to the *Independent*, while Leonora's sudden collapse and prescribed need for rest had been run by the *Mail*. The biggest shock so far had come with the resignation of the head of the European Central Bank, who'd held a press conference in Brussels announcing that ill health was the major factor in his decision to step down. It was all no more than the spouting of hot air before the real volcano erupted.

Now, as Elliot and Erwin finished their meals and ordered more coffee, they continued discussing the structure and intent of the syndicate, going over everything in the minutest detail, scrolling up and down the screens of their laptops, checking that each piece of the puzzle was either in place, or ready to go in once it had been vetted for accuracy, and cleared by lawyers. The task was painstaking and complicated to the extreme, and required the kind of concentration that made their heads spin. However, thanks to the back-up efforts of Maykin's people in New York, Elliot's team in London and a selected group of currency experts worldwide, it was finally coming together in a way that was going to shake Europe to its very core.

Finally, his vision blurred by fatigue, Elliot sat back and glanced at the date on his watch. 'You know, I reckon there's a chance we can make it for Thursday,' he said.

Erwin nodded agreement. 'We just need some final feedback from the lawyers, a few more sessions going over it again, and a couple of bullet-proof vests.'

Elliot's smile was grim. 'Publicity is protection,' he reminded him.

'We like to think,' Erwin added. 'But hey, don't worry, if they do take us out, we'll go knowing our names have gone down in history.'

Elliot cast him a look, then, stifling a yawn, closed down his laptop and tucked it into the back of the seat in front. 'See if you can get some shuteye before we arrive,' he said, getting up. 'You need to be in a fit state to drive.'

Returning to his own seat, he fastened his seat belt and ran a hand over his exhausted, unshaven face. After a while he closed his eyes, but as sleep rose up to claim him, he was suddenly jolted awake by the sharp explosion of a gunshot. It took only seconds for him to realize it had happened in his head, not in reality. Nevertheless, his heart was pounding and a thin film of sweat had broken out on his skin. It had been like this since it had happened, though occasionally he managed some sleep before the nightmare of hearing that gun go off blasted him from a dream into the real world.

He'd known, even before Stan had thrown a rock through the bedroom window to break them in, what the two shots meant. What he hadn't been prepared for, though, was the blonde woman sprawled across the bed with half her head missing, and the moment of absolute conviction that he was looking at Laurie. In all his life he'd never forget the wrenching horror that had seared through him then, or the denial that had made him cry out. Within seconds he'd realized it was Beth, but the relief was only fleeting for there had been two shots and there was no sign of Laurie.

He'd found her on the ground in the sitting room, half hidden by the cushioned seat of a sofa. She wasn't moving. There was nothing to say she was alive, and dread of what he was going to find when he moved the cushion had made him hold back. In the end, it was Stan who lifted it and, seeing her terrified eyes staring up at them, Elliot threw himself to the ground and grabbed her into his arms. 'Oh thank God, thank God, thank God,' he cried, holding her tight. He knew he was crushing her, that he was sobbing like a fool, but he couldn't let go. She was alive. That was all that mattered – until, realizing she could be injured, he loosened his embrace and drew back to look at her.

'Are you hurt?' he asked, his eyes dark with fear again.

She shook her head, still too traumatized to speak.

He pulled her close and pressed his mouth to her hair. 'I love you,' he whispered. 'I love you so much. If anything had happened to you . . .' His voice had been swallowed by the relief of her being alive; of having the chance to tell her that any doubts he might have had were over, even before this. He'd been planning to tell her that night how sorry he was, how much he loved her. 'Please forgive me,' he'd choked. 'Please say you forgive me and I swear I'll never hurt you again.'

It was probably because of how certain he'd been she was dead that he was still finding it hard to believe that she wasn't. He had been *so* sure that, even now, as she worked quietly beside him on her computer, he had to touch her just to make sure she was there.

Turning to look at him she smiled and kissed his fingers as they brushed over her lips. 'OK?' she asked softly.

He nodded. He couldn't speak. Fatigue was making him emotional, and right now it would be easy to believe she was an apparition, for the plane had broken through the cloud, so the sun was casting a radiant glow around her hair, and the lustrous blue of her eyes seemed almost deep enough to fall into. Yet her irrepressible air of chaos made her real, and the memory of how she felt in his arms turned his heart inside out. How could he have tried to keep her shut out when he'd always known he never could.

'How's it going?' he asked, nodding towards her computer.

'OK,' she answered. Then, leaning towards him, she pressed her mouth gently to his.

He'd kissed and held her a lot since that nightmare day, lying with her on her hotel room bed after long, gruelling hours of police interrogation, when she'd had to relive, over and over, why she'd been at Beth's house, what they'd discussed and what had happened. The sofa cushion she'd seized to protect herself, after shoving Beth back against the wall, had saved her life, there was no question about that, though whether Beth had realized it, no one would ever know. It was pure terror that had made Laurie stay rooted to the floor, even though she'd heard Beth walking away. Then it was shock, and unmitigated horror that had kept her there, for the sound of Beth firing again had invoked such terrible images of Lysette's final moments that she'd been unable to move. It was only after Elliot had lifted her into his arms, that she'd dared to breathe again, and then awful, animal sounds began coming from her as she tried to catch her breath. They'd clung together then, so hard, and with such relief, that they'd only let go when the police and rescue services arrived.

In the days that followed, after Laurie had been treated for shock, a swarm of reporters and detectives had flown in from

London to talk to them all, but most particularly to her. Then Georgie and Bruce had arrived to take Beth's body home. That had been the hardest time of all for Laurie, as she'd held Georgie in her arms and cried with her.

'I can't believe she's dead,' Georgie had whispered, her voice cracked with grief. 'I just can't make myself accept it. I should have come to get her. I knew she needed me . . .'

'You can't blame yourself,' Laurie told her. 'She wouldn't want that.'

'I know. But she only really had me.'

Laurie pulled her back into an embrace as they cried some more. 'Have you spoken to Colin?' she asked after a while.

'No. Bruce has. They should be releasing him some time next week.'

Laurie was picturing him the last time she'd seen him, desolate and defeated, yet still confident enough in Beth's feelings to say, 'Believe me, if she knew something that would put them here instead of me, she wouldn't keep it to herself.' What a shock all this must have been for him, and knowing that it was his treatment of her that had driven her to such despair had to be making it all so much worse.

'How did he take it?' she asked.

'I don't know, I didn't ask,' Georgie answered.

Laurie was surprised by the coldness of the response, but said nothing. Obviously Georgie was angry, and in her shoes maybe she'd be blaming Colin too.

'I wonder if he'll go to Heather now,' Georgie said. Then, seeming not to want to dwell on that, she dabbed her eyes and took more tissues from the box on the bed. 'We're going to cremate her and bury the ashes in our little church,' she said. 'I spoke to her parents . . . I don't think they'll come for the funeral.'

Laurie hardly knew what to say to that.

'Her mother's a terrible woman,' Georgie said. 'You always think even the worst people have some kind of redeeming feature, but in all the years I've known her I've never seen one in Joyce. It's because of her that Beth has such a dreadful inferiority complex. Who wouldn't with a mother like that?' Looking down at her sodden, shredded tissues, she said, 'I know this has to be very difficult for Sophie Long's family and believe me, it's not that I don't feel for them, but I want to ask you, when you write about this, please don't let people think of Beth as just a cold-blooded killer. Maybe to some that's what she'll always be, but there was so much more to her. She was so beautiful and gentle really, so willing to love, but afraid of it too. What she did, that's just not who she really was.'

'Please don't worry,' Laurie said. 'When we talked, on that last day, I saw how deeply she'd been hurt, how little more she could take.' Feeling her eyes fill with tears again, she said, 'I'll never forget her.'

'No, don't let's ever forget her,' Georgie agreed.

Laurie wasn't sure now if she and Georgie would stay in touch, though they'd promised to. Initially they'd have to, of course, while Laurie wrote the story, but later it was almost inevitable they would drift apart.

'What are you thinking about?' Elliot asked, his eyes searching hers.

Her eyebrows went up. 'What do you think? This story's all-consuming.'

His expression became more intense as, tilting her face up to his, he said, 'As soon as it's done, we're going to make time for us.'

She nodded, then a teasing light came into her eyes as she said, 'I'm not sure I can wait that long.' She was about to kiss him when Max Erwin came to stand over them.

'We're not home and dry yet,' he said to Elliot. 'I was just going through what I thought were non-urgent emails, and there's one I think you should take a look at.'

Colin was walking towards Bruce and Georgie. Behind him was the glowering edifice of the prison, ahead a future he could hardly begin to imagine. He was, he knew, a shadow of the man who'd been arrested five months ago, a ghost about to revisit a world that had changed for ever.

As he drew closer Georgie's face was becoming clearer. His legs felt weak; a faint sun stung his eyes. He was aware of the sporadic birdsong around him, and the rumble of distant traffic. He could feel a slight chill in the air, and smell the damp street. His footsteps made no sound as he walked; over his shoulder was a small bag containing his belongings.

Georgie looked nothing like Beth, yet he knew when he spoke to her it would be as though he was speaking to Beth. He wondered how she would respond, and was almost afraid to find out, though he doubted anything could make him feel worse than he already did.

Bruce was reaching for his hand, waiting to welcome him back. His good and patient friend who'd stood by him through this, and had misinformed the press today so that he could escape the fuss. It would only be temporary, they both knew that, but of all the things he was most grateful to Bruce for, it was this.

Bracing himself, he turned to Georgie, hoping she understood how hard this was for him too. He knew what he was going to say, he'd been rehearsing it all night, but now, confronted by her, he felt the words being choked back in his throat. He took a breath, tried again to speak, but no sound came out. Then his shoulders began to shake, and terrible soul-wrenching sobs tore from his chest.

'It's all right,' she said, putting her hands on his shoulders. 'It's going to be all right.'

'Beth!' he cried. 'Beth, oh Beth, please forgive me.'

'Sssh.' Georgie wept too. 'It'll be all right.'

He was shaking his head. 'It was all my fault,' he gasped. 'I never meant to hurt her.'

'Let's talk about this at home,' Bruce said gently.

The journey back to Chelsea took less than twenty minutes, by which time Colin's grief had subsided a little, and Georgie was perhaps more ready to listen than she'd been before.

'I always thought,' Colin said, as Bruce put a large Scotch in front of him, 'that I'd celebrate the day I was released, that I'd be so relieved I'd drink champagne all night. I never imagined . . .' His voice faltered, and as though to cover it he took a mouthful of whisky.

'Better go easy on that,' Bruce advised. 'It's been a while.'

Colin nodded, and looked down at the rich amber liquid.

Georgie's eyes were expressionless as she watched him. Though she could see how difficult he was finding this, and could even on one level feel sorry for him, on another she knew she wasn't going to help him at all.

'Ever since you told me about Beth,' he said, his voice dropping to a whisper on his wife's name, 'since I got the news . . .' He swallowed hard and tried again. 'I've lain awake at night, wanting to get out of that place so badly. Yet I was dreading it too, like I've never dreaded anything in my life, because I knew that once I was out I'd have to find a way of dealing with the truth – that two women are dead because of me. One of them my own wife.' His eyes came up to Georgie's, showing just how devastated and bewildered he was inside. 'I loved her,' he said brokenly. 'I know you might find that hard to believe, but it's true. She was so much a part of my life, we were so close in so many ways . . . All that doesn't just go away because you fall in love with someone else. It doesn't mean you stop caring. I never stopped caring.'

Georgie looked at Bruce. Did she need to spell out just how appalling a husband this man had been? How selfishly he had behaved over the years? How especially insensitive, even brutal he had been in the last few months?

'I told myself a clean break would be easier,' he said. 'And I had to protect her from Gatling, or I thought I did . . . But the truth is, I was using it as an excuse not to see her. I didn't want to deal with her pain. I was afraid of it, because I knew I couldn't resist it. It was why I'd never been able to end our marriage before. I couldn't bear to hurt her, yet it was all I ever seemed to do.'

Georgie's face was pinched. 'Aren't you angry about what she tried to do to you?' she said.

He shook his head. 'How can I be when things have turned out the way they have?'

Georgie's eyes dropped to her hands wrapped around her glass. She knew he was hoping for her forgiveness, that in some surrogate way she, as though she were Beth, would set him free from the blame. But she wasn't Beth. She was immune to his charms, unmoved by his show of grief and regret, because were it not for him and the despicable way he had treated his wife, she wouldn't be blaming herself for having let Beth down at the end. 'What will you do now?' she asked finally.

Though his dismay showed at not receiving even a glimmer of the comfort he'd hoped for, he knew in his heart that it was still much too soon. A lot of time would have to pass, and even then there were no guarantees. 'Heather's in Ireland,' he said. 'She got in touch a couple of days ago, as soon as she heard they were releasing me.'

Georgie's eyes came up. The mention of Heather had made her so tense it hurt.

'I'd really like you to meet her,' he said. 'I think the two of you would get on well.'

Though Georgie didn't move, the disgust that had raised every barrier in her was more than visible. That he could think she'd even consider meeting Heather Dance, never mind befriending her, only went to show how utterly self-centred and delusional he was.

'It's perhaps a bit soon,' Bruce said.

Colin nodded. 'Yes, of course,' he said. 'Sorry.'

Georgie was taking in his gaunt, still-handsome face, red-rimmed eyes and clothes that bagged over his almost skeletal frame. He might not be guilty of murder, but as far as she was concerned, the list of his other crimes was long, and almost equally as heinous. It was because of them that both Beth and Sophie Long had died, and no amount of remorse on his part was going to change that. He was accountable, and he knew it, yet he was still here, his life irrevocably altered it was true, even to some degree ruined, but he'd survive. He'd build a new life with Heather, become a full-time father, and very soon Beth would be all but forgotten.

'I can't help wondering,' she said, feeling herself start to shake, 'how long it will be before you start cheating on Heather.'

He looked as though he'd been kicked. 'I know I deserve that,' he said, 'but I swear, this has changed me. From now on I'll never cheat on a woman again.'

Georgie's nostrils flared with anger. 'Then who is Jackie Peters?' she challenged, feeling Bruce's hand close on her shoulder.

Colin's face immediately coloured. 'I don't . . . I . . .' he stammered. 'She's someone who visited me in prison. That's what she does, visit people in prison.'

'So all the time Beth was tearing herself to pieces because you wouldn't let her visit, you were allowing this *stranger* –'

'It wasn't like that,' he cut in. 'She only visited me twice, towards the end.'

'And now you've arranged to have lunch with her tomorrow.'

'She suggested it. What could I say?'

'No?' Georgie spat. 'Have you ever tried it where a woman's concerned?'

'Georgie, please –'

'Save it for Heather, Colin. Let her deal with your lies. I've already lost my best friend because of them, so I sure as hell don't want to hear any more.' She got to her feet, shaken by her outburst, for it was unlike her to speak so bluntly. 'You're pathetic, do you know that?' she suddenly cried, rounding on him again. 'You're weak, spineless, self-centred and totally insensitive to anyone's needs except your own. Not even one day out of prison and already you're involved with two women, and you've got the nerve to give one of them *my* phone number. Where's it going to end, Colin? How many more people are going to have to get hurt before *you* learn to control that monstrosity inside your pants? Or before you own up to the fact that you're responsible for everything that happened. *Everything*, because she'd be alive now, if it weren't for you. So would Sophie Long.'

Colin's face was stricken, his eyes darting between her and Bruce, as though Bruce might come to his rescue. 'I'm sorry,' he said. 'Georgie, I'm so sorry. I'll cancel the lunch with Jackie. Give me the phone, I'll do it right now.'

'But there'll be others, won't there? We both know that, because you're incapable of resisting. So let me tell you this: after Jackie Peters called here today, I called Laurie Forbes and Elliot Russell. They might be in Mexico, but they've got colleagues right here in London who they were more than happy to put me on to. So you can expect to see your cosy little lunch with Miss Peters on the front page of Friday's *Sun*. And I'm going to keep doing it, Colin. Every time I hear about you and some new dalliance, or whatever you call it, you're going to find it all over the papers. Colin Ashby, the man who can't keep it in his trousers! They'll turn you into a laughing stock – a stigma for any decent-thinking woman; a byword for dirty old man. So don't think you've got away with anything here, Colin, or that you ever will again. The press is on your case now, and so, my friend, am I.'

Though the suddenness of change of pace had at first been bewildering, it had taken little time for the almost glutinous humidity of Playita to reduce the stress and urgency they'd brought with them to a reasonable, unpanicked desire to complete the job. Though they worked constantly, throughout the day and night, the heavy, languorous air and perpetual motion of the waves slowed their thoughts as surely as it slowed their bodies – though the remoteness and calm seemed to allow an objectivity it would have been hard to muster in the frenzy of LA.

Max's cleverly designed casa was set back from the beach, enclosed by the thick, succulent foliage of a rain forest. Its sand-coloured walls curved around an inner courtyard, where a waterfall splashed over rocks into a deep lagoon pool, and the garden was crowded with dense, rubbery leaves, and purple, red and gold flowers. At one end of the courtyard were the kitchen and sitting room, whose walls were shaped like an inverted 9, with the kitchen in the circle and the sitting room spread out in the tail. There was no front wall to the sitting room, so the springy grass and shrubbery were as much a part of it as the heavy wood furniture and clay-tiled floors. Elliot and Max worked at a long oval table, mobile phones beside their computers, stacks of documents spilling out of the hi-tech printer and fax Max kept at the house. Every now and again one or other would get up and go and dive into the pool to cool off, ease the tension from their limbs, and give themselves some moments to reflect.

On the opposite side of the courtyard, tucked in behind twisting vines and climbing bougainvillaea, were the round bedroom bungalows, whose outer walls were washed rusty pink and whose roofs were like fans of red tiles. Inside, the decor ranged from ochre yellow to leaf green to dazzling blue. Bright Mexican tiles surrounded the showers and added their own kind of sprightliness to the walls and cupboards. Laurie had set up a small card table in the bigger of the two bedrooms, having pushed the large oak bed to one side, so that the mosquito net could tumble down around her.

As she worked small lizards scuttled around in the shadows while exotic birds chirruped and hooted in the trees outside. Pulling everything together, from the day she'd first met Beth Ashby, to the way her bosses had blocked the story, to how she'd been attacked in her own home and later abducted off the street, to having her parents threatened, to ultimately losing her job, then the details of her final meeting with Beth was having a profound effect on her. In a way it was as though it was happening all over again, and each time she looked up, when Elliot came in with a drink, or if her mobile phone rang, she was slightly startled by her surroundings, for they felt so removed from the events she was writing about that for a few disoriented moments she couldn't be sure where she was.

Though she was managing more sleep than Elliot or Max, taking herself into the other bedroom where she could lie on a single bed beneath a net and a fan, her naps were still short, for the damp, penetrating heat seemed to stir her memories into weirdly disturbing dreams. Occasionally she woke up to find Elliot on the next bed, his expression stern in sleep, yet the vulnerability of his closed eyes and loosely clenched hands never failed to make her heartbeat quicken. Sometimes she would just lie there, watching him, longing to go and lie with him, but he needed what little sleep he could get, and with Max still there such physical closeness would only add to their growing frustration.

It was on the morning of the fourth day that she finally finished Beth's story. After emailing it to Elliot to read when he could, she peeled off her shorts and wearing only the briefest of bikinis, she wandered out to the pool and slipped quietly into the sparkling water. Though she swam several lengths, she soon had to stop, for it was as though the weight of Beth was pulling her down and stealing her breath. She moved into the shade and sat in a deck chair. Though she couldn't see them behind a luxuriant hibiscus bush, she could hear Elliot and Max talking, and somewhere, from a villa nearby, came the unmistakably vibrant sounds of Mexican music. Her heart felt fragile and full. Being here, in this almost limbo-like world, had made it possible for her to think about Beth in a less painful way than when she'd been in LA,

510

though all the time she'd been writing, it was as though Beth was watching her from the shadows, pressing her for sympathy and understanding, and maybe even forgiveness.

Now, sitting here, shielded by a jungle of exotic trees and flowers, she felt Beth's power finally starting to ebb, for the story was no longer exclusively theirs, holding them together with invisible bonds. Soon Elliot would read it, then Max, then editors in New York and London – then the rest of the world. It felt right to let it go, though she knew that in their way they would always be linked now.

A shadow fell over her and her heart tightened as she looked up into Elliot's face. Weariness showed in his eyes, as distinctly as the two-day stubble on his chin. His body, too, seemed tired, yet its strength was as immutable as the blue sky that framed him, and the chemistry they shared was like the powerful tow of the sea. Under his scrutiny all her senses responded, causing desire to slake a long, painful path through her most intimate parts, and a tiny breath of pleasure to escape her lips.

Dropping down in front of her he folded his arms on her knees and looked up at her. 'Are you OK?' he asked quietly.

She nodded and reached out to touch his face. He turned his mouth into her palm and kissed it.

'Have you finished?' she asked.

'Just about.' His eyes came back to hers and she felt herself moving into a tide of longing. Taking her hand he pulled her forward and covered her lips with his own. She knew he was as aroused as she was, and heard him moan softly as she spread her hands over the hard muscles of his chest. Her legs were parted, her knees resting against his hips. His hands moved to her shoulders, down over her breasts to her waist. Then, sitting back on his heels, he took her hands and said, 'Max is leaving tonight.'

'I know,' she whispered.

Their eyes held each other's with a potency that needed no words, until, slowly bringing her mouth back to his, he penetrated with his tongue, and moved his fingers so gently over her nipples that she wanted to cry out.

Later, after the stories had been read, checked, re-edited and read again, at Max's suggestion they took a laptop and mobile down to the beach where they ordered margaritas from a bar, then sat under a thatched palapa to wait for their drinks to arrive. The sand was hot underfoot, the ocean heaved and soughed on to the shore, and white clouds, like a mystical mountain range, floated slowly over the horizon. A few locals were repairing nets, or trapping crabs, while a handful of intrepid surfers made the most of the surging tide.

Laurie was sitting beside Elliot. They both wore shorts and the light touch of their legs burned like a caress. She watched his hands, long, elegant, yet strong, as he attached his phone to the computer. As soon as the drinks arrived, he would make the connection to submit their stories.

Max was grinning. 'If they could see us now,' he commented.

Elliot and Laurie laughed, as they imagined those who would receive the stories, and where they were at that moment: so far removed in time, distance and even culture, that it was curious, even difficult to associate the two worlds and how they were about to connect.

A waiter arrived with three salted-rim glasses containing the potent cocktail. After setting them down, with a bowl of fresh guacamole and taco chips, he left menus and returned to the bar.

Elliot began dialling the Puerto Vallarta access number.

Laurie's breath was shallow, her eyes were watchful and amused. Max was grave, and tapped the ground with one heel. His glance met Laurie's and his unshaven face showed a glimpse of sardonic humour. After the squeal and crush of connection Elliot looked up from the screen. The sun was beating down; a dozen pelicans swooped in perfect formation. 'Are we ready for this?' he said.

Laurie's fingers slid down the stem of her glass. It was hard to reconcile the complex gravity of their stories with the sublime simplicity of where they were.

'Go for it, man,' Max responded.

Elliot positioned the cursor over *send*, then, with a quick flick of his thumb, the stories were simultaneously transmitted to *The Times* in London, the *Wall Street Journal* in New York, and Tom Maykin at his Upper West Side condo. They also went to Elliot's team in docklands, and certain contacts in the Bahamas, Hong Kong and Switzerland. In her mind Laurie likened it to setting free a flock of wild birds. None could be captured again, and what effect they might have on the world at large could only be guessed at. She could almost hear the string-bound bundles of newspapers thudding to the ground throughout Britain and the US, dropping like the birds' dead bodies, before they were opened to reveal the ugly truth behind the currency inflations, the high-powered syndicate that had devised the scheme, and the lonely British woman whose despair at her husband's infidelity had perversely brought it all to light.

'*Vérité sans peur*,' Elliot said quietly.

'Truth without fear,' Laurie translated for Max.

They raised their glasses, faces sombre, yet eyes betraying humour and intrigue.

'To us,' Max declared.

'To us,' Elliot and Laurie echoed, and they drank.

Laurie's eyes closed as the tequila and lime stung her taste buds. For some reason the dreamy ballad coming from inside the bar made her think of Beth, and she wondered what it had been like for her and Colin at the beginning. As it was for her and Elliot now? Intense, breathless, rife with erotic fantasy and wonderfully romantic dreams?

Elliot's tone was droll as he unplugged the phone, and shut down the computer. 'If they change anything now, the lawsuits are theirs,' he said. His leg was still against hers and as she drank again she tensed with the pleasure of his hand coming to rest on her thigh.

'Do you think they will?' she asked.

'Change anything? Of course. They won't be able to resist.'

She was shaking her head in amazement. 'I always imagined,' she said, 'that if I were ever involved in anything this big I'd either be submitting it from the hub of the action, or right there in the craziness of a newsroom. Have you ever submitted anything like this before? I mean, so cut off from it all.'

Elliot smiled. 'No. I can't say I have.'

'What about you, Max?'

'Me neither,' he responded, stretching out his legs. 'But it's kind of cool.'

They laughed, then after a while Elliot said, 'So what next for you, Max?'

Max put down his glass. 'I'll tell you what next for me,' he said, linking his hands behind his head. 'I'm going after Hank Wingate. The shots I sent you of Beth's injuries? I took them with one purpose in mind, to nail the bastard that did it.' His eyes closed as he turned his face to the evening sun. 'That Texan son-of-a-bitch is sure to have done something like it before, so now I'm on his case, and guess what, he's going to jail.'

Laurie clinked her glass against his. 'Power to you,' she said.

'And tonight?' Elliot said. 'I know your plane's going to Mexico City.'

'Final destination, Buenos Aires,' Max replied. 'Eloise is there.'

'Eloise?' Laurie echoed.

'My wife. The casa's hers.'

'The one we're staying at?'

Max nodded. 'She designed it. It's what she does.'

It was incredible, Laurie was thinking, how other people's reality could be something so entirely different than imagined, though Max having a wife would account for the unmistakably feminine touches in the casa, like the matching napkins and table mats, the expensive hand-painted plates, the sumptuous pillows and unusual art, the absence of hard corners, and dozens of candleholders that wended a path through the sitting room, courtyard and bedrooms. She smiled secretly to herself, as she recalled the easy communication she'd had with the maid, Sylva, that morning about those holders.

They finished their drinks slowly, seeming reluctant to part now the time was approaching. Eventually they strolled back along the beach, warm waves foaming round their ankles, palms arching high overhead, while they continued to discuss the story and guess at its effects. The path home wound through the hot, dusty village, where evening was bringing music and people from the protective shade of their homes, and the delicious smell of freshly roasting corn wafted in the still, humid air. They stopped at a stall selling earthenware

514

pots; then at another with skipping ropes, fake leather sandals and second-hand music tapes. As Laurie browsed Max and Elliot kicked a ball with a group of teenage boys.

'How long before you guys put your phones on again?' Max asked, as they walked on across a bridge where children splashed in the sandy-bottomed creek, and unfettered horses grazed beside it.

Elliot's hand reached for Laurie's. 'At least a couple of days,' he responded.

She gave an answering squeeze, and leaned in closer to his shoulder. The time for them was fast approaching and despite her nerves a very strong part of her was wishing they'd arranged for a taxi to take Max to the airport.

However, when Max was loading his bags into the rented Jeep half an hour later, and Elliot held her very close as they kissed a temporary goodbye, she felt glad of the hour she now had to prepare, for she wanted to make this the most special night of their lives – so far.

After listening to the Jeep jolting away down the narrow dirt road she went first to the larger of the two bedrooms, where Elliot had already moved the bed back into place, and took a cool, refreshing shower, before wrapping herself in a flimsy sarong and clipping her hair on top of her head. Then she checked her face in a mirror that was lit by the coloured lights of a paper toucan lamp. Her eyes were shining, and the delicate glow on her skin was like burnished honey.

Her heart was pounding a faster beat as she wound her way across the courtyard to the kitchen where she found the boxes of candles Sylva had smuggled in that morning. The holders, spread out all over the house and garden, were in tall, handcrafted stands, or round, filigree pots, jazzy ceramic dishes, Aztec pyramids, and moulded granite slabs. They decorated pillars, tables, rocks, the pool edge, the steps to the bedrooms and the bedrooms themselves. After filling them all she returned to the kitchen, not ready to light them yet, she'd wait until just before he was due to get back.

The barbecue was already set up for him to grill the swordfish Sylva had left in the fridge, and since he was the gourmet cook Laurie had happily agreed to leave it to him.

Her contribution was merely to prepare a salad and set the table. Her hands weren't quite steady as she broke apart a crisp, curly lettuce. Her head was whirring with so many thoughts and her chest becoming so tight, that she poured herself some wine to relax. Though she'd been planning this virtually since they'd arrived, wanting to make everything as beautiful and romantic as possible, now that it was upon her she was feeling much too apprehensive, and even daunted by the thought of his worldliness which would make her own small experiences seem almost naïve by comparison. She took another comforting gulp of wine, then went back to the bedroom to get the tapes she'd bought earlier in the village. The fact that they'd been there had been too auspicious to ignore.

Going back to the kitchen she drank some more wine, then washed the lettuce in a bowl of iced water. She guessed he'd have dropped Max off by now so would be on his way back, and almost gasped at the sudden onslaught of nerves that the time was now so close. Recalling the journey in from the airport she pictured him at the wheel of the open-topped Jeep, his dark hair blowing in the wind as he passed the bull ring, then the sea-view cemetery, roadside cafés and artisans' stalls, before speeding through long arches of overhanging trees, funnels of light brightening the road ahead. He'd have one hand on the wheel, an elbow resting on the doorframe where the window should be. She could see his face, taut with concentration, and knew that his thoughts were on her. Again her insides caught, this time on the desire that scooped her up like prey. No matter how much more experienced he was than her, she knew he wanted her tonight, and whatever he had to teach her, she would willingly learn, for she'd never felt such a physical longing for a man in her life.

By the time she finished lighting all the candles, and turned off the lamps she knew he should arrive any minute. Not even a breath of air whispered through the garden, nor did a single cloud darken the half-moon. The only movement was the shimmering reflection of tiny white flames in the pool, and on the shiny surfaces of leaves.

Minutes later she heard the Jeep pull up outside and the engine die. As the car door closed she pushed a button on the

516

tape player and the room filled with the magical opening to
'*E lucevan le stelle*', from Puccini's *Tosca*. Already transported
by the music, she turned to face the door, and took a step back
into the candlelit foliage of a pink hibiscus. Her hand was
resting where her sarong was tied over her breasts; her breath
was so shallow and her heart so full that she could feel herself
starting to tremble.

His key barely made a noise in the lock as Carreras's
majestic voice joined with the music, and as the door opened
her throat caught on his surprise at the music, then the
candles, then the vision of her, almost dreamlike, in the shell
of foliage across the room. Carreras decrescendoed. Her hand
moved and her sarong fell to the ground.

As the door closed behind him the Italian love song began
to build again, its passion filling the air as he moved towards
her, never taking his eyes from hers. She stepped forward to
meet him, her heart buoyed by music and love.

He gazed far into her eyes, showing her without words
how deeply he felt, how poignant this moment was for him
too. Reaching behind her, he removed the clip from her hair
and watched it fall around her shoulders. She put a hand on
his chest, and as the aria reached its peak his mouth touched
hers with such searing tenderness she felt her own start to
shake.

The heat of the music flared around them as he stood back
to remove his clothes. Then, naked, he pulled her to him, his
hands feeling her nudity as his skin embraced it too. Their
bodies were bathed in soft, golden light, his so dark and
masculine, hers so slender and female. His hands slipped
down over her hips, then spanned her waist, bringing her
harder to his erection. His lips moved to her neck and
shoulders, then they watched his hands as they moved to her
breasts, cupping their fullness, and feeling their weight. She
lifted her mouth to his, and he drew her lips between his own,
sucking them and biting them gently, until lowering his head,
he did the same to her nipples. Her back arched towards him
and her fingers slid into his hair, as her breath caught on the
eroticism of their reflections in the mirror beside them.

His movements seemed as fluid as the music as he stood
behind her, and turned her so that they could both look at her

reflected nudity and watch his hands as they explored it. Her head fell back on his shoulder as his fingers touched her nipples so lightly that the biting desire for more made her gasp. He squeezed them hard, and groaning she turned her face into his neck. The scent of him inflamed her, and as his mouth sought hers, she kissed him with her lips and tongue until his hands on her breasts made her pleasure so heavy she could barely support it.

Turning back to the mirror she looked at his reflection. Behind her his erection was hard and strong and she wanted it so badly she was ready to beg. Taking it he pushed it gently between her thighs, then they watched as his hands descended to her waist, over the soft skin of her belly to the place that was so ready for his touch she was almost afraid to feel it.

'You're perfect,' he whispered. She raised her eyes to his in the mirror, then sobbed as his fingers opened her and began to stroke her, too gently to make her come, but enough to take her so close she could hardly bear it. Then, almost in time with the music, he scooped her up in his arms, carried her to the heavy oak table, and pushing aside the place mats and napkins, he laid her down amongst the candles.

She looked up at him, and felt so full of emotion that no words would come. Her legs were parted, he was standing between them and she knew that at any moment he would enter her. Leaning over her he kissed each of her breasts, her belly, then the place where his tongue could exploit her harshly. She moaned and sobbed beneath him, grasping his hands hard and opening her legs wide. The music was now pulsing through her with the same relentless force as the sensations. The sounds were as tangible as touch, the orchestra as powerful as the climax she was nearing. She gasped and cried out, then tightened her grasp on him, so hard that he could make no mistake about how far he had taken her.

He stood up and looked down at her. She was dazed by sensation, so close to the brink, yet starting to fall away with the diminuendo. He watched her, waiting for her eyes to come to his. When they did, the opening bars to *Si, mi chiamano Mimi* began, and as the exquisite female voice merged with Carreras's powerful tenor in one of *La Bohème's* most stirring arias, she felt him moving slowly, inexorably into her.

She watched his face, and held his hands, every muscle tensed with the pleasure of him filling her. Already he was so big inside her that she could feel him taking her in a way she'd never been taken before. His eyes remained on hers as he raised her knees, and pulled her right to the table's edge. He pushed again until finally he was all the way in, then easing back he began the sublime penetration all over again. He did it again, and again. Slowly, tenderly, lovingly. Rotating his hips, then rocking them, watching her face, kissing her hands until the music suddenly galvanized his movements and he thrust into her, so hard that she cried out – and he kept her crying out as the rhythm carried them in a frenzy of harmony and sensation, to a tremendous, explosive climax that seemed to have no end.

Lifting her up, he held her and kissed her mouth. The seed was still bursting from him, the pulsing grip of her inner muscles hadn't even begun to subside. The opera swirled around them as they clung together, their bodies damp with sweat and bruised with love. The candles flickered, the moon gleamed above and the pool shone like glass. There was no way for either of them to express the beauty of this, their first experience together. They knew only that the other felt its power too, and that nothing they had imagined had even come close to being this good.

When at last he stopped kissing her, and looked down into her eyes, she smiled blearily up at him.

'I love you,' he whispered.

'No more doubts?'

He shook his head. 'They were never real.'

Her eyes were mischievous. 'But I almost had to get killed to bring you to your senses.'

For a long time they just looked at each other, cherishing the moments as they passed, feeling the emotions in their hearts, occasionally kissing, never wanting to let go. Then, holding his face between her hands, and feeling the strength of him still there inside her, she said, 'I'm going to love Puccini for ever.'

His eyes were suffused with humour, then his mouth closed brutally on hers and the turbulence of renewed desire

519

moved between them like the opening gusts of a storm. Lifting her up with her legs around his waist he carried her to the grassy mattress next to the pool and laid her down.

'I bought *two* tapes today,' she told him as he lay on his side next to her.

'Oh?' He was watching his hand moving over her belly.

She waited for his eyes to come to hers, then smiled as she said, 'The other one's Wagner.'

Humour was deep in his voice as he said, 'So while the world reverberates to the shock of our revelations, we're here making love to *Tristan und Isolde*?'

'Nothing so tame.'

His eyebrows flickered upwards, then, guessing, his face tightened with desire. 'If I'm right,' he said, 'then you know what it means.'

'It's why I chose it,' she responded.

For a while they only looked at each other, imagining the eroticism of what was to come, knowing the positions they would take, and feeling its promise beating through them with a harsh and brazen power. Letting her go, he lay on his back, gazing up at the stars, as she went to change the tape. Then the first triumphal sounds of Wagner's greatest master-piece began.

'Do you realize,' she said, coming back to kneel beside him, 'that in England the papers are about to hit the stands?'

He was already reaching for her, moving behind her to cover her body with his. 'Then I guess we could say,' he murmured, as the music's rousing drama began to encircle them, 'that the opera really is about to begin.'

Silent Truths

Susan Lewis was born and brought up in Bristol. While pursuing a successful career in television she started to write, and her first novel, *A Class Apart*, became an instant bestseller, as did its successor, *Dance While You Can*. She gave up her job to write full-time and *Silent Truths* is her fourteenth bestselling novel. She now divides her time between her homes in London and Los Angeles